OTHER BOOKS BY JANE SMILEY

Barn Blind

At Paradise Gate

Duplicate Keys

The Age of Grief

The
Greenlanders

The GReen

anders

JANE SMILEY

ALFRED A. KNOPF

NEW YORK

1988

THIS IS A BORZOI BOOK
PUBLISHED BY ALFRED A. KNOPF, INC.

Library of Congress Cataloging-in-Publication Data

Smiley, Jane.
The Greenlanders.
1. Greenland—History—Fiction.   I. Title.
PS3569.M39G7   1988   813'.54   87-40494
ISBN 0-394-55120-6

Manufactured in the United States of America

FIRST EDITION

The Greenlanders was conceived while I was in Iceland, in 1976 and 1977, on a
Fulbright-Hays Full Grant for Study Abroad. I am indebted to the program for
that support.

I also wish to thank Iowa State University for generously supporting this
project at every stage.

J. S.

*This book is fondly dedicated to Elizabeth Stern,
Duncan Campbell, Frank Ponzi, and to the memory of
Knud-Erik Holm-Pedersen.*

þar munu eftir
undrsamligar
gullnar töflur
í grasi finnask,
þærs í árdaga
áttar höfðu.

Afterwards they will find the chessmen,
marvelous and golden in the grass,
just where the ancient gods
had dropped them.

"Völuspá"
("The Sayings of the Prophetess")

CONTENTS

LIST OF CHARACTERS

Erlend Ketilsson, his quarrelsome son

    Vigdis, Erlend's wife or mistress

    Thordis, Vigdis' daughter

    Their sons: Geir, Kollbein, Hallvard, Jon Andres (born 1374)

GARDAR FOLK (priests):

Ivar Bardarson, Norwegian, caretaker of the Episcopal See of Gardar

Bishop Alf, bishop of Gardar, from Stavanger district, in Norway

Sira Jon, priest, nephew of Alf

Sira Petur, a priest hastily ordained in Norway after the Black Death

Sira Pall Hallvardsson, another priest in Alf's entourage, of mixed
Icelandic and Flemish descent

Sira Audun, a Greenlander, designated a priest but not officially
ordained

Sira Eindridi Andresson, another Greenlander, Sira Audun's cousin,
designated but not ordained

Sira Andres, son of Sira Eindridi

Larus the Prophet, a Greenlander, originally a cowherd

SOLAR FELL FOLK:

Ragnvald Einarsson, first owner of Solar Fell

    St. Olaf the Greenlander, his grandson

Bjorn Bollason, from Dyrnes, second owner of Solar Fell

    Signy, his wife

    Sigrid, their daughter

    Their sons, Bolli, Sigurd, Hoskuld, Arni

ICELANDERS:

Bjorn Einarsson Jorsalfari
 Solveig, his wife
 Einar, his foster-son

Snorri, captain of an Icelandic ship

Thorstein Olafsson, a teller of tales

Thorgrim Solvason, a prominent Icelander
 Steinunn Hrafnsdottir, Thorgrim's wife
 Thorunn Hrafnsdottir, Steinunn's sister

NORWEGIANS:

Thorleif, ship's captain, called the Magnificent by the Greenlanders

Skuli Gudmundsson, a boy on Thorleif's ship, later a hirdman of Kollbein Sigurdsson

Kollbein Sigurdsson, last representative of the Norwegian king to Greenland, 1373–1376

Riches

Asgeir Gunnarsson farmed at Gunnars Stead near Undir Hofdi church in Austfjord. His homefield was nearly as large as the homefield at Gardar, where the absent bishop had his seat, and he had another large field as well. From the time he took over the farm upon the death of his father, this Asgeir had a great reputation among the Greenlanders for pride. It happened that when he was a young man he went off on the king's knarr to Norway, and when he returned to Gunnars Stead two years later, he brought with him an Icelandic wife, whose name was Helga Ingvadottir. She carried with her two wallhangings and six white ewes with black faces, as well as other valuable goods, and for pride folk said that Asgeir was well matched in her.

Asgeir built a special pen for these Icelandic ewes at the edge of his second field, and this pen was visible from the steading. Each morning Asgeir liked to open the door of the steading and gaze out upon his ewes cropping the rich grass of his second field, and when Helga brought him his bowl of sourmilk, he would turn and set his eyes upon her elaborate headdress and the silver brooches that lay against her throat. Thus he would contemplate his luck. About this time, Helga Ingvadottir gave birth to a child who was named Margret, and who was a sturdy, quiet child and a great source of pride to the mother.

Also visible from the door of the steading was the turf hut belonging to Thorunn Jorundsdottir, and the bit of land surrounding this hut cut a notch in the Gunnars Stead property where it met the property of Ketil Erlendsson, Asgeir's nearest neighbor. This Thorunn was an old woman, who kept one cow and only a few sheep and goats. She supplemented her meager provisions by going about to nearby farms and begging for some of this and some of that. She was also given much to whispering, and folk in the district were not disinclined to hear what she had to say, although they were disinclined to speak of it.

There was nothing about this Thorunn that Helga Ingvadottir cared for, neither her whispering, nor her begging, nor the sight of her hovel on the horizon, nor the way that the one cow and the few sheep and goats often strayed among Gunnars Stead beasts. One day Thorunn came to Gunnars Stead, as she was in the habit of doing, and asked Helga for some of the new milk. Helga, who was standing in the doorway of the dairy, with basins of new milk all about her, refused this request, for recently she had felt another child quicken within her, and it was well known among the Greenlanders that a woman hoping for a boy child must drink only new milk. Thorunn glanced about at the basins of milk and went away muttering. Later, when Asgeir returned to the steading for his evening meat, Helga spoke bitterly against the old woman, until Asgeir demanded silence.

But it seemed the case that Thorunn had indeed cursed the Gunnars Stead folk, for not long after this, one of Asgeir's horses stepped in a hole and broke his leg, and had to have his throat cut, and then, after the servants had filled in the hole, another of the horses stepped in the same hole, and broke the selfsame leg, and had to have his throat cut, as well. And then Helga Ingvadottir came to her time, but the birth did not go well, and though the child lived, the mother did not. This was in the year 1352, by the reckoning of the stick calendar at Gardar.

Asgeir named the child Gunnar, for there had been a Gunnar or an Asgeir at Gunnars Stead since the time of Erik the Red, when Erik gave his friend Hafgrim all of Austfjord and the northern part of Vatna Hverfi district, the richest district in all of Greenland, and Hafgrim gave a piece to the first Gunnar, his cousin. The child Gunnar was not especially small and not especially large. His nurse was a servingwoman whose name was Ingrid. Margret was by this time some seven winters old.

The child Gunnar did not grow well, and when he should have been walking, he was only sitting up, and when he should have been playing with the other children about the farmstead, Margret was still carrying him about in a sling upon her back. Asgeir regretted naming the child Gunnar, and spoke of changing it to Ingvi.

Asgeir Gunnarsson had a brother who also lived at Gunnars Stead, who was named Hauk. Hauk had no wife, and was very fond of all sorts of hunting and snaring and fishing. He had been to the Northsetur, far to the north of the western settlement, where Greenlanders liked to hunt walrus and narwhal and polar bear, such large animals as were very valuable to the bishop and to the ships that came from the archbishop of Nidaros and the king in Norway. He sought the icy, waste districts both summer and winter, and his skills made Gunnars Stead especially prosperous. He spoke little. Asgeir said his brother could make the killing of a polar bear sound like a day at the butter churn. Hauk was the taller of the two brothers, very straight-limbed and fair-looking. Asgeir often urged him to find himself a wife, but Hauk said nothing to these suggestions, as he said nothing to most suggestions. He was well liked among the Greenlanders for his skills, and not blamed for his independent ways, for the Greenlanders live far out on the western ocean, and know what it is to depend upon themselves in all things.

One day Asgeir gathered together a group of men. Toward dusk, they surrounded Thorunn's little steading and called her out. When she came, carrying a basin and muttering in her usual fashion, Asgeir said that he was tired of her curses, and he killed her with his sheep-shearing knife. Gunnar was three winters old. Now he began to walk and to act more like other children. Asgeir stopped talking of changing his name to Ingvi. Folk in the district said little of this killing. Thorunn had a niece with a young daughter who lived in Petursvik at Ketils Fjord, far to the south, but no male relatives to exact revenge. It was clear enough that she had put a spell over the child, and many praised Asgeir for his decisive action, including especially Hauk Gunnarsson, who had been away in Isafjord and not present at the killing. After Thorunn was buried near Undir Hofdi church, Asgeir sent his servants to her steading and had them tear it down, and he gave the cow and the sheep to Nikolaus, the priest at Undir Hofdi church, along with all of Thorunn's house furnishings. In this way, the boundary between Gunnars Stead and Ketils Stead was straightened, and the unsightly steading could no longer be seen from the doorway at Gunnars Stead. After these events, it seemed to Asgeir that he had renewed his good luck, and he was much pleased with himself.

It was Margret's habit and pleasure as a child to walk about in the hills above the farmstead looking for herbs and bilberries, and most of the time she would carry Gunnar with her in a sling, for at eleven winters of age she was tall and strong, taller than Ingrid by far and not so much shorter than Asgeir himself. It happened on one such day a year after the killing of Thorunn the witch that Margret strayed beyond her usual range, and Gunnar, tired from playing among the tiny, trickling streams and tangles of birch scrub, fell into a deep sleep. It was well past the time for evening meat when Margret carried the sleeping child back to the farmstead, and she looked for a beating from Ingrid, but instead she found the farmstead deserted and everything quiet.

The nurse Ingrid was a great storyteller, and she had told Margret many stories of the skraelings and their evil ways, and of the sad lives of little girls whom the skraelings stole and took with them into the north, farther north than the Northsetur, where Hauk Gunnarsson hunted for walrus and narwhal. Now Margret sat with her back against the turf of the steading and contemplated how the babies of these little girls would never be baptized, and would be taken out in the dark of winter and left to the elements. These little girls would be beaten if they dared to pray, and would have to submit to any man who wanted them. They would never bathe from year to year, and would wear only animal skins, and when they died they would have no final sacraments, and so they would spend eternal life in the same darkness and cold, and with the same sort of devilish companions as the skraelings. The fact was, that it was not unusual for Margret to give herself over to thoughts such as these, for though they frightened her, they also drew her. It made no difference that Asgeir laughed at Ingrid's tales, and declared that she had never seen a skraeling in her life (for the skraelings did not come near the Norse farms and never had), nor that Hauk Gunnarsson himself had frequent intercourse with the demons, and admired their hunting skills and the warmth of their garments. On the other hand, Margret had heard Asgeir and Ivar Bardarson, the priest who had Gardar in his charge until the coming of the new bishop, speaking of what had befallen the western settlement, for Ivar Bardarson had taken some men and gone there in a boat and found all of the farms abandoned and all of the livestock dead or scattered to the wastelands. And she had heard them mention skraelings more than once. She got up, ostensibly to find Gunnar some bits of dried fish and butter, for he was whimpering with hunger, but really to look around the corners of the steading. There was no one, man nor demon, to be seen. Dusk was falling. She sat down and took Gunnar upon her lap. He began to eat, and she dozed off.

The two children were awakened by the glare of torches and the sound of Asgeir's rolling voice. "Well," he said, "here are the only folk along the whole of Einars Fjord who know nothing of the great event." He smiled in the flickering light of the torches. "A ship has come, my daughter, and though it brings no bishop, we will not send it back for one without unloading it first."

Now folk crowded into the steading, not only Gunnars Stead folk, but Ketils Stead folk, too, for this event was interesting enough to draw the whole neighborhood together for talk and speculation. Gunnar sat open-eyed at the bench while Margret, Ingrid, and the servingmaids dished up sourmilk and other refreshments for the guests. Ketil Erlendsson spoke up. "Even so, it is but a single ship, and not sent of the king, either."

"Nor of the bishop," said one of the other men.

Asgeir said, "But it is large enough for there to be a bit of something for each of us." He laughed. "Something, it is certain, that we did not know we needed before this."

Now a man spoke whom Gunnar had never seen before, dark and sour-looking, with odd, crinkly hair. "The news is that King Magnus has given the throne to King Hakon now, though Magnus still lives." He spoke angrily, and Gunnar's cousin, Thorkel, said with a grin, "Erlend Ketilsson, you sound as if he might have given the throne to you, had events gone another way." Gunnar had heard the name of the man, Erlend Ketilsson, many times, and widened his eyes in the flickering light to get a good look at him. His gaze seemed to fall upon Erlend like the touch of a hand, for the young man turned at once and stared back. Now Gunnar raised his palms to his face and pulled his cheeks down, until his eyes were staring out of the sockets, then he thrust forth his tongue, nearly to the roots. It was the work of a moment. Thorkel saw him and laughed aloud. Erlend scowled. Ketil said, "That won't be the only news, you may be sure, and the rest of it will be worse."

"Few goods and bad news," said Asgeir, "but I am content. That is enough for me, if there is nothing else." The other men nodded and ate up the sourmilk and went off.

The next day, all the Greenlanders flocked to Gardar to catch sight of the Norwegians and to trade the goods they had been hoarding for many years. The captain of the traders, a Bergen man named Thorleif, seemed to laugh all the time. He roared with laughter at the sight of the Greenlanders' tradegoods: sealskins and walrus tusks and lengths of homespun fabric, piles of sheepskins and reindeer skins and long twisted narwhal tusks. He came near to folk and peered at them, then laughed. The sailors seemed too sober by comparison, and hardly had a word to say. They stared at the Greenlanders, in fact, and stood like dolts around the Gardar field, as if they had never seen a cathedral, or a byre, or a hall such as the great Gardar hall, or sheep and goats and cattle grazing about the hillsides, or horses in their pens, or the landing spot, or the fjord itself, or the high dark mountains that rose all about. When Ivar Bardarson brought out cheese and sourmilk and boiled reindeer meat and dried sealmeat—a feast, in the view of most of the Greenlanders—they gazed at that for a long time before they began to eat it.

Asgeir said to Thorleif, "Are your men such farmboys that they've never seen wealth like this before?" and Gunnar thought Thorleif would choke from laughing at this joke.

"Nay, Greenlander," he finally replied. "It is only what they have heard about this place. Some folk say that all Greenlanders are a little bluish, which is why you are called Greenlanders. And other folk say that you live on a diet of ice and salt water, and such a diet sustains you through your being accustomed to it."

Now Asgeir grinned a wide grin, and said, "These things may be true of Herjolfsnes men, for they live far to the south and keep to themselves. You will have to see for yourself."

"Perhaps I will. Our voyage was not so short that I can return this summer, as I had hoped." Thorleif looked about and laughed again. Asgeir said, "Most folk do not laugh at the prospect of a Greenland winter."

"But they may laugh at the prospect of telling tales upon it for the rest of their lives."

The trading went quickly, and there was little fighting. Farmers from as far away as Siglufjord and Alptafjord appeared with their goods, and Thorleif seemed always to have more to offer. The Gunnars Stead folk had much to trade, because Asgeir had raised and sheared many sheep and Hauk had been three times to the Northsetur. The large boat they brought to Gardar was full of walrus hide rope, vats of blubber, feathers, down, and hides. When Thorleif returned a second time to negotiate about the tusks, Asgeir made him sit down and brought out a round of cheese. "Now, shipmaster," he said, "you must try this, if you think the Greenlanders live upon salt water and ice, and then you must tell me some news. We Greenlanders have been pushing these goods out of our way for ten years now. It is you who have the real wealth, and that is news of other places."

"That is such a coin as you might be sorry to receive, when you have heard what I have to tell."

"Nevertheless, you must tell it."

"Has a great pestilence not come to you here in Greenland?"

"No more than usual, though not so many years ago bad conditions drove folk out of the western settlement, and they have settled among us here."

"The hand of God has not fallen heavily upon you?"

"Shipmaster, the hand of God rests heavily upon the Greenlanders, and that is a fact."

Now the two were interrupted by an acquaintance of Asgeir's, named Lavrans Kollgrimsson, of Hvalsey Fjord. Folk considered Lavrans rather foolish, but good-hearted, and Asgeir shared in this estimate. He offered Lavrans a bit of cheese.

"Nay," said Lavrans. "I am here about this bearskin business, and will stand before this Norwegian until he gives me what I desire."

Thorleif replied, "Old man, you are a fool. Folk tell me you had considerable trouble for this bearhide, and yet all you want for it is a length of red silk, no wheel hubs nor pitch nor iron goods."

"It would have been a great thing to send a live bear back to the king of Norway, as Greenlanders did in former days, but the animal died in my cowbyre, though not before it maimed a servant of mine. Nevertheless, I have my heart set on this bit of shining red, for no one in all of Greenland has such a possession. My wife is with child again, and it is no secret that she has lost the other three. Perhaps it will be good luck to have this banner from afar waving over her bedcloset when she comes to her time. I cannot be dissuaded." And so Thorleif agreed to trade the silk, which he had brought for the see of Gardar, to Lavrans Kollgrimsson, a poor farmer from a poor district. Folk said Lavrans had gotten little for the trouble he had taken with the bear, but Lavrans, as always, paid no attention to the opinions of his neighbors. Now Osmund Thordarson, of Brattahlid, who also had a bearskin, and furthermore, a big one he had taken from the bear in the wilds, got two sacks of oatseed, one iron ax head, a vat of pitch, and a knife with a steel blade. But Osmund was known as a lucky man, who stepped forward and spoke up in all things. His mother's brother, Gizur Gizursson, was the lawspeaker, but it was well known that Osmund knew the laws better than any man in Brattahlid district.

What with the trading and bargaining, it was well toward nightfall before Thorleif had the breath to tell his news, and then it was wondrous news indeed. For the wrath of God had indeed descended upon the Norwegians, and not only upon them, but upon all others in the world as well, man and woman and child, rich and poor, country folk and town folk. It was such an ill that no one had ever seen the like of it: there were families, said Thorleif, who were healthy at dinner and died before daybreak, all together; there were whole districts, where every soul in every parish, excepting only one child or one old man, died within days. The streets of Bergen were less crowded during the sailing season, he said to Asgeir, who had been there, than they had once been in the dead of winter. Every sailor had lost parents or children or wife or brother; every sailor had seen the trains of penitents going from town to town, raising a great roar of prayers and alms-begging. Thorleif had seen the death ship itself, a little ship that floated into Bergen harbor from England—all of the sailors had the mark of death upon them, and then all were dead, and then folk in the town began to die off, and others fled, but the pestilence followed them into every valley and up every fjord. And there was more: poisoned wells and folk burned at the stake, priests found dead upon their altars and corpuses lying in the streets with no one to gather them into their graves, or to say a last prayer over them. Had none of this touched the Greenlanders? It had not. The sailors marveled at this, but in their turn, the Greenlanders were struck speechless and went off to their homes and considered these tidings for many days.

Ivar Bardarson, who was a great friend of Asgeir, found Thorleif an entertaining companion, and brought him to Vatna Hverfi to visit with Asgeir rather often, and Asgeir answered Thorleif's questions with glee. How was it the Greenlanders were so big and fat? (Plenty of sealmeat.) How did they do without bread? (Plenty of sealmeat.) Why did their houses have so many rooms and passageways? (The better to be warmed by seal oil lamps.) Why were the sheep and goats so big and the cows and horses so small? (Because they always had been so, since Erik the Red brought his shiploads of settlers from the west coast of Iceland.) What did the Greenlanders do for a bishop? (They waited, as they had been waiting for ten years, since the death of the last bishop, Arni.) Why did the Greenlanders have no ships? (The law of the king and a dearth of wood.) Nor did they have any cats, or chickens, or pigs, though some farmers had a fine breed of deerhound that Thorleif admired. The Greenlanders were so poor in weapons, how did they manage to hunt? (Even the best hunters, like Hauk Gunnarsson, used snares and traps more than spears or arrows.) Nor did they have any swords. Thorleif marveled. "There are other ways to settle disputes," Asgeir told him, "and Greenlanders prefer the peaceable ones no more than anyone else."

"And how," Thorleif said more than once, "have you escaped this pestilence that haunts the rest of the world?" For this, Asgeir had no answer.

Some sailors wintered in Vatna Hverfi district, and one of these, a boy named Skuli Gudmundsson, stayed at Gunnars Stead. He was very deft, and he always had a bit of wood in his hands, or some soapstone. He carved Margret a spindle whorl in the shape of a grinning face, which Ingrid said was sinful and idolatrous. For Asgeir he carved a set of chessmen. Even so, he had little to say of interest, for he had lived at his father's farm near Bergen until the very day he went off with Thorleif on the ship to Greenland.

It happened that the autumn of this year was an especially prosperous one for Asgeir. The grass stood high in the fields, there were many lambs to be slaughtered, Hauk brought back so much sealmeat and blubber from the autumn seal hunt that the drying racks bowed beneath it, and so Asgeir declared his intention to give a Yule feast for the priest Ivar Bardarson, Thorleif, and his cousin, Thorkel Gellison, who had just come into possession of his steading in the southern part of Vatna Hverfi district. And it was the case that Asgeir had given no feast at Gunnars Stead since his homecoming feast to celebrate his marriage to Helga Ingvadottir.

One night, when Hauk and Ingrid and the other members of the household were sitting about, Asgeir went to the storeroom and came back with a vat of honey, which he had gotten from Thorleif in exchange for two walrus tusks. The others sat forward where they were dozing or occupying themselves with game counters, and Hauk said, "It seems to me that we are not about to dish this onto our sourmilk."

"Nay, indeed," said Asgeir, and he mixed all of this honey, which was a great quantity, with some fresh water and with some measures full of rotten bilberries, and then he put it away.

Ingrid looked at him, and said, "This mead-making will have ill results."

"It will be a good surprise for Ivar Bardarson," replied Asgeir.

"You think to impress the shipmaster with the acquirements of the Greenlanders. Greenlanders always run after folk from other lands as if they were saints in heaven."

"We know what is suitable to a feast, as others do, and if we may supply it, then it is pleasant to do so."

"At least we will see," said Ingrid, "who has the head for drink and who does not."

Now Hauk spoke up and said, "Will the Ketils Stead folk be invited to the feast?"

"If they are not," replied Asgeir, "then Ketil will stand upon his fence and count our guests as they come into the steading, and in his opinion, he will be counting the heads of his enemies. It is better to have him inside the steading, where we can look upon him." It was a fact that though Ketils Stead lay hard by Gunnars Stead, Asgeir and Ketil were ill-assorted neighbors, and always found much to disagree about.

Hauk smiled, and Asgeir looked at him briefly, then said, "My brother, it seems to me that you are looking for a reason to absent yourself from the gathering, and seek the wastelands, even in the dead of winter."

"It is certain that there are not a few pursuits I prefer to sitting about the steading with a lot of folk, stifling from the lamps and the talk."

"Even so, you will not find a wife in the wastelands, unless she is a ghost or a snow demon."

Hauk made no reply, and Ingrid spoke up and said, "A wife would be ashamed to go with a man who wears feathered birdskins next to his flesh, as skraelings do."

"And an old woman should be ashamed," said Asgeir, "to notice a young man's undergarments," and he laughed merrily, for he was much pleased at the prospect of his feast, and it seemed to him that he had repaid Ingrid handily for her prediction concerning the mead.

Now the day of the feast came around, and many folk came from Gardar and other farmsteads to Gunnars Stead, and it was Margret's task to help with the serving, but also, of course, to keep her eye on Gunnar. She sat him at a bench with Skuli and Jona Vigmundsdottir, the wife of Thorkel. Margret was a little shy of Jona, though Jona was but a few years older, in part because Jona was married, but largely because Jona had been born in the western settlement. Those folk had come in many small boats, hugging their sheep and goats to their breasts and sitting on what remained of their wealth, carrying tales of year after year of bad weather—rain and ice all winter, wind and wind-blown sand all summer, fights at the Northsetur hunting grounds between Norsemen with their axes and skraelings with their bows and arrows. They had arrived thin and remained thin, most of them, moving to vacated farms in the southern parts of the eastern settlement, or taking service in Brattahlid or at Gardar. Once, Asgeir said, it was the western settlement where the wealthy Greenlanders lived, but now not even the attractions of the Northsetur, where men went to hunt narwhal, polar bear, and walrus, could compensate for the dwindling of stock in the homefield. Men must eat mutton and cheese and drink milk. A diet of wild food makes them demons. Now only a few of the hardiest souls, like Hauk, went to the Northsetur, and most folk sought the eastern wastelands, though the game there was not as plentiful.

Even the fact that Jona had been married at such an early age betrayed her as a westerner, for these farmers from the west were anxious to get their daughters off their hands, and find them places at other folks' tables. Gunnar sat across from her, and Margret set a big basin of sourmilk and a small one of honey between them. Jona had one child, Skeggi, some two winters old, who sat beside her. Gunnar passed the time making faces at the child, and Skeggi, who was a bold, defiant boy, only laughed at whatever Gunnar attempted. Soon some young men from Gardar took places at the bench, and when Margret brought them basins to eat from, they said their names were Olaf Finnbogason and Halldor Karlson. Halldor was another of the boys from the ship, and he and Skuli were much pleased to see one another.

Margret knew of Olaf, though she had never seen him. He was a boy from Brattahlid, whose father had died on a seal hunt one year, and his mother had sent him to Gardar to be made a priest. He was a quiet boy, thick and short of stature, about Margret's own age. His spoon, which he took out of his spooncase rather furtively, was of Greenlandic horn, and a bit of the bowl was broken off, too. The sailor boys had wooden spoons, and Skuli's, especially beautiful, was of carved Norwegian ashwood, decorated with clusters of grapes. Margret had admired it before. She went off to serve some other folk, then sat down beside Gunnar to eat her own meat.

Skuli and Halldor had dipped portions of honey onto their sourmilk, and Halldor was saying, in a loud voice, "Who are these Greenlanders that they have never tasted honey before?" To Olaf, he said, "Just because of the color, you think it is horse piss?"

Olaf sat silent, red-faced, and Halldor and Skuli began to laugh. Gunnar joined them. Margret spooned some of the honey onto her sourmilk, and looked encouragingly across at Olaf, but he ignored her. Just then there was a commotion, and Ivar Bardarson could be seen taking something from the sack he had brought. There were three of them, large and roundish, like stones, and about the color of stone, too. The guests muttered and laughed. Ivar Bardarson had brought bread, something most Greenlanders had never seen, for Greenlanders have neither grain nor yeast, and make do with dried sealmeat for their butter. Asgeir stood up with a shout, and called for his servant to bring in the vat. It was a great success. Ivar and Asgeir had each surprised the other, and the guests were more than eager. The Norwegians had tasted no drink in half a year. Some of the Greenlanders had never tasted drink in their lives, as there are no beehives, nor grapes, nor barley in Greenland and men can refresh themselves only with water and milk.

When Margret returned to her place, Olaf was silent, and Jona was talking with Skuli about the voyage.

"How long was your journey?" she said.

"Six weeks, by Thorleif's stick calendar."

"Is that long for such a journey?"

"We were hungry enough when we got here." Skuli and Halldor grinned.

"Were there storms?"

Halldor replied, "Thorleif says that there must be as many storms in every crossing as the ship can bear." Suddenly, Olaf Finnbogason grabbed the basin of honey and poured its entire contents over his meat.

"Ho! Greenlander!" shouted Halldor, loudly enough to attract the attention of folk at other benches. "You have doused your meat in the horse piss and left none for the rest of us!" And he brought his fist down on Olaf's spoon, which lay between the two of them. The handle of the spoon broke off at the bowl. First Gunnar, then Skeggi, then even Jona began to laugh at Olaf's embarrassment, for his face truly flushed purple to his hairline. Other folk smiled and called out. Margret stood up, but really she didn't know what to do, because all of the Gunnars Stead spoons were being used for serving, and anyway, it was customary for a man to carry his own spoon about with him. Just then, Skuli Gudmundsson exclaimed, "Halldor, it is always the case that you make more trouble than pleasure," and he reached his foot under the eating board and kicked Halldor backwards off the bench. Then, amidst the gasping and laughter of the guests, he pushed his ashwood spoon across to Olaf and said, "Have this one, Olaf Finnbogason. It is carved of sturdy wood, and will fit in your spooncase, to boot." Olaf muttered his thanks, and stared at the elaborate spoon, but did not pick it up.

The steading was in a great uproar. It seemed to Margret that everyone was shouting, and she was not surprised when Gunnar climbed upon her lap and nestled fearfully there. All about, men were calling out to one another, smiling, scowling, and pouring down the mead, which Margret herself had tasted and found too sweet. Asgeir's face was as florid and shiny as anyone's, and Margret could see him, thumping the shipmaster repeatedly on the back. Margret had never seen her father behave in this way. Margret hugged Gunnar tightly.

Now it happened that Ingrid appeared and herded the children, including Jona and Skuli and Halldor, into one of the other rooms of the steading, where there were two bedclosets. All sat down in the doorways of the bedclosets and prepared to listen to a tale.

Ingrid told them one of her best, the tale of Thorgils the foster son of Orrabein. Even Jona sat open-mouthed at the familiar story of the big ship leaving Iceland with Thorgils and his folk, some thirty of them. They sailed late in the season into a huge storm, and the seas were so high that heaven itself disappeared from sight, unless you were to lie down in the bottom of the boat and look straight up. Two thralls were carried overboard by waves and another would have been had Thorgils not caught him by the shirt just as the wave took him. It happened that the storm lasted many days and nights, which proved that it was a magical storm, the fruit of a curse, and indeed they were cursed, for they were cast up on the eastern coast of Greenland, far from the settlements, and their ship was broken up in the ice floes. Before the onset of winter, Thorgils and his folk managed to build a booth and to kill some of the many seals that frequented the area, and indeed, the seals were not seals, because they smiled like men and came close to the booth. The folk inside could hear the swishing and flapping of the seals as they walked round and round the booth. But men have to eat, so they did eat the sealmeat, although Thorgils' old mother said that they were the souls of the men who had been washed overboard. In that year many of Thorgils' party died of the bleeding disease, but Thorgils' wife gave birth to a son, who was called Thorbjorn.

One day Thorgils sent his steward to fish with the thralls, while he himself climbed up to the nearest icefield to get a view of the pack ice. When he returned, he found the steward and thralls to have disappeared, taking the ship's boat and all the stores of food. Thorgils' wife, they discovered, lay upon a bench in the booth, murdered, and the baby was suckling the corpus.

At this, though all Greenlanders know the story quite well, for it is a true story, the children let out little cries, and Margret shivered.

Thorgils took his knife and cut into his own nipple and put the baby to suck. First came blood, then clear serum, then, at last, milk, and Thorgils suckled his own child thereafter, and discovered for himself what is possible in Greenland, where folk must learn new ways, or die.

Now the outcry in the hall had settled down, and Ingrid said that it was far past bedtime. The hall of the farmhouse was in great disarray, with benches pushed back and overturned and men and women slumped where they sat, asleep. Ingrid looked about. "Indeed, it is unlikely that this will be the only mess to clean up from this mead drinking."

Sometime later, the news got about the district that Sigrun Ketilsdottir had been raped by one of Thorleif's men, Ragnar Einarsson, on the night of the feast. Some folk said that Ragnar might not have been the first accused, had Sigrun been differently disposed in the past, but others said that Thorleif's men did not all comport themselves as well as they might, and, furthermore, sailors are what they are.

It happened that one day Ketil and his son Erlend surprised Ragnar in the southern part of the district, where he was overwintering with some Greenlanders, and they abducted him to Ketils Stead and beat him. Only the intervention of their servants prevented them from killing the sailor in anger, thereby having to pay compensation rather than receiving it.

Now it was well into Lent, but Ivar Bardarson left Gardar and came to Gunnars Stead on skis, and he and Asgeir decided between them that the case must be settled quietly in Vatna Hverfi district, and not taken to the Thing, where most cases were settled. No need to let matters stew until the summer, said Ivar, for it was not such a large incident, although Ketil might make it so. Ketil was well known to be a litigious man. The two went early the next morning around the hill to Ketils Stead, and the result was that Ketil received some compensation for the rape of his daughter, amounting to six large sheep, six goats, and three good milking cows from Asgeir, since the drink served at his feast had gone to Ragnar's head, and from Thorleif's store of untraded goods he received a small amount of barley seed, a vat of pitch, and four iron wheel hubs. Ragnar was allowed to leave Ketils Stead and return to Gardar, where, some folk said, Thorleif ought to finish what Ketil and Erlend had begun. But Thorleif simply laughed at Ragnar's stupidity and did nothing.

As soon as the snow melted and the grass greened in the spring, Asgeir had the south end of the cowbyre torn down. The cows were carried out into the homefield. This spring there was no hay left at all, but the grass turned early, and a few of the younger cows were able to stand up almost as soon as Asgeir and Hauk set them down. Others were not so sturdy, but Asgeir said that they would eat their way back to health, and put Gunnar and some of the other boys to pulling the moist grass and carrying it to the leaner beasts. After four days all the cows but one old one were on their feet and grazing in the homefield. That was not much of a loss for one winter, and the sheep and goats, too, had lasted well, without sickness. Skuli Gudmundsson said that his father, and other farmers in his district in Norway, did not hold with walling up the cows for the winter, and Asgeir was surprised at this, for it is well known among the Greenlanders that in addition to winter grass being unsuitable for a cow's stomach, winter light hurts their eyes and has been known to blind more sensitive beasts. Skuli said he had never heard such things.

Margret was extremely fond of her uncle, Hauk Gunnarsson, and in this spring, as Hauk was not going often to the wastelands, they spent a good deal of time together in the hills above the farmstead. They were of like temperament, and sometimes they went for an entire day without speaking. Such days were a relief to Margret, for the nurse Ingrid was always chiding her to speak up, or to adopt softer ways, for soon enough she would be wanting a husband, and it was good to develop pleasing habits early.

Hauk's hunting prowess was well known among the Greenlanders, and Asgeir had joked more than once that he was not going to be the one who probed into what skraeling tricks his brother might have taken up. There was no telling what a Christian man could learn from the demons in the north. Nor did Margret ask questions, but she watched with eager, though veiled, curiosity, every time he set a snare or a trap, every time he fingered a bit of a plant, or plucked it and put it in his pocket. She followed in like manner his gliding, calm, and silent gait, and emulated the utter stillness of his posture when he paused to listen for the sound of a hare or a fox in the underbrush. She had seen him, in other times, bend suddenly and pick up a hare by the leg or a fox by the neck, but he denigrated his own skills—skraelings, he said, could stand still as a stone over a seal's breathing hole, sometimes for two days and nights, and even then have the wit to sense the seal rising through the water and fling a harpoon suddenly downward to make the kill. A skraeling man could walk over ice in the fjord so quietly that the seals swimming below would not hear him, sharp as they were. "It may be," he said, "that we Greenlanders, with our sheep and our cows and our great stone churches are not so well off as we think, and the skraelings, with their howling dogs and everlasting moving about are not so badly off as we think." And that was all Margret ever heard him say on the subject.

One day, the sailor boy, Skuli, came up to Margret and handed her a bird cage that he had made from willow withes, and he told her only that her uncle had asked him to make it, and showed him the proper shape. Margret thanked him for his work, and her uncle came up behind her, and nodded at it, but he did not say what it was for. Some days later, when Margret was in the hills with Hauk, and he was laying snares for ptarmigan, she saw him do a thing that she had never seen a man do, and that was to reach out to a lark perched on a branch of birch and take the bird in his hand. Then he closed his other hand gently over it, and put it in his pocket. When they returned to the steading, he took it, still living, out of his pocket, and put it in Margret's cage. "Now," he said, "when the bird sings to you, think of his song as your uncle telling you a tale, for if it had been up to me to choose a shape to be born in, I would have chosen such a shape as this."

Now Skuli went back to Gardar, and he gave Gunnar a great parting gift, such a gift as belonged to no child in the eastern settlement—a carved model of Thorleif's ship, with six men sitting in it and a sail made of gray wadmal that could be taken down and put up again, and Thorleif himself standing in the bow. The tiny mouth of the figure was open, as if it were laughing. He also had a small gift for Asgeir, a tiny knob of soapstone in the shape of a seal, as smooth and shiny and wet-looking as the real thing, Asgeir said.

Thorleif and his men were hard at work tarring and repairing their ship, and sewing up rents in the sail, even though there was still a great deal of drift ice in Eriks Fjord. Thorleif, Asgeir, and Ivar Bardarson spoke of the winter, as men must when they meet for the first time in the spring. The hall at Gardar had been covered, almost completely, by a snowdrift, all through Yuletide and a while thereafter. "Not so bad," said Ivar, though Thorleif rolled his eyes. Had not an old couple in Isafjord died of cold inside their own steading, with seal oil still in the lamps? "Isafjord folk," said Asgeir, "expect the worst and, often as not, receive it."

The feast of St. Hallvard came on and Margret was twelve winters old. Thorleif, for all his declarations, lingered at Gardar, and his sailors were about Vatna Hverfi district, still. Margret, Ingrid said, must stop her wandering about the hillsides and tend to her weaving and her spinning and to the making of such provisions as all women devote their lives to. And Gunnar. Asgeir glowered down at Gunnar. Gunnar must not grow up sitting about the steading and telling tales to the servingwomen, but must turn his hand to such farm work as he was capable of.

And this, too, was to be the case, that Gunnar was not to sleep in Margret's bedcloset any longer. He might sleep with Karl, one of the younger servants, or by himself.

"Not even dogs sleep by themselves," said Gunnar. But he would not sleep with Karl, and so he lay by himself every night in the big bedcloset that had horseheads carved upon it.

Now it happened that the young man Olaf Finnbogason came around the hill from the landing place at Undir Hofdi church, and Asgeir said that he had come to teach Gunnar to read, and that Gunnar could have Olaf in his bedcloset with him if he cared to. And Gunnar took a small soapstone basin off the eating board and threw it against the stones of the wall, but he was not punished, and everyone went out of the steading, and when Gunnar came out later, they were all hard at work.

Olaf received as payment from Asgeir a new shirt, new stockings, and new shoes. He was given a bedcloset, a place at the bench, and his own cup and trencher. He brought the ashwood spoon that Skuli had given him and two books from Gardar. For seven days he sat with Gunnar for a while each morning and showed him the books. Gunnar said that they were poor things, and teased Olaf unceasingly about going outside, or eating something, or getting a drink, or any of a number of activities that Gunnar preferred to puzzling out the words that Olaf set for him. Finally, Asgeir said that they might put the books away for a day or so. On that day, Olaf helped manure the homefield, and Gunnar helped scrape the second field for seeding with the barley and oatseed Thorleif had traded to them. On the following day, Asgeir awoke early to find that the cows had broken into the homefield, and the farm folk spent most of the day rounding up cows and repairing the stone fence. After that, Asgeir said that reading was a winter amusement, but that Olaf needn't return to Gardar until the old priest asked for him.

Sigrun Ketilsdottir was now far along with her child by Ragnar Einarsson. It was also the case that Ketil's flock had been hard hit by disease during the winter, and five of the six sheep he had received as compensation had died. Of this event, Erlend Ketilsson, who liked to go about the district and put his feet under other folk's tables, had much to say. Asgeir shrugged his shoulders and pointed to his own healthy flock. Many folk said that Ketil had not been blessed in his children. Only luck, they said, had preserved Sigrun from motherhood before this, and Erlend was a blowhard and a complainer. Nevertheless, folk thought that Ragnar Einarsson would do well to marry Sigrun and settle at Ketils Stead, or even to take Sigrun back with him to Norway. Sigrun herself said, "Folk live prosperously in Norway as well as in Greenland." But Thorleif said that as far as he knew, none of his sailors had come to Greenland to find a wife. It was certain that Thorleif and his sailors were eager to begin their return journey. Their ship was fully repaired and made ready, and Thorleif was collecting provisions and finishing his trading.

It was the custom, from time to time, for Greenlanders from all parts of the eastern settlement to gather far to the south, at the mouth of Alptafjord, where there were great birdcliffs, and many eggs in the spring. Asgeir, for one, considered these eggs a treat, and there was always the opportunity for much talk with folk from the south. In this spring, he was moved to go to the egg gathering for the first time in a number of years, and declared that Margret and Gunnar would go along. They would stay with Thord Magnusson in Siglufjord, near the hot springs. Thorkel Gellison, too, would go.

The nesting sites were on the seaward face of the island. West of this island, Thorkel told Gunnar, was Markland. The open ocean, which Gunnar had never seen before, was deep and blue, and it beat against the birdcliffs with a roar. There was no birch scrub, nor any other vegetation—the cliffs glared white in the high sunlight, alive and teeming with skuas and gulls. The skies resounded with bird cries and the rush of beating wings.

Gunnar carried a small willow basket full of moss with a loop to hang it over his shoulder, and Asgeir firmly grasped him by the hand and pulled him up the slippery rockfaces toward the nesting grounds. Ahead of them, Kristin, the wife of Thord Magnusson, and her two children scattered over the cliff. Kristin was very quick. She would raise her basket and shout, then bend down and pick up one or two of the eggs in the nest, which she would weigh in her hand and hold up to the sunlight. Some she kept and others she set back into the nest. Asgeir said to Gunnar that these were too old—the birds inside them had already begun to grow. He picked one up and weighed it in his hand, then cracked it. Inside was a yellow mass with feet and a beak that Gunnar could make out. Asgeir picked up another and held it up to the light for Gunnar. There were no shadows through the translucent shell. Asgeir nodded and Gunnar placed it in his basket. When, a while later, Gunnar showed Asgeir that he had gathered ten good eggs, Asgeir looked at him and said, "My son, were there eggs to be gathered every day, I might have some hope for you."

Sometime later, Asgeir took Gunnar by the hand and eased him down the side of the cliff. Below him, drawn up on the strand, were many other boats from many other farms in the eastern settlement. Folk were standing about on the sand, talking and eating. Emboldened by Asgeir's praise, Gunnar said, "My father, can all of these folk be Greenlanders?"

"By Ivar Bardarson's estimation, there are some hundred and ninety farms in the eastern settlement alone, and that was before the coming of folk from the west, too. Ivar Bardarson has talked of writing a great account of the Greenlanders, through which all the folk of the world will learn what is really the case with us."

"Then Ivar Bardarson has learned to read, like Olaf?"

"And to write a fair hand and make pictures for decorating his words. It is a fine skill."

Gunnar sat with his sealmeat and his pieces of cheese and pondered this.

Now someone came down the cliff, shouting that a party of men had cornered Thorleif and one of his sailors, who were also gathering eggs on the cliffs, and were threatening to kill the Norwegians. Asgeir set down his dish and said, "It is always the case with Ketil Erlendsson that he carries his discontents with him wherever he goes." And he and Thorkel and Thord and some other men picked up what small weapons they had amongst them and went off.

It happened a few days later that Ivar Bardarson appeared at Gunnars Stead with Thorleif. The shipmaster had a large bruise on his face and walked with a limp. Asgeir and Ivar sat him down at his refreshments, and then sat down with him, one on either side. Thorleif was not laughing. Asgeir said, "Eat your meat, my Thorleif, and listen to this. The woman gets bigger, and Ketil says that she is worth more now. A vat of pitch and two wheel hubs, as well as six more healthy sheep."

Thorleif shifted in his seat. "Ragnar has been paid no compensation."

"And it seems to me," said Asgeir, "that the trades I made last summer have been costly ones, when I add in these payments over the winter."

"Even so, Ragnar received nothing for his first beating, and now he has been beaten again," said Thorleif. "Perhaps the Greenlanders are in the habit of these beatings. Even so, I do not pay out my goods for the pleasure of limping about. And Ragnar is a valuable man to me."

"This business has made ill dealings in the district. Ketil's eyes are opened to every imagined slight."

Thorleif shrugged. "We are off soon enough."

Ivar said, "Others are annoyed as well as Ketil. Your sailors have eaten a great deal over the winter. Folk would like to see what they are getting for this."

Thorleif made a gesture to push away his trencher, but Asgeir filled it again with a smile, and said, "Indeed, enjoy yourself, shipmaster."

Early the next morning, when Thorleif was asleep, some men began to gather outside the farmstead. They carried various knives and clubs and other weapons, and spoke quietly among themselves. When Ingrid arose and saw them, she roused Gunnar and Margret, and hurried them to the bath house, but she could not stop Gunnar from watching. In fact, there turned out to be no fighting. When Thorleif came out of the steading to wash himself, he stood still before the array, then laughed loudly enough. Later, the Greenlanders dispersed. When Hauk Gunnarsson returned two days later from the wastelands, Asgeir told him that Thorleif and his sailors and a party of Greenlanders would be traveling to Markland for the purpose of bringing back timber, for Ketil had demanded this further compensation, and many Greenlanders were eager to take advantage of such a trip as had not been made in years.

Once the journey had been decided on, Thorleif regained his good humor, saying to Ivar Bardarson that a journey to Markland would last him even more years in the telling than a journey to Greenland. It was well known that the forests of Markland were rich in sable, black bear, marten, and other desirable furs, and Thorleif looked forward to making his fortune. The ship had been readied to return to Norway, and so the journey was quickly begun. Many boats accompanied it to Herjolfsnes, and many pairs of eyes watched the red and white sails disappear under the horizon. The Greenlanders who went along included Hauk Gunnarsson, Odd, the brother of Thord of Siglufjord, Osmund Thordarson, who had been to Markland once before, Ketil Erlendsson, and his son Erlend. But it may be fairly said that all the Greenlanders were tempted to go, for every Greenlander knows of the famous adventures of Leif Eriksson and his kin, and of the paradise to be found in the west.

One day toward the middle of summer, when the ship had been gone for a little time, a servingwoman came from Ketils Stead to Gunnars Stead, seeking Ingrid, with word that Sigrun Ketilsdottir had come to her confinement, and that the women of the farm were unable to bring on the birth. She went off with them in spite of the ill feeling between the two farmsteads, and Margret went with her.

Ketils Stead was a large farm with a number of advantages. Austfjord lapped at the foot of the homefield and there was excellent fishing right outside the farmhouse. The homefield, though, had a northerly slope, and was late, every year, to turn green. Ketil's horses were seaweed eaters, which, Asgeir said, made them hard to handle. Ketils Stead was within sight of another farm, which belonged to the church at Undir Hofdi. For this reason, Ketil tended to look to Gunnars Stead when he coveted more land, or so Asgeir often said.

Sigrun Ketilsdottir was white, and except for her large belly, as bony as a cow at the end of winter. She lay with her eyes closed between the pains, and each pain seemed to wring her out. The women sat about her. Ingrid went up and took her hand and said, "My Sigrun, it seems to me that the child will be a big one, for it has been eating you up from the inside. But it will sleep well and thrive, once it is born." Sigrun nodded and was taken with another pain. Behind her, Margret heard one of the farm women mutter, "She has been seized by ghosts, no matter what folk say about sleeping and thriving." And another woman said, "This child here has more flesh on her bones."

It seemed to Margret that Sigrun's belly lay over her like a whale, smothering her, for no matter how the women pulled her up, or propped her, Sigrun sank down without strength beneath the weight. The first pains had come at evening meat, two nights before, and the waters shortly after that. Margret gleaned from the farm women's whispered conversation that they had little hope for either mother or child.

But Ingrid had a good reputation in the district for delivering at difficult births, and she went about her business in the usual fashion. She smoothed the coverlet and untangled Sigrun's gown, made sure there were no knots in her clothes. The door and the window to the steading were open, and the women walked in and out with their spinning. Sometimes Ingrid offered the laboring girl a warm drink of ground dulse mixed with some other herbs. She slipped a small knife under the straw of the bedcloset, to cut the pains. The afternoon went on, and toward suppertime, Ingrid reached into Sigrun and felt the baby's head with the tips of three of her fingers. The servingwomen ran to get a clean sheepskin for catching the baby, and Ingrid sent for Nikolaus the Priest from Undir Hofdi. Sigrun had ceased screaming, although anyone could see the contractions under her gown. But they seemed not to be a part of the woman in the bedcloset, whose eyes were almost closed, and who let the warm hearty seaweed mixture dribble out of the corners of her mouth nearly as fast as the servingwoman could pour it in. All the women were full of sighs now. Night fell, and Nikolaus the old priest came after his evening meat and stood beside the bedcloset and prayed in a way that told everyone the outcome.

The women held Sigrun up by the shoulders and the back to ease the passage of the baby, and she was utterly without strength. The baby was born, caught on the sheepskin, and wrapped quickly in a length of fine wadmal. It was not large at all, and it frightened Margret to look at it, with its slanting eyes and black hair growing all down its back. After it was born, Sigrun began to pour forth bright red blood, drenching her shift and the straw of the bedcloset, and then she was dead.

The child was taken to Vigdis, one of the farm women who had given birth to a child in the late winter, and put to the breast, but Vigdis said that it didn't know how to suck, and finally the women had to drip ewe's milk into its little mouth through the shaft of an eagle's quill. Nikolaus the Priest christened the baby Ketil and agreed that it would die.

But the child did not die, as it happened, and Vigdis succeeded in feeding it full of rich ewe's milk. Not only that, it passed two large black stools, and in all ways began to look more like any other child. Vigdis and her own baby, Thordis, who was fat and cheerful, moved into the steading with the new one. Now it was reported that for three nights running, the ghost of Sigrun walked about the farmstead and came inside to seize the baby. And so Vigdis placed her own Thordis in the cradle, and when Sigrun laid hands upon her, Thordis screamed lustily, and Vigdis leapt from her bed and wrestled the ghost to the ground, saying, "Sigrun, your child has been baptized in the name of Christ, and must live." After this, Sigrun's ghost departed from Ketils Stead, and Vigdis was widely praised for her resourcefulness.

In Markland, meanwhile, the travelers were commending themselves on how well their journey had gone—fair winds, excellent hunting, and much timber to be found in those dark, dense forests, and the only signs of skraelings were at least a year old. Each night, the sailors sat about the fire they had made, and the Greenlanders sat about the fire they had made, but these fires were not so far apart that the two parties could not speak in a friendly way to one another, nor reply to observations the other party might make. Men's trenchers were so full of roast meat that they could not eat it all, and all were content.

One night, Thorleif asked what manner of beings these skraelings were, and Osmund Thordarson, the only man who had traveled to Markland before, replied that he had never seen skraelings in Markland, himself, but the tales of them were that they were large and fierce. Early expeditions to the Markland coast had seen much fighting. Surely Thorleif had heard of Karlsefni's famous voyage, when men had hoped to settle in Markland and build farms there? Thorleif had not. The short of it was that Karlsefni found the land rich and mild—the cattle stayed out in the fields all winter, for one thing, as there was no snow—but in the spring skraelings came in fleets of canoes, waving staves that made a great whistling noise, and they came with many, many skins, anxious to trade, especially for red cloths, and as always with skraelings, the Norsemen could cut the cloth into smaller and smaller pieces, but the skraelings would trade as much for the small as for the large. And then Karlsefni's bull came out of the woods and bellowed, and the skraelings ran off in terror.

The Norsemen laughed at the ignorance of these demons, but, Osmund said, they were not laughing so heartily when the skraelings returned three days later, and in greater numbers—numbers so great that the water was black with their boats, and this time they were waving their staves in the other direction, and they stormed upon the land and attacked, and they had so many and such strange weapons, and they knew so well how to use them, that the Norsemen took to their heels this time, and, Osmund reminded Thorleif, this was in early days, when iron wasn't so scarce, and all men carried axes and swords and shields, as well.

There was with the party a woman named Freydis, who was the daughter of Erik the Red and the sister of Leif the Lucky, and she had been resting in her booth. When she heard the commotion, it was said, she came out of the booth and shouted her contempt after the fleeing Norsemen, but they did not turn to aid her, so she made her way after them, though she was with child and feeling poorly. The skraelings pursued her. But the fact was that she happened upon the corpus of one of the Norsemen, and she grabbed the sword from his hand and turned. The skraelings were nearly upon her, but she pulled the front of her gown back from her breasts, and beat the flat of the sword upon her chest, yelling all the while, and the skraelings were frightened by this display, and fled.

Thorleif found this tale very diverting.

"The case is," said Osmund, "that Greenlanders have been back and forth to Markland time and again since then, and the skraelings in Markland have always been just as numerous and unpredictable as they were in the beginning, and the Greenlanders have been steadily less numerous and less well armed, so it is not a land that Greenlanders feel at home in, though it is a more welcoming land than their home."

Now Hauk Gunnarsson spoke up, and said that the skraelings in the waste parts of Greenland were not so fierce nor so strange as these Markland skraelings, and by this time it was late, and so the party of travelers rolled up in their furs and slept.

The next night, Osmund Thordarson spoke up again, and said, "Indeed, Markland is rich enough, though dark withal. And we have found what we sought here."

The men greeted this remark with silence.

Osmund went on. "But few folk have seen such a land as Vinland, which lies to the south."

"Even so," said Thorleif, "I can see far enough. Small islands, narrow straits, and upthrusting rocks make for bad sailing."

The men continued silent, sleepy with their meat.

Now Erlend Ketilsson sat up and leaned forward in the firelight. "It seems to me that this Norwegian has come by a great deal of praise in this past year. What a fine man, what a fine ship, what a lot of goods he has brought us." He fell silent, and some of the Greenlanders set their bowls beside them on the sand. "Mostly, though, folk chatter about what a fine sailor the fellow is, how he might sail through the eye of a Nuremburg needle if he wished. Now this Thorleif sits back and eats up this praise like sourmilk with berries in it."

There was a long pause, when all of the men, Norwegians and Greenlanders alike, were silent, and the silence was filled with the dark sounds of the great Markland forest, and then Thorleif laughed in his usual way, but loudly, and so suddenly that men started in their places. But he made no reply to Erlend, and shortly men went to their rest.

In the morning, Thorleif said, "If this place called Vinland is so rich, it may be that such poor folk as ourselves will want to trade it for Bergen, where many Germans are getting themselves in, or Gardar, even, though Gardar is said by the Greenlanders to be next door to Paradise. But we cannot make this trade until we see the famous spot, can we?"

"It seems to me," said Odd of Siglufjord, "that we would do well to finish our work here and return to Gardar. Only yesterday we considered ourselves rich men, for all the furs and timber we have gotten. And these tales of the skraelings do not make me want to encounter them."

Thorleif looked at Hauk Gunnarsson, but Hauk said nothing, so Thorleif said, "This morning we are poor men again. We are like folk who have gobbled up a lot of rich meat and then hear that a better feast is laid elsewhere."

Osmund pressed them. "We have seen no signs of skraelings in this district, and though men have died seeking Vinland, what sort of men are we if we don't take a look? It is said that the waving grass is as high as a man's waist, and wild grapes are only the best of all the berries to be found there. The cove is full of swimming fish and shellfish of all kinds, and the reindeer herds take days to move past. And all the sorts of timber needed for building a ship grow together in one place."

Erlend said, "Leif the Lucky found himself the Garden of Eden, and that's a fact."

But Odd said, "No priest has ever been to Vinland itself, only to Markland, and so it is not easy to know about the Garden of Eden."

Now Thorleif looked at Hauk again, and Hauk looked at him, and said, "I would like to see it."

So they stacked the piles of timber and buried the furs against scavengers and set out, and for the first day, the sailing was easy and swift. On the second day, however, a storm blew up so suddenly that they had no time to put in among the treacherous islets and chains of rocks, and they were caught. The storm lasted well into the night, the ship was thrown against many rocks, and its planking was dented and cracked. The mast came down, and Ketil Erlendsson and a sailor, Lavrans with the black beard, were killed outright. The lookout was thrown into the sea and drowned, and another sailor was thrown by a wave against the side of the ship with such force that his arm was shattered.

After this misadventure, there was no peace within the group. The lookout had been a sharp-sighted and well-liked man, and Lavrans was related to some of the other sailors. They were not pleased with his death. Ketil, the sailors said, had gotten his deserts for instigating this ill-omened trip to Markland, and for having raised such a flirtatious daughter in the first place. Erlend, they said, was a troublemaker, and it was like the Greenlanders to be influenced by such a person. Thorleif did not put a stop to these arguments, but for himself, he only said, "I am not the first man to seek good fortune and find ill."

The land was well wooded, and materials for repairs were not far to seek. While the sailors went about this business, the Greenlanders lashed together a large vat, filled it with water, dismembered the corpuses, and set to boiling the flesh off the bones so that they could be carried back to Gardar and buried in consecrated ground. Two sailors explored the shore, but the body of the drowned man did not appear, so one of the Greenlanders carved him a runestick, and put this in the sack with the others' bones for burial at the church. By the time the ship was repaired, the Greenlanders and the sailors had little to say to one another.

Thorleif sailed north along the coast, putting in from time to time to look for game or fish, but everything seemed to have vanished, as if by some curse. When, after six days, they found the timber and furs they had gathered, these treasures now seemed somehow of little worth and yet cumbersome. Hauk and a few men went snaring game in this spot, but had no luck. After some debate, because of the lateness of the year, the ship set out with few provisions, only some fresh water and a bit of dried meat. The sailors taunted the Greenlanders, saying, "Tell us your tales, now." But the only tales the Greenlanders knew were of ships that had missed Greenland entirely and found themselves in Iceland, or, worse, Ireland, after weeks of drifting. Had not Thorvald, a mighty Viking hero who sailed with Karlsefni on his famous voyage, been swept to Ireland and enslaved there?

After three days of slow and careful sailing, Thorleif brought them to Bear Island for the night, and here a fight broke out between two of the sailors and two of the Greenlanders, a man from Herjolfsnes and Erlend Ketilsson. Erlend lost two teeth. Osmund tried to prevail on Thorleif to stop the fight, but Thorleif said, "A stopped fight must start again, when men are angrier. If they break each other's bones now, they must kill each other later." In the morning, the travelers awoke, hungry again, to discover that Hauk Gunnarsson had disappeared.

Of all the people on the voyage, Hauk Gunnarsson was friendly only toward Odd from Siglufjord, whom he had known from boyhood. The others he rarely spoke to or even looked at, and the Greenlanders, familiar with Hauk Gunnarsson's ways, did not take this amiss. The sailors, however, spoke ill of Hauk, and accused him of being haughty. One man, especially, named Koll, whose temper was inflamed by the death of his cousin Lavrans, seemed to take great pleasure in baiting Hauk at mealtimes and times of rest. The humor of this fellow Koll was not improved by the diminishing food stocks, but Thorleif exerted no restraint, for that was not his way. Now Koll began suggesting that they would not soon get another wind as good as the one then blowing, and they had better set forth, for obviously, Hauk Gunnarsson had been swept away, or lured away by trolls. The Greenlanders scoffed at this, and replied that Hauk was no doubt hunting.

And, indeed, Hauk Gunnarsson had seen a wealth of birds flying around the cliffs of the island, and had set out to snare some, the work of a morning, but once he was away from the ship, he saw many signs of bears. The tale of his hunting trip is a famous one, for after men ceased going to the Northsetur, the hunting of bears grew rare in Greenland, and few men knew how to come upon them, lure them into the water, and kill them as they were swimming, for unlike the skraelings, the Greenlanders were not adept with skin boats, and did not especially enjoy ice hunting, or sea hunting. Hauk Gunnarsson was crouched down, setting a snare for a bird when he smelled the odor of bear, and then a small she-bear and her single cub came over the cliff near where he was hidden in a cleft. As he stood still, the bear came closer, neither smelling nor seeing him, and he silently removed a loop of walrus hide from his belt, tossed it over the bear's head, and quickly wrapped it around a protruding rock, jerking the bear's head backward. Then he quickly grabbed his short spear and drove it down into the bear's breast, and so quickly did all of this happen that the she-bear made no noise and the cub, foraging farther down the cliffside, did not even look around. After that, Hauk waited behind the she-bear for the cub to return, and when it did, Hauk took the loop of walrus hide, and dropped it over the neck of the cub, as with a dog. The other end he tied to the paw of the she-bear, and then the cub followed along when Hauk dragged the she-bear back to the landing spot, where it was nearly nightfall, and the Greenlanders and the sailors were disputing about whether to sail or not.

The sight of the bear, and the prospect of roast meat, quieted all voices. The cub Hauk gave to Thorleif, who poured the water out of his largest cask and put the bear cub in it. And that is how it happened that one last tamed bear cub came to Bergen, and ended eventually in the Castle of Mehun-sur-Yevre, for the Duke of Berry was a collector of wild animals, and this bear, it is said, lived for many years, and died long after Hauk Gunnarsson himself.

From Bear Island it is six days sail to Greenland, but Thorleif was thrown off course by two storms, and the trip took twice as long. Nonetheless, Thorleif was happy enough to get there with his ship in one piece, for, he said, "With a ship, Bergen is a little closer than it is without a ship."

Hauk cured the hide of the she-bear, and threw it over his bedstead, and this bear hide stayed with the Gunnars Stead folk for many years. Ketil's bones and skull were buried near the grave of Sigrun at Undir Hofdi, and the bones and skull of Lavrans the sailor, as well as the runestick of the drowned man, were interred at Gardar. Many were shocked at the death of Ketil, for he was a prosperous man who had always had pretty good luck. Some said that it was always ill luck to name a child for a living man. Nevertheless, the man Ketil was dead, and the child Ketil Ragnarsson was said to be weakly and ill-favored. After Erlend returned, the farm woman Vigdis remained at the farmhouse with her child Thordis, and she and Erlend lived together as husband and wife, although no priest married them. Erlend, who was cross-grained by nature, became even gloomier, and no one saw the Ketils Stead folk from season to season.

Hauk Gunnarsson had little mind to hunt that season, although he prospered on the autumn seal hunt and snared plenty of birds. For the first time in many years, he helped with the autumn farm work, and with the gathering of seaweed and berries for fodder and storage. He did not prepare for a winter voyage to the hunting grounds, and when the hay was in and the cows were sealed up and the sheep were down from the hills, he sat sometimes with Gunnar and Olaf and looked over their shoulders at the reading books. At Yule, Gunnar took to sleeping in Hauk Gunnarsson's bedcloset and became less friendly than he had been toward Margret and Ingrid.

After Yule, the weather, especially around Gardar, grew very fierce, and there were deep snows so that the sheep could not paw down to the grass. Even the huge stocks of hay that Ivar Bardarson took off his fields were rapidly depleted, and many were glad at a sudden and profound thaw. Asgeir, however, shook his head suspiciously, and indeed, the thaw was quickly followed by a hard frost, which turned the fields to ice and drove the sheep toward the fjords in search of seaweed or other fodder. Many of them lost their footing on the icy cliffs and fell into the sea, where they were drowned or swept away. Ivar Bardarson estimated that he lost a quarter of the Gardar sheep in this way, and two or three of his best horses. Other farmers lost more. At Gunnars Stead, the blizzards were so thick that five sheep suffocated with the snow driven into their mouths and nostrils from all directions, and when the fodder gave out, and even the oat hay from the second field, four cows starved to death. The horses ate what the family ate, especially dried meat and seaweed. One of the servingwomen died from a fall on the ice and one of the shepherds was lost in a storm. It was still unusually cold at egg gathering time, but then the weather broke, and the summer was high and hot. Gunnar was now six years old, and Asgeir spoke of sending Margret down to Siglufjord, to live with Kristin the wife of Thord and learn how women must use their time.

Thorleif made his ship ready for departure. Early in the summer, shortly after egg gathering, the people from Gunnars Stead went over to Gardar to make a few last trades, and watch the loading of goods onto the ship. Now Ivar Bardarson had the Gardar servingmen remove the east wall of the largest storehouse, both turf and stone, for the first time in ten years, and this took a whole day. Then the servingmen and the sailors began carrying things to the ship. The children stood staring, and the adults soon did, too, asking each other who would have thought Greenland to have such wealth. A hundred and twenty-four pairs of walrus tusks wrapped in fine wadmal of a reddish brown color went in first, for they were ivory, and extremely valuable, said Ivar Bardarson, and formed the greater part of the tithe owed by the Gardar bishopric to the pope for the last ten years. Amongst these went forty-nine twisted narwhal tusks, and then, on top of these, cushioning and protecting them, went the two polar bear hides of Lavrans Kollgrimsson and Osmund Thordarson, and three more that men had gotten in the days before the end of the western settlement. These, too, were very valuable, and would probably go to the archbishop in Nidaros or even to the pope himself. On top of these, from one side of the ship to the other and almost from end to end, were laid coils of walrus hide rope, and on top of these, rolls and rolls of woven wadmal, in many shades. Gunnar pointed out to Margret the distinct Gunnars Stead shade, a deep brownish purple, exactly similar to the color of the clothes they were wearing, and Margret said that some of these lengths had certainly been woven by Helga Ingvadottir and gone as Asgeir's tithe to the bishopric. Now the roomy hull of the ship was nearly full, so the sailors laid the planking of the deck over the goods. On top of the planking went piles of reindeer hides and sealskins, blue and white fox furs, a cage containing six white falcons, leather bags full of seal blubber and vats of whale oil, leather bags of dried sealmeat, some butter and sourmilk for the return voyage, and wheels of cheeses for the archbishop of Nidaros from the farms at Gardar. In a special place was a large package wrapped in yellowish wadmal that contained, people said, the furs Thorleif brought from Markland that could not be found in Greenland, and finally, the bear was brought with his cage, where he would spend his time on the journey, although he had been largely tamed by one of Ivar Bardarson's serving youths, who was going along. In addition, a Greenlander from Herjolfsnes was going to learn to be a sailor, and Odd, the brother of Thord from Siglufjord, thought that a fortune might be made with Thorleif. Gunnar asked Hauk if he, too, was going, for Asgeir kept saying that a single man without children would do well to see the world, but Hauk thought little of the world he had heard about, although he said that he would surely go if he could be certain that Thorleif's ship would be blown off course to Vinland. Thorleif was only three sailors short of a full crew (for in addition to Lavrans and the lookout, two sailors had died of a fever). Skuli and another boy had filled out considerably in Greenland, and so he had few worries. They set out, and many people said good riddance. Ingrid said that in her grandmother's youth two and three ships would come to the Greenlanders every season, but Asgeir said this could not have been even in those days, when, everyone knew, Greenland was on the shores of Paradise.

In the summer that Thorleif's ship went back to Bergen, Margret Asgeirsdottir went with Kristin the wife of Thord Magnusson to Siglufjord, and Hauk Gunnarsson declared that it was high time his nephew Gunnar learned to come upon birds and snare them, for even the bones of birds were useful around the farm for needles and hooks, not to mention their meat, feathers, and down. Hauk sat across the table from Gunnar, looking at him. "The birds about the farmstead are wary enough, not like birds in the Northsetur or in Markland, who come to perch on your arms and head if you sit still long enough. But they can still be caught, with a little care." Gunnar nodded, but it seemed to him a tedious thing, to walk about, far up into the hills. Not even the dogs accompanied them, for Hauk preferred to hunt without dogs, as skraelings do.

The two left Vatna Hverfi and hiked westward, up into the mountains behind the church, taking their meat for the day; Hauk refused to carry Gunnar as Margret had, and made him match his own pace as well. When Gunnar was not a little annoyed by this, Hauk met his complaints with even-tempered silence, so that they fell off, and then ceased altogether with the speed and effort of the walking. Once Gunnar yawned. Just then, Hauk said, as if to himself, "All the farm folk will be out in the fields, spreading manure and forking it into the ground. There is a back-breaking day's work, in my opinion." Gunnar plodded behind him.

Soon they had reached barren pebbly ground above the low bilberry bushes that Gunnar knew from his walks with Margret. Here and there, in clefts, grew low birches and scrub willow. Hauk settled himself in one of these clefts without a word, and began fashioning bird snares out of seal gut. These he lay on the ground, covered with pebbles and leaves and neatly attached to bent willow twigs, then he moved Gunnar away, to another cleft, and sat patiently amongst the underbrush. Gunnar, who did not dare speak, fell into a doze. After a while, he was aroused by a loud cackling chorus, and he lifted his head to see his uncle wringing the necks of four brown ptarmigan and lashing them together with a strip of walrus hide. Then he picked up the other snares and beckoned Gunnar to follow him to another spot. Once Hauk said, "Seal gut is the best to use for making snares." Sometime after that he said, "Ptarmigan are good in the winter only for starving men, because their winter flesh is bitter and unappetizing." Gunnar nodded and yawned. He looked with longing at Hauk's pouch of food, for he had seen Ingrid fill it with goat's cheese and dried meat.

When they returned late that evening, Asgeir and Ingrid had already gone to their beds. Hauk hung his thirteen ptarmigan from the eaves of the farmstead, and Gunnar fell asleep on the bench over his evening meat. And so it went on in this wise for four more days, until Hauk told Asgeir that Gunnar had little bent for hunting, and was clumsy and noisy about even the simplest tasks. Although Asgeir did not talk about this, the farm folk said among themselves that he was very angry at the way in which Gunnar was growing up, for Olaf, too, had had no luck in imposing learning on the child, and he was hardly industrious around the farm. He kept to himself, and refused to play with the other children. Nor did he make friends of the horses, as children sometimes did. His early loquacity had vanished, although he could sometimes be heard in Hauk's bedcloset, relating stories to his uncle in an excited tone. All in all, he was lazy and unsociable and he and Asgeir stayed far from each other. Asgeir often had Olaf with him, for Olaf was now grown into a heavyset, low-browed fellow, not much to look at, Asgeir said, but with a natural farmer's touch, especially with the cows. Asgeir was in no hurry to send him back to Gardar and see him become a priest, and Olaf himself did not often speak of Gardar, where, it was said, the priests had to make do without butter, and without milk to drink, while at Gunnars Stead there was plenty of meat of all kinds, and cheese and butter and gathered berries and herbs. At the end of the summer half year, Margret returned from Siglufjord, and the family sat quietly at Gunnars Stead through the winter.

Now it happened in the spring, some four years after the coming of Thorleif, that another ship arrived at Gardar, but this was not a merchant ship, and it carried nothing except a few presents for Ivar Bardarson, some altar furnishings for the cathedral, and news of England, for the master of the ship was an English monk named Nicholas, who had come to Green-land out of curiosity. At the news of this, there was a great deal of talk about curiosity. The bishop, folk said, wasn't even curious about his lands or his farms, much less about his flock, for it had now been twenty years since the death of the last bishop, and many who didn't care to be were surely in a state of mortal sin without knowing it, and a monk could come from England out of mere curiosity, but a bishop could not come to do God's work.

Nevertheless, the Monk Nicholas was a charming man with many stories to tell about the Church, and about life in England since the Great Death and in other places, such as France and among the Dutch, for he was a well-traveled man. Some said that his stories were not those of most monks, for he also knew what the women were wearing and how rich men were furnishing their houses. He asked many questions of the Greenlanders, and encouraged Ivar Bardarson not only to tell him everything he had learned about the eastern settlement and the western settlement, but was eager for him to write it down, as he had spoken of, for, Nicholas said, the people of Europe hardly believed that Greenland existed anymore. And this was the beginning of Ivar Bardarson's project, which lasted the follow-ing winter.

Now it happened one day that the Monk Nicholas appeared at Gunnars Stead, and sought out Hauk Gunnarsson, who was snaring rabbits in the hills, and he was full of questions: How many days' sail was it to the Northsetur? What was the sailing weather like at this time of the year? Was it true that Ivar Bardarson and some men had rowed a boat to the western settlement in six days? How far to the north had Hauk ever gone? What sort of folk were the skraelings there? Did they speak their prayers backward and recoil at the sign of the cross? Was it their clothing that was furry, or were they themselves covered with fur, like beasts? Where was it that the ice turned to fire in the north, as it must according to old books? And all Hauk said to any of these questions about the northern regions was "I know not. The hunting is good there." Later, after Nicholas went back to Gardar, Hauk said, "This fellow seems a fool to me. Any man may hunt in the northern regions, and prosper, but these notions of his have no purpose."

"You may say," Asgeir returned, "that the English are often thus: they talk merely to talk, and go idly on great journeys merely to see the sights."

Some days after this, Nicholas appeared again, and he found Hauk at his morning meat, and he sat down with him at once, and leaned forward and pushed his trencher aside, although Hauk had just been eating from it, and he said, "Hauk Gunnarsson, it is my fixed intention to sail north this summer, and I desire your guidance." Hauk laughed, and said that it was too late in the summer for such a journey.

"But," said Nicholas, "it is my fixed intention to find the Greenland bottoms, and to see such skraelings as may be found, for that is why I have come to Greenland."

Hauk laughed again, and said that he must put off his intention, for it was no one else's intention to comply.

And Nicholas returned a few days later, and he said that he had found a crew of Greenlanders who wished to hunt in the old hunting grounds, and the most prominent of these was Osmund Thordarson, of Brattahlid. Eindridi Gudmundsson and Sigurd Sighvatsson were also eager to go, for they had prospered in the north before. Indeed, many folk remembered the prosperity of the old days, when men went north every year and brought back quantities of walrus hide and narwhal horn, and the settlement was rich in items that the archbishop of Nidaros and the merchants of Bergen cared for. Thorleif had carried away what was stored in the bishop's storehouse, and now folk were hard pressed to pay in sheepskins, cheeses, and wadmal what they had once paid in hides and ropes and horns. Hauk said to Asgeir that Nicholas was like a madman with this project. "The bottoms will be full of drift ice, and soon, anyway, there will be little to see in the dark, whether of ice turning to fire, or skraelings turning to demons." And now Nicholas came again, with Osmund, and they said that the ship was ready. Osmund walked off a little to the side with Hauk, and he said, "The voyage to the Northsetur is little like a voyage to Markland, for the winds are usually favorable, and there is no lack of provisions. Are there not sheep and goats still in the pastures of the western settlement? Indeed, my friend," said Osmund, "you are strangely unwilling, when you yourself have often gone off to the north any time of the year, and stayed there." Now Asgeir came up to them, and he had been talking with Nicholas, and he said, "My brother, will not the sailors be Greenlanders, all except for Nicholas himself? Greenlanders know something about the ways of the ice. And a few walrus tusks and narwhal horns might ease the difficulty of the tithe. It is seven cows we lost last winter, and the sheep cast fewer lambs than they have been doing." And so Hauk Gunnarsson was persuaded to take ship with the Englishman, and guide it north so that Nicholas could have a look at things.

Seven days after leaving Gardar, the ship's crew put in to Lysufjord in the western settlement and rowed to the Sandnes church, where they drew the boat up onto the strand and looked about for a place to rest for a day. The farmsteads were deserted and many roofs and walls had fallen in. The hay in the fields was sometimes thick, but in other places, sand had drifted in. The sheep and goats that the Greenlanders had hoped to find were dead, or had wandered away, but there were many cod in the fjord, and voyagers ate well and bedded down in a large farmstead of many rooms. One man found a spindle whorl and a loom weight where he was sleeping, and he kept them, although many said such abandoned things were ill-omened and would bring misfortune to the journey. In the night, Hauk Gunnarsson, who had said little since leaving Gardar, woke up shouting with an evil dream. In it, he said, a giantess with the face of a walrus was found on a piece of ice, dismembering and eating a little boy, although the boy was still alive. At the telling of this dream, many of the Greenlanders declared that the wisest course would be to end their journey and return to the eastern settlement, but the Monk Nicholas scoffed at their fears, saying that not all dreams were visions, and that many dreams were the result of the previous day's activities, or of something the dreamer chanced to eat. In fact, he said, the coming of the dream in the early part of the night showed that it could not be a vision, for the old books all said that visions could come only toward morning. Nicholas was a man of great learning, and Hauk Gunnarsson declared that he was perfectly willing to go on, and so after another day in the settlement, they rowed out of Lysufjord and began their journey north, away from the settlements and the homes of men.

They coasted north for some days, frequently harpoooning seals or snaring birds or sighting polar bears and reindeer. The Monk Nicholas charted the height of the sun using a peculiar instrument that none of the Greenlanders were allowed to touch, for it was rare and very costly, said Nicholas, and was called an astrolabe. From time to time they sighted the skin boats of skraelings at a distance, but they could not come close enough to the little boats for Nicholas to satisfy his curiosity about these beings.

Now they came to a walrus island that some of the older men had visited before, and they saw that many walrus were hauled out on this island, piled high on top of one another, males, females, and half grown calves, scores upon scores. It seemed to the Greenlanders that this was what they had come north for, to make a walrus kill, and they began talking among themselves about how to go about this hunt. The case was that only Hauk Gunnarsson, Sigurd Sighvatsson, and Eindridi Gudmundsson had knowledge of walrus hunting, but the others were even more eager to try their skill, and so Hauk gave them a plan, and this is what they did.

Some little while before high tide, but after dark, they rowed the boat up to the island and clambered onto the ledge, which stood about two ells above the surface of the water, but would stand about eight ells above the water at low tide. The walruses were in their autumn humor, which is phlegmatic and inattentive, but even so, a few of the bulls would be raising their giant heads and gazing about at all times, so the Greenlanders got down upon their stomachs, and slithered from the shore into the group, and they went without speaking, and were still if any nearby bull lifted his gaze.

Now it happened that the men had spread out, and had their longest spears ready in their hands, and they looked to Hauk, who gave them a signal, and when he gave this signal, the men leaped up and began to run among the walruses, spearing them in their chests and drawing forth their heart's blood, for this is the way a walrus must be killed, not with blows to the head, like seals, for every walrus has a head like a stone, and is invulnerable there. And as soon as the first blows were struck, the walruses all roused themselves and began to heave about, with a great bellowing and scraping of flesh over rock. Some of these beasts did go toward the water, and the men made sure to stay out of their way, but other beasts, in their confusion, went away from the water, and the men pursued them and speared them and the wet rocks were soon slippery with blood. And it was the case that Sigurd Sighvatsson stumbled and fell in front of two bull walruses, and he was speared with their tusks and crushed with their weight, but all of the other Greenlanders kept their feet and no other men were lost.

Now the sun began to come up, and the men began to parley among themselves about the butchering of the beasts, for though a good length of walrus hide rope is a valuable thing, folk get it only at the cost of great inconvenience, at the cost of bathing in the blood of these animals. On the other hand, men may quickly go among their kill and chop off the tusks and faces of the beasts, and half of the Greenlanders wished to arrange things in this way, while others wished to take the rope. Now Hauk Gunnarsson said, "We may butcher until the tide rises again, and take the tusks, or we may butcher until the tide rises the second time and take some of the rope, but by the time of the second high tide, we will expect company, and so we must set lookouts on the shore to watch for bears," for it is the case that in the north, bears come together for one thing only, and that is to eat the walruses that men have killed for them.

But the Greenlanders could not decide, and wasted time wrangling among themselves, and so the first high tide passed before all of the tusks had been cut off, and then it seemed just as well to take some of the hide, so three men stripped down and went among the walruses in their undergarments and began to slice off the skin. And the blood poured forth, and steam rose around the beasts, keeping the butchers warm enough, and soon the men were red and gory from head to toe. Hauk Gunnarsson did not help with this work, but stayed near the shoreline, watching after bears, for he thought he might kill one in the water, but in this he had no luck. Now the tide rose again, and bears began crawling out of the sea, and the men took what trophies they had gained, and went to the boat, and jumped down into it. But when all the men were in the boat, and they had begun to pull away from the shore, it was discovered that the bones of Sigurd Sighvatsson had been left behind through greed for walrus trophies and fear of bears. And this was considered very ill luck, to leave the corpus of a man as food for bears, and to take none of his bones back to Gardar for proper burial.

Nicholas wanted to go farther and farther north, even though the Greenlanders assured him that soon the ship would come to the land at the foot of the Greenland bottom, and they pointed out to him the way that the shore turned westward, and the western shore, too, could be seen in fine weather. And it did seem that they had reached the end of the ocean fjord, and Nicholas was about to turn back, when one morning they awoke to find themselves in a wide fjord or riverlike body of water with a strong current. According to Nicholas, the direction of this fjord headed due north. But night had returned to the land by this time, and the Greenlanders were hesitant about entering far into this northward-tending fjord. When it was time to sleep, Nicholas took Osmund aside, and spoke with him for a long time, keeping him awake, for Nicholas, it appeared, needed no sleep, and was again like a madman about his project, and he harried and chattered at Osmund and Hauk and the rest of the Greenlanders, until they finally agreed to go a day's sail to the north. And that day, many

narwhal were sighted, and in addition four polar bears, and so the Greenlanders thought that hunting might be good here.

They moved forward, avoiding the drift ice, hunting one day for
every day that they sailed, and the Greenlanders were pretty well satisfied,
and at last they came into open sea, and Nicholas said that they were at
the top of the world, judging by the stars and the sun, but the Greenlanders
were inclined to think that they had merely found another large bay. Here
the ship turned around and began to head southward. Now, although it
was only a few days after their northward sailing, the fjord was much fuller
of pack ice, and leads between the floes opened and closed in a matter of
moments. Ice, as every Greenlander knew, could suddenly begin heaving
and exploding into the air as if flung up by the curses of witches and trolls.
From time to time the men had to get out of the ship and drag it over
the ice to open water. It was on one of these trips that they encountered
a group of skraelings in sledges drawn by packs of wolves. These people
could not be approached because of the howling of these wolves, until one
skraeling went amongst his pack and beat at them with a bone club. The
skraelings were carrying piles of narwhal hides and tusks, which the
Greenlanders eyed enviously, but only Hauk Gunnarsson consented to
approach them, for, he said, he knew some of their devilish tongue from
earlier journeys to the north. In the end, the skraelings traded a considerable
number of horns and some seal blubber for two iron-tipped spears and three
of the Englishman's iron-bladed knives, and they appeared to consider
themselves well repaid. One of these knives had a tempered blade and a
silver handle with the figure of St. Matthew on it, and some of the
Greenlanders laughed at the thought of a skraeling with such a knife.
Nicholas grumbled that Hauk would have traded away all of his astronomical instruments, but nevertheless he appeared well pleased with his look
at the devilish skraeling peoples, and declared them certainly to be denizens
of hell, as the old books said. He made the Greenlanders promise to have
the narwhal horns blessed at the cathedral as soon as Gardar was reached.

Now the Greenlanders were anxious to return home, for the days
were shortening quickly, but the ship got among some islands that none
of the Greenlanders had ever seen, where the currents were strong and the
ice thick and deceptive. The ship was fog- and icebound many times, and
the travelers began to despair of their lives at the approach of winter. Only
Nicholas and Hauk Gunnarsson were confident, the one because of the
mercy of God, for which he prayed loudly and long every day, and the
other because he had wintered in the north before, and knew that there
would be much game, even in the dark of the long winter night. But the

others were not as confident, and pressed for continuing the journey south at every possible opportunity.

Now they were having to pull the ship out of the water and across the ice many times in a day, and in the white waste it was hard to tell which way was safe to go, although because of Nicholas' astronomical instruments, they always knew which direction was south and which direction was east. Two men would walk a distance ahead of the ship, where they could be seen but not shouted to, and where they could see but not shout to each other, and they would test the stability of the ice and look for leads between floes. Each man except Nicholas had to do this, for the Monk Nicholas knew nothing about ice. This worked well for many days, and the Greenlanders began to be hopeful that they would find open water and make their way back to the eastern settlement. One of these times, when Hauk Gunnarsson was walking ahead and Njal Ingvason to his left, two slabs of pack ice shook, then smashed together and apart, and Hauk Gunnarsson disappeared. A day later his corpus was found, and it had been thrown by the impact some three or four ells high on an ice cliff, so that men had to climb to it, and carry it down. Shortly after this, the travelers found the ocean, and were able to sail south, first to the western settlement, and then to Gardar, and Hauk Gunnarsson's bones were buried at Vatna Hverfi, close under the southern wall of the church.

Concerning this summer there was another tale about the people at Gunnars Stead that was repeated around the settlement, although not in the hearing of Asgeir Gunnarsson, and this was that one morning Gunnar rose early, although it was his custom to sleep as long as possible, and then he spent a great deal of time pulling the furs and cloaks off the bed and putting them back on, until they had been arranged to his satisfaction. That evening after the meal, he went to the bedcloset he shared with his uncle and seemed to go to sleep, except that when the others went to their rest, they could hear him talking excitedly, as if to Hauk, but of course, Hauk was with Nicholas in the north. The next day everything was as usual, and Asgeir did not ask the boy about his night, nor did the boy volunteer any information, but when the ship returned with the dead man, Gunnar of Gunnars Stead seemed in no way surprised. After this, the great prosperity of Gunnars Stead was diminished, for Asgeir was not an avid hunter, and he had to depend more and more on the wealth he could raise on his land. But indeed, he had a great deal of land, and even now considered himself a lucky man.

The Monk Nicholas stayed with Ivar Bardarson during the winter and the next, and all of this time he was making measurements and notations with the instruments he had brought. The English sailors thought little of the Greenlanders at first, and especially disliked the meat and other foods they had to eat, for, they said, dried meat was no substitute for bread, and milk was no substitute for wine and beer, which the English sailors were much accustomed to. Folk said that they grew fat enough on the Greenlanders' food, anyway, and at the end of the second winter they were not loath to take away as much as they could load into their small ship. After they had left, not a few pointed out that the Greenlanders had made a poor bargain with this particular churchman, for they had received little more than a few items for the cathedral in exchange for almost two years room and board, and in addition, the monk's foolish quest had cost the settlement two good men it could ill afford to lose—a third if you counted the departure of Ivar Bardarson the priest, who, after twenty years at Gardar overseeing the bishop's farm and the cathedral, had decided to return to Norway.

Nicholas' talk, he told Asgeir, had given him a great longing for Nidaros, where he had spent some years in his youth, and for Bremen, the scene of his schooling. He was getting to be an old man, and soon he feared he would be too old ever to leave Gardar, and so he left. Many people pointed out that Gizur Gizursson, the lawspeaker who lived at Brattahlid, who had allowed Ivar to take care of the business of the eastern settlement for twenty years, was much older than Ivar, too old, it was said, to remember much about the law or about settling disputes. And now there was much more grumbling about the failure of the arch-bishop to send a bishop to Gardar, for there was no one in the settlement who could take a strong hand either in behalf of the Church or in behalf of the king. People began to notice how the churches were in disrepair and how the precious altar furnishings were tarnished and bent or broken in many of the churches, and this was because Ivar Bardarson had come only to husband the goods of the bishopric, he had been given no right to expend them. In the same way, it was said, the souls of the folk were tarnished with sin and bent from improper practices, and broken with despair that a new bishop would ever come, and some threatened to return to the old religion of Thor and Odin and Frey, although their neighbors laughed at them and said that those beliefs were in even greater disrepair. And so it continued for the Greenlanders, with some good years and some cold ones, for six more summers, and then a ship arrived from Norway, and on it was Bishop Alf, who had come to take over the see at Gardar, and rectify those errors the souls of Greenland might have fallen into.

Asgeir was among the first of the farmers to go to Gardar after the
arrival of the new bishop, and he carried many gifts: a pair of narwhal
horns he had held in reserve from Hauk's last trip, many thick sheepskins
in a number of shades, rolls of fine wadmal, and an excellent cup carved
by his father, Gunnar Asgeirsson, from a walrus tusk in the time of the
last bishop. The bishop, he reported, accepted these graciously, saying that
the Greenlanders had brought him handsome items for his household.

Alf was an older man than Asgeir had expected, almost as old as Ivar
Bardarson would be, but taller and thinner, with cheekbones like red
knobs, and eyes the pale color of the spring sky above the fjords. He did
not, Asgeir told Ingrid, have the easy ways of a man much accustomed to
good fellowship, and talked of Greenland as if it were at the end of the
earth, or as if the Greenlanders were trolls of some sort. When Asgeir made
a joke about men returning to the old faith in Thor and Odin, the new
bishop had thought he was serious, and Asgeir had felt awkward and had
fallen to making explanations. In addition, the ship that had carried him
was a small one, and had few goods, only some pitch and some oatseed,
and not enough of either for all the farmsteads in Eriks Fjord, much less
the whole settlement. There were also some wheel rims, and hubs and axles
that Asgeir had his eye on, but a number of farmers had been there, and
all had seen the dearth of goods.

Nonetheless, the bishop did have some young priests with him,
properly ordained by the archbishop himself, and all properly trained, with
only one of the three an older man who had been rushed into the priesthood after the Great Death, for the plague had returned again to Norway
and England and the rest of Europe around the time of Ivar Bardarson's
departure, but no one was able to tell Asgeir whether his friend had fallen
victim to it. He had also asked after Thorleif, for now the Greenlanders
often talked of Thorleif and his wondrous ship, his bottomless store of
goods, and everything exactly what was needed by every man, but no one
had heard of Thorleif, either, or Skuli, or any of the other sailors anyone
could remember.

These young priests had brought many books with them for the
Gardar library, and it was said among everyone who visited the new bishop
that Gardar would soon be a busy, bustling place, as it had been in the time
of the old bishop, and, Asgeir said, soon Olaf Finnbogason would have
to go back, because people there would suddenly remember him and
wonder where he had gotten to. Olaf laughed at this, but the farm folk
said he was little minded to spend his time puzzling over books he had
never read with strangers he had never met.

Margret was now twenty-three, tall and fair in coloring, and she had been well taught by Kristin in her summers at Siglufjord all the skills of a good farm wife. She went about in shoes and stockings and gowns she herself had woven, dyed, and sewed together, with her hair held in bands she had fashioned in the evenings out of brightly colored yarns. In addition, she had learned of Ingrid many of the uses of herbs and plants, for childbirth and for the curing of the springtime bleeding disease and many things besides. She worked every day with the other women, spinning and weaving and making cheese and butter, and there was no reason why she had not been married, or even betrothed, but she was not. It was true that Helga Ingvadottir had reached the age of twenty-four before coming to Greenland with Asgeir, but she had been a stiff-necked, opinionated woman, and unpleased by the men she knew. Kristin told Asgeir that Margret did not know how to be alluring, and Asgeir said that his wealth should be alluring enough, but indeed, everyone knew that along with the wealth and the capable wife must come the son.

Gunnar was now sixteen, and although he was tall and handsome, he was entirely useless around the farmstead, as he had always been. He could be put to chinking fences or manuring the fields, and he did this simple work cheerfully but slowly, always tempting whoever was working with him to do Gunnar's share as well as his own. He slept long nights, even in the height of summer, and sometimes fell asleep during the day. He was never taken hunting because he could not be quiet or still. He spent many of his days sitting with Ingrid by the fire, for the nurse was extremely old now, stiff in the joints, almost blind, and close to death, and Gunnar was her only friend, and only he took pains to make sure that her meat suited her and that she was warm. Many days they spent mumbling between themselves while the others were in the storehouses or in the fields, and Gunnar even resorted to spinning wool, like a woman, in order to earn his place at the table, for Ingrid said that he must do something. Asgeir said that all men do what they do and seek their own fate, but others in the settlement said that he had ill luck in his children. The servingfolk treated Gunnar as if he were weak-minded, always laughing at him or speaking to him in loud voices, and this was so much the custom that Asgeir did not object, nor Margret, nor even Gunnar himself.

Among the priests who came to Greenland with Bishop Alf was Pall Hallvardsson, who was sent to Vatna Hverfi to assist Nikolaus, the priest at Undir Hofdi church, who, like all the other Greenland priests, was now rather old, although still hale and outspoken. Sira Pall Hallvardsson was not Norwegian, but Flemish, although his father had been an Icelander and had traveled to Greenland once himself, as a boy on a trading ship, in the time of the last bishop. Few priests, Pall Hallvardsson told Asgeir, actually requested duties in Greenland, and so when he had spoken of his wishes, the archbishop had been happy to grant them. Pall Hallvardsson had studied at Ghent, and had been in the care and service of the Church since the death of his mother of the plague shortly after his birth.

Of the other two priests Sira Jon was about the age of Margret and was the bishop's nephew. Folk said of him that he made a special point of deferring to the bishop "even about the taste of his broth." Petur was the plague priest, nearly as old as Asgeir, although newly ordained. He did not push himself forward, and many in the settlement said this was proper, for there was grumbling that after so many years the archbishop should send an old man to a place where there were already plenty of old men.

At the end of summer, when the flocks were brought down from the mountains, a messenger went to all the farmsteads in Vatna Hverfi and Einars Fjord up to Gardar and invited the farmers and their folk to a great feast to be held at Ketils Stead. Asgeir was no friend of Erlend, nor were many who had had dealings with Ketils Stead since the death of Ketil in Markland, for Erlend was a hard man, and his wife Vigdis was no gentler. They were always ready to dispute over little things like stray sheep and vats of milk. Nonetheless, the messenger promised a great feast, for Erlend had many sheep to kill before winter. The bishop and the new priests also intended to come, after saying a celebratory mass at Undir Hofdi church, which the bishop had not yet done.

And indeed, the bishop seemed well pleased with Erlend's feast, for Erlend and Vigdis made much of him and his party, seating the bishop in the high seat, and giving him the choicest bits of meat. Every time the bishop spoke, Erlend looked out over the company, and they fell silent, even though many were too far from the bishop to hear what he said. The two children, Vigdis' Thordis and Ketil, and a third, Geir, were dressed up in white gowns with their hair tied back in red and white woven bands, and they had been instructed to serve the bishop his meat. Every time he took something, they knelt and thanked him for taking it. The bishop seemed well pleased by this obeisance, and the other Greenlanders tried to suppress their smiles. Erlend sat to one side of the bishop and Vigdis sat to the other, and beside each of them sat people Asgeir didn't recognize, but Osmund whispered to him that they were friends of Erlend's from Petursvik, far to the south, and had taken to spending a great deal of time at Ketils Stead. Osmund said that Asgeir should certainly know them, for the woman was Hjordis, the niece of Thorunn, the old witch, the girl was her daughter, Oddny, and the man was Hjordis' husband, Sigmund. Asgeir laughed through his teeth and declared that this was a bad sign indeed, and afterward said nothing more about it.

In the winter, for the first time in years, a Yuletide mass was held at the Cathedral of St. Nikolaus, and the Greenlanders could see that it had been newly and beautifully fitted out, with new tapestries and a new altar cloth and chalice. The bishop had brought magnificent robes with him, and he had taught some of the Gardar boys beautiful melodies for the mass. People said that this had gone on with the old bishop as well, but the notes for the songs had been lost in the time of Ivar Bardarson. Other masses were held at the New Year and the feast of the Circumcision, and the bishop wore still other robes and preached a great loud sermon on heresy and sin and lapses from proper practice. Now, he shouted, had the souls of the Greenlanders fallen into sin? Indeed they had, and for this the Church was greatly to blame, but that Holy Mother had at last heard the loud crying out of these souls, and now in the person of himself, she cried back to them to turn away from old ways, and to return to obedience and vigilance against evil. This was considered a good topic for a New Year sermon.

In subsequent services, during Lent, the bishop spoke eloquently of the visitations of the plague in Norway and Germany, and the terrible sinfulness of the people that offended God so that He punished them, and how this could befall any sinful people at any time, through the will of God. God was so merciful, the bishop said, that He had seen the plight of His people in Greenland, and the way that they were bereft of guidance, and He had held His hand, but now their shepherd, the bishop himself, had come, and God would hold them to the true path with rod and scourge, just as He did the rest of the world. As a result of these sermons, a number of men and women went to the monastery at Arosvik and the nunnery near Vagar Church, and the buildings had to be put in order to house them. It was this half year that Sigmund Sigmundsson of Petursvik with the help of Erlend Ketilsson brought suit in front of the bishop against Asgeir Gunnarsson for the killing fourteen years earlier of Thorunn Jorundsdottir, who had lived at Undir Hofdi for many years.

At this time the Greenlanders had three types of law, the Thing law, the bishop's law, and the king's law, of which the last two were sometimes combined, depending upon whether the bishop or the representative of the king was living in Greenland. Thing law and the law of the bishop were intended to concern the different matters of secular law and Church law, but sometimes the Thing was less powerful, and sometimes the bishop was not in residence, and so the men of most of the fjords settled disputes among themselves, and this was a habit the Greenlanders had gotten into since the death of the last bishop and the aging of the lawspeaker Gizur, who lived at Brattahlid.

The first thing Asgeir did was to go to Gizur, at Brattahlid, for a few days. When he got back, a message was taken to Ketils Stead by one of the Brattahlid men that Sigmund's suit was illegal because killings were matters for the Thing, and Sigmund had not brought it up at the Thing, which was just then ended. A few days later, Sigmund sent a message to Gizur, to the bishop, and to Asgeir that Thorunn had been killed outside her cottage on church property, and that this property had been appropriated by Asgeir, who had had illegal use of it and had not paid the tithe on it for many years. Asgeir then went to the bishop and spoke in private to him and to Nikolaus the Priest at Undir Hofdi. After that, a message was sent to Erlend that Asgeir, thanks to the hunting skills of Hauk, had paid his tithe and his Peter's pence in full for all these years, and that the killing was thus not an ecclesiastical matter, but a Thing matter, and Sigmund was welcome to press his suit the following year at the Thing in the usual fashion. Erlend greeted this message with silence at first, but then, just as people had ceased talking of the matter, Sigmund let it be known that Thorunn had been accused of witchcraft and had been killed as a witch without church inquiry, and therefore, her killing was a matter for the bishop. The bishop and the lawspeaker agreed that this was so, and Asgeir began seeking followers and supporters in the case.

The day that the bishop set aside for hearing the case came during the spring manuring time, just after lambing, when late lambs were still being born. Nevertheless, when Asgeir gathered his supporters on the field in front of the cathedral at Gardar, they were numerous, and many had come from distant farms in Hrafns Fjord and Siglufjord. These men did as men do at the Thing, to ensure that fighting will not break out, that is, they put all their weapons together in a pile and went about unarmed. Of Sigmund's supporters, which were rather few, only Erlend was a prosperous farmer with much land. The others were like Sigmund, small farmers from the south, some of whom had lived originally in the western settlement. The two groups had little to say to one another, but there was no fighting, as there might have been at the Thing. Erlend spoke for Sigmund and Asgeir spoke for himself, although Gizur the lawspeaker put in a word for him from time to time.

Now the bishop came out in front of the door to the cathedral and looked about, and he said, "To whom do all these men gathered here belong?"

And Asgeir replied, "They are their own men, but they are my supporters in this case."

"Whose ever men they may be," said Erlend, contentiously, "six of them prevented me from drawing my boat up onto the strand, and threatened to pitch me into the water along with Sigmund."

Asgeir declared, "Your own bad dealings with folk over trifles have gained you that reward, as everyone knows. It was not for me to suggest that my supporters should prevent the case, for I have no need of that."

The bishop now said, "We must know what sort of person this Thorunn was."

"This old woman was in the habit of casting spells upon my sheep," said Asgeir, "and especially on two fine horses I had, so that each of these two, Flosi and Gulli, stepped into the selfsame hole and broke the selfsame leg, although my men were careful to fill the hole after the first event. And Thorunn caused this to happen because she was much put out, as my wife, Helga Ingvadottir, had refused her milk when she had come about the place seeking some. But all folk know that a wife who is wishing to conceive a son must save her cows' first milk for her own drink." He looked about at the men upon the grass, and said, "Others, too, once felt the weight of Thorunn's curses, and she let it be known about the district that she would cast spells for love and death. But even so, it was that case that I killed her for this, that she cursed my child Gunnar so that he was unable to walk and went upon all fours, even into his third year. And the best proof of this fact is that as soon as the woman was killed, the boy got up onto his feet and went about as other children."

"Nay," said Erlend. "This Thorunn was no witch, but an old woman of little prosperity or power, and Helga Ingvadottir spoke all over the district of how poor and ugly the steading was, and how it ought to be done away with. It seems to me that Asgeir Gunnarsson wanted only this, to bring that plot into his own fields, which he has done, even though on one long side, the plot fronts the homefield at Ketils Stead, and on one short side, it fronts the lands of Undir Hofdi church. No curses could have been proved against the old woman, and so there was no church inquiry." Erlend looked at Asgeir in his sour way. "And if we are talking of things that are well known in the district, then we must talk of the boy Gunnar, who is as slow now as then, and whose wits are dim. This killing may have been announced, as should be the case in law, but it was unjustified, and therefore Hjordis and Oddny, through Sigmund from Petursvik and myself, are demanding compensation from Asgeir."

"Who was there in Greenland at the time," said Asgeir, "with the learning or the jurisdiction to uncover witchcraft and punish it? If there is no bishop, then the Greenlanders must settle their own disputes, and always have."

Gizur nodded. "This is certainly true," he said.

"And this, too, is true," said Asgeir, "Sigmund would have had little luck with his friend Erlend in persuading him to bring this suit, if Erlend lived in another district, in a spot where he could not look out his front door and covet the fields of his neighbor at Gunnars Stead. Or he might have brought a suit against someone else, for some other imaginary crime." And Asgeir showed his teeth in a bitter smile.

The bishop turned to Sira Jon, and spoke to him quietly for a few minutes, and then asked these questions, "Had Thorunn ever been heard to speak ill of Jesus Christ, or seen to spit upon and otherwise defame any image of Christ?"

Gizur and Asgeir stood silent.

"Had the woman ever been seen to fly out at night, or to turn into a cat or a goat or any other unclean beast?"

Gizur and Asgeir stood silent, for they had no knowledge of such doings.

"This Thorunn," said the bishop, "has she ever consorted with groups of demons, or was she ever seen to disinter the bodies of buried men or cause the disappearance of children?"

At length Asgeir said, "The witch was friendless enough, except for this niece Hjordis, and she moved to the south some twenty winters ago."

The bishop declared that he would go into the church and pray over his decision. As he went to the church, he stopped and again looked out over Asgeir's supporters loitering on the grass, and Asgeir said that this look was ill-omened, and that he did not expect it to go well with him.

The bishop stayed in the church for most of the day, sometimes calling Jon to him, or Gizur the lawspeaker. Margret, Gunnar, and Olaf sat together with Osmund and Thord from Siglufjord, but Asgeir did not stay with them, and instead went from group to group, speaking good-humoredly and making jokes. Erlend and his party kept to themselves and stayed near their boat on the shore.

Toward dusk, the bishop came out and stood on a hillock in front of the cathedral, and began to preach a sermon.

A servant, the bishop said, goes out of his master's steading in the depths of winter. It is a clear, frosty day, so that he can walk easily on the crust of the snow, and the moon is full, so that even before daylight all objects are visible to him. His work is simple. He wishes only to feed the cows and the horses some hay and to bring a vat of sourmilk from the storehouse back to the steading, where the household awaits. His life is a good one, for he is a servant on a prosperous farm, where he is well fed and rarely beaten, and his master watches him carefully, and is just but merciful.

At once a cloud passes in front of the moon and a great wind comes up and the stars are hidden and a storm begins. The servant can only just see the byre in the darkness, and he directs his steps there with difficulty, on account of the storm. He is greatly afraid, for he hears, he thinks, voices crying out to him, and he recollects a dream that he, or perhaps someone else of the household, has had, about a walking ghost who tears the eyes out of the heads of men if they try to see, and tears out their throats if they try to speak. The servant is so afraid that he can hardly move, yet he knows that the cows and the horses will starve if he doesn't give them their feed. He says a Hail Mary and then cries out to our Lord Jesus Christ, and the storm only grows worse and the cries louder, so that he is buffeted about and no longer knows where he is, near the byre or near the storehouses or near the bathhouse. Now he gets down on his knees and prays fervently to Christ to preserve him, and he is preserved, but at the same time the storm increases in power, and there are great crashes of thunder and repeated flashes of lightning, so that the man is sorely afraid and he calls on Thor to save him, promising Thor the sacrifice of a good sheep or a goat or even a cow, although these are his master's animals, if Thor will only make the storm diminish a wit. And the storm does diminish, and the servant thanks Thor and declares that Thor is more powerful than Jesus Christ.

And then the servant makes his way into the byre in the darkness, and he sees a man amongst the cows, and he thinks that the man is stealing a cow, and so, in the darkness, with the howling of the storm and the crying of many voices in his ears, the servant sneaks up behind the man in the byre and he bashes him on the head with a great club that has come into his hand, perhaps thanks to Thor, and the intruder falls senseless to the ground. And then the storm subsides, and members of the household come out with torches and lamps looking for their faithful and hardworking servant, and they find him in the byre, and they discover that he has beaten and killed, not an intruder, but the master's only son, who has seen the hunger of the livestock and begun to feed them. And the bishop declared that this is a true tale, one that took place on a farm in Vik, when the bishop himself was a boy on the neighboring farmstead. And now Asgeir turned to Thorkel Gellison, who was standing beside him and said, "This case will be the death of me, and that is truth."

"Thus it is," said the bishop, looking at Asgeir, "that the servant succumbed to two temptations. First of these was the temptation to think that our Lord Jesus Christ was powerless, although his prayer was promptly answered, and he was spared. This was the temptation that led Thorunn into sorcery and casting spells. But the other temptation, the temptation to act ignorantly on behalf of his master, was a more powerful and still more evil temptation, for any man can recant his belief in demons such as Thor, but no man can undo the murder of his master's only son.

"It may be," the bishop went on, "that the killing of Thorunn was duly announced, so that Asgeir is not guilty of murder, and therefore not subject to a sentence of outlawry. And it may be that Thorunn was a sorceress, and guilty of casting injurious spells. After fourteen years these things cannot clearly be proven. There is no evidence that the old woman abjured her savior, made a pact with the devil, or engaged in witchcraft as it has recently been defined among the Italians and the Germans and the French by the holy inquisitors of the Church."

The bishop paused and looked around the Gardar field at Asgeir's many supporters. "And in this case, too," he said, "Asgeir Gunnarsson shows a fondness for force, and a desire to sway our decision by a show of strength. We do not care for such threats. Those who threaten do so because they fear that they do not have right on their side."

"Asgeir himself," the bishop said, "is a beloved member of our flock, and now, at the end of a long winter, when the shepherd has been absent from the flock for many months, many of the sheep have lost the way, and some have strayed farther into the mountains than others, and are in danger of being forever lost. Asgeir, who treats all subjects lightly and with merriment, is one of these.

"The spring has come, however, and the shepherd in his strength has returned. He goes out among the wastelands to seek his sheep, and his desire is not to punish them, but to bring them into the fold, and to assure their safety, thus," the bishop declared, "we will be merciful in our sentence." The muttering among those standing in the field ceased so that even the lapping of the waters of the fjord on the hull of Erlend's little boat could be heard.

"Asgeir," said the bishop, "is the possessor of two great fields. Of these, he will be allowed to keep for himself and his heirs the larger homefield, but he must surrender up the second field to the Gardar church, and the hay on this field will be divided as follows: A third part to the see of Gardar, a third part to Undir Hofdi church, and a third part to Sigmund and Oddny and their heirs, the whole to be administered by Erlend Ketilsson, as the nearest neighbor, for a commission of one-fifth of all the hay grown on the field. After nine years, Asgeir may purchase the field back for a price to be set by the bishop at a later date, and if he is unable to do so, any man of the settlement may purchase the field." Then the bishop said prayers, and went away, and the group on the Gardar field began to take up their weapons and go off, for it was now dark, and people were hungry for their supper.

After this, the spring seal hunt went forward, and Asgeir's piece of ill luck was the topic of much talk there, and men were perplexed at such a result, namely that they should not be able to act in their own behalf without punishment. Later, in the fall, Asgeir slaughtered many lambs and calves and one of his horses, for he said that he would not have the hay to bring them through the winter. Erlend Ketilsson harvested the hay on the second field with great trouble, for it was distant from his storehouse and from his other field. Nikolaus the Priest of Undir Hofdi church sent over three of his servingmen to help with the harvesting. The crop from the field was excellent, and much of it went to Erlend himself, because the bishop allowed him to take the Gardar third as well as his own fifth part in exchange for some of Vigdis' tablet weaving and three soapstone basins. This extra hay made a huge pile outside Erlend's storehouse, and folk said that it would be a long time before his horses ate seaweed again. These were not things Asgeir spoke of, except to say, once, with a laugh as he was putting on his shirt in the morning, "I find I grow thinner and much diminished," but he had as much flesh upon his bones as always.

Now in this winter, he spent much of his time with Olaf, and at Yule time he made Olaf his foster son, for Olaf's mother had died. After Yule, there was a great thaw, followed by a hard freeze, so that the sheep went long distances looking for twigs and tufts of grass. Some even wandered out onto the frozen lake and had to be carefully herded back. Once, when doing this, Asgeir went through the ice. Others were nearby, but no one heard him call out. Some people said that he did not call out at all. When Olaf and one of the servingmen found him toward dusk, his corpus was frozen solid, with his arms wrapped around his chest and his eyes and mouth wide open. They had to build a fire in the bathhouse and lay him out there so that he could thaw. And that was the death of Asgeir Gunnarsson of Gunnars Stead. He was buried next to his brother, Hauk, close under the south side of Undir Hofdi church, and many said that the food provided at his funeral was the most delicious and most plentiful of any funeral in years, for Margret Asgeirsdottir had spent her summers with Kristin, the wife of Thord, who was well known to be one of the most skilled and liberal farmer's wives in all the settlement. Thorkel Gellison spoke all over the district of what Asgeir had said to him at the end of the bishop's sermon, that the case would be the death of him.

Not long after the death of Asgeir Gunnarsson by drowning and freezing, Bishop Alf declared the souls of the Greenlanders to be in imminent peril of damnation, for, he said, not one man in five made the proper observances of fast days, especially during the forty days of Lent. It was said that Sira Jon had discovered servingmen of the bishop's own table eating quantities of meat, and with great reveling, when they should have been fasting and meditating upon the suffering of the Lord Jesus Christ. The bishop was especially interested in the skraelings, and preached not a few long sermons on demons and devils and heathens, and declared that sinful contact of Christian men with she-devils was as black as darkest night in the eyes of our Lord, and after this the Greenlanders began to look about themselves and see the skraelings with different eyes. A few men, indeed, left off going among the skraeling women, but others did not, although their visits were now not so open nor so frequent.

In these years it had gotten so that the Greenlanders met the skraelings more and more often, especially hunting in the waste districts, and men and demons came to blows from time to time, but most folk said that the skraelings were happiest on the open ocean, in their skin boats. The best sign of their demon nature was that the fiercest storms could do them no harm. Men had seen skraelings in their boats disappear completely under the waves, and reappear again many ells away and be none the worse. Many said that the most frightening thing about the skraelings was their deceptive habit of smiling at everything, and that their very quietness was a sign of what plans they were hatching against the Christian Greenlanders. There was much talk of these things, but the end result was that those who wanted to trade with the skraelings did so, and those who were afraid to did not.

After first declaring that there must be no contact, the bishop changed his mind and said that it was the duty of all Christians to strive to bring the heathen to Christ. Three men brought skraeling women home, had them baptized, and married them, and some men said that these women made good-humored and willing wives, less self-willed than Christian women. These women lived peacefully among the farms of the settlement. So it was that at Gardar the talk was all of the skraelings and their ways, and among themselves the Greenlanders got a deal of amusement from this.

One woman who was not married was Margret Asgeirsdottir of Gunnars Stead. A certain Arnkel, from a farmstead in Siglufjord, had declared his intention to marry her, but then nothing was heard of this, and Arnkel returned to his steading. Folk in Vatna Hverfi district said how handsome Margret was and how large her marriage portion would have been had Asgeir managed to hold on to all of his farm, but now any man taking on Margret could well be taking on a family of dependents who would drain his own wealth. It was true that Gunnar and Margret were rich in fine things, for the men of their lineage had been abroad and the women had been skilled craftswomen, but there were more fine things inside the farmhouse than there were sheep in the fields or cows in the byre. Folk also remembered how proud and determined to have her own way Helga Ingvadottir had been, and sometimes these habits, it was said, did not appear until a woman had her own house and dairy. Arnkel told people in Siglufjord that he had had some conversations with the woman, but in fact she made him uneasy, with her way of waiting to speak a long moment after he had spoken, and keeping her eyes on his face the whole time, so that he was tempted to say more and more, and ended up feeling that he was a simpleton.

Another thing Margret did that was not usual for a woman was to go off into the mountains above Gunnars Stead in all seasons and come home with not only herbs and medicinal plants, but also birds she had snared and eggs she had gathered. Like her uncle Hauk, she was outside more than inside, and always in pursuit of some quarry. Five willow cages hung from the beams in the Gunnars Stead farmhouse, and in them were Margret's little birds, wheatears and larks, who chattered and clamored all winter in a way that most of the neighbors considered unlucky and unpleasant.

The farm folk at Gunnars Stead were considerably diminished in the spring after Asgeir's death, so that only Margret, Gunnar, Olaf, and Ingrid were left, along with one shepherd, Hrafn, and two women servants, Hrafn's wife Maria, and Gudrun, a young girl. There were also two menservants to help Olaf with the farming. Hrafn and Maria had two children, boys, who went with their father into the sheep meadows early in the summer. Ingrid now spent her days and nights in her bedcloset, for she could no longer stand, or even sit up. No torches or lamps were brought to her, because she didn't know night from day, and she would sometimes call out to Gunnar to bring her some sourmilk and dried sealmeat mashed with butter for her breakfast or her dinner when breakfast or dinner was long past. Gunnar always did so, and Ingrid would tell him fragments of old stories that he remembered from his childhood. At other times Nikolaus the Undir Hofdi priest and his "wife" would sit with her and pray with her, for she hadn't been to the church in a number of years.

The farmstead belonged to Gunnar, but he did as little work in the fields as ever, and cared as little for the sheep, although he sometimes rode one of the old horses, leaving the two younger ones to Olaf. The amount of yarn he spun in his idle time was more than Gudrun and Maria had time to weave into cloth, and so he learned to dye and weave, and laughed, too, when people laughed at this. Folk in the district said that Gunnars Stead was an upside down household, and considered this unlucky, but indeed, the winters after the coming of the bishop were so cold and stormy, and the summers so short that every household in the settlement did things in ways that had never been done before. Only the folk at Gardar and at a few other farmsteads had enough hay and other provisions to last through these cold springs, and many Greenlanders were so weakened by hunger and the bleeding disease that they succumbed to vomiting and coughing ills as if they were plagues.

It seemed that nothing could induce Gunnar to work. If it was cold, he would lie silently under his polar bear coverlet until it warmed up, rather than look for driftwood. If he was hungry, he would wait until Ingrid called out for food, and then eat whatever she left. Whenever anything was lost, no matter how valuable, he would declare that it would turn up sometime. He wore whatever shirts and stockings no one else seemed to want, although he knew well how to stitch these things himself. He said that Yule would soon come around, or Easter, or the first day of winter, or some other occasion for the giving of gifts, and then he would get a new shirt from someone, and he could easily wait until then. The result was that the servants began to emulate him, and little work got done on the farm. Fences fell down, turves fell from their places, buildings began to crumble. The storehouses emptied and were not filled again, the bath house fell into disuse, the cows and horses were sent out to look for food when the fields were covered with ice. Neither Gunnar nor Olaf went on the spring seal hunt or the autumn seal hunt. All of Olaf's efforts could not lift the curse of Gunnar's laziness, although he himself had become a skilled farmer and was like Asgeir had been in his energy. Things went like this for more than a year after the death of Asgeir, and the neighbors declared that soon Gunnar and Margret would have to go out as servants, for they could hardly keep themselves in this way for another summer, much less another winter.

Now the time came around for the Thing, and Gunnar declared that he was nineteen years old and ready to journey to Gardar and find out what it was necessary for men to do. He stitched himself a new shirt and new stockings, and took one of the servingmen with him, and, to tell briefly what happened, he returned home seven days later with the news that he had agreed to take a wife, Birgitta Lavransdottir, of Hvalsey Fjord, who was fourteen years old, and who brought as her marriage portion two sheep and a roll of red silk.

Folk said that it was obvious that Lavrans Kollgrimsson hadn't been to Gunnars Stead in many a year, or else he did not care much for his daughter. Others declared, though, that Lavrans himself was a poor man, although he farmed good Hvalsey land, and getting old, so that any marriage would be a good one for a child as headstrong as Birgitta Lavransdottir.

Birgitta Lavransdottir was considered quite fair among the Greenlanders, red-cheeked and well fed, blond like Gunnar, but of low stature, so that she came up only to the middle of his breast, and only as high as Margret's shoulder. The marriage was held at the new church in Hvalsey Fjord and the marriage feast at Lavrans Stead, which sat above the water of the inner arm of Hvalsey Fjord, directly across from the church, which was called after St. Birgitta, and had been built by the Hvalsey Fjord folk in the reign of King Sverri. Gunnar presented Birgitta with many fine gifts, including a silver comb his grandfather Gunnar had gotten in Ireland and the boat with its sailors carved from birchwood that Skuli Gudmundsson had given him when he was a boy. Birgitta seemed especially pleased with this toy, and with the thick gray cloak Margret sewed for her. They came to Vatna Hverfi with their sheep and their bolt of silk in Lavrans' boat, rowing slowly up Einars Fjord on a day in late summer when the fjord was as still and bright, people said, as water in a goblet. The bellowing of the two sheep carried across the water into every farmstead, and even the dip of Gunnar's oars could be heard in an eerie way, so that many families spoke of the passing of this little boat as they sat down that evening to their meat.

Now it was the case that the Gunnars Stead folk had a pleasant feast in honor of the coming of Birgitta Lavransdottir, and when all were sitting contented at their trenchers after eating their fill, Gunnar said to Margret, "Where is it that Birgitta Lavransdottir will be sleeping now that she is living here?" At this Olaf and Maria, the wife of Hrafn, burst out laughing.

Birgitta looked up, her eyes full of curiosity, and Margret looked at her. Now she sent Olaf and Maria from the steading, and gazed upon her brother and the child who was his wife. Birgitta's headdress, the prerogative of a married woman, sat heavily on her small head, and slightly askew. Margret turned to Gunnar. "My own bedcloset," she said, "is the largest. I will make a place for her there." And she got up and showed Birgitta the bedcloset, with its carvings of angelica leaves and its little shelf that ran all around the head, for putting down a seal oil lamp or such other things as the sleeper might care to have near him during the night.

On this shelf Birgitta set about arranging her wedding gifts in a row, the silver comb, a necklace of glass beads, an ivory spindle weight carved to look like a seal with its head up and the thread coming out of its mouth, a small knife with a beaten iron handle, and two or three woven colored bands to be worn with her headdress, as well as the little ship. Next to these she stacked her folded undergarments and stockings, and beside these she set her new shoes, then, after saying her prayers, she lay down and pulled her new gray cloak up to her chin, turned her face toward her new things and fell asleep.

Of all those living in the house, Olaf was the most like Asgeir had been. He got up early each morning and took his meal of dried reindeer meat and sourmilk into the fields and began to work at whatever there was to be done. In the spring, it was he and Hrafn who carried the cows into the homefield. It was he who hitched up the horses to the cart and carried manure out. It was Olaf who dragged the birch sapling over the manure to break it up and mix it with the soil, then Olaf who repaired the fences to keep the cows from eating the new shoots of grass. At sheep shearing time, he found Hrafn in the hills with the sheep, helped him with the shearing, then dragged home the bundles of wool for Maria and Gudrun to wash and comb. He also helped with the milking and the making of cheeses and butter. At the end of summer, he scythed the grass and Maria and Gudrun raked it, then he bundled the hay and piled it in front of the cowbyre.

One day a man called Audun came from Gardar to Gunnars Stead with a message that the bishop wished to see Olaf, and wished him to return to Gardar at once with the messenger. Olaf sent the messenger into the farmstead for some refreshment, then lingered over his work until it was almost dark and too late to begin the journey.

This Audun was a fellow from the south, and throughout the evening he complained jokingly about having to spend the night in such a poor place, sleeping on the floor with only a single reindeer hide to wrap himself up in, his head under the table and his feet nearly out the door. Gardar, he said, was quite magnificent now that the bishop was in residence. "Indeed," he said, "many of the boys do no farm work at all anymore, but spend their days making parchment from the hides of calves and learning to copy manuscripts, and making bearberry ink. There are boys who spend their time singing, three boys, and it seems to me their voices sound angelically sweet. Sira Jon is the master of this, and when he sings a bit, to show these boys what they must do, all the copyists and parchments makers stop what they are doing, for the sake of hearing it. The bishop himself watches over the copyists, and Sira Pall Hallvardsson goes in and out, and Sira Petur, too, although these priests are most often away at Brattahlid, or Isafjord." As Audun was rattling on, Olaf put his few things in a bundle, his ashwood spoon, his books, the cup Asgeir had given him, and his newest stockings, breeches, and shoes. When the time came in the morning for the two men to go around the hill to Undir Hofdi church, Olaf said to Gunnar, "It seems to me that I would rather have my feet out the door than have my head full of singing." And he said to Margret, "I do not see how the sheep will come down from the hills or the cows will be walled into the cowbyre if I am not here to do it."

"And that," said Margret, watching him go off, "is the end of Olaf."

Olaf had not been to Gardar now for fourteen years, and the bishop's farm had indeed changed. Nothing that was not immediately needed was kept in the house, for all of these rooms that had once held vats and basins and hides and rolls of cloth now held priests and boys. Olaf was shown to one of them, where he found a pallet woven of reeds on the dirt floor covered with two reindeer hides, one to sleep on and one to sleep underneath. There were also two small shelves, one holding an oil lamp and another for books. On this one Olaf placed his cup, his spoon and his three small volumes, which he had not looked into in six years. He did not look into them now, for the bindings and pages were stiff as if stuck together. If the bishop asked for them, he would certainly see that they were ready to fall apart.

Olaf had seen the bishop once, from a distance, at the judgment of Asgeir Gunnarsson. Otherwise he had kept away from Gardar and from all visitors to Gunnars Stead who might carry tales of him back to the bishop. Now that he was here, though, it was obvious that everyone was perfectly familiar with him, that all had expected him back sooner or later, that his hopes had been those of an infant, who covers his eyes and thinks he cannot be seen.

Olaf came out of the residence into the sunlight in time to see the bishop's cows being led in a double row from the byre, where they had been milked, to the field. There were fifty of them, and already in the field were numerous calves and heifers. They were good cows, fat and dark-colored, and the two servants carrying the vats of milk around to the dairy had plenty to do, but they were all servants—the boys with the cows, the boys carrying the milk, the cowman and his assistant standing in the doorway of the byre. No priests among them, for all the priests were inside the residence, reading and writing by the light of smoky little lamps. But this was not true, either, for Pall Hallvardsson came up behind him. "So, now you have come, my Olaf," he said. "Folk here have been looking for you for these fourteen winters." He grinned.

"Well," said Olaf, and he brought out a cheese Margret had sent to the bishop as a gift. Pall Hallvardsson held the cheese aloft in the light, and declared, "These Gunnars Stead cheeses are too good for mere priests, are they not? As white and melting as a cheese could be." And Olaf could not keep himself from sighing, for indeed he had a great love of eating and had eaten well at Gunnars Stead for fourteen years.

Then Pall Hallvardsson took Olaf inside and sat him down at a table with a few of the smaller boys and their books. He told the boys that Olaf would help them with their reading, but Olaf's eyes were still dazzled by the sunshine, and his thick fingers could not get used to turning pages again, and so the result was that the boys grew rowdy and Jon, at another table across the room, had to come over and quiet them, and now he met Olaf, which he had not done before. He said, "Oh, so you are Olaf!" as if there had been much talk about him, both good and bad. After Jon went away, the small boys settled down and read their work, but Olaf could not tell if they read correctly or not, for he could not see the letters well enough to make out the words.

Although there was much activity and talk in the great room, the day seemed long and tedious to Olaf, and his bones ached from sitting. Everyone got up twice to file into the church for services, and there was no food until after vespers, when it was nearly dark. Olaf felt much hungrier than usual, and grew sorry that he had given Pall Hallvardsson Margret's cheese instead of hiding it in his room, or at least keeping a piece in his pocket. Dinner was just enough to fill your mouth once, as Asgeir would have said, and so, as tired as he was, Olaf knew he would sleep poorly. His wakefulness, however, did not make it any easier to get up for matins in the cold dark. He had neither the devotion of Pall Hallvardsson nor the habits of an old priest, who could shuffle into the cathedral and sit upright in his seat without appearing to be awake at all. Even so, when he returned to his cell after services he lay wake until morning thinking of the personal peculiarities of the cows and sheep and horses at Gunnars Stead that only he knew of, and had forgotten to mention before leaving. And who would take note of them, anyway?

After nones, the bishop requested Olaf's presence in his room, where he ran his finger down a page of a book, and recited to Olaf Olaf's own history, the death of his father, the departure of his mother and sister to Ketils Fjord, where both had since died of the coughing sickness, the nature of his duties at Gardar in the time of Ivar Bardarson, his education and his assignment, by Ivar, to Gunnars Stead, for the purpose of teaching Gunnar Asgeirsson to read. From time to time the bishop would look up at him, and Olaf would nod. "And now," said the bishop, "has Gunnar Asgeirsson learned to read?"

"Nay," said Olaf, in his rough growl. "Asgeir Gunnarsson ended the reading lessons when Gunnar showed no inclination for them."

"And why were you not sent back then, when your services were no longer of use?"

And Olaf did not reply, for indeed he did not know. Finally he said, "Sira, I was but a child myself at that time, and Ivar Bardarson did not send for me."

"What did you do then, my Olaf, for fourteen years, at Gunnars Stead?"

"Sira, I tended the cows and helped around the farmstead," said Olaf.

Now the bishop turned away and walked across the room, and then returned, and he said, "Asgeir Gunnarsson was a man who did as he pleased," but he said it in a low, angry voice, not as Asgeir had said it of himself, with a shout and a grin. Olaf muttered that Asgeir had made him his foster son after the death of his mother, but the bishop made no reply to this, and Olaf wasn't sure he had heard.

The bishop now turned away again, and stood with his back to Olaf, regarding the chair that sat in one corner of his chamber, and Olaf saw that this was a magnificent chair, with a triangular seat and figures carved into the back and arms, but his eyes could not make out the figures, they had grown so unused to the dim light of indoors. "There is such a great need of priests to do the work of God," said the bishop, "as there has never been since the days of the Apostles." He spun around, and Olaf stepped back. "For the earth is ravaged and decimated by the Great Death, so that the see of Nidaros itself—well, once, my Olaf, there were three hundred priests there, lifting their prayers to Heaven and adding figures in the books." He smiled briefly. "Know you how many there are these days? How many there were before myself and Sira Jon and Sira Pall Hallvardsson and Sira Petur were ripped away?" Olaf shook his head. "Three dozen or fewer. Indeed, up every fjord in Norway whole parishes have been lost, save only a child found in the woods sometimes. Other times whole tracts of land have been swept clean by death." He looked Olaf up and down, and went on. "Now is the time for men such as Petur, who are willing but untrained, to come forward and devote themselves to God's work, or men such as Pall Hallvardsson, foreigners and orphans, to leave those they love, lands and people, and go to where they are needed. We ourself expected to live out our years in Stavanger, close to the district of our birth, but now we are across the northern sea, at Gardar." Olaf nodded.

The bishop returned to his seat and smiled at Olaf. He opened his eyes wide and they protruded suddenly, causing Olaf to step back another half step. "Even so," said the bishop, "the wonderful mercy of our Lord is such that it provides materials for men to work with in these black days, among the farthest waves of the western ocean." He looked down again at the page in his book and read from it what was written there, perhaps by Ivar Bardarson himself. "Olaf Finnbogason," he said, "came to us late as a student, but he reads very well and is learning to write in a large but careful hand." Now the bishop really smiled. Not at Olaf, but to himself, as a man smiles who is making a barrel, when he fits the last stave into place. "Who better than you, my Olaf," he went on, "to bring along the little boys while you yourself study for your long-awaited ordination?"

"Indeed, Sira, I have done no reading in many years. It seems to me that my eyes have grown used to distances. Also, my hands are roughened from much farm work." He spoke in his usual muttering growl, and the bishop seemed not to hear him, or, perhaps, to understand him. After a brief time, Olaf said, more loudly, "Sira, as a boy, God gave me the gift of a prodigious memory, so that when a passage was read aloud to me, I could repeat it word for word, but I could make little of the writing, nor did I understand what I was saying if the passage was in Latin."

Now the bishop looked at him, and said, "The priest is the mouthpiece of God, and the Lord speaks through him, although he himself does not understand what the Lord is saying. The Word is a wine that does not spill even when the cup is broken." His eyelids dropped over his eyes and he looked more kindly at Olaf, saying in a softer voice, "You may trust the Lord to inspire you."

Thus Olaf was dismissed, but he did not go. He said, loudly, "Sira, I am betrothed to Margret Asgeirsdottir, and we have been together as husband and wife."

Now the bishop looked up, surprised, and said that he had not heard this before, but indeed, he had not spoken to Nikolaus, the priest of Undir Hofdi church, in some weeks. Olaf replied that the betrothal had not yet been announced to Nikolaus, but only to Gunnar, as master of Gunnars Stead, and to Ingrid, out of thought of her great age. At this, the bishop stood and approached Olaf and his eyes blazed out of their sockets like stars and sought Olaf's own. Olaf settled himself on his legs, as he would to curb a restive bull, and after a moment the bishop turned away, dismissing Olaf to his cell and asking him to send in Sira Jon.

On the day of Olaf's departure, Margret Asgeirsdottir went up into the mountains above Vatna Hverfi, and Gunnar sat with his wife Birgitta in the sunlight in front of the farmstead and told her stories.

After milking the cows, Maria and Gudrun sat themselves nearby, and listened to Gunnar along with Birgitta. Once in a while one of them or Gunnar himself would get up and carry something to Ingrid. After telling his tales, Gunnar lay back in the grass and fell asleep, while the two servingwomen went about their work in the storehouse and the dairy. Birgitta Lavransdottir removed her headdress, which she found heavy and uncomfortable, and began to pull her silver comb through her hair, which was blonde, though darker than Gunnar's, and hung to her waist. While Gunnar slept, she braided and bound it in various ways, getting up now and then to look at her reflection in a barrel of water which stood under the eave of the house.

At this time, just after her marriage, Birgitta Lavransdottir was only fourteen winters old, but she was well known among the folk who lived around Hvalsey Fjord for being outspoken and confident in her opinions, for indeed, Lavrans was a wasteful man who had been unable to indulge his only child in much else besides her opinions. On such things as the colors of her clothing or the arrangement of her hair and belongings she was very definite, and she offered notions about much else besides that sometimes made men laugh behind their hands, and Lavrans with them. Everyone around Hvalsey agreed, however, that Birgitta was extremely sharp-sighted and keen of hearing, and she knew about the coming of visitors and the migrations of birds and fish before anyone else did. People thought of these things later, after Birgitta related what she had seen on the homefield at Gunnars Stead while the servingwomen were at their work and Gunnar was sleeping beside her.

The first thing Birgitta noticed was a circle of yellow and white flowers at some distance, on a little hump of the field. Although it was late in the season, almost the beginning of the winter half year, these appeared to be anemones and goldthread. The sun shone full upon them. Then Birgitta beheld a woman in a white gown and white headdress walking among the anemones, and at first she thought that this was Margret, returning from her sojourn, but she recollected that Margret wore a brown cloak, and also this woman was not carrying a bag of any type. At this moment, Birgitta looked away, at Gunnar, to see if he might be waking up, and when she looked back she saw that the woman carried in her arms a child of about one winter's age, also clothed in white. As Birgitta watched, the woman lifted the child to her face and kissed it, then set it among the flowers on the grass. The child laughed, then stood up carefully and staggered forward with its arms in the air. At this, Birgitta thought the pair must be from Ketils Stead, or another of the neighboring farms, for she was new in the district and had not yet met everyone. But the strange thing was that as the child staggered and stumbled forward, more anemones and goldthread sprang up at its feet, and the bright sunlight followed.

Just then Maria called from the dairy house to ask Birgitta to find her something. Birgitta did not catch what this thing was, and, distracted, she looked away. When she looked back the mother and child were gone.

Soon enough Margret did return, and it was not until the household was seated at their evening meat that Birgitta, in her usual confident tones, related what she had seen in the homefield. And this was the first vision that came to Birgitta Lavransdottir of Gunnars Stead, who was later well known for having second sight.

On the morning of the third day after the departure of Olaf, Sira Jon and Pall Hallvardsson his colleague set out in the early morning from Gardar in the bishop's small boat. Both priests were big in the shoulders and good at rowing, and they glided swiftly through the waters of Einars Fjord, easily avoiding the ice that was beginning to form there. They landed at Undir Hofdi church and left their boat there with Nikolaus the Priest, then walked to Gunnars Stead, arriving well before mid-day. The folk at Gunnars Stead were only just rising, and Birgitta still wore her nightdress. Gunnar was with Ingrid, trying to induce her to taste a bit of sourmilk. Margret met the two priests at the door.

It did not seem to the two priests that she was surprised to see them, and from this Sira Pall Hallvardsson deduced that she knew what Olaf had communicated to the bishop, but then she began talking unaccountably, saying, "Indeed, Sira Jon, each of the farm folk has looked carefully over the homefield, and found nothing, but you may ask the girl herself."

Birgitta spoke in her usual confident tones. "Whether you may see them now or not, the case is that there were anemones and goldthread in the homefield, first a ring of them, then a train of them, where the two walked."

Sira Jon drew himself up and looked down upon the shorter woman, and said, "What two were these, my child?"

Margret spoke. "A mother and a child, and the babe was in a white shirt, and the mother was in a white cloak. But it is more likely, in my opinion, to have been Thora Bengtsdottir, who has twin daughters, and lives in this district."

"My sister, it was no pair of twins that I saw," said Birgitta, and she went away to put on her gown and her shoes. Sira Pall Hallvardsson looked at Sira Jon and saw that he had flushed to his hairline and that his hand that lay across the front of his robe trembled slightly. At once, Sira Jon said in a loud voice, "I have heard of this before, three instances, indeed. And in Norway alone the Virgin has appeared to young girls who were known to friends of mine. One of these girls lived on a farm in the Trondelag, and two of them in Jaemtland. And these flowers, how they appeared, that is a mark of this miracle. These spring flowers. This girl in the Trondelag picked wild strawberries out of the snow and carried them home, and these strawberries are kept carefully in a reliquary at her parish church." Margret and Sira Pall Hallvardsson looked steadily at him, and he dropped his eyes, saying, "Indeed, I have not seen them, but we may tramp about the homefield and gaze upon the spot, may we not?"

And so they did so, and the discussion of Olaf was slow in beginning. Sira Jon could not prevent himself from turning all talk to this vision, and he plagued Birgitta with questions until she went off to the dairy and closed herself inside. Finally, Pall Hallvardsson asked Margret outright, "Is it true, my girl, that you are betrothed to Olaf Finnbogason?" And without a blink, Margret declared, "Indeed, Sira Pall, this has been the case these four weeks." The servingmaid, who had been standing behind Margret, picked up some cheeses and went out.

Now Pall Hallvardsson, with Sira Jon trailing after him, sought out Gunnar in the fields and asked whether this betrothal "between Margret Asgeirsdottir and Olaf Finnbogason" had been duly announced to him, and Gunnar said, "It seems to me that I have heard of this," and he said these words steadily, without turning his gaze away from Pall Hallvardsson's face.

"When is the marriage to take place?" said Sira Jon, suddenly.

"Yuletide, when Lavrans Kollgrimsson will come for the feasting," declared Gunnar, now gazing steadily at Sira Jon.

"Even so," said Sira Jon, "we must speak to Ingrid, to see if these tidings have been announced to her."

Now Gunnar stepped in front of Sira Jon, where he had turned to go toward the steading, and he drew himself up and said, mildly, and with a smile on his face, "My old nurse sleeps most of the day, and she is very weak, and you may not go to her."

And Sira Jon glanced about himself, so that his eye fell on the spot of the homefield where the Virgin had walked with Her Child, and he did not press the point. Not long after this, the priests made ready to leave, because they wanted to finish their rowing back to Gardar before nightfall. Thus it was that Olaf returned to Gunnars Stead, but many people said that had Jon asked the question he was supposed to ask, which was, did Margret Asgeirsdottir know of any reason why Olaf Finnbogason should not continue his studies and be ordained a priest, Margret Asgeirsdottir would not have known how to answer.

When Olaf returned, he said only that there were fifty milk cows at Gardar, and they were fat and shining and sleek, and that the horses had thick manes and big haunches, and that all the animals ate better than the priests.

At Yule, in the presence of Lavrans and his folk, the wedding of Margret Asgeirsdottir and Olaf Finnbogason was held. At this time Lavrans had much talk with his daughter Birgitta, and the result was that Birgitta moved her wedding gifts into Gunnar's bedcloset and crept under Hauk's great polar bear hide with her husband. Shortly after Yule Ingrid Magnusdottir died in her sleep, and she was buried beside Hauk Gunnarsson, her favorite nursling, at the south end of Undir Hofdi church.

In the spring, Olaf and the folk of Gunnars Stead had the reward of their thrifty fast, and that was the birth of seven calves, including a fine bull calf, and of nineteen lambs. Three of these Olaf traded to Magnus Arnason of Nes in Austervik for a young mare. This mare was of a peculiar color, grayish with a dark strip down the middle of her back. Olaf named her Mikla, and he was very fond of her.

Ketils Stead was now the largest farm in Vatna Hverfi district, for Erlend Ketilsson was a hardworking farmer and his wife, Vigdis, no less so. Five children lived with them: Thordis (Vigdis' daughter), Ketil Ragnarsson, who was known as the Unlucky, Geir Erlendsson, Kollbein Erlendsson, and Hallvard Erlendsson. Vigdis had also lost two others, both girls, shortly after birth. Vigdis had grown very stout by this time, and her daughter Thordis, it was said, looked as much like Vigdis had once looked as to be her twin sister. Only Ketil the Unlucky looked like Erlend's lineage. The rest were fair and sturdy, with wide round faces and large teeth like Vigdis, and they were considered by many to be a very handsome family. Thordis, although not Erlend's daughter, was much sought after, for Erlend had pledged her a large marriage portion, and anyone could see that, like Vigdis, she would be a healthy, hardworking wife. Since they lived near to the church, they attended every mass, and Thordis often wore a long reddish robe with a high tight waist of her own design and making. Many in the district spoke of how good a farmer Erlend had turned out to be, and many numbered themselves among Erlend's and Vigdis' friends, although nearly everyone agreed that the folk at Ketils Stead could be unusually petty and exacting.

During the summer after the marriage of Olaf and Margret, a large number of skraelings began lingering near Ketils Stead, for it was a prosperous farm overlooking the fjord. Almost every day skin boats of the skraelings could be seen on the water, or drawn up on the shore, and the skraelings would make fires and cook on Erlend's land. Once one of Erlend's good ewes was slaughtered and cooked by these skraelings, but more often they simply fished in the fjord. Erlend was one of the Greenlanders who had never learned any words of the skraeling tongue, and Vigdis knew nothing of it, either, so that when Erlend went out to meet them and order them from his land he could speak to them only as he would to another Norseman. They always greeted him gaily, with much friendliness and laughter, but always acted as if they hadn't the least understanding of what he was saying or what he meant. A few neighbors laughed at this, for it was well known that skraelings often understood much of the Norse tongue. Erlend's was not the only steading used in this way by the skraelings, but because they were so exacting, Vigdis and Erlend minded it more than anyone else, as if, folk said, something more than just the one ewe had been stolen from them every time the skraelings set foot upon their land.

In addition to this, one of the skraeling boys often followed Thordis around, sometimes from a distance and sometimes closer at hand, although if the girl were to wave him away and make faces, the boy would run off in seeming fright. Neighbors who knew something of the skraelings declared that these demons especially admired stoutness in a woman. And it was true that there were no women among the skraelings quite as imposing as Vigdis and Thordis.

Vigdis declared that demons could not be bribed, for, as she had heard from Nikolaus the Priest, if a demon thought that he could get something from you, he would always come back for more, until he had reduced your wealth to nothing. Therefore, said Vigdis, she would give the demons no milk and no cheese, as some of the farmsteads did, and she would receive none of their goods into her storehouses. A few Greenlanders had gotten into the habit of trading cloth and butter to the skraelings for hides and tusks that the Greenlanders could no longer get through hunting, since journeys to the Northsetur had ended. But Vigdis would have none of these.

Erlend said that the demons must be frightened away, and he persuaded Hafgrim Hafgrimsson of Eriks Fjord, who had married a skraeling woman, to come and talk to the skraelings for him. Hafgrim did this, and he told the skraelings that Erlend and Vigdis would injure or kill anyone found on Ketils Stead thereafter, and for a day or so the skraelings stayed away, but then they returned, like maggots to a rotting carcase, and of course Erlend had no power to have them killed, because the Greenlanders had few weapons at this time, and had fallen far from the warrior days of Erik the Red or Egil Skallagrimsson and had little prowess in battle.

Erlend's already irritable nature was not improved by the summer's difficulties with the skraelings, and when, in the autumn, they departed as mysteriously as they had come, he was not made any more pleasant by their absence. And one day in the autumn, Mikla, the new mare from Gunnars Stead, was found in Erlend's horsefield with his stallion. Erlend determined that the mare was in season, and when he led the horse back to Gunnars Stead, he demanded of Gunnar the payment of two good lambs for the breeding, for, he said, a foal by his stallion would be better than any horse Gunnar had, and it was right that Gunnar should pay well for the privilege. At this Gunnar laughed and said, "Neither Ketil Erlendsson nor Erlend Ketilsson paid Thorleif for the breeding of Ketil the Unlucky, and I would follow the same rule. Unruly mares who stray get to keep what they find." Erlend was little pleased with this reply, and came toward Gunnar as if to strike him, but then Olaf appeared nearby, in the doorway of the dairy, and Erlend stepped back, saying, "After all, there will be time enough at the Thing to discuss the matter." Gunnar's remark went around the district, and folk considered it neatly said. But men cajoled Erlend into dropping his suit before the spring, because in that time breeding arrangements between farms were quite informal, and Erlend's horse was not considered such a good horse as to deserve payment for his services. Nonetheless, the ill feeling between the two farms, which had seemed to subside a little, now flourished again, and it was a bad business.

In this autumn, Gizur the lawspeaker of Brattahlid died. He was very old, and left no children, and so at the Thing the Greenlanders chose Osmund Thordarson, who lived at another large farm at the head of Eriks Fjord, to be the lawspeaker. Osmund was an enterprising fellow, a good friend of Bishop Alf, and the nephew of Gizur Gizursson. Few cases now came to the Thing, and farmers from the distant fjords began to declare that they had too much to do to make the long trip. Gardar was more centrally located, and so folk seeking conversation and trade began going more and more to Gardar for Easter, which came just before the beginning of spring work, and for the feast of St. Michael, which came after haying and the autumn seal hunt. Many also went at Yule on skis, if the fjords were frozen solid and the snow had a good crust on it. All who came noted the changes that had taken place at Gardar, and most were pleased, for although there was more bending of the knee than before, not only to the bishop, but to Jon his vicar, there was also so much activity, so many priests and boys going hither and thither, so many well-favored beasts, so many buildings that had been put into good repair, and so many new and beautiful things in the residence and in the cathedral, that the Greenlanders said to one another that the Church would never abandon them again.

Bit by bit, the bishop had learned the ways of the Greenlanders, and often judged cases as the Greenlanders themselves would have judged them. The only thing to be said against him was that he was somewhat too strict about fast days, and not quite strict enough about the "wife" of Nikolaus of Undir Hofdi church, who was really his concubine, but had lived with him for so long that she went about with him openly, and even spoke for him on all subjects, including those of proper practices and observances. In addition to this, one of the Gardar servingwomen began spending time with Petur, the plague priest, who, it was said, had once been married. The bishop allowed this, too, and, in fact, Petur still ministered to as many or more of the Greenlanders than he had before, for he was considered a kindly man, discreet, and a merciful confessor.

Pall Hallvardsson came often to Gunnars Stead, and became friends with, first, Birgitta Lavransdottir, who chattered and joked with him as a child might, and then with Gunnar and the rest of the household. He especially enjoyed hearing Gunnar tell the tales he had learned from Ingrid, and once in a while he would tell a tale of his own, which the folk enjoyed although they were strange narratives about people with odd names who lived in lands far to the south, where there was no snow at all. The Gunnars Stead folk praised Pall Hallvardsson for being a good teller of tales, but he only laughed and said that he had read the tales of other men in books, and at that he hardly remembered the details. Gunnar declared that he was surprised to hear of such books, because the only books he had ever seen contained prayers and lists of rules, nothing else. Such were the books Olaf had carried with him when he first came to Gunnars Stead. Pall Hallvardsson said that he would bring with him on his next visit a book of excellent tales that he himself owned, and this he did. The book was called in Latin "Metamorphoses," and from it Pall Hallvardsson related a tale, rendering the Latin into Norse as he spoke. This was a book he happened to have, he said, but there were other books in the bishop's library, and some of these were already written in Norse, both histories of the Norsemen and histories of others translated by Icelandic monks at Skalholt and Holar.

Now Gunnar quit his spinning and came over to Pall Hallvardsson and took the book into his hands. It was more elaborate than Olaf's books had been, with small pictures on some of the pages in faded but attractive colors. Pall Hallvardsson said that he himself had copied the book as a student, and that a friend of his had drawn the small pictures. This had taken place in Ghent, among the Belgians. After a while, Gunnar handed back the book and asked to hear another of the stories, and so Pall Hallvardsson leafed through the pages, found one, and began again to translate what he found there. It was a story about a fox and a cock, and Olaf and Birgitta found it very funny. Gunnar laughed, but said it was a child's story, not like the tales of Icelanders and Greenlanders he had had from Ingrid. Pall Hallvardsson asked for one of these, and so Gunnar related the tale of Atli, as they tell it among the Greenlanders, where it is very well known and one of the favorite tales.

There was a woman called Gudrun, he said, and she was the sister of Gunnar and Hogni, who were great heroes and very wealthy men in the time of Egil Skallagrimsson and Erik the Red. Gudrun, he said, was married to a rich farmer called Atli, who lived in the east, according to the tale, but this probably meant the east of Iceland, since there is no other mention of this Atli among the Greenlanders. Atli, too, had a great farmstead with a multitude of sheep and cows and horses, as well as rich furnishings inside a large farmhouse with high wooden beams, as high as those at Gardar, and many rooms. He also had many servants, but even so, he was not content, and was resolved to have the wealth of his wife's brothers, which was in the form of gold and silver. And so he ordered his wife to invite her brothers to the Yuletide feast, and since he kept his designs a secret, she did so, and they came alone on their horses to the farmstead of their sister's husband, eager in anticipation of great feasting, with much beer and ale as well as meat.

As soon as Gudrun led them into the farmhouse, Atli's servants seized the two men and tied them up, and Atli came to them and demanded to know where the treasure was hidden, and Atli threatened Gunnar with death, and with the death of his brother if he did not tell, but Gunnar did not tell. Then Atli told Gunnar that Hogni had indeed been killed, and that there was no use holding out, for Hogni had divulged the whereabouts of the treasure before dying, and so Gunnar said for Atli's servants to bring him Hogni's heart on a trencher. Since the servants had not killed Hogni, for he was a prodigious fighter, they seized one of their own men and put him to death and cut out his heart, which they brought to Gunnar. The heart, however, quivered on the trencher, and Gunnar declared that this was not Hogni's heart, but the heart of a coward, and so Atli himself subdued Hogni, and cut out his heart and brought it to Gunnar. And Gunnar recognized the stout heart of his brother, and declared that now he would never speak, because now only he knew the secret. At this he took his own knife and cut out his own tongue. Then Atli and his men seized Gunnar and threw him into a snake pit, where he was done to death by adders and other poisonous snakes.

That night Atli went to his bed very drunk, and did not notice the sword that his wife had placed between them. And after he was asleep, she rose up and plunged the blade into him. Then she opened the door of the farmstead, roused all the dogs and sent them outside, and burned Atli and his servants in their beds.

Gunnar paced back and forth while telling this tale, for it was one of his favorites, and he got great enjoyment from it. At the end of it, Pall Hallvardsson smiled. "This is a bloody tale," he said, "not much fit for a priest, except as an exemplum of the lives of men before the coming of Christ as their Savior."

"Is it not true," asked Gunnar, in an agitated voice, "that men are still very greedy and murderous, even those who go to the church every Sunday and make themselves good friends with the priests?"

"If there are such men, even so," said Sira Pall, "God thinks ill of a man who cherishes an enemy in his breast, and fondles the injuries done to him by others as if they are treasured possessions."

"It seems to me that Gudrun's tale is a fine one, for when I tell it, my breast swells for the injuries done to her, and her bold resolve in avenging herself." After this, they stopped talking of this tale, and Gunnar asked Pall Hallvardsson to show him some of the pictures and the words in his little book.

Now Nikolaus the Priest became very ill, and took to his bed for almost the entire winter. This illness was the occasion for even more frequent visits by Pall Hallvardsson, for he was sent by the bishop to care for the parishioners of Vatna Hverfi, which was a populous district. On one of these visits he brought with him a book of tales written in the Norse tongue, and he began to teach Gunnar to read, and Gunnar was a much more avid student than he had been many years before with Olaf. The result was that by the time Nikolaus the Priest was on his feet again in the spring, and Pall Hallvardsson stopped coming, Gunnar could read most of the book he had brought, and Birgitta, who was younger and sharper-eyed, could read all of it, so that between them they knew all of Pall Hallvardsson's tales better than he did. When this became known in the district, there was much talk, for everyone knew Gunnar Asgeirsson to be lazy and dull. Some attributed his new knowledge to the vision of Our Lady in the Gunnars Stead homefield, and others said that he was merely coming late to his wits. Most people talked about it for a little while and then forgot the whole thing, for, they said, knowledge of reading was small and useless knowledge, anyway, and without Olaf no books would keep the Gunnars Stead folk from starving as they nearly had done before.

In this winter there was a great sickness, and many people died. The course of the illness was swift, lasting only three or four days, and often it was the old people and the children who survived and those in the strength of their years who died. The first sign was always great vomiting, so that the victim could not keep the least drop of sourmilk or bit of meat inside, but must heave it all up as soon as he tasted it. Accompanying this was a great fever, so that the person seemed to be aflame within his flesh, and could not stand the touch of any hand on his cheek or even the weight of the lightest coverlet. In these signs it was not a little like other vomiting ills that came every so often, but much more severe.

One of the first to take sick and die was Thordis of Ketils Stead, and at her funeral, Pall Hallvardsson, who was still sharing the duties of Nikolaus the Priest, preached a sermon about Thordis' red dress and her lively ways, that had seemed to bode years of good health and prosperity, and had brought her nothing but the grave. And so, he said, are we all. And people of the district were much cast down by the weight of this sermon and there was much talk of the plague in Norway. Also at Ketils Stead, Geir Erlendsson died of the sickness, and then people began taking sick and dying everywhere in the district, usually one or two at each farmstead. At Gunnars Stead, Maria, the wife of Hrafn, died, and Birgitta and Olaf got sick, but managed to survive, although Birgitta was very weak, and stayed near to her bed for many days. Petur, the plague priest, also died, and two of the bishop's singing boys, and two of the other boys as well, so that services were not so elaborate as they had been. Pall Hallvardsson and the bishop himself also fell ill, but Pall Hallvardsson would take nothing but water from a tarn high in the mountains, and soon recovered, and so the bishop followed his example and recovered also.

The sickness did not depart from the Greenlanders until after Easter, and many farms were left with but one or two recuperating folk to work the fields, tend to the lambing and calving, and oversee all the spring work, so in this spring, a few farms were abandoned, as it happened never to be worked again, and on many others calves and lambs and kids were lost through neglect and the grass was left to grow in the fields however it might. In this summer, Gunnar first left his spinning and his lazy ways and worked long days in the fields doing tasks he was unaccustomed to and had little talent for.

Shortly before the morning meal, he would come to Olaf in his bedcloset and ask what was to be done that day, and Olaf would say, for example, that Gunnar should walk along the south wall of the homefield and replace any stones that might have fallen, and Gunnar would exclaim at what quick work that would be and go out into the chill morning light. But the walking would be heavy in the snow, and the stones weighty and difficult to fit, so that some he managed to put back would fall out again as he turned away. At last, toward mid-day, Birgitta would go out with his food and find him staring at a stone, seeking to find the proper turning for it with his eyes, and she would come in and say that he was doing well enough, and would surely finish very soon. Or he would be set to rake up the manure in the cowbyre, and he would rake it up under the feet of the cows themselves, so that they would flatten and scatter it before he was finished. When the grass turned green shortly after Easter, it was Gunnar who took down the last vestiges of the byre wall and carried the cows into the homefield. Hrafn and his sons, who did not take the sickness, assisted the ewes at lambing, but Gunnar had to deliver the three calves, one of whom presented hind legs first and was lost, but Hrafn and Olaf, who rose weakly from his bed, managed between them to save the cow. Now Olaf began getting up more frequently and coming out of the farmhouse, and then he began turning his hand to a little work, helping Gunnar here and there, more and more often, especially after Hrafn and his sons herded the sheep into the hill pastures and Gunnar and Olaf were alone on the farm, and the result was that when haying came around, Gunnar had not lain late in his bed one morning since the beginning of Lent, and there was much laughter about this.

When in the summer the representative and ombudsman of King Hakon and Queen Margarethe arrived in a ship from Norway, he found the settlement much depleted. The king's two farms, Foss in the south, and Thjodhilds Stead, in Kambstead Fjord, had fallen into great disrepair, and Kollbein Sigurdsson, for that was the name of this ombudsman, was not a little put out to find that the Greenlanders could not rebuild his buildings and dig out his water system at once. He kept his great tapestries rolled up and his golden vessels wrapped and put away at Gardar, and worked his fields along with his sailors. He was a man of choleric temper who had left a prosperous district in Norway and come to Greenland after incurring the displeasure of Queen Margarethe herself, it was said, though the full tale of this did not get about quickly enough to suit the curiosity of the Greenlanders.

Many farmers in Vatna Hverfi district and in the district of Hrafns Fjord declared that there was much to be said for settling one's disputes within the district and being well out of sight of the king's tax gatherer, no matter how highly the king himself was held in respect.

Not long after the arrival of the ship, a man in sailor's clothing appeared at Gunnars Stead and declared that he was known there, but neither Birgitta nor Gunnar nor Olaf recognized his face or his name, although they gave him refreshment and invited him to stay for the night, as decent folk do with travelers. Margret was away in the mountains, gathering herbs, for Birgitta was with child, and the child, said Margret, did not seem to be thriving. As it was summer, Margret did not return until late, after Olaf and Birgitta had gone to their bedclosets. Only Gunnar was sitting up with the sailor, asking him of his adventures in Norway and elsewhere, and telling him of the deaths of Asgeir and Ingrid. They were sitting out of doors in the long rays of the late sun when Margret appeared carrying her bag and striding toward them. After a few moments, she stopped, turned, and disappeared. Some time later, she came up behind them, from the direction of the steading, and she set on the bench before them Gunnar's little boat, still neatly carved, but now missing two sailors and the high knob of the bowsprit. Then she said, even before Gunnar could speak, "Good evening, Skuli Gudmundsson, welcome to Gunnars Stead." Now Gunnar, too, remembered who Skuli was, for the little boat had been his favorite plaything as a child, and he embraced the visitor.

Skuli grinned, and withdrew from his pocket the presents that he had brought from Norway: four ornately carved wooden cups, made, Skuli said, of olive wood from Jerusalem, and a small sharp knife with a silver handle Skuli had brought to Asgeir but now gave to Gunnar. To Margret, Skuli told the news of Thorleif and others she remembered. The tale of Thorleif was the unluckiest, for shortly after his return to Bergen from Greenland, he had fallen afoul of a group of merchants there known as the Hanseatic Brotherhood. These were Germans who hoped to take all of the Bergen trade for themselves, and who dealt harshly with other traders when they thought they could get away with it. This group of foreigners numbered three or more thousand, according to some, and they carried arms, refused to marry, and kept to themselves. When Thorleif returned from Greenland with his ship fully laden, his cargo had been so rich that the archbishop of Nidaros himself had insured its safety, but after the cargo was disposed of, Thorleif was at the mercy of this Hanseatic Brotherhood, who treacherously burned his ship to the waterline, and then, when he had another ship built with the money he had made from the Greenland venture, they raided the shipyard and cut the throats of the guards who were watching it, and destroyed it with axes, so that not one splinter of wood adhered to another. After this Thorleif was much discouraged, and talked of taking passage to England, but then he died in the Great Death of the year 1362. At this tale, Margret was much cast down, and she and Skuli spoke of Thorleif's loud laugh and defiant ways, and Margret said that no ship had ever come again so full of treasures as Thorleif's ship. Skuli recollected the voyage of Thorleif and Hauk Gunnarsson to Markland, and Margret told him of the English monk Nicholas, and Hauk's death among the ice floes of the Greenland bottoms.

Skuli told of himself. After returning from Greenland, Skuli had gone back to his father's small farm and farmed for a year or two, but the work seemed stupid to him after his travels, and peasants to help with the work were hard to find and asked wages that only the best men in the district were able to pay, so Skuli's father had gone into the service of a prosperous cousin, and Skuli had attached himself to another man of the district, who was anxious to make his fortune with the new young king, Hakon, and Queen Margarethe, although she preferred Danes and Germans around her. Thus Skuli had spent many of the last years in great houses, doing what he was told, and he had married the daughter of another man such as himself, of no lineage, but serviceable abilities. Her name was Hrefna, and she had borne him four boys. But, unluckily, Hrefna had died in a more recent childbirth, of a daughter who also died, and the little boys had gone to Hrefna's brother, who had a large farm in the Trondelag, and was not dependent for his meat on the whims of others. Now he was in the service of this very powerful man, Kollbein Sigurdsson, who meant to make much of his Greenland service to the king, and after this journey, Skuli would go back to his father's farm near Bergen with some wealth and try it again, for his father had died and the farm now belonged to him.

By this time the sun had approached the horizon and begun upward again, and the birds, after a brief quiet, had started their raucous calling again. Gunnar had fallen asleep. Margret showed Skuli a place to sleep, but she herself stayed up sorting through what she had gathered and hanging bunches of plants from the beams of the farmhouse. It was said in the district that Margret knew many things about the qualities and powers of plants, though her knowledge was not so deep as Ingrid's had been. Soon Olaf rose, and Margret put his morning meat before him, with an extra measure of butter for his dried meat, and then she went to him and sat close beside him in a way that was unusual. Now Olaf looked at his wife and laughed and said, "Have you been trying your own potions, then, so that you have blinded yourself to my low brow and swarthy looks?" Margret had no answer for this, and Olaf went outside.

There was a man who had a large farm on the north side of Eriks Fjord, and this farm was called Solar Fell, because of the southern slope of the fields there. It was just across Eriks Fjord from the Gardar landing, and the folk from Solar Fell had more intercourse with the Gardar folk than they had with anyone else. It was a prosperous farm, and Ragnvald Einarsson, the master of this farm, had many folk, and six healthy sons. One day during the harvest, one of the sons, a grown man by the name of Vestein who had a reputation as a simple fellow, espied a lone skraeling in his skin boat, paddling up out in Eriks Fjord and playing with his bow and arrows. This Vestein began to shout to the skraeling from the shore, saying in the skraeling tongue, "Let's see whether you can hit me from so far away." There was at this time a large group of skraelings settled about halfway up Isafjord, behind Solar Fell, and so many of the Greenlanders who lived nearby knew something of the skraeling tongue, and these farmers were enriched by the goods the skraelings had to trade, for the demons seemed to hold their own goods very cheaply, and the Greenlanders' goods very dear.

When the skraeling paid little attention to Vestein, he jumped up from his net and began to call out more loudly, so that Ragnvald himself came out of the cowbyre. Vestein was now calling out and jumping around, and other folk from the farmstead stopped their work to look, until at last Ragnvald shouted to the skraeling, "Go ahead, since he wants it so, and take good aim!" and it is true that many fathers wish to teach their sons what foolishness is by allowing them to feel its effects. The skraeling nocked his bird arrow, and indeed he did take good aim, for the tip entered Vestein at the base of his throat, and he fell down dead. Ragnvald ran down to the shore and gathered Vestein into his arms, but he called out to the skraeling in the boat, "We cast no blame on you, since you have only done what you were told to do!" Nonetheless, many of the skraelings that had settled nearby went away shortly thereafter.

Of this incident there was much talk among the Greenlanders, and blame fell on all three parties, but especially on the skraeling, for being so ready to slay a Christian. Vigdis and Erlend said that the first victim of the skraelings might have been anyone, might have been one of their sons, or their folk, in fact, during the summer when the skraelings spent so much time at Ketils Stead. When Lavrans Kollgrimsson came to visit his daughter at Gunnars Stead, he reported that Vebjorn and Oli, Vestein's brothers, had spoken ill of their father in the hearing of many, and called him a coward for his speech to the skraeling, and some folk in Hvalsey Fjord and Brattahlid district were saying that the skraeling had shot his arrow at Vestein without provocation.

After a few days of talk, it was no little difficulty to sort out the actual case of things, and the talk had gotten into every ear, including that of Kollbein Sigurdsson at Thjodhilds Stead in Kambstead Fjord, and though it was the middle of harvest, Kollbein decided to take some men and make a visit to Ragnvald, for the sake of inquiring into this matter in the name of the king.

It was the case that most of the Greenlanders did not know what to make of Kollbein Sigurdsson. He always went about in bright clothing, as did the courtiers he had brought with him, and he kept things magnificently at Thjodhilds Stead, so that Greenlanders who visited there reported a great quantity of all sorts of meat, beautiful tapestries on the walls, and lovely furnishings lying here and there about the place. But, indeed, all was in great disorder, and in the midst of the magnificence, Kollbein always took folk aside and complained of how quickly his livestock were dwindling, or how poor the harvest from his fields looked to be, or how stingy the Greenlanders were with the sealmeat and reindeer meat they allowed him. And he always spoke of one thing, and that was the Northsetur, where men had once gained a wealth of walrus ivory, and narwhal tusks, and polar bear skins and white falcons. In addition to this, it seemed to the Greenlanders that he was always looking for amusement at other folk's tables. When he was invited, he never failed to bring most of his household.

On the evening of Kollbein's arrival (with five of his men and six horses) at Solar Fell, Ragnvald gave him a great feast and showed him over the farm, and Kollbein was much impressed with it. He spoke not at all of the matter of Vestein, but only of Ragnvald's numbers of sheep and goats and cattle, and of the drying racks that stood about everywhere, and of the magnificence of the steading, and of the good looks of Ragnvald's wife and his sons.

However, on the morning of the second day, Kollbein sequestered himself with Ragnvald, and again in the afternoon, until the time of the evening meal.

On the morning of the third day, Kollbein spoke at length to Vebjorn and Oli, one in the morning and one in the afternoon.

On the morning of the fourth day, Kollbein spoke again with Ragnvald, and in the afternoon, he sat with one of his men, then took a nap.

On the fifth day, each man or woman who had knowledge of the incident came to Kollbein in the bath house, where he sat, and spoke about what he or she had seen.

On the sixth day there was a large feast in the middle of the day. The skraelings had moved off, and Ragnvald showed no inclination to pursue them, and so the result of Kollbein's visit was that Vebjorn and Oli apologized to Ragnvald in the presence of Kollbein. During these days, Kollbein's five men and their six horses all ate heartily of Ragnvald's stores and provisions, and many in the district said that by now Ragnvald had surely been sufficiently punished for having one foolish son in six.

In this fall, after the seal hunt, the farmers of Brattahlid district and Dyrnes district went to the bishop and gained permission for a great reindeer hunt on Hreiney, an island that stood at the mouth of Einars Fjord, and was teeming with reindeer at this time of year. Every fall, most farmers went to hunt the reindeer here and there in the pastures north of the settlement, or on the islands at the mouth of the fjords, but for a number of years there had been no great reindeer hunt, and the bishop had not given permission for the taking of animals on Hreiney. In this year, however, he listened closely to the farmers' tales of hardship, and declared that he shared their fears about the coming winter after so many deaths in the spring and such a poor harvest in the summer. He also ruled that one animal in ten would go to the church. Many thought that this was a stiff price, with the tithe on top as well, but others spoke glowingly of the abundance of reindeer on the island, and cared little for the price.

Gunnar and Hrafn the shepherd, who was not bad at hunting, were to go along to claim the Gunnars Stead share, and Olaf was to stay behind and care for the farm animals. Gunnar found all the tools on the farm, and all the weapons and knives, and arrayed them on the grass in front of the farmhouse for repair and sharpening. Many of these instruments had belonged to Hauk Gunnarsson—two small spears and one large one, three hand knives with long blades, although the blade of one of these was moon-shaped with use and sharpening, a large bow and eighteen long arrows, nine tipped in iron and nine tipped in sharpened bone, and a small bow and eight blunt arrows, for hunting birds, a hatchet, two larger knives, and nets of various sizes. There were also two other hand knives that had belonged to Asgeir, and two more small bows that had belonged to Asgeir and his father Gunnar Asgeirsson. The sheep-shearing knife with which Asgeir had killed Thorunn the witch could not be found. Hrafn had his own bow and arrows and a large sheep-shearing knife with a handle made of carved reindeer antler.

After sharpening and greasing the weapons, Gunnar and Olaf turned to the two Gunnars Stead boats. Both of these were ancient in age, and small enough, but both were put together of planks sawed from Markland timber, rather than of driftwood covered by sealskins. The better of the two had been taken apart and rebuilt just before the coming of the bishop by Asgeir, his steward, and a man from Isafjord named Koll the shipbuilder, who had a good reputation for this work, as well as for making barrels and house beams. Both boats were seaworthy enough to be rowed out of the fjord into the sea, and both would be taken on the hunt, for some farmsteads no longer had boats in good repair. For these two boats Olaf and Gunnar made seal tar, by digging a large pit near the bath house, and filling it with seal blubber, which they then boiled by dropping in burning stones. When this cooled, they smeared it over the bottoms of the boats to make them watertight and slippery. No one had carried pitch to the Greenlanders in many years, since the time of Thorleif, but many men said that seal tar was as good for this work.

Hreiney was the only place in Greenland where reindeer pits had been dug as they are in Norway, for the Greenlanders had many ways of killing a few reindeer, and reindeer were abundant near most districts. These reindeer pits were considered very valuable, however, and often in former times, men would go from Gardar to Hreiney and clear them out. This had not been done for many years. Most men in the district, however, declared that there would be little trouble with the pits, for they were well made and deep. Thirty-nine farms sent men and hounds to the hunt, and from Gardar set forth Pall Hallvardsson the priest and two servingmen who were skilled with game. There were forty-one small boats, almost all of them plank-built. At this, Gunnar exclaimed to Hrafn, "I had not thought the Greenlanders' were so well provided with boats. Thus it looked when Harald Harfagri set out for England, do you not think so?"

"I don't know about that," said Hrafn, "but we will be badly off if we have Harald's luck."

It was now that time of year when the days are half light and half darkness, and the ice is beginning to form again in the fjords. The fleet of boats arrived at the jetty on the island, where the sea cuts deeply between Hreiney and Stone-ey, just as the sun was rising behind Einars Fjord. They drew the many boats up on the strand, and spread out to seek the largest herds of deer, but indeed, at this time of year, Hreiney is one large herd of deer from end to end, and they had not far to seek. Gunnar stared with amazement, for he had heard of such numbers only in tales of Markland and Vinland. The hunters were in high spirits, and some rushed in among the deer with spears, greedy to take them as soon as they could. It was in this way that the young man Thorbjorn Thorgilsson was injured, through the panicked trampling of the deer, so that he always walked lamely and his breath came with the sound of twigs scraping together forever after this until the end of his life. Others had better luck, and five deer were killed before Hoskuld Hrutsson, of Dyrnes, and Osmund Thordarson of Brattahlid, who had arranged the hunt, could find the old pits.

The pits, a series of seven, were overgrown with willow scrub, and partially filled with sand, but Osmund declared that they were serviceable enough. Now the men walked some distance in a large half-circle, so that they could come up in a line behind the beasts and move them toward the pits. At first it seemed that they would have little success with this plan, for the reindeer were so plentiful that no part of the herd would move toward the pits, but the herd simply seethed and turned upon itself. At last, however, one group became frightened and broke away, and the Greenlanders were able to turn them toward the pits with deerhounds and arrows. Soon the animals were running, and the Greenlanders and their dogs after them, shouting, waving their weapons, and making a great din. At the pits, another group of men was waiting, wearing their deerskin hoods, and hiding in makeshift blinds. Gunnar and Hrafn now hid with these men, near the lip of the first pit, which had been disguised with willow brush and turves. As the first animals of the stampede stopped here, they threw up their heads and tried to turn, but the rush behind them was too great, and they slid and toppled into the first pit. Others clambered after and over them, only to fall into the second pit, or the third. There was a great bellowing. Gunnar, Hrafn, and the rest of the men ran forward after the herd had passed, and laid about themselves with spears, knives, and axes, trying to kill as many of the animals as possible before they could struggle to their feet and out of the pit, but always wary of the tossing antlers and the kicking hindquarters. Soon Gunnar, who was bruised and pummeled by the struggling of the deer, was standing in blood up to his knees.

This was the hunt on the first day. Because of the disrepair that the pits had gotten into, many deer who might have been taken got away. After the animals who had been killed were gutted and counted, it was discovered that there weren't even enough for one to each farmstead, with the bishop's price and the bishop's tithe, so Osmund and Hoskuld and Pall Hallvardsson took counsel among themselves and decided to try another way of hunting that had often been used in the western settlement, where deer were even more abundant than they were in the eastern settlement.

The next morning, before light, the men pulled half their boats into the water just beside the strand, and in each boat sat one man with a pair of oars and another with a weapon. Other men once again made a half-circle and came up behind a group of deer, this one a very large group with many head, and these they herded toward the boats, without letting them near the flat beach, but forcing them, with many yells and much clatter, to run over a high cliff near where the boats were waiting, so that the animals soon found themselves swimming in the sea. Now the men in the boats, and others with them, carrying clubs and spears and arrows, rowed among the deer and grabbed them by the antlers, jerking back their heads and cutting their throats or thrusting spears into their necks. The runners on land also got into the other boats and helped with this work. Soon the sea was boiling with the thrashing of the beasts, and red with their blood. Many deer were taken this way, although some were lost through sinking before they could be taken into the boats and carried to land. When all of these reindeer were counted, it was discovered that five would go to each farmstead and more than forty to the bishop, although some complained that the sea did not belong to the bishop, and so Gardar should only receive a price for using the pits. Others said that it was the island itself that belonged to the bishop, and therefore the reindeer on it, and anyway, there was small likelihood that the bishop, if asked to decide the case, would decide against himself.

Of the hunters, no one was killed, and only Thorbjorn was badly hurt, although three others had been gored or kicked by the struggling deer. The Greenlanders spent the rest of the day gutting the deer, and toward dusk, the fleet of laden boats made its way up Einars Fjord toward Vatna Hverfi and Gardar. Gunnar had little to say, but rowed with Hrafn at the rear of the flotilla.

Now for a few days all farm work was put aside so that the reindeer could be taken care of. Olaf stretched the hides fur side down on the grass of the homefield, and Margret hung strips of meat up to dry on the drying racks. The bones were boiled clean and stacked in the storehouse along with the antlers. The hooves were boiled for broth, and the heads skinned and singed like sheeps' heads, and the blood ran out and was made into blood puddings, and of these Birgitta was required to sup on twice daily, which she didn't mind, as she was especially fond of blood puddings. The meat from this hunt, and from the seal hunt earlier, was especially welcome to the Greenlanders in this year, for there were not as many sheep to slaughter as there had been, and when people visited from farm to farm they spoke of hunting in this way every year, for indeed, after the dozens of deer taken, Hreiney was still as full of deer as the ocean is of water after a dipperful is lifted out, and they remarked at the plenitude of game and sea animals in their land and gave thanks for God's bounty in the western ocean.

In these days the weather smiled on the folk preparing their deer, for the sky was high and clear and day after day the sun sparkled on the fields and on the blue icebergs floating in the fjords. A brisk, dry wind blew steadily from the east and the meat dried on the racks in less than a day. People were well able to work at night, for the moon shone brightly, unringed and full. Each night the northern lights waved and fluttered in the midheaven. On one of these nights, Birgitta Lavransdottir arose from her bed cupboard soaked to the waist with her waters, and Margret arose with her, and gave her a little sourmilk mixed with honey. Then they sat down with their spinning to await the coming of the pains, but after many hours and into the day they did not come. After the morning meal, Birgitta took off her headdress and brushed and arranged her hair, then she went to her bedcloset. Margret went outside to oversee the boiling of the reindeer bones, for these would later be of great use to the farmstead. With Birgitta she left Svava Vigmundsdottir, an old nurse who had come to Gunnars Stead from Kristin in Siglufjord, who was an ugly old woman indeed, with a humped back and one walleye, but knowledgeable about children nonetheless, and experienced at births.

After the evening meal, Svava said that Birgitta must be made to walk about, for sometimes this would bring on the pains, but Birgitta refused to walk, and indeed, it seemed as though she could barely stand upright. Then Svava said that once in such a case as this, she had seen a man go to lie with his wife, and soon afterward the pains had come on and the baby had been born, but Margret said that Gunnar and Birgitta would not like this, and she feared to ask them. While they were talking, Birgitta fell asleep and she slept until sunrise, but when she awoke, the pains still had not come on. At this, Svava and Margret lifted her from her bed and made her go back and forth between her room and Margret's, but they were supporting her, and her legs hardly moved.

Now the girl began to toss her head and mutter, and her cheeks became very red and warm to the touch. When they laid her in her bed, a foul odor rose around her, so that Margret was not a little reluctant to raise her shift. When Margret gave her sips of cool water from a cup, she eagerly took some, but then tossed her hand so that the rest flew onto the floor. Gunnar now came in, looked at the girl on the bed, and went out again. After a while, he came back with the "wife" of Nikolaus the Priest and two of her servants. This woman went up to Birgitta at once and undid the top of her shift. Then she placed her hands on Birgitta's breasts and began to rub vigorously, although Birgitta cried out and shook her head and tried to push her away. When the priest's wife no longer had the strength to do it, one of her servants stepped in for her, and then Margret, and then the wife again. Svava held her hand on Birgitta's belly, and the other servant stood by the girl's face with a bit of cloth, wiping away tears and sweat. After some time, Svava felt the belly go rigid beneath her hand, and then again a little while later. But the women did not stop their rubbing, for Nikolaus' "wife" said that if they did, the pains would stop, too, and the baby would never be born—she had heard that some babies had to be cut out of their mothers, though of course she had never seen this.

It was well into the night when Svava declared that she could just see the top of the baby's head for the first time, and almost morning before the baby was born, a boy as small as a puppy, his nostrils flaring and his chest heaving like a horse that had just run itself into a sweat. The "wife" took one look and whispered to her servant, who ran for Nikolaus the Priest. Margret bent down and asked Birgitta if she wanted to see the baby, but Birgitta could not speak, and lay there with her eyes closed, so Margret walked back and forth with the baby, who heaved and trembled and sometimes gave out little cries. Svava blew gently in its face, and after a while, they carried it out to Gunnar and asked him what the name would be, and he said Asgeir. And then the priest arrived just as the baby lay still in Margret's arms, and he baptized him with the name Asgeir Gunnarsson, and then after a moment he blessed him and prayed over him, and then wrapped the baby up tightly in a piece of wadmal and laid him in his cradle, and Gunnar bent down over him, and then stood up and said that they would bury him near the farmstead, where other infants had been buried in past times, and that he and Olaf would do this in the morning.

Now folk left the steading, and Gunnar went to his bedcloset, but Margret and Svava could not sleep and sat down at the table for some refreshment, and Margret said, "Do you remember the birth of Ketil the Unlucky?"

"Nay," said Svava, "but you may say that most children are unlucky for the women who give them life. I have seen enough hard births in my time. They are ill to speak of."

"Kristin has four children, and there are folk with more than that."

"Even so, I have taken care of others' children since I was twelve winters old, and it is no accident, nor the result of my ugliness that I have never known a man, because more often than not, a Christian woman gives up her life to her child, if not the first, then a later one. Hafgrim Hafgrimsson has three children about him now, and the woman hardly lay down for the births, folk say. These skraelings are different, and it matters not whether they are baptized."

"But folk will be married, and then they must have children."

"Nay," said Svava, "it seems to me that folk wish only one thing above all, and that is to have goods for themselves, to hold and to keep, and then they are surprised at the cost of these goods, for this cost is either almost more than they can pay, or more than they can pay." Now she fell silent for a space, and then she gazed at Margret across the table and said, "I have gone from steading to steading all my life, and never taken things for my own, and I have no regrets."

After this, it was many days before Birgitta Lavransdottir was able to get up on her feet again. Svava went back to Siglufjord and a servant of Nikolaus the Priest came in the days to help take care of the girl. When Margret spoke of the baby, and its death, Birgitta looked at her for a long time, and then said she was little surprised, for on the day of Svava Vigmundsdottir's coming, she had seen Margret run off and come back with a strange woman, and then, as quickly as an eye blink, the woman had turned into a blazing fire, and Margret had put her hand in the fire and brought it forth burning like a torch, and Birgitta had been so afraid that she had fallen down in a faint. Since then she had had little hope for the baby, and was grateful enough to God that he had spared her life, for

she had looked forward to death with certainty. Afterwards, Margret and
Birgitta did not speak of these things again, and neither mentioned this to
Gunnar. At Yule, Birgitta was strong enough to be churched again, and
she went forth on her own two feet, wearing the gray cloak she had
received at her wedding, and leading her husband, at her left, and her father
Lavrans at her right. And that was the tale of Gunnar's firstborn son.

The folk at Gunnars Stead were much diverted at this time by the visits
of Skuli Gudmundsson, whose duties on the king's farm at Thjodhilds
Stead were rather light. Skuli had much to say, about the court in Norway
where he had lived for many years, and about Kollbein the ombudsman,
and he had a way of telling these stories that made their subjects seem
foolish. Margret sometimes teased him, wondering in what sly ways he
spoke of Gunnars Stead when he was at Thjodhilds Stead, but Skuli knit
his brows and feigned ignorance of this.

He also told them what sorts of things folk were wearing at Queen
Margarethe's court, for, he said, the court always dressed in a rich and
colorful way even when they had no meat for the table and no wood for
the fire. Queen Margarethe herself, Skuli said, was low and dark, not at
all pretty, though all of the courtiers said she was, but she had an attentive
way about her that showed she knew where to step. King Hakon was more
handsome, like his father Magnus, and in Skuli's view, this caused folk to
pay attention to him when they might better be watching the queen, and
indeed, this very thing had overtaken Kollbein the ombudsman, who had
been a tax collector in the Trondelag and had made a rich man of himself.
He had purchased two estates for next to nothing, though they were much
improved with good byres, rich chapels, and water systems in excellent
repair. It was the queen who noted the richness of these estates and
compared them to the relative leanness of the tax collections for these years.
Although Kollbein had in fact purchased these estates for much less than
it appeared, and probably had not cheated the treasury, he had spent so
much time flattering the king and so little flattering the queen, that the
queen had turned a displeased ear to his protestations when he made them,
and sent him off to Greenland as his punishment, placing some Danes upon
his farms as "stewards."

"We should pity him for these hardships," said Margret, "but folk
only laugh at him."

"He knows not what to do with Thjodhilds Stead and Foss," said
Skuli, "though they are goodly pieces of land. He chatters on and on only

about bearskins and walrus tusks. And he has slaughtered nearly all the sheep that the Greenlanders gave him. It doesn't seem to the sailors that the Greenlanders will be so generous again. We all look forward to empty bellies."

Now Olaf spoke up, and said, "This Kollbein is the king's tax collector, is he not? He must know that there are farms in other districts, and that generosity has little to do with it, come to that."

Formerly, Skuli had spoken of his dead wife, and especially of his four sons, but now he did not do this as much, because, perhaps, of the recent death of the baby Asgeir Gunnarsson. He acted very kindly toward Birgitta Lavransdottir, and carved her a small round box with a lid out of the base of a large reindeer antler. Around it marched the figures of a polar bear and a seal and a man with a bow and arrow. For Margret, he carved six sharp needles out of bird bones, and they were very cleverly done, so that the eye of a needle was hardly wider than the body, although big enough to carry seal-gut thread. Although these gifts were remarkable to the Gunnars Stead folk, Skuli hardly paused in his talk while he made them. In return, Margret and Birgitta sewed Skuli a pair of purplish stockings from the thickest and warmest Gunnars Stead wadmal, woven by Gunnar himself, and Skuli was considered by the folk at Gunnars Stead to be an old and good friend.

Pall Hallvardsson, too, continued to visit, and Skuli's stories sometimes aroused him to remember ones he hadn't told before, about his childhood among Belgian priests, and the things he had learned there about singing and illuminating manuscripts. From time to time, though, he and Skuli discussed the Great Death and the sinfulness of cities, where unprotected folk passing through the ways at night were as likely as not to be beaten and stripped of their possessions, if not killed, and where such abundance of food as the Greenlanders knew except in the severest winters was never known to anyone but the highest folk.

"As for abundance," said Margret, from her great loom, "anyone who has come to the Greenlanders after the time of Ivar Bardarson, and since men stopped hunting in the Northsetur, has never known abundance. It took a whole summer's day to carry all of the Greenlanders' goods out of the bishop's storehouses when Thorleif departed for Norway, and this was not only wealth, but also meat and sourmilk and blubber and eggs and other good things to eat. Thorleif himself said to my father Asgeir that the ship sat so low in the water that the sailors would have to eat their way to Bergen."

"That was a fat trip, indeed," said Skuli, with a laugh, "not like our

crossing with Kollbein Sigurdsson, for all that he is the king's representative. It seems to me that the queen must have purposely stinted him on
money for provisions so that the sailors would grumble the whole journey." And so the talk went on many evenings, while Margret and Birgitta
wove and spun, and Skuli carved this and that, and Gunnar repaired such
furnishings as needed his attention.

Once, in very early winter, when Margret was in the hills above
Vatna Hverfi laying partridge snares, a man came upon her suddenly, and
gave her a fright. He was wearing a shirt and hood of very thick sheepskin
that fell forward over his face, so that she didn't know him, and when he
stepped out from a willow cleft, where he had been doing something, she
jumped back and gave a cry. As she stepped back, her foot rolled with a
loose stone, so that she would have fallen, except that the man caught her
elbow and held her up.

There was a man at this time living above Vatna Hverfi district, who
had committed the crime of killing his cousin over a horse fight, and had
been outlawed for three years by the Thing, although in Greenland outlaws
were allowed to live at the fringes of the settlement, sometimes among the
skraelings and sometimes not, since there was no going abroad as there had
been in the old days. This man was named Thorir the Black-browed, and
so, when Margret regained her balance, she said, "Thank you, Thorir
Sigmundsson," and backed away from him, for it was not known how he
had been enduring his time of outlawry. Nonetheless, although she was
afraid, she took three fat ptarmigan from her pouch and laid them side by
side on a flat rock at her feet, saying, "You would do me a great favor
by accepting these poor birds, Thorir Sigmundsson." Then she backed
away, slowly, not taking her eyes off the outlaw and feeling her way with
her feet. The man neither looked at her, nor picked up the birds, and after
a while she was out of his sight and she ran the rest of the way to Gunnars
Stead.

The next evening, when she came into the farmhouse from the
dairy, the three birds, all neatly plucked, were lying on the bench beside
the fire. Margret went at once to the door and surveyed the homefield
for signs of the outlawed man, for there were many reasons why such
visits were not a little to be feared, and the fact that they were contrary
to the law was not the least of these. Vigdis, the wife of Erlend, for one,
would be glad of something new to bring against the Gunnars Stead
folk. Aside from this, an outlawed man living above Isafjord had gained
entrance to an isolated farmstead and stolen a great deal of food from
both the kitchen and the storehouse, although the tale that he had killed

a member of the family had turned out to be false. But there were no signs of anyone except Olaf and Skuli, who were standing near the cowbyre. Margret took the birds outside around the house and buried them in the midden with a spade.

After that, Birgitta came from her bedcloset, and the two women prepared the evening meal of reindeer meat seethed in broth, sourmilk, and dulse mixed with butter and spread on dried meat. Soon Olaf came in and sat before his trencher, and looked at it once, and said, "What more is there to eat, then? I am looking for a good roast ptarmigan."

Birgitta laughed. "You may look for it as hard as you please, but you are not likely to find it until we have all eaten our fill of reindeer meat."

Olaf looked around again. The roasting spit was standing upright, unused, near the fire. The only birds in the room were the wheatears and larks in Margret's willow cages. "Well," demanded Olaf, "where are these birds Skuli Gudmundsson has brought us, plucked and bled? I laid them on the bench myself."

Now Margret looked at Skuli, who laughed heartily in his beard. "Indeed," he said, "I have heard that from time to time a ghost may come between a gift and its recipient, and so it is considered the better course to place it in the hands of the one you are giving it to."

Olaf growled, "Anything is possible, but truly I have been looking forward to roast fowl all afternoon."

Later that evening, Margret went to Skuli, and said that it ill behooved him, especially as one of the ombudsman's men, to consort with outlawed men and in reply, Skuli went outside and carried in a large sheepskin shirt with attached hood, and declared to Margret that she should admire the thing, poor as it was, for one of the young women at Thjodhilds Stead had sewed it for him, and he expected to be very warm in the winter. At this, Margret reddened and turned away, and what had befallen the three birds on the bench remained a mystery that the Gunnars Stead folk talked about for a day or so afterward.

In this fall, Gunnar and Hrafn counted a hundred and sixty-two sheep and goats, thirty-four cows, and four horses, including Mikla, that now belonged to Gunnars Stead. Also in this fall, Hrafn brought home a new wife from another farmstead in Vatna Hverfi, named Katla. In age, Katla fell somewhere between Birgitta and Margret, but much of the time she spoke nonsense, and so the Gunnars Stead folk considered her silly. She was good-natured, however, and worked well if someone stood near her and helped her keep her mind on her tasks. Now Hrafn came to Gunnar and asked if one of the outbuildings could be put in good order for himself and his new wife. The boys, who were now eleven and nine, would continue to sleep off the cowbyre, as Hrafn had done when married to Maria. Maria had been born at Gunnars Stead in Asgeir Gunnarsson's time, and had preferred to sleep in the farmstead where she always had slept, but this was not suitable for a stranger, Hrafn explained. Now Olaf and Gunnar went around to all the buildings with Hrafn, trying to choose a large enough one that would take only a little fixing up, for Gunnar did not care to hire anyone to help with this work, although neither he nor Olaf was especially clever at building.

Soon a building was chosen, of about ten ells long and eight ells wide, that had once been used as a storehouse in the time of Gunnar Asgeirsson, the father of Asgeir. The masonry in this building was still in good repair, and turves could be easily cut nearby. In addition, the east wall of this house was built into the side of a hill, so that the only real difficulty would be replacing two rotten beams under the roof. When Olaf stuck his finger into them, the wood crumbled away into powder. Now Gunnar had to bethink himself where he might get two stout beams, and what he would have to pay for them. The next time that Pall Hallvardsson and Skuli were visiting, Gunnar leaned back in his seat after the evening meal and declared, casually, that he was thinking of building, if he could find the wood to build with. Pall Hallvardsson said that he had heard that others were thinking of building, too, not only Kollbein the ombudsman, who was always thinking of something, but a farmer of Eriks Fjord, who wanted to put up a new storehouse, and a farmer near Gardar, who wanted to add two rooms to his house. He didn't know about the men of Vatna Hverfi or the southern districts, but it was common knowledge that wood was in short supply, and that old houses would have to be taken down before new ones could be put up. Gunnar made no reply to this, and afterwards, they spoke of other things.

Now, whenever Gunnar met another farmer or went to church, he mentioned casually that he was thinking of building, if he could get the wood to build, and one by one he began to hear of who else wanted wood and who had wood to trade, and there were more of the former than there were of the latter. After this, Gunnar and Olaf went around to the Gunnars Stead buildings again and tried to decide what could be torn down, so that they could use their own wood, but the buildings not in use were so old that their beams were much like the two beams in Hrafn's house, so that some bargain had to be made with someone, and many Gunnar asked in the district declared that it would have to be made with Erlend, for indeed, Erlend still had six great beams of wood from Markland that had never been used, and this was more than any other farmer had, but Gunnar said that he would not go to Erlend.

Now Lavrans and his servants came from Hvalsey district to visit with Birgitta, and Lavrans declared that a farmer in his district had one beam of wood in excellent condition that he would trade for four good heifers bred to the Gunnars Stead bull, and Gunnar asked if Lavrans had seen the wood, and Lavrans said that he had, and that the man was not lying about its soundness, although it was only about eight ells long. Gunnar agreed to the deal, if the man, who was a prosperous farmer with many servants, would send the beam to Vatna Hverfi and take the heifers back himself, and Lavrans guaranteed for this.

Now Gunnar heard that Erik Thorleifsson had found wood to build his storehouse from a farmer in Isafjord, and that he had traded for eight beams, enough for the storehouse and more, and Gunnar said angrily that this seemed rather greedy to him, but Pall Hallvardsson said that the tale was that he had paid six cows apiece for the beams, and that they were old and not especially sound. After this, there was news from Thord Magnusson of Siglufjord that a beam could be had in Alptafjord, but Gunnar declared that he knew of no way he could get it in one of his own small boats, and the farmer who owned the wood had no boat. Now there was no news for a while, and Hrafn came to Gunnar and said that Katla was complaining day and night of sleeping beside the cowbyre, and Hrafn asked that Gunnar go to Erlend and get the wood from him, but Gunnar did not agree to do this. Instead, he and Olaf and Skuli repaired what they could of the new building, hoping other news would come.

It was getting well toward Yule, and the ground began to be frozen with hoarfrost every day, although there had as yet been no snow. The cows were still grazing in the homefield, and had not as yet been walled into the byre. On one of these days, Gunnar looked out to see Vigdis approaching, and he turned to Olaf and said, "A strange ship is sailing in the Gunnars Stead waters."

Now Olaf looked out, and replied, "It is an ill-omened ship to be sure, and a switch in the wind is unlikely to carry it away."

Margret came out of the storehouse, and went up to Vigdis and took her into the steading. A little while later, Gunnar wandered past the door to the steading, which was closed, and feigned stumbling, so that he bumped against it. Margret opened it. Inside, Vigdis was sitting on a bench, drinking a cup of sourmilk. In front of her were various other refreshments. Margret glanced at Gunnar and lifted her eyebrows. Gunnar entered and sat down. Vigdis looked him up and down without smiling or scowling, and finished her milk deliberately, not forgetting afterwards to wipe her upper lip with the sleeve of her gown. At last she said, politely, "It seems to me that I have heard of the death of the child Asgeir Gunnarsson."

Gunnar nodded.

"It is an unlucky year for children."

Gunnar nodded again.

Now she pushed the cup away from her and the other things to eat and looked at Margret, but said to Gunnar, "There is a tale in the district that you are thinking of building and that you have found beams in Alptafjord."

"Indeed, there is a sound beam to be had in Alptafjord, for a small trade."

"Alptafjord is far away, though."

"Not far from the bird cliffs where my father used to take us for eggs."

"Egg laying time is even farther away."

Gunnar shrugged.

Vigdis looked at him. "It's fine to be indifferent when you can. The tale is that Katla is not indifferent."

"There are bedclosets at Gunnars Stead that go empty at night. Katla doesn't need to ask the neighbors to find out such things for her."

"Five cows is not a lot for a beam that is close at hand."

"Does someone in the district need a beam?"

"There is a half-built house on a farm in the district that could be weathertight before Yule."

Now Gunnar settled his back against the wall of the farmhouse, and let his eyes close. After a long time, he said, "We have a new building on our farm, just by chance. But we don't need any beams." Then he was silent for a long time, as if he had fallen asleep. After a while, Vigdis motioned to Margret to help her to her feet. As Margret did so, Vigdis said, "It is my opinion that the Gunnars Stead folk have done little in this matter to make friends, and all in the district know how Gunnar Asgeirsson cherishes ancient disagreements." She glanced once or twice at Gunnar, but his eyes did not open. Margret accompanied her a little way on her walk back to Ketils Stead. Soon, Gunnar returned to the new building, and set about helping Olaf put turves into place. The ground was too frozen, now, to cut new ones, and Olaf declared that it was a bad time of year for such work. That evening, after eating, Gunnar declared that if Hrafn's sons were old enough to sleep alone beside the cowbyre when their father was across the field in a new building, then they could sleep alone there if their father and Katla were sleeping in Ingrid's old bedcloset, and Hrafn agreed that this was so, and in this way Katla and Hrafn moved into the farmhouse for the winter.

Now Yuletide came on, and since the ground was hard and good for traveling, and there had as yet been snow only to the north, in Isafjord, many more souls than usual went to the cathedral at Gardar for the Christmas mass and feasting. Since the fjords were frozen over, many traveled on skates made from reindeer bones, and others traveled on horseback, and the horses were turned out in the giant Gardar homefield. Of the Gunnars Stead folk, only Olaf and Hrafn's sons stayed behind to look after the livestock. Olaf declared that Gardar was too busy for him, and too full of the bishop. Then Margret said that she, too, would stay behind, but went after all, because Birgitta Lavransdottir wanted her to.

Now it happened for the first time that many of the Greenlanders got a good look at Kollbein Sigurdsson and his retainers and sailors, who sat together near Kollbein's high seat. Margret saw that Kollbein was a dark man with a round face and small round eyes, who dressed in furs, like the bishop, but wore them casually, half thrown off his shoulder, rather than for warmth. Skuli, Margret saw, sat next to him, and repeatedly, Kollbein turned to Margret's friend and asked him who those present might be. Once or twice his eyes fell on Margret herself, and once she saw Skuli's lips make the words "Margret Asgeirsdottir," but although her friend was looking right at her, his glance did not distinguish her in any way. Kollbein's gaze slid quickly past Gunnar, but lingered on the more prosperous farmers, such as Erlend Ketilsson, until it was almost a stare. Birgitta Lavransdottir, the sharp-eyed, was watching Kollbein, too, and now she whispered to Margret that the ombudsman looked as if he were counting Erlend's head of cattle as they filed into the byre for winter. Erlend and Vigdis were regarding, with smiles, the bishop and Jon the Priest, to whom they had brought six Ketils Stead cheeses.

In fact, the gifts brought by the Greenlanders to Gardar made a great array, though there was an especially large number of things of humble home manufacture—lengths of wadmal, sheepskins, and some fancy weaving in the form of bands for the decoration of vestments. This was not a year in which the benches of Gardar Hall were piled with bear hides and walrus ivory and silver from Ireland and manuscripts from Normandy and York and silk from Italy and wine from France, as they had once been, when Greenlanders traveled widely in every direction. Even so, the farmers and their wives nodded and gaped at the collection and spoke, as they had done after the reindeer hunt, of the richness of their home.

Now the bishop stood and made his blessing over the feast, and his voice, though unusually low, was still penetrating, and his eyes, when he looked out over the assembled guests, blazed forth with their usual light. "Lord," he breathed, "bless especially the bread and wine the safe arrival of Kollbein Sigurdsson has brought us. And bless Kollbein himself, who is the honored representative of the great King Hakon, his wife Queen Margarethe, and the old King Magnus, who sometimes seem to forget their loyal subjects in Greenland, but this year have remembered them so fittingly. And we beg, oh Lord, thy special blessing also for the meat of the reindeer from the great hunt on Hreiney, which reminds us all of your abundance everywhere in creation. For the other, more usual fare, we also ask thy blessing, for this is the meat that thy souls live by, from day to day, sometimes plentiful and sometimes spare, but always sufficient unto our needs." And at this point the bishop seemed to fall back into his high seat, and the voice of Sira Jon rang out, "For this and all our blessings, O Lord, we thank thee." Here Margret craned her neck for a look at the bishop, as did everyone around her. But the bishop weakly motioned all to begin, and soon the hall was resounding with the clamor of the feast.

Soon it seemed to Margret, with the passing of the basins and the bread that the hall had grown very hot and smoky, and that the voices of Gunnar and Birgitta beside her were at once too loud to bear and too soft to be understood, for truly she was like her uncle Hauk in this, that she did not care for feasting and large groups of folk. She stood up and found her way outside.

The great Gardar homefield, hard and glistening with frost, spread down to the strand and the pale, luminous ice, and Margret took some deep breaths of the fresh air. And now she turned and discovered Skuli approaching, and he was dressed in his blue and red court dress and his hair was neatly done up in blue and red bands. He seemed to Margret very fair, as fair as he had seemed to her many years before, when he had stayed at Gunnars Stead and carved for her a spindle in the shape of a grinning face, which she shrank from using, but kept with her in her pocket for many years. As he approached her, he seemed to her much fairer than Olaf Finnbogason, and that distant time much closer to the present than all of the intervening years.

Now Skuli came up to her and stood near her, and said, "Margret Asgeirsdottir, it seemed to me that you grew pale in the hall, and left the feast suddenly. Are you ill? Have you been made ill by the bread? Indeed, it is ill enough bread."

"Nay." Now she turned away from him and looked out over the Gardar homefield, toward the giant cowbyre, where many Gardar cows were cozily walled up, waiting for spring. At this, Skuli stepped back and said in a more usual voice, "Gardar has prospered in the years since the coming of the bishop, though others have not, I know."

"It is true that others have not, and folk lay the blame here and there. But it seems to me that the bishop is like a storm or an act of God, whose coming might be for good or ill, and I have no bitterness against him, though my Gunnar may. It is something not often talked about."

Now, as they looked, servants came out of the storehouses, carrying hay to the cowbyre on large hides, dragging them over the frozen ground. Skuli remarked that the Greenlanders' way of transporting feed still amused him, but Margret interrupted him. "Know you the tale of Olaf's return to Gunnars Stead?"

"Nay."

"It happened one day that this Audun, who is now a priest, came from Gardar to get Olaf, who was to continue his studies for the priesthood and be made a priest by the bishop, and Olaf had to go away after many years at Gunnars Stead. On the first day of Olaf's departure, our folk milled about like sheep, not only Gunnar and Birgitta, who was but a child then; I myself barely remembered how to serve the meals and stir the whey, things I have done since I was five winters old. Gunnar had sat down at once and told a story, and Birgitta and the servants spent the whole morning listening to him. I went into the hills to set snares and gather herbs, but my snares tangled and I gathered nothing." She looked at Skuli. He was very handsome. She went on, "Now I was in despair, for I saw that the great farm of my fathers had fallen into the hands of fools, and that Gunnar and I and Birgitta, a guiltless child, would quickly starve. And we went on at this rate for two more days, so that little was done, though good luck would have it that the beasts were still grazing in the hills. It does not seem to me that we would have had the wit even to feed them, had it been a different time of year.

"And then on the third day, the priests Jon and Pall Hallvardsson came to us, and I knew at once that they were coming about Olaf, although they spoke for a long time of another matter. And we had this bit of luck, that Pall Hallvardsson, who was a friend, spoke first, and asked me directly if I was betrothed to Olaf, and I saw in his glance a message that Olaf was as unhappy at Gardar as we were to have him there, and so I said I was. And one of the servingwomen slipped out and carried this news to Gunnar, so that when Jon spoke to him, he, too, attested to a proper betrothal. And so, a day or so later, Olaf returned, and we didn't starve after all, but prospered, even in this year, when hardly anyone in the eastern settlement can say the same."

"It seems to me that you have not done ill to take such a talented husbandman into the family, but in the court of Queen Margarethe and in other great houses in Norway and Denmark, it is not considered ill for a man to admire a married woman, to recognize something graceful in her figure, for example, or to see something precious in the color of her eyes." Now he touched one of her braids with his finger, and said, "Indeed, it is rare for a woman's hair to grow heavier and paler after girlhood, but your braids are thicker than a man's wrist and as pale as hay in the sunlight."

Now Margret felt her face grow hot, and said, "At Gunnars Stead, the married women are sometimes careless of our headdresses, and this is a shame to us."

"Nonetheless, a man's eyes do no harm to a virtuous woman, and those things he might do in her honor or for her benefit are no compromise to her."

"Now it seems to me that we have been talking too long and will be missed from the feast." And she turned and went inside without looking at him again.

In this year after Yule, the weather grew very cold, and a great deal of snow fell, so that the horses and sheep could not paw through it to the grass beneath. Because of the vomiting ill a year before, there were few extra hands for chasing sheep who strayed toward the fjords or for gathering seaweed as feed. Many sat beside their fires wrapped in cloaks and furs and declared that God would have to take care of the sheep this year. In some low, moist places, the cowbyres were almost entirely covered in drifting snow, and holes to the breathing vents had to be dug and redug. In other ways, too, the winter seemed especially fierce, and this was a great topic of conversation until the feast of St. Thorfinn, when a very perplexing thing occurred in Eriks Fjord. There was a farmer named Helgi Grimsson, who had a small farm called Mel, where he lived with his son. One day this Helgi went out after a blizzard to seek his sheep, and found them not far from the farmstead, twenty-six of them, and all had had their throats cut, and they lay frozen in the snow.

Shortly after this, Helgi dreamed the same dream for two nights in a row, and that was that a rank of fire came marching up his hillside homefield like an army of men, and burned everything in its path, including Helgi, who both saw himself burn and felt the burning. On the second morning of this dream, Helgi took down the south wall of his cowbyre, in spite of the snow, and led his four cows outside and fed them some hay. That evening, he refused to put the cows back, although he could not say why. In the night, a fire began in the cowbyre, and burnt up all the dung and dried turf in the byre, but through Helgi's cleverness, the cows were saved. Now Helgi refused to live any longer at Mel, and went to Gardar as a servant, giving his son over to the bishop to be trained as a priest. These events were much discussed, and many watched for similar happenings at Gardar once Helgi and the boy were in residence, but all remained quiet. And so spring came on.

One day just before the beginning of the spring work, Gunnar took one of the horses and went to Gardar, where he spent the night. The next day, he spoke to his usual friends, but was also seen in discussion with the farmer Helgi. Then he came home. The result was that after the spring work was completed, and the sheep were in their summer pasture and the fjords were free of ice, four beams were brought to Gunnars Stead in the large boat belonging to Osmund Thordarson, and these were from the farmhouse at Mel, for Helgi had decided to tear down the ill-omened house, and Gunnar had bought the beams for one cow apiece. These cows were taken over to Gardar in the same boat, and kept in the Gardar herd along with Helgi's other cows. Now many folk in Vatna Hverfi said that Gunnar had made a good bargain, and had not had to travel far to make it, but others said that the calculated insult to Erlend Ketilsson weighed heavily against Gunnar's thrift. Olaf and Gunnar now fixed up the old outbuilding for Hrafn and Katla, and Gunnar let it be known that he had three beams of wood to trade. The peculiar happenings at Mel were never explained, though folk spoke of them for a good while.

Skuli Gudmundsson was little impressed by Kollbein Sigurdsson, who complained unceasingly of the discomforts of Thjodhilds Stead, which were certainly greater than those of the court or either of Kollbein's two estates in Norway, and also greater than all but the poorest farms of the Greenlanders. Kollbein was always scheming for invitations to Gardar or Brattahlid and always asking about the prosperous farmers of other districts—how big were their houses, how much hay did they have for the winter, how many sheep and cows and horses and servants. He spoke always of an accounting—the king would have to know what these Greenlanders had, and how much they owed to him, through his trusted tax collector, but beyond sitting with his clerk, an Englishman named Martin of Chester, from time to time, he made no effort to do this accounting, but frittered away what his neighbors gave him for his support.

After a while, these sessions with Martin became fewer, and the king with his court seemed farther and farther away.

Of Kollbein's retainers, all were sailors and city men by birth except Skuli and two others, brothers who were a farmer's sons named Egil and Erik from the Vestfold. These three often commented on what fine farms Thjodhilds Stead and Foss had once been, with large, well-manured fields, sturdy buildings, and a good water supply, but it was beyond their strength to farm it by themselves, as heedless as Kollbein was, and the result was that Egil and Erik, like Skuli, preferred to be away from Thjodhilds Stead as much as they could.

In this spring, Skuli Gudmundsson began to meet Margret Asgeirs-dottir in the hills above Vatna Hverfi where she was accustomed to roam, setting snares and gathering herbs. Always he spoke about her figure and her countenance in a way that she had never heard before, and after a little, it got to be something that she was consumingly curious to hear. Or he told her tales of life with Kollbein that made her laugh, or tales of Norway and the court of Hakon and Margarethe that dazzled her, or simple bits about himself and his thoughts that intrigued her. Always he made her gifts. His hands were never idle.

These meetings, which were neither frequent nor infrequent, had no effect on Skuli's visits to the Gunnars Stead folk, who welcomed him as readily as ever, and who were especially glad of his assistance in the building of the new house. Only Margret dreaded his coming, but only she looked for him, and was cast down when three days went by without a visit. Sometimes Birgitta, the sharp-eyed, looked at her and declared that she seemed feverish and anxious. With the building and the lambing and the calving and the birth of a large gray foal to his favorite mare, Mikla, as well as the other work that had to be done about the farm, Olaf Finnbogason was often out of the house. Olaf had now grown to be quite round, but he was reputed a very strong man, and he was sometimes called to other farms to tame unruly bulls and stallions. His large belly was hard and his thighs muscular from seventeen years of farm work.

Skuli looked not at all like Olaf. Where one was dark, the other was fair. Where one's strength was in his legs and hips, the other's was in his arms and shoulders. Where one cut his hair short and went bareheaded, the other wore his hair to his shoulders with a colorful cap as it was done in Norway, at the court. Where one spoke infrequently, and then only to make a joke, the other spoke often, about every subject. Where one had lived only at Gardar and at Gunnars Stead, the other had lived in many places and seen many more. Where one would be a

Greenlander all of his life, following the same habits until he died, the other would soon be gone, as he had left before. Where one's work was always to be done and redone through the round of the year, the other fashioned now this cunning knife handle, now that clever chess piece, things that could be taken up in the hand and looked on with pleasure over and over. Where one saw the homefield and the byre and the farmhouse and the dairy and the family with Margret among them, the other saw only Margret, or, at times, he didn't see Margret at all, but instead her hair and her eyes and her hands and her breasts, or the swell of her hips and the sway of her gait, or even smaller things, such as the fall of her cloak at one moment or the turning of her head at another. After being with him, Margret, too, saw these things—her wrist, her skirt swinging about her, and she felt a puzzlement and an exhilaration that, as it faded, she yearned to feel again.

Skuli, too, was deeply curious about Margret Asgeirsdottir, and felt keenly the change that had occurred in her between the visit of Thorleif and the visit of Kollbein, so that she was like two beings to him, a woman and a ghost of a girl or a girl and a ghost of a woman. The result was that when he was not with her he wanted to see her and assuage his curiosity, but when he was with her his curiosity was not assuaged but heightened, so that he cataloged this and that about her, but in speaking of it, lost it, and had to speak of something else. He regretted that he was not a learned man, for he had heard poems written to ladies, extolling their virtues, but he could not remember them. And he had heard a sermon once, which took as its text the Sayings of King Solomon about the Church, but these, too, he had never learned, and he was ashamed to approach Sira Pall Hallvardsson with such a request, asking the priest to inflame him with Holy Writ.

In addition to this, Margret was so unlike his wife that when he was with the Greenland woman, he could not stop remembering the other. He remembered her, and his sons, as he had been unable to do by himself, and he longed for them more and more freshly, until it seemed that only Margret, who looked and acted nothing like his wife had done (for the one was teasing and talkative and the other quiet and serious) could assuage the stab and twist of such longing. The result was that in the spring, after the ground had warmed up and Margret's herb gathering afforded her a daily excuse for forays into the hills, Skuli and Margret lay together as man and wife, and Margret admitted that she had never in fact been with Olaf in this way since she was given at her marriage feast by her brother Gunnar Asgeirsson.

Of Gunnar Asgeirsson and his wife Birgitta Lavransdottir there is this
to say, that they ceased entirely to be children in the winter after the death
of the baby. Gunnar was now twenty-two years old and fully grown, as
big as Hauk Gunnarsson and more similar to him in appearance than to
Asgeir, with long arms and legs and something of Hauk's graceful way of
moving, although he still had no skill at hunting or trapping. For him,
Birgitta Lavransdottir was a fitting companion, and folk said they made
a handsome enough couple. Birgitta was short but not slight, agile and
strong for a woman. Her hair had darkened and thinned, and she no longer
forgot her headdress. She was seventeen years old.

One day in the spring, she called Katla to her and she gave her two
lengths of wadmal for gowns, and another length for clothes for Hrafn's
sons. Then she gave her a handsome carved horn spoon in a clasped case,
and praised her for her good work and faithful service. Now they went
into the dairy and counted the cheeses and lumps of butter and tubs of
sourmilk, and Birgitta declared that in the time of Asgeir Gunnarsson, there
had been such an abundance of these things that another storehouse was
needed in addition to the dairy, just to hold the summer's produce. Then
they went to the storehouse where the dried sealmeat was kept, and the
store was greatly depleted, for the end of winter had passed and spring was
only just begun, and Birgitta declared that, soon enough, dried sealmeat
would mount to the ceiling, year around, so that ugly or rotten bits could
be thrown away without a second thought. After this they looked into vats
of seal blubber, both melted and pickled, and racks of dried reindeer meat,
and other dried meats. Then they got out all the rolls of wadmal and all
the hides and sheepskins, and Birgitta looked carefully at everything before
having it put back. Then she walked around the farm and looked carefully
at the buildings, and the livestock, and the two boats, and the wheeled cart,
and the stone walls around the homefield, and then she walked across the
homefield and gazed for a long time at Erlend's field, which his servants
were manuring, but which had for generations been the Gunnars Stead
second field and had supplied Gunnars Stead with all that could be called
wealth—everything above a sufficiency. She was at this for two days.

Now she was sitting at her evening meat, and she said to Gunnar, "A
poor man is like a farmer who farms on a low island. When the river rises
over his fields, he counts himself lucky to have his sheep, for he has moved
them higher, and when the river carries away his sheep, he congratulates
himself for leading the cows onto the roof of the cowbyre and letting them
graze there, and after the drowning of the cows, he thanks the Lord that
he has a boat to put his children in. When the boat is swamped and the

children swept away, he considers himself lucky to be able to swim, and he loves his luck all the way until his strength gives out and he, too, goes under. But a rich man is a man with forethought enough to farm high on the shore, who never speaks of luck, and expects the river to flood every year."

"This is probably true enough," said Gunnar.

Now Birgitta looked at him, and said, "I asked Lavrans at Easter when his father used to carry the cows out of the cowbyre, and he said that this used to be at the beginning of the summer nights, but once or twice much earlier than that, close to the beginning of Lent. Now, we often cannot carry the cows out before the feast of St. Hallvard, and never as early as Lent. Once we carried the cows out in the week after Easter and counted ourselves fortunate to do it."

"I have heard such things myself, but often old men misremember."

"There is another tale you might care to hear."

"I might."

Birgitta lifted her eyes to his, and said, "More often than not, Lavrans' father, this Kollgrim, did not carry his cows into the field at all, but led them, for in those days the hay always lasted through the winter, and the cows themselves went to it and finished it off in the spring."

"This might indeed be true."

Now Birgitta said, "A rising flood can take many forms."

After this, Gunnar, too, got into the habit of overlooking the work on Erlend's field, and Birgitta became as irritable about waste as Vigdis was reputed to be, so that the folk at Gunnars Stead sometimes laughed and called her over to look at their trenchers when they had finished eating their meat. However, she was not niggardly, and fed everyone generously, for she had taken over much of the cooking from Margret, with Katla as her helper. In this summer, she sent Hrafn's older boy to Hvalsey Fjord with twenty ewes and lambs, and there these beasts grazed on Lavrans' rich pasturage, and this was a practice that continued for many years, so that in some years there were more Gunnars Stead sheep at Lavrans Stead than there were Lavrans Stead sheep. The Gunnars Stead flock grew very large, and approached the size of Asgeir's flock in the days of Helga Ingvadottir's ewes, but many more had to be slaughtered in the autumn than Asgeir had been in the habit of slaughtering, for lack of winter hay.

Also in this spring, Birgitta and Katla walked to the church every Sunday that there was a service there, and Birgitta grew friendly with some women of the district for the first time since coming into Vatna Hverfi. After this, many praised her looks and quickness, for she showed herself anxious to ask the advice of these women about everything from cooking to conceiving healthy children, and she often lamented her ignorance compared to their wisdom. Some now said that the dull-witted Gunnar was fortunate to find such a wife, but others said that it was possible that the husband was not as dull-witted as he had always appeared.

One day Margret met Skuli in the hills, and as usual they spoke of many things, until they fell to discussing the queen, Margarethe, and her ladies of the court. The one thing important to these women, declared Skuli, was their dress, and they strove always to wear bright colors, beautiful furs, and flattering headdresses, which were not unlike Margret's headdress in shape and purpose, but much unlike it in effect, for men's eyes were caused to look toward the heads of these women, rather than to look away. The colors, purple, red, rose, for example, seemed to touch the cheeks of the ladies and make them more beautiful. Other things were daring, too, such as necklines cut to reveal the swell of the breasts, and then veiled with a fine tissue, or waists set high and pulled tight. The queen especially preferred sleeves that were tight at the shoulder then flowed more loosely to the hand, and sometimes hung almost to the floor. In winter these would be trimmed with furs of various colors, from Russia, perhaps, and in summer they would be cut and embroidered, and in fact it was this sort of work that his wife had done for Margarethe. Skuli spoke idly, while watching Margret tie snares, and even when he talked of his wife, his tone was light. In France, he had heard, the fashion was for other things more outlandish still—shoes a man could barely walk in, a robe that was more like a shirt, with stockings a different color on each leg. He went on in this vein for a while, then began speaking of dogs, for King Hakon had a great pack of Irish wolfhounds that looked like wolves themselves, but roamed the palace freely, terrifying visitors. Soon it was time to part, and Margret, swaying gracefully under her load of small animals and other gatherings, went off without looking back. Skuli took his dinner and spent the night, as he often did, at Undir Hofdi church, for the "wife" of old Sira Nikolaus was particularly fond of him.

That night, Margret took a small seal blubber lamp and stole from her bedcloset after everyone else had gone to sleep. Now she went from chest to chest, opening, searching carefully, and closing, but all the chests were newly cleaned and rearranged after Birgitta's inventory. At last, however, Margret found and drew forth the roll of red silk from Bergen that Birgitta had brought with her as her marriage portion. Debate arose from time to time as to what might be done with this silk. Once in a while,

Gunnar suggested that they give it to the bishop or to Undir Hofdi church as part of their tithe, but at these times, Birgitta always wanted to save it for their children. When Birgitta was bent upon donating it, as she had been after seeing the Virgin and Child strolling in the homefield, or after the death of the baby, it was Gunnar who wanted to save it, and so nothing had been done with it. It was, after all, the only cloth of its kind in Vatna Hverfi district. Margret laid it across her cheek and wrapped it around her neck, then rolled it up and put it away again, this time in her own chest. She seemed to herself to be in a kind of fever that only the coolness of the silk could quench.

Now she watched for a time when everyone would be away from the farmstead, and this came soon enough, the next time Birgitta and Katla walked over to Undir Hofdi church for services, for Gunnar had gone to Gardar and Olaf was up in the hills with Hrafn and his sons, shearing the sheep. Now Margret found the silk, spread it out, and fell upon it as if in a fury, and in very little time she had cut it into pieces for a gown. Now she sat back and the fever was quenched, and she saw what she had done and became sorely afraid, so she rolled up the pieces and put them away again in her chest.

Not long after this, she met Skuli once again in the mountains, and he was wearing an especially colorful suit of light blue and green, while Margret was wearing her same gown of purplish Gunnars Stead wadmal, and Margret asked him, as if idly, "How came you by clothing of such outlandish colors?"

Skuli stepped back and looked down at himself and laughed. "My former master would be little obliged to you for your words, since every retainer on his estate wore such colors every day, except those engaged in field work. Such bright dress is much thought of in Norway now, and no one goes about like a Viking princess as you do." After this, he took her in his arms, and they spoke no more of dress, but their lovemaking did nothing to abate the fever that was once more upon Margret, and she parted with Skuli quickly and returned home.

Now the farmstead was well populated, for everyone was about, especially Birgitta, who was in and out of the house, chattering and asking questions. For this reason, Margret stayed far from her chest, although it glowed in her eyes like an ember, and drew her much as Skuli did. First there was the preparation of the evening meal, and then the eating of it, and after this Gunnar and Olaf sat over their trenchers and talked at length about Olaf's sheep shearing. Then Birgitta sat at Gunnar's elbow and asked

him for a tale, so he told the tale of the two women, Gudrid Thorbjarnar-
dottir and Freydis Eriksdottir, both of whom were related to Leif Eriksson,
the lucky.

Now this is a famous story among the Greenlanders, for it treats of
some of their favorite subjects, namely Vinland, and the kin of Erik the
Red. And in this story, there is a good woman and a bad woman, and so
folk often tell it as a lesson concerning the wills of women, for Freydis
Eriksdottir was always resolved to have her will, and caused the deaths of
a number of men, as well as herself killing seven women with an ax.
Though this story went on for a long time, and Olaf and Hrafn fell asleep
and Katla went off to her house, Margret could not leave off listening,
although it seemed unbearable to her. Gunnar finished the story, thus, "For
Gudrid things went much differently, for she had three husbands, all of
whom died wealthy, and each was followed by another handsomer and
more agreeable than the last, until Gudrid died in her bed with her sons,
including Snorri, who had been born in Vinland, about her." And Birgitta
pinched his arm and yawned, and said, "I didn't foresee such a long story.
Indeed," she smiled, "Vigdis would like this tale, for I'm sure she fancies
herself such a woman as Gudrid is, prosperous and pious. But, Gunnar, you
must tell me, how is it that those seven women that Freydis murdered stood
still for it, and how is it that twenty men stood about and watched it? This
Freydis must have been fierce indeed." Gunnar shrugged and laughed and
so the two went to their bedcloset, and their talking died down after a bit.

After this Margret went to her chest and opened it and drew forth
a piece of red silk and a spindle whorl and she began to pull threads from
the silk and spin them together into sewing thread. Such work was easily
done in the half light of the spring night, and her hands worked quickly,
sometimes spinning and sometimes winding the spun thread onto a length
of reindeer antler. Once or twice she got up to put away the pieces of silk
that she was not spinning from, but each time she sat down again with the
tissue in her hand. After she was done, and had spun all of the threads
together, she sat with the roll in her hands. Just before Olaf got up for
the morning work, she put everything away again.

As usual, Olaf went out while Margret dished up his morning meal.
There were many things she could say to him when he returned, about how
Asgeir had loved him, and how familiar and necessary he was about
Gunnars Stead, and about her gratitude at the way he had saved them from
starvation before, and the way they depended on him to do so even now.
Some of these things she formed with her lips, trying out how she would
say them when he was sitting before her. But when he was sitting before

her, scooping up his sourmilk with a piece of dried sealmeat, she said none of these things, for these things could not be said to this Olaf, who tied a band of wadmal around his head to keep the sweat out of his eyes, and whose shoulders hunched over his trencher as if to protect it from polar bears. Soon enough, telling her he would be manuring the homefield for the rest of the day, he pushed himself to his feet and went out, carrying a skin bag full of cheese and dried reindeer meat.

Margret ran to her chest and drew forth the pieces of silk. It seemed the only virtue now to sew them together as quickly as possible. She took fine stitches with Skuli's finest needle, and the thread she had spun pulled through the silk as if it were water. Birgitta and Gunnar arose late, laughing, and she had sewn a long seam.

One day not long after this, she went into the mountains wearing her cloak, although the sun was warm on the scree of the mountain sides, and then she lingered here and there in some of the clefts where Skuli had a habit of meeting her. Now she saw him at the bottom of the hill, looking back over his shoulder toward Undir Hofdi church. Then he turned and began again to climb the path. He was wearing simple blue clothing that she had seen many times before, and an ornate band of blue and white tablet weaving around his hair, which hung luxuriantly to his shoulders. He climbed confidently, knowing where to step without looking. From time to time he picked up twigs and threw them down again. No wood in Greenland except driftwood was satisfactory for carving, but Margret smiled that he liked to handle bits of it anyway. Now he looked up, and perhaps caught sight of her, for he seemed to smile and quicken his pace. Margret stepped out of sight into a copse of willow brush, removed her cloak, and waited. The red dress was too long, and fell in folds over her shoes, a good fashion for court ladies with nothing to do, of little use in Greenland, but it pleased her, the flow of the red silk and the cool sway of it against her skin.

Now came the crunch of Skuli's foot on the scree, a foot she could see, shod in blue, then another one. He spoke her name. She reached forward and pushed aside some branches of willow brush and his face was so close that it startled her and she snorted. He turned toward her, and at first his face had no expression, and then she saw his jaw drop and his eyes widen into perfect admiration and surprise, such as she had never seen on his or any face before in her life, and at the same time that she knew this as sin and vanity she also fell into the terror of never seeing such a look on his face again.

On this afternoon, the two stayed together much longer than usual, walking back and forth along the side of the hill and talking of many things. Skuli told Margret of two or three men of the court, who had fallen deeply in love with ladies who were married to other men, and one of these men was the brother of the king of Sweden. By subterfuge, the knight and his lady saw one another two or three times during the year, and the rest of the time the lady stayed with her husband and children and the knight governed his estates, and it was said by all that the good sense with which he did all of his works was the direct result of the love that he felt for the lady, and the way in which that love showed him the proper love of God, so that he was never cruel toward his tenants, and was always hospitable and openhanded to strangers and visitors. And she, too, was without anger or pride or envy or sloth, and was considered an excellent wife and loving mother, and this love between the two lasted many years, until the lady's children were grown and her hair was gray. But when, at last, the Great Death came upon the world, and the lady was lying ill and ready to repent of all her sins, the only sin she could not repent freely of was her love for the king's brother, and so she held this in her heart, and died unshriven of that sin, and her maids feared for her soul, until not long after her death, when her corpus lay on its bier and the maids were washing it, there arose from it a great fragrance, as of the purest flowers in spring, so that it filled the lady's steading with a pleasing odor, and this fragrance continued in the lady's chamber for many years after she was buried, and was seen as a sign of her virtue. And no one who was about her during her last days died of the contagion, for the fragrance served to repel bad airs from the steading.

There was another story, said Skuli, of a poor man who went on a crusade against the Turks, and he, too, was much in love with the wife of a fellow knight, who stayed home. And this man was made very bold in his crusade, so that he slew great numbers of the infidel, and was rewarded with many lands back in Denmark, where his concubine lived, but his love for the lady moved him to give away these prizes to the Church, and keep for himself only his horse and a sufficiency of plunder so that he could provide for his manservant and himself. It so happened that after twenty years of fighting, he was grievously wounded and near to death when his servant carried him from the field, but he grieved more over the knowledge that he had nothing to send back to his lady as a reminder of himself and a keepsake except a fragment of a green banner that he had won in the day's battle. This the servant vowed to take to the lady, and he did so, traveling for five more years. But when he had made his return, he discovered that the lady was dead, and when he found her tomb near the church, he saw that she had died on the selfsame day as the knight had died, and that hanging from her tomb was an unfaded sleeve of the same color of green as the banner, and the fragment of the banner fit into the sleeve as if they had been cut from the same cloth. Margret could not hear enough of such stories, and when Skuli came to the end of the ones he knew, she begged him to repeat them, which he gladly did. When she returned to Gunnars Stead, the evening meal was finished, and all the Gunnars Stead folk were asleep. Margret was not a little pleased with this great piece of luck.

Now Skuli persuaded Kollbein Sigurdsson to allow him to lodge at Undir Hofdi church, in order to help the old priest, Nikolaus, with the summer work. Kollbein was not a little reluctant to do this, since he had great plans of his own for Skuli's time, but Skuli pointed out to him that Nikolaus' steading was within easy visiting distance of all the farms in Vatna Hverfi, and it would be convenient from there to judge the wealth of the district. Kollbein declared that indeed this was so, and allowed Skuli's departure. Even so, Skuli put off the move for a few days, and seemed to himself almost afraid, and yet he found the thought of Margret Asgeirsdottir irresistibly alluring, as if she had changed into a person he had never seen before. In the red dress, she seemed to burst forth like a phoenix, burning up everything around her, more beautiful than any court lady he had ever seen, and yet not proud at all, as frightened by him as he was by her. The stories he told her came out of him willy-nilly, ones he knew fairly well and ones he barely remembered hearing, and they gave him a feeling of intoxication that he had never had in Greenland before, for the lack of beer and ale. If she showed the least mote of doubt, he felt himself swell with the knowledge that everything he said was perfect truth. But then it seemed to him after a while that she never showed any doubt at all.

In this same spring, Pall Hallvardsson the Priest and Jon the Priest had a disagreement about some of the revenues of Hvalsey church, where Pall Hallvardsson was now living and preaching. With the great snows of the past two winters, the church and especially the priest's house had fallen into disrepair, so that rain and wind came in upon the parishioners as they knelt at their prayers, and in addition, three of the six rooms of Pall Hallvardsson's house were unusable most of the time. Gunnar Asgeirsson agreed to supply three beams of wood and some men in Hvalsey Fjord agreed to work at repairing the church and at least one room of the priest's house, if these services could be applied against the tithe and the Peter's pence that were owed to Gardar. But Jon declared that the bishop could not afford to forgo these revenues, for Gardar itself was in poorer straits than it had been before the sickness. Jon said that the most important endeavor was to rebuild Gardar to the same degree of richness and splendor as two years before, for the greater glory of God, and that temporary repairs of Hvalsey church would do until the following year. The men of Hvalsey Fjord were greatly angered by this, for they said that it showed in what little esteem they and their families were held by the men at Gardar, and in addition to this, it showed how little Jon, and perhaps others, had learned about Greenland since coming, for it took no time at all for a Greenland building, once the wind and windborne sand got in, to be utterly laid waste, and at least those at Gardar had four solid walls about them when they worshiped.

One day Pall Hallvardsson got on his horse and rode to Gardar, and met with Jon, for although he was accustomed to bowing to the other man, he was also much disturbed at the complaints of his parishioners. Now when Pall Hallvardsson was announced, Jon retired to his cell and put on a red monsignor's gown and the ring and the other paraphernalia of his rank, so that Pall Hallvardsson would know that it was permissible for him to seek redress, but that the power for giving or withholding lay with Jon, especially now, when the bishop was weak and ill. When the servant showed Pall Hallvardsson to Jon's working chamber, Jon was sitting very upright in his seat. Pall Hallvardsson went to him and kissed his ring, and asked politely after his health and that of the bishop.

Jon looked down upon him. "The bishop finds it difficult to throw off his illness of the spring, and keeps mostly to his bed and is often dozing. It is in our power these days to make all but the most important decisions." He closed his eyes once, in exasperation. "We have not seen fit to disturb his peace with the unreasonable demands of the Hvalsey Fjord farmers."

"A day's row from Hvalsey church is a long row, and once inside the solid walls of Gardar, a man might find it difficult to see how a church could be in such disrepair as to drench the worshipers in a sudden shower or to render them windblown and uncomfortable in a stiff onshore breeze. Gardar is low and warm and damp, but St. Birgitta's is higher and more exposed, and closer to the open sea."

"Gardar does indeed look rich to some, but those who left before the vomiting ill cannot know how the daily life of the place has changed. So many have died off that copying manuscripts and singing have ceased altogether. Services in the cathedral are stark and poor things, and shameful offerings to the glory of God and His Son. The bishop is not so aware of this falling off, thanks be to God." He fell silent abruptly, and then went on, "As much wealth as possible has to be gathered at Gardar before the summer's end. In fact"—he looked Pall Hallvardsson full in the face—"we do the Hvalsey Fjorders a favor in not requiring more revenues than usual of them, but allowing them to use the extra that might have been required for repairing their own church. And your house is very large, whether it have three rooms or six."

"Do the Greenlanders have extra to give? Every farm is hard pressed, it seems to me."

"No more is being required than the farmers are able to pay. The bishop, in his generosity, gave a great boon before Yule when he allowed the farmers to hunt reindeer on Hreiney. Every farm that participated is rich in meat and hides. But even if this were not true, we have noticed more than once that the farmers of Greenland pay great attention to the wealth of the earth, but little to the riches of Heaven. More than one farm is nearly as wealthy as Gardar, and every farmer schemes to get more goods for himself. Almost no one gives freely to the church, or the king. All live as if they were their own men, here and in eternity."

"This is true, that the Greenlanders are much accustomed to holding their own opinions and doing as they please."

"Now when they have the chance to glorify God in His earthly temple, they grumble and mutter more even than the French, although they sacrifice themselves far less than the French, and although, in fact, the building they dare to call a cathedral would be as nothing among the French, or among the English or the Germans, or any people you could name on the face of the earth."

"The Greenlanders are much unlike the French."

Now Jon stood up, and his visage was dark with indignation. Pall Hallvardsson raised his hand and said quietly, "Brother, it seems to me that you have persuaded yourself that these Greenlanders deserve your anger, and that you are about to speak in haste of things that should be considered carefully, especially in light of the fact that it is likely that you and I will die here among the Greenlanders, and never again visit or live among the French or the Germans, or even the Norwegians."

Jon seated himself again and was silent for many minutes, and then at last he said in a low voice, "Brother, it is many weeks since I have been confessed," and together the two men went into the cathedral.

Now Sira Jon knelt behind the gray wadmal curtain of the confessional, and he spoke in low, passionate tones. "It seems to me," he said, "that there are two sins that rise like twins in my heart, and that these are anger and pride. These demands of the Hvalsey Fjorders touch me closely on these two points, for what they withhold, it seems to me, will end in the humbling of Gardar and of the bishop himself, and I am his steward these days."

Now he was silent for a long while, and Pall Hallvardsson listened to him shift and groan at his place. "Whatever our feelings, the bishop is fixed in his views on the proper wealth of the Church, is he not? He deplores the heretical meanness of such as the Franciscans, does he not? It is true that the peculiar place of the Greenlanders on the face of the earth has spared them that baneful influence, but it also gives them such pride in themselves!" And now he groaned loudly, and declared, "You see in my tones this anger that mortifies me? That I wrestle with every day? Every time I have aught to do with a Greenlander? It is given to me, of all the bishop's men, to gather goods for the tithe, and so it is given to me to witness the trickery and reluctance and stubbornness of the farmers. Indeed, they become deafer and deafer when I name to them the sums they really owe, and more forgetful as the day of payment approaches. I am not taking these gifts for myself, am I? Is not God Himself the recipient? Why think they that they are losing something? Know they not that they are building up treasure in Heaven?

"But such anger is not my deepest sin, rather this sin is something I know Greenlanders see in me, and are right to despise." And now his voice rose: "For I am humiliated to be here, at Gardar, when I should be at Nidaros or even Paris. I have been trained for that, not this. Oh, brother, what means it that just before sleep, or just waking, I often see myself in such a cathedral as at Rheims, as if from on high, a tiny insect carrying a taper from light to light, and simultaneously I see the huge vault of the ceiling, the interlaced fans receding and disappearing into the gloom, and there seems in such a place no room for pride, and the great space of the cathedral is filled with the glory of God, and I am as a fly in this space, happily attending my functions, and thinking only the simplest of thoughts. This picture comes to me unbidden. Though I push this picture away, it comes to me, driving out whatever better thoughts are there, and the result is that the stony gloom of Gardar and its turf smell seem paltry to me, a shame to God and His Son, this crude altar and these ragged tapestries! Thus pride and humiliation partake of each other, and the thing that I long for seems at times pure and at times defiled by my longing."

"In the fertile soil of the Greenland fjords, there is an eighth mortal sin that sprouts, and that is the sin of yearning. A man's only resource is to turn his yearning more and more toward God and death."

"Oh, I am but a young man, just twenty-nine winters old. Is that not too young to be yearning for death? Most men care for women or riches or good food, but through long habit I care not for these. May I have no pleasures of the simplest sort? no glimpses of orchards in bloom nor of the carved faces of the saints? nor the feel of leather and parchment volumes weighing in my hands? nor the sound of sacred music in my ears, but only the everlasting noise of sheep and of the wind whistling around the buildings, and with this the complaints of the Greenlanders, who think that God and His Son live far away in Rome, and cannot see them?"

"And yet, the Great Death has never come here, although it has visited and revisited all those places of which you speak. God must see in them some virtue that you do not."

"Yes, and I see in these speeches that I strive to repent without repenting, and that I seek to love something that I don't love." And that was the end of their conversation on this subject, and Jon neither asked for nor received absolution. Later, after the evening meal, when they spoke again of the Hvalsey church, Jon repeated that the revenues must be forthcoming, and had changed his views on the matter in no way. When Pall Hallvardsson spoke of these things to his parishioners, they declared that they would reckon up the value of their work, and withhold exactly that much from the tithe, and in this resolve they were determined and nothing Pall Hallvardsson said could move them.

News of these doings came to the Gunnars Stead folk with Lavrans and his servant when they came to Vatna Hverfi, for Birgitta was carrying a child again and Lavrans visited frequently, bringing dishes and remedies that the women neighboring Lavrans Stead thought might be successful in bringing about a healthy birth. But this time it appeared that few remedies were necessary, for Birgitta filled out nicely, like a cow let loose in the homefield, said Lavrans, and her cheeks were pink and fat as well as her belly, and her hair also seemed to thicken and shine. Now the women Birgitta met at church predicted the birth of a girl, for, they said, this was the way with some, to fight the boys and flourish with the girls, or to fight the girls and flourish with the boys. Others denied this, and remarked that many babies had died in the year of the vomiting ill, both girls and boys, and some born dead hardly looking like babies at all. The fact was that folk would see what they wished to see, but it was God Himself who gave babies and took them away.

It was also said among the women that Vigdis, the wife of Erlend, was taking a great interest in this baby, especially considering the enmity between Gunnar and Erlend, and that she was often asking after Birgitta—how she looked or how she seemed to be feeling—and it was true that when Birgitta was in church, she occasionally raised her eyes and met the gaze of the older woman, who looked her up and down at her leisure, then turned away. Now it came into Birgitta's mind that Vigdis might be wanting to put a spell on the baby, and she grew afraid to go to church, although she and Katla had gotten into the habit of going every week. One day walking home after church, Birgitta asked Katla if evil spells could actually be cast inside the sacred walls, but Katla could not say. The women talked about Vigdis between themselves all the way home, but Birgitta hesitated to speak to Gunnar, fearing his reaction. After that, Birgitta decided to consult Nikolaus the Priest, but he was past understanding the talk of anyone but his "wife," and, as this woman was a good friend of Vigdis, Birgitta only declared that she had come to make an offering for the health of her baby, and she left the two cheeses she had brought on the altar. When Lavrans came again, she persuaded him to take her back to Hvalsey Fjord in his boat, so that she could visit with her old friends and look after her twenty-four ewes and lambs that were grazing the fields of Lavrans Stead.

Now Birgitta stayed at her father's farm for many days, and this was the first long visit she had made there since her marriage. She talked at length with her father's old steward about her sheep, and he praised their size and hardihood, and the rate at which the lambs were growing. Against Lavrans' wishes, Birgitta went out into the hill pastures behind the farm with the man, whose name was Jonas, and looked at every sheep and lamb, and Jonas told her which of these would do well over the winter and which would be best to slaughter for meat. Birgitta listened well to these remarks and watched carefully where Jonas pointed. Jonas was said to be a peculiar man, for he had been found more than once cast face down upon the grass, his clothing wet with rain and his sheep far and wide, sometimes the worse for mischief. Then he would rise up and have no memory of how long it had been since he last took notice, whether less than a day or more. And so, though possessed of much lore about the raising and breeding of sheep, he could find work with few farmers, or perhaps only one, Lavrans, who was generally thought a careless man. But Jonas knew nothing about the casting of spells.

Another day, Birgitta followed her father's dairy maid about, a young woman named Kristin, who was ill-favored and club-footed, but knew well enough about making cheese and butter. This woman was a little older than Birgitta, and Birgitta had resorted much to her friendship as they were growing up, but now she seemed shy of Birgitta, and would hardly speak to her of news about Lavrans Stead or Hvalsey Fjord, much less of casting spells.

Finally, after some days of hesitation, Birgitta went across the water to St. Birgitta's church and sought out Pall Hallvardsson, who greeted her jovially, and was much pleased with her looks. They talked briefly of Gunnars Stead and the folk at Vatna Hverfi, and Birgitta said she had been to visit with Nikolaus the Priest, but that he had not been able to hear her or to make out her greetings, but Pall Hallvardsson did not ask her why she had been to see the priest. After this, they spoke of Lavrans, and his livestock, and his fears for Birgitta's new child, although Birgitta declared that she did not share these fears, except in one particular, but Pall Hallvardsson did not ask about this particular and instead began talking of other people in the district that he had recently seen. Birgitta listened patiently while he spoke, but could not have said, even at the moment, of whom or what he was speaking. Then there was something about Gardar and Jon the Priest and the men of Hvalsey Fjord, but Birgitta did not hear this, either, and Pall Hallvardsson declared that he might as well be giving a sermon, since she was nearly asleep at his news, and Birgitta laughed at this but still could not talk of what she had come to discuss, and so, after a few minutes, she bid the priest farewell and returned to her father's farmstead.

At this time, Birgitta had been at Lavrans Stead for eight or nine days, so that there was little more for her to do there, and much work, especially in the dairy, calling her back to Gunnars Stead, but a dream came to her once during the day, when she did not even know that she was quite asleep, and in the dream Vigdis appeared, and she was so fat that she covered Vatna Hverfi district. After this dream, Birgitta was even more reluctant to return to her home, but she went about Lavrans Stead as if distracted, not sitting for more than an eye blink, but unable to work at anything useful, always going out and in, sometimes wandering toward the church and sometimes wandering away from it. One night she would sleep as if dead well into the morning light, and the next she would be up and down so that the servants complained and yawned at their next day's work. Now Lavrans went out of the farmstead and reappeared not long afterward with Sira Pall Hallvardsson, and he closed the priest and his daughter in the dairy together and barred the door and said that they could come out when the girl was cured of this fretfulness.

Birgitta declared in her opinionated way that Vigdis Markusdottir of Ketils Stead was visiting her in her dreams, and striving to cast the evil eye upon Birgitta's unborn child, and she would feel safe only when she had come upon a suitable charm against these endeavors.

"Are you not ashamed of seeking evil where there is none, my Birgitta?" And although he spoke to her in a low and soothing voice, Sira Pall's eyes flashed in the dim light as if he were exceedingly angry with her. Birgitta lifted her head and thrust out her chin. "Think you of the Virgin, into whose womb the Lord Jesus Christ miraculously came through the agency of the Holy Spirit. Mary's eyes were cast down and her thoughts within, for she trusted the Lord and rejoiced in her soul. Nor did she look about for enemies, conjuring up baseless fears and slandering her neighbors, but instead the love for all men grew in her as the child grew."

"I have heard this tale."

Pall Hallvardsson took her hand in his and lifted it up so that she could see it in the ray of light that came in through the single high window in Lavrans' dairy. "Just as this hand might come into the light through the will of Pall Hallvardsson or Birgitta herself, so Birgitta can will her fears into the light of the Virgin's care, for prayer is the arm and the shoulder and the strength that does such a simple deed, and the virtuous heart turns to prayer even as a thirsty person turns to water."

"This must be so, if the priest says that it is so."

Now Pall Hallvardsson leaned forward and spoke more quietly in Birgitta's ear. "The race of the Asgeirssons," he said, "is known to be a wayward and self-reliant lineage. In addition to this, many in the district speak of the enmity between Gunnar Asgeirsson and Erlend Ketilsson, and say that this enmity is cherished more carefully in the heart of Gunnar Asgeirsson than it is in the heart of his neighbor." He paused. "True enough, Erlend is a choleric man, but a hasty one as well, and not as hard as he might appear on the surface."

"I have no knowledge of this, but Gunnar sees a few things very well, namely whose servants they are who scuttle about on a certain large field, and whose cart it is that they drag here and there, and whose byre it is that receives the thick hay taken off the field in the autumn. Never once has this cart turned toward the Gunnars Stead byre in what some might call a neighborly fashion."

Now Sira Pall Hallvardsson grew very wrathful. "It seems to me that the Gunnars Stead folk are much to blame in this, that they stand looking over this field and drinking in the actions of guiltless folk who act only in the interests of the bishop and the justice he brought to the Greenlanders. Have you become as folk to whom gall tastes as sweet as wine?"

At this Birgitta dropped her eyes and spoke no more, but only kissed Pall Hallvardsson's ring when her father came to let the pair out of the dairy. And Sira Pall Hallvardsson said to Lavrans later, "The heart of a woman is known only to God, and a great enigma to those to whom it is given to guide these eternal strangers through life." And the two men shook their heads in rueful agreement on this score. Early the next morning, Birgitta returned to Gunnars Stead, and thereafter she went about her work with great steadiness and purpose. The Hvalsey Fjord folk, and Lavrans among them, agreed that of all the priests, Pall Hallvardsson was the wisest and the most to be trusted, and sometimes they spoke among themselves of what would happen if the bishop were to die.

Not long after this, Birgitta went to Gunnar where he was dredging a canal through the homefield, for Gunnar and Olaf had decided to enlarge the farmstead's water system, and she spoke to him at length of Vigdis and her designs, and the result of this was that Birgitta and Katla stopped visiting Undir Hofdi church and Birgitta stayed quietly at home for the rest of her term. One day Gunnar rode away from the farm early in the morning and did not return until the late summer dusk. Sometime later, there was talk in the district that one of Erlend's thirty cows had been meddled with, so that her ears and her teats had been nicked with a knife, and a wide band had been tied tightly around her eyes and she had been led into the lake, which was quite cold, and tied there overnight, facing Erlend's farmhouse. By the time of the seal hunt, the talk subsided, and just after the beginning of the winter half year, a daughter was born to Birgitta, and she was named Gunnhild, and everything went well with her. Shortly thereafter, on the feast of St. Andrew, a son was born to Vigdis at Ketils Stead, and this was a great surprise, for Vigdis had grown so stout that the coming of the child had gone unnoticed. This child was named Jon Andres, and he did well enough considering that Vigdis was something close to forty winters of age.

It so happened that shortly after the beginning of Lent, Margret Asgeirsdottir felt the quickening of life within her, and she calculated that the child would be born around the feast of Mary Magdalen, but she said nothing of this, neither to any of the Gunnars Stead folk nor to Skuli Gudmundsson, who visited from time to time.

It was Skuli's habit, when he lived in Vatna Hverfi district, to ride from farm to farm and stay at each for some days, for he was considered the representative of Kollbein Sigurdsson, who was the representative of the king. He had at first intended to stay at Undir Hofdi church, with Nikolaus and his "wife," but this elderly couple was hard put to take care of his needs, and yet were too polite to allow him to take care of himself. He told Margret that awaking in his bedcloset to the sound of Unn's slow, hobbling step as she approached with a bowl of sourmilk and knowing that she would be hurt if he arose to help her, or even appeared not to be asleep when she came up to him, was no little difficulty for him.

The other farmers greeted him suspiciously, at first, and, though showing all the forms of hospitality, were also ostentatious about the hardship his coming made for them, giving his horse what appeared to be the last of the hay, scraping the bottom of the cooking pots to make the evening meat go around, declaring that certain healthy cows belonged, not to the farmers themselves, but to neighbors. Skuli, however, did not appear to be counting the livestock or surveying the farmsteads, or looking longer than was polite at the fine possessions inside the houses, and after a while, after it was discovered how handy he was at fashioning some needles or carving gamepieces or repairing anything made of wood, the hay and food became more plentiful and milk appeared on the table that was yellow and full of cream. One result of this was that Margret was able to see him more often, as he was always in the district. Another result was that others were looking out for him more, especially those with marriageable daughters, and more often noting his whereabouts.

Many folk considered that of all the districts, Vatna Hverfi district was the most favored, because of the multitude of lakes, large and small, that brightened every cleft and hollow. Of these, two were very large, and most of the farmsteads were scattered about the shores of these two. Gunnars Stead, however, and Ketils Stead were situated to the north of these lakes, each on a smaller lake of its own. Although more isolated, these farmsteads were also on the way from Vatna Hverfi district to both Gardar and Undir Hofdi church, and so travelers to these places often passed by, and sometimes stopped for refreshment. This had been a great practice in the time of Gunnar Asgeirsson and his son Asgeir Gunnarsson, when the farm was large and prosperous and the farmers fond of company, but since the death of Asgeir, travelers had found the hospitality there more haphazard and the host a less jovial companion, and so most people in the district stopped at Ketils Stead. Although Erlend Ketilsson was not a generous man by nature, he knew the power of the reports travelers carry with them, about what they find when they stop. In addition to this, Vigdis was very fond of news, and often spoke of how far away from things Ketils Stead was. The result was that the way from Vatna Hverfi to the church and the fjord bypassed Gunnars Stead entirely, and the folk there often didn't see others for days on end. Skuli Gudmundsson was much taken by this remoteness, and often commented that when he was at Gunnars Stead, it was as if he were not in the district at all.

Skuli was possessed of a very fine horse, strong and quick and on the large side, but not exceptionally good-looking or distinctively marked. Margret said that this horse brought them good luck, and she was very fond of it, although Skuli remembered the beautiful matched red horses of King Hakon, which came from Flanders and were extremely large, and he sometimes regretted that his horse was so humble-looking. Since living in the district, he had seen most of the horses owned by most of the farmers, and all of the good ones, for the farmers liked to bring out their horses most of all, more than their sleekest cows or woolliest sheep, or even their children, and parade them for the admiration of visitors. It so happened that he conceived a desire for a dark gray stallion owned by Thorkel Gellison. Thorkel was well aware of the value of his beast, for the animal was big and aggressive as well as good-looking, and Thorkel got good payments for breeding, as well as much pleasure from horsefighting with his neighbors. Skuli spoke of this horse very warmly and frequently, and sang his praises whenever he could.

The result of this was that the horse got to be in great demand for breeding, and brought Thorkel much wealth, so that one day, when Skuli was staying in the southern part of the district, Thorkel came to Skuli and offered to breed the horse for free to one of his mares, and give Skuli the resulting foal. Skuli thanked him, but said that he had a mare in mind that he considered the best mare in the district, and this was Mikla, Olaf Finnbogason's mare of Gunnars Stead. Now Thorkel agreed to allow Skuli to borrow the horse and take him to Gunnars Stead for the breeding and bring him back at his leisure. A few days later, Skuli rode the horse to Gunnars Stead, and the horse was as delightful as Skuli had suspected. Skuli's own horse was to stay at Hestur Stead, awaiting his return. When Skuli rode into the farmyard, Margret Asgeirsdottir came up to him, and said, "My Skuli, you have thrown away your luck, for it seems to me that this gray horse will be your death." Skuli laughed at this. "The beast is only borrowed," he said, and, as there was no one about, he kissed her on the lips, then went to find Olaf.

In the time since Skuli had moved into the district, Margret had learned to cover her feelings completely, even from the sharp eyes of Birgitta Lavransdottir, so that she felt herself to be two persons as a fur-lined cloak is two cloaks—humble, brownish wadmal on the outside, with a modest hood and simple bone buttons, but thick, glittering white foxskin underneath. Her passion had not faded and could not, she discov-

ered, be sated by Skuli's presence. It was not diminished by his reverence
for appearances (as exemplified by the two horses) nor his carelessness
about them (casting her dangerous glances in the presence of Birgitta, or
even Olaf). In the year of their liaison, he had grown inordinately proud,
Margret thought, and yet his brilliant dress and wild sociability excited her,
even as his striking appearance mounted on the gray horse riding into the
farmyard filled her with admiration she was hard put to contain.

Olaf was much impressed by the horse, and anxious to make the
match with Mikla, but, he said, it would be some time before the mare
would come into heat, for she was often later than other horses, and she
had only just borne her new foal. About this Skuli was not disappointed,
since he would thus get to keep the stallion that much longer, and he
intended to do Thorkel the good turn of getting other breeding fees while
the animal was in the area. The horse was not turned out with the others,
but kept carefully in the horsebyre, and Skuli checked him three times
every day for scratches and tiny injuries.

Bit by bit in the course of his year with Margret, Skuli had come
to view some things in a different light, and this was especially true since
his coming to Vatna Hverfi. For reasons of economy, or simple laziness,
Kollbein Sigurdsson neither came to Vatna Hverfi district nor sent messengers to his representative, and for much of the time there was no news at
all from Foss and Thjodhilds Stead. Skuli's tie to Kollbein and through him
to the court of the king in Norway seemed to loosen, seemed to lighten,
almost to disappear. Now he hardly remembered his dead wife, or even
his children, or his land on the hillside near Bergen. His friendship with
Margret seemed as much a marriage to him as his doings in the district
seemed his business. He took as great an interest in the livestock of some
of the farmers as he would have in his own, and was earnest in his advice.
In the same way, Thorkel Gellison's stud horse seemed to him to be his
own while it was in his care, and he showed great pride in it.

It seemed to Skuli that this life could last forever, or could shade
gently into a similar one that included Margret as his acknowledged spouse,
some children by her, ownership of a Vatna Hverfi farmstead, and a race
of horses in the byre that were descended from Mikla and the gray stud.
From time to time he suggested this to Margret, and she saw that in
unguarded moments, he acted as if these impossibilities were already accomplished. Olaf, for example, was so friendly with Skuli that Margret
could see that Skuli often forgot that Olaf was her husband. And now they
were much thrown together by the planned breeding of the stallion and
the mare.

Gunnhild was a strong-minded and active child who consumed all of Birgitta's attention and most of Svava Vigmundsdottir's as well, for Svava had returned to Gunnars Stead just before the birth. The two women were much occupied in concocting enticing viands for the child, as well as in following her about and preserving her from danger, for Svava declared that she had never seen a child with such a penchant for things she was not allowed. Also in this year, Easter came early and was followed by the sudden breakup of the ice in the fjord and the early greening of the mountain pastures. Olaf and Gunnar were much pleased by this, and assisted Hrafn and his sons in taking most of the livestock, which now numbered six horses, eighteen cows, and a hundred and five sheep and goats, up into the hills. Twenty of the best ewes and their lambs were once again removed to Hvalsey Fjord, and this was a three-day trip. So it was that Margret was left alone about the farm to do as she wished, and so it was that she and Skuli often resorted to their accustomed trysting spot. Skuli seemed not to notice the coming of the child. Their habit was that Skuli left early in the morning on his gray horse, and Margret walked off some time later. When they met, the horse would be hobbled and left to graze as he might.

It so happened that one day some travelers brought a tale to Vigdis at Ketils Stead that Thorkel Gellison's gray stud was often seen wandering in the mountains north of Gunnars Stead, and one of these travelers made a verse,

> *The gray stallion seeks mares where there are none,*
> *But the hirdman seeking wives knows where to look.*

Vigdis had borne many children, and the activities of Jon Andres were not so interesting to her as to exclude other amusements. So it was that she asked all of those who passed by what they knew of the goings-on at Gunnars Stead, and soon enough she knew who the wife in the verse might be. The verse itself she never repeated, but neither did she forbid her servants or children to repeat it. She had not forgotten how they had found the half-frozen, blindfolded cow in the lake, nor the insult intended, nor the probable perpetrators.

Sometime after this, Gunnar was sitting beside the small lake on the shores of which Gunnars Stead was situated, and he was repairing a seal net. Hrafn's wife Katla came up to him and, looking down at him, repeated the verse that was by now common knowledge throughout the district. Gunnar said nothing and continued to repair the net. He sat there for most of the day, and by the time of the evening meal, the net was in perfect condition. He put it away and went inside to eat. At the table, he asked Birgitta where Margret might be. Birgitta replied that Margret had gone to snare ptarmigan in the hills. After this, Gunnar asked where Skuli might be. Birgitta replied that Skuli had taken the gray horse to the farm of Axel Njalsson, which was less than a short morning's ride from Gunnars Stead. Now Olaf looked up from his trencher and looked at Gunnar. They finished their meal. Afterward they went to find Katla, and, somewhat frightened, she repeated the rhyme to Olaf. A little later, Margret returned with five birds. Skuli came back the next morning.

The Gunnars Stead folk were still sitting at their morning meat, when Skuli came into the steading and Gunnar greeted him and said, "You are always here and there, my friend. Where do you next intend to seek the king's revenues?"

"I have not yet visited the farm of Stein Sigmundsson."

"That is a poor place," said Gunnar. "I doubt that he is eager for your visit." The two men laughed together. "You are such a good friend to us that we would prefer it if you lingered about Gunnars Stead, at least until the breeding of the mare."

"It would hardly be ill to partake of such meat and such talk as I am accustomed to at Gunnars Stead, that is the truth," said Skuli, with a grin.

And now Margret said, "Is not the round of your business of first consideration, Skuli Gudmundsson?" But Skuli laughed and stretched himself on the bench, and reached for the basin of sourmilk. "Indeed," he said, "I have already done more business for Kollbein in this district than he has done for himself in all the other districts together."

Margret fell silent.

After this, for a few days, everyone, including Margret, stayed about the farm buildings, and Margret declared that the storehouses were sufficiently stocked with hanging birds and drying herbs. She followed the child as she crawled from place to place, and related to Birgitta tales from Gunnar's infancy, but indeed, Gunnhild was much unlike Gunnar except in looks. Birgitta was very proud of her, and carefully arranged the house and the yard outside the steading for her safety and entertainment, even though Gunnar and Olaf were much put out to find their tools and supplies hidden away in odd or distant spots. The child was never struck, or even spoken sharply to, and for this reason, perhaps, she was very merry. One morning, just after the morning meal, Skuli rode away on the gray stallion.

After his departure, the morning went very slowly. With great effort, Margret listened to Birgitta and to Svava, although their talk did little but annoy her. She went to the storehouse and puttered among her herbs and the other provisions she found there. She spun a little wool and sat for a time at the loom. She followed the baby about, and walked around the periphery of the homefield, but there was little to do, and what there was she was not familiar with, as she had spent nearly every summer day in the hills since well before the death of Asgeir. In addition, there was some danger in falling too often under the gaze of Birgitta Lavransdottir, for Margret's waist was growing rounder, and straining the seams of her everyday dress (concerning this, she was somewhat afraid to let the seams out, for the dress was so well worn that new sewing would immediately declare itself). In addition to this, every moment brought her the thought of Skuli in the hills, wandering about their favorite places, wishing for her as she wished for him.

Now Margret went to her cages of birds, and began to speak to the birds while giving them water and sweeping out. She had six birds in three cages—two pairs of larks and one pair of wheatears. As she looked at them, she thought, as she sometimes did when Skuli was not around and never did when he was around, of how miserably she had given herself to temptation, and how little she had resisted at every point, but gladly had gone into his arms the first time, and more gladly each time since. She thought what a sinner she had become in the eyes of the Lord, and how gaily she had embraced her sin, so that the last year had fled by so quickly that time seemed really not to have passed at all, and she seemed to herself exactly the same guiltless soul that she had been. At once she hungered for the year not to have passed, for herself to be again the truly guiltless person she had been, but not, she realized, so that she might resist temptation, only so that she might have again each moment of the last year. After this, she took each bird on her finger and spoke to it, then, when she was finished with this, she fetched her cloak, put it on, and went out into the hills. Skuli was there, waiting for her, and she expected Gunnar and Olaf, as well, but they were not to be seen. Now their meetings grew as bold as before.

Soon, Ketil the Unlucky, who had grown into a clever man, but of sour and mocking temperament, made up another verse,

> *The landless stranger in colored clothing has only*
> *The bushy hillside where he can plow the blond whore.*
> *The Greenlanders are getting careless*
> *when they trade their horses and their wives*
> *For so little.*

Soon after this verse was made, Hrafn and Olaf began shearing the sheep in the summer pastures. Katla went with Olaf to visit her husband and help with the washing of the wool. When Olaf returned, he took Gunnar aside and had speech with him on this matter, and recited the verse to Gunnar. He also declared that Hrafn had threatened to find himself another place unless this matter were seen to, for it was a great shame to all the folk of the steading to have such verses going about, and the master and the husband powerless to do anything.

Now Gunnar thought silently for a few minutes. Then he said to Olaf, "My Olaf, I am well known to be a lazy man, and what a lazy man likes best is for each morning and evening and nighttime to pass as each before it has, and to turn his lazy hand always to the work that he has turned it to before, to watch, with his lazy gaze, the same cows, the same sheep, the same horses, and the same folk going from place to place about the farm, from sunlight into shade and back out again, as they always have. A lazy man must always shrink from a new task, especially from work that he has no practice in, such as killing and burying a friend."

"But I have never been lazy, and I, too, am unsure of undertaking this task."

And the two men sat there, and they did not hesitate to weep, but after they wept, they went to their store of tools and chose two axes, and sharpened them carefully, and then they set them beside the door of the farmstead, and called out the farm folk and told them the news. When they had finished speaking, and repeated both of the verses, Birgitta, who was holding little Gunnhild in her arms, said, "It is obvious that the two of you are such cowards that you need the permission of your servants to do what needs to be done." Then Olaf mounted Mikla and Gunnar mounted his old horse, Noddi, and they tied their axes to their saddles and rode away.

Margret and Skuli were sitting side by side on the hill, talking. Skuli wore his blue and green court suit and Margret the red silk dress she had made herself, and worn from time to time since. The gray horse grazed a little way off, and was brightly visible, because of the way his shining coat cast back the sunlight, from a long way off. Margret was little surprised to see Gunnar and Olaf, as she had been anticipating them for some time, but she was surprised to see that Skuli greeted their appearance with expectation not unequal to hers. He stood up and whistled to the gray horse as he was in the habit of doing with his own horse, but the stallion paid no heed, and walked farther off. Skuli walked toward him, making low clucking noises, for his only weapon, a knife, was fixed to the saddle.

The horse trotted away. Now it was easy to see that Gunnar and Olaf had
caught sight of Margret's bright dress, for they began to gallop up the
slope. The stallion lifted his head at the sound of hooves, then whinnied
loudly and began to trot toward his fellows. A few minutes later, Olaf
caught the horse and tied him to a twisted birch tree. Gunnar and Olaf
came forward at a trot. Skuli walked forward, then stood still in the middle
of the slope.

He was wearing his green cap, and his bright hair lay smoothly on
his shoulders. Now as Olaf neared him, with Gunnar a little behind, he
raised his ax and dealt the Norwegian a hard, glancing blow on the side
of the head. As the man fell, Gunnar finished him off with another blow
to the back of the neck. Blood spurted forth into the willow scrub. Now
Gunnar and Olaf approached Margret, and their horses and legs were
spattered with fresh blood. With his hand, Gunnar wiped some of this
blood on Margret's cheek, and turned away.

Olaf dismounted in front of his wife. "Now," he said, looking her
up and down, "my eyes are opened, and I see that this shame will soon
bear fruit." And then he spat in her face. After this, he turned and galloped
after the other man, and the first thing they did was to go to Ketils Stead,
which was the nearest farm, and announce the killing of Skuli Gudmundsson, as was required in the laws.

Kollbein Sigurdsson was much angered by the killing of Skuli
Gudmundsson, and sought the counsel of many prosperous farmers in
trying to decide what action to press and where to press it—at the Thing,
under his own jurisdiction as representative of the king, or at Gardar, under
the jurisdiction of the bishop. Skuli Gudmundsson, he said, had been one
of his finest-looking men, and the retinue was much meaner without him.
Many of the farmers around Thjodhilds Stead considered that the wisest
course was to support Kollbein in the matter, and seek full outlawry for
Gunnar Asgeirsson and Olaf Finnbogason. But the farmers who lived
farther away, and the bishop as well, considered that Gunnar and Olaf had
been within their rights, and that it was Skuli who had risked outlawry
in pursuing his liaison with a married woman.

The time of the Thing came quickly upon the heels of the killing,
but the four days of the assembly went by one after the other and no action
was brought against Gunnar and Olaf, although Kollbein kept busy going
from farmer to farmer, and talking, always, in a quiet earnest voice. Every
farmer, except Kollbein's nearest neighbors, declared that yes, the killing
might be considered deplorable by some, but that, on the other hand, the
killing of a Norwegian should not necessarily come between Greenlanders,

especially the killing of a thief who came to a farmstead as a friend. None of the arguments Kollbein advanced concerning Skuli's position as his representative in the Vatna Hverfi district, and his position as representative of the king, impressed the Greenlanders with their power, and Gunnar's and Olaf's supporters thronged Gunnar's booth, which was new and made of distinctively marked almost white reindeer hides, and they also appeared to be everywhere about the Thing. Now it happened that on the morning of the last day before the Thing was to break up, the booth was gone. Seeing this, a neighbor of Kollbein suggested that Kollbein might have luck with his suit if he brought it before the court when the defenders were absent.

Although the Greenlander spoke in jest, Kollbein took him at his word, and hastily presented the suit at the end of the last day. He asked that Gunnar Asgeirsson and Olaf Finnbogason, of Gunnars Stead in Vatna Hverfi, be declared outlaws, with all their property confiscated, for the killing of Skuli Gudmundsson, hirdman and representative of Kollbein Sigurdsson, himself direct representative of the king, and he asked, as was his right, that the presiding judges, of which there were thirteen—three from each district to the north and south and one from Gardar—vote on the verdict at once, before the adjournment of the session. His supporters felt that this was cleverly done, and might win what was generally considered to be a very weak case. The judges had just begun to speak among themselves, when a large group of men, led by Thord of Siglufjord and Thorkel Gellison of Vatna Hverfi, and including Gunnar and Olaf, charged onto the law field and demanded a hearing. The tale of Margret Asgeirsdottir and Skuli Gudmundsson was then told, and the judges declined all penalties, and Kollbein Sigurdsson was greatly discomfited by what he called outmoded practices, for the Thing had long wielded no power in Norway or even in Iceland, where the power of the king ruled. After this the Greenlanders were much pleased, and showed even less respect for Kollbein, and some farmers even went so far as to dictate to the ombudsman concerning the ordering of his lands and livestock, and to deny him new animals when he had disposed of his others in a foolish way. The notion of taking down the new white booth and hiding above the Gardar law field on the last day in hopes that Kollbein would submit his suit had been Gunnar's and folk considered it very clever.

One day just after the Thing, Gunnar set out with Margret in the Gunnars Stead boat. They took with them five ewes and some household goods. At the end of the morning, they arrived at Gardar, but they did not stop to talk, only carried their goods on their backs and herded their sheep the short distance across Gardar peninsula to where the bishop kept his Eriks Fjord boat, which they borrowed. Now they rowed for most of the rest of the day, until they could see the red stone buildings of Brattahlid across the fjord to the north, and a gray glacial river to the south. The sheep lay still in the bottom of the boat, and though from time to time Margret sought Gunnar's face, he would not look at her. When they came to a small landing place, Gunnar sat quietly in the boat while Margret took all of her belongings out and set them upon the pebbly shore. Then she led forth the ewes. As soon as they were unloaded, Gunnar pushed the boat off, and began to row away, and as they parted, neither looked at the other, nor made any valediction.

This farm belonged to Gardar, for the lineage that had owned it had died out two generations before. In addition to the tithe, Margret was obliged to pay another tenth of her yearly produce as rent. In exchange for this, Pall Hallvardsson, Jon, or Audun (who was one of three Green-landers who had been made priests by the bishop) was to row out to her three times each year, at Easter, at Yule, and near St. Michael's mass, and confess her and give her communion. These arrangements were made by Gunnar with Jon, and were considered unusual, more unusual than either adultery or killings.

The red silk gown disappeared. It was not to be found in any of the Gunnars Stead chests. No bits of it or of the remnants of the fabric were used to decorate Gunnhild's little dresses. It did not appear on any altar or sewn into the vestments of any priest. It was not among the items sent to Lavrans Stead, for Birgitta had packed those herself, not allowing Margret to touch anything until it was time for her to take it out of the boat. Folk said that Birgitta was not a little parsimonious, giving Margret the oldest and most easily spared pots and bits of furniture. One article only was thick and richly made, and that was the white cloak Margret had given Birgitta as a bridal gift.

The little farm, called Steinstraumstead, Margret found to be in great disrepair. Of the three rooms in the house, only one had all four walls, and none was dry or cozy or tightly roofed. The storeroom, being the smallest, was the easiest to put in good order, and this Margret quickly did—setting stones, cutting and replacing turves, clearing the floor with a wooden spade and a broom made of willow brush tightly bound with reindeer sinew. The room was dark and cramped, however, and one oil lamp rendered it smoky and warm, so Margret spent little time there once it was clean and she had arranged her stores. After this she surveyed the byre, which had once been tightly built, with stalls for four cows. As she had no cows, though, and intended to have none, she could leave the byre much as it was, only clearing a protected spot for whatever hay and seaweed she would be able to find, and piling turves along the north wall to shelter her five sheep in the worst of the winter storms. Her own room presented more difficulties, for it was large and nearly roofless and the built-in bedcloset (for there was one, although it was roughly made) was staved in on two sides. For some days, she left these things as they were, and merely followed her sheep in their new pastures, first along the river and then in the other direction, which led toward the bottom of Eriks Fjord. These new walks were some pleasure to her, and though she brought the sheep back at the end of each day, it was only to sleep a little, milk the ewes, and then set off again. The child within her moved but little while she was walking, and sometimes she was seized with the certainty that it had died. When she sat, however, or lay down to sleep, it rolled and jumped until she had to get up.

The hillside, once a little cultivated, although never as rich as Gunnars Stead or any other farm in Vatna Hverfi, was much overrun with herbs and other plants, including ones that she had seen little of in Vatna Hverfi. The fjord, down a little slope from her door, was full of cod and ocean-going trout, although the glacial stream for which the steading was named was cloudy with silt and contained few fish. The strand was narrow and pebbly, and sloped abruptly upward. She had no boat.

The child was little trouble to her. The pains and discomforts of pregnancy, such as Birgitta and Svava spoke about, were absent. Birgitta, in particular, had often complained of the baby's head catching her just below the heart so that she had no air for walking, and sometimes even for speaking. Another time, rather toward the end of Birgitta's term, the girl had been seized with a sudden long pain, lasting most of the morning and running from her heart down to her legs. It was the child turning upside-down to be born, she said, and worse by far than any of the pains of confinement. Svava recalled of Kristin of Siglufjord that her feet burst out of her shoes, and her legs could not fit into her stockings, and at times it seemed that the skin itself would burst, for her toes were as big as loom weights, and this with every child, from the first quickening to the birth. There were worse things, and Svava knew most of them. Such discomforts as she and Birgitta spoke about were almost laughable, but even these Margret didn't have. She was simply herself, with a large belly, in a loose dress, well able to follow her sheep as far as they wished to wander.

One day a rather large piece of driftwood, V-shaped and rounded at both ends, as if it had been drifting for many years, was caught below the farmhouse on the strand, and her first thought upon seeing it was that Skuli Gudmundsson could make good use of it, for it was a large piece of wood, six or eight ells long and at least an ell broad in the widest spot, and no branches at all, and she remembered how he had spoken of carving her a chair with fish for arms and a whale in low relief across the back, but a good piece of wood had never come to him for such a project. And now she was taken with longing for him in such a way as she hadn't yet been since his death, for the piece of wood below her began to take the shape of two wiggling fish, curved and shining, caught in the piece of wood as if in ice, or amber, or water itself made solid. The two fish seemed to arch and writhe for freedom, as they do in a net being pulled from the water, and Margret could not drag her gaze away from them. When after a small space, they ceased moving and resolved themselves once again into the two halves of the piece of driftwood, she was seized with such grief that she began screaming and screaming, until at last she fell forward in a fit, and it was thus that it came to her what changes had been wrought around her, that Skuli Gudmundsson was dead and she was to be alone with her child for the rest of her life.

Before this, in the time since the killing, she had thought of little except what she would be taking to Steinstraumstead and how she would be living there. During the killing itself, and the retrieval and burial of the corpus, and during the time she spent at Undir Hofdi and Gunnars Stead before moving, she had felt calm, as if dead, but not unhappy. She had followed many commands—Birgitta's commands to free her little birds and rip apart, seam by seam, the red gown, Pall Hallvardsson's commands to pray for God's forgiveness and to beg for the forgiveness of her husband and brother, as well as that of Kollbein Sigurdsson for luring his hirdman into sin and death. Even Olaf had commanded her. He had commanded her to sleep in Ingrid's old bedcloset and never to be inside when he was, nor outside when he was. She had done every task set her day after day, and then fallen into such sleeps as she had never known before, dreamless and black. Then she had come to Steinstraumstead, following Gunnar's commands not to speak to him and not to look into what Birgitta had packed for her until he was away.

After her coming, there was such novelty and labor to establishing herself that she had thought of little, and dreamed of nothing still, but now, after seeing the fish caught in the driftwood, dreams came to her every night of Skuli Gudmundsson, whole and beautiful, sometimes as if he had been resurrected, more often as if there had been no killing. The yearning for him that she had never been without after their first meetings doubled and redoubled, so that she could not sit or walk or run or lie down or pray or eat or sleep or set one stone on top of another. She thought of tales she had heard of fiery demons that sometimes got into folk, so that they looked the same, but when they died, as they always must, their insides were black and putrid, unlike the flesh of godly souls. A few Greenlanders maintained that the skraelings were such folk, others declared that they were not, that these things were more often seen far to the south, in hot places. However it came about, Margret thought that the entrance of such a demon would surely feel much as her longing felt, and would be as difficult to relieve. The V-shaped piece of driftwood sat as if enchanted on the tiny strip of strand for many days. Storms and high tides seemed only to lift it higher, never to carry it off. Margret grow both afraid of it and fond of it, but she never approached it or touched it.

One day when Margret returned from pasturing her sheep, she saw that a small boat was pulled up on the strand, and that an old woman and a young man were sitting on the hillside in front of the farmstead. These folk were Marta Thordardottir, the sister of Osmund Thordarson, the lawspeaker, and her son, Isleif Isleifsson. Both lived in the Brattahlid district, and Isleif was one of the Greenlanders who had been made a priest by the bishop. Marta was not an old woman, but her husband had died during a coughing sickness. Now she lived in great state on the farm of Osmund at Brattahlid and her other son, Ragnleif, farmed her old farm. Now Margret approached her visitors and welcomed them to Steinstraumstead, and invited them to take some ewe's milk as refreshment. They greeted her in a friendly fashion, and Marta said, "My Margret, you little resemble my friend Helga Ingvadottir. All the Gunnars Stead lineage has looked just the same for generation after generation, with never a soul who resembles the mother's line."

"It seems to me that I know your face well, too, Marta Thordardottir, though I have not seen you for many years."

Isleif was not unhandsome, with fair hair and straight teeth, but Margret saw that his eyes were weak, for he habitually narrowed them when he looked at anything, as if to bring it into focus. He said, "And I would know you, Margret, from the warm tales that Pall Hallvardsson relates of your many virtues."

After they had finished their milk and Marta had wiped her mouth with the hem of her sleeve and settled herself on the hillside, she asked Margret when she expected to be confined. Margret said that she had once calculated St. Mary Magdalen's mass, but that she had since lost track of the dates, and did not now know how soon this would be. Isleif said that they had just passed the feast of Sts. Peter and Paul, and so Margret's date would be some twenty days off. Neither Marta nor Isleif spoke to her with contempt, but as they spoke of these things, Margret sat with her eyes cast down, feeling shame that she felt not a whit of when she was alone. Marta now invited Margret to come to Brattahlid, where she lived, and to stay there as she wished, and the child would be fostered by Osmund, or, if Margret preferred, by Ragnleif, or even Isleif, on behalf of the church. "Otherwise," she said, "all of the folk of the Brattahlid district, but especially friends of Asgeir Gunnarsson and his father, will feel it to be a shame on them that Margret Asgeirsdottir is living so poorly, in danger from starvation or accident or even the skraelings, and on such a tiny steading so close by."

Now Margret looked up, into Marta's gaze, to see if this was a command, but Marta and Isleif were smiling at her, and she saw that it would be possible to refuse, but that if she did so, the offer would not be made again. Finally, she said, "The case lies thus, that I have brought shame enough to my brother and husband, as well as to myself and my child. Through my own wish, I left Vatna Hverfi and came to this poor steading, although it is true that my brother and husband wished nothing else than this. It seems to me that such a course as my coming to live at Brattahlid would speak ill of my folk to all of the Greenlanders, and people would say that they had left me to wander from place to place, seeking charity. Also, they must say that I had traded on my sin and gained a statelier home than I deserved."

Seeing the direction of Margret's response, Marta said, "But no woman can be brought to bed in solitude, without midwives, or a priest. Such a thing courts death and worse, and your folk are greatly to blame for putting you in such peril."

Margret smiled. "Peril to me has not been our foremost concern, and, to speak the truth, things that haven't yet happened always seem the farthest away."

"It seems to you now that all will go well."

"Or, that whatever will happen will be good enough." But she could see that these words were unpleasing to Marta and Isleif, both. She dropped her eyes again. After a few moments, she said, "I have no wish for a solitary confinement, although about this, as about much else, I have been careless. But I also have no wish to leave Steinstraumstead, and my five sheep, and my little house, for there is much to be done with it before the winter, and each day I do some little thing."

At this, Marta Thordardottir sat silent for a while, gazing across the fjord at the cloud shadows moving across the face of Brattahlid. Finally she sighed, and said, "The trip across the fjord is not such a great one, and one of the servingmen from Brattahlid might make it each morning until the birth of the child, and after that we may talk again about the arrangement of your affairs. But still this seems to me the less satisfactory course." Margret was much pleased by this, and she took Marta Thordardottir's hand and kissed her fingers, and thanked her heartily. Then Sira Isleif spoke with Margret and confessed her and prayed with her, and the two visitors went into their boat and rowed back to Brattahlid, and Margret watched them the entire way. But after this, she felt much ashamed, and longed even more painfully for Skuli Gudmundsson. It was said that Osmund Thordarson was not a little displeased that one of his servants should take the time for such an errand every morning, but that in this business as always, his sister must have her way.

Margret Asgeirsdottir was brought to bed of a boy, and all went well with him. He was christened by Sira Isleif, and his name was Jonas Skulason. A girl came to live with Margret, whose name was Asta Thorbergsdottir, and this girl was so strong that she liked to compete with boys and men in swimming contests and other tests of strength, although she was past the age of marrying. Many laughed at her, and Osmund said that he was well rid of her, although she was his cousin's granddaughter. In addition, a carpenter and another of Osmund's servants came one day and repaired Margret's bedcloset and the roof of the room where she and Asta slept. Margret was very grateful to Marta Thordardottir for all of these benefits, and loved her as a daughter her mother forever after this until Marta's death.

One day Olaf Finnbogason took the small Gunnars Stead boat, and rowed to Gardar. As he had not been there in four summers, he was much surprised at the change he found, although, as before, folk greeted him in a familiar way, as if he had been gone only a few days. Here, of course, the hay crop on the huge homefield was as green and thick as ever—so thick that a man could hardly find the earth under the grass with his fingers. But there were few servants, boys, or priests running from here to there. The herd of cattle had diminished somewhat—about thirty cows and fifteen calves grazed on the hillside above the homefield. Even so, they were lovely big beasts, with shining red rumps and patches of white spreading like snow over their necks and shoulders. The Gardar bull grazed in a separate pen, as big as a rowboat and vigilant, able to graze and watch the comings and goings of the cows at the same time. He eyed Olaf. Olaf found much to admire in the animal—the Gunnars

Stead bull was old and mild, and Olaf was fond of him, but it seemed to him that it would be a fine thing to care for this beast, a daily test of wills dangerous not to win. After looking for a long while at the bull, Olaf approached the hall.

Only a single figure leaned over some writing, and there was no singing. Sira Pall Hallvardsson lived now at Hvalsey Fjord, and Olaf did not know this man, who was dressed as a priest. A servingwoman named Anna Jonsdottir came up to him wiping her hands on her gown, and greeted him by name and asked him his business. Olaf inquired after the bishop. Anna replied that the bishop was sleeping, but that Sira Jon was anyway in the habit of receiving all visitors and she took him off with her to find the priest.

When Sira Jon came forward, Olaf pulled off his hat and, with little grace, dropped to his knees and kissed the priest's ring. Jon looked at Olaf for a long moment, and then declared, "Olaf Finnbogason, you are so changed that I would not have known you, although I remember you well from your earlier visit."

"Many say this of me, and ask me if I have been ill, but I have not," said Olaf. Now Sira Jon asked for the news of Gunnars Stead, and sent Anna Jonsdottir away for a bowl of milk and other refreshments, and he invited Olaf into his chamber. The man's clothing was so soiled and humble that Jon could not forbear staring at it, for the folk at Gunnars Stead were known for dressing well, in the thick, purplish Gunnars Stead wadmal that was so desirable. Even folk who laughed at Gunnar's womanish weaving were not slow to trade for some of it when they could. The two men sat without talking until Olaf had finished his meal. Olaf kept his eyes down and ate carefully, for even though those who knew him as a child at Gardar had died long ago, Gardar reminded him of how he had been teased for eating like a beast, snorting and snuffling into his food as if he had never seen a spoon in his life.

After eating, Olaf pushed away his bowl and turned to Sira Jon. "I beg you," he said, "to prevail upon the bishop to let me be made a priest now, for I am but thirty winters old, and that is of an age with Petur, the plague priest, when he began his training."

Jon sat back and stared at him.

Still with his eyes down, Olaf went on, "Once I had everything by memory, every book that I was read, word for word, so that even though my eyes may be ill-suited for reading now, I know what should be said, and when to say it. Those things I have forgotten, I might learn again, for though my memory is not what it was, it is still larger than is common, and a trial would prove it." He looked up. "My mother did intend me for a priest, after all, as the bishop himself well knows."

Sira Jon cleared his throat. "It is true," he said, "that of the seven churches in the eastern settlement, only four, including Gardar, have resident priests, and Sira Nikolaus at Undir Hofdi would surely have retired before now if such things were ordered in Greenland as they are in Norway. But why have you changed your mind? Why do you so suddenly wish to serve God, when you did not have this wish before?"

"Indeed, Sira, I do not think that I knew my own wishes before, because I was young, and I blindly shunned the sign of God. I have since found cause to regret my mistake, and I seek with all my heart to correct it." As he spoke, he pressed his spoon against a drop of sourmilk and brought it to his tongue. Sira Jon turned away, and called for Anna to take away the vessels.

After she had left again, Jon addressed Olaf as follows: "It is well known that the bishop has been unwell, both during this summer and for much of the last winter. Such business as I do from day to day is beyond his strength, although he thinks clearly and often on more important matters, and we have great hope of his returning to health. Until this event, no new students can begin, for only the bishop can divine the true nature of their calling, and only he can conduct their religious training. When they are trained, only he can ordain them and guide their progress. Greenland is full of boys who will repay their training with years of service." His voice faded into silence, but the import of this last was not lost on Olaf. They sat quietly again.

After a bit, Olaf said, "I might also come to Gardar as a servant. I have the reputation of a good cowman in the Vatna Hverfi district, and I am often called for when something goes wrong at a calving or a bull is difficult to handle. In fact"—Olaf smiled—"I noticed the Gardar bull as I was coming to the residence. The like of such an animal I have never seen before, and not just his size and strength, but his spirit, the way his gaze seeks everything, and the way his skin quivers over his flesh in the sunlight."

Sira Jon frowned and said, "You speak more warmly of the bull now than you spoke before of the Lord."

Olaf fell silent again, and Jon got up and began to pace around the room. Finally he told Olaf that he would pray over a decision and send him a message. Olaf stood up and put on his cap. When Jon turned to him, Olaf said, "From these words I know that there is no place for me at

Gardar," and he spoke in his usual low, rough tones, so that he sounded angry. Then he walked out.

And now, Sira Jon, who had been pleased enough to receive Olaf and entertain his supplications, was seized with such anger that he desired to run after the other man and give him his death blow. He remembered nothing of Olaf's words or demeanor, but only his disrespectful attire and sullen manner of speaking. This was not the first such fit to overtake the priest. As gently as possible, he closed the door of his chamber and threw himself full length before the carved ivory crucifix on the eastern wall, although Satan himself prevented his eyes from lifting to the lovely somber face of the Christ, just as he prevented Jon's soul from rising out of the fire and shame of his anger. This anger appeared to him as a pool at the bottom of an abyss, and each day of his life in Greenland was spent in threading his way around this flaming tarn on a narrow and rock-strewn ledge. Many days Satan threw him in, propelling him with slight and unexpected provocations, and these days did not get fewer, nor did the fire burn less fiercely. Worse, these angers went unconfessed and unabsolved, as Jon could not bring himself to portray their full intensity to the bishop for some reasons nor to Pall Hallvardsson, for other reasons.

Now he lay on the floor in a state of rigid supplication for a long while, never lifting his eyes to the crucifix but knowing it, even as he knew the knock of Anna Jonsdottir, who was calling him to the bishop. He had, in the past few days, ceased fighting Satan, and now only hoped to contain him within this chamber and within his corpus.

The bishop sat beside his bedcloset in a chair that had been carved for him by his brother in Norway when they were both young men, and had gone with him everywhere. Now it had come to Greenland, and he sat heavily against the back rail instead of upright, disdaining support, as he had always done. At the front of one of the arms was carved the face of a pig, for St. Anthony, and at the front of the other, a lion, for St. Jerome. The bishop's eyes were half open, and Anna Jonsdottir was speaking to him as she put morsels of steamed fish into his mouth. "These are good bits, indeed," she said. "Just as your excellency likes them, with a bit of thyme and butter." His jaws worked intermittently, but nothing dropped out, and when his mouth was full, he swallowed. "Not the least bone," she said, and it was true, she was especially careful about removing even the smallest bones. When this delayed her feeding, he groaned, as if the wait were unbearable. Sometimes she put a cup of milk to his lips, and he sipped it. At last his arm flew up, signaling that he had had enough. Anna snatched the trencher away, so that it wouldn't be knocked across

the room, as had happened, and she helped the bishop up, for he had slid
far down. He opened his eyes wider. "There you are," she said, "that bit
of fish has strengthened you," though privately she thought that folk did
better with seal blubber and reindeer meat. The front of his gown was
covered with a white napkin, and this she took away. Now it would be
time for the coming of Sira Jon, and she cocked her ear for the other man's
step. Bishop Alf, too, appeared to be listening, although it was well known
to the servingwomen in the residence that he could hardly hear anything
anymore. Anna herself had once dropped some utensils and a heavy iron
pot, through stumbling over an unevenness in the paving of the floor, and
the bishop, sitting in his chair, hadn't flinched at all. Now Anna turned
from the bishop and began arranging the furs and rugs in his bedcloset.
Her nose twisted from the smell.

Sira Jon came in, his face white but his manner bustling, and Anna
curtsied and moved back toward the wall. Jon began talking at once, saying
how well his grace looked today, and that he hoped the bishop had had
a pleasant meal. He always talked to the bishop in this way, without
stopping for an answer to any of the questions he asked, and without
looking into the bishop's face. Even so, he appeared to Anna to think that
the bishop heard him, and that the two were following each other's
thoughts. Indeed, it was true enough that even before his illness the bishop
had spoken little but expected Jon to know his thoughts. The servingwomen often gossiped among themselves about how peculiar these
Norwegians were, and some attributed their behavior to this, that they
were Norwegian, and others declared that it was because of their clerical
training. Soon Sira Jon signaled to Anna that she could leave, for he had
weighty matters to discuss with the older man in private.

It was always thus that Jon came to his uncle, and always thus that
he sat on a low stool at the older man's feet. When the bishop had been
confined to his bedcloset, Jon had sat on this same three-legged stool beside
the bishop's head and leaned in to catch whatever words the bishop uttered.
When the bishop had been well and in his high seat, Jon had sat on this
same stool with his eyes down, making a similar report. When the bishop,
then not a bishop but a simple priest, had come to his sister's home in
Stavanger district, the boy Jon had sat below him thus, and reported upon
his progress in learning and holiness.

Now he began with the beasts. "My uncle," he said without looking
up, "I have it from the herdsman's boy that two lambs have been taken
by foxes, and this is one fewer than last year. All of the cows are in good
health, and the illness that struck the herd in the spring has, by the grace

of God, run its course. Alas, only fifteen calves have survived, but all of them good-sized beasts, as if the sickness culled the weaklings. Surely this, too, shows the care of the Lord for His servants. Stein expects to bring every calf and every cow through the winter. Of the horses, there is this to say, that Lofti is a little lame in the left hind leg and Nonni's eye still runs with matter, although nothing can be found in it, nor any scratch. So much for the beasts, with them all is as well as can be expected." And in this way Sira Jon went on talking about first the servingwomen, then the servingmen, then the boys (of which there were but two, but very good boys, from prosperous Brattahlid families, who had brought much property with them), then the assistant priest, Audun, the Greenlander who had been set to the work of making a copy of the liturgical calendar as his first project (although his hand had little grace or beauty, it was clear and readable, perhaps a quality more necessary among the Greenlanders than other qualities).

Above his head, his uncle groaned and shuffled, but it was not Jon's habit to raise his eyes. Then he spoke of Olaf, although not by name, saying, "It is the case that an older man has come as an applicant, wishing to be trained as a priest, but indeed, he shows little respect for the Lord or His servants, being dressed in tattered, soiled clothes and greedy for food rather than for knowledge of the ways of the Lord." Here, Jon paused, but the bishop said nothing. "The man," Jon said, "looks to be unskillful in any but the most menial work, and has no property that he might bring with him to enrich the see. Altogether, considering recent straitened circumstances, a place that might be opened to another should not be opened to this man." Again Jon fell silent, for the bishop had from time to time chastened him for being hard and fastidious, and dazzled by the surfaces of things. But now the bishop said nothing, and it is a saying in old books that in silence there is approval.

Now Jon enlarged upon a project that he had cherished for some time. "My uncle, the feast of St. Bartholomew is near at hand, and I wish to say mass in the cathedral on this day, and to clean the cathedral and repair and polish all of the altar furniture with this in view, and not only that, but also to bring out some of the rarely used drapery and vestments." The bishop made no response, and it occurred to Jon that in silence there might also be disapproval, and he said, "This would be an occasion to announce the Lord and His coming more strongly to the Greenlanders, especially as the time is approaching when rents and tithes are to be paid. Such a mass and celebration I have cherished in my heart for some time, as a way of bringing the Greenlanders to thoughts of the Lord, for this is the time farthest from Yule and Easter, and the thoughts of the Greenlanders are wholly fixed on the harvest and the seal hunt and the slaughter of livestock. Indeed, it seems to me that they show the fury of pagans in this slaughter." Here, thinking of these things, Jon expected the Devil to fling him into the lake of anger, but it did not occur; he passed safely on.

Now he sat below the bishop in silence for some little while, and then he got to his knees and prayed, and, as always in the company of his uncle, his heart lifted upward, and the words of his prayers flew out of his mouth like birds, and his soul slipped easily into the contemplation of the Lord, and this was the great holiness of the bishop, that his presence cast light upon those around him like sunbeams, and the soul rode these beams as a ship sailing upwards to heaven. It was this more than anything else that prevented Jon from revealing his sin to the bishop, although the bishop was his confessor—in the presence of the bishop it was a task of no little difficulty to recall the substance of his sin. It was as his mother had always declared—the holiness of Sira Alf drove out all else, as the sun drives out darkness, and so it was far better to confess the worst sins, the thickest and darkest sins, to another sort of priest, a man of greater melancholy, as the boy Jon's parish priest had been. And after this praying, Jon kissed the bishop's ring and went out.

Anna Jonsdottir found the bishop much slumped down in his seat, and to all appearances asleep. She helped him into his bedcloset and pulled the cloaks and furs up to his chin, for he was beginning to shiver. And so, the bishop went on in much this way, some days better and some days not so well, and it was said by the Greenlanders that he was certainly mending, and would be saying mass again by the beginning of the winter nights, or by Yule, perhaps.

In this autumn, the skraelings returned to Eriks Fjord and Isafjord, and set up their camps and fished and traded with the Norsemen as if the killing of Vestein had never taken place. They had much to trade in the way of furs and especially tusks, and most of the farmers were glad enough to see them, and praised their virtues as hunters and fishermen. But toward Yule a skraeling in his skin boat and carrying his hunting tools paddled near to the shore at Solar Fell. This time a man named Solmund Skeggjason, who was the husband of Ragnvald Einarsson's daughter Gudny, was gathering shells and driftwood along the strand. It was after mid-day, and the sun glared off the water of the fjord into his eyes, and so he didn't catch sight of the skraeling. As he stood up with his basket, the skraeling threw his spear and it lodged in Solmund's viscera and he fell down. The skraeling paddled swiftly away and Solmund sat up and pulled the shaft from his belly, but the spearhead was barbed, for hunting walrus, and it lodged in the flesh. Now Solmund began to creep toward the farmhouse, which was up a steep slope, and when he got to the doorway, he scratched at it. When Ragnvald opened the door, his son-in-law fell inside, saying, "My father, I have gathered a spearhead during my labors, but now I cannot find it again." At this, the man died, and he was carried into the house.

Now activities became very unusual at Ragnvald's steading. Each time one of the sons or a servingman or a neighbor came to the house, the door would open to let him in, but no one came out. And this was also unusual, that the skraelings didn't move off, but stayed in their camps and attended to their business as usual, and none of those who traded with the skraelings heard anything of this killing, and so it was afterwards said that the skraeling had kept this news to himself, and not told his chief about it. It was also the case that the skraelings were living in their winter dwelling houses, which were neatly built stone huts, and not so easy to carry off, or to leave, at this time of the year, as skin booths.

Sometime after the killing, when the fjord was full of ice from shore to shore, the Greenlanders in a group of twenty-two men surprised the skraelings at their camp, and caught a group, including the killer, inside their hut. There were seven men and boys and four women. One of the men ran out, and was killed with an ax, and after this the Greenlanders drove all of the skraelings out by setting fire to brush at the windows and doors of the booth, so that the demons were overcome by smoke, and the skraelings were killed as they tried to escape. However, two of the skrael-ings escaped under cover of smoke and darkness, and ran out onto the ice of the fjord. They ran all the way across to the opposite shore, although one of them kept falling. Opposite to Solar Fell were two beaches, one a flat, pebbly peninsula forming a little harbor, and the other the steep scree of a mountain. The Norsemen chased the two skraelings toward the steeper beach, and the one who had kept falling down was caught and killed. The other managed to climb up the slippery slope about twelve or fifteen ells. Now Ragnvald came up to the dead one and grabbed his left arm and cut it off with one blow of his ax, and then he raised it high and shouted, "Skraeling! As long as you live, surely you won't forget your brother!" And then it was dark, and the Norsemen went home, leaving the bodies of the demons out in the ice and snow. When the Norsemen awoke the next day, the skraelings were gone from Eriks Fjord, and by the next day they were gone from Isafjord, and no more was seen of them during that winter.

Kollbein Sigurdsson was much put out by Ragnvald's actions and said that they endangered the whole settlement, for now he expected that the skraelings would return from the north soon enough, and more of them than the Greenlanders would know what to do with. Others, especially those who had profited by the recent trading, also disapproved of the course the Solar Fell folk had taken, but more said that Ragnvald had earned the second killing by not avenging the death of Vestein, so that the demons had considered themselves free to do as they wished. The years-old killing of Erlend Ketilsson's ewe was recalled, as well as other thefts and little conflicts, and these were said to show a pattern of increasing audacity. The Greenlanders pointed to the huts of the skraelings, which were empty but tightly built and known to be warm and dry—warmer, in fact, than a Norseman could tolerate, for the skraelings, both men and women, were known to sit about savagely naked—and declared that the way these huts had been built and then left showed a plan, first to take over the farms and pastures of the Greenlanders, and second to go for reinforcements and return. And so Kollbein and the Greenlanders came around to agreement on what was to be expected, but continued to disagree on how Ragnvald and his men should have acquitted themselves. Discussion of this topic raged throughout the winter, and hordes of skraelings in fleets of skin boats were looked for each day, but such a thing did not come to pass, and the settlement was quiet.

This winter was a time of great hunger, especially for the beasts, for the dry harvest had been sparse and the hay poor in quality, and then the snows came early and deep, around Eriks Fjord in particular, so that it was hard, and then impossible, for the sheep to paw through to their forage. Three times before Yule Margret Asgeirsdottir went on skis across Eriks Fjord with Asta Thorbergsdottir, carrying the child tied in a cloak on her back, as she had carried Gunnar as a young girl. Each time she dragged home as much hay as Marta could give her, but the last time she saw that she dared not ask again without putting the Brattahlid beasts at risk. In addition to the hay, Marta gave her a large quantity of dried reindeer meat, but this, too, Margret saw was ill-spared, for the Brattahlid folk were numerous. After this, Margret declared to Asta that they would not cross the fjord again, but would be sparing of what they had and pray for God's bounty. Now the Gunnars Stead ewes died, and under the thick wool, Margret could feel the ribs and spine as if there weren't any flesh on the animals at all. Sometime before the beginning of Lent, a servingman from Brattahlid came to them with a few provisions—some butter, cheese, and dried sealmeat. Margret saw that he was gaunt and exhausted from the crossing, which in other years folk did for pleasure on fine winter days.

The child Jonas was now nearly half a year old, with just the finest down on his domed head, which Asta declared signified a thick mane of fair hair to come. Asta was very fond of the infant, and chattered about him to Margret from morning until bedtime. Her examination of his parts brought those same parts of his father so vividly into Margret's imagination that Skuli seemed to inhabit their tiny dwelling like the folk in old stories who refused to stay in their graves, but rode roof peaks and guarded doorways, tormenting the living inhabitants of the steading. Asta was eloquent on the subject of the boy's hands, which were large and, according to her, unusually dexterous. He certainly liked above all things to take bits of stuff into his hands and gaze upon them. But this was too much like Skuli and his eternal carving, and Margret found in his evident pleasure a burning pain to go with the pain of her dreams, which continued unabated to resurrect the Norwegian each night so that he died again each morning, only to be replaced by his son at the breast, suckling furiously.

After the visit of Marta's servingman, the two women ate but a single meal each day, and this consisted of two morsels of dried reindeer meat for Margret and one for Asta, a bit of cheese for each, some pieces of dried seal blubber for Margret, and a small bowl of sourmilk mixed with dried, powdered seaweed. Even with the seal blubber, which folk said always assured a copious milk supply, Jonas began to suckle more often, so that he was almost always at the breast, and still grew thinner, and he was smaller than he had been at the beginning of winter. Now Asta spoke less of the boy and always of the food at Marta Thordardottir's table, where, she said, every meal was a feast, and all the servingfolk ate as much as they pleased.

One day Margret put Jonas on her back and declared that she was going to snare some ptarmigan, for the weather was fine and without snow or high winds for the first time in many days. As always now, the child moaned to be at the breast, but soon he fell asleep with the motion of Margret's skis over the snow. Ptarmigan signs were easy to spot, and made the water come in her mouth as soon as she saw them, so that she had to sit down, panting, at the thought of food, though winter ptarmigan were often bitter to eat. Ptarmigan, she knew, were always fat as demons, even in the snowiest winters. Her fingers trembled as she tied her snares, and she was unaccountably clumsy, fouling her lines and crushing the snow and flailing about. After only five snares, and still just within sight of the steading, she grew so tired that she could think only of sleep, and she was ready to lie down in the snow and nap, but Jonas awoke screaming to suck, and this aroused her. Such a distance as she was from the farmstead she had trotted past without thought in the summer, but it now formed the limit of her strength, and even her determination. She took Jonas from her back and brought forth her breast to give him suck, but after the briefest while, he put back his head and screamed, and she could see no milk on his lips, nor was her breast full and hard as it once had been. Slowly, for she was very fatigued, she arranged herself and the child so that he could suckle the other breast, but this, too, had nothing. Now she rubbed some snow between her hands until it began to melt, and touched it to his lips. He took this greedily, so she gave it to him again, and he was satisfied for a while. When he stopped howling, her eyes closed, for she could keep them open no longer.

It so happened that Asta thought so hard about ptarmigan roasting on a spit that it was as if she could hear the popping of the fat and smell the fragrance of the cooking meat. Soon she became impatient, and arose from her bedstead and went to the door, but Margret was not coming, so she went back to her bed and lay down. But then it seemed to her that she heard shouting, as if of men over their trenchers, and she went to the door again to look out. All was white waste, and she ate some of this snow. She went back to her bed and lay down, but as soon as she had pulled up her furs for warmth, the sound and fragrance of the roasting birds drove her out again, and to the door, and it came to her that Margret had caught some birds, and was roasting them on the hillside, so that she might have them all to herself. At this, Asta donned her cloak and shoes and went out of the steading. Now she followed Margret's track, and the snow was deep and powdery, causing her to stumble about, for she had forgotten to put on her skis. And when she came to where Margret and Jonas sat, slumped and sleeping, with no ptarmigan roasting on a spit, popping and browning, she burst into tears and began shaking Margret by the shoulders.

Now Jonas suckled at the breast all the time, night and morning, but it seemed that the only time he got anything was just after Margret awoke. Other times in the day, when he was hungry, they gave him snow, and they ate much snow themselves, and Asta sometimes said that hers tasted like sourmilk with bilberries, but Margret said that hers never tasted like this, although such a thing was pleasant to think of. Jonas no longer played such games as he was accustomed to, nor did he try to sit or creep, as he had, but only sometimes did he take something in his hand and look at it while he worked at the breast, but soon enough it would fall from his hand, for his grip had no strength. One day they ate the last of the seal blubber, and soon after that the last of the cheese and butter. Now their provisions consisted of a few pieces of dried reindeer meat, a little sourmilk, and some angelica stalks, and they each ate one bit of dried meat every day and a mouthful of sourmilk, and otherwise they lay under their furs in the bedstead, all together, for any touch of the cold made them shiver so that they could not hold a spoon. Margret's breasts were so flat that they looked as though they had never been, except that the nipples were raw from the constant sucking of the child. And one of these days, when Margret awoke in the morning after a long sleep, Jonas was still asleep in the crook of her arm, with his hand slipped into the slit of her dress and outspread on her skin, and his arm was as thin as the bones of birds, though his belly was round and fat, and she saw that he was, indeed, not asleep, but that the life had passed from him in the night, and she put her hand over his hand that rested against her skin and she wrapped him more tightly in her cloak and lay there quietly, waiting for Asta to awaken.

One day after this, the servingman came from Brattahlid with news, and he found Margret and Asta dozing in the bedcloset, as was their habit, and they were so exhausted that they could not by any means sit up. Margret asked him if it was Lent yet, and he laughed and declared that it was nearly Easter. The other news he brought was that a whale had stranded on the ice near the mouth of Eriks Fjord some two days previously, and all the men of the settlement were engaged in carving up the great leviathan, and he bore with him some other provisions, sent by Marta Thordardottir to last them until the whale flesh had been carried home.

At this Easter the Greenlanders rejoiced greatly in resurrection, they said, and not only the resurrection of the Lord. The dead in Eriks Fjord and Isafjord, where the snows had been deepest, numbered fifteen, while in Vatna Hverfi district and south, the weather had been milder, and only cattle had died off from lack of fodder. Jonas Skulason was blessed and buried at the east side of Thjodhilds church at Brattahlid, for this was what Marta Thordardottir insisted upon, although Osmund her brother spoke against it.

In this spring it happened that not long before Easter, another child was born to Birgitta Lavransdottir, and this girl was blessed and baptized with the name Helga, after Helga Ingvadottir. Helga Gunnarsdottir was not so jolly as her sister Gunnhild, but cried and complained every day, and all day, until midsummer, when, as if by a miracle she was relieved of her pain through a mixture of sheep's urine and angelica leaves warmed and rubbed onto her belly, and then tied tightly with a band, so that every day this treatment was done to little Helga, for fear that the pains would return, and Birgitta continued this for a long time, until the child was four winters old. After the infant's recovery, Birgitta began to gain the reputation of skill in healing, and to go about to other farms in the district suggesting remedies for various ills, especially those of children. As she always brought with her large pieces of the good Gunnars Stead cheeses and lengths of thick Gunnars Stead wadmal (for she greatly believed in the efficacy of wrapping the affected part tightly in cloths), she got to be not a little sought out for her skills. Folk said that what she did for the belly made up for everything else, and in any case, that was usually harmless enough.

Unn, the "wife" of Nikolaus the Priest, was now so old and blind that she could hardly step out of the priest's house and wouldn't know the difference between a fistula and a fever anyway. Even so, some women visited her when they were ill, for she was much pleased to give advice. It was said that Nikolaus and his "wife" were ninety years old, nearing a hundred, in fact, and could easily remember the days of King Erik, but if this was true, it was something they never spoke of. It was also said that Nikolaus and Unn were somewhat over sixty years in age, that is that they could remember only as far back as King Magnus, which was no rare thing at all, but even so, it was said that these two were the oldest folk in the eastern settlement.

In this summer, Kollbein Sigurdsson, because of the boredom of his sailors in Greenland, agreed to give a fine prize to the winner of a swimming contest. This prize was to be either a richly colored wallhanging or a carved ivory altar with two hinged leaves and small enough to be slipped into a pocket, as the winner might choose, and in addition there was to be a great feast to last three days, with a swimming contest each day, so that the winner would not be known until the last day. The site chosen was at the hot springs in Hrafns Fjord. Greenlanders were not much used to swimming, except those who lived in the vicinity of the hot springs, for the water in Greenland is colder than in Iceland or other places, and a man can freeze to death even in the summer, but the Norwegian sailors were eager to show off their skills.

As it happened, other contests were added to the swimming contests, and these were ones, such as rowing, that the Greenlanders excelled in, but Kollbein declared that the prize should go only to swimmers. From this as from the ombudsman's every other action, it was known that the Norwegian was niggardly and foolish. Even so, when the time for the contests was at hand, most of the folk from most of the farmsteads were not a little pleased to congregate in Hrafns Fjord and enjoy the hot springs and the feasting.

On the first day, there were two contests of endurance, one of swimming back and forth in the cold waters of Hrafns Fjord until the arms and legs were so cold that they could no longer be moved and the men were hauled out and taken to the hot springs to be revived. The winner of this contest was a sailor by the name of Egil Halldorsson. The second contest involved how long a man could hold his breath under water. In this game, a man would be held down by two other men while two judges counted the time, and when the man began fighting and flailing he would be let up for breath. Each man got three chances, and the winner of this contest was the young son of Thord and Kristin of Siglufjord, whose name was Ingvi Thordarson. After these contests, the benches were set up outside the booths, and everyone ate with much appetite. When the benches were taken away, the sailors began to chant a number of their songs and to dance in a circle. These songs were bawdy, but tuneful and pleasant. After this, a man named Steinthor, who had traveled to the feast from Isafjord, brought out a flute he had carved from a narwhal tusk, and played it for a while. Other Greenlanders sang their Greenlandic songs, and Gunnar Asgeirsson and Axel Njalsson each told a tale. Kollbein Sigurdsson declared that this was good entertainment for a place so lacking in beer and other joy-inducing refreshments.

On the second day, participants in the contests had to dive, first for a heavy marked stone, which they were to bring up, and then for a small soapstone weight, which they were to find and bring up. Many participated in these contests, and so many were able to bring up the great stone that the game had to be repeated three times, each time with a bulkier and more awkward weight. This contest was also won by Egil Halldorsson, for he was the most accomplished of the sailors in these sorts of sports. Another sailor, named Olaf Bogulfsson, won the test of finding the small loom-weight. After this six rowboats made a race from one farmer's jetty across the fjord and back. This race was won by a Greenlandic boat. After these events there was feasting, as well, and the talk turned to past feasts, especially to the great feast at Gunnars Stead, where all, even the women, had gotten much intoxicated with Asgeir's mead, and the result had been the rape of Sigrun Ketilsdottir and all that followed it. The Norwegians spoke with longing of feasts in their own home districts, and with such conversation the evening ended.

Now on the third day there was but a single contest, but it took all day. All those participating were to go together into the spring and attempt to hold each other under the water until the wiliest man with the strongest lungs was the last one left. If this ended up to be Egil Halldorsson, then he would win the prize, but if another man should be strongest, then he and Egil would at once, without resting, run a foot race between two designated points, and that would show the strongest man. It so happened that Kollbein Sigurdsson insisted on participating in this contest, much against the advice of his English accountant, Martin of Chester, and his other friends, both Greenlanders and Norwegians.

The spring chosen was large and deep, but not so warm as the others. In spots it was so deep that no one had ever touched the bottom, and everywhere it was deep enough so that no man could be weighed down or pinned against the bottom by another. At a signal from one of Kollbein's party, all of the men leaped into the water, which at once began to seethe with the jumping, diving, and arm swinging of the contestants. For a while, everyone struggled with great spirit, and no one raised his hand to show that he was ready to come out, for this was the rule, that each man was the best judge of his own strength and wind. Certain strong older men, who were not competing, stood around the edge of the pool to gather up those who might be rendered senseless during the contest. Folk always consider such a game to be amusing, and there was not a little shouting and calling out from the spectators. After a certain while, hands began going up, and men started being pulled, sputtering and spitting water, from the pool. Soon there were four men where there had been thirty, and these were Egil Halldorsson, two other sailors, and a big man from Siglufjord named Starkad the Strong.

One of the sailors had a thick black beard, and Starkad at once swam up to him from behind and grabbed his beard, pulled his head back, and submerged him. This sailor now brought his legs up to his head and attempted to kick at Starkad with his heels, but he could not get his beard free of the Greenlander's fingers and began to swing his arms. Soon his hand went up, and Starkad let go his grip. The man had taken in much water, and came out coughing. He flung himself on the grass and heaved. In the meantime, Egil swam up to the other sailor and brought his legs tightly around the other man's waist, hooking his feet together so that his clasp could not be broken. Then he grasped the other man by the ears and pushed his face under while pulling the rest of him down with his legs. This sailor, who was Egil's friend and familiar with his trick, brought the sides of his hands hard into Egil's ribs, causing him to let go, but now Egil caught the man around the jaw and teeth, and grabbed his tongue, so that he could not bite, and he forced the man under the water. He still clasped the man around the waist with his legs. Very soon the man's hand went up, and he was pulled from the pool. Now the contest was between Egil and

Starkad, and Starkad was the larger of the two men, one of the largest men in Greenland, and it was generally thought that the Greenlanders were larger than the Norwegians on the whole. Starkad was also known to be a good runner, and folk said that it would be a fine thing for a prize such as Kollbein had offered to come into the possession of a Greenlander.

As soon as Egil let go of his opponent, Starkad was upon him, and he took his hair in one hand and his nose in the other and forced the Norwegian's face into the water, but Egil brought his legs up underwater and dealt Starkad a hard blow in the groin, so that the Greenlander relinquished the sailor's nose and he took a breath. Now Egil's arms came down on Starkad's shoulders, and pushed him a little under the water, then, quick as an eyeblink, his legs came up and grasped the Greenlander about the head. He hooked his feet and there seemed to be little hope for the Greenlander, as his opponent's body was out of reach. He went under, and the water grew quiet. After this, there was a long moment when Starkad was striving to break the other man's hold, and he succeeded in doing this, but he did not appear at the surface, and Egil found himself treading water alone in the middle of the pool. Just then, Starkad came up again, took a breath, and went down again. When he surfaced the second time, he carried a large object which showed itself to be the corpus of Kollbein Sigurdsson.

This threw the assembled throng into a great stir. Starkad and Egil carried the ombudsman from the water and laid him upon the grass. Folk recalled when he had last been seen, and contestants recalled their struggles with him, but all alleged that they had hardly touched the man, for fear of his office, but had held him under a little, to go along with the game, and then let him up. Several men attested that they had seen others act in this courteous fashion. Starkad the Strong related how as Egil had forced him under, he had pushed off downwards and felt the flesh of the ombudsman, lying on the bottom of the pool, with his foot. The ombudsman was lifted up and made to give forth the water in his gullet, but this did not revive him.

There was a law in Greenland in those times that a drowned man, if recovered from the waters and not frozen, was to be placed before the altar of St. Nikolaus at the cathedral for six days, for St. Nikolaus was the patron of sailors and drowned men, and more than a few such unfortunates had been brought back from death through the intercession of the saint. But some of the Norwegians and some of the Greenlanders fell into a dispute about the quickest and best way of carrying the ombudsman back to Gardar, the Norwegians desiring to row out Hrafns Fjord, around the peninsula, and up Einars Fjord, and the Greenlanders wishing to take a smaller boat up the streams and ponds of Vatna Hverfi, which would mean that the corpus would have to be carried part of the way, but would get there in one day rather than two. This dispute soon grew acrimonious, and the Norwegians declared that the Greenlanders intended disrespect to the ombudsman, while the Greenlanders scoffed at the ignorance of the Norwegians, who knew nothing of the treacheries of the open sea at this time of year, especially if challenged in a small boat such as those that were the only ones to be had in Hrafns Fjord just then. After this, the Norwegians began accusing those Greenlanders of blindness and stupidity, whose task it had been to watch for contestants in distress, and some of the men fell to fighting and there was no one with sufficient authority to halt the fray, for Osmund Thordarson the lawspeaker had stayed at home in Eriks Fjord, and the bishop, of course, was at Gardar. Now the fight spread all over the field, and some women standing together were knocked down and the corpus itself was stepped on, so that the fighters desisted and were shamefaced.

The corpus was put into a small boat with four oarsmen, two Greenlanders and two Norwegians, and was rowed up Hrafns Fjord to the waterfall to the south of Vatna Hverfi district, and from there by various streams and lakes, it went to Einars Fjord and Gardar, where it lay before the altar but did not revive, and so the ombudsman was buried on the south side of the cathedral, and there was much discussion concerning who would now be the representative of the king in Norway. Martin of Chester and the Norwegians considered that this post should fall to another Norwegian, but among themselves the Greenlanders declared that with Kollbein Sigurdsson and Skuli Gudmundsson both dead, there was little to make of King Hakon and Queen Margarethe in Greenland.

Soon enough the end of summer came round, and the Norwegians looked about themselves at the snowy waste, and in the spring they set sail for Bergen. The Greenlanders considered their ship to be poorly provisioned and ill-repaired, and no Greenlanders chose to go off with them. In later years it was said by some that the ship had been wrecked on the ice at Cap Farvel, and that pieces of it had drifted back to Herjolfsnes, and others said that the ship had come to Norway late in the year, all aboard safe. But these tales were merely Greenlanders' tales and the truth of the matter was never discovered.

And it came to pass that a year to the day after the death of Kollbein Sigurdsson, that is, two days before the mass of St. Bartholomew, the servingwoman Anna Jonsdottir discovered Bishop Alf dead in his bed when she went to him in the morning, and she saw that his eyes were open wide and his hands gripping the coverlet so tightly that she could not take it from them. Anna stood quietly near the bedcloset for a long while, for though she was an old woman and had seen many dead folk, as had every Greenlander, she had never known such a one as Sira Jon, priest or layman, and she shrank not a little from carrying her news to him. The talk among the servants was that he didn't even know how ill the bishop was, so little notice did he seem to take of the old man, but each day spoke to him of all the episcopal concerns. Nor did he prepare his uncle to meet the Lord of Heaven, as the servingwomen considered that he should, saying prayers with him or confessing the old man's sins, but he chattered on and on about masses or cattle or the weather or the accounts, as if Alf had not left that behind him months or years past. Anna looked at the bishop's face and the grip of his hands. It was said among the Greenlanders that every man saw something in his mortal moment. Anna always imagined seeing her brother Bjartur, who had drowned as a boy, standing among the saints.

Anna went out of the room and found the priest, Audun, and gave him the news. Before she could suggest that he tell Sira Jon, he said, "Sira Jon will want to know that. He is sitting in the great hall," and he slipped into his chamber and closed the door behind him.

Anna went across the yard to the kitchen house, where the women were making soap. Now the other five women looked at Anna in the face, and after a moment she nodded, and the other women sat back from their soapmaking, and shook their heads and were greatly downcast and one of them, a girl with a harelip, said, "The Lord retreats from us," but an older woman declared that such words were foolish, for the Lord never retreated from those who loved him. Now Anna went toward the great hall.

Sira Jon sat at a table under the window, bending over his account book and squinting. For a moment he put his face in his hand, and then he went back to his work. As always he was neatly attired, his robes clean and carefully arranged, much more colorful than the clothing of the Greenlanders. She stepped in front of him, and he smiled at her. So it was that she sometimes had summoned him into the bishop's presence. Now she said, "Sira, I have gone to the bishop this morning, and I have found him in his bed. I saw that he has been gathered to the saints."

Sira Jon sat gazing upon her, his smile still fixed on his face, and he sat thus for so long that Anna grew afraid, but then he said, "Thank you, Anna Jonsdottir, I will go to him. You may return to the other women and begin the preparations for laying out the corpus." Anna curtsied and began to move away, when all at once the priest closed his eyes and groaned, saying, "Lord, Thou hast retreated from us indeed," and Anna was so startled that she stumbled backward. Now Sira Jon stood up and began to stagger in the direction of the bishop's chamber and he looked to have lost his senses. Anna ran to the door of Sira Audun's chamber and beat upon it, calling the young priest's name, but there was no answer, until Anna declared aloud that she was well aware that the Greenlander was inside. He came sheepishly to the door.

They found Sira Jon in the bishop's chamber, with the door open. He had closed the dead man's eyes, and was now praying loudly, and Sira Audun stepped inside the room and began to pray with the older priest, but at the sound of his voice, Sira Jon looked around and glared at him so bitterly that he rose with as much dignity as possible and went out past Anna, declaring that there were many things to be done. Anna went to the cooking house, and the women left their soapmaking for other tasks. Some of the servingmen set out by horse and by boat for Brattahlid, Vatna Hverfi, Hvalsey Fjord, and other districts, to carry the news. The Greenlanders, who had not had a glimpse of the bishop in two summers, were little surprised. Sira Pall Hallvardsson accompanied the Hvalsey Fjord messenger back to Gardar, arriving late in the evening. Sira Jon, he was told, was still with the bishop's corpus, and had declared that he intended to carry it into the cathedral and place it before the altar of the saint and pray for its revival, through a miracle.

Sira Jon could not stay away from the women who were laying out the body, and he walked around and around them, pulling his hair and wringing his hands, talking not about the bishop, but about the power of relics. He spoke in matter-of-fact tones, but tears ran down his cheeks. "Why do the Greenlanders not have some blood of St. Nikolaus," he said. "This is a great scandal, to have as the only relics belonging to the see the last joint of the littlest finger of the left hand of St. Olaf." The women made no reply, and Sira Jon seemed to need none, but went on, "The relics of a powerful saint like St. Nikolaus, now they give off a potency that is like a fragrance, in that it spreads through the space around the relics, and makes oil lamps burn more brightly, and gems grow purer and more deeply colored." His voice gained strength and passion. "Objects placed near by grow heavier. Such things have been measured. We need this sort of power here in Greenland, where every endeavor is fraught with more risk than elsewhere." He stopped and gazed down upon the corpus. "What can the tip of a finger do?" He let out a great cry, and began pacing again. The women did not know what to make of him.

In his former chamber, on a pile of reindeer hides taken from the storehouses, Sira Pall Hallvardsson awakened and sat up. On the east wall of the room was a small metal cross. He knelt before it and said his morning prayers, concluding with a long thanksgiving for the mercy of the Lord upon Bishop Alf, who yearned, as all men do, to come into the house of the Lord after stumbling about for years in the wastelands of the sublunary world. Pall Hallvardsson had not seen Gardar since assisting Jon the previous summer at his St. Bartholomew's mass, for there had been no Yuletide feast, and Pall Hallvardsson had celebrated Easter at Hvalsey church. After prayers, he straightened his clothing and went out into the yard to wash.

In this summer, the grass on the homefield was as thick as it had been in any year, and the cattle in their pen were numerous and glossy. Five boats, ranging in size from one-oarsman to eight-oarsmen, were tied up in Einars Fjord. As he watched, ten men and boys ran toward the cattle pen with neatly coopered buckets and one-legged stools and began upon the milking. After the thin prosperity of Hvalsey Fjord, such sights made a man dizzy. Soon the yoked pails were being carried at a run to the dairy, where the milk was poured into large vats, and the milkers ran back to the field, seeking without the least hesitation each unmilked cow, and missing none. After what seemed to be the briefest while, they washed out their pails and went into the kitchen house for their morning meal. Of all the men and women he saw, Pall Hallvardsson could pick out no more than half a dozen whose names he knew.

After washing his face and hands in the cold water of the washing vat, he took a simple wooden comb out of his pocket and ran it through his hair. He did not look either prosperous or polished. The great church of St. Birgitta at Hvalsey Fjord, the newest in the settlement and, aside from the cathedral, the finest, was about all the folk in that district could support. The lands around the church were rather small and the mountains behind them high and rough. Recent repairs to the church roof had, in the end, meant short rations for Pall Hallvardsson, in that the parishioners added less to what he could raise himself in the way of wadmal or furnishings, although there was enough food for himself and his beasts and the two servants he had with him. One of the servants, whose name was Magnus the Bent because of his humped back, was an excellent fisherman and hunter of game. These were Sira Pall's blessings. Sira Jon, however, would soon greet him dressed in red silk, sitting in the bishop's high seat, with many fine things arrayed about him, and he would have little respect for such a brown mended robe and hood as Pall Hallvardsson was wearing. He would, in fact, look above his head and allow his eyes to fall on Pall's humble form only with reluctance. After he considered these things, Pall

Hallvardsson asked for forgiveness for the sin of anger, and went off to find the other priest.

Come upon him suddenly he could not, for two servants and Audun delayed him and escorted him in, so that indeed Sira Jon was in the high seat, and he was arrayed magnificently, surrounded by whale oil lamps which glittered on the eye but made it hard at first to see about the room. Pall Hallvardsson approached the high seat. He said, "Our grief is eased by the sure knowledge of the love with which our Lord has received him into Heaven."

Sira Jon nodded.

"As for ourselves, although it is late in the season, it may be that a ship will arrive in answer to our prayers and carry this news to Nidaros." He smiled. "Isn't it true for us in Greenland that ships always come from the Lord, bringing His grace to us, and sometimes His trials of our spirit? If any place is the perfect picture of the world, it must be Greenland."

Sira Jon spoke in a low voice. "This is true, at the least, that no veil of beauty hides the evils from our sight."

"And yet, these Greenlanders declare it a fresh and lovely spot, in the way that all men look about themselves at the earth and think themselves at home."

"And all are deceived." Jon spoke this in such a bitter tone that Pall Hallvardsson stepped closer. Jon sat up straighter and appeared to press himself against the back of the seat.

Pall Hallvardsson stepped back, and went on in an even voice. "It must be said that Gardar is thriving with your stewardship. The Greenlanders say that they have the Garden of Eden in their midst."

"The new bishop, whoever he may be, must bring with him some relics. The see is far too poor in such things, and folk suffer from it."

"Perhaps—"

"In Nidaros when I was a boy, an old man was carried on his bier into the cathedral, and set for a moment near the bones of St. Olaf so that the tomb could be opened, and in this moment St. Olaf in his mercy gave him life again, and after that he lived in the chapter house as a lay brother for eleven years, so that he was eighty-four years old when he died, and this was an attested miracle."

"All, of course, have heard of such things, but not every man can hope to escape death."

"No right-thinking man hopes to escape his reunion with our Lord, but alas, those on earth who have great needs dearly wish that death would—" He stopped, then went on. "May the Lord look down with mercy on His helpless flock." At last he looked at Pall Hallvardsson, and for a long moment, then said, "Sira Pall Hallvardsson, you are welcome to sit down. Sorrow makes me careless."

Pall Hallvardsson drew a stool forward from under the table beside him and settled himself upon it. This table was piled with the books in which Pall Hallvardsson knew that Jon had always kept the accounts. There were three of them, so large that a year's business usually took only a spread of two pages, in Jon's minuscule hand. The books themselves were valuable enough—most writing in Greenland was done on rolls of parchment, and all books were owned by the bishopric or folk who had been across the ocean. It had been the bishop's wish that some of the Greenlandic boys would learn the art of bookbinding, but with the vomiting ill and one thing and another, this had not come to pass. Although there was plenty of calfskin and goatskin in Greenland, manuscripts illuminated at Gardar or in the monastery were poorly bound things, crude and easily damaged.

Pall Hallvardsson said, "I well remember these nine summers past, when we embarked with the bishop for Greenland, and all the treasures he carried with him. Only he guessed how low a state things would have come to. St. Nikolaus Church was a great cold place, with the wallhangings tattered and black with mildew and a fungus growing over the stones, and the altar furnishings tarnished and dinted, and the servants and other folk careless about their work and the dishonor they brought to the Lord's house. He brought such a change upon the state of Greenland that his loss need not destroy it, or take us back to earlier days. It may be that we long for the magnificence that speaks the glory of the Lord, so that what we have seems poor to us, but the Lord sees our means and our endeavors as well as our handiwork."

Sira Jon turned his eyes upon the other priest and said, "Every day, summer and winter, I have gone into the chamber of Bishop Alf and sat below him and imparted to him all the intelligence of the day." He stopped, then went on, "And for many days he has not seen fit to speak to me, or to raise his hand as a sign, and this was my only prayer and hope, that once before death he would hear my voice and know my presence. Had he cast his gaze upon me, I would have been surfeited. Had his hand moved under mine, I would have been content, but nothing came. His flesh was cold and shrinking to my touch. No prayer, no multitude of prayers brought the slightest flicker of his eyelid."

"Sometimes men are so very old and ill——"

"My uncle had but sixty-two winters. He came to this place a strong and vigorous man. Once, you may not know, and not as a young man, he went on skis from Stavanger to Nidaros, accompanied only by a dog, and this took him but seventeen days in the depths of winter. When he lived among the Flemings, a walk from Ghent to Bruges was little to him, not worthy of remark. My mother, too, was known for the hardiness of her sanguine nature. It was said that her cousin refused to die in the Great Death, but recovered even as he was being carted to the burial pits."

Pall Hallvardsson made no response.

"This may or may not be a true account. Many tales were abroad during the Great Death."

Pall Hallvardsson nodded, then said, "Is it not the case that all who survived that time, even you and I, who were but little children, have received God's grace, and a sign that our work on earth was worthy?"

"Perhaps, but the import of the signs granted us by the Lord during the Great Death is much debated. What can be said about signs and portents, after all? The fate of men is to yearn for an answer from the Lord." After speaking thus, Sira Jon sighed a deep sigh.

Now Sira Pall Hallvardsson shifted on his stool, for he had never heard such speeches from the other priest. After a while, he said, "I recall as well the three priests the bishop saw fit to carry with him. It has often occurred to me that the first lost and least regarded of us was in fact the straightest and most solid. After Sira Petur's death, I was even less eager for this day." Jon gave an audible sniff. "The Lord has laid upon the hands of any priest a deal of work, but I say humbly that this work in the western ocean is work that not a few would shirk. Not a few did, after all, when Bishop Alf was seeking priests to accompany him. The folk about us are unlike even those with whom they share a tongue, Norwegians. They are half-wild, like horses left in the mountains to fend for themselves. They have made their own paths through the wilderness, and they balk at being led. And anyone who would lead them must sometimes confess that the paths they have made are as good as or better than those he would bring them to. They are not, perhaps, men of our world, as men in France or men in Flanders or Germany are, though they seek after the fashions and ways of the world and consider themselves like us. But they are new men and Vikings at the same time. This was something that Petur didn't have to think of or to be told. For myself, every time I am among them, I must consider everything very carefully, as if I were learning a new tongue, except that each day it gets no less difficult. For you, please pardon me if I say that you expect them to mold themselves and their habits to yours. But they are like horses who come when they are called because such peculiar noises arouse their curiosity, although the farmer esteems himself for the success of his training." Sira Jon sat still as a post. "And now I must speak hardly to you, for guiding these folk has come to you and not to me. Before Bishop Alf, twenty-six years went by after the death of Bishop Arni. It was always true when Bishop Alf spoke of the Lord, he spoke of Him as the king of Heaven, whose steward upon earth the bishop was, so that the power of God's law flowed through him and into the settlement of the Greenlanders. And the Greenlanders, for the most part, saw the rightness and truth of this, and brought their disputes and crimes to his wisdom. But you never speak of God's law. You speak only of His love and His displeasure, and signs from Him, as if He were but your Heavenly Father and not your Heavenly King." Now he stopped, and waited for a reply.

Sira Jon spoke. "You have little experience with many servants or a large establishment. You were raised among monks. You would not know what to do with the means at Gardar, or how to rule the men."

Pall Hallvardsson stood up. "This is indeed true, and about this I will never contradict you, nor will I ever challenge your authority at Gardar or among the Greenlanders. I am pleased to place in your hands my faith and my friendship, and I ask only to serve the see as you consider fit."

Now Jon inhaled deeply, and looked at Pall Hallvardsson with a flicker of pleasure. "On such a day as this, there is no little difficulty in attending to all that folk wish to say to us. But this speech is clear and easy to grasp, and we thank you for it. It shall be the staff that steadies our steps."

Now Sira Pall Hallvardsson went out and found the room where the bishop had been laid out, and he got to his knees at the feet of the corpus and said many prayers. After a few days he returned to Hvalsey Fjord for the seal hunt. The death of the bishop was the subject of great talk among the Greenlanders, especially in light of how young he had been next to Sira Nikolaus and his "wife." Some folk laughed and said that Sira Nikolaus would come to be the bishop after all, if he hung on long enough. Folk found it reassuring that activities at Gardar went on as before, with no change or diminishment, for all greatly feared even the slightest falling off, declaring that this would betoken only a steeper decline into the godlessness of the earlier time. Families hurried to send their sons to Gardar for training, and some of these were taken on and taught some letters. There were, perhaps, fewer feasts and masses, but folk said that this was less important than other things, namely the richness of the Gardar hay crop, the good repair of the buildings, and the state of the beasts. Although he was not the bishop, Sira Jon began wearing bits of Bishop Alf's apparel, and speaking to folk with more of the distance and formality that the bishop had used, and the Greenlanders spoke of this with approval, and recalled how lowly Ivar Bardarson had held himself, so that others, too, held him lowly, and his office.

It was a fact that Erlend Ketilsson was one of the two or three most prosperous farmers south of Gardar. He farmed not only Ketils Stead, but also two other farms in Vatna Hverfi. Sigmund Sigmundsson of Petursvik, the husband of Thorunn's niece, had died during the vomiting ill, willing his farm to Erlend as well, for, folk said, the case Erlend had won for him against Asgeir Gunnarsson had made his rotten dried sealmeat taste like roast lamb and his sourmilk taste like wine to him, and he had never considered himself a poor man again. Nonetheless, the farm fell waste, for Petursvik was far away, and the folk there hard put, and Erlend could not find anyone to do the farming for him.

When folk died, or farms were abandoned, as had happened more and more after the vomiting ill and the famine, people came to Erlend and Vigdis first, asking to be put to work and bringing their livestock and their goods, and most of these folk Erlend and Vigdis took in. Erlend was as tight-lipped as ever, and Vigdis as stern, and in addition folk were made to work long hours, but, it was said, folk always work long hours, and at Ketils Stead, the hours ended in a full trencher. In addition to this, wherever many folk gather, there is talk, and jesting, and tale-telling, no matter whether the master gains enjoyment or not. Erlend had many friends.

It happened that in this year the seal hunt was especially lucky, with many seals taken and no man killed, nor even injured, and so folk prepared for the winter with more confidence than they had in recent years. At Gunnars Stead, a third child was conceived, and Birgitta Lavransdottir had such experience at these things now that she went about her business unfatigued and full of joy, for it came to her in a dream that the child was a boy. Svava Vigmundsdottir had become a regular member of the Gunnars Stead household, and two chests of her treasures had been carried from Siglufjord to Gunnars Stead. She was given Margret Asgeirsdottir's bedcloset, and Olaf went to the one Ingrid had used.

Folk in Vatna Hverfi no longer spoke of the dull wits of Gunnar Asgeirsson, but declared that although others had sometimes doubted Gunnar's future, they had never done so, but had always considered that the shrewdness of Asgeir Gunnarsson and his brother Hauk would surface

in the boy sooner or later. Gunnar was not as powerful or prosperous as
the richest men in the district, but the storehouses were nearly as full as
they had been in Asgeir's time, and far better disposed, for Birgitta Lavransdottir, it was said, was the sort of wife who must always know what
she has. Concerning the killing of Skuli Gudmundsson, it was widely
remarked that he was a Norwegian after all, and given to wearing peculiar
bright clothing, as all of the ombudsman's men had been, and in addition
had been given too little to do by his lord. Did not Norwegians who came
to Greenland always turn out thus—idle and troublemaking? That he had
gone forward to his death without cowardice, however, was something to
be praised.

And of course Skuli had done Thorkel Gellison a great turn, for after
the killing, his was the only stallion anyone cared to breed their mares to,
although it must be said that most of the farmers came to him shamefacedly
and as if looking after other business. Thorkel kept the great gray horse
in a round pen just in front of the door to his steading, and always
conducted business in the open doorway, and it always happened that after
talk of other things, the visitor would remark at how attractive the horse
was, and Thorkel would declare the animal an unlucky one, who had
caused the death of a man, and then the other would remark that even so,
it was a fine horse indeed, and they would walk forward and lean upon
the wall of the pen. Thorkel grew very rich.

Gunnar was a very fair man, as fair as Olaf Finnbogason was ugly,
and at least a head taller than his foster brother. He still busied himself
spinning and weaving and sewing and tale-telling during the long dark
months of winter, and his dress was somewhat peculiar, as he devised it
himself. One time his hood would have a face piece with slits for the eyes.
Another time his gown would have patch pockets of different sizes stitched
all down the front, and into these pockets he would put his tools. Another
time his gown would be very short, as the Norwegians had worn theirs,
and his hose very thick, or his shoes would have peculiar flaps and fasten-
ings. He tried weaving oddly colored threads into the Gunnars Stead
wadmal and sometimes the Gunnars Stead folk appeared in outlandish
stripes. Concerning all of this, Birgitta Lavransdottir said nothing and
seemed to have no thoughts. When Gunnar wore stripes that ran from arm
to arm, or even from neck to knee, Birgitta wore them as well, and dressed
little Gunnhild and Helga in them. She even wore gowns that Gunnar
contrived for her, although she did not make Katla or the other servants
put on such things.

Birgitta had six servants about her now, including Svava. Besides Hrafn and his sons, Gunnar and Olaf had taken on a new man with a great fondness for hunting and fishing, who looked to have skraeling blood in him, though his name was Finn Thormodsson and he spoke and dressed as a Norseman. He was somewhat old, and had come from the western settlement as a boy of twelve. He had never owned land in the eastern settlement, but had moved from farmstead to farmstead and working at gametaking and tanning skins. After the famine, such men had come to be greatly in demand, for it was said by some that a man's cattle could no longer carry him through the winter as they once had. Gunnar considered himself lucky to have Finn, and he treated him well.

All these folk sat at Gunnars Stead during the winter, and helped Gunnar to gather together the goods that would be needed for the payment that would regain Asgeir's second field. Birgitta and the women servants had been busy at their tablet weaving for two winters, and had produced a green and white altar cloth with a wide border, that depicted the angel speaking to the Virgin Mary of the coming of the Lord. Olaf had gotten together a great pile of sheepskins, half of them white and half black, and the dairy had furnished two dozen large round cheeses. There were reindeer hides from the great hunt and bags of seal blubber. But the man Finn had done something few had done since the end of the Northsetur, and that was to procure a narwhal tusk and a white hawk, which he was training. These were very desirable and valuable goods, and Gunnar expected that Sira Jon would be pleased with them, even though he was not friends with the Gunnars Stead folk.

Days passed quietly at Gunnars Stead, and the winter was no colder than previous ones, Lent no longer, and Easter no warmer. The sheep were just beginning to lamb when the time arrived for Gunnar to take his goods to Gardar and reclaim Asgeir's second field. The custom was in such cases that on the day nine years to the day after the sentence was passed, the guilty man or his heirs would appear with goods to a value already fixed upon, pay them over, and receive his rights again, but if he did not appear on this day, then he was to lose his rights permanently and the duty of the bishop, or in this case, his representative, was to dispose of the confiscated property as he saw fit. Everyone in the district knew which day this was to be—two days before the feast of St. Hallvard of Oslo—and Pall Hallvardsson went forth himself to Gardar to make sure of Sira Jon.

Now it happened that on the evening before the day of the journey, the goods were placed in chests and all things were made ready, as Gunnar and Olaf intended to stay at Gardar for two or three days, and then the folk went to their bedclosets and slept.

After dark, some men came over the hill from the south, and they were servants of Erlend Ketilsson, led by Ketil the Unlucky, who was now a young man with an evil reputation about the district. There were six in the band. The first thing they did was to drag the two small Gunnars Stead boats north over the hill to the waters of the fjord, where they set them adrift. After this, they returned to Gunnars Stead and began to round up the four horses, thinking to take them into the mountains and hobble them where they would be difficult to find, but it so happened that the mare Mikla would not at first allow herself to be caught, and when she was caught through the effort of four of the men, she began whinnying and fighting so that Ketil took out his knife and cut her throat and left her lying in the horse pen. The other horses were taken off and left at the spot where Skuli Gudmundsson had met his death. The Gunnars Stead folk slept as if under a spell.

Now it was almost morning. Ketil's last act was to open the fence of the sheep pen and drive the flock into the homefield, where the grass was new and the earth wet from snow melt. When, a while later, Olaf rose to make ready for his journey, he found livestock scattered everywhere.

At Ketils Stead, Erlend and Vigdis made ready their goods, and had them carried to their boat, which was moored near the church in Einars Fjord, and sometime in the morning, they, too, along with Ketil and their steward, set out for Gardar, arriving just after mid-day. Now everyone at Gardar sat still and waited for the appearance of Gunnar and Olaf, but the day went on and then declined into darkness, and they neither came themselves nor sent a message. Pall Hallvardsson sat with Sira Jon so that Erlend might not get at him, and the two priests stayed up through the whole night until the morning light, but day did not shine upon the folk from Gunnars Stead, and Sira Jon came out into the hall and greeted Erlend and Vigdis, and received their goods, but asked them to stay one more day in case Gunnar might show up, for Pall Hallvardsson was determined that Gunnar not be cheated or tricked.

But on this day, the day before the feast of St. Hallvard, a great storm blew off the ice cap so that no journeys could be made, and folk were hard put even to go from the farmstead to the byre, and the ewes at Gardar chose this day to drop their lambs, and so there was a great stir there. This storm lasted all that day and all the next, and then Erlend and Vigdis made ready to go back to Ketils Stead, and as there still had been no message from Gunnar, they were awarded the great field, to have entirely as their own. It happened that as they rowed back to Vatna Hverfi, they espied the two Gunnars Stead boats, smashed to pieces by the storm.

When they arrived at Ketils Stead, Erlend's shepherd came up to him and took him to one side, and he remarked that a certain gray mare with a dark stripe down her back had been discovered in the horse pen at Gunnars Stead with her throat slit, and at this news, Erlend took Ketil into the dairy house and began to beat him. Erlend was a big, heavy man with large hands, and Ketil was a slight fellow better known for his sour wit than his strength. And Erlend said, "It is certain truth that you are indeed an unlucky fellow, and you have brought our lineage nothing but evil since the day you were born. When you and Vigdis set your heads together, every man can be sure that mischance will follow." And Ketil lay recuperating from this beating for many weeks. Vigdis only remarked to Erlend, "Most men are pleased to get what they want, especially if it means felling an enemy at the same time." To this, Erlend replied, "Ill luck only can follow such an unlucky fellow as Ketil Ragnarsson, and you will know this better than anyone one of these days."

About his misfortunes Gunnar spoke little. One day he took the narwhal tusk to Axel Njalsson, a powerful man, and traded it for a small boat made from the remains of an old ship, and in very good condition. Another day he took the altar cloth the women had made and decorated to Thorkel Gellison in the southern part of the district, and came back a few days later leading a handsome mare who was in foal to the famous gray stallion. The white hawk was set free. The other goods in their chests were put away and not spoken of. The homefield dried up, but it took much labor to break up the hard clods churned up by the sheep, and the hay crop was set back a week or so. Gunnar and Finn Thormodsson could frequently be seen conferring, but the subject of their talk was unknown even to Birgitta, even to Olaf. Olaf buried Mikla on the hillside above the byre, and set up a small cairn over the grave. After that, he worked all the time that he wasn't sleeping, and never took meals with the rest of the farm folk. It was said in the district that he minded the death of the mare more than the departure of his wife, but if he did, it was not something he mentioned to anyone.

Now Gunnar set about arranging his case for the Thing. He named witnesses to attest that he was summoning Erlend Ketilsson of Ketils Stead to lesser outlawry for the destruction of property in the form of the hay crop of his homefield, and for greater outlawry for the destruction of property in the form of two serviceable boats and one excellent breeding and riding mare. Then Gunnar and Olaf went about the district, looking for supporters in the case. At first these suits looked promising, for Axel Njalsson agreed to support the Gunnars Stead folk, and he was a rich and powerful man. In addition, Thorkel Gellison and a neighbor of his said they would aid Gunnar, for they were from a part of the district where Erlend owned no property. But the other men of the district, especially those who lived on the steadings around the shores of the great lakes, Antler Lake and Broad Lake, had little wish to offend Erlend, to whom they went every winter for hay when their own provisions ran short. In addition, a few recalled the mutilation of a certain Ketils Stead cow. So it was that Gunnar rode from farm to farm dressed in his best, most pleasing clothing, and he was received cordially in all places, but he ended as he had begun, with the support of three men and the knowledge that all of the others in the district could not fail to support Erlend and destroy his case.

Now Gunnar took his new boat and went to Hvalsey Fjord and stayed with Lavrans for a few days. On the first day they spoke only of the Gunnars Stead folk and especially Birgitta, for Lavrans could never speak enough of Birgitta and her health and her neat ways and her many talents. She expected her confinement, Gunnar remarked, around St. Bartholomew's Day.

On the second day they spoke of the events at Gunnars Stead, the killing of the mare, the destruction of the boats, and the trampling of the homefield, and Lavrans declared that of all of these, the last was the most serious, and he said to Gunnar, "How have you declared this case?"

"I have asked for greater outlawry for the smashing of the boats and the killing of the mare, who was excellent both for breeding and riding, and I have asked for lesser outlawry for the trampling of the homefield."

Lavrans shook his head, and said, "My son, you have asked the lesser penalty for the greater offense, and it may be that Erlend will catch this procedural flaw, because he has a great reputation for knowledge of the law. We will see what comes of this." Then Lavrans went to his bedcloset for the night.

There were six farmsteads in Hvalsey Fjord near Lavrans Stead, and the next day Lavrans went out and gained the support of these six farmers, poor though they were, but the difficulty was that Gunnar had to go after him and give presents. "These two rolls of wadmal, for your wife who is pregnant," or "This ivory-handled knife with silver chasing in thanks for your services to my wife's father in the instance of his illness," for it was the case in these times that it was an offense against the court to offer payment for support. Lavrans' counsel, however, was that gifts need have nothing to do with cases, when all men were agreeable. On the fourth day, Gunnar returned to Gunnars Stead and waited for the Thing.

Although there were some killings from Brattahlid to be brought before the Thing court in addition to Gunnar's case, the men involved were neither powerful nor rich, and folk were far more taken with the case against Erlend, especially as Erlend came to the Thing field in great state, and set up four large booths for his many supporters. Erlend was seen to be a fine man now, for his hair was nearly white, and he had lost the lowering dark looks of his younger days. He spoke to everyone at the Thing, even to Gunnar, in good-humored, loud tones, and was everywhere in evidence. He had a long conference with Sira Jon in the middle of one day, escorting him with great ceremony from the hall to his booth, and seating him inside on the high seat with the flap of the booth open to passersby. The result of all of this was that when Gunnar made his suit, the thirteen judges did not even hesitate to decide against him, on the grounds that his procedures were flawed, and none could gainsay this, for such was the law of Greenland. After this the Thing broke up and everyone returned home.

It happened that one evening, just after midsummer, Gunnar and Birgitta were outside the farmstead with Gunnhild and Helga at the end of a fine day. The two little girls were busy trying to entice one of Olaf's sheep dogs, an ancient bitch named Nalli, to come to them. Nalli sat on her haunches looking past them toward where Olaf had disappeared into the byre. When they came near her, she stood up and moved away, then sat down again. Birgitta walked to and fro. As she walked one way, her spindle twirled downward, drawing the thread out of the wool she carried. As she walked the other way, she wound the new thread onto the shaft of the spindle. Since growing so great with this child she spun a quantity of wool, for she only felt at ease when she was walking about. Gunnar sat near her with a large pile of shearings, carding bits of grass and twigs out of them. Now he looked up at her and remarked that if her scissors were at hand, he would like to have her cut his hair. Gunnar's hair was thick and very fair, for he wore no hat in the sun, only a thin band about his forehead.

Birgitta put down her spinning and went for the case that held the scissors, as well as a piece of cloth for his shoulders and a stool for him to sit on. She possessed a fine ivory comb, made in Bergen and neatly carved, which was also kept in a case. This comb had come to her through her mother and was missing only two teeth. Now Gunnar sat down on the stool and Birgitta began to comb his hair upon his shoulders. Nalli stood up and trotted down the hillside before the farmstead and Gunnhild began to run after her, and little Helga after her. Many times the smaller child tumbled and rolled, and each time her sister came back and set her on her feet again. The dog came to the shore of the lake and began toward the byre, far outdistancing the girls, who stopped and sat down among the wild flowers on the hillside. Now Gunnar said, "Some would say that we have fallen on evil days."

"No doubt some do say it," replied Birgitta.

"Some say that there is little hope now of Gunnars Stead regaining the place it once had among the farms of Vatna Hverfi. It is true that Hafgrim himself, who came with Erik to Greenland, gave this farmstead to Gunnar Asgeirsson, and there was always one great field to feed folk and one great field to grow prosperous on."

Birgitta took out the scissors and began to snip along the bottom fringe of Gunnar's hair. She said, "Some would say that in these days, one field feeds you in the summer and the other feeds you in the winter. The richest farms eat some of their breeding stock before the winter is over, not only middling farms such as ours."

Now Birgitta went to put away the scissors, but Gunnar stopped her, and asked her to cut more off. Then he said, "Even so, the evilest days have not come when one can look upon one's children tumbling about and laughing, and see one's wife as you are, and sit upon one's own stool for the pleasure of a haircut."

Birgitta smiled.

"Gunnhild is much like you. She looks about her, and sees what her eyes fall upon. She laughs little but smiles often, and she takes great pains over her dress and her hair. When I am with her, it seems to me that she is my favored child."

Birgitta caught her comb in the hair and lifted it up, then snipped off what the comb held.

"Then Helga comes to me and climbs upon my lap and speaks nonsense exactly as if it were gossip, and looks into my face for a reply, and it seems to me that she is my favored child, although she is as unlike Gunnhild as she could be."

Now Gunnar's hair fell evenly to the middle of his neck, and Birgitta once again went to put away her scissors, but he stopped her and asked her to cut it shorter. Then he went on. "Soon," he said, "another child will be brought to me, a boy, as you have told me from your dreams, and this child will be as different from the others as can be, and as appealing. And yet, I find lately that I do not look for this with pleasure, but only with fear, for the evilest days are yet to come, and not far off."

Now Birgitta had cut the hair very short, so that it looked like a priest's fringe, and she put away the scissors. Gunnar ran his hands over the bristles. She said, "These things may come to pass as you say, for only you know your intentions."

"Sira Pall Hallvardsson is right in this, that there is such pleasure in enmity that after a while it cannot be left off even if one would will it. Another thing is also true, that when a quarrel is new, one's friends hold one back, and give cool advice, but when it is long-standing, folk put off its end and goad the rivals."

"If by this you mean that there is talk of what goes on about the district, and everyone must add a bit and let nothing go unremarked upon, that is indeed true."

Gunnar turned and looked at her, but her eye was always partly on the two little girls, who were now plodding slowly up the hill. "It may come to pass that Lavrans will regret giving you to me, as folk said he would at the time."

"It may, but if so, then he should come to me and find out what I think, as he did at the time. This is my thought, that for every soul, something must come to pass, and for everything that does come to pass, every soul can imagine many things that might have come to pass, all of them less evil than what actually fell out. Folk must have something to think on, or they would be unable to hope for Heaven or remember Paradise."

And to this Gunnar made no reply, but carried the stool and the cloth inside. Soon after this, Birgitta and Gunnhild and Helga went to the bedcloset and made ready for sleep. Birgitta did not ask, as she always did, when Gunnar would be coming to bed. A while later, as dusk was falling, he went out.

Beside the cowbyre Gunnar encountered seven men, and besides Olaf and Finn Thormodsson, these were Axel Njalsson and his two sons Bessi and Arni and in addition to them Thorkel Gellison and his son Skeggi. Each of these men carried no weapons, but each carried a spade and Finn carried a bundle of something tied together and wrapped in a reindeer hide. Now they went to Asgeir's second field, as it was still called around Gunnars Stead, and began to dig a long, deep ditch across the edge of the

field, like a reindeer pit, but wider. The men were strong and the work
went quickly. After it was deep enough, Finn went along the length of
the ditch, and distributed the contents of his bundle, which turned out to
be the antlers of reindeer and also the ribs, sharpened at one end to a keen
point. After he had finished, the men laid willow brush thinly across the
opening, and, on top of that, mats of grass woven by Finn to look like
turf.

Now it was not long before sunrise, and the men went to Ketils Stead,
where they loosed all of the cows, and one of these Gunnar killed, and
slit open its belly, and inside he placed a little figure of a man carved of
soapstone. Now the band of men stood off a little ways while Gunnar and
Olaf went to the doors of the farmhouse, for it was a large building with
two doors, and they pounded on them, shouting, "Rise, sleepers, rise! The
cows have gotten into the homefield!" The first one out was Kollbein
Erlendsson, in his nightshirt and to him Gunnar sang out the following
verse:

In the farmyard lies a pregnant beast
Within, there sits the son of a whore.
How black is the cooking pot?
How leaky is the kettle?

Now Hallvard Erlendsson came forth, followed by two servingmen,
and Gunnar and Olaf backed away, for they could see that the servingmen
were armed with axes. Soon enough Ketil Ragnarsson himself came out,
and he too carried an ax, and he was the first to see the effigy of himself
in the cow's belly. Now everyone was up and attempting to herd the cows
out of the homefield, but the Ketils Stead herd was large and the cows
lively and independent. The band of folk from Gunnars Stead were barely
within sight by the time that Erlend's sons and Ketil had armed themselves
and their men and begun to chase them.

Gunnar's men moved slowly, staying well within sight, and calling
out to the others from time to time, so that Ketil was soon beside himself
with rage. Now Gunnar and the others came to the second field and began
to walk across it. Gunnar looked about himself and remarked to Olaf that
it was still a beautiful piece of ground, and Olaf nodded. After this, Gunnar
began to run, and Ketil's folk to run after him, and the pursuers appeared
to be gaining. The Gunnars Stead folk ran between the ditches, on the
narrow paths they had left, but in the blue light of early sunrise, these were

not so visible to the others, and, much like reindeer, they fell through the brush and into the pits, Ketil, Kollbein, and Hallvard first, for they were in the lead, and one of their servants after, for he was just behind Ketil, and fell upon him, but the others had been a step slower, and were able to stop themselves.

And it happened that the three brothers were impaled upon the stakes in the pits, and Gunnar and his men ran back to the pits, and prevented the Ketils Stead servants from aiding the dying men. There was great groaning until the men died. When this had happened, Gunnar and his men went to a nearby farm, where the folk were just rising for the day, and they announced the killings of Ketil Ragnarsson, Kollbein Erlendsson, and Hallvard Erlendsson.

At Gunnars Stead, the servingfolk came out of their sleeping places and Birgitta saw that Olaf and Finn were not among them, and she bade the women to begin putting all of the housewares into chests, and the children's clothing and toys. And after they had done this, she went to Svava Vigmundsdottir and bade her to return to Kristin in Siglufjord, and then she went around to each of the other maids, and sent them on their ways to other farmsteads. Then she bade the men to begin carrying the chests to the new Gunnars Stead boat where it sat in Austfjord. And by the time Gunnar returned with the news of the deaths, the farmstead was empty of furnishings.

Gunnar gave his four horses to the men who had helped him—two to Axel and his sons, and two to Thorkel and Skeggi. Olaf called his five sheep dogs to him, and he killed the three old ones, including Nalli. After this Gunnar, Olaf, Birgitta, Finn, Gunnhild, and Helga went to the boat and embarked, and they rowed to Hvalsey Fjord and announced the killings. And after this they lived at Lavrans Stead in Hvalsey Fjord, and Gunnars Stead was the following year confiscated by the Thing and awarded to Erlend. This farm Erlend gave to Vigdis, so that it would, he said, remind her of the consequences of her schemes. Erlend had asked in his case for greater outlawry and death for Gunnar, but certain powerful men, led by Thorkel Gellison, said of Gunnar that he had been greatly provoked by damages done to him through the agency of Ketil Ragnarsson, and so he was only sentenced to lesser outlawry, which meant the payment of compensation, for there was no going abroad.

Lavrans' farmstead at Hvalsey Fjord was smaller and poorer than Gunnars Stead had been, but the fact was that all of Birgitta's best livestock was there, now numbering some fifty or sixty beasts. These, with Lavrans' own flock, made a sizable holding. And Finn Thormodsson was with them.

It was here that the boy she expected was born to Birgitta, and at the last minute before the baptism, she recalled Asgeir Gunnarsson, the child who had died, and the name seemed ill-omened to her. So she told the priest to name him after Lavrans' father, that was, Kollgrim. And Kollgrim Gunnarsson was a fat and bonny babe, and all went well with him.

The Devil

It happened in the autumn of this year 1378 that Ragnvald Einarsson, who lived with his folk at Solar Fell in Eriks Fjord, grew very suspicious and apprehensive, so that he often saw apparitions among the icebergs in the fjord, and he was never so happy during the whole summer as when the fjord was free of ice, and never so haunted as in the time after the seal hunt, when icebergs, small and large, began to calve and cluster between his farmstead and the two beaches where he had killed one skraeling and allowed the other to escape. Tidings that Ragnvald Einarsson was spirit-ridden were greeted with much interest all around Eriks Fjord and Gardar, for Ragnvald was a prosperous and powerful man.

Now one day toward the end of the summer half year, some days after St. Michael's mass, folk at Solar Fell were engaged in making preparations for the winter, and were busy slaughtering sheep. On this day, Ragnvald's spirits seemed to lift, and he no longer stared out into the fjord, but instead admired his fat sheep and handsome children, including especially his young grandson, Olaf Vebjarnarson, who had been born the previous fall. Late in the morning, one of Ragnvald's servingmen came to him and declared that he had seen a strange boat in the water, such a boat as appeared and then disappeared, neither a skin boat, as skraelings paddle, nor a wooden boat, as Norsemen row. Ragnvald said that this would be a peculiar sight indeed, and laughed heartily at the idea. However, his children and servingfolk grew uneasy, and began casting glances toward the fjord.

Sometime after this, when most of the sheep had been slaughtered, Ragnvald's folk built a fire and began singeing the hair off the heads of the slaughtered sheep. Ragnvald himself oversaw this operation, in the company of his wife, who was a sturdy, gray-haired woman named Svanhild Erlingsdottir, and had produced five sons and three daughters for Ragnvald. When this job had been done, and the sheeps' heads carried into the storehouse, the folk went inside for their evening meal, leaving one servingman, Gaut, tending the fire and boiling a large vat of water for washing wadmal cloth. All of a sudden, Gaut ran to the door of the house and shouted that the skraelings were coming, and all of Ragnvald's folk streamed out of the house, but they saw nothing. Ragnvald himself reassured them, saying, "It is only that the ice is so thick in the fjord." They went back to their meal, and Gaut back to his work.

While Gaut was engaged in putting driftwood on the fire, a strange iceberg floated to shore, and figures silently slipped out of it and silently ran up the strand, and one of these figures, who were skraelings after all, dealt Gaut a blow on the head with a rock. Blood and gray matter spilled out onto the turf. Then the skraelings grabbed the burning faggots from the fire and carried these and some other brush they had brought with them to Ragnvald's farmhouse and set the turf afire. And the turf went up very quickly, for it was the end of summer: little rain had come yet, and no snow.

The skraelings were diabolical in this, that they filled the doorway with brush and whale oil–dipped faggots, so that those who attempted to escape by the door were burned to death. Among these was Svanhild. It happened, however, that Ragnvald himself escaped through a back passage with his grandson Olaf in his arms, and he fled at first up the hills toward Isafjord, but the skraelings cut off that route, and so he turned and ran along the fjord toward Brattahlid with the child screaming in his arms. Many skraelings pursued him, both on foot and in skin boats, and he grew despairing, for he saw that they had many arrows in their quivers. Ragnvald was sure of death, both for himself and for his grandson, and much talk had gone around of what the skraelings were known to do with the children of men, such as roast them like sealmeat and drink their blood, and so, fearing such a fate for his beloved grandson, Ragnvald came to the fjord and threw the child into the water, while at the same time repeating the last prayers, as it is spelled out in the laws. The child drowned, but was assured of Heaven, and Ragnvald ran on. As it turned out, the skraelings were unable to catch him, and he came to the farms of Brattahlid district. The number of those killed, including Olaf Vebjarnarson, amounted to fifteen. A large band of skraelings settled at Ragnvald's steading, and took prisoner two of Ragnvald's shepherd boys.

Those Greenlanders who were in the habit of trading with the skraelings soon had news of this fight from the demons they traded with, and this was, that a certain warrior by the name of Kissabi was resolved to kill Ragnvald himself, for Ragnvald had killed his brother, cut off the brother's arm, and shamed Kissabi with it. Other than this, it was discovered that two of the skraelings had been killed in this fight. During this winter, Ragnvald moved to the southern fork of Hrafns Fjord and took over an abandoned farm there. As many of his children and folk as had survived the attack at Solar Fell came to live with him, and this included two daughters and one son and one daughter's husband and nine serving-folk. One of these daughters was named Gudny, and her husband had been the Solmund who was shot by the arrow of the second skraeling when he was innocently gathering shells. She was now married to a man named Halldor Grimsson, and these two lived with their baby son Grim at Hrafns Fjord with Ragnvald.

Folk in every district spoke about this attack until Yule, through Lent, and past Easter, for it was the greatest event to take place in Greenland for many years, and now folk looked upon the skraelings with renewed fear and contempt. Some men, Erlend Ketilsson among them, gained great respect from this attack, for Erlend had always refused to trade with the skraelings and to learn any of their language, for, he said, those who speak the tongue of the devil will soon be doing the devil's work. Vigdis, too, spoke of this, and she said that she looked for the great conflict between Goodness and Evil in her own lifetime, when the skraelings would come down from the north in myriads and overrun the farms of men, and they would cease to look like men, as they did now, but be revealed as giants and trolls. At this time there was a prayer that began to be repeated during services, and this prayer went:

> Lord, we see Thee in Thy might,
> Higher than the cliffs of white,
> Greater than the ocean gales,
> Thou who mad'st both bear and whale.
> We call to Thee, Father and Son,
> Look down upon these lowly ones,
> Scattered thinly in these hills,
> Beset by demons and devils.

This prayer was the work of the Greenlander priest Sira Audun, and was highly thought of by every one of the Greenlanders.

Certain men thought differently than Erlend did, those who had grown rich trading with the skraelings, or were married to skraeling women and had their wives' mothers with them on their farmsteads. These men remarked on how exactly the skraelings' attack had matched Ragnvald's attack upon the skraelings after the killing of Solmund; but the killing of Solmund was itself a sore subject, as it had been unprovoked.

Another tale much repeated was the tale of the drowning of Olaf Vebjarnarson, and Ragnvald was greatly praised for his course of action, although much pitied for the extremity of desperation he had found himself in. There began to be talk of how little Olaf might be made a saint for this, and Sira Jon declared that there had to be evidence of miracles. Some declared that a holy glow emanated from the water where Olaf was drowned.

The case was that the Greenlanders could do nothing about the skraelings living at Solar Fell, as they did not have enough weapons to make a proper attack, not enough boats to come by sea nor enough skis to come over the hill from Isafjord, and so it was judged better to leave the skraelings be through the winter. By spring hot blood had cooled, and men thought more carefully of the bloodshed and death that would be involved in such an undertaking. Ragnvald, after all, lived far to the south, at Hrafns Fjord, and was not present to excite the anger of the other farmers.

Ragnvald was much downcast through the winter, and so spirit-ridden that he could neither sleep nor pay attention to his tasks, but woke up screaming every night and often entertained the ghosts of his sons and his wife, who had followed him southward.

The folk at Hvalsey Fjord were much concerned with these events, for there were fewer farms there, and the district was more subject than others to the comings and goings of groups of skraelings. For many years a band of skraelings had been in the habit of hunting whales at the mouth of Einars Fjord, where there are many islands. It was the practice of these demons to hide among a group of small islands in their skin boats, and one sign of their diabolical nature was that they could rest quietly in these boats even in rough seas for long periods of time if they knew that a family of leviathans was approaching. Greenlanders had once or twice gone with them, but it was impossible for men to sit so quietly as these skraelings. At the approach of the great sea beasts, the hunters would fix their harpoons, and then, quick as lightning, the barbed spear would hurtle into the flesh of any whale that surfaced. And then the other boats would descend upon the place like a flock of wheatears, and the demons would kill the beast with their harpoons and tie their boats together and float the beast to others standing on the shore. Some of the Greenlanders were much envious of this sort of hunting, for one whale could feed many folk for many days, but this sort of hunting is not in the nature of men, and whales come to Christians only by the grace of God.

This latter point had sometimes been the object of much debate among the folk of Hvalsey Fjord, for folk disagreed about whether whalemeat traded from the skraelings was wholesome to eat without being blessed, or even after being blessed. Sometimes folk grew sick from it and sometimes they did not. Sira Pall Hallvardsson had learned nothing of this at his school among the Flemish, and folk were greatly surprised at this, that such an important question was unconsidered by learned men. But the fact was that the farmers of Hvalsey Fjord always kept by some whalemeat traded from the skraelings, and this flesh spelled the difference between life and death at the end of the winter.

Much else about living in Hvalsey Fjord was different from the ways of Vatna Hverfi district. Folk used boats much more than they used horses, and in fact there was only one horse in the district, but every farm had two or more boats, and there was much discussion about the best ways of keeping these boats watertight and in good repair. Men vied about their boats just as men in Vatna Hverfi district vied about their horses. Another Hvalsey Fjord habit was to depend upon the fjord for a great number of fish, and there were times when the folk of the district ate nothing but fish day after day, for both morning meat and evening meat. Gunnhild Gunnarsdottir, for one, thought little of this custom, and was often discontented. For their part, natives of Hvalsey Fjord were much surprised at the quantity of ewe's milk Birgitta gave her children to drink and predicted that children nourished in such a fashion would soon suffer an excess of blood.

Nor were there so many good herbs growing about the farms, for the slopes above the farmsteads were steep and rocky and the strip of ground beside the water narrow. Often the peaks were clad in morning mists and the winds that blew these mists away, if they came off the ocean to the west, were brisk and chill. For this reason, farm buildings had smaller rooms and were themselves smaller, for folk had to go off in their boats to cut turves, and the turves had to be set thickly about the stone walls, for the wind, especially in the late winter, when folk are hungry, could seek out the smallest chinks and bring frost into the house.

The folk of Hvalsey Fjord were ready builders, Gunnar found, and when they were not tinkering with their boats, they were climbing about on their houses and outbuildings, repairing this or rebuilding that. It was for this reason that Hvalsey Fjord had such a great church, the newest and most beautiful in Greenland. The builders had done an unusual thing. They had ground up the shells of mussels and mixed these with water and put this into the spaces between the stones of the walls, so that these walls, on the inside, were very smooth, and did not need to be covered with wallhangings. They had also built an arched window in the east wall of the church, which not even Gardar Cathedral had, and from the feast of St. Eskil forward until the feast of St. Thomas, the morning sun rose in this window and lit the church with a dazzling light. Birgitta was much pleased with this church, and with Sira Pall Hallvardsson, who had lived there for many years now, and as Lavrans Stead was situated just across the water from the church, she spent not a little time there, and soon came to the position of overseeing the disposition of church furnishings and also of Sira Pall Hallvardsson's household.

Lavrans' house was a steading of fourteen rooms, if the two partly open sheep byres and the three storage rooms were counted. All of these rooms were connected, and could be reached without going out of doors. In addition to this, all of the servants slept in bedclosets in the house, so that there were twelve people sleeping in the house, and such close quarters were unusual for the Vatna Hverfi folk, even Birgitta, who was now accustomed to a more spacious life. Added to this were the perennial crying of the sheep after they were brought in for the winter and the smells of the stored provisions, the privy, which was also within the walls, and of the sheep themselves. Lavrans' steading had no bath house, and folk from all over the district were accustomed to using the bath house at the church.

One day when a storm was raging outside, Olaf came in from his work, and he was in a black temper, and he said, "These farmers of Hvalsey Fjord are beggarly folk, for though they have good land and plenty of beasts, they go out in all weathers, and care not if they are sleeping outside or in. Just now I saw Orm Guttormsson out upon the fjord in his larger boat, and it seemed to me that he would kill himself."

"I am very fond of Orm," said Birgitta, "and it is a great pleasure to me to have him as a neighbor again." And she put her hand over Lavrans' hand, where it was resting on the planks of the table.

"Even so," said Olaf, "in these Hvalsey Fjord steadings the folk are always stumbling over each other and there is hardly the elbow room to lift your spoon."

"It seems to me," said Birgitta, "that you are always overflowing with complaints," and her eyes flashed at him, so that Lavrans saw that they would soon fall to bickering, and he settled himself on his stool and told a tale.

There was a man, said Lavrans, whose name was Thorbjorn, and he lived with his folk in the oldest house in the district, a house that had been built by a relative of his many years before, when folk first came to Hvalsey

Fjord. This was a long house, such as they build in Norway and Iceland, and it had many sturdy buildings around it, and Thorbjorn's ancestor had retrieved many beams from the shores of Markland, for men in those days were great seafarers, and thought little of going to Markland for a load or two of wood. These beams were hewn into staves and porches and attached to the buildings, and carved with fantastic designs, and folk admired them a great deal, and came from other districts to look over these carvings. The carver, in fact, was a Norwegian called Bjarni the Easterner, and he went back to his home district after coming to Greenland, and made a name for himself there as a carver. The result was that in every respect, this Hvalsey Fjord steading came to look exactly like those of the great lords of Norway, with an outer court and an inner court and separate buildings for every activity, except that the buildings were built of Greenland stone, and only faced on the outside with staves. This ancestor would have no turf.

Now it happened that the folk at this steading strove to live in every way as they live in Norway, with hangings on the walls and lots of chairs and the livestock scattered all over the countryside, and they lived so for two generations, in much greater magnificence than anyone else in Hvalsey Fjord. Each generation was full of seafarers, and these men brought a wealth of goods with them at the end of every journey. They fought in many wars, especially those between the kings and the nobles of Norway, and they received rich rewards, and their women rocked the children back and forth in cradles mounted with gold and silver and swaddled them in brightly colored silk. They went often enough to Markland that they had much to trade in the way of marten furs and black bear skins and, of course, great beams of wood were always piled in the outer courtyard of the farmstead, so much wood that these folk thought nothing of burning it on their winter fires to drive away the cold.

Soon enough other houses were being built in Hvalsey Fjord, for the other districts were getting full, especially Vatna Hverfi district. These new farmers, however, were not so wealthy as Thorbjorn's lineage, and they built more humbly, with stone surrounded by turf and all the buildings linked together, for sheep on the north and cows on the south are like the low glow of a whale oil lamp—you only notice when they are gone that the house is darker than dark and colder than cold.

It happened that these folk who were Thorbjorn's kin became steeped in pride, for they were thought considerable men even in Norway, and were the first Greenlanders to be so honored. One of these kings (here Lavrans shook his head, for he could not remember the name of this king)

made one of these men a lord at the Norwegian court. Earl Skeggi he was
to be called, but it happened that this king was killed in battle, and Skeggi
remained Skeggi the Greenlander. In this year, when Skeggi almost became
an earl, Thorbjorn was some fifteen winters old, and of all his kin he was
the most proud, although he was a sickly fellow and left the warrior's life
to his uncles and brothers. Thorbjorn stayed in Greenland and oversaw the
farmstead, and he was considered clever at it.

One autumn, two ships containing all of the brothers and uncles set
out from Norway, hoping to come to Greenland by the beginning of
winter, and the short tale of this is that both ships were lost, one at Cap
Farvel and one only the Lord Himself knows where, because it vanished.
Thus it was that of all the men in his family, which numbered eight strong
fellows and Thorbjorn, only Thorbjorn was left.

The family were greatly grieved of course, but Thorbjorn saw that
the many cattle were taken care of and the women kept up the household
economy, and so they considered themselves happy enough, and the farm
was so rich, with such an abundance of goods, that it seemed to everyone
that life on this steading could go on as it had forever. But of course, it
went on as it had for only two winters, and at the end of the second winter,
servingmen began pulling down the carved staves and throwing them upon
the fire, for folk hate to be cold when they are hungry, and almost all of
the cows and sheep had been slaughtered except those Thorbjorn wanted
to use for breeding. These were folk who had never been hungry before,
and they thought that if they had food, they had best eat it all and have
a full stomach, as if a full stomach would last longer before it longed to
be full again, and so, although they were plump and pink of cheek,
Thorbjorn's folk were always complaining of hunger pains and begging
him to slaughter a sheep or a cow, for something was bound to happen
that would replace the cow or sheep. Thorbjorn himself was sure of this,
also, and still looked for the vanished ship that had carried his brothers and
uncles to their doom. He spoke often of what would be on this ship, and
how his folk would be saved when it came. But in that summer after the
second winter it still did not come, and in the autumn, all of the servants
had to be sent away, and Thorbjorn himself undertook to care for the
beasts.

At the beginning of this third winter all of the carved staves of all
of the outbuildings had been used up, and so Thorbjorn began pulling
down the staves around the main house, and these lasted for a few weeks,
although the fires got smaller and smaller. After that, he pulled down the
decorations inside the steading and burned them, and these lasted about a

week. Then he threw on the carved chairs, with their arms in the shape of lions' heads and hounds' heads and their feet in the shape of claws. At one chair per day, these chairs lasted twenty days. At Yule, Thorbjorn began breaking up the bedclosets and throwing that wood on the fire, and there were so many of these that Thorbjorn was sure they would last until spring and the return of the second ship. The gold-embossed cradles went on the fire, and benches and barrels—Thorbjorn's folk drove him on as if under a spell of frenzy, for they were never warm, and talked always of how warm they had been a few years before. The wallhangings went on the fire, the trenchers, and, at last, all of the bedclosets, and still it wasn't spring, and there was no warmth in the air, and the fresh breezes of Hvalsey Fjord blew into every crevice and chink, and the folk were nearly mad with the cold.

It happened that Thorbjorn still had two cows and one bull, and he went out one day to the byre to feed them. It was about twenty steps to the byre from the farmstead, and as Thorbjorn was making his way, a great storm blew up, suddenly, as storms do in Hvalsey Fjord, and in the midst of this storm, Thorbjorn saw that there was a man standing beside the byre, wrapped in a beautiful cloak of marten fur from Markland. The man came up to him, and spoke to him, and his words could be readily made out, even in the din of the storm, and the man said, "Thorbjorn, you need a little steading cloaked in turf. I have one, may I give it to you?" And Thorbjorn said, "Nay, a big hall is a fine thing to look at."

And so the man said, "Thorbjorn, I have some sheep trotters in my pouch here. You might seethe them up and eat them." And Thorbjorn said, "Hungry though I am, I have never cared for sheepsfoot. That is poor man's fare."

And the man said, "Here in my pouch I also have this bit of a lamp. You might put some seal oil in it, and have both light and warmth."

"Nay," said Thorbjorn, "the smell of seal oil turns my nose."

Now the man laughed and said, "Thorbjorn, thy neighbors have been eager to help you in your trouble." And Thorbjorn said, "They are lowly men, these neighbors, and none of them has been made into an earl by the Norwegian king. It is for us to help them, not for them to help us." And so this man, who was the Devil himself, opened his great black cloak and said, "My Thorbjorn, the light of your pride has been like a beacon in the darkness to me, and I have come to take you for my own. You can go with me now. Your folk, I assure you, will follow shortly, one by one." And that was the last of Thorbjorn.

Now all the assembled folk who were listening to Lavrans' tale laughed at this, and Lavrans himself laughed, and Birgitta said, "Indeed, my father, there was never such a lordly family in Hvalsey Fjord as this one." Lavrans grinned and raised little Helga onto his lap. But Olaf was not made more contented by this tale, and he sulked about all winter.

On moonlit winter nights, Gunnar got into the habit of skiing or skating across the fjord and spending the evening in conversation with Sira Pall Hallvardsson. And it happened that one of these nights, he asked the priest what he remembered of the ways of Europeans, for now that he was no longer at Gunnars Stead, Gunnar declared, he had a new longing to go on ship as his father had done, when he traveled to Norway and the Orkney Isles and Iceland, and returned with Helga Ingvadottir, Gunnar's mother.

Sira Pall Hallvardsson now laughed heartily, and when Gunnar asked him why he was laughing, he said that in his many winters in Greenland, he had never been led to recall his youth or his education, for no Greenlander had asked him about it before this.

"It is true," said Gunnar, "that we Greenlanders are like most men in this, we think that what is important is what is taking place in Greenland. And the men of Hvalsey Fjord are the same. To them, the disputes of Vatna Hverfi are small things, hardly worthy of remark, even though Vatna Hverfi is a larger district with greater farms and richer men."

Sira Pall Hallvardsson said, "And the men of Vatna Hverfi consider that Eriks Fjord has lost much of its importance in late years." Now Gunnar and the priest both laughed. Gunnar said, "When we went to the south, to Kollbein Sigurdsson's swimming contest at the hot springs, the farmers of the south were a little perplexed by us and our concerns, and thought of Kollbein as a peculiar and insignificant man, although he was the ombudsman of the king. It seems to me that folk have smaller minds than they once did, in the days of my grandfather Gunnar Asgeirsson. My father, too, was a great one for having news of distant places."

Now Pall Hallvardsson grew sober, and nodded, and said that all things were worse than they had been, that the decline of men from a state of grace was proven by Church authorities. Gunnar said, "My wife and her father say that even the weather is worse, and every year worse, although Finn declares that of seals and birds and other game there are such numbers as he has never seen before. I know this, that in earlier days, a man who wished to take ship and sail away for wealth and adventure had but to wait a year or so, and now he may see the birth of many children before he sees a single ship."

Some time after this, Sira Pall Hallvardsson began to speak of his school, for he could remember nothing before this school, although it was said that his mother had been the daughter of a Flemish cloth dyer and his father an Icelander who was part owner of a small ship, and who had visited Greenland as a young man, before Bishop Arni died. But these people, Pall Hallvardsson's mother and father, along with her parents and brother, all died during the Great Death, as did many of the folk of Tournai, where they dwelt. But Pall Hallvardsson had been taken to the Augustinians of Drongen, and this entire monastery had been spared by a miracle of prayer and fasting, so that no monk or servingman or school-child had died during the whole of the first visitation of the Great Death.

"Flanders," Pall Hallvardsson declared, "is such a place as can hardly be imagined by Greenlanders, or even by folk such as myself, whose eye has become familiar with the wastes of the western ocean. In Flanders, a man did not wait for folk to visit him, or look out his door for them, squinting into the breeze and making of every shadow the longed-for guest, but was instead so beset with folk that he might rather wish to be left alone to hold his thoughts in peace. And all of these folk were seized with aims and desires many times every day, for the very commerce that they had among themselves put them in a frenzy of conflicting notions. All men rushed about as fast as possible, and in addition spoke quickly. Well, these things are outlandish for me to think upon now, but when I was a boy they seemed ordinary. I spent enough time bemoaning the tedium of Drongen. How I longed to be taken along when the cellarer of the monastery went to do business in Ghent, which was not far away."

Gunnar said, "Was this Ghent another and larger monastery, then?"

Pall Hallvardsson's eyes opened wide, and he ran his hands over his head. Finally he said, "No, indeed. Ghent is such a compounding of mankind and buildings and animals and machines and noises and smells and sights and colors that it might seem to be Hell at one moment and Heaven at the next." Then he considered for a moment and added, "Or Hell to one man and Heaven to the next. For folk lie about in the street who have neither arms nor legs, but only a voice to cry out to those passing for alms, and children raise their faces to you as you pass and they are lepers, with no noses and great sores eating into their flesh, and many of these folk have no homes, but only lean against a particular bit of wall, day and night, summer and winter, until they are no longer there, and have died and been tossed into mass graves, for these cities spawn cities of the dead, as well."

Gunnar said, "But there is Heaven, too?"

"Of a sort. There are houses where rich men have gathered together belongings of such grace and beauty of form that the eye rather eats them up than looks at them. Many statues might be placed about a garden where flowering trees and a carpet of blossoms perfume the air, and fountains spew mists into sky, and amidst it all, a dwelling rises thirty ells with towers and winding staircases and banners afloat and the sunlight bouncing off a galaxy of window lights. Such a thing might be called heaven, or paradise, although those men who dwell within are fallen, as all men are, through the sin of Adam."

Now Gunnar reflected for a moment, and asked, "When as a child you looked out in the morning, what did you look out upon?"

Sira Pall Hallvardsson closed his eyes. "Neither mountains nor oceans, neither sheep nor fish drying racks, but always this, a little space of green between the dormitory and the church which was a neat pattern of herbs and vegetables planted in the form of a cross with four equal arms inside a circle which was itself inside a square, and behind this a row of ancient apricot trees set against the church wall. Along the edge of this garden ran a paved path, and upon this path, no matter how early I might look out, I would see robed monks or else servingmen going among the dormitory and the kitchen house and the church and the rectory offices, and if the stones of this path were not flat and smooth and clean, it was said that in this way the path to heaven was strewn with snares and overgrown with sin, unless all were to exercise the utmost vigilance, and so the little boys went out and tore up the grass and moss growing between the stones, and swept the stones carefully with bunches of twigs. That is one thing I remember clearly."

"Where did the sheep pasture, then? Were they never allowed into this homefield?"

Pall Hallvardsson smiled. "I was a grown man and had gone far from this place before I ever saw a sheep, although the monks kept two cows and a few chickens and geese for eggs. On the other side of this church there was a small hospital for old men, and beyond that a row of houses. In front of the church ran a road paved with flagstones and along the other side of that was another row of houses, so, you see, sheep would have had to look far and wide for the merest blade of grass. And when I lifted my eyes, I saw towers, but never mountains, for the earth was as flat as the surface of the fjord in midsummer, and ran this way as far as a man could see in any direction."

Sometimes Gunnar related these wonders to Olaf as they were repairing the stone fences, or to Birgitta as they lay with little Kollgrim between them in the bedcloset. But Olaf merely grunted at the news that Pall Hallvardsson had never seen a sheep until he was a grown man, and said,

"It is true that he goes among his sheep in this way, like a man stepping into a cold pond on a spring morning, as if he would rather not." Birgitta listened with more care, but then asked Gunnar questions he could not answer, such as where were the mothers of these children whose noses were gone, or what folk did inside these rows of houses, or how, with things cramped together in this wise, children were able to get such air and sunlight as they needed to grow? And did each family keep a cow when there was no pasture, and what did folk eat in such a place? Some turnips, some bread, oats cooked with water, greens, wine, and beer, said Gunnar after his next talk with Sira Pall Hallvardsson, and Birgitta replied that she had never heard of such things before, and pitied folk if they were true, for though winter famine and hardship were the lot of Greenlanders and all northern folk, yet at the end of the famine, when a ptarmigan was roasting on the spit, or reindeer meat seething in a stew, such odors arose as were nearly rich enough to fill the belly, and how could some oats boiled with water do the same? And after this, when Helga complained of her whalemeat or her fish seethed with milk into a kind of soup, Birgitta asked her if she would like to eat oats boiled with water, as cows eat, and people in the East, or green grass, for according to Sira Pall Hallvardsson, such greens were their daily meat, as well. The result of this was that Helga ate without complaint.

One day before Yule, a man came from Sira Jon at Gardar, with greetings, and a neatly carved soapstone ewer, the work of one of the Gardar servants. There was other news from the south as well, for the skraeling Kissabi had succeeded in killing Ragnvald Einarsson at his new home in Hrafns Fjord, after casting a demon spell upon him and causing him to fall to the ground in fear. Then the skraeling had shot an arrow at him from a close distance, and this arrow had lodged in Ragnvald's throat, and Ragnvald's folk had themselves been thrown into such a state by this spell that they had been too frightened to defend themselves, and allowed Kissabi to come into the steading and kill the daughter, Gudny, as well, and her little son who was at the breast. And when this devil had cut off Ragnvald's arm and raised it above his head and shouted a great curse in the skraeling tongue, they had not known what to do, and allowed him to get away. Folk who traded with the skraelings said that he was already gone off to the wastes of the east, where he had disappeared among the hordes of his fellows, and he would probably never be seen again. When he heard this, Gunnar only said that it surprised him that a respected man such as Ragnvald should have fallen so low, and proved himself so cowardly. Lavrans continued to trade with the skraeling man he had always traded with, and Finn consorted with the demons as much as ever, but Yule was not held with any great joy, either at the steading or in the church of St. Birgitta, or anywhere else in Hvalsey Fjord.

And this was another piece of news, that Isleif Isleifsson had come to Sira Jon from Brattahlid and told him in secret that Margret Asgeirsdottir had gone mad at her little steading. But Gunnar would hear no more of this news, and forbade Pall Hallvardsson from relating it to him, and went out of the door of the house. Birgitta was just then taking Kollgrim from the breast. Now she sat him upon her knee and looked up toward the roof, saying, "Where is my Kollgrim? Where is my boy Kollgrim?" Now she looked behind herself and said again, "Where is my little Kollgrim?" Gunnhild and Helga peeked out from the bedcloset where they were keeping warm and began to laugh, and Birgitta looked over her other shoulder and spoke in a louder voice, "Where is that little boy? Oh, Kollgrim, where are you?" And at this the little boy managed to creep toward her face and grab her chin, bringing her eyes to his. "Ah! My Kollgrim! There you are! Why do you run off like that, where your mother can't find you?" Now Gunnhild and Helga were jumping up and down and laughing, and Lavrans and the priest were laughing, too, and Sira Pall Hallvardsson leaned forward and looked in Kollgrim's face, so that Kollgrim opened his eyes wide and stared back and then pinched the priest's nose.

But when Sira Pall Hallvardsson got up to leave at dusk, Birgitta put Kollgrim into the bedcloset with his sisters, and followed the priest out into the snow, and she declared that it was her hope that Margret Asgeirsdottir was not afflicted with a frenzy, nor left alone in her suffering, for it was said that devils sought out those who were alone and entered into them and possessed their souls, and this was something folk who lived far from others must fear above all things.

Sira Pall Hallvardsson tied the thongs of his skis without speaking. Now he stood and looked down at her and took a pole in each hand, and asked what news the Gunnars Stead folk had had of Margret since their parting with her, and Birgitta said that none had come to her ears. Did Birgitta know of the death of the boy Jonas Skulason of starvation, perchance? Birgitta replied that she did not, nor had she known how the boy was baptized, or whether, indeed, it had been a boy or a girl. Sira Pall Hallvardsson glanced across the ice at the church, then back at Birgitta, and said, "This thing I told Gunnar Asgeirsson was overheard by a serving-woman, and related to two or three people before it came to me through my visitor from Gardar, and so the cup is much cracked, and most of the truth has spilled out before it was our turn to drink. Isleif Isleifsson lives at Brattahlid with his mother, Marta, the sister of Osmund the lawspeaker. They are prosperous folk. It is said that Margret Asgeirsdottir is spending the winter with these folk." After this, he skied away, and Birgitta returned to the house. Gunnar came back after the evening meat had been cleared from the table and folk had gone to their beds.

Birgitta lay with her eyes closed and her cloak wrapped tightly about herself and Kollgrim. In the next bedcloset, Thora, the servingmaid, lay with the little girls, for the frost in these last nights since Yule had been especially deep. Gunnar piled turves against the bottom of the door to keep out the draft and renewed the seal oil in the lamp that always burned through the night, then slipped under the polar bear skin. After a moment he said, "Where is she?" Birgitta replied, "With Marta the sister of Osmund Thordarson." And this was all that passed between them.

At this Yule, Margret Asgeirsdottir and Asta Thorbergsdottir gathered their things together and removed themselves to Brattahlid, where they went to work serving Marta Thordardottir. Margret was to weave her a large piece of fine two-by-two wadmal and then to decorate this with a wide band of tablet weaving, such as she had learned to make from Kristin of Siglufjord. It was agreed that after the mass of St. Hallvard, Margret would return to Steinstraumstead with Asta and twenty of the Brattahlid sheep for pasturing above the little farm. In the autumn she would bring the ewes and the lambs back to Brattahlid, and spend another winter there, weaving and spinning. Marta was much pleased with this arrangement for, she said, anyone who had been taught by Kristin of Siglufjord would know the patterns Kristin's mother had learned as a child in Jaemtland, and she spoke of this woman, Ashild, who had been most jealous of her skills at the tablet and loom, and had never allowed her servants to see how she threw her shuttle or set up her warp. And Marta spoke so much about this woman Ashild that Margret was persuaded, and she spent her days at the great Brattahlid loom.

But she spoke little, and had little flesh on her bones, and even after staying among the Brattahlid folk from St. Andrew's mass to the feast of St. Stephen, she looked to be starving, and so Isleif had gone, without consulting Marta Thordardottir, to Sira Jon just before Yule, and declared that the woman was mad with melancholy, but that it was not the habit of Marta to note such things, nor, said folk in the district, to consider the views of her son, Isleif, with much seriousness. Since Osmund always paid heed only to his sister, he, too, had no concern for the young woman, and cared little where she was sitting or where she was staring, but only that she was out of the way. And Isleif asked Sira Jon what he, as the woman's priest, might do to encourage her to look to God for help.

It was not Sira Jon's wont to leave Gardar during the winter, for Gardar was low and damp and warm and everywhere else in Greenland was high and dry and chill. And so Sira Jon told Isleif that it did not sound to him as though the woman was making any trouble for these folk at Brattahlid, but was calm and self-contained, and Isleif said that this was so, and Sira Jon declared that it would be best to watch her, and see if the grace of the Lord came to her in the course of the spring. To this Isleif replied that it might happen that she would starve herself before the spring was over, but Sira Jon said that this could not be done, that treatises of the Church showed that the flesh must cling to the flesh, and could not become spirit through an act of will, and so the body could not deprive itself of life, but the woman must eat in the end. To this Isleif replied that she might be possessed with a devil, and Sira Jon inquired after her behavior. But she was not speaking aloud in strange tongues, nor averting her eyes from the Cross nor turning her prayers backward, and so she could not be possessed in this way, although Jon admitted that such slackness as she showed was as a door left ajar for demons, true enough. And to every question Isleif made, Sira Jon answered with the observations of such authorities as would know about these things, and so Sira Isleif went back to Brattahlid somewhat confused in his thoughts, but reassured.

And so it happened that Sira Jon grew very restless during Lent and complained bitterly of the winter cold, although others of the Greenlanders were remarking that this winter was less difficult than others, with a thaw in January, so that the sheep could get to some forage, and then another deep snow, but no ice storm such as every district had been receiving every winter, not once but three times and more. The priest was displeased at every bit of news, whether good, such as the news that there would be plenty of hay for the winter and some left over to give to more desperate folk, or bad, such as the news that two cows had gone through the ice of the big Gardar pond and been lost. He always looked out for folk from Brattahlid, and when they came, he asked them about the madwoman living with Marta Thordardottir, and sometimes they had news of her and sometimes they did not. For Lent, Sira Jon set himself a strict regimen of fasting and prayer, so that he grew very thin and big-eyed, and Sira Audun was left to look after the daily business of the household, although folk said that after so many years, the servingwoman Anna Jonsdottir looked after all the business that needed to be looked after. Sira Audun, it was said, was working at composing another hymn, or perhaps some other sort of verse.

At Easter, Sira Jon broke his fast and celebrated the Resurrection of the Lord in the company of Sira Pall Hallvardsson at Gardar. It happened that after the meal, Sira Pall whispered to Sira Audun that all the folk must go from the table, leaving only Sira Jon, and after a time, this was accomplished. When they were alone, Sira Pall Hallvardsson went and sat close beside the other priest, and he said, "My brother, do you recall the time we rowed the big Gardar boat together to Undir Hofdi church? I sat in the bow, and marveled at the power of your stroke."

"Young men have pride in their strength as maidens have pride in their beauty, but all forms of pride are sinful. It seems to me that the task of old men such as we are now is to repent of the pride they had in their youth."

"It seems to me that you repent at the expense of your own flesh."

Now Sira Jon turned and looked at Sira Pall for the first time, and Sira Pall saw in his face a look of both fear and bitterness. Sira Jon said, "Is our own flesh not the first thing that we must repent of?"

"Even so, it is not possible to live in Greenland without a goodly store of flesh. It is the Lord's mercy upon His beasts here that He gives them a goodly layer of fat and a pleasant, rounded form. So He is merciful to the men of the place, as well, for they are bigger than other men, and sturdier."

Sira Jon sat stubbornly silent.

Now Sira Pall spoke in a low soothing voice, and said, "My brother, you are more learned than I am, but it seems to me that the Lord asks two things of men, and one of these is penitence, devotion, and sacrifice, but the other is the wise husbandry of the goods of the world, for the care of His servants and their charges. But the Lord does not ask both things from a single man. Instead He has made room in His church for both St. Francis and St. Augustine, and neither one sits before the other at the foot of His throne."

Now Sira Jon sat for a long time, at first staring at Sira Pall, and then staring away. Finally, he said, "When meat sticks in the throat, it must be spit out, and when prayers burn within, their smoke must fly upward."

And Sira Pall said, "Will you not speak to me of what is troubling you?"

And Sira Jon sat silent, and would not speak.

Soon after Easter, the ice broke up in Eriks Fjord, as it always does, in the space of a day or so, and a warm wind off the glacier blew the ice to the mouth of the fjord and out into the ocean. And soon after this, Sira Jon and three Gardar servingmen took the big Gardar boat, and they went to Brattahlid and made a visit to Osmund Thordarson.

Sira Jon went with his men into the farmsteading and the table was set up for them, and several women brought them food. None of these was Margret Asgeirsdottir. Isleif, he was told, was visiting his brother Ragnleif and conducting masses there. Nothing was said of the madwoman. After the eating was over, Marta Thordardottir took the priest to the high seat, and sat him there, then, in her commanding way, she began to quiz him about news from Gardar and the other districts. And this wish he had to know of Margret Asgeirsdottir was so great that he could in no way speak of it. His desire for knowledge of her felt unaccountably so like a sin that even when Marta herself mentioned the name and showed Sira Jon the lovely piece of cloth Margret had woven and decorated in the course of the winter, he could not ask, and Marta did not say, whether the woman had died or had gone away, or was simply not present in the room. The four men rowed back to Gardar after the evening meat, and made their way from the Eriks Fjord jetty to the residence in the dark, and even as they were walking along, it came to Sira Jon how he might have asked after the woman, what his manner might have been, and his words, and he thought of what he would say upon his return to Brattahlid—how he would incline his head and refer to Margret Asgeirsdottir as "that woman you had with you in the winter, what was her name? I believe Sira Isleif mentioned her to me."

The fact was that Margret Asgeirsdottir had indeed served Sira Jon at his meat, but that in looking for the tall blond girl claimed ten years before by Olaf Finnbogason, he had overlooked a certain old woman, as he thought she was, although she was but of an age with himself. If, however, he had not rushed away, but stayed the night with Osmund, he would have known her from her dreams, for every night she awoke either weeping or calling out, and it was said that Skuli Gudmundsson prevented her from sleeping out of malice, for it is the case that even ghosts who were formerly gentle and considerate folk become ferocious and hateful after death. Nevertheless, although talk of this went about, Skuli neither appeared to nor harmed anyone other than Margret Asgeirsdottir, and so no one cared to do anything about it, for it was said, a man could draw the anger of ghosts upon himself by meddling. In addition to this, Margret never spoke of her dreams nor identified her tormentor, and so no one felt called upon to bring the topic up, not even Sira Isleif.

Now it happened that some days after Sira Jon's visit, around the mass of St. Hallvard, Margret and Asta returned to Steinstraumstead with a flock of twenty sheep and ewes and began putting things in order there. Where Margret seemed to have grown smaller, Asta Thorbergsdottir seemed to have grown larger, and her strength, always that of a man, now seemed equal to that of two men. Cutting turves and piling them up was as nothing to her, and she hardly grunted when lifting the heaviest stones. Her arms were so long and so strong that she could carry two struggling sheep with no trouble, and her hips were wide as the beam of a boat. It was her habit always to ask Margret Asgeirsdottir for advice and instructions, and always to look to her if someone else, even Marta Thordardottir, asked her to perform any service. On the day when they rowed across Eriks Fjord to Steinstraumstead, they found upon the shore a deserted arrangement of stones, such as skraelings build when they desire to cook, and Asta went over to these stones, and kicked them apart with her foot, and found another large boulder and lifted it and set it among these stones, but the two women said nothing of this, but only went about sweeping out the steading and moving into it.

Some days after their coming, they looked out in the morning and discovered three skin boats pulled up on the shore and another two out in the fjord. There were some twelve or fifteen skraeling men and boys on the shore and in the boats, but after a short while, they pushed the beached boats back into the water and paddled swiftly away. Margret was not a little afraid of these signs, for in addition to the news of Ragnvald Einarsson, she knew well from the stories of her childhood the sorts of indignities skraelings were prepared to perpetrate upon the children of men, especially the female children, and she did not hesitate to relate them to Asta.

It was true, she said, that they took particular pleasure in preventing the worship of the Lord among their captives, and often cast spells upon these unfortunates so that they forgot all of their prayers. It was also said by some, including her old nurse, Ingrid, that the feet of these demons were covered with fur, as was their skin inside their clothing, and this was the reason they could endure such cold as they did. Only their hands and faces were hairless, but these didn't freeze, either, for some reason, and even in the bitterest cold the demons went without hoods or mittens. Asta looked fixedly at the fjord where the skin boats had turned into specks in the distance. She made no response, but went down the hillside and kicked the cooking stones even farther apart. After this, they saw nothing of the skraelings for a long while.

It happened that one day around the feast of St. Jon, Margret and Asta set about shearing the twenty ewes that they had brought with them to Steinstraumstead. Asta was good at this work, but Margret was clumsy, for Hrafn and Olaf did the shearing at Gunnars Stead, and so it was Margret's task to take the fleeces and lay them across the side of the hill, to cool and loosen so that they could be broken into wool for spinning. These fleeces were laid out for the space of one day, then rolled up at nightfall and put away. With the bleating of the ewes and the crying of the lambs, there was such a clamor that neither Asta nor Margret, who was farther down the hillside, noticed the approach of two skin boats until they were drawn up on the shore and the skraelings in them had already gotten out and begun to cook their meal over a fire they built. This group of demons included three men, a young woman, an old woman, and two children, and these children came up the hillside and surprised Margret at her work so that she cried out. Now the young woman appeared behind them and took their hands and backed away. Unlike the children of men, these children stared into Margret's face as a cat might, never needing to blink or turn away. The demon woman smiled and nodded.

Now Asta came down the hillside carrying the sheep shears and two of the demon men came up from the shore, one of them carrying a bow and some arrows. This man appeared to be younger even than the young woman, perhaps eighteen or nineteen winters old. He stopped as if startled by the sight of Asta Thorbergsdottir, and let his gaze wander over her. Seeing this, Asta raised her shears above her head and brandished them, and the skraelings and their young turned and went down the hillside. But the young man looked back twice at Asta, although she scowled mightily at him. Now a sheep scampered down the slope, and Margret and Asta saw that the three unshorn ewes had escaped from the ewe fold and scattered themselves among the shorn ewes, and that the fleeces were in danger of being stepped on and broken, so they began to run about the slope chasing the sheep back to the fold. They thought no more of the skraeling group until the next morning, when Asta stepped out of the steading and discovered a fine sealskin upon the doorstone that could only have come from the skraelings. This she carried down to the strand and pitched into the fjord. After that, she went to the cooking spot and scattered the stones once again.

Now it was usual during the summer days that Margret would take the sheep back into the hills behind Steinstraumstead that overlooked the stony creek known as Steinstraum, and were well watered by the glacier, so that they were green all summer, and she would herd them out each morning and back each evening, and also gather angelica and other herbs such as she found and put them in her sack. It was true that in spite of the fact that Margret had lost her girlish appearance, she was still little burdened by pain of the hips or any of the other ills of maturity, and she stepped about the hills with as much speed and grace as she always had. It was also true that such movement was a pleasure to her in all weathers, for the sunlight and the breezes and the rain drove away thoughts of past things. This had been a great trial to her, that the cloth she had fashioned for Marta Thordardottir had been all woven of memories and regrets, so that when Marta brought it out to admire it, the very smell of it brought Margret grief, and she foresaw that this would be the case again in the coming winter and every succeeding one, that her memories, all alike but eternally repeating themselves, would cluster about her as she sat quietly at the loom and bear down upon her and smother her. And yet, Marta was herself growing old and her sight was dimming, so that if she wished to have Margret about her, Margret desired to fulfill her wish.

Going with the sheep, however, was so like her childhood wanderings in the mountains above Gunnars Stead that it seemed to her that she was returned to that time, and the ghostly figure she sometimes caught sight of just ahead of her or half hidden among the scrub birch was only her father's brother, Hauk Gunnarsson, setting bird snares. And this figure was so quiet and elusive, as Hauk himself had been, that its appearance hardly even surprised her. It was true, she sometimes said to Asta, that her father's brother had visited every part of the eastern settlement, and must have known Steinstraumstead and the stony river as well as anywhere else. At the end of each day with the sheep, Margret returned to the steading to receive her dreams, and as night fell, grew melancholy, so that she did not welcome talk with Asta, and Asta did not offer it.

Perhaps as a result of these habits, Margret came and went without knowing that Asta was much oppressed by the attentions of the young skraeling man. He came every day alone in a fine skin boat, and at first he was content to demonstrate his skills to Asta, she thought for her admiration. He was agile in the skin boat, and capable of great speed and almost magical maneuvers. Of course, she dared not look at them at first, but kept to her work of cheesemaking, spinning, and repair of the turf and stonework about the little steading, but in the end it was difficult never to look, for his feats were such as she had never seen before performed by men. And as the devil tempts folk little by little out of the path of the Lord, so these sights tempted Asta Thorbergsdottir first to glance and then to stare and then to come down upon the strand and gaze out into the fjord, where demon and boat together acted like playful fish, leaping in and out of the water, disappearing and reappearing in the waves, shooting from one place to another. At least, so these things appeared to the sight of Asta Thorbergsdottir, but she would not have admitted them to others, for fear of being thought possessed. But even so, when the skraeling approached the shore, Asta had the sense to run up the hillside, and in addition to this, to cast away every gift that the devil left for her, no matter how desirable some little trinket might be, for the fact was that the beauty of such things hid their corrupt nature—were someone to cut open a hunk of whalemeat, for example, such a hunk left as a gift by a demon, one would find it crawling with maggots, and what was more, even gifts not naturally prone to such transformations, a bone needle or a piece of walrus tusk, were transformed by the skraelings into crawling and corrupt objects.

After some days of this, she was willing to admit that the way this corruption came about was not intended by the skraelings themselves, but came as a result of their demon natures. Even so, she resolutely threw everything away and brandished whatever might be in her hand when the skraeling appeared in as threatening a fashion as she could muster. Also, on some days she looked for Sira Isleif to come and relieve her fears, or at least stiffen her resistance against this skraeling, for, say what one wished, she had come to look for his gifts and his antics in the fjord. Life at Steinstraumstead, especially after the winter at Brattahlid, was a solitary undertaking. Other days she feared that Sira Isleif's visit might be upon them, and that he would castigate her sin in paying any notice to this devil at all, and she turned over in her thoughts what she might say in her own defense, but the fact was, that for deserting the ways of God, even in thoughts, there is no defense. And so she wished away the visit of Sira Isleif on these days.

Margret and Asta were in the habit of arising with the sun to milk the ewes, then eating a bit of dried sealmeat together before Margret drove the animals to their pasture, and on one such morning it came to Asta that she should speak of her distress to the other woman, for she had come far from the days of kicking apart the skraelings' stone cooking spot, and although she had seen the young woman and the two children only that once, she remembered their faces clearly, but not with the fear or hatred that she remembered feeling at the time. At morning meat she held in her hand a little trinket, a man carved in the skraeling fashion from a bit of

ivory, with a few incised lines to depict his parka and his fur boots and
his eye slits. This trinket she had been unable to make herself cast away,
and yet it weighed heavily upon her soul. In addition to this, she knew
that the skraeling was hiding in wait for Margret's departure, as he had
for each of the last few mornings, and that he would appear, smiling, as
soon as the little flock disappeared over the brow of the hill. Were she to
put the charm upon the tiny table she had made for them, Margret, she
knew, would lift her eyes from it to Asta's own face, and she would be
preserved, and yet she kept it tight and warm in the palm of her hand.

For her part, Margret Asgeirsdottir was still in the grip of her
dreams, as she was every morning, and looked upon the face of Asta
Thorbergsdottir with the same sense of distance as she always did. She
longed to be off.

Now it happened that shortly after Margret went away, Asta stepped
out of the steading with the intention of going to the privy, and the
skraeling leapt out from behind the corner of the house and grabbed Asta
by the arm. Then he took her wrist and squeezed it, so that her hand opened
and disclosed the ivory figure. At once the skraeling gave a great shout
and began to grin in a diabolical fashion, and then, greatly to Asta's
surprise, he grabbed her hair at the nape of her neck and began jerking her
about him, attempting to throw her down upon the ground. With his
other hand, he slapped her bottom, not hard, but like Thorkel Gellison
slapping the flanks of a favorite mare. Asta readily saw that she was a good
deal taller than the demon, and probably heavier as well, though like all
skraelings, he was clothed in furs summer and winter. Now she turned
toward him and grabbed him around the chest as folk do in wrestling
contests, and squeezed him as hard as she could, all the while listening with
her head jerked back by his hand gripping her hair for the crack of his ribs.
This never came, but she did manage to drive the wind out of him and
overpower him so that he fell to his knees and his face grew red and
swollen. She, in turn, was nearly overpowered by the rank odor of seal
blubber on his hands and face, but she pushed him away and turned and
ran up the hillside. Sometime later, she looked out and saw that his skin
boat was gone, and this was a good example indeed of the wages of
walking with the devil, for some of her hair had come out in a large patch
and the back of her head throbbed painfully. In the evening, she spoke of
this misadventure to Margret, and wept mightily in remorse at her weakness. But when they awakened on the second day, it was to discover not
just the one skraeling, but a whole group of them standing about outside
the steading, all men.

Margret stood inside the doorway and Asta behind her with a weighty soapstone lamp concealed in each of her hands. One of the men, who had graying hair and a little beard upon his chin, stepped forward and addressed Margret as follows, "Old woman, where are your men?" His Norse tongue was almost unintelligible, and Margret stepped forward two paces so that she could make it out. The men stepped back.

She said, "We have no men here." Now Asta stepped in front of her and lifted the pieces of stone above her head as if to throw them. The group of men conferred among themselves, and the leader spoke once again. He said, "It is a shame to all men when they have to do business with women."

Margret shrugged and turned to go inside the house.

"Even so," he went on, "a certain young man finds his heart set upon this young woman here, for she is a fine fat girl, and he can hardly keep his eyes off her, and so he wishes to take her for his first wife."

"I think," said Margret, "that I don't understand your words." And indeed, much of what he had said had escaped her, but it appeared that he was asking to have Asta Thorbergsdottir marry the young skraeling who had pulled her hair out.

The demon spoke more slowly, gesturing at the young skraeling, who stepped forward. "This fellow, Quimiak, wishes to have your girl for his wife."

Margret and Asta looked at each other.

"He is a good hunter and a prosperous man. Soon he will have another wife to help her, and her life will be an easy one, although it is true that he is young to marry."

Margret turned to Asta and said, "I think he is marrying someone else, too."

"This courtship has gone on for many days, and Quimiak is most anxious to bring it to a conclusion."

Now Margret spoke loudly to the older skraeling. "My friend and I must consult together about this." She waved her hand toward the bottom of the slope, and the leader said a few words. Soon the skraelings were out of sight of the house, although the breeze carried sounds of their talking to the two women. Margret and Asta sat down upon a stone that lay against the south wall of the steading, and a little time passed before they began to converse. At last Margret said, "It seems to me that things have passed that I have known nothing of."

Now Asta smiled and said, "And it seems to me that things have passed that I have known nothing of, as well." And they sat silently for another short time.

Margret said, "This is the smallest of steadings, and will never support both of us in both summer and winter, and in addition to that, Marta Thordardottir is growing old, and I doubt that Isleif or Ragnleif will greet us with such pleasure as Marta does every autumn."

"And though it may not be able to support two, yet one would not be able to live in such a lonely spot."

"That may be or may not be."

"No one knows how the skraelings live. And this one smelled like an old sealskin that hasn't been cleaned properly, and yet—" But she fell silent.

"And yet?"

"And yet, like as not one such as I will get few enough offers from others."

"But skraelings aren't men. They are demons, and do the work of Satan."

"Many men marry skraeling women and father children. Their wives' mothers come to live with them on their steadings."

"And all are baptized, and they live as Norsemen, and change their names, and worship in church as others do."

"I was greatly fond of Jonas Skulason, that is a fact."

"My father's brother, Hauk Gunnarsson, used to go to the Northsetur as a young man, and he had much to do with skraelings, and he used to say that these folk, for he considered them folk and not demons, were used to traveling great distances in the darkest part of winter, and in fact in the places where they go, the sun never shines after the winter nights."

"Why is it that they make these journeys?"

"They have no sheep, and spend all of their time hunting walrus and whale and seal and bears."

"It may be that they are never hungry."

"It may be. My father's brother was not a little impressed with their skills."

"Hauk Gunnarsson was himself well known as a hunter."

"It may be that they are never hungry." Now Margret looked steadily at Asta and said, "Sira Pall Hallvardsson would say one thing, and that is, what availeth a man to gain the world if he loseth his soul? And it may be that the children of God are meant to go hungry in this world. It is not for us to walk with demons in order to have full bellies."

"It is true that as few priests as we have among us here, there are fewer than that in the wastelands. And we know nothing of these folk. And yet, I think often of little Jonas. More often now than I did."

Margret looked at Asta, then out toward the fjord. Finally she said, "The pain of such thoughts always turns to pleasure, and the pleasure of them always turns to pain, it seems to me." Now they stood up and walked down the slope, and the skraelings turned to them at the sound of their steps, and Margret declared to the older man that Asta would speak for herself, then Asta said, "It is true that a daughter leaves her folk and takes up the ways of a husband's folk, as skraeling women have come to live among the Greenlanders. But a daughter of God must not turn away from Him, and embrace unholy ways."

Now the older skraeling spoke to Quimiak, and then said to Margret, "This girl is oddly unwilling, since she received Quimiak's gift, and kept it with her in her hand. When a girl does this, that means she has accepted a man for her husband, and is willing to go away with him. Does this woman demand more gifts?"

Most of this talk was intelligible to Margret and she answered as follows, "It is true that we are not familiar with your ways, and the girl may have done one thing and meant another. For this you should blame our ignorance and forgive us. But it was not her intention to encourage this Quimiak, and she has no desire to marry him." Now she looked at Asta, and the two women were a little afraid, for the skraelings numbered half a dozen at least, and all carried such skraeling weapons as bows and arrows and harpoons.

The bearded man took Quimiak aside and began to parley with him, and Quimiak looked often and admiringly at Asta. He was not tall, but he was straight-limbed and clothed in fine furs, finer than those of some of the other men, although they were older than he was. Margret saw Asta looking at him, and stepped back into the house with Asta by the hand. Asta declared that it might happen this time as she had heard it had happened with others, that the demons would try to steal her away by force, and Margret did not know how to respond to this observation. But the skraelings did not try to steal her away, rather the older man came away from his talk with Quimiak and addressed Margret with thanks for listening to their plea, and then all of the skraelings slipped silently down the slope, and in an eye blink they were in their skin boats in the middle of the fjord. On this day, Margret kept the sheep folded, and did not take them to their pasture, and Asta went about her business in somewhat low spirits.

It happened that some days after this Margret and Asta were looking out for Sira Isleif, who was to come to them on the feast of Mary Magdalen and confess them and administer communion. Because of the priest's dim sight, the two women always looked for him rather than suffering him to thread his way up the slope from the strand, for the scrub willow was thick and treacherous, and few paths had been worn in it. And so one morning they were looking out and spied a small boat in the fjord with two rowers in it, and when it came to shore, Sira Isleif was not one of these men, but Sira Jon from Gardar was. Margret was much put out by this chance, for she and Asta had been gathering dried sheep's dung from the fold to spread on a bit of flat ground near the steading that Margret thought to use as a homefield. In addition to this, there was nothing prepared to give the priest to refresh himself. Sira Isleif liked to sit inside the steading and gossip with the women as they prepared him something, but someone such as Sira Jon, Margret knew, expected to be led to the high seat and have various meats placed before him for him to pick and choose among.

Now the priest and his servant began to climb the slope, and Margret wiped her hands upon her gown and stepped forward to greet them and show them the faint path. But when she came to the priest and inclined her head courteously, he only stopped and stared at her so that she was discountenanced and forgot to say the proper words of greeting. The servant declared in a loud voice that Sira Jon had come to visit the unfortunate Margret Asgeirsdottir and her servant Asta Thorbergsdottir. And they began to climb again and soon they came to the tiny steading, where, once again, Sira Jon stared about himself, first at Margret and then at her dwelling place and then at her sheep, who were scattered about the slope, foraging among the scrub. Now Margret offered such food as she had on hand—some dried sealmeat and dried reindeer meat with new butter and that day's ewe's milk, humble fare indeed. But the two men ate greedily. As a last dish, she placed before them sweet dried bilberries, and they ate these, too, always turning to look at Margret as she moved about the tiny room.

After the meal, Margret said to the priest, "Sira Jon, it is our hope that you have come to confess us and give us communion, for we are in a state of sin here, as men are everywhere, and we have been looking eagerly for Sira Isleif."

Now Sira Jon smiled and nodded, and took Margret off away from the steading and bid her to kneel down and make her confession. And after she was finished he asked her, "Have you more to say to me, or any other sins to confess, or even any news for me, or questions, or any wish to confide in me?" He pressed her so with these inquiries that Margret began to look toward the steading for Sira Jon's servant and Asta, but they were lost in conversation, and afforded her no aid. Finally, Sira Jon declared, "It is said, my child, that you are afflicted with dreams and melancholia."

Margret said nothing.

"It may be that you wish to speak to me about these dreams."

But Margret did not reply to this, either.

Now Sira Jon became somewhat agitated, and said, "You come from a prideful lineage, and wayward. Your brother has killed men and been driven from his patrimony and only narrowly escaped outlawry. You choose to live apart from folk, and disdain their aid. The Lord looks with little kindness upon such doings, and his punishment is swift and sure. It is truly said that pride is the greatest sin."

Now Margret spoke softly, and said, "My dreams are as those of others, and my melancholy is such as comes and goes, which seems to me not unusual. The snares of pride are many and much tangled together. You may truly say that I fail to avoid them."

Now Sira Jon grew gentler and leaned toward Margret. "My child, do you not grow desperate with loneliness in this place, so that it seems to you that voices speak or faces appear where you know there can be none?"

"It may be——"

"Or perhaps you hear a kind of screaming above the wind, as of souls in torment, as if, perhaps, the mouth of Hell were yawning open and men were given to hear the crying of the Damned?"

"This has not——"

Now Sira Jon's voice fell to a whisper, "Or it could be that the Devil himself speaks into your ear as you are thinking of other things and tempts you, toward what you could not say, for his words can hardly be distinguished, and yet they fill you with longing? Is this not something that happens to you?"

"Nay. My father's brother sometimes walks among the birches, back in the mountains where I take the sheep, but it seems to me that he was so foolishly fond of these wild places that he cannot forsake them even in death."

Sira Jon looked up the slope as if seeking traces of Hauk Gunnarsson, then looked into Margret's face so sharply that she was forced to drop her eyes. She declared in a low voice, "Ingrid our nurse used to tell many tales of folk who stalked their own steadings out of inordinate love for them, and my father's brother was as fond of these wild places as other men are of their steadings——"

"What does he look like? What do you see?"

"I know not what to say. Shadows among the birches, a bit of color afar, white or the purplish color of Gunnars Stead wadmal. These are not things I have pondered much."

Sira Jon leaned so close to Margret that his face was nearly touching hers and spoke in a whisper. "It is said that those who cannot lie in their graves are horrible of aspect, covered with blood, perhaps, or mutilated."

"This is not for me to say——"

"It is said that you are mad. I would help you if you would let me." Great drops of perspiration burst out upon the priest's forehead and a bright red spot appeared in each of his cheeks.

"Perhaps folk do say that. It is true that I was once greatly tried, but——" Here Margret stopped speaking, for Sira Jon had slumped forward in a faint.

Now Margret ran to the servant, and brought him to Sira Jon, hoping that he would give her some explanation for this, but he only looked down at the priest where he lay upon the turf, and said nothing. After a bit Sira Jon revived, and sat up, and looked about, and it seemed to Margret that he was much surprised to find himself where he was. But indeed, he was an odd man, for he only thanked her for her hospitality and gave her his ring to kiss, and went off without a word about his fit. Margret was much perplexed, and through the winter she sometimes considered the meaning of the priest's visit, but she mentioned it to no one at Brattahlid.

And it so happened that in the summer of 1381 a certain ship carrying Norwegian traders did arrive, a ship blown off course from Iceland, and the folk from this ship stayed at Herjolfsnes in the south. Still another ship appeared in the following summer, although much damaged, while the folk of the first ship were still at Herjolfsnes, and the folk on the new ship stayed for the winter at Brattahlid, and the captains of both these ships agreed to take the news of the bishop's death to the chapter at Nidaros, and as payment for this favor, Sira Jon gave each captain something of worth. To the master of the first ship, which was called *Olafssuden,* he gave a pair of walrus tusks, and to the captain of the damaged ship, which was called *Thorlakssuden,* he gave a pair of white falcons, and these were the items of greatest value among the Gardar stores, for the wealth of Gardar was not as it had been, but even so, these shipmasters seemed little impressed with their gifts and the Greenlanders said that these Norwegians thought very well of themselves.

When it came time for the *Olafssuden* to return to Norway (the *Thorlakssuden* could not be repaired with such materials as were at hand), the two shipmasters went about getting provisions for their journey. In every instance when they were offered other goods for trade, they refused them, and denigrated their value, and maintained that they wished to keep their own goods for trade in Iceland. For the provisions they needed, they offered very little in the way of seed or pitch or iron goods or wood, much less than the Greenlanders considered their cheeses and dried reindeer flesh and dried sealmeat to be worth, and these two men were said to be stiff-necked and hard. Other shipmasters, especially Thorleif, were warmly recalled, and Thorleif's ship as well, for it had been long and wide and deep and had carried such an abundance of goods and treasures that every Greenlander had been satisfied.

In the last days before the departure of these two in the summer of 1383, the master of the *Thorlakssuden,* a man by the name of Markus Arason, went about gathering payments for the wooden beams and laps of his broken ship, and those who refused to pay were told that they would have none of the driftage. This was contrary to the law of Greenland, which at this time said that driftwood was the property of that man whose strand it caught upon, but the *Olafssuden*'s master declared that he cared nothing for the law of Greenland, and that the ship would be burned to the water line if not paid for. And indeed, on the evening before the departure of the *Olafssuden,* the *Thorlakssuden* was broken apart with axes, and folk who had paid the Norwegian were given their beams and laps, and the rest of the wood was burned in a great bonfire, and his sailors stood about the fire with their axes to prevent anyone from throwing water upon it. And the Greenlanders considered this a great crime, but they were unable to prevent the departure of the *Olafssuden,* and this event was spoken of for some years.

Another topic of discussion among the Greenlanders was this, that following the killings of the Erlendssons by Gunnar Asgeirsson there occurred seven more killings in the course of five winters, and this was a greater number of killings than folk expected, and in addition to this, there were robberies and some rapes, and the desecration of the churchyard at the church in Herjolfsnes. Not all of these killings were properly announced, and in four of the cases, the killers went undiscovered, or at least, unpunished, for it is truly said that folk know more than they speak about. It was also true that those who desecrated the churchyard were thought to be sailors from the *Thorlakssuden,* and after the departure of the Norwegian's men, it was a pleasure to the Greenlanders to blame these folk for all sorts of things.

But another thing was also true, and this was that the Greenlanders felt the absence of the bishop and, as far as that went, of the king's ombudsman Kollbein Sigurdsson, and disputes were too often decided between men on the spot, without the counsel of the prosperous farmers of a district. Since the coming of Bishop Alf, fewer and fewer men had bothered to make the long journeys that they had once made, either to Gardar at Yule and Easter for the celebration in the cathedral, or to Brattahlid just after the mass of St. Jon the Baptist in the summer, and Osmund Thordarson, the lawspeaker himself, declared that there was little he could do to persuade men to leave their farms in the middle of summer when there was much work to be done. Others said, perhaps truly, that there was little that Osmund tried to do, in fact. But the result was that some years Osmund was left to recite the laws to not more than two dozen men, and few cases were brought and only half of the thirteen district judges were present at any rate.

Sometimes folk declared that this was a great scandal, and other times they said that after all no murders had occurred in their district, or near their steadings, or only one, and the killer was known and would not kill again, for this is also true, that no matter how evil times become, they are not so evil as they might be, and even Erlend and Vigdis lived from day to day, and did their work, and carried on much as before, and if this was possible for them, then how much more possible would it be for others, who had not suffered as they had? Even so, there came to be some little dissatisfaction with Osmund Thordarson. He was too genial, or too careless, or too old—each complaint was different, but every man had one.

It happened that about two summers after the departure of the *Olafssuden,* another ship appeared in Einars Fjord, a large, richly painted vessel with a beautiful red and gold sail. Its master, a prosperous Icelander by the name of Bjorn Einarsson, was called Jorsalfari, or "Jerusalem traveler," for he had taken a ship to Jerusalem and to many other places as well, including Rome and Spain as well as the more usual places. What was especially interesting to the Greenlanders was that his wife was with him, a woman who was very richly and fashionably dressed. A scribe traveled with him as well, his foster son Einar, who wrote down all of Bjorn's adventures and all of his discoveries.

In addition to Bjorn Einarsson's beautiful ship, there were three others in the party, and each of these three was a serviceable, seaworthy craft, and the Greenlanders were not a little impressed with the array they made. It was soon apparent that Bjorn was a man possessed of great luck. He was red-faced, portly, and high-spirited, and he himself said that he was much pleased at coming to Greenland, for though, he told Sira Jon, he had been heading for Iceland, Greenland was a place that few came to, a place lost to the considerations of men, especially since the coming of the Great Death and its subsequent visitations. And he went on in this vein. Sira Jon made him and his wife and foster son greatly welcome, and the sailors were sent with gifts out among the Greenlanders, and they had a lot to tell, much of it about Bjorn Einarsson, for he was a man whom talk clustered about wherever he went.

The first thing Bjorn did was ask who had the best horses in Greenland, and he was told about Thorkel Gellison of Hestur Stead and about Magnus Arnason of Nes and about Ragnleif Isleifsson of Brattahlid, who had the best horses in the northern part of the settlement, and he took four rowers and his wife and foster son in the big Gardar boat and went first to Brattahlid and then to Vatna Hverfi district, and at each of these places he traded for a fine pair of horses for himself and his wife, to be kept for him whenever he desired to come from Gardar and ride about the district. At Brattahlid he traded a fine pair of silver candlesticks, and with these a pair of iron wheel hubs to pay for the horses' keep. To Thorkel Gellison he gave a carved ivory crucifix, and with this a bag of rye seed to pay for the keeping of the animals. And folk were surprised at Thorkel Gellison, for he allowed himself to be traded out of his favorite gray mare and a roan stallion that some said was better even than the famous gray. But Thorkel said to his steward that this Icelander would neither be staying in Greenland nor taking horses with him on a sea journey, and it would do the beasts good to be sat on by a man of luck.

Bjorn's wife, whose name was Solveig Ogmundsdottir, was not very pretty. Nevertheless, she wore such clothing and headdresses as Greenland women had never seen before, embroidered in gold and silver, with gold threads woven through the silk. Her shoes were especially delightful, as colorful as the dresses, and soft and dainty. She had a special pair of shoes for going about in muddy weather, and these were made of violet leather and wood, with designs of birds and flowers painted on them. She was glad to display these things to folk who were interested, and although she spoke in an odd, and perhaps affected, manner, there was little gossip about her except as praised her wealth and her apparel and her courtesy. In the winter after their arrival, Solveig gave birth to a boy, and he was cared for by two children who were skraeling children. These had been rescued from an islet at the mouth of Eriks Fjord, and they were very fond of Solveig and Bjorn. They went about with them everywhere, and lived with them at Gardar, and of this peculiar arrangement, Sira Jon said nothing.

Of news, this was the greatest piece, that now there were two popes, one in Rome, whom some folk considered to be a madman, and another in Avignon, among the French, whom some considered to be the tool of the king of France, and far from the sight of God, and this schism was some seven years old. Sira Jon asked if Pope Urban was no longer the pope, then, for the crew of the *Thorlakssuden* had spoken of that election, and of the return of Gregory to Rome some years before, and Bjorn replied that indeed, Urban was still in Rome, and considered to be pope by Norwegians and Englishmen and the Holy Roman Emperor, but that there was a Pope Clement in Avignon who had gained the support of the French and the Scots and the king of Castile, and this Clement had all the old cardinals with him, and Urban's cardinals were all new ones, created by himself, and what was worse, each pope was busy excommunicating everyone loyal to the other one; whole towns and regions had been excommunicated, and among the people of the countryside there was no assurance that rites performed were in any way effective. Bjorn himself had little to say of this matter, for he had been to Rome and seen it for what it was, a crowded, miserable rubble, where decent folk might be set upon and beaten even unto death for no reason, for a few coins or a trinket. And this was also true, that every cardinal kept fighting men about him, and more than one had used various pretexts for ordering the slaughter of innocent folk; indeed, this other pope, Clement, had ordered the slaughter of the citizens of a certain town, called by the Italians Cesena. The case was as follows, that the cardinal accepted hostages, and freed them as a sign of goodwill, and then called out his English mercenaries, and had the gates of the city barred and then for the space of three days and nights, these Englishmen had become as berserks, frenzied with killing and laying waste, for when all is said and done, Englishmen are well known to be ungodly folk. It was said that upwards of ten thousand or more of the folk were put to the sword, as many or more as died in the Great Death, Bjorn did not know how many. And more fled. And many fine things were broken apart and burned and stolen.

This news cast Sira Jon sorely down, and he said to Bjorn that among the hopes of men, that small one of the Greenlanders, the hope for a new bishop, must now be blasted. After this, to give him some cheer, Bjorn spoke of his journey to Jerusalem. There, he said, the sun shone so bright and hot that folk had to remain within their houses during the day so as not to be burned up or faint at their tasks, and in addition to this, the countryside around the town was much parched with the excess of heat. Nevertheless, the place shone with the beauty of holiness, and a man could wander there among the holy places for many years, and never see his fill of them, for nearly every step that a man took was in the footsteps of Abraham, or David, or Joshua, who caused the destruction of Jericho, so that what had been a great city was now a little village, as Bjorn had seen for himself, or Jon the Baptist, or Our Lady, or Jesus Christ and Peter and the other disciples. At times when Bjorn himself could not remember this or that, his foster son Einar supplied the information, for Einar had gone on all these travels and written everything down, and Bjorn had fostered him with this in mind.

Einar told folk the tale of the Saracens, who were called Mohamme-dans, and who own Jerusalem through the sins and failings of Christian men, for it is well known that God took Jerusalem from the Christians because they do not follow his laws, so that such wealth as King Baldwin showed to King Sigurd when he came to Jerusalem, when his brother Eystein was king of Norway, no longer belongs to Christians, but to the Saracen sultan. Everyone knows the tale of how Baldwin had rich cloths laid upon the road to Jerusalem, to test the pride of Sigurd, and Sigurd rode his horse over them as if they were dirt and told all his men to do the same, so that Baldwin was much impressed. But now these Mohamme-dans have all this wealth for themselves, through the justice of God.

These Mohammedans, Einar said, look forward eagerly to Paradise, and say that in Paradise every man shall have eighty wives, all maidens, and shall lie with them every day and always find them maidens again. And other than that, they have their laws in a book called *Alkoran,* and one of these laws is that they shall fast and keep from their wives a whole month every year, and another of these is that Jesus was never crucified, but was changed by the Lord into Judas, who was crucified for him, and that Jesus came to heaven without dying, for it would be injustice for God to bring Jesus to be crucified with no guilt upon Him, so it could not be. Another of these laws says that Jesus was not the Son of God, but a great prophet, like Moses and Abraham, and that another prophet was Mo-hammed, who was the messenger of God. Because they know much of the Virgin and of Jesus and of the gospels, they are easily converted to proper faith, when they are shown how to understand it properly. And it is not only in Paradise that they have many wives, but on earth too, for Mohammed said that this was just. But now these men take many more than is proper, and concubines as well. Such practices were much spoken of by the Greenlanders, being so strange. And Einar said this, that when men in this country saw the wealth of Bjorn Einarsson Jorsalfari, they offered him beautiful women for his wives and concubines, but Bjorn always said to them that Solveig was as six wives to him already. And these Mohammedans were much surprised by Solveig, for she went with her face uncovered, whereas women in these parts went covered from head to foot.

One tale that Sira Jon was eager to hear was that of Bjorn's travels to Bethlehem, and Bjorn did remember a great deal about this little city, which, he said, was long and narrow and surrounded by a sturdy wall. And Bethlehem was set in a pleasant district of plains and woodland and a lovely church which was set on the place where Jesus was born. Inside this church, exactly at the spot, could be found a rich chapel, painted with silver, gold, azure, crimson, and all the colors a man could think of. Three paces from this is the crib, and beside that the spot where the star fell from the heavens that led the three kings to worship the new babe. Here Einar interrupted and declared that although these kings are known to Christians as Balthazar, Melchior, and Gaspar, they are known to other peoples by other names, to wit, the Greeks call them Galgalathe, Malgalathe, and Saraphie, but the Jews call them otherwise in Hebrew: Appelius, Amerrius, and Damasus. These kings, Bjorn said, had a miraculous journey, for everyone in the holy places will tell you that they met each other in a city called Cassak, which is further east from Jerusalem by fifty-three days' journey, and yet they arrived in Bethlehem after twelve days.

But there are other things in Bethlehem, also, namely the charnel house of the Innocents, where the bones of all the babes who were slaughtered by Herod are kept, and near that the tomb of St. Jerome, and outside this tomb sits the chair St. Jerome sat upon while he was translating the Bible and the Psalter from Hebrew into Latin. And near to this church is the church of St. Nicholas, where the Virgin rested after giving birth, and in these red marble stones can be seen the white traces of her milk, for when she came here, her breasts were full and painful, and she milked them and the milk fell on the red stones. Bjorn had seen this for himself. Bjorn had considered Bethlehem a very fine city, and much admired the vineyards round about, for Bethlehem is inhabited solely by Christians, who make good wine. Here Einar broke in again and explained that the Mohammedans drink no wine because their prophet, Mohammed, is said to have killed a holy man in drink. They also, Einar said, eat no pork, for they consider swine to be men's brothers, and though the Greenlanders quizzed him about this, Einar declared it to be true. Such were some of the marvels related by Bjorn Einarsson Jorsalfari and his foster son when they came to Greenland. The Greenlanders could not get enough of their tales.

One day Bjorn and Einar and some servingmen went on a skiing trip to Vatna Hverfi and Hvalsey Fjord, where they visited St. Birgitta's church, for they had heard of its fair proportions and excellent stonework, and Bjorn wanted to make acquaintance with Sira Pall Hallvardsson. When Pall Hallvardsson brought them into the church, Birgitta Lavrans-dottir was there with her daughter Gunnhild, who was some eleven winters old. In addition to Gunnhild, Helga, and Kollgrim, Birgitta now had two more daughters, Astrid and Maria, and she was far gone with a sixth child. Although there had been some news of the travelers from other districts, this was the first time Birgitta had seen Bjorn, and she and Gunnhild curtsied politely. Gunnhild stared mightily at the man's clothing, for it was full of many colors, and his hat touched the top of the doorway as he came into St. Birgitta's church. Bjorn in turn stared mightily at Gunnhild, for she was growing into a handsome child, as tall and blond as Gunnar's lineage, but with the round softness of Birgitta. At the sight of her, Bjorn laughed and said, "I had thought there were no trees in Greenland," and Birgitta smiled and said, "Such trees as there are grow in clefts and valleys far from the paths of men." And so it came about that Pall Hallvardsson and Bjorn and Einar were invited to visit Lavrans Stead and have a sight of all the Gunnarsdottirs, who were all much like Gunnhild, although Birgitta considered Gunnhild the handsomest, and of Kollgrim, who was no different, except a boy and therefore more troublesome and more delightful.

Lavrans Stead was somewhat bigger now than it had been, with two new rooms, a small one for storage and a large one for bedding down all of the children. Lavrans himself was old and much bent with the joint ill, and suffering greatly in the winter from the cold, which always makes the joint ill more painful. It was the duty of Gunnhild and Helga to sit beside him and fetch things for him and prevent Kollgrim from teasing him, for Kollgrim was a great tease, and could be persuaded to leave no one alone. Olaf said he was possessed with an imp who could be seen winking out of the boy's eyes from time to time, but Birgitta said that Olaf had grown sour from the day they left Gunnars Stead, and Gunnar said nothing. Bjorn and Einar were full of praise for the children, for their height and for their fat cheeks, and Birgitta declared that through the efforts of Finn Thormodsson, Gunnar's family had not yet gone hungry through a single

Lenten season, although other families in the district had not been so fortunate, and she said this in such a way that Gunnar laughed at her and declared that she was swollen, not with another child, but with pride.

It happened in the early spring, sometime around the feast of the Virgin, that a group of men who were all prosperous farmers, and from every district, went to Gardar where Bjorn Einarsson was staying and proposed to him that he should undertake the position and duties of district judge and revenue officer for the Norwegian king. And the men offered Bjorn the following compensation: the right to farm Foss and Thjodhilds Stead and in addition one hundred and thirty legs of mutton, as well as other valuable wares. Some folk said that the Greenlanders were too dazzled by the wealth and energy of the Icelander, and that such difficulties as Greenlanders found themselves in, they themselves could relieve without the expense of the mutton and other goods. But others said that Kollbein Sigurdsson had left the two farmsteads in poor condition, and Bjorn was an energetic man with many servants and sailors who could be easily put to work. These folk also looked at Bjorn's ships and his goods and his character, and declared that such a man would be a valuable fellow to have about, but would hardly stay if there was no compensation through revenue gathering or other means. And so Bjorn Einarsson Jorsalfari, a famous and singular man, was induced to remain in Greenland when he had intended to depart. In this year, he traded a great deal for the goods of the Greenlanders, for his ships were full of desirable cargo, and there were Greenlandic stuffs that he wanted to have for himself or to carry back to Bergen for trade. And, in addition to this, it was the Greenlanders' law, passed at the Thing after the departure of the *Olafssuden,* that visiting ships had to take trade goods with them and not only provisions. Another thing also happened, and this was that those Greenlanders who had been trading quietly with the skraelings since the death of Ragnvald began talking more about it, and bringing out their goods, and some of these goods—ivories, fine furs—pleased Bjorn immensely.

In the later spring, after Bjorn and his folk were installed at their farm, Einar, Bjorn's foster son, came to Hvalsey Fjord with the intention of visiting Pall Hallvardsson and showing him some of the writing he had done on his journeys with Bjorn, for he was well trained and had a fine hand. Pall Hallvardsson kept six manuscripts at St. Birgitta's church, four of which he had written out himself, including the little book he had taught Gunnar Asgeirsson to read out of, another which he had received as a gift upon his ordination, and still another, this one very small, which he had purchased as a young man in Ghent, and this one was his favorite, for it contained twelve small pictures, one for each month of the year, showing what folk did as the days of the year went by.

After this, Einar let Pall Hallvardsson look over his writings, and they were extensive, covering many rolls of parchment, and Einar said that he was much afraid to let these rolls out of his possession to have them copied, and yet he himself did not have the time to copy them. While Einar was beside him, Pall Hallvardsson read aloud what Einar had written down about Spain, France, and England, and Einar interrupted him and added bits and pieces that he remembered, for example, that the fellow called Wat the Tiler, who brought about the burning and smashing of a great palace in London, had called for the breakup of church lands, so that poor folk would have them and priests and bishops and even archbishops would be sent upon the roads, begging, and furthermore, these words were not surprising to Englishmen, and were often in the mouths of others who were more respectable. But Einar and Bjorn and Solveig had had to stay indoors during these disruptions, for it was the practice of these wild peasant folk to hunt down men from foreign countries and club them to death. Pall Hallvardsson replied that there had recently been more killings in Greenland, as well, a sure sign of the sinfulness of man and the evil of the times, but Einar declared that such killings as these done in England were not like killings among men who had enmity for one another because of feuding; they were more like a plague or a curse of God, for the killers came in a group and were fired with a frenzy such as a Berserk might be, and their victim's every action, of meekness or challenge, inflamed them further, and the only thing that quelled them was fear for their lives, when they saw that armored knights on horseback were about to go among them with swords and spears. At this, they would begin to run away, and trample each other and in turn get trampled by the plunging horses, and all this time the knights would be laughing and cheering, for they, too, were inflamed with hatred as with a madness. Now Pall Hallvardsson and Einar fell silent, contemplating the English, who in all stories appear to glory in slaughter, as it is said by the poet, Thorkel Skallason:

> *It is true that killing in England*
> *Will be a long time ending.*

And so Einar Bjarnarfostri stayed for some days at Hvalsey Fjord as a guest of Sira Pall Hallvardsson, and each day he met Gunnhild Gunnarsdottir, and he greatly admired her looks and demeanor, and the result was that on the last day of his visit, he approached Gunnar Asgeirsson and asked to be betrothed to the child, though she was but twelve winters old.

"Everyone can see," Einar declared, "that my foster father Bjorn is a wealthy man, and possessed of great luck. I have land of my own in Iceland, close by Bjorn's farm in Reykholar, and I have servingmen to work it, and servingwomen to ease the labor of my wife. In addition to this, my wife would be a great friend and cherished relation of Solveig Ogmundsdottir, who would surely act as a mother to the girl." And he smiled, for it was clear to him that such an offer as his for any Greenland girl, even a girl as handsome as Gunnhild, would not come again.

All of this time, Gunnar was sitting apart on a rock, repairing a fishing net, and he continued to work at the project until it was finished, then he put it aside. Now he looked up at Einar and said, "Because we are Greenlanders does not mean that we don't know the forms of such things. No man comes without friends to the household of the woman he desires, unless he thinks that the household is of little importance." He got up and carried his net across the yard into the boathouse, and Einar saw that he was much offended. The next day, Einar returned to Gardar, and there was no more talk of this matter.

One day later in the spring, when the hillsides had begun to green up and only small icebergs floated in the fjord, Birgitta was pacing back and forth in front of the farmstead, spinning. Her time was near, and she was very great with child; it was intolerable for her to be within the steading. And as she was walking back and forth, she looked toward the water, where the five children were gathering seaweed, even Maria, the youngest, who was but two winters old. As she looked at them, and thought of the child within her, they seemed to vanish, so that their cries to one another were silenced and the strand was empty and the sea behind it cold and gray. Now Birgitta dropped her spindle and put her face in her hands, and when she looked up again, the water of the fjord was blue and the children had reappeared, as they were before, running about and dropping bits of seaweed into the yellow basket. Sometime later, Gunnar and Olaf came down from the sheepfold, and Birgitta took Gunnar's elbow and held it until Olaf washed himself and went inside, then she said to Gunnar, "This man Einar is something above thirty winters old, and has had one wife already, but he is much accomplished and allied to a great man. Perhaps Bjorn will not go from Greenland at all. Perhaps these farms here are better than those he has in Iceland."

Gunnar stood gazing upon the children, who had begun to drag the basket up the hillside. He said, "A man with four ships must leave."

Now they were silent for a space, and then Birgitta said, "It seems to me that Gunnhild is fated to go with him, for just now I saw her vanish before me." After this, they did not discuss the matter again.

Now the summer came on, and Birgitta gave birth to yet another daughter, and she was baptized with the name Johanna, and she was the largest of all the children, and born with a full head of hair and a tooth in her lower jaw, and people spoke of this, for such children, it is said, come into the world with ideas of their own. Birgitta found in herself an unaccountable dislike for this child, and left its care much to Gunnhild and Helga. Johanna was born while Olaf, Gunnar, and Finn were away for the seal hunt, and when Gunnar returned he looked for a long time at the baby and she lay awake without crying and looked back at him, and he declared himself pleased with her, and from this time Johanna stuck to her father as Kollgrim had always followed after his mother.

Of Kollgrim, there is this to say, that he was a great wanderer, and he was known at all the farmsteads round about and at Pall Hallvardsson's priesthouse across the water. It happened at this time, while Gunnar was away hunting for seals and Birgitta was occupied with Johanna, that Kollgrim was walking past a neighboring farmstead and two boys, Hrolf and Hakon, came out of the byre with their dog, who was a large deerhound by breed, but not fully grown. This dog, seeing Kollgrim, broke away from the two boys and ran at Kollgrim, baring its teeth and knocking him down. Now Kollgrim felt a stone beside his hand and picked it up and brought it down hard on the dog's head, so that the dog's skull was broken and the dog died. Then the boys came up, and Kollgrim jumped to his feet, declaring it was unneighborly to set such a beast upon a guiltless passerby, and he fell upon Hrolf, the older boy, although without the stone, and he beat him. This boy was not quite Kollgrim's age, and certainly not his size. Hakon ran to get a servingman, as the farmer, Harald, was also away on the seal hunt. This servingman was carrying a staff, and struck Kollgrim with it on the side of the head, and at this the boys ceased fighting.

When Gunnar and Harald returned from the seal hunt, Gunnar paid Harald two sealskins as compensation for the death of the dog and the beating of Hrolf. Birgitta was much annoyed to get nothing for the dog attack and the blow to Kollgrim's head, and Gunnar and Birgitta had words about this. In addition, Kollgrim was forbidden visiting Haralds Stead, but he went there often anyway, for it seemed that now he would not or could not forbear teasing this boy Hrolf, as he had teased his grandfather and his sisters and Olaf and everyone else.

One day shortly after this, Birgitta sat down beside Lavrans, who now stayed beside the fire, for he was some sixty-five winters old or more. This was the first time Birgitta had gotten up after her confinement, and she carried the new baby with her to show to her father. For a little while, Lavrans held the child in his arms and admired her size and her clothing, for Birgitta had woven a new white shawl for her, and decorated it with handsome woven bands. Then Birgitta leaned over his shoulder and put her finger in the infant's mouth and felt around gently until she found the tiny tooth, and she said, "Don't folk say that such a tooth brings ill luck to the whole lineage?"

Lavrans replied, "Such a thing was never spoken in my hearing, but it may be."

"I am afraid for the others."

Now Lavrans looked at her for a while, and then he said, "Such pride as I had in you, which folk laughed at, and such doting as I fell into, which folk once marveled at, you show tenfold, and fivefold for the boy alone. The priests say it is a sin to love a child more than God Himself. The truth is that God is jealous and powerful and well pleased to take our cherished idols for His own."

"I can't help it that they fill up my eyes with their beauty and winsome ways."

Now Lavrans waited for a long time, then he spoke in a low voice. "One at least blinds your sight. One at least has brought you some ill luck already, more than a newborn babe has brought you. One at least will do much harm before he does good, because the devil draws him on."

"He is lively, indeed, but not ill disposed."

"He is disposed to do as he pleases until everyone around him is displeased. Then he is content."

Now Birgitta stood up, and she was much offended, and she took the new baby from her father and put her in the bedcloset, and after this Birgitta chatted little with her father, and always spoke to him in a cool and formal tone of voice.

In the middle of the summer, sometime around the feast of St. Benedikt, a ship painted bright colors and sporting a red and white sail rode into Hvalsey Fjord, and stood off Lavrans' tiny landing until Gunnar, who was herding sheep down by the water, motioned it to approach. This was a ship belonging, of course, to Bjorn Einarsson, and Bjorn and Einar and twelve other men, including Thorkel Gellison, disembarked. Gunnar made them welcome and asked after the news in Vatna Hverfi district and at Gardar, and Thorkel told him the following tale:

At the previous Yule, Vigdis, the wife of Erlend Ketilsson, declared herself divorced from Erlend, although they had never been married by a priest, and moved away from Ketils Stead and installed herself with a steward and six servants and Jon Andres Erlendsson at Gunnars Stead, and when folk, such as beggars and travelers, came about looking for hospitality and gossip, she sent them off speedily without either. Erlend, on the other hand, seemed willing to entertain everyone in the district, and sent out messengers inviting folk to not one but two feasts, except that when folk arrived for the first of these feasts, Erlend had made no preparations, and acted as if he had invited no one, and when folk arrived for the second of these feasts, more to see what was going on than in the expectation of festivities, he served up much food, but it was all nearly rotten or badly cooked, and he spent the whole time making much of one of his servants, a fat, gap-toothed girl who dressed herself in all of Vigdis' finest gowns, and all at once, one on top of the other.

After these feasts, Vigdis stopped being so unfriendly, and indeed, invited folk to Gunnars Stead and made them talk of Erlend and Ketils Stead and this servingmaid until they were hoarse, for she couldn't get enough of any tale. And in addition to this, she had her servants take down the stone wall around the great field Erlend had won from Asgeir and Gunnar, and rebuild it so that the field was again part of Gunnars Stead, and any of Erlend's servants who were found trying to manure the field were driven off by Vigdis' servants.

And after Thorkel told this tale, which the Lavrans Stead folk found very interesting, Bjorn took Gunnar aside and asked for Gunnhild Gunnarsdottir as a bride for Einar his foster son, and he listed all of Einar's assets in Iceland and said also that he had given Einar the very ship that they had sailed in to Hvalsey Fjord, which was a large enough ship for seafaring, but nimble and neat. And Gunnar replied, as all men do, that he would leave the decision to his daughter, though he had no doubt that she would agree, but he made one condition, on account of the girl's age, that she stay at home, only betrothed, until she was the age that Birgitta had been on her marriage, and, should Bjorn choose to leave Greenland before that time, that she would go away under the protection of Solveig Ogmundsdottir, and live with her as a daughter until she reached the proper age. Bjorn and Einar agreed to this condition, and after that, the men from the ship stayed for two days, feasting and celebrating the betrothal.

When it came time for them to leave, Gunnar had a great desire to go with them on the ship, although it was only going to Gardar, and it was arranged that he and Sira Pall Hallvardsson would go on the ship and then return in Gunnar's big boat, which would be towed along behind. And Gunnar agreed to return some five days hence, the night before Sira Pall Hallvardsson held his Sunday service. At the last minute it was agreed that Kollgrim would go along.

When they went onto the ship, Gunnar was much impressed, for the ship was deeper and wider than she looked from the outside, and had room for a fair number of goods. In addition to this, she was built of six different kinds of wood, including a tall, straight Norwegian fir trunk for the mast. The pieces of the keel were neatly joined, and the strakes nailed to the hull with wooden pegs. This ship, Bjorn declared, had never been damaged, for it was but six years old. Indeed, the carving along the gunwales and the prow, of leaping fish entwined with galloping reindeer, was fresh and sharp. All of the lines and casks and planking and other equipment was of the finest sort.

Passage to Gardar, out of Hvalsey Fjord and up Einars Fjord to the Gardar landing, took but half a day, for Bjorn caught a good wind, and the ship sailed quickly. As a rule, men from Hvalsey Fjord counted on two days when rowing to Gardar, and would stop for the night at Sudarstrand, where men from Vatna Hverfi kept a landing and some pasturage.

When they arrived at Gardar, they saw that Sira Jon had been looking out for them, for he himself ran down to the landing place and began at once greeting Bjorn Einarsson and asking him questions. Before the ship was even drawn up on the strand, he was hurrying everyone up to the Gardar hall for food and other refreshments. Sometime later he began asking Bjorn how long he would be staying, and how quickly he cared to return to the farms he had been given, and it was apparent to Gunnar that Sira Jon did not mean to let the other man go.

Sira Jon was much older-looking now. What hair he had about the sides of his head was nearly gray, and his cheeks had sunk so that his eyes blazed out somewhat as Bishop Alf's had done. But he did not draw himself up proudly, as his uncle had, and instead seemed to hang his head before Bjorn as a dog does before its master. His face composed itself into youthful smiles and eager looks, and Gunnar saw Pall Hallvardsson watching him from afar. After eating he took Bjorn aside and showed him the accounts and told him the news of Gardar even though Bjorn had only been away for some ten days or so. He also spoke loudly of a dream that had come to him the night before. In this dream, which all about were able to hear, Sira Jon was transported to the cathedral at Nidaros, except that this cathedral was more magnificent even than that one, and looked as Bishop

Alf had often described the great cathedrals he had known as a young man. In this cathedral, hundreds of folk in brilliant clothing sat bowed in prayer, and the colored light of the surrounding glass played over them. Now, at the far end, a great priest arose, and this was the archbishop of Nidaros, although his name was never mentioned, and he declared as he stood before them that he was consecrating his greatest bishop and sending him to Greenland in a giant ship, and this ship would be carrying to Greenland all manner of wealth, from the most mundane sorts of seed and tar to the richest and most beautiful of golden vessels and wallhangings, and he lifted one of these last up, and the colors of the glass penetrated it, and glowed within it. And then, as if by a miracle, Sira Jon had seen himself running down to the landing and greeting this bishop and making him welcome, and he had risen from the dream and prayed a great prayer of thanks to the Lord for communicating his purposes to Sira Jon, for this dream bore all the marks of a prophecy, namely that he dreamt it in the morning, and that he had eaten nothing before going to bed but the blandest and mildest of foods.

Now, after this, Sira Jon and the others expressed the hope that these things were indeed true, and that a new bishop would be arriving soon, and some folk spoke of the dream in one way, as a prophecy, and others spoke of it in another way, as a delusion, but Bjorn only listened and nodded and did not enter into gossip concerning the dream. After these events, Bjorn and Einar approached Sira Jon with the news of Einar's betrothal to Gunnhild Gunnarsdottir, and then Gunnar stepped forward and greeted Sira Jon and was greeted politely in return, except that after every sentence Sira Jon glanced at Bjorn as he had once glanced at Bishop Alf. Then Gunnar brought Kollgrim forward and introduced him, for Kollgrim had never visited Gardar before, and Kollgrim stepped up boldly, kissed Sira Jon's ring, and then, rather than stepping back, stood and stared freely into the priest's face, with his eyes wide open and challenging, for indeed, Kollgrim had never learned to veil his gaze in a courteous manner. Gunnar stood to the side of him, and a little behind, and did not interfere, but only watched the priest and the boy with evident amusement. When Sira Jon finally turned away, somewhat agitated, Gunnar only smiled and said to Sira Pall Hallvardsson, "So, we are not made better friends by this branch of the Asgeir lineage." Sira Pall Hallvardsson shook his head with disapproval.

Shortly after this, it got to be time for everyone on the place to retire, for the three priests, with Pall Hallvardsson, kept canonical hours, and so Gunnar and Kollgrim were shown a small chamber with a seal oil dish for

light and heat and a pile of reindeer hides on the floor for them to sleep
upon and wrap themselves in. Kollgrim was very disdainful of these
provisions and declared that the floor stank, although no one had inhabited
the room in a number of winters and Gunnar did not find the room
unusually dirty. By the dim, flickering light of the lamp, Gunnar spread
out the reindeer skins to make a soft bed for his son, then tucked others
tightly about the boy. Finally, he lay down and settled himself to go to
sleep, but Kollgrim would take no rest. He bounced and fidgeted, threw
off his coverings, and turned awry so that his foot was in Gunnar's belly.
Gunnar sat up and looked at him by the light of the lamp and saw that,
though his eyes were open, the boy was nearly asleep. Gunnar lay down
again. But still the boy wiggled beside him so that every time sleep came,
Kollgrim sent it off again. Gunnar sat up. Kollgrim was still in this state
of open-eyed dreaming that he had been in before, and Gunnar found this
oddly provoking, although as a rule, he did not often allow himself to be
provoked to anger about anything. It was true that when he was angered,
it was Kollgrim more often than not who had caused it. Now the boy cried
out pettishly in his sleep, as if put out by something, and Gunnar leaned
over and shook him until he seemed to wake up, but when Gunnar spoke
his name in a sharp voice, the boy made no response. Gunnar shook him
again. Kollgrim's eyes closed. At last, Gunnar dealt the boy a blow upon
the side of the head, and he woke up.

If there needed to be any proof that an imp was in partial possession
of the child, then this was it, that after jumping about so, and causing such
difficulty, Kollgrim opened his eyes, with their fan of lashes, and looked
at Gunnar in guileless question, as innocent and well disposed as any child
could be, as Johanna herself looked when she awakened between Birgitta
and Gunnar in the morning. Now Gunnar said, "It is true, boy, that my
father Asgeir was greatly disappointed with me, and went about asking
whether he could change my name from Gunnar, which was the name of
his father, to Ingvi, which was a strange name, and the name of a stranger,
my mother's father in Iceland. But it seems to me that he would have been
much pleased with the likes of you, for you bustle about, even in your
sleep, as Asgeir bustled about from dawn to dark on the longest days."

"Lavrans sits all day in his chair beside the fire."

"Lavrans is close to seventy winters old, and much afflicted in his
joints. But my father was some forty-five or forty-eight winters when he
died, still a young man with bright yellow hair, although he seemed to
me at the time as old and set in his ways and bitter to me as Lavrans does
to you."

"Did he greet you angrily, as Lavrans does me?"

"Every time he saw me, his countenance fell, for all folk considered me a do-nothing, and it is true that it seemed for a time as if a sleeping curse was upon me, especially after my father's brother was killed on the ice far to the north."

"Did he go among the skraelings?"

"Hauk Gunnarsson went often among the skraelings, and was not averse to their ways. He wore the skins of birds for his underclothing, and my old nurse was greatly scandalized at such a thing. But folk didn't speak of the skraelings then as they do now, for the skraelings hadn't shown their true devilish natures, and hadn't killed Christians as they have now. Nor were they about in such numbers as they are now. Hauk Gunnarsson ate his meat raw sometimes, at the end of winter, as skraelings do, and foxes and bears, and he said it wasn't a sin to do so, but a necessity in the far north, where the world is white from year's end to year's end."

"Lavrans is a do-nothing, and yet everyone serves him, day and night."

"After a long day, folk rest at night. After a long summer, folk play games and sit about in the winter. After a long life folk sit about the fire and stay warm, for the chill of death is upon them, and even the thickest bearskin can't keep off the shivering."

"But folk say that Lavrans was never prosperous or hardworking, and that is why Lavrans Stead is so mean. And Gunnhild sometimes speaks of Gunnars Stead at night in bed, and she says that the fields and the lakes there were like the meadows of Paradise."

"It is true that Gunnars Stead is a fine farm, and any man would long from time to time for such a place. But when I see Lavrans beside the fire, I am fond of him, for this reason, that one time, after the death of Asgeir Gunnarsson, I went to the Thing at Gardar, and I had few friends, if any, and my booth was small and made of a piece of wadmal, not of white reindeer skins, as it is now. Although my father was Asgeir Gunnarsson and I lived at the great farm of Gunnars Stead, men pushed past me without seeing me, or they looked me up and down and recollected what was said about me and laughed into their beards. And so it happened that I wandered away from the Thing field, and I saw a young girl standing on the hillside, right on the hillside out there, where the Gardar stream runs down, before it divides and flows into the homefield."

"Was that girl my mother?"

"Indeed it was she, and she had just passed her fourteenth birthday. And now it happened that as I was looking at her, she turned her head and looked at me, and from that long way, I could see the blue color of her eyes, and I climbed the hill toward her, gazing at her eyes the whole way. She was not like any other girl I had known, for my sister was tall and much inside herself, and her hair was always braided perfectly, as if her head had been carved from stone, but Birgitta was slight and not a little disheveled. However, she looked at things as if her soul went out to them and fixed upon them. And so I went and sat down on the hillside next to her, and we talked and became friends, and it seemed to me that this young girl and only she would have the strength to save me and make me a man.

"The next day was the last day of the Thing, and all morning men were striking their booths and taking to their boats and leaving, and I knew that I should go to Lavrans, but I had no friends to take with me, and I was afraid. I also knew that Lavrans lived far away, in Hvalsey Fjord at the mouth of the fjord, and that the Hvalsey Fjorders were usually the first to leave. But I walked about in fear and did not approach him, and before long almost everyone was gone, and it was time for me to go, too, for I had come in a boat with a man from Vatna Hverfi who was eager to leave. Finally I saw that Lavrans' booth was still up, but that his servants were beginning to take it down, so in a panic I ran to where he was packing up his belongings, and I said that Birgitta Lavransdottir was my only friend in the whole world and I wished to have her for my wife. Now another man such as Asgeir or even myself as I am now, with five handsome daughters, might have knocked me down for such a speech, but Lavrans has never acted as other men do. He only smiled and looked at me with a gaze that was somehow like Birgitta's and somehow different, and less, perhaps, since Birgitta has second sight and Lavrans doesn't, and he said that such a thing was not as he had desired when the child was born, for then King Hakon had been an unmarried man, and available, but now, alas, the news was that King Hakon had taken Queen Margarethe to his wife, and so Birgitta Lavransdottir would have to look elsewhere, and in short, he gave her to me, and she did as I thought she would, though she was but a child, and I even more of a child, though five winters older."

Now Kollgrim yawned and declared that this was a nice tale for Gunnar to tell, but not as nice as the tale of the Sandnes polar bear, who used to speak to folk at a big farm in the western settlement just as they were falling asleep or waking from sleep, and tell them what the animals said about them. Kollgrim fell asleep against him, and Gunnar slipped him among the reindeer hides. Then he carried two or three hides away from the boy and settled himself down. The rooms at Gardar were so well turfed that the tiny lamp and their breath were enough to keep them warm all night.

There was much activity at Gardar, of animals and men and farm business and church business and other business. The news of Sira Jon's dream seemed to imbue everyone with a fresh sense of haste, and folk ran here and there, straightening, polishing, shining, and arranging, as if the new bishop's ship had already been sighted in the fjord. Even so, Gunnar felt a great longing for Lavrans Stead come upon him, so that every conversation seemed tedious to him, and all the news he gathered stale and dubious. Kollgrim was especially tiresome, for he refused to stay among the other children, and was always going among the cattle or wetting himself in the water below the landing spot. The day stretched out in length, and Gunnar spent much of it down by the water, admiring Einar's ship. Even among Bjorn's larger ones, this one attracted the eye by its trim lines.

For Sira Pall Hallvardsson, the day seemed to pass with painful quickness, for there was much to talk about, and not only to Sira Jon, with whom Pall Hallvardsson, of course, had business, but also with Sira Audun and the other boys and with folk from other districts who were visiting for various reasons. In fact, for the first time ever, Sira Pall Hallvardsson could not help conceiving something of a horror against returning to Hvalsey Fjord and the loneliness there. As a young man new in Greenland he had gone from district to district, filling in for absent priests and visiting many farmsteads, but now Sira Audun and an assistant, Gizur, did this, and they complained bitterly about it. It was hard to find boats, and hard to persuade folk to lend servants as rowers, and harder still to come to the churches, most of which had fallen into bad repair, especially in the southern part of the settlement, so that Sira Audun had written a verse, as follows:

> Men who come to cut turf with the priest
> Men who come to lift stones with the priest
> Women who come to sweep sand out of the church
> Women who change broken lamps for whole ones
> All these are as blessed as the kneelers;
> our Lord hears loudly their voiceless prayers.

But Sira Pall Hallvardsson expected that the younger man merely longed to be among the comforts of Gardar, and it was true, that being himself a Greenlander, Sira Audun would hardly be received with the sort of curiosity that had opened doors to himself. Sira Audun's father was a man well known in the south for parsimonious dealings with his neighbors, and perhaps Sira Audun was something like his father, or seen to be, which amounted to the same thing. Nonetheless, his hymns and verses were pleasing.

And now, the night before, Sira Audun had sat upon the tall stool in his room, where he entertained Sira Pall Hallvardsson for a few minutes, and he had said, "Indeed, brother, I little like to be away from here, and I always leave with a sense of apprehension and return with a sense of foreboding. I begin looking out for the buildings as soon as they can be seen, or for messengers sent out to meet me."

"What is it you fear, then?" said Sira Pall.

"Not that he will harm others."

Sira Pall did not need to ask who it might be who wouldn't harm others. He said, "He is busy and has all the threads of the bishopric sorted out in his hand."

"Even so."

"So what is it you fear?"

But Sira Audun could not say. Sira Pall walked off calmly, as if dismissing such concerns from his thoughts, but when he went in for his interview with Sira Jon, he could not help looking at him closely.

Of the condition of the church and steading at Hvalsey Fjord, the condition of the poor folk under the church's protection, and the size of the revenues he had received so far in the year from the Hvalsey Fjorders he spoke at length. He was careful to figure in repairs to St. Birgitta's sheep fold as well as the services of the younger Lavrans Stead ram, an animal of Birgitta Lavransdottir's own breeding, who produced exceptionally fine offspring even if the ewe was not very large or thick of wool. Sira Jon became annoyed with these items, and declared, "Is it in such bits and pieces that you expect the church to eke out her due?" but Sira Pall Hallvardsson was not disconcerted, and said only "Yes" in a mild and soothing tone of voice. In addition to these things enumerated, Sira Pall Hallvardsson went on, St. Birgitta's church had a great excess of whale meat and whale oil left over from the winter, and these commodities could easily be transported to Gardar for use there.

"Such oil always burns with a stink that is repellent to us, worse even than seal oil. And the meat is good only for dogs after a day or so, even if it has been dried."

After his report, Sira Pall Hallvardsson knelt before the other priest, thinking that the other man would never accommodate himself to life among the Greenlanders, and then he made his confession, and among the sins he confessed was covetousness toward Einar, the foster son of Bjorn Jorsalfari, for even on such a journey as the visitors were on, Einar went daily among writings and books and manuscripts as Pall Hallvardsson hadn't seen since his boyhood in Ghent, and he spoke of authors, and recited fragments of poetry in Latin and Norse and German as set Pall Hallvardsson's heart afire with longing. In addition to this, Einar was now betrothed to the child Gunnhild Gunnarsdottir, a child Pall Hallvardsson had always known well and felt much love for, as she was beautiful and good-natured and like unto her mother in the calmness of her temperament. And these thoughts of the books and the girl, not to mention the travels, tormented his thoughts, although he liked Einar well enough.

This confession seemed, for a time, to render Sira Jon speechless, for he said nothing, and his silence drew Sira Pall Hallvardsson onward, to speak more and more fully of what it was that he envied of the Icelander. Now, Sira Jon cut him short with a brief sentence of absolution, then suddenly ran off, and some while later, Pall Hallvardsson heard him speaking to one of the servingwomen. At the evening meal, he presided with his customary aplomb, only, as usual, glancing often at Bjorn, who was eating beside him. When Pall Hallvardsson came out of the hall, Einar was nearby, in the yard, and Pall Hallvardsson went up to him, for indeed, he could not stay away from the man, for as folk say, when envy does not engender hatred, it engenders love, and this was what happened to Sira Pall Hallvardsson.

There were folk who did not care for Einar, for he was always ready to contradict what was being said, and to take a greater part in the conversation than some thought proper. In addition to this, he could not forbear correcting folk. If a man declared that a cool but rainy summer was better for the hay than a sunny but dry one, Einar was sure to insist the opposite. After this, a few would offer stories of the starvation of eight winters before, when no rain at all fell until after the hay crop was all burned up, but Einar persisted with tales of the grass rotting in the fields and the hooves of livestock softening and disintegrating, and the weight of his stories was so great that talk would stop.

Or discussion would arise of the efficacy of certain relics. St. Olaf's finger bone at Gardar would be recalled to have cured a madness, and Einar would declare that the relics of St. Olaf were well known for curing scrofula and other skin ills, but not for curing madness. At this someone would assert that his father or grandfather had been there when the cure took place, or was a member of the household, at which Einar would declare that in that case, it must not be the finger bone of St. Olaf, but of some other saint, perhaps St. Hallvard, or even a saint from Germany or France, such as St. Clothilda or St. Otto, and folk did not know how to answer these notions, for they had not heard of these saints, and hesitated to admit it. It was true that Einar's tales had this effect on people, that when he was finished speaking, they were reluctant to admit how little they knew in comparison to him. It was also the case that he often corrected his foster father when Bjorn related tales or made talk, but Bjorn did not mind, and indeed, thanked the younger man for remembering things he himself had forgotten.

Nevertheless, like Bjorn, Einar was a generous and interested man, as free with tales and trinkets from abroad as he was with advice. Best of all, he was of the sort of sanguine temperament that doesn't recognize when it is giving offense, and so he felt no enmity for others, and received none. When folk heard of the betrothal to Gunnhild Gunnarsdottir, they cocked their heads wisely and declared among themselves that the Gunnar Stead lineage would certainly bring some much needed pulchritude to the lineage of the Icelanders. But mostly it was a lucky match for Gunnar, who was a man of little luck, after all.

Now Einar began to talk to Sira Pall Hallvardsson of the cattle before them in the Gardar pen. These cattle now numbered about forty, including spring calves, who were just being weaned, and Einar was not much impressed with them; he had seen better in Denmark, Germany, even Iceland. And now he told a tale of Iceland, in which someone he knew desecrated a small chapel by using it for a lambing fold in the early spring. And this man lived near a volcano, and one day some vapors rose out of the volcano in the gray cloud and settled upon the farmer's pastures, and after this his cattle and sheep grew quickly, but in distorted and monstrous ways—their teeth grew out of their mouths so that they could not feed, and their hooves grew long and curved backward toward their pasterns and one or two legs grew more quickly than the others, so that the animals could not stand or walk and were in great pain, so that those who didn't die the farmer had to kill himself and he was reduced to a beggar and had to go out to the farms of other folk as a servingman.

Sira Pall Hallvardsson had no tale to match this one, so he only said that when he first came out to Greenland, there had been almost a hundred cattle in the pasture, all fat and glossy, with these same lovely white marks upon them. And the Gardar sheep had numbered in the hundreds, and of all possible colors, and in addition there had been many goats, ten horses, a half dozen or so pigs, and many dogs, both of the reindeer hunting breed

and of a smaller black and white breed that was sometimes used by herders
to ease their work, but these were no longer found much at Gardar or
Brattahlid, though more in the southern parts of Vatna Hverfi district.

Einar declared that these deer hunting dogs were fine beasts, but not
as fine as those you might see among the Irish, dogs whose backs came up
to a man's waist and who were coursed against wolves as large as themselves. And now he told about Ireland, where everything is greater than
everywhere else—the grass is greener, the wolves and dogs and horses are
larger, the hermits more austere, the folk more violent, the women more
beautiful, the rich men richer and the poor men poorer. And so he went
on, and it seemed to Sira Pall Hallvardsson that he was lolling in a wealth
of words. Now the great bell of Gardar began to toll vespers and Einar
and Pall Hallvardsson strolled toward the cathedral, talking of the Irish.

In the morning, as they were rowing in Einars Fjord, which was still
and blue so that the icebergs sat in the water like stones, Pall Hallvardsson
said to Gunnar that the tale was that along with Margret and her servingwoman, Asta, there was a boychild of some three or four winters of age
running about, and it seemed to folk that he was dark-haired and flat of
cheek, as if he were of skraeling lineage, and Gunnar made no response
to this, for it was his habit never to speak of Margret and never to act as
if he had heard her spoken of. When, at the end of the next day, they rowed
up to the landing place at Lavrans Stead, he was much pleased to see his
wife and daughters, though not as pleased as he expected to be. And that
evening, telling the news, Lavrans Stead seemed quiet and small to him,
and he could not help a longing for the business and wealth of Gardar.

It was true that a child lived at Steinstraumstead with Margret and
Asta, and his name was Sigurd. He was the son of Asta Thorbergsdottir.
The father of this child was the skraeling boy who had once asked her hand
in marriage. He had two wives who were skraelings and spent most of his
time in the east or the north, or at any rate away from Steinstraumstead,
but he visited Asta two times each year, once at Yule time, at Brattahlid,
when he brought with him rich gifts of sealmeat, furs, and walrus tusks
and once in the summer, when he brought child's clothing fashioned by
his two wives as well as other provisions such as he had gathered in his
summer hunting. He spoke no Norse, and he always came by himself. Asta
spoke none of the skraeling tongue. But she dressed herself carefully for
these visits, prepared rich foods, and looked out eagerly for his skin boat.
Although his name was Quimiak, she called him Koll.

Of Sigurd, both she and Margret were very fond. He had no regular
tasks and was carried everywhere by one or the other of the women and

was made to eat only what he wished to eat and was allowed to speak out no matter who was speaking, and the two women fell silent to hear what he had to say, although it was also true that as a rule he was laconic in the manner of skraeling children. He was not handsome, but he was big and strong, like Asta, and looked much like her, except for his straight black hair. He thought very well of himself, Brattahlid folk said.

Of other matters at Steinstraumstead, there is this to say, that Asta and Margret had made of the place a simple but comfortable steading, and by living with great austerity, they managed to stay there from the time when the ice broke up in Eriks Fjord almost until Yule every year. Margret had gotten for herself ten ewes, and from their milk she made an excellent quantity of cheese, for the pasturage above the tiny steading was rich and little used. All the steadings up that side of Eriks Fjord were abandoned and she could pasture them for a great distance along the fjord and also as far back into the mountains as the glacier. At Yule they went with her across the fjord to Brattahlid and were bred to Osmund's ram. Also in the summer she spun a great deal of wool and in the winter she wove this into wadmal for the use of folk at Brattahlid, as well as for clothing for herself, Asta, and Sigurd. She was quick at the loom, and was pleased to show the Brattahlid servants what she remembered of the patterns Kristin the wife of Thord of Siglufjord had taught her long ago. Her hair was completely white and her body as thin and hard as a whale bone. She was some forty winters old, and still suffered little if at all from the joint ill. She no longer complained of her dreams. She no longer had recourse to Sira Isleif, and had not taken communion or made a confession in three summers. Sira Isleif was afraid to approach her concerning this matter, for he was a timid man, especially since the death of Marta Thordardottir some two winters before.

Some things were changed at Steinstraumstead, and one of these happened as follows: one day when Sigurd was sitting at his meat, he knocked over his cup of ewe's milk and spilled it into the moss that lay upon the floor of the steading. At once he began to cry, because he was very fond of this drink, and sorry to lose his. Now it happened that Asta, without speaking or considering, took up the other cup of ewe's milk at the table and placed it in front of Sigurd, and he drank it down. This cup of milk belonged to Margret, and at once Asta realized this, and was stricken with mortification, and she and Margret gazed upon each other's faces without speaking for some moments. Then Margret smiled, for she was amused, and she said, "Although you are my servant, Asta, it seems to me that you grow to fill every nook of this place, and all things here flow to Sigurd. We spend our days consulting his pleasure as servants do a peevish master. You grow and flourish as richly as a patch of angelica by the side of a clear stream, but it seems to me that I shrink and harden and shrink and harden, and when I die I will be as a small pebble, and this is not frightening to me, but pleasant."

And Asta, because she had her child beside her, leaning into her so that she could feel the warmth of his body against hers, was somewhat offended by this remark and offered no reply. When Sigurd jumped up and wandered out of the steading, she, too, got up, and went to the vat of ewe's milk from that morning and dipped up another cupful for Margret. This Margret drank, and all of the rest of the evening, Asta dogged Margret's steps and helped her with tasks she was accustomed to doing herself and quieted Sigurd or sent him out of the way when he seemed to be annoying Margret, but by awakening time the next morning these things were forgotten, and Asta went back to thinking first of Sigurd in all things. Margret took some cheese and followed the sheep for the entire day, eating bilberries as she went about the hillsides, and this was a great pleasure to her.

At the farmstead, Asta had begun to look for Koll's visit, for it was at this time of the summer and in such weather, brisk and bright, that he often came to her. This waiting was little agreeable to her, for fear was mixed with eagerness so that she alternately dreaded and yearned for the first sudden meeting. On the one hand, she had grown familiar with and almost fond of Koll's face, so that it seemed as commonplace to her as any Norse face she knew. On the other hand, she had not gotten accustomed to the smell that arose from his clothing and his hands and his hair, and this came over her like a miasma, freshly each time. Fortunately, however, it seemed to go away after he had been near her for a while. Koll also seemed to share her fondness for Sigurd, whom he called by a name in the skraeling tongue. He always brought the boy exquisite gifts, finer even than those he had brought Asta to win her. The boy slept between two snowy white bearskins and as a baby had been swaddled in a length pieced from the fur of blue and white foxes. There were also carvings of ivory and two lamps of the skraeling style as well as various weapons and tools that Asta thought little of but kept for the boy.

As a balance to this anticipation, Asta had a great fear of Koll's other fondnesses when he saw her, for he came for the purpose of having intercourse, that was plain to see, and this activity seemed odd and not a little shocking. She had learned at his first reappearance, about a year after the marriage proposal, that to run or scream merely inflamed him and gave him greater strength. And yet the penetration itself, the pinning of her arms and the writhing of his flesh against her made her gasp and choke. This was a thing he wished to do many times during each visit. Each time he did it, Asta thought of Sira Isleif and regretted her sin, for this was sin indeed, but after each time was over, it seemed a small thing in retrospect, and little to pay for such boons as Sigurd and the gifts and, even, the fondness of Koll himself, who slapped her flanks and laughed at her flesh, and chattered about it in the skraeling tongue as if it were a thing of great beauty and pride to him.

Now she sat Sigurd in front of the steading with a basin of water and some other vessels, both whole and broken, and Sigurd set about pouring the water back and forth among the vessels. Then Asta went into the steading and carried out all of the skins of the two beds, and laid them on the hillside in the sun. Then she gathered some birch branches and lashed them together with a willow whip and began to beat the skins so that the fleas and lice rose out of them as well as dirt and dust. After that, she took a comb and set about combing the remaining vermin out of Sigurd's bearskins, and this was something she did four or five times in a summer, more often than most folk, because she was very particular about such things.

As she was engaged in this, Sigurd got up from his play and came over to the furs and began to lie down upon them and roll around on them, laughing merrily, for they were soft and clean and sweet to the skin, and though he was undoing her work, Asta was incapable of wrath at her son, and she merely laughed with him and knelt down and ruffled his hair and put her face close to his and looked at him. His mother's admiration moved the boy to jump up and begin running back and forth on the flat place in front of the steading, as fast as he could. Then he began to gather small stones and toss them down the hill toward the water, for it was his fixed desire to stand just in front of the steading and throw a stone so that it went into the water, although the strip of hillside was some fifty paces in width. He threw these stones with great intensity of thought, one after the other. Asta went back to her work, and finished combing the skins and began to carry them indoors.

In the shade of the steading was a vat of ewe's milk from the morning, and beside it a smaller one from the evening before. Asta went over to these and looked at the milk, then gathered some small pieces of driftwood and a clump of sheep's dung and built a small fire. On this she set a soapstone pot, and into that she poured the night's milk, letting it heat until she could just barely endure to touch it with her finger. Then she poured it out into the morning's milk. Now she went into the steading and got a small basin of buttermilk from the butter making of the day before, and poured it into the milk. After this she took Sigurd farther down the slope so that there would be no chance of his coming against the vat of milk or disturbing it in any way. She sat with him on the lower slope, looking across to Brattahlid, and she played with him a game that involved their four hands, where she put one of her hands down upon her leg, and he covered it with one of his, and she covered his, and he put his on top. Then she removed her bottom hand and put it on top, and he did the same, and they did this, taking turns, faster and faster. This was the one game Asta could remember playing as a child, and Sigurd enjoyed it very much and could go very fast without becoming confused. Then Asta got up and returned up the hill and gazed upon the vat of milk, and she put her finger into the mixture so that a hole was made that filled up with whey, and from this she knew that the curds were ready to be cut. She went into the steading and returned with a long blade made from the shoulder bone of a reindeer and sharpened, and she cut the curd four times, not hesitating to remove such pieces as Sigurd had a desire for, for fresh curd was a favorite treat with him. And so she went on with the cheesemaking, until the end of the day, when she set the cheese to drip over the vat, wrapped in a piece of clean wadmal and hanging from the eves of the steading by a hook made from a reindeer antler. And on this day, Koll made no appearance.

Margret returned with the sheep and folded them, and Sigurd went to her and was pleased to see her and carried to her some stones of peculiar shapes and made a gift of them to her. In return she presented him with an ancient ram's horn she had found near the old steading farther up the fjord, and when she came into the steading she could see that Koll had not yet come, and of this she was somewhat glad, for it seemed to her when he did come that it fell upon her as mistress to put a stop to these visits, and yet she could not bring herself to do it, and made many excuses and so he came like this every half year, drawing mistress and servant deeper and deeper into sin.

And after Sigurd went to the bedcloset, the two women sat spinning just outside the door of the steading, by the light of the late sun, and though they did this almost every night of the year, even at Brattahlid, these recent nights they did something else, also, and that was wait. And this new thing that they did made the customary spinning seem especially tedious and difficult. Margret saw that this is how it is that folk are made to desire what they know they should not have, they are made to wait for it, so that when it comes, no matter how dark and full of sin and repellent it is, they are glad enough to welcome it.

It happened that Bjorn Einarsson Jorsalfari stayed among the Greenlanders year after year, and he performed his office as the king's revenue officer just as they wished he might, for he took little revenue from them, and none that he did not pay for with some goods as the Greenlanders wished to have. He traded from time to time with the skraelings and got from them good wares. In addition to this, he saw to the punishment of two men who killed a third man, in the southern part of Vatna Hverfi district, and also of a man who killed his wife out of anger, a man who lived behind Brattahlid where the river came down to Isafjord. There were some boys who smashed up the boat of a neighbor, who were required by Bjorn to put the boat in good order, and there was other business that he did in the southern region, at Herjolfsnes, having to do with a dispute over a stranded whale (for Herjolfsnes sits at the outer reaches of Herjolfs Fjord, and the folk there often have such disputes) and at Arosvik he settled a dispute between the farmers and the church concerning services owed to the church, although the church building itself was in great disrepair and Sira Audun had refused to preach there, insisting instead that the Arosvik folk, of which there were about forty, journey to Petursvik for services. Bjorn Einarsson reprimanded both the folk of Arosvik and Sira Audun and made peace between them, and he decided other cases as well, in as judicious a manner as could be wished for. When he didn't sail away by the end of the second summer, folk ceased speculating when he would leave Greenland. He was much liked by all.

It happened that during Lent of Bjorn's third winter in Greenland there was a hunger similar to the hunger of twelve winters before, only it struck differently, so that the folk in Vatna Hverfi and to the south were greatly affected but the folk at Brattahlid and at Gardar and at Hvalsey Fjord, where the summer weather had been drier and brighter, were not so affected. And the first person to die in this famine was Erlend Ketilsson. This is how it came about. It was still the case that Erlend and Vigdis were living apart, the one at Ketils Stead and the other at Gunnars Stead, and some of the servants were living with one and some were living with the other, except that Erlend's servants had a habit of leaving him and going off to Gunnars Stead, for matters were better ordered there, and Vigdis, for all her niggardly ways, treated all fairly. There was much intercourse between the servants of both places, and when the servants who had stayed with Erlend gossiped with those who had gone with Vigdis, they were often persuaded to change places. Vigdis was much pleased by this, and rewarded any who came to her with extra food and pleasant tasks. In the meantime, she spoke evil of the servingmaid Ulfhild, who had recently had a daughter by Erlend.

Now this Ulfhild was only some eighteen winters in age, and the daughter of a servingwoman herself, and it was easy to see that she was not a little defeated by the variety of business at Ketils Stead. She did not see how it happened that the storehouses that had once been full had become empty and the servants who had once sat happily at the benches with their trenchers were now departed. As for Erlend, folk said that he fell upon the girl without resting or ceasing, even in the sinful time when she was with child. His antics raised a good deal of laughter about the district, and folk recalled how quickly Vigdis herself had produced a daughter and four sons, although only one of these was still alive.

At Gunnars Stead, though the summer was a cool and damp one, Vigdis' folk were out early and busily, manuring the fields where they could and making expeditions to the fjord for seaweed and to the hillside for angelica and bilberries. At Ketils Stead there was none of this, and what work the remaining servants did was done late and with little will, for the servants saw the idleness of the master and mimicked it.

The short tale of this is that Ketils Stead sheep were lost, cheeses went unmade, cows died in calving because no one was there to help them. Birds in the mountains went unsnared, herbs and berries went ungathered, and Ulfhild gave out things from the storehouses in the middle of summer. Still, everyone in the district was much taken with surprise when Erlend failed to send out messengers with invitations to the usual Ketils Stead feast, and were surprised again when only a few of the Ketils Stead folk appeared at Undir Hofdi church for the Yule services of Sira Audun. But it was also true that Erlend now drove people off sometimes when they came toward Ketils Stead, and so no one cared to go there. It was said that any number of new young women would have no effect on Erlend's temper, which used to be sour, was sour now, and would always be sour. In this fashion the days went by before and after Yule, until at last Vigdis yielded and sent one of her servingmen to Ketils Stead with a message, and this man went on skis and found the door to the steading drifted shut with snow, and when he got it open, he discovered only the dogs alive, and that because they had been gnawing the bones of the folk, which numbered five—Erlend, Ulfhild, two elderly servingmen, and the babe. And this was a tale told avidly in Vatna Hverfi district for a few weeks, until it became clear during Lent that this tale might not be the last such of the winter.

This mischance was followed by another one, this one in Hrafns Fjord and Siglufjord, where the nuns' cloister and the monastery lay. Here it happened that the January thaw was followed by a driving storm of rain that drenched the sheep that had been let out to forage, and filled their eyes and noses so that they were maddened and panicked, and many of them fell over cliffs into the fjords or stumbled into clefts and broke their necks and died, and by the time the rain was over and folk had found their lost sheep, the carcases were rotten from the warm weather, and so Thord Magnusson of Siglufjord and four other farmers and their men went north to Vatna Hverfi district on horseback, although the mud was very deep, and they went seeking food from the Vatna Hverfi folk, who had little to spare. After this Thord and his friends and two men from Vatna Hverfi district went on skates to Gardar, though after the thaw it was considered by many that the ice in Einars Fjord would be treacherous and thin. But Thord would not be dissuaded, and the men arrived at Gardar safely, and at Gardar all was much as usual, and folk were getting up from their meat sated before the meat was gone. Now Sira Jon sent a messenger to Bjorn Einarsson at Thjodhilds Stead and some three days later twelve Eriks Fjord farmers and twenty servants besides appeared dragging sledges over the ice, and these sledges were laden with dried meat and cheese and sour butter, and to this Sira Jon added what he could, which was not a little, and thus the folk of the south were saved, and only those at Ketils Stead and three more who lived at outlying farms, including one outlaw, died in this hunger.

Now the spring came on, and the ice broke up under the winds off the inland ice, and was swept out of the fjords. The farms of the south were much diminished of their sheep and goats and especially cattle, and it happened that some farms were abandoned at Alptafjord and at the head of Ketils Fjord and the folk from these farms moved their belongings down the fjord to Herjolfsnes, where there dwelt a rich and powerful family, still after many generations the lineage of Herjolf and Bjarni Herjolfsson, who was the first man to sight Markland. These Herjolfsnes folk, because their steading had been built near the ocean, had bad years that were stormier and good years that were more prosperous than most folk, and in addition to this, they were a family of sailors. Herjolfsnes was always the first landing place for ships that came to Greenland and the last for ships that were leaving. The folk of Herjolfsnes wore the most outlandish clothing, and prided themselves on attending to what was going on elsewhere in the world of men. The head of this family was named Snaebjorn and he had three sons named Ari, Sigtrygg, and Flosi. All of these men were experienced sealers and whalers, and the Herjolfsnes folk relished sealmeat and whalemeat even more than the Hvalsey Fjord folk. They also had some knowledge of the ways of the skraelings in their skin boats, but, of course, little of their skills, for these are reserved to demons and closed to the minds of men. Nevertheless, between the seals and the whales and the bird cliffs and the coming of ships from afar, the Herjolfsnes folk lived a life that was somewhat peculiar, and it was said in other districts that the hunger back in Alptafjord must have been severe to drive those folk to Herjolfsnes.

Another thing that happened after this hunger was that Bjorn Einarsson Jorsalafari declared his intention of remaining year round at Thjodhilds Stead, which was in Kambstead Fjord, at the back of Hvalsey Fjord, instead of spending part of the year at one farm and part of the year at the other, for he hadn't enough men to make something of both farmsteads, and he preferred the location of Thjodhilds Stead, for it gave his ships easy access to the sea but also to Gardar and Brattahlid. For this reason it happened that Gunnhild Gunnarsdottir would be within a day's walk of her own home when she went to stay with Solveig for the summer. She was now fourteen winters in age, and it was necessary to take this course for her to learn the ways of her new family, who after all were not Greenlanders and would for this reason do things differently from the Greenland way.

Gunnhild was now half a head taller than her mother and fully grown, so that she seemed to be three or four winters older than she was. She held herself with pride and reserve, which also made her seem less girlish, and she knew well how to spin and weave and sew and make cheese and butter and look after small children, and so when she came to Birgitta one day, after Birgitta had nursed Johanna and took the baby into her arms, Birgitta smiled at her and declared that she carried the little one with as much ease as if it were her own.

"Perhaps, then," said Gunnhild, "I might stay home for another summer, because Johanna is happier with me than she is with Helga, and she cries after me when I leave her."

Birgitta smiled now and said, "Even so, Johanna is learning to walk, and everyone knows that the first thing a baby does when she learns to walk is she walks away from those who care for her. And that is a good time for parting."

"Lavrans says you were not sent off before you were married."

"But, indeed, I was wed at your age, and, in addition, Gunnars Stead daughters always went off, and then it is not so burdensome to them when they leave for good. It is the way with you that you are always reluctant to begin with, but happy when the beginning is over. I have more faith in you than I do in Helga, who rushes into things and is afterward filled with regret."

"Helga can't persuade Kollgrim or Astrid to do their tasks."

"When you are away, she will learn how."

Now Johanna, who had been sitting on Gunnhild's hip, leaned forward and cried to be put down, and so Gunnhild set her on her feet and she took a few steps to the bedcloset and began to walk around it, holding on and looking to Birgitta and Gunnhild for praise. Gunnhild was distracted by this from her thoughts and began to laugh, and Birgitta jumped up and made her escape, for indeed, the plans that they had made for Gunnhild made her somewhat uneasy, and she found it not a little difficult to talk to the child. Since the betrothal and Bjorn's move to Thjodhilds Stead there had been some visiting back and forth, with feasting and tale-telling and the usual amusements. The case was that Birgitta and her family did their best to show themselves happy and welcoming to the Thjodhilds Stead folk, and Bjorn and Solveig did the same, and yet, when Birgitta and Gunnar went to the other farmstead, they were annoyed by the stiffness of things, and Solveig's affected manner, and when Bjorn and Solveig visited, Birgitta could see that they, and especially Solveig, were attempting to overlook this and that, out of conscious generosity. Always Solveig's eyes went around the room with veiled dismay, and then fell upon Gunnhild, and Birgitta could see that the other woman was thinking that at least the girl was lovely to look at. Solveig herself was not, and Birgitta found this increasingly disturbing, for each time she saw the other woman she seemed to see only her jiggling chin or the peculiar way she sniffed and blinked when she was talking. During and after these times, she prayed mightily for the grace to look past Solveig's earthly appearance to her soul within, for the woman was as kind as she could be, but the next time Birgitta always failed again.

Einar, too, had an unattractive feature which Birgitta saw that others did not see as she did, and this was a habitual squint from reading and writing. Even Gunnhild had not really seen this thing, but a girl does not see with the clarity of a wife, Birgitta well knew. When she herself had been betrothed and then married to Gunnar, she had been aware mostly of Gunnar's clothes, and the gifts he gave her, and the gifts her father gave her, and her own clothes, and the weight of the sheep against her in the boat as they rowed to Vatna Hverfi, and then again the odd sense of sleeping in a different bedcloset from the one she was used to and the figure next to her that was Margret and not the Lavrans Stead dairy maid, whom she had slept with for some years before moving to Gunnars Stead.

And for a while she had been filled with hatred for all these folk and their ways, and had longed only for visits from her father, but when the first of these came, Lavrans had told her in hard terms, it seemed to her, that it was necessary and proper for a woman to sleep in bed with her husband, and he had chastised her and then himself, and had been very ashamed of the arrangements that had been made at Gunnars Stead. And Birgitta had learned that this thing that they had done after the marriage, fumbling and painful, was not something folk did once, but often, except that it got less painful and somewhat less fumbling. At the beginning she had been pleased with the relief that being with child gave her, and then she had been indifferent, and then between Maria and Johanna, it had seemed a pleasant thing, though rare enough with Astrid and Maria sleeping in the bedcloset between herself and Gunnar.

But it was well known that the years it took to settle into a new family and to learn to tolerate the husband and his ways and his say over everything could not be few, and so it was also well known that a girl should begin early, before her own habits were formed. It was not a secret to Birgitta that there had been much gossip in Vatna Hverfi district about Margret Asgeirsdottir, and folk had said more than once that by the time of her late marriage she was much accustomed to having her own way, and so when Skuli Gudmundsson presented himself, she had her own way in that, and after his death, she ordered things so that she continued to have her own way, in spite of her sin. Though Birgitta had not taken part in this gossip, she largely agreed with it, and deplored the way Margret had behaved. In addition to this, it was clear that Olaf would now be a different sort, less cross-grained with everyone, had Margret not fallen into such unrestrained habits. These things, however, were not such as Birgitta could speak of to Gunnhild, for they were beyond the understanding of a child.

As for Gunnhild, when Birgitta left the steading, she continued to watch over Johanna, and tried to entice her away from the bedcloset and across the room, which was not very big, with smiles and encouragement. Some time later it happened that Kollgrim came into the steading, and whereas Johanna had carefully ignored Gunnhild's entreaties, she turned as soon as she saw the boy and toddled straight to him, a matter of some four steps. And when he picked the child up and gave her into the arms of Gunnhild, then left the steading again, Johanna began to cry after him, and this led Gunnhild herself to weep.

Some days later, Gunnar accompanied Gunnhild to Thjodhilds Stead. They rowed across Hvalsey Fjord to the farm of Orm Guttormsson, who lived in a valley on a neck of land between Hvalsey Fjord and Kambstead Fjord. After refreshing themselves and hearing Orm's news, they walked through the valley to Kambstead Fjord, then along the side of the fjord, and through another valley to Thjodhilds Stead, where Einar, Bjorn, Solveig, the new baby, and some men and servants were awaiting them. This was a journey of about half a day. Solveig offered them further refreshment, including excellent goat cheese, such as Asgeir had been fond of, and sourmilk with honey and berries. After this, Gunnar was put in a good humor, and he began to speak with Einar about his manuscripts and writings. Solveig took Gunnhild away and showed her her sleeping closet and her chest and acquainted her with the other folk about the farmstead. The fields had a northerly slope, and there was much ice to be seen in the fjord.

Einar and Gunnar sat at a bench in one of the rooms of the steading and Einar took down some of the writings he had most recently completed. They were about the districts of Greenland. Gunnar read slowly aloud as follows:

"Of these many Greenland districts, one of the largest and most populous is Vatna Hverfi district, which contains some twenty farms in the north part of the district and some fifteen farms in the south part of the district, and these farms are set rather close together, by the standards of Iceland, but the land of this district is so rich and the lakes so numerous that all the farms make a good enough living. This district has but one church, called Undir Hofdi, and this is not one of the larger churches of Greenland, for it was built many years ago and has not been rebuilt or expanded as others have. The folk of this district keep many cows and horses, as well as sheep. Some of the wealthier farmers of this district are Thorkel Gellison, Erlend Ketilsson, and Magnus Arnason."

Now Gunnar stopped reading and asked Einar if he had written in this way about every district, and Einar said that he had. "But," said Gunnar, "Erlend has died in the past winter, and you have said nothing of it." But Einar smiled and said that he was little interested in such tales, about men no one knew. When he came back to Iceland, this is what folk would wish to know, about the size of the farms and the life folk made on them. Now Gunnar sat silently for a while. Then he said, "Formerly, when the bishop was alive, boys at Gardar made parchment and learned to write upon it, but now I fear that only Sira Audun has this skill."

"It may be so. Gardar does not seem to me to be a thriving place under the direction of the priest Jon. But it may be that the new bishop will appear soon."

"It may be, indeed." And Gunnar fingered a bit of the parchment. "I have heard that the making of parchment is a difficult thing, asking much skill."

"Most men have such skills. They are a farmer's skills." He lifted up a roll and put it down. "Forming the letters, this is the skill of a priest. Forming the ideas is a rarer thing."

"For now, some would be content to make the parchment."

"It is easily taught."

And in this way Gunnar was kept from his evening meat, for he passed so much time at Thjodhilds Stead watching Einar stretch a sheepskin by laces onto a frame he had carried with him from Iceland, and then shave it with a handsome rounded knife that he did not return to Lavrans Stead until all the people there had gone to their bedclosets. After this, he got into the habit of going off to Thjodhilds Stead whenever he could borrow time from the summer's tasks. Gunnhild seemed to him well enough employed. Whenever he saw her, she was going from the dairy to the steading or the storehouse to the dairy, or she was sitting with the baby and the two skraeling children who nursed him, or she was spinning and talking with Solveig about this or that. She knew better than to make much of his visits or to ask to accompany him back to Lavrans Stead, even for a few nights. And so the summer passed quietly, and there were no killings or other disturbances in the district and Bjorn Einarsson stayed home for the most part after the end of the Thing.

And the winter, too, passed quietly, except that Gunnar was engaged in stretching his own sheepskins over a frame he had made of whale bone, and shaving them with a curved knife sharpened from the shoulder blade of a reindeer, and Gunnhild, who returned at the end of the summer nights, helped him with this work. These tools worked surprisingly well, so that his parchments were smooth and pale and took the merest stroke of bearberry ink, and after Yule he began to write upon them in a large and awkward hand, and the first thing he wrote was as follows:

"A man named Erlend Ketilsson lived at Ketils Stead in Vatna Hverfi district, in much conflict with his neighbors. All considered him an ill-tempered and quarrelsome fellow. He was a very prosperous farmer, with a large steading and many outbuildings. Through his entire life he fornicated with a servant woman named Vigdis, and when she grew old, he chose another to fornicate with. As a result of his sin, he and his servant and the child of his servant and two others starved to death at a certain Yule season and were partly eaten by their dogs."

Gunnar was much dissatisfied with this writing and scraped it off the parchment. As for Gunnhild, she was much dissatisfied with everything about Lavrans Stead, and complained without ceasing of how cramped the rooms were, and how humble all the household arrangements. Tales of Solveig and the baby and Bjorn were always on her lips, so that Helga and Kollgrim tormented her with mockery of the way Solveig blinked and talked and took turns breaking into each other's conversation with corrections and other remarks, as was Einar's habit. Even Johanna was unpleasing to Gunnhild, for she greeted her oldest sister as a stranger after so much time, and clung to Astrid, who was a very playful nurse, and fond of games and silliness.

It happened that a few days before Yule there was a great battle among the three older children, in which all ended up weeping, and it was clear to Birgitta that although Helga and especially Kollgrim were excessively teasing toward Gunnhild, she had brought this upon herself by condemning their ways and their clothes and everything about them for the previous two days, and doing her best to make them seem mean and unworthy in their own eyes. Now when they had all been sent to separate bedclosets, Gunnar came to Birgitta in great anger and complained of the uproar, and of Gunnhild especially. Birgitta took a deep breath, and glanced about the room, at her father sleeping by the fire, and the smoky lights cast by the lamps against the turfing of the walls, and at such cloths and tapestries as they had put up to help keep out the wind. A few stools were stacked in the corner and the floor was a heap of moss and much else that didn't bear looking into, and she saw these things, it seemed to her, with Solveig's eyes, and Gunnhild's, and she sighed. Then she turned to Gunnar and declared that as a child of but fifteen years, Gunnhild could not be asked to keep two things in her mind at once, namely the Thjodhilds Stead way and the Lavrans Stead way. And since one had to make way for the other, it was necessary that the old go out and the new come in. The result of this was that on the feast of St. Stephen, Gunnhild and Gunnar went on skis across the fjord and over the hills to Thjodhilds Stead, and Gunnhild stayed there, as a maiden, and came home no more. And this was also the case, that in the disorder of departure, she never once looked over her shoulder, nor did she see her brother and sisters and mother waving after her, but she only went forward, looking for her new home, and this came to Birgitta as an unaccountable grief, no matter how she prayed and told herself that this was the pain of bearing daughters, and folk must always accustom themselves to it. At midsummer, Bjorn Einarsson declared that he was becoming intolerably restless, and had made up his mind to return to Iceland and Norway. And, as his decision was so sudden, there was no time for Gunnhild's wedding feast, but Solveig promised that she should have a brilliant one in Iceland.

And one thing that happened after Bjorn Einarsson, Einar, Solveig, the baby, Gunnhild, and the others left in their four neat ships was that the farmer Orm Guttormsson agreed to take some of Bjorn's ewes and lambs in trade for a number of sheepskins equal to the number of ewes, but it happened that his seal nets became fouled together, and he was unable to make the trip to Thjodhilds Stead until the day after Bjorn's departure. When he got there, he expected to find the sheep folded, and he did, but before taking them home, he made up his mind to look about the steading and see if anything else had been left behind that might be useful, for Bjorn and his family had a great quantity of belongings. And he did find something, a nicely carved lamp, of small size, good for lighting, though not for heat. And he also found something else, the corpuses of the two skraeling children who had nursed Solveig's baby. It seemed to Orm that they had climbed an outcropping overlooking Thjodhilds inlet, and pitched themselves into the fjord. The boy's corpus floated in the shallows, catching on the strand, and the girl's was caught by the headdress on some rocks. Orm did not quite know what to do with these corpuses, and so he fished them from the sea and put them in the cowbyre, then a day or so later, he came to Sira Pall Hallvardsson and told of his discovery. These children had been baptized with the names of Josef and Maria, and so Sira Pall Hallvardsson went with Orm and Gunnar and another man and found the corpuses. There was some talk about whether these two children should be buried at the church or not, for it was the law among the Greenlanders that this was prohibited if they had done away with themselves. And so the men spent the greater part of a day walking back and forth around the steading, and looking at the places Orm had found them, and hearing Orm tell his tale over and over.

"Perhaps," Gunnar said, "these children merely ran into the water, and were seized by the cold," for Kambstead Fjord was close to freezing at all times of the year. But no, it was apparent that their bodies were broken from falling, as Orm had said.

"Perhaps," said Hakon, the fourth man, "they merely climbed upon the rock to get a last look at the ships as they sailed away." And it did seem possible that they might have clutched at each other and in this way pulled each other down, but when Sira Pall Hallvardsson climbed the rock, he saw that the ascent was so easy and full of holds and places to stand that no man could simply slip down into the water.

Now Orm said, "Only I have seen them, and only we have spoken of this. When folk ask, we can tell them that they fell from the rock." But Sira Pall Hallvardsson looked gloomy, and he shook his head, for indeed, the eye of God sees all, including acts of false mercy. And so these skraeling children, Maria and Josef, were buried a bow shot beyond the homefield wall of Thjodhilds Stead, in sight of the fjord, among some rocks and away from the watercourse that ran down to the steading. Sira Pall Hallvardsson spoke over them, and all of the men were rendered oddly despondent.

Walking back to Orm Guttormsson's farm, Sira Pall Hallvardsson and Gunnar fell to talking of Gunnhild. "Never in Greenland," said Pall Hallvardsson, "can there have been many maidens such as Gunnhild, so fair as to take a man's breath, and yet withal as modest as an alpine blossom and as skillful at her tasks as a maiden twice her age."

Gunnar smiled a little, thinking of Gunnhild's quarrels with Helga and Kollgrim, but said only, "Birgitta Lavransdottir has taken her going much to heart, for indeed, we packed her things up and gave to her sisters what she did not need as if she were going to the grave. We must not hide from ourselves the knowledge that we are likely never to see her again."

"It may be that Bjorn will return, or Einar."

"Folk say that."

"Bjorn himself said it. Perhaps he will go to Norway and gain the ear of the king and queen. They would surely let him come back, for it is not every revenue officer and ombudsman who wishes to come here." And the two men smiled at the memory of Kollbein Sigurdsson.

"Perhaps," said Gunnar, "but Bjorn himself told me that it is common knowledge among sailing folk that the seas get more treacherous every year. He said that twenty ships used to leave Bergen for Iceland each summer, but now Bergen is much shrunk, and those who send the ships, as folk have said before, are uninterested in Iceland or Greenland, for they are Germans, not Norsemen."

"It is true that Germans care little for the sea, though they care greatly for trade."

"Perhaps folk will see what Bjorn carries back from Greenland and long to have it themselves. That has happened before."

"Perhaps," said Sira Pall Hallvardsson, "Bjorn will long to have more."

Now Gunnar cast him a glance. "Did you not see in the last half year of Bjorn's stay that look of a man who has eaten his fill? Who turns from the table half-disgusted at the dishes still remaining? Birgitta Lavransdottir says that Bjorn is a man with a great appetite for new things, not so much for accustomed things." He sighed. "Nay, it is best for those such as ourselves, who send our children after what we once wished to have, to make up our minds to give these children up." Now he spoke in a lower voice. "And even if Bjorn or Einar did return, it is the lives of married women that are the most slippery."

"Then," said Sira Pall Hallvardsson, "we must satisfy ourselves with the knowledge of our heavenly meeting."

"We must, indeed. But it seems to me that this thing is hard for a father to do, and for one reason, that much of what draws me to them is the manner in which the passing days flit across them, so that they are themselves and yet not the same as they were. When we put off our flesh and appear in the raiment of our eternal souls, perhaps we shall long for this earthly quality."

"It is promised that we shall long for nothing." And Sira Pall Hallvardsson spoke with such longing that Gunnar glanced at him sharply, and when he came home he declared to Birgitta that Sira Pall Hallvardsson was in love with Gunnhild. But Birgitta was more interested to hear of the skraeling children, and she pondered what Gunnar told her of them for a long time, and then, as they were getting under the old bearskin in their bedcloset, she said, "It seems to me that even such grief as theirs was hardly great enough for this event, and I am frightened." But Gunnar did not know how to answer this remark, and said nothing.

After the departure of Bjorn Einarsson Jorsalfari, it fell to Osmund Thordarson to take up his position as lawspeaker again, and he did this with the help of his nephew Isleif. On the one hand, folk didn't care for this unorthodox procedure, but on the other, it was easy to see that Osmund was on his last legs and ready for death, and there was no other farmer of the Brattahlid district who wished to take up the position of lawspeaker. Fridjon, the son of Gizur, the former lawspeaker, had never learned the laws, and was too old to begin, although he was a prosperous man, and Ragnleif, the brother of Isleif, considered that he had too much work to do on his steading, although folk said he had no more than any other man. It was easy to see that the position would fall to Isleif, and soon, for Osmund was old and Isleif knew the laws, but Isleif was a priest, and nearly blind, and without powerful friends in other districts. Osmund called a special Thing in the autumn after Bjorn left, and on each of three days, with the help of Isleif, he spoke one-third of the laws in a weak, reedy voice. There were twenty farmers and their servants and men there to hear him, all of them from Brattahlid, Vatna Hverfi, and Dyrnes districts. Sira Jon was there, along with Sira Pall Hallvardsson and Gunnar Asgeirsson, who came on the second day. And just after the ending of the Thing, there was a storm in Eriks Fjord, and the boat carrying the three farmers and their servants from Dyrnes district was capsized and broken up, and all the men were drowned and all the wood of the boat was swept out of the fjord by the winds and lost.

Upon hearing this news from Sira Pall Hallvardsson, who had it from Orm Guttormsson, who had relatives in Dyrnes district, Birgitta Lavransdottir became much cast down, and wished only to remain in her bedcloset all day, although these men were unknown to her. The autumn work was left to others. And on the third day, Gunnar came to her and asked her to get up and went away again, but she did not get up, and when it was time for the evening meat, she got up neither to prepare it nor to eat what was prepared by Helga and the servingmaid. And during the evening Gunnar said nothing about this, nor did he show anger toward Birgitta; nevertheless, he was much disturbed. Lavrans dozed beside the fire. Olaf sat over the chessboard with Kollgrim. Helga and the servingwomen sat spinning, and Astrid and Maria played a game with Johanna, in which the little girl was spun about and then sent staggering from one sister to the other, and all three children shouted with laughter. Finally, when it appeared that Kollgrim was about to give to Olaf's patience the uttermost test, Gunnar began the following tale:

It happened in the time of Erik the Red that there lived in Greenland a young woman named Skadi, who had come on one of Erik's ships with her father, Thorir. And this man Thorir chose as his steading a large piece of land in the western settlement, and indeed, he and Skadi were the first folk to live there. In addition to this, they chose a piece of land in the north part of that settlement, far from the church and near to the inland ice, for Thorir was a great hunter and he and his daughter much preferred the land of ice and snow. This Thorir was a big, strong fellow, and likewise his daughter was as big as a man, with huge arms and huge legs, but also huge breasts and long flowing hair, and she was not unpretty, for a certain type. Thorir was a simple fellow, and it happened once that when he was visiting Erik at Brattahlid, a man named Larus tricked him into stealing three silver apples from one of Erik's chests and giving them to him, Larus.

It is well known to all that Erik the Red was a wrathful and impatient man, and when he was told by one of the servingwomen that

Thorir had stolen these apples, which were very valuable, and prized very highly by their owner, he went to Thorir and dealt him a heavy blow with his sword, for in those days all Norsemen carried swords, and many had the knowledge of tempering and sharpening a keen blade, and Thorir was badly injured from this blow and soon died, although Erik had repented of his anger and himself nursed the man. Now Erik said to his wife Thjodhild that something must be done for the daughter Skadi, for she would be full of revenge when she heard the news of the death of her father, and of course such news would travel, even as far as Thoristead, and quickly as the blink of an eye or the taking of a breath. And sure enough, some days later, Skadi appeared in the six-oared boat, and she was rowing the boat by herself, she was that strong.

Skadi rowed up Eriks Fjord, and all along the way, the folk in the farms could hear great bellowing as she wept and sighed after Thorir, her father. Now she pulled up to the Brattahlid jetty, and called Erik out of his steading. When he appeared before her, before she could speak, he said, "Now Skadi, what is the price of your father's death? I have much gold, and I will give you self-judgment."

But Skadi said, "My father was a great hunter and a rich man. And I am his only heir. Your gold is worthless to me." And all this time she was casting her eye upon Leif the Lucky, who was by all accounts very fair to behold. And Erik said, "What will you have, then? For I am very repentant of my wrath."

"I will settle for a husband and a bellyful of laughter," said Skadi, and she looked again, with longing, at Leif. But Erik had other plans for Leif, and Leif himself was little inclined toward the woman, who indeed stood some half a head taller than he did. So Erik said, "Then you may choose any man you would have, with this provision, you must choose according to their feet, and you may not see the man you have married until after the bridal." Skadi agreed to this, and all the men of the farmstead stood behind a tapestry, and Skadi chose the most shapely pair of feet, and she was married. But her husband turned out to be not Leif the Lucky but another man, Erik's best ship pilot, a man by the name of Njord. He was a fine man, but weather-beaten and somewhat old, for he had been on the sea all of his life. Skadi declared that she had been tricked, and was much angered. Njord, on the other hand, was pleased with his wife, and smiled upon her with warmth and kindness. She stepped back and opened her mouth, and he said, "Take care, wife. Remember that these are the first words of your marriage." And so Skadi remained silent, and Erik said to her, "You have found a good husband, and such a one as would not be tricked by Larus. Indeed, you might have chosen Larus, had you been less lucky."

"But," said Skadi, 'I have no laughter, and I expect none, now."

"Bring out Larus," said Erik. Some men did so. "Now," said Erik, "it is up to you to make this woman laugh, as you are the author of her grief."

"She does not look to be the laughing sort, sir," was Larus' reply.

"Then your payment will be all the greater," said Erik.

"But let me first tell you what happened to me," said Larus to Erik, and he took a thin strap of walrus hide out of his pocket. "Remember that you told me to take that goat over there and tie him in the upper pasture?" Now Larus looked at Skadi. "You know how goats are, my dear. Wayward and independent." He went across the field to the goat and tied one end of the strap to the goat's beard. "But of course I had other things to carry, as one always does, and so I could only think of one way to lead the goat." He tied the other end of the strap to his testicles. "And this was the case, too, that it was early morning, and the flies and fleas were biting something fierce." And just then the goat jumped away, and the strap between the two of them tightened. Larus gave out a great squawk and pulled back. Now the goat became annoyed with this, as goats do, and he began to step backward, and Larus, too, began to step backward, and soon the strap was tight enough to sing when plucked. And now the goat shook its head and Larus stepped backward again, and he grew red in the face and squawked again. Then he said, "Truly, master, this is an unhealthy way to lead a goat," and suddenly the goat lost his footing, then caught it again, and ran at Larus and knocked him down right into the arms of Skadi, who laughed aloud. And then she forgave him for causing the death of her father.

Now Gunnar paused, for he had heard a sound from the bedcloset where Birgitta lay in the dark, but there was no other sound after the first one. The story was finished, and the folk went to their bedclosets, and Birgitta gave no sign that she had heard the story, except that in the morning she got up and went about her tasks, although all could see that she was still in low spirits.

The winter nights came on, and Gunnar began again to sit over his parchment, and as he did this, he too felt a longing for Gunnhild, who only one year before had helped him at this task of parchment making. And then he noticed another thing, and that was that his thoughts were led through Gunnhild to Margret Asgeirsdottir, whom Gunnhild somewhat resembled in stature and manner, and as he sat quietly over his work, the two became a little mixed up in his thoughts—Gunnhild as she had been a year before and Margret as she had been many many years before, when she was thirteen and Gunnar was six winters of age, as Astrid was now, and Hauk Gunnarsson would come and go, and Ingrid and his father stood above him at every turn.

Asta had given birth to another child by the skraeling, and this girl, Bryndis, was now one winter old and more. During the year since her birth, Margret had spent a great deal of time with Sigurd, who was now some seven winters old and more. The reason for this was that Bryndis had been born so small that Asta could fit her in the palm of her hand, and the two women had considered that the child would surely die. Sira Isleif, who came with his servants in answer to the signal fire they made, gave the child baptism and last rites at the same time. Koll, who had stayed not far off, waiting for the birth of another son, was little pleased at such a daughter, and Asta had expressed some fear that he would steal the child and expose it, as skraelings were known to do with girl children. But indeed, Bryndis suckled heartily and slept soundly in the robe of foxskins, and did not die after all, but grew and sat up and crept and walked, just as other children do. She looked like Sigurd, though tiny, and she was exquisite in her tininess, like an ivory miniature. Asta was very fond of her and carried her about on her back, as skraelings do, for when Koll saw that the child would live, he arranged a harness for the baby as his wives used. Then he went off, as always.

Sigurd stayed beside Margret, and was little trouble. In the winter, at Brattahlid, she taught him to spin, and he sat beside her loom, spinning bits of different colored wools together. In the summer, she took him into the mountains with her and showed him the patches of blueberries, where they ate their fill. From time to time she gathered other green things, and she explained the uses of these to him and he listened carefully. He was not like other children she had known, who hung upon her, chattering, or else ran off and got into mischief. He was as silent by nature as she was, but withal very observant and attentive. When he grew playful, it was with an inward sort of amusement at her or at some other unusual event. At these times he would laugh and laugh to himself until Margret had to laugh as well, although she rarely knew what she was laughing at. He was not popular at Brattahlid, and in the fall after the departure of Bjorn Einarsson, Margret put off their moving to the estate across the fjord day after day.

Now that Marta Thordardottir was dead, Margret had little desire to live among Osmund's family. Osmund's young wife, Gudrunn, was a meek, hiding sort of person who nevertheless had strong likes and dislikes, and it happened, as it often does, that after her husband's sister died, it turned out that she disliked all those things that the other woman had liked. Osmund himself was palsied and old, particularly since the special autumn Thing, for the saying of the laws had been beyond his strength, and he spent much of the rest of the autumn in his bedcloset. Sira Isleif stayed among his mother's brother's family and gave services and buried folk at Thjodhilds church, but he was no longer honored as he had once been. Gudrunn blamed him for his dim eyesight, and thought him clumsy and troublesome, and was, in addition, annoyed with him for his pride in himself. Soon enough it would be time for him to go off to live with Ragnleif, but then the trek to Thjodhilds church would be longer and his duties more difficult, and so he was putting off this move. In the meantime, he was not especially welcoming toward Margret, for after the death of Marta, she had ceased accepting his ministrations or counsel.

As she put off the trip from day to day, it seemed to Margret just possible that they might winter at Steinstraumstead, if they prepared for it for the entire previous summer and if the winter was a short, snowy one, and if some large pieces of driftwood could be obtained and if they surrounded the tiny steading with another course of turf and if, to be honest, Koll appeared after Yule with extra provisions. Except that he would look for them at Brattahlid. And this was another provocation to Gudrunn, the yearly visit of Koll, whom she called, "that servingmaid's demon." In this view, as in no other, she was supported by Sira Isleif.

And so the first winter nights came, but this was earlier than Margret had ever gone to Brattahlid. And then, according to the stick calendar Margret had made herself, came the mass of St. Kolumban, and soon enough after that the feast of St. Andrew. Always by this time in past years they had made their passage across the fjord. In early years, in fact, Marta had sent servingmen for them, to help them over the ice, for the fjord was well iced up, a smooth surface for skating or skiing. But still the coldest part of the winter had not set in, and the four of them were comfortable enough. Another few days went by, and it was the feast of St. Nikolaus; Advent had begun. They sat down at their morning meat and Margret saw that there were but three cheeses and some dried sealmeat remaining, and in addition to this, the sheep could no longer paw through the snow to any grass, as the snow was too deep. Margret said, "We will take two of these cheeses to Gudrunn Jonsdottir tomorrow." Asta nodded.

But on the next day, they awoke to a snowstorm that blanketed sight and this storm continued for still another day, and on the morning of the third day there was but a single cheese to be taken to Brattahlid, and a wedge cut out of it to boot. Margret considered, as she had never done in the days of Marta Thordardottir, how she might make her party welcome, or at least avoid scorn until she could finish some weaving. She went through her belongings to find some little gift, and her hand came upon some tablet weaving, a border for a shawl in bluish-gray and white, and she folded this up and put it in her bundle.

The two women had decided that Asta would carry Bryndis and some other articles on her back, and also drag behind her a sealskin bag full of necessities. Margret and Sigurd would herd the five sheep before themselves, and the trip would take a morning or a little more. When they got outside the steading, however, they saw that the snow was much deeper now than when they had made their plans, and that Sigurd would have to go on someone's back, namely Margret's, although he was almost too large for her to carry. And so they strapped on their short skis and made their way, with the sheep in front of them, down the hillside to the fjord. Sigurd sat in a piece of wadmal tied around Margret's back and neck, as Gunnar had done once. The sheep were weak from hunger, which had this advantage, that they did not care to frisk away or wander off, but this disadvantage, that even under the best circumstances, one or more of them might not make it all the way to Brattahlid. On a day in summer, the red buildings of Brattahlid were clearly visible across the fjord, and shadows playing on the hillside, and sometimes, folk moving back and forth across it, but on such a day as this, when whiteness shrouded every surface, no sight of the goal drew them forward, or carried their eyes out of their heads, making the way seem short.

Only once did Margret dare look back at Steinstraumstead, and when she did, she saw that her own hillside loomed above her. Momentarily it seemed to her that the ice she was walking on was slipping backwards underneath her feet, so that no matter how she stepped forward, the ice carried her back. She shook off this feeling and looked at Bryndis, shrouded in the foxskins so that nothing of her skin could be seen, only the movement of the fox fur as she breathed against it. She would be sleeping with Asta's walking, and warm in the furs. Margret turned her mind upon this, the sight of the little girl sleeping warmly among the furs, and she thought about it with absorption, so that when she had to go off to bring a sheep closer into the group, she longed for the sight of Bryndis asleep as if it were her own warm bedcloset or a seat beside a fire. On her back, Sigurd sat still and calm, as Gunnar never had. Now Asta forged forward in front of the sheep, breaking a path through drifted snow. Margret saw that good luck alone would carry them across the fjord, and she could not help giving herself up to contemplating her luck, which was little enough, all things considered. But then the thought of Skuli Gudmundsson came to her, and with it something that her father had often said, that a man's luck shows itself differently to him than it does to his neighbors. And in the midst of these thoughts she saw that they were more than halfway across the fjord.

Not long after this, one of the ewes stumbled and fell down, and then did not get up. Margret called out to Asta, who turned and saw the sheep, which was lying on its side with its eyes closed. And Asta made her way back to the sheep, and hefted it into the crook of her arm and began to carry it forward. But then another sheep fell over, and there was no carrying two. Margret went to the second sheep and began to coax it to its feet, and briefly it stood up, while she was slapping it and urging it, for sheep are fearful beasts and they distrust the touch of hands. But after stumbling a step or two, the second ewe fell into the snow again, and Margret saw that it would have to be left there to freeze to death.

In this way they trudged forward, and some time later they came to the Brattahlid jetty, and Margret began to look about for a servingman or someone else to help them, for indeed she felt like falling down herself from the weight of Sigurd Kolsson on her back, but no one was there, so they began the steep climb to Osmund's steading, only stopping at the cowbyre to fold the sheep in with the others that were already folded there, and to gather for them a few handfuls of hay from the stack in front of the byre. And it was the case with Margret that the sight of the buildings filled her, not with the desire to go forward into them, but with the false assurance that if she were to founder just where she was standing, she would be discovered and preserved. And from this she knew that she had nearly died on this journey across the fjord. Asta, too, labored painfully up the hillside, and looked about for folk but saw none.

And now it happened that they came to the door of the large steading, and still they had seen no one in the byres, no one in the storehouses, no one in the dairy, no one gathering snow to be melted for drinking water. Asta put her shoulder against the door and it swung open, and she stepped inside with Margret just behind her. The room was warm and humid, but dark, for no lamps had been lit. Margret and Asta stood still and peered about. In the master bedcloset, a figure rustled among the furs, and then a thin, high voice said, "Who is it? Who has come?" And Margret said, in a low voice, to Asta, "This stench I remember from many years ago. This is the stench of the vomiting ill, and, no doubt, partly the stench of death." Then she spoke up and said, "It is Margret Asgeirsdottir and Asta Thorbergsdottir. We have a great fear of what we have discovered here."

"You would have done better," said the thin voice of Gudrunn Jonsdottir, "to have stayed where you were, even starving, than to have come here," and her voice faded away as she fell back into the bedcloset. Now Asta put Bryndis in her foxskins down on the bench, and Sigurd huddled beside her, and Asta covered them with whatever furs she could find, so that they would get their warmth back, and then she and Margret went about the bedclosets and took note of the inhabitants, and these were dead: Osmund, his daughter, two servingwomen, and a servingman; Gudrunn seemed well enough, while her son, Ozur, appeared to be sleeping. A servingwoman and three servingmen were weak, but recovering, for it is the case with the vomiting ill that its course is straight. If a man goes to the bottom of it and does not find death, he will come up again with time.

And now it was with some dread that Margret and Asta began to minister to the living and see to the dead. Asta carried Osmund and the others out and buried them in a snowbank for the time being. Margret went to the storehouses and brought out dried reindeer meat and sourmilk. The first of these she seethed in broth, and with this she cooked some pieces of mutton, and she also found some salt to add to it, for Brattahlid was a rich farm, and sometimes in the summer when a fire was built for other purposes, such as butchering or washing clothes, the servingmaids made salt from the water of the fjord. In addition to these things, she found much dried dulse and dried angelica, and these, too, she added to the broth, so that it was thick and smooth and nourishing, and on this food, first the broth, then the bits of meat, then the sourmilk, the folk of the steading began to revive. Sira Isleif, they said, had gone off with one servingman to Ragnleif's steading, upon hearing that Ragnleif was ill. This was some six or seven days before.

After feeding the folk, Margret and Asta went about and washed them with heated water, for all of them were covered with vomit and other dirt. Then they washed the floors and benches and beat out the furs in all the bedclosets and brought snow into the steading for clear, clean water. And these tasks took all of the rest of the day and part of the night, so that the two women were much fatigued when they at last went to the bedcloset they were accustomed to sharing. They lay with Sigurd on the inside, beside Asta, and Bryndis in her foxskins between them. Now Margret said to Asta, "Have you heard the tale of Sigurd Njalsson, when he was in the Northsetur and discovered the ship of Arnbjorn the Norwegian in the time of Bishop Arnald?" But Asta had not heard this tale. Margret said, "Here is what Sigurd said, 'There is nothing more certain than that the foul air of a closed room where men have died of sickness is utterly destructive.'" And Asta said, "If he is right, then we will find it out soon enough." And the two women went to sleep.

The next days passed in this way, with much cooking and some cleaning, and some feeding of the beasts, for Brattahlid had a large byre full of cows. Six horses ran about in a walled-in field, and the sheep were fed in a protected fold, for Brattahlid had plenty of fodder, as Gardar did. And each day one visitor or more would come from one of the surrounding farms to bring the news and ask for provisions, and at every farm one or two were dead, though not so many as at Brattahlid. From each of these messengers Margret asked news of Sira Isleif or his servingman, but no one knew of events at Ragnleif's steading. To all of these folk she handed out sealmeat and blubber with a generous hand, until Gudrunn was well enough to sit up and give these things away herself. Gudrunn was much cast down by the death of her daughter, who had been a very pretty and appealing child, less so by the death of Osmund, for this she said she had expected all autumn. She clung to Ozur, who clung to her, and Margret saw that they would not be easily roused to take charge of the steading.

And now, by the Brattahlid calendar, which Sira Isleif himself had made, the time for Yule came on, although by Margret's calendar it was still some eight days off, and Gudrunn asked Margret and Asta to slaughter and roast two sheep for the feast, as was always done at Brattahlid, and indeed on most of the wealthier farms, for Yule. And it was as they were getting ready to do this, building the fire, that Asta began to vomit, and so she was taken with the vomiting ill, and shortly after her the child Bryndis, and within three days they were dead. And now one of the servingmen was pretty fully recovered, and he carried Asta out of the steading and buried her with Bryndis in her arms in the snowbank beside the others. Margret was not subject to the sickness at any time, and Sigurd became only a little ill, but managed to hold onto his food, and this, Margret told Gudrunn, was the way folk recovered, by keeping their food inside them to fortify them. As there still had been no news from Ragnleif's steading, a servingman who had a daughter living there went off to see how things stood with those folk.

One day Gudrunn was sitting up in her bed and sipping some broth, and she said to Margret, "How is it that you go about your business with such strength when you have just lately looked upon the death of Asta

Thorbergsdottir? But folk say that this is not the first death you have looked upon."

Margret did not reply.

"Folk say you looked upon the death of your lover with indifference though his blood spurted over your dress." But she spoke in a neutral voice, as if merely curious.

Margret said, "Everyone has many chances to practice with death. If you have not, then you are indeed rare among the Greenlanders."

"It is practice, then, that makes you cold?"

Margret turned back the sleeve of her gown and exposed her arm. The flesh was thin and wiry, the skin white and dry. Margret lifted her arm toward Gudrunn. "Many deaths have worn me down, and soon I will be as bony and hard as Death himself. Then I will be cold indeed." She took the basin that had contained the broth and turned away.

On this same day, the servingman returned from Ragnleif's steading, and this was his news, that Ragnleif had not been ill, after all, only somewhat injured from a fall on the ice, but some five or six days after the coming of Sira Isleif, many at the steading had fallen sick all at once, with only Sira Isleif, who remained healthy, and one old servingman to take care of them. The short tale was this, that Ragnleif's wife, Finna, and his youngest child, Steinthor, as well as a servingmaid and her child and two serving boys who were brothers, all of these had died, but all the others were recovering. And this, too, had happened, that in the midst of the sickness some unknown men had broken into Ragnleif's storehouse and taken all of the mutton and dried reindeer meat and a moiety of the sourmilk, so that provisions were low at the other farmstead. And at this news, Gudrunn grew angry at Margret and berated her for handing out foodstuffs to all and sundry with such a generous hand, for now they would suffer the curse of seeing strangers fat and satisfied while near kin went hungry.

On the day after this, a messenger arrived from Gardar, carrying news for Osmund Thordarson from Sira Jon, but he was not much surprised to discover the fate of Osmund, he said, for such an outcome had been speculated about at Gardar. It was said that a farmer who had a place at Dyrnes would take over two abandoned farms not far from Solar Fell and become lawspeaker. And the other gossip was that the vomiting ill had struck hard at Hvalsey Fjord, where some twenty were dead, and in the southern part of Vatna Hverfi, and around Herjolfsnes. Six had died at Gardar and thirty survived. And Gudrunn counted up the dead they had heard of in Brattahlid and Isafjord, and this came to about twenty-five.

Gudrunn said, "There will be others in the lonelier steadings that we will hear of after Easter." But indeed, this was little the case, and the greatest death occurred at the largest farms, in the most thickly populated districts. After the messenger had spoken to Gudrunn, Margret took him aside and asked about Gunnar and Birgitta, who lived at Lavrans Stead in Hvalsey Fjord, but the boy had not heard their names among the names of the dead. "What then," she said, "of this name, Olaf Finnbogason?" and the boy said this was not the name of one of the dead. Of Vatna Hverfi, he rattled on. He told her that Sira Nikolaus, of Undir Hofdi church, had been taken, as well as his "wife." And folk estimated that he was a hundred years old. At least this was true, that when they carried him out, he was as shriveled as a child.

Not the least curse of this general sickness was that it took place so early in the winter, and folk and beasts had to endure many weeks of snow and storming before the coming of spring. Many who were weakened died, and beasts on many farms went hungry for too long too early in the season for them to survive, and so this was a bad winter, with deaths and bouts of hunger stretching past Easter. At Hvalsey Fjord, Orm Guttormsson was among the dead, and Astrid Gunnarsdottir and Maria Gunnarsdottir, one in the morning of the mass of St. Stephen and the other in that evening, and after their corpuses had been wrapped and set into a snowbank, Birgitta came to Gunnar and told him of the sight she had seen these many months before, of all of the children vanishing before her eyes as they were gathering seaweed beside the water. And she said, "It may be that I am being punished for my pride, for I was much taken with Gunnhild's beauty, and Astrid's lightheartedness and Maria's fondness for me, so that now I am afraid to look upon the others, and I seek ways to humble my pride in them and avert this punishment."

Gunnar asked if she had spoken to anyone of this sight, especially to Sira Pall Hallvardsson, and Birgitta said that she had not, that she had feared to talk of it. And Gunnar said, "Surely the priest can give you a penance, or some prayers to say."

"But," said Birgitta, "when I saw this disappearance I had Johanna within me, and it happened that she jumped with glee that I should see it, and therefore it seems that she carries ill luck with her, and spreads it like a contagion, though not suffering from it herself."

"And it gives you little love for her, that is plain to see."

"It seems to me that she will live and they will die, just as she, of all of them, has not become ill in this sickness, and she goes about to all the bedclosets and looks in upon them with a curious and unwearying eye."

But Gunnar would not admit that this sickness was any different than any other spell of the vomiting ill had been, where many live and some die and no man can say ahead of time which way it will go for him. Even so, Birgitta would not be freed of her notion that Johanna was an uncanny child, and she avoided her when she could.

Now it happened that the spring came on, and Sira Jon sent out messengers to every district with the news that he would hold an Easter mass and a feast at Gardar, to celebrate the Resurrection of the Lord and the resurrection of all the souls of the dead into heavenly life, for, the messenger declared, Sira Jon often spoke to the folk at Gardar, and declared that God had much in store for those who suffered among the wastes of the earth, and toiled there for His glory.

There was a woman at Gardar named Olof, who was the daughter of Anna Jonsdottir, who had been in charge of the housekeeping at the steading, and Olof, although she was but twenty winters old or so when Anna herself died in the first year of Bjorn Einarsson's coming, had taken over her mother's position and now had the care of Sira Jon and Sira Audun, and the cleaning of the bishop's chamber, which she carried out with great pains every three days or so, under Sira Jon's orders, in anticipation of the new bishop. Sira Jon himself had moved into a tiny, dark chamber, much unlike his former room, and all of the furniture in this room consisted of some furs and lengths of wadmal and a small lamp, and this place was only large enough for him to stand up and lie down in, and he seemed to Olof to like it very much, for he spent a great deal of time there.

Sira Jon often fell into a state which the folk at Gardar referred to as "out of sorts," and when he was in this condition he was especially alert to every sound and every trick of the light, and he looked at his servants as if searching through them. In these times, only Olof could approach him, and also in these times, he would go to his tiny chamber and come out again somewhat relieved. He would be especially impatient with his steward, a man about his age, whose name was Petur, and rage at him no matter what the news was; whether two cows had calved handsomely or whether seventeen lambs and goats had died, Jon took both sorts of news with equal anger. And so it came about that the servants at Gardar watched their master with even more vigilance than is usual among servants, and the great topic of conversation every morning and every evening was how Sira Jon seemed to be. Sira Audun often

arranged his trips to other districts suddenly, when the general opinion
was that Sira Jon was out of sorts. Folk considered that the two priests
were not friends, although not yet enemies.

During the sickness it was the case that most people at Gardar fell
ill, but some did not. Sira Jon did not, and Sira Audun did, although he
recovered, and Petur the steward did not, and Olof did, and when this
happened, Sira Jon went one day to where Petur was standing among the
sheep, and he berated Petur. "Indeed," he said, "you are beset with devils
and abandoned by the Lord, and therefore it is you, Petur, who should die
and take up your abode in Hell." And then he declared, "It has come to
me in a dream that the beasts of the field and the fjord are going to rise
up and conquer, and you will be trampled by horses, then gored by cows,
then trod upon by scores of sheep, and crushed in the embrace of a walrus,
then carried to the depths of the sea by a whale, but even after all of these
things are done, there will still be a stone of evil in you, and so you will
be carried off to the icy wastes and left there." And Petur, although a strong
man, was somewhat frightened by this speech, and began to walk away
from his master, which enraged Sira Jon even further, so that his voice,
which had been low, and directed to Petur alone, now rose, and all nearby
could hear it, and another man, an old servingman, led the priest away.
Someone went to find Sira Audun, and though the door to his chamber
was closed, he did not answer a knock, and could not be found. When Olof
got up from her sickbed, Sira Jon improved, and he gave Petur some
sheepskins. It was this miracle, the recovery of Olof, that prompted Sira
Jon to celebrate Easter with a feast.

Sira Jon was much delighted with the coming occasion, and seemed
hardly out of sorts at all. He especially enjoyed going among the storage
chests and taking out the handsome silks and wallhangings, and adorning
the altar and the walls of the cathedral with them. For his own wear he
took out two separate suits of vestments, one white, shot with gold
thread, for the early mass, and one gold with scarlet borders for the later
mass. These articles had been carefully kept, and so were in good condition except for one or two small rents where the cloth had worn away.
After the vestments, he went among all the altar furniture that had ever
been gathered, and found the very best pieces, without dents or missing
bits, and he cleaned these himself, with fine, pure sand brought in some
years before especially for the purpose. After that he went to the kitchen
house and among the storehouses, and he looked upon all of the stored
food and ancient vessels of wine, and he brought out vats of honey, and
wine from the time of Bishop Arni.

As the time grew closer, it seemed that he even wanted to look in upon the rooms where the guests would be staying, and watch the serving-women beat out the reindeer skins and sweep down the floors. But as Good Friday drew on, Sira Jon seemed to Olof to grow more and more out of sorts, so that the servingfolk were afraid of his coming, and Petur the steward would not go into his presence. Now Olof went to Sira Audun's chamber and beat upon the door so that he could not ignore her, and after some while of this beating and calling, he opened the door and let her in. And Olof told Sira Audun what she wished to do to assure good masses and a pleasant feast, but she said that she could not do this thing by herself, for Sira Jon was her master and she was a servant and a woman to boot. Sira Audun was greatly reluctant, and Olof sat with him for almost an entire morning, and would not leave his room, although he ordered her to. This was on the morning of Good Friday. At last, because of duties that Sira Audun needed to perform, he agreed with Olof, and she went away.

That night, Olof carried an especially rich dinner to Sira Jon in his room, with many kinds of food and in greater quantity than he could eat, and then she went out, closing the door, as usual. Sira Audun then barred the door so that the other priest could not open it, and Sira Jon stayed in there, sometimes crying out and sometimes silent, until dawn on Easter morning. When they let him out, he was not out of sorts at all. So it was that all the folk who came to Gardar for the feast were much pleased with Sira Jon, and remarked at how calm he seemed, and even Sira Pall Hallvardsson was happy with the other priest's demeanor.

It happened that many folk carried with them the best gifts that they could afford, and placed them on the altar in front of the finger bone of St. Olaf as a thank-offering for bringing them through the winter. Thorkel Gellison gave a stool, carved from olive wood from Jerusalem, that his great-grandfather had carried from Ireland, where it had come from the crusades, and this stool had many fantastic beasts carved upon it in the Eastern manner. Thorkel was pleased to have survived the winter with his wife.

Snaebjorn Bjarnarson of Herjolfsnes and his two sons who had not died made the gift of a French ivory folding altar, which men of their family had always carried with them on sea journeys, and which had afforded them great good luck. These men gave thanks for the survival of their children, eleven in all, though Siggtryg and two of the wives had died.

Magnus Arnason could not bring his gift inside the church, for it was a large and handsome roan stallion, some five winters old and well broke to both drawing and riding, the best of Magnus' fine group of horses, and one of the best of the offspring of Thorkel Gellison's old gray stallion. Magnus gave thanks for the life of his concubine and his other servants as well, for his skraeling-born wife had died many years before.

Bjorn Bollason, the new lawspeaker, gave a chair for the priest to sit in during the mass, and carved along the back of this chair, which was made from driftwood gathered over a number of seasons, were an eagle and a bear, for St. Jon and St. Kolumban. This was the most magnificent gift, as was appropriate, and many folk pressed in to get a look at it.

Vigdis of Gunnars Stead and Ketils Stead gave a soapstone bowl, shaped and carved with twelve figures holding hands, and these were the twelve apostles. There had once been a face in the bottom of the bowl, the face of Jesus, but Vigdis had this face smoothed away because she declared that it was a sin to cover such a face with sourmilk or broth. This bowl had been among the furniture at Ketils Stead for as long as anyone knew, and its origin and maker were lost.

Ragnleif and his uncle's wife, Gudrunn Jonsdottir, gave a gift together, and this was a pair of walrus tusks that Osmund Thordarson had owned for many years, since the last time a party of men went to the Northsetur, and also these two announced that it was their fixed intention to wed each other at the following Yule, and while some folk disapproved of the haste with which they went about their courtship, others said that the time of courteous formalities was past for Greenlanders, and that a woman and a large steading should not be without a strong farmer for the summer's work.

Gunnar Asgeirsson and Birgitta Lavransdottir made a gift of a length of red silk, sewn into a priest's cope. Folk saw that much elaborate stitching concealed where the lengths had been pieced out.

Other gifts, of wadmal and weaving and furs and sealskins, were plentiful as well, and many were given by unknown folk, in the dark of the night, and among these was a lovely carved olive wood cup wrapped in a woven blue and white border. And after Margret Asgeirsdottir placed these with the other things, she owned nothing more that had once belonged to Skuli Gudmundsson.

After the giving of the gifts, Sira Jon conducted the first mass, with Sira Audun assisting him, and Sira Audun spoke the following prayer:

> *Lord, we lie in our turf houses,*
> *As in graves covered with snow,*

And our prayers rise to you as loudly
As the voices of the dead.

Lord, You break the ice for us,
And call forth the green grass,
And so we rise out of our houses
And come forth singing.

But folk did not consider this prayer as good as others of Sira Audun's, and only a few praised it.

Now at this feast, the great topic of talk besides the sickness and the harsh winter was Bjorn Einarsson, and folk recalled how he had acted and the belongings he had brought with him, and the articles of dress Solveig had worn about in every sort of weather. Folk who were interested in ships and boats, as the Hvalsey Fjord folk were, recalled the trim lines and fine carving of his four ships. Folk from Vatna Hverfi recalled the expert way that he had chosen for himself the very best horses in the district. Thord of Siglufjord recalled the types of food he had sent during the hunger of 1388—only wholesome and delicate and tasty items, nothing from the back of the storehouse. Gardar folk recalled his tales of Rome and Jerusalem and France and Iceland, and the way that Einar always stood by to correct and add to these tales. Sira Audun recalled some jokes that Bjorn had made while settling his dispute with the Alptafjorders about where they should worship, and others were led to recall Kollbein Sigurdsson, and his wooden-headed manner of doing the same thing, so that everyone felt cheated when Kollbein was through, and everyone felt benefited when Bjorn was through. Those who had not known Bjorn, or had seen him only from afar, related to their neighbors what they had heard about him. This became a topic of controversy, whether Bjorn in his four ships had carried as many goods to Greenland as Thorleif had in his one ship, and there was great disagreement about this. The result of this was that at the end of the evening, it seemed to folk that visitors such as Bjorn were too good to be true, and some doubted in their minds that he and his ships and his tales had ever really been among them, or declared that he couldn't have been a man, but must have been a ghost or an angel or a devil sent to try or to bless the Greenlanders, and as they went back to their booths and chambers, folk recalled other uncanny things, both those that they had not seen and those that they had seen.

After the visitors passed a short while resting, they got up in the dark and went to another mass, where Sira Jon wore the gold vestments, and

Sira Audun repeated his prayer from the morning, so that most folk were confirmed in their dislike of it, while some praised it even more than they had, perhaps as a way of amusing themselves at the expense of their neighbors.

After this second mass, there were more refreshments laid upon the tables of the hall, and folk took their trenchers and sat about on benches next to the walls or sat upon the floor, and the business of this gathering was to exchange news and make plans, or to tell tales. And Sira Jon sat in his high seat with a bowl of sourmilk and a carved spoon, looking out over the rest of the folk, so that some of the more prosperous farmers came over and sat near him, as was only proper. But he did not fall to eating, and so the other farmers were unable to eat themselves, and sat politely waiting. Soon Sira Jon began to gaze upon the farmers one by one, so that each man hesitated to return the gaze and seem unfriendly, and some of these men looked about for Sira Pall Hallvardsson or Sira Audun or Olof to come among them, but Olof was at the serving table, Sira Pall Hallvardsson was speaking with a group of farmers from Vatna Hverfi, and Sira Audun was nowhere to be seen. Finally, Thorkel Gellison spoke up and said, "Priest, thy bowl contains goodly victuals, and it must be that thou art hungry, after thy great efforts," and folk noticed that Thorkel used the formal mode of address and praised him for such skill. Nevertheless, Sira Jon only looked at his bowl, and did not eat from it. And now, just when Thorkel was opening his mouth to speak again, Sira Jon spoke and said, "I have a tale to tell," and this was Sira Jon's tale:

It happened, he said, that there was a young man named Alf, from Stavanger Fjord, in Norway. When he was twenty-seven winters of age, he made a journey to Denmark and then to Aachen, in Germany, and there he went to the palace of the bishop, and asked to see the prelate, but the guards at the door beat him and sent him away. And so the next day at the same time, he returned and asked to see the bishop, and once again the guards beat him, only this time with sticks, and sent him off. And still he went, on the third day, and as soon as they saw him, the guards fell upon him, and were about to beat him, when the bishop went out of the gate with a hunting party, and he saw what was taking place and had his steward call off the guards. Now this German bishop rode over to Alf on his horse, and looked at him, and saw such holiness in his eyes that he dismounted from his horse and had the young man carried into the bishop's palace, and there, while Alf was recovering from his beatings, the two men held discourses about holy matters, and the bishop was much impressed by Alf's understanding of everything pertaining to the Church, so that when he had recovered, the bishop put him in major orders, and installed him in a benefice he then had in his gift. And Sira Alf lived in this way for six years, until he was thirty-three, which was the age of the Lord Jesus Christ when He was crucified for our sins at Jerusalem. And all of this is known and written down in the annals of the bishopric of Aachen. And in addition to this, folk at Aachen considered that their bishop was transformed by the coming of Sira Alf, from a young man sunk in sin to a holy and virtuous personage, and this was thought a miracle, for in the previous year, this bishop had fathered four bastards and provided each of them with benefices, although they were but newborn babies. And Sira Alf declared this, that the name of Aachen had come to him in a dream, as he was walking down a road, and before this he had not known that name at all.

Those listening began to look around and shift in their seats, for they little believed such things of Bishop Alf, who had been good enough as a bishop, but no saint, and had performed no miracles in Greenland. Some also began to eat, because it is not considered improper to eat when a tale is being told. Sira Jon went on.

Now it came time for Sira Alf to leave Aachen, although the bishop and many other folk were loath to see him depart, and gave him many rich gifts, which he in turn gave to the cathedral there at Aachen, keeping only a few things for himself. It happened that he set out for Bremen, intending to go from there northward to Bergen, and from there to Nidaros.

And so, on a day in springtime he set out toward Bremen in his priest's robe, and leading a donkey, and loaded on the donkey were many gifts for the bishops he would meet upon the way, but Alf refused guards, saying that the Lord would guard him. The first day passed uneventfully, until he came to a certain shrine, where he intended to make a pilgrimage. There it happened that at dusk a beautiful woman approached him, dressed in the richest and most colorful garments, and she began to speak to him shyly and innocently, but he saw at once through her deceptive manner, and knew her for a whore, and he began to speak to her in a loving fashion, and he prevailed on her so that she put off her rich clothing and put on a simple wadmal robe, and she consecrated herself to the Lord then and there. And the next morning Sira Alf went on.

It so happened that toward dusk of the second day, it became clear that Sira Alf and the donkey would have to spend the night upon the roads, for they were far from any town. And so Sira Alf found a secluded spot and hobbled the donkey, and got down upon his knees to make his evening prayers. And while he was in the midst of these prayers, thieves came and began to unload the donkey and take away the treasures that Sira Alf was carrying with him, but Sira Alf was so holy and so sunk in his prayers that he didn't notice what was happening. And now, when the donkey was unloaded, and relieved of even its most precious burden, which was a reliquary containing the jawbone of Joseph of Arimathea, it began to bray loudly, as if crying out, so loudly that a man's hair might stand up on end, but instead of getting up from his prayers, Sira Alf called, "Oh, faithless beast, your cries are wasted, for they will never change the hearts of our persecutors, nor will they call up helpers for us. Better that you pray to the Lord who created you that He move the feelings of these thieves!" and so Sira Alf continued in his praying, and the donkey fell silent. But then it happened that when the priest arose in the morning, the two packs were sitting, neatly tied together, beside the road, and nothing had been taken from them. He loaded them onto the donkey's back and set out.

And now, on this third day, they came to the town of Cologne, where there is a great and beautiful cathedral. And at dusk they went through the city gates as they were closing, and began toward the cathedral. But as soon as Sira Alf got into the city, he was set upon by murderers, who carried daggers, and these folk declared their intention of killing the priest and stealing his goods, and to that end they threw him to the stones of the street and raised their weapons. But Sira Alf looked at them steadily, and did not cry out in fear, only saying in a low voice to the donkey, "So we are brought nearer to the hope of Heaven." And it happened just then that a storm broke out above their heads, and a bolt of lightning came down and struck the leader of this gang of murderers, so that he was knocked down and rendered blind. And the others of the gang were greatly afraid and they stepped backward and allowed Sira Alf to get up. And the Norwegian laid about himself with his fists, and many of the murdering band were knocked insensible, and so Sira Alf continued to the precincts of the cathedral, where the bishop himself was waiting to greet him. The bishop said three dreams had come to him of Sira Alf, a dream of a whore, a dream of thieves, and a dream of murderers, and in each instance Sira Alf had done the work of a holy man, for a holy man is one who turns away from sin, one who relies on the Lord, and one who battles the enemies of the Lord with all the means at his command. And Sira Alf was received into the cathedral, and he lived there for one year, discoursing with the bishop and assisting at masses in that beautiful temple.

Now Sira Jon fell silent, and began to eat the sourmilk he had in his bowl, and the assembled folk considered this a pleasant tale, and one well told, whether this Alf was the Alf they knew or not. And now folk recollected that Sira Jon had been among them for some twenty-three winters, although it hardly seemed so long, and they praised him for his feast and for his stewardship of Gardar, which he had maintained in greater state than Ivar Bardarson had done when he was steward. And, with much talk along these lines, folk went to their beds.

After this feast the spring came on, and it was a hot one that turned the grass suddenly, and there was little rain, but there was so much snowmelt from the previous winter that the fields were rich and thick. Now the time came for Margret Asgeirsdottir to return to Steinstraumstead with Sigurd, and she readied her belongings. On the day of her departure, as she was speaking with one of the servingmen about how she wished to load the boat and how much she had to carry, Gudrunn Jonsdottir came to her and said this, "Things have changed here now, for Osmund has died, and this farm of his is poorer than it was in the time of Marta Thordardottir. In addition to that, most of the folk are removing themselves to Ragnleif's steading, where you are unknown and have few friends. For these reasons, you must find another winter place, or take yourself back to your brother in Hvalsey Fjord, which seems to me the best course of action. But in order that folk will not think me an ungenerous woman, I am sending with you as your own seven ewes, not only five, and all of these ewes have lambs at their sides." And she stood by for Margret to thank her. And Margret said, "This news is not unexpected, for you have treated me with little respect during my time here, although I nursed all of the folk in this steading back to health when I found them dying. Two more ewes than I am accustomed to receiving is little enough payment for the death of Asta Thorbergsdottir, in my view." And then the ewes were led down the hillside and carried into the boat, and Margret went off.

But it happened that the Lord was not finished with the Greenlanders, for after the feast, some folk who had been there fell ill with the stomach ill, wherein folk vomit and spend much time in the privy and sweat and have great pain in their bellies. Those folk who had it first were from Vatna Hverfi district and Dyrnes district, and soon after the feast, others in these districts had the disease as well, and some old people and some children died from it. Then the disease came to Brattahlid and Hvalsey Fjord, and after that to the south, to Herjolfsnes, and though few died, the great result of the disease was that folk were in their privies when they should have been manuring their fields and after that many were unable to join the summer seal hunt, and fewer seals were taken. But even so, the grass in the fields looked so thick and rich that the priests spoke in church of the way that the Lord takes things from us and then gives them back in other forms. At Lavrans Stead, everyone had it but only Lavrans was much devastated by the disease, and died after three days, and folk round about marveled at how shrunk he had become in so brief a time, for his skin lay over his bones wrinkled and loose, and he had no flesh to speak of, although he had always been a sturdy man. Of the other households in Hvalsey Fjord, Sira Pall Hallvardsson's household had it the worst, and folk who didn't go much to church had it the least, and many remarked on the peculiarity of this.

At Lavrans Stead it was the habit of Finn, Gunnar, and Olaf to go on the seal hunt, but in this year Gunnar and Olaf were laid low by the stomach ill, and so Finn was to go alone, as his case had been mild and he had already recovered. Kollgrim was not quite twelve winters of age, but he was tall and large, built as Hauk Gunnarsson had been, and he came to Birgitta and begged her to allow him to go off with Finn on the seal hunt. Birgitta declared that he could not, but then he tormented her so relentlessly for the next three days that at last she relented, but without telling Gunnar, who had little faith in Kollgrim's good conduct and even less in Finn's ability to control the boy, for Finn was often amused at Kollgrim's teasing and saw no reason to curb him.

Nonetheless, Kollgrim came of his own accord to his mother just before the departure and vowed that he would do as Finn instructed him and would remember himself and try hard not to shame the Lavrans Stead family, for, as Birgitta often said, Kollgrim was not ill-meaning, and only tended to get carried away, and after doing evil, he felt greater remorse than anyone. Such were her excuses for him. Even so, she felt little faith that he would participate in the seal hunt without causing trouble, and she regretted having given in to his whims.

On the evening after the departure, Gunnar came to himself and felt somewhat better than he had, and he called to Helga to bring him some food in his bedcloset, for it is the effect of the stomach ill to make folk so hungry that some folk call it the hunger ill, and yet however hungry folk become, they dread to eat, for no one can tell beforehand if the food will burn and torment him or not. In this case, Gunnar was pleased to discover that he could indeed eat his broth, which was very hot and savory—guillemot that Finn had snared, seethed with a seal flipper for fat, and seasoned with herbs. While he was eating Helga sat beside him and began to chatter about Johanna, who had gotten into the carded wool and scattered it about the main room of the steading while Birgitta was in the privy, and then, frightened at what she had done, she had gotten out

Birgitta's spindle and attempted to spin it into thread, so that she had tangled everything together, unspun wool and spun wool and dirt. Helga found this very amusing, and Gunnar, too, began to laugh at the thought. After he had finished his food, Gunnar told Helga to send Kollgrim to him, for he had some instructions for the boy, and Helga cast down her eyes, so that Gunnar demanded to know what sort of trouble Kollgrim had gotten into, and Helga said, "None, that we know of, but Birgitta is greatly afraid, for she allowed him to go with Finn on the seal hunt."

Now Gunnar leaped out of the bedcloset, in spite of the pains in his belly, and began shouting for Birgitta, who came in from the dairy, where she had been cutting cheese curds. And Birgitta, too, cast down her eyes, for she knew the source of Gunnar's anger. And after this, for the next six days, Gunnar refused to speak to Birgitta, and the two waited in fear for news of the seal hunt. And no knowledge of any sort came to Birgitta, in dreams or awake, and this made her a bit sanguine for a good outcome.

It was the custom of the Greenlanders to row their boats to the mouth of Alptafjord and hide there among the islands until the seals began to appear from the south in their great numbers. Then the boats would move outward in a line, and go among the seals and try to force groups of them into small inlets and fjords, where they could be speared or clubbed and dragged quickly out before they sank. For this work, Finn was not ready to be amused, or to allow any transgressions on the part of Kollgrim Gunnarsson, and it happened that he tied the boy by his hands to the gunwale of the boat and bade him only to watch. And Kollgrim was tied thus for three days, and only let go at night, when boats were pulled out of the water and folk were engaged in butchering and boiling down blubber. And when he let Kollgrim go, Finn only said that Kollgrim should be ready for the boat when the time came to depart, for it was not possible for Finn to wait for him and allow the seals to get far past them. And so Kollgrim was on his own at night.

On one of these nights, Kollgrim was going among the camps of men and looking about, and some folk called him over and asked his name, as often happened. He gazed boldly upon them and said that all who knew anything knew that he was Kollgrim Gunnarsson of Lavrans Stead in Hvalsey Fjord, and that he had been brought along by the hunter Finn Thormodsson, surely they knew of him, to help in the seal hunt. Now the men laughed, and one of them said, "Is your father, Gunnar, then, a famous man, though he dwells on but a poor steading that came to him through his wife?"

"Any man may be tricked out of his patrimony, and that is a fact. Certain folk, who have the second sight, see that it will return to us."

"It seems to me that Gunnar Asgeirsson is but a murderer and a fool, and Vatna Hverfi district is the more pleasant for his leaving." These men continued to laugh, and none more loudly than the man who was speaking.

Now Kollgrim stooped and picked up a large rock, and raised his arm to throw it, but another man, who was standing not far off, caught his arm and deflected the missile so that it hit a nearby boulder with a sharp smack.

Now the man who had been talking said, "The pup is like to the dog, then. Well, here is one you should meet." And he stepped aside to reveal another man sitting on a rock behind him, eating his meat. This man now looked up. He was a burly dark fellow, but withal he had such a beautiful countenance that Kollgrim was content to look upon him for a few moments. The loud man yelled at him, "This is the one to throw your rock at, boy, this is the fellow who lives at Gunnars Stead, Jon Andres Erlendsson, and a wild fellow he is. 'Tis not a rock that will stop him if he cares to have something he wants."

"Right now, Ofeig Thorkelsson, what I wish to have is my meat, and you are making a great deal of noise," said Jon Andres. Then he looked at Kollgrim. It was the case that although Kollgrim was large for his age, he was still a boy. Jon Andres Erlendsson was just become a man, with a man's stature and a man's breadth. He looked sternly at Kollgrim for some moments while spooning up his food, then he put aside his bowl and said, "Do you know, boy, that your father injured my three brothers, so that they lay in torment before they were fortunate enough to die, and that this fellow Finn Thormodsson was the fiend who concocted the scheme of their destruction?"

"I know that your father and mother gave three sons so that they might have our great steading. It was a small price to pay, or so folk said at the time." But indeed, Kollgrim could not take his eyes off Jon Andres. "Here is another tale. That your father and his second whore were gnawed by dogs. What neighbor do you blame for that?"

Now the man Ofeig began to laugh again, and he said, "I truly think this boy is half fox. He would rather bite than live."

Now Kollgrim looked at him, "Are you intending to kill me, then, Ofeig Thorkelsson? Will it be by pushing my head into your belly and suffocating me?" And it was the case that Ofeig was somewhat fat. Now Kollgrim stooped again and picked up another rock.

Now Jon Andres spoke up and said, "It is not my wish to start a fight with a boy. You came upon us unexpectedly, and we only wished to know who you might be, little thinking that it would have anything to do with us. You had best go back to Finn Thormodsson and forget that we have met."

Now Kollgrim glanced around, and in the late dusk, for this was not long before the feast of St. Kolumkilli and the days were very long, he saw some birds down by the shore, picking among the leavings of the Greenlanders, and he shouted and raised his arm, and the birds lifted a little off the strand, and he threw the rock and felled one of them, as Finn had taught him to do. And after this he turned to Jon Andres and said, "This is the sort of boy that I am," and he walked off, but as if reluctantly, and he looked back two or three times. One of the men with Ofeig, whose name was Mar, went down to the water and picked up the bird. When he brought it back to Ofeig, they saw that its head was smashed in.

The next morning Finn Thormodsson tied Kollgrim's hands to the gunwale of the boat once again, and they set out. On this, the third day, it was intended that the seals would be herded into Hvalsey Fjord and Kambstead Fjord, but it was the custom that all the hunters would follow the seals until the end of the hunt, to make sure that the northerly farmsteads would have as much sealmeat as the southerly ones. Even so, Finn intended to stop at Lavrans Stead and get another suit of clothes for himself, as the ones he was wearing were wet and soaked with blood and melted blubber.

Before the sun was well up, they were nearly to Lavrans Stead, and Finn looked at Kollgrim and said, "It may be that Gunnar is up and about after the passage of these days, and it may be that he will seize you and prevent you from going on the rest of the hunt."

Kollgrim replied, "Do you wish that he will?"

Now Finn smiled, showing lots of teeth, and said, "You are no trouble to me, however you seem to folk from other districts."

"It may be that folk from other districts will not insult me and threaten me again."

"Or it may be that they will be led by mischief into doing whatever they please. Folk from other districts often act in unaccountable ways."

"Even so, this hunting life is agreeable to me. I wonder that my father and Olaf don't like it."

And so Finn put Kollgrim out of the boat on shore some distance from the Lavrans Stead jetty, and told him that he would return shortly, and so he did, in other clothes, and bringing clothes for Kollgrim as well. And when Kollgrim climbed into the boat, Finn tied his hands to the gunwale and they rowed in silence back out the mouth of the fjord, and this detour had taken them but a short while, and Finn caught up quickly to the line of boats that was herding seals into the islands at the mouth of Eriks Fjord, and he didn't speak of what he had found at Lavrans Stead, although Kollgrim looked at him with curiosity and eagerness.

Now they brought a pod of seals to a very good bay, wide at the mouth and then narrowing sharply and ending in a low sandy beach. Only a few boats were needed to drive many seals out of the water and up onto the strand, where they would lie, mildly awaiting the strokes of the Greenlanders' spears. But even so, the wide mouth of the bay was deceptively deep, and men who had hunted before never speared seals in the water here, for they were sure to sink at once, and carry spears with them. Now it happened that someone in a boat near Finn's boat succumbed to the temptation of the boiling seals around him, for a man could reach out and touch their slick bodies, and he poked his spear into the back of the seal nearest him—a succulent, half-grown beast. But the seal now twisted and pulled the spear out of the man's hands, and without thinking, the man reached for it, and was pitched by his leaping boat into the water, among the seething of the pod of seals. And this disturbance seemed to arouse some of the seals, and more than half of the pod turned and broke through the line of boats, and made for the open sea, so that the catch was considerably diminished, and in addition to this, the man and his spear were lost and his boat was tossed against a rock by the swimming of the seals, and caved in.

In the midst of this, Finn leaned forward and untied Kollgrim's hands, so that he could balance himself better in the boat, and when they had driven the seals up onto the strand, Finn handed the boy a short spear, and so Kollgrim went among the prostrate beasts and stabbed them in their throats, and the blood spurted out over his spear and his hands, so that the spear grew slippery and hard to grasp, and Kollgrim seized a large rock and began smashing this weapon down upon the heads of the seals, large and small, white and brown. After he was finished, Finn and another hunter came to him and praised him highly, for he had killed some twenty-five beasts, enough for the farmstead to live on through the autumn at least until Yule. And now Finn said, "So it is become true, what I told Gunnar Asgeirsson this morning, that you are more a help than a hindrance on the trip."

The next day they followed the seals to the most northerly of the settlements, where men lived very poorly and depended almost entirely upon seals and stranded whales for sustenance, and had few dogs, and no church at all, and the next day after that, they returned to Hvalsey Fjord with some fifteen beasts, in the boat and in tow, not so many as folk had hoped there would be, but indeed to Kollgrim it seemed that he was mired in blubber and lost in a mountain of sealmeat. Finn told Gunnar that Kollgrim had caused no trouble and attracted none, and Gunnar looked upon his son with unaccustomed pleasure for many days after this.

Soon came St. Bartholomew's mass and the sun stayed high and hot, but the grass in Hvalsey Fjord seemed to draw moisture up from the depths of the earth, for it continued green and thick, and so it was in other districts, too, and in this summer Gunnar allowed Kollgrim to go off with Finn more and more, for snaring birds or catching hares and foxes, and it happened that Kollgrim especially liked to hunt in Einars Fjord, though the best hunting was not to be found there, and on these hunts, Kollgrim caught glimpses of Undir Hofdi church and Gunnars Stead and Ketils Stead and the folk who went about these farms, and Finn saw this curiosity, but after all he said nothing of it to Gunnar and the summer passed uneventfully and in the fall the sheep were very fat and healthy and toward the beginning of the winter nights the stomach ill passed from the Greenlanders entirely, and no one had it or knew anyone who had it, and at the beginning of this winter there were more feasts than usual.

Margret Asgeirsdottir stayed with Sigurd at Steinstraumstead only until the end of the summer nights, then she herded her sheep along the northerly shore of Eriks Fjord and across the river there at the head of the fjord that was known as Braided River, and then she herded them down the southerly side of the fjord, with her other belongings on her back and Sigurd by the hand, and she stopped at each steading and offered her services weaving and five of her twelve ewes and lambs as payment for winter boarding, and before she came to Brattahlid she went over land along the river and asked at the inland farms between Eriks Fjord and Isafjord, and it happened that she found a place with an old couple who had a foolish son and some servingmen but no servingwomen. And this is where Margret and Sigurd stayed for the winter. As it happened, though, she was too silent for the old woman, who was always looking for someone to talk to and to share news with, and they agreed in the spring that this would not be a customary arrangement but that Margret might return if she failed to find herself another place in that fall.

Also in this winter, Gunnar continued with his parchment making and his writing, as he had done for the two previous winters, and he was somewhat more pleased with his hand and his words than he had been. In this winter he wrote down what he remembered of Hauk Gunnarsson, and his trips to the Northsetur and to Markland, and his journey with the English Monk Nicholas into the far north. But indeed, this was painstaking work, not such a great pleasure as spinning and weaving, his old winter occupations, had been, and not so appreciated by Birgitta Lavransdottir, who complained of the mess, nor by Olaf Finnbogason, who thought it an endeavor of little worth.

Now in this summer Sigurd Kolsson was nine winters old and more, and he looked to be strong and big, as Asta had been. He was a great help to Margret around Steinstraumstead, and she was very fond of him. He had a certain way about him that was unusual, of seeming to step back from each event or object and take it in for a moment before acting. It seemed to Margret that this considering manner must be an inheritance from Quimiak, whom Asta had called Koll. Quimiak himself she had not seen in about two years, since before the death of Asta Thorbergsdottir, and she did not really expect to see him again, as skraelings were like wild animals in this, that they appeared for many seasons in a row and then, inexplicably, disappeared, perhaps to reappear again and perhaps not. Folk sometimes spoke of the vanishing of the reindeer, and even the vanishing of such as foxes and hares, after they had been everywhere only the year before. At any rate, Margret did not wonder about Quimiak, and only remembered him from time to time when she was gazing upon Sigurd.

Steinstraumstead was falling down. Many hard winters had damaged the turf about the walls of the steading so that it crumbled away at a touch and blew away in the breeze and washed away in the rain. Margret had neither the means nor the knowledge to cut turf, even as inexpertly as Asta had done from time to time for repairs. Other things that they had been given upon coming here, or that Margret had brought with her, such as basins and coverlets and spoons, were in equal disrepair, and the folk Margret had stayed with the previous winter had had none themselves to give her, and indeed, the old man had sighed at the departure of Margret's five ewes, though she had left him three yearling sheep, a ram and two ewes. The woman had taken all of the agreed-upon weaving and put it away in her chests, and not offered any of it to Margret on her departure, as even Gudrunn did at Brattahlid, but it was the case that this family's clothes were poor and threadbare, and through the joint ill the old woman had been unable to weave, or even to spin, for many years. At any rate, all of Margret's and Sigurd's things, from their clothing (for Margret had no loom at Steinstraumstead) to their steading, had come bit by bit to a state of disrepair, and between the woman and the boy there was neither the skill nor the energy to put much to rights. The ewes dropped four healthy lambs and gave plentifully of their milk, though, and so Margret made lots of cheeses.

And in the middle of the summer, a boat came from Brattahlid, from Sira Isleif, who sent word that he was now entirely blind and confined within doors, for the light gave him throbbing headaches, but he sent his goodwill to Margret and also a boatload of dried sealmeat from the hunt, which had been especially good this year. He also said that he would send another boatload of reindeer meat in the autumn. The servant had much gossip of Ragnleif and Gudrunn, who, he said, were not suited to each other, but happy enough in the size of their farm, and this was what kept them together. Sira Isleif, he said, was so little thought of by Gudrunn, in spite of the fact that he was Ragnleif's brother, that sometimes he didn't even get his dinner, as an oversight, and then when someone pointed it out, Gudrunn would say, "Well, he can eat more in the morning, then," and not let any of the servants rectify the matter. It was true that Sira Isleif had become a querulous and complaining dependent who had little to contribute to the work on the steading, but indeed, there was too much work, with all the fields, no respite from raking manure, manuring the fields, forking it in, repairing fences, herding sheep, making cheese. Too few servants and too much land.

Now Margret wondered aloud whether Gudrunn might need some help in the autumn, but the servingman gazed upon her skeptically and said that she should go elsewhere, for all of Marta Thordardottir's former favorites had a hard time of it, and were blamed for everything that went wrong, and Ragnleif had no control over this, or over much else, even the treatment of his only remaining daughter by his first wife, who acted the part of a servant herself, though she was but ten years old. Now they sat silently for a while, and then Margret said aloud, "How was it that Sira Isleif could send such a quantity of sealmeat, then?"

The servingman shrugged and smiled. After a moment, he said, "Sira Isleif has one or two friends among the servingfolk, it might be said, who have their own schemes for this and that."

"But Gudrunn Jonsdottir will be angry with you."

"But indeed, there is plenty of work to do about the place, and experience is valuable. She will only be angry, she won't act upon her anger."

Now their talk turned to others. Among the guests about the place recently, the new lawspeaker had turned up and been greatly honored. He was a very young man, not more than twenty-five winters or so, this Bjorn

Bollason. Already he had a daughter and two sons by his wife, who was some five winters older than he. He was a proud man, well dressed and haughty, but for all that much interested in Sira Isleif, with whom he had spent most of his visit, and it turned out that Sira Isleif had been teaching him some of the laws, for he did not know half of what he needed to know. It was said that Gudrunn planned to send Sira Isleif to the man in the winter, since he was so fond of him, and Sira Isleif was not loath to go. But nothing of these things had actually been spoken aloud, only in whispers among the servants. "However low folk have fallen," said the servingman, whose hair was gray and who had a habit of rubbing his fingers, for they were afflicted with the joint ill, "sending away a priest and a brother and a blind man into the care of strangers is still something they hesitate before doing."

After the servingman departed, with a promise to listen for word of any farms that needed servants during the winter, Margret told Sigurd that she felt uncommonly low, for this was the effect of unexpected company, to leave you more in silence than you had been, and farther from others. Such a thing as this Margret could not remember ever having spoken of to anyone, not even Skuli Gudmundsson, for she had always been of a taciturn bent, so much so that all the folk she had ever known complained of it, but indeed, unlike all the folk she had ever known, Sigurd was nearly as reticent as she was, and so if talk was to be made, she had to help make it.

Also unlike all the folk she had ever known, Sigurd occasionally aroused her to anger, and most often it happened in the same way, that the boy would take a notion to do something and would not be moved from this, no matter what sort of work needed to be begun or finished about the steading. One time, Margret had finished milking the ewes and had set the milk on the shady side of the steading, and was ready to go off with the sheep to their pasture. One of the younger ewes took a fright, for Margret made a noise behind her, and she veered away from where the others were standing, and Margret looked about for Sigurd to herd the beast back in. She saw that the boy had taken to pitching stones into the water and called him over, but indeed, he had no intention of stopping his game, or even acknowledging her shout, but stood there tossing rocks as if entranced. Another instance, later in the summer, took place in the early morning, when the boy would not rise from his bed, but lay there with his eyes open, ignoring her, and on this occasion she gave in to the temptation to strike him, not, after all, when he refused to help her, but when he showed no interest in his morning meat. But indeed, he went his own way even so, as all folk do, whether they are fully grown or not, and Margret resolved upon no more blows.

Shortly after this incident, Quimiak reappeared. He was now a much changed fellow, no longer with anything of a boy about him, and on his upper lip he sported a few long threads of mustache in the skraeling fashion. His furs were very rich. He bounded up the hill as Margret was folding the sheep for the night and without speaking to her, for skraelings do not like to look at or speak to women if they don't have to, he searched all about the steading, and opened the door of the little house. Margret saw that he was looking for Asta and Bryndis, and she gestured to him that they were dead of sickness. Now he stood there staring at her for a long moment, and it seemed to Margret that he was much disturbed by this news. Just then, Sigurd came from behind the steading.

Now Quimiak smiled broadly, as if surprised, and Margret saw that he had understood the boy to be dead, as well. Sigurd, not being used to visitors, perhaps, or not recognizing the skraeling, ran over to Margret and pressed against her robe. At this, Quimiak stepped up to her and took the boy by the shoulders and pulled him away from her and turned him about, and Margret said, "Indeed, child, you must stand up straight, for this is your father, whom you have seen many times before and should remember." Quimiak was much pleased with the boy, and pinched his flesh between his forefinger and thumb, then ran his hand down the boy's side, then put his hand on top of the boy's head, and regarded how tall Sigurd was. Then he began talking in the skraeling tongue and smiling. After this, he pulled something from underneath his fur shirt, and this was a smaller shirt, in the same style as his own, and made of white rabbit and blue fox skins sewn together in a pattern of chevrons. This he handed to Sigurd, who looked at Margret as he took it. Margret said, "This is a handsome gift, Sigurd, and your father has brought it to you from the Northsetur or the eastern lands. Other children do not have such things." Sigurd thanked Quimiak in the Norse tongue, and Quimiak seemed to understand the gist of his reply.

Now Quimiak held out his hand, and, with a look at Margret, Sigurd placed his within it. Thinking that this was some sort of skraeling custom, Margret nodded and smiled, but then she was surprised to see Quimiak begin half to lead and half to drag Sigurd down the hillside toward his skin boat. When Sigurd balked, Quimiak picked him up with ease and began to carry him. At this, Sigurd began to shout to Margret, but it was as if she could not respond or move, as if she were entranced by a spell, and she suddenly remembered the same sensation from the killing of Skuli

Gudmundsson as freshly as if that death were but a day old and not some sixteen summers in the past. It was not until they were nearly at the boat that it came to her that she could run after them, and so she did, across the trackless willow scrub that caught at her feet and made her stumble, and she, too, was crying out, but Quimiak paid no heed, and simply put the screaming boy into the skin boat. Margret fell down and got up again, and by the time she was to the water, the skin boat was far out into the fjord, and Sigurd's frightened voice came back to her, amplified by the water, calling for her to come and to save him and to help him, and the sound of these cries lasted almost as long as she could see the boat.

In this same summer, a pair of messengers came to St. Birgitta's church from Gardar, and they were the steward Petur and the serving-woman Olof, and they spoke to Sira Pall Hallvardsson for an afternoon, an evening, and a morning, and the result was that Sira Pall Hallvardsson got into the Gardar boat and returned with them to the bishop's residence. It could not be said that the Hvalsey Fjord folk were much surprised by these events, but they were put out even so, as they had become used to much activity about the church, and more than a few of the farmers visited Sira Pall Hallvardsson rather often.

When Sira Pall Hallvardsson came to Gardar, he found Sira Jon locked in his chamber, as Olof had said he would, and when Olof unlocked the door and he went in, Sira Pall Hallvardsson's nose turned at the odor of the tiny place. Sira Jon had nothing on, and his flesh was covered with scratches that he had made with his own fingernails before Olof had had the sense to cut them. When Sira Pall Hallvardsson entered, Sira Jon, who had been sitting by the wall, stood up and approached with his old haughty manner. Sira Pall Hallvardsson greeted him. He had never seen a man go naked in Greenland except to swim in the hot springs of the south, such was the coolness of the climate. Now Sira Jon gave him the episcopal kiss on his cheek and held out his hand for Sira Pall Hallvardsson to kiss. To get down upon his knee and kiss the other man's ring, or in this case, his finger, for there was no ring, was something Sira Pall Hallvardsson had never been asked to do before. He did it with difficulty, for his knees were much affected by the joint ill. The mad priest stood shamelessly and apparently unchilled, for his arms hung loosely at his sides though his skin was bluish. Sira Pall Hallvardsson rose to his feet. The top of his head brushed a beam of the ceiling.

Now Sira Jon said, "Welcome, then, Pall Hallvardsson. You are come to ask for money, I suspect, as you are always wanting to improve your church at the expense of everything else in the bishopric."

"No, indeed, the church is in good repair, and even the priest's house is——"

"It was a sight to see, indeed."

"What was that?"

"After they carried him out, such rot! Mice were living in the bedcloset, and indeed, making use of his hair for their nests and his clothing for their litters. Folk say he was a hundred and fifty years old, and she wasn't far behind. They say that only such a disease as the vomiting ill could have killed him, because of the relics in the church."

"The relics in the church?"

"Those stolen from Gardar when Bishop Arni died. That's why they lived so long. They kept the relics in their bedcloset. The bedcloset glowed from the holy radiance. Many people saw it. But then some mice carried off the relics to their nesting site away from the steading, and the vomiting ill came on, and they were as mortal as anyone, the demons." Now he began to laugh.

"These tales seem to me to be rumors inflated by the passage of time. It is true that Sira Nikolaus and his wife lived in poor conditions and to a great age, but everything folk say about them is not truth."

"Indeed?" Sira Jon smiled. "Well, it is a habit of yours to tell me what is true and what is false, and to correct me at every turn, and to contradict everything I say, with that respectful tone, and to deny me. False humility and priggishness are sins, as well."

"As well as what?"

"No doubt you would like to know, for it is generally thought that you are a nosy fellow."

"Would it soothe you to have confession, or to pray with me?"

"Even the boards were rotten, and chewed away by mice. And listen to this. The dogs were gnawing on their bones."

"Sira Nikolaus didn't keep any dogs." And so the conversation went on in this vein, sometimes about Sira Nikolaus and sometimes about how Pall Hallvardsson had betrayed Sira Jon at every turn in the last twenty-five years. What seemed most peculiar to Pall Hallvardsson was not the other priest's manner, or even, in the end, his nakedness, but the persuasiveness of his case against himself, for indeed, he saw now that his secret sin for all these years had been the pleasure he took in setting the other man right, in undermining his self-confidence and stature among the Greenlanders. Even, perhaps, in seeing him go wrong with them and then turn away in amusement. At last Sira Jon asked Pall Hallvardsson what he was lingering for, and Pall Hallvardsson went off to find Sira Audun.

Now when he had knocked twice upon Sira Audun's door without any response and was turning away to seek him elsewhere, Olof appeared and said to him in a low voice, "Indeed, he is in there, but he will say that he was sleeping, or he didn't hear you knocking so softly, or he was sunk in his work, or he was at prayer. You must beat upon the door so that in the end he cannot stand it any longer and knows that he can't wait you out." And she approached the door and struck it with great force over and over, and after some two dozen blows, the door opened a bit and Sira Audun peeped out. When he saw Olof, he opened his mouth to speak, but when he saw Pall Hallvardsson, he stepped back and allowed him in. When Olof looked as though she, too, might enter, he closed the door hastily in her face.

Sira Audun's was a cell Pall Hallvardsson had not visited before, and, though small, it was very neatly contrived, with a small lamp for light, a large lamp for heat, an old door set up as a desk, and a pleasantly carved three-legged stool beside it. The dirt floor was covered with two layers of reindeer skins, and more furs were piled in the corner for a bed. Some hooks had been made of antler pieces, and Sira Audun's other robe and some additional clothing hung from these. In a line on a shelf that occurred naturally in the stone wall were a series of figures carved out of walrus teeth. These numbered thirteen, and Pall Hallvardsson could see that they were Christ and His apostles, each carrying his particular emblem, two crossed keys, a winged lion, but they were dressed as Greenlanders. Pall Hallvardsson stood admiring them. It soon became apparent that each man wished the other to speak first. At length Sira Audun said, "I was sleeping, for I have been to the churches of the south. Indeed, I am set to go to Dyrnes tomorrow or the day after."

"You went to the south when this had happened?"

"As it was, I happened to leave a day or so before the worst. Olof and I thought that he was getting better."

"But that very night, I am told, was the night that he raged through the cathedral and tore down the hangings and went about the steading unclothed for the first time, so that Petur could not approach him, nor any of the other servingmen, but only Olof, a young girl——"

"It cannot be said that I have had any soothing effect on him heretofore. When others cannot approach, neither can I."

"But, indeed, you left his fate to servants and boys, so that the shame of his madness was known to everyone."

Now it looked as though Sira Audun intended to continue his protests, for he scowled and thrust his hands into the pockets of his robe, but then he said only, "I am to blame, indeed, and I thank you for your castigation of my faults." After that, though, he went over to his stool and sat upon it and leaned over his work as if Pall Hallvardsson were no longer there, and Pall Hallvardsson saw that it would indeed be a long time before he returned to Hvalsey Fjord, and that his wish, of leaving the administration of the bishopric in the hands of Sira Audun, was a vain one. So he went out again without speaking and found Olof waiting for him.

Now he began, with some reluctance, to look into the affairs of the place, and to speak to Petur and Olof and the other servants as a master might, and to ask them about their work. At Hvalsey Fjord this had not been his way, for at the last his only servants had been Magnus the Bent and his servingwoman Gunna, who had the help of her niece, who lived not far off, at St. Birgitta's farm, and each dweller on the steading had known what work there was to be done, and Pall Hallvardsson had done his accounts by this method—what was meant for Gardar and as tithings and Peter's pence he put in one cupboard, and what was meant for himself and the others who lived with him, he put in another cupboard, and for each item that he put in one cupboard, he put the same thing in the other cupboard, and when the church cupboard was full, he carried those things to Sira Jon at Gardar, to be stored there, and if Sira Jon was disappointed and complained of the poor quality of the offerings, he carried some extra from the other cupboard the next time. Now it happened that every so often it seemed to him that he ought to make a list of what was in each cupboard, but after a few days of this list making, other tasks seemed more important, and the list making fell off.

Now he looked at Sira Jon's account books, and he saw that they were meticulously kept, with entries even from the day that he tore the hangings down in the cathedral. The health of all of the cows and sheep and goats and horses and servants was duly noted down. Meat and sourmilk taken from the storehouse for the morning meal was marked. A length of wadmal given to one of the servingmen was entered, and so on for every day since the day Jon and Alf and Petur and Pall Hallvardsson had arrived from Bergen on the ship. Each year had a single finely written-over page, and at the end of every quarter, numbers of goods for use and for the archbishop at Nidaros were totted up. Sira Jon's hand was so fine that Pall Hallvardsson could hardly make it out, and though he sat in the light of the window for a good while, staring at the books, Sira Jon's method for coming to the figures he wrote down escaped Pall Hallvardsson completely, although at first glance it had seemed simple enough. But indeed, Pall Hallvardsson reflected that he was some forty-five winters old now, and his eyes were dimming, and when he said the mass, it was from memory.

After he had been at this task for some little while, he began to look around himself at the great Gardar hall, from where he sat in one corner. It was a space with which he was perfectly familiar, but now he saw it afresh. Over the stone floor lay fresh moss, that would have to be carted in every two or three weeks—or oftener, for Pall Hallvardsson did not know how often the moss was swept out and renewed, but it was a prodigious quantity of moss. Above his head spread the wooden beams of the ceiling, ancient fir beams brought from Norway, carved like ship masts and black with the smoke of almost three hundred years. Would they break? Would they burn? Would they turn out to be rotten while they were under his care? The Hvalsey Fjorders were always after this and that at St. Birgitta's church—stopping rot before it started, or repairing turves while they still held their shape—but St. Birgitta's was a new church, only some eighty or ninety years old, and an object of great pride. Folk strolled about Gardar, admiring it and accepting it as if it were permanent. There were no records in Sira Jon's books of repairs to the cathedral in twenty-five years. Perhaps, indeed, it was built for the ages, but perhaps these ages were about to end? Indeed, the moss of the floor, deep and dry, could spell the end of the beams of the roof, also dry, should a fire get started.

And the tapestries and hangings about the walls. They were tattered enough. Here and there the tatters were neatly stitched, but not everywhere. Even from where he was sitting he could see that repairs of some of the hangings would involve stitching stitches to stitches, and the best needlewomen in Greenland could not necessarily make such repairs handsome. Some of the tears offended the sight. Christ shouldering His cross, taking a taste of water, except that the cup was rent from the Lord's lips and the cupbearer hung in a fold turned toward the stone. Sira Pall Hallvardsson got up to touch it, but saw when he approached that the wool would not stand touching. On another hanging, St. Lucy stood with her arms held out, but her dish of eyes was gone. And how did one dispose of such things as these, if he were to order them taken down? There of course would be rules, but if he had ever learned them, he did not know them now. He had never been trained for administration.

The stone of the walls looked permanent enough, but he knew from his experience at St. Birgitta's that a wet summer followed by a cold winter produced networks of cracks in the stones as if by magic. The very turf that kept in the winter warmth held moisture against the outside of the stone until far into the summer. Even stone did not last here as it did in

Europe, but shattered and crumbled. And yet, a building without turf in Greenland would be as cold as the winter itself, and no man could stand it.

Now there were the benches where the servingfolk assembled for their meals and took their leisure in the evenings. Gardar was filled with folk. He might look in Sira Jon's book and discover how many, since that was duly noted, as well, but he knew that the number would daunt him. These folk, whose names he did not even know, would soon be coming to him for instructions in their work. Was that the worst, since he had no idea of what their work was? Sooner than that, they would be finding their places for their evening meal, and was that the worst, since he would be liable for their clothing and nourishment and the health of their souls?

Now, seeing him looking about, Olof, who had been standing just outside the doorway, entered and came toward the priest. She stood respectfully, and cast her eyes down. She said, "Gudleif and Bjarni have gotten into a fight, Sira, and Bjarni has injured his shoulder, so that he can no longer pick up the large vats for Ingibjorg. The steward Petur wishes to have them beaten for fighting, but Sira Jon always said that I should come to him before folk were to be punished in that way."

"Who are Gudleif and Bjarni and Ingibjorg?"

"Ingibjorg is the cook, and Bjarni is her helper. Gudleif is Bjarni's older brother, and he is somewhat dim of wits, which is why Petur would like to have him beaten, but he dare not beat the one without beating the other, or Gudleif will be inflamed, and fight with Bjarni again as soon as they are alone."

"What do you usually do with them?"

"Sometimes they are beaten and sometimes not, depending upon Sira Jon's temper."

"Does Bjarni have a chamber?"

"He sleeps in the kitchen, Sira, and takes care of the fire in the night. Gudleif sleeps in the cowbyre with the other cowmen."

"Give Bjarni a place to rest, and send Gudleif to me."

"In the hall here? Sira Jon didn't like the outdoor servants coming into the hall."

"Where did he talk to them, then?"

"He only talked to Petur."

"He may come to me in the doorway."

And so he went to the doorway, but he quickly saw that this was a mistake, for many servants were gathered in the yard, perhaps because of the fight, and his conversation with Gudleif was going to have many witnesses.

Now a man approached the doorway, and the others standing about made way for him. He was of low stature, with big shoulders and a thick yellow beard, although when he took off his cap, Pall Hallvardsson saw that he had little hair on his head. He looked Pall Hallvardsson quickly and shrewdly in the face, then cast his eyes downward. Pall Hallvardsson said, in a voice rather too loud, "So Gudleif, the story is that you have been fighting with your brother."

"Ay, Sira, and I am little regretful, except that I did not stave his head in for him. I have few enough things of my own, that he should go among my stockings and mittens and make free with them, and then leave them about in the weather."

"This seems a small thing to kill a brother for, if you indeed wish that you had crushed in his head."

"Is it so to you then, that this is a small thing?" Gudleif looked at Pall Hallvardsson full in the face. "Had he better rummaged with my wife? For he did that too, though the neither of them will admit to it but they lie and dissemble, and say naught when they should be speaking fast, and speak fast when they should be saying naught. You'll tell me that's a small thing, too, surely."

"No, it is not a small thing at all, but now you have put out the cook, for she has no one to carry the vats for her."

"Indeed, Sira, so it is that my wife speaks to me, always throwing the cook at me, for the cook is fond of this snake Bjarni, and gives him bits of this and that and he revels my wife with them and draws her love away from me. But a cowman gives nothing and gains nothing except shit on his shoes, so that he can't even come into the hall to eat as the others do, but must hang about the doorway with his trencher in his hands."

"Gudleif, you should know that it is not here that we shall get our reward, but—"

"Yes, Sira, it is not here. These words are true enough." And now he turned away, and it seemed to Pall Hallvardsson that they both knew that he would not have spoken in this manner to Sira Jon. And so Pall Hallvardsson drew himself up, but it was difficult to do so, and he raised his voice, and this, too, was a labor, and he called Gudleif back to him, and he said, "Gudleif, you have not been dismissed from my presence. The steward Petur wants to have you beaten for this fighting, for he thinks that otherwise you will not learn to stay away from Bjarni."

"Nay, Sira, I will not learn this. I will never learn this until Bjarni has learned what is his and what is mine, so have me beaten indeed, for it matters not to me." Now the man walked quickly down the hillside away from the hall, but the eyes of the folk did not follow him, they stayed upon Sira Pall Hallvardsson, and it seemed to him that they were measuring him with interest and pleasure, for it is a characteristic of the Greenlanders that they get the greatest pleasure out of a curious event, of which many opinions can be held and exchanged. Sira Pall Hallvardsson turned and went back into the hall. Olof came to him, and he said, "Is Bjarni meddling with Gudleif's wife?"

"Folk say something to that effect."

"Indeed, then, have them both beaten." Olof went away, and Sira Pall Hallvardsson looked once again around the room, and did not wonder that Sira Jon had always felt far from heaven here. But Bishop Alf? A picture of the bishop giving a sermon came into Pall Hallvardsson's mind, of the old man's eyes protruding in their fiery stare, of the neatness of his toilet, and the care he took of his sleeves and collars. He had been Pall Hallvardsson's confessor, but never had he said a word, only listened in cool silence to what Pall Hallvardsson had to say, then given the prescribed penance and absolution in clipped, cool tones. He had been a man of such forbidding coolness that he hardly even aroused gossip, much less, until now, contemplation. But where, indeed, had he thought himself to be when he looked about him at the Gardar hall, and heard the Greenlanders in the yard?

The next day, Sira Pall Hallvardsson went once again to Sira Jon in his cell, and had conversation with him, and this became their routine. Sira Jon stood carefully to greet the other priest when he entered, and held out his hand for it to be kissed, and then he would retreat again to his corner, and begin to talk, and sometimes Sira Pall Hallvardsson would understand the references of this conversation and sometimes he would not, and when he did not, Sira Jon would mock him with his ignorance. Concerning the accounts, or Sira Jon's methods, or information of any kind concerning the administration of the bishopric, the mad priest was entirely and gleefully uncommunicative, and declared that such secrets as these were not for the ears of someone like Pall Hallvardsson. But still Pall Hallvardsson went in for his visit, and could not stay away. Sira Jon never covered his nakedness for the entire summer, and his skin became crusted with sores from sleeping on the damp ground. He did not admit to Sira Pall Hallvardsson that he noticed or cared, although sometimes Sira Pall Hallvardsson found him weeping, and considered that these might be the tears of pain. About other matters, matters brought to him by Petur or Olof, Pall Hallvardsson got into the habit of saying, "Do as you think should be done." In the winter, he promised himself, when there is always much leisure in Greenland, he would learn about the workings of the bishopric, and how to control what was used and what was saved and what was done and not done. And so the summer went on, and there were many tales among the Greenlanders of Sira Jon's adventures as a madman, for some folk said that he saw visions of what was to come, and rained down curses upon the heads of his enemies, and others said that he had become as a child, and could no longer speak or walk or feed himself, and others said that he came upon the servingwomen in their beds at night and lay with them, whether they would or no. Every district had its own tales, and these lasted through the winter, for the winter was neither mild nor severe, and there was little else to talk about.

After the reindeer hunt, Margret's friend came to her from Isleif with some parcels of reindeer meat and such hides as he could get for her, not beautiful or distinctively marked, but serviceable enough. Margret, who had been looking out for him and had seen his boat out in the water, was waiting at the tiny Steinstraumstead jetty with her sheep and her cheeses and a packet of clothing, and when he came upon the strand, she prevented him from unloading his articles, but asked him to take her across, for she was ready to quit Steinstraumstead for the winter, and, indeed, for good, for the steading needed more care than she had in her to give it. And as they crossed Eriks Fjord, the servingman told her of some other farms abandoned this year—three or four in the valley leading to Isafjord, two more in Isafjord itself, and two on the way to Solar Fell, although it was also true that the skraelings had moved off from Solar Fell, and the farm of Ragnvald had been claimed by Bjorn Bollason the lawspeaker. There was other gossip, too, enough to keep them occupied for the trip, and the servingman rubbed his fingers and rowed more and more slowly, apparently because of his joint ill, but really, Margret suspected, because he had intended to have the day to himself for a good gossip with her, and she had cut his time short. She opened one of her bags, and took out a cheese, and they sat in the middle of Eriks Fjord talking and eating bits of cheese.

He told her about Sira Jon. "The eyes started from his head and his arms swiveled in their sockets, showing to anyone who cares to see it that the fellow is possessed of the devil and there can be no two opinions about it. And indeed, what help is there if the chief priest himself lies open to evil like a trencher on a bench? And so Sira Pall Hallvardsson is in charge, and perhaps, you might go there. Weren't you a friend of Sira Pall Hallvardsson once?"

"And what do folk say of Sira Pall Hallvardsson?" asked Margret.

The man smiled. "The servingfolk say that he is timid enough for them, and lets them do as they please. It seems to me that everyone expected the new bishop a long time ago, and will be glad enough when he gets here. But folk have been expecting new bishops for most of my life, and only one has ever come."

Margret sat looking out over the water. Icebergs were beginning to gather in the fjord, blue underneath, white on top.

"Or you might follow Sira Isleif to Bjorn Bollason the lawspeaker, for Bjorn Bollason is greedy for help."

"So she has sent him off, then?"

"Not just yet. Folk say that any priest in the house is better than none after all, especially through the winter, when folk are dying and need to be ministered to, and it is better not to have to go out, but only to go among the bedclosets in your stocking feet. But Bjorn Bollason is urging her, and promises to send two or three of his folk in exchange, plus other gifts. It seems to me that her only hesitation has to do with the difference between what she considers enough and what Bjorn Bollason considers too much. She looks about her folk and tries to foresee who is going to die this winter!" He laughed. "Her son looks healthy enough, and it is not at all sure that she would send for a priest for Ragnleif!" He laughed again, and Margret smiled. "But indeed, folk who go there on errands say that Bjorn Bollason's place is a merry one, and the masters do much to ingratiate themselves with the servants, as if the servants might go elsewhere, as indeed they might, that is true enough these days. That would be a good place for you."

"Nay, Sira Isleif would attend too much to his lost sheep. Neither of these crowded steadings interests me. I have never been to Isafjord."

"Isafjord is a bitter place, and it would be well if you never went there."

"It is not so far off from Eriks Fjord, only over the hills a bit."

"But that bit is enough. The whole place slopes northward, and the fjord is full of ice winter and summer. Folk who were born there, with lots of land, long to get out. It is truly said that a small farm in Vatna Hverfi district is like unto an estate in Isafjord."

"Even so, I am curious to go there."

Now the servingman picked up the oars to the boat and looked

Margret full in the face. Then he said, "It is true enough that we are old, you and I, for your hair is as white as can be and my fingers are bent and my hips ache all the time now, day and night, winter and summer. But even so, there are many abandoned farmsteads these days, and some in happy locations, and it would please me to wed you and go to one of these places."

"Do you know that I am married already to Olaf Finnbogason of Hvalsey Fjord? Have you heard that he has died?"

"Folk don't hear much of the Hvalsey Fjorders, but I have not heard that anyone of that name has died." After this they rowed in silence to the Brattahlid jetty, and Margret got out of the boat with her things, and packed them onto her back, and then for some days, she herded her sheep, which numbered nine this year, to Isafjord, and there she found herself a place for the winter at a large but somewhat ramshackle steading owned by a man named Eyvind, who had four daughters. As all folk do who are going into service, Margret gave her sheep and her cheeses and her reindeer hides and her meat to Eyvind as a pledge of her service, and he promised to return the value of these goods to her should she have to go elsewhere in the future. And all this time she looked out for Quimiak and Sigurd, for it was said everywhere that of all the districts of Greenland, the skraelings preferred Isafjord district, and spent a great deal of time there, winter and summer.

It was true that the Isafjorders were unlike any folk that Margret had known before. Eyvind and his daughters were small and dark, and the eldest daughter, although only eighteen winters old, was already stooped from the joint ill. Eyvind himself bragged of having had the joint ill very badly in his shoulder, so that his arm had been frozen for a time in the socket, but then spring had come and he had gone out and done the spring work with especial vigor, and his arm had freed itself. When Margret remarked that his shoulder looked peculiar as if the arm had come out of the socket, Eyvind laughed and said that indeed it had, and that had been the purpose of his vigor. And now he raised his arm above his head and lowered it again. "Now, old woman," he said, "it may be that a man can have pain or he can have death, and surely in Isafjord a man with one arm is facing death. But the priests tell us that we must not choose death, if we have any hope of Heaven, and so I chose that my shoulder should swim freely in my flesh as payment for life, and so it does, and so I live, and when it swims too far, we nudge it back where it came from!" Now Eyvind laughed and his daughters laughed with him, and indeed, they laughed at many things, pinched and small and gray as they were. Food about the place was spare and always had been, although Eyvind had as much land to his steading as Asgeir had had in his best days.

The daughters were named Finna, Anna, Brenna, and Freydis. Their mother and brother had died in the recent stomach ill. After a messenger had come from Brattahlid to all the farmsteads of Isafjord to see how folk were faring, some of those who had been hale fell ill, and these two and three of the servingfolk had died. The four daughters were pleased to speak every day of the qualities of Heaven and to picture for each other the sort of life the souls of their mother and brother were leading. Each day they would sit over their small meals and begin:

"What do you think our mother is eating?" said Finna.

"Milk and honey is what the priest says," said Anna.

"But surely other things, too," said Finna.

"Oh, yes," said Brenna. "Bread and grapes and calves' meat, I would say."

"And what," said Finna, "will she make at her weaving today?"

"The thread will be mostly gold, I think," said Anna. "But with some silver twisted in."

"It seems to me that the angels would like a nice two-by-two twill." Everyone laughed merrily.

"Do you think," said Brenna, "that the shuttle flies back and forth of its own accord?"

"Perhaps," said Freydis, "she is finished as soon as she begins, or as soon as she thinks of the pattern."

"Maybe there is other thread, thread the colors of the rainbow," said Anna.

Some days they would talk all morning about exactly how warm Heaven might be. It could not be warm enough so that souls went naked, or could it? If souls went naked, then why all the weaving, and if there was no weaving then how did souls occupy themselves? And in addition to this, Hell was said to be hot and cold, so it must be that Heaven was warm and cool, and then they would talk about whether it was as warm as a hillside with the sun shining right upon it, or as cool as a cool sunny day in the summer, with a breeze blowing or without a breeze blowing, with lots of ice in the fjord or without very much ice in the fjord. And so their talk went on and on, as lively as could be, and it seemed to Margret sometimes that she could see the mother Hjordis in the fields of Heaven, or the streets of Heaven. Some folk said that Heaven was a holy city, as Jerusalem was, and so the daughters would imagine what a city was, and what Jerusalem was, and what a heavenly city Jerusalem might be. The folk at Eyvind's steading chattered all the time, and Margret thought of something that Ingrid had said often when she was a child, of poor folk, that "They have words for meat and little else."

Eyvind was practiced at getting through the winter, and had a routine of sheep killing through Yule and fasting through Lent that left him with three cows and twelve ewes with their lambs in the spring. In Lent, the whole household did as Margret and Asta had done during their winter at Steinstraumstead, that is, they stayed in bed under the coverlets and furs, half asleep and very hungry, saving what they could for an Easter feast. At the seal hunting time, Eyvind could hardly drag himself out of the steading, but he did so anyway, in the same way that he had made his shoulder work, and he returned with great quantities of meat and fat and everyone got up and ate some, and then more the next day, for, as they did this same thing every year, they knew about the sin of gluttony and the payment such sin exacted. And so it went at Eyvinds Stead in Isafjord, and when Margret spoke from time to time of other ways, the daughters and even Eyvind himself marveled at the peculiarities of folk elsewhere. Though Margret saw a number of skraelings during the winter and the following summer, none of them were Quimiak or any of his wives, nor indeed, the much-loved Sigurd Kolsson. Nonetheless, she decided to stay with Eyvind and his daughters, for she liked them very much, and considered their steading a good place for her.

Now it came time for the Thing, and one morning Eyvind said, "Well, I will go this year, though I haven't gone in so many summers that I have lost count. But indeed, this year I have three or four daughters to marry out of Isafjord, and it will also be a pleasure to see the new lawspeaker. I have seen them all in my time, Gizur Gizurarson and Bishop Alf and Ivar Bardarson himself, and Osmund Thordarson." And so the daughters got out their finest items of clothing and put them on and began the walk to Brattahlid, for Eyvind had no horses, as there are no horses in Isafjord. The land can no longer support them, though it is said that there were many horses there at one time. The daughters asked Margret to go with them, and she had no wish to refuse, but only to wrap up in her cloak and stay out of the light of folk's attention.

When they got to Brattahlid and encountered others traveling toward the Thing, Eyvind found them places in one of the Brattahlid boats that was going to Gardar, and Margret spoke politely to her former associates when they spoke to her, but mostly she occupied herself in soothing the impatience of Brenna and Freydis, who had never been so far from Isafjord before, and in consoling Finna and Anna, who had earlier been pleased with their clothing, but now were less pleased, when they saw the finery of the wealthy folk from Brattahlid. But, said Margret, it was true enough that some of that finery was stitched from wadmal she had dyed and woven herself while living with Marta, Osmund, and Gudrunn, and it would please her to weave such things for the Eyvindsdottirs, too, and so they passed the time of the boat ride to Gardar talking of weaving patterns and colors and such dyeing plants as there were about Eyvind's steading. Finna and Anna contented themselves, as women do, with the knowledge that even if they received no offers at this Thing, they would be far better dressed at the next one.

When they came to the Eriks Fjord jetty that belonged to the bishopric, everyone drew their boats up onto the strand or tied them to the rocks that jutted out of the water on the north side of the landing place. Now these northerners began to walk over the hill to Gardar, and to meet others who had come before them, and to linger and look back over the water for others who were behind, and there was a great deal of gossip and talk, and folk, especially womenfolk, saw relatives and friends that they hadn't seen for many summers. It seemed to Margret that everyone had looked about themselves and thought as Eyvind had thought, that after many years of not going to the Thing, this was a good year to do so, if only to get a look at Bjorn Bollason and his family and his style of speaking and his knowledge of the laws. And as they were walking, an old man that Margret did not recognize told a tale of Osmund Thordarson that Margret had never heard before, and this is how it went:

There was a Greenlander named Oskar Ospaksson who had come to Greenland from Iceland as a small boy, for his father was a poor man in Iceland, and in addition to that had received a sentence of lesser outlawry for attacking a wealthy man. Ospak saw that there was little for him in Iceland, so he came to Greenland, thinking to take to hunting in the Northsetur and make himself a wealthy man, and so he had done so, bringing his son Oskar, but leaving behind his wife. And Ospak and Oskar lived in Greenland for some fifteen summers, mostly in the western settlement, which was closer to the Northsetur. And Ospak was not a bad hunter, and Oskar was not either, although he was hardly so good as he thought himself, for no man could be. These men had one great advantage, and that was that they had had the foresight to bring with them many iron weapons—swords and spears and crossbows with iron-tipped arrows—indeed, Ospak had sold off his patrimony for these weapons, and they were the making of him.

Now it happened when Oskar was some twenty-five winters old, that Ospak grew ill and died suddenly one winter, and Oskar was left alone, and he found just how much he was lacking, as men do when they have only one companion and that companion dies. So Oskar went to the Thing of the western settlement in search of a wife, but none of the girls was to Oskar's liking, and so he took his boat, which was an open boat he had built himself from driftwood found in the Northsetur, and he rowed to the eastern settlement, where the Thing had already broken up. But he was a man of some resourcefulness, and he carried with him a stock of fine goods from the Northsetur, and he used these goods to gain himself hospitality at all the best houses in Brattahlid and Vatna Hverfi districts, and at Herjolfsnes as well, and he saw many good-looking young women. After the winter had gone by, he looked within his heart and saw there that his fancy was for a young woman named Oddny, who was the daughter of the wealthiest man in Herjolfsnes, and of course she thought little of him, for the Herjolfsnes folk are very proud, refined, and outlandish, and look more to Norway and France than they do to the western settlement for the things they desire.

Now this fellow Oskar was very importunate, so much so that Oddny lost patience and told her father that he had to do something to rid her of this hairy fellow. Oddny's father, who was a man named Kalf, feared to offend such an unpredictable fellow as Oskar, so he made him a vow, that if he would do something that he had never done before, to prove that he was indeed the best hunter in Greenland, he would give him Oddny's hand. Oskar asked what this thing might be, and Kalf declared that it would be to go to Markland and bring goods back from there for Oddny's bridal gift, for as valued as Greenland goods were in Norway at the time, so much more so were goods from Markland. But Kalf knew that there were no ships in Greenland, as none had come at that time in about three years, and so he expected that this would be an impossible task, and he and Oddny were confident that they would now be rid of the northerner.

This was at the end of winter, during Lent, and after hearing these words, Oskar went off and was not heard of for a while, and the folk at Herjolfsnes were pleased enough at that. But then the summer began, and it was just time for the seal hunt, and shortly after the seal hunt was over, news came to Kalf that Oskar had persuaded seventeen men to go with him in his open boat to Markland. And Kalf laughed at this and declared that Oskar had chosen death, not Oddny's hand.

One of these men who chose to go to Markland was Osmund

Thordarson, who was then about twenty-two winters of age, and a big strong fellow, though not much of a hunter. He was a good rower, though, so Oskar consented to his coming, and he was the youngest fellow on the boat. Such a thing as this had never been done before, to take an open boat to Markland, and many folk considered Oskar exceptionally foolhardy, but it must be said that he had little trouble finding folk to go with him, especially folk from the west, who never lived as comfortably as folk in the east.

Now it did seem that Kalf and Oddny would be out of luck, for the men in the boat had exceptionally good weather, and came to the forests of Markland in a very short time, some twenty days or so, with nine men rowing half the time and the other nine rowing the other half of the time, and when they got there, they had good hunting and no encounters with the skraelings, and they got so many furs that Oskar tore the benches out of the boat and piled furs where they had been, and the men sat on these for the trip homeward. Now it happened that one night Osmund came to Oskar and said, "It seems to me that our luck is about to turn and unless we prepare ourselves properly, we will lose all these riches that we have already counted as ours and already used to pay for many things in our mind's eye." But because Osmund was the youngest man on the voyage, Oskar merely smiled upon him and paid him little heed. Perhaps, as Osmund said, Oskar considered Oddny to be his, and in his dreams he was already enjoying her. At any rate, there was little to bear out Osmund's prediction, for the good weather and the good luck held, and they cast off from Markland around the time of the feast of Mary Magdalen, as they thought, for Oskar carried a stick calendar that he had made the previous winter. And they had good weather and rowed vigorously, and by this time Oskar was already counting his sons and daughters.

After some days it happened that some of the men sighted flocks of birds off in the distance, and Oskar thought that he was close to Greenland indeed, and as Herjolfsnes is the first stopping place in Greenland, he began to brag about how he would row into the harborage at Kalf's steading and throw the furs on the ground in front of the old man, and then claim his wife, but as he was speaking, the birds all disappeared, and within moments a great storm blew up, a storm such as would swamp a ship, much less an open boat that should have been used for coasting from farmstead to farmstead among the fjords of the eastern settlement. The little boat shipped a great deal of water, and the men were often in fear of their lives, and it happened that Osmund, who was indeed prepared, raised his voice in prayer both to the Lord and the Virgin, and also to St. Nikolaus, who once saved a boatload of sailors and since has often interceded for them. And so Osmund rowed and prayed and prayed and rowed, and after some time, the storm died down, but indeed, there was no sign of land, and none of the men recognized anything, for there was nothing to recognize, only open sea and the occasional iceberg. And so they drifted and rowed for many days, and their supply of water began to run low, and with his lips now parched, Osmund raised his voice in prayer again.

Now Oskar lamented his fate, and began to blame Oddny and declared that her hand was little worth such a trial. After a few days, and when they were in great fear of their lives, they awakened one morning to discover that they had drifted within sight of land—great black cliffs and green valleys. And this land was Borgarfjord in the west of Iceland, and they were not a little glad to see it, and they took up their oars with renewed strength, though they were greatly debilitated by their journey, and they rowed into Borgarfjord.

It happened that the farmer who controlled much of the land along the southern shores of Borgarfjord was a man named Elias Egilsson, and he and his folk came down to the fjord to greet the newcomers. And when Elias Egilsson the Icelander saw the open boat, he was not a little amazed at the journey the Greenlanders had undertaken, and he doubted their words, but when Oskar, in his brash way, began to lift out the furs he had gotten in Markland and show them off, Elias Egilsson was seized by greed, for indeed he saw that the eighteen Greenlanders were much weakened by hunger, and from their tale he knew that it would be assumed that they had been lost at sea. He could take the furs, which were tied up in bundles, and declare that they had washed ashore on his strand, and he therefore had the rights over them. And so he told his servants to say nothing of the coming of these visitors. But to the visitors he showed nothing but open hospitality, and all of the Greenlanders were taken in, and congratulated themselves on their luck. All except Osmund Thordarson, who saw at once that Elias was planning to tempt them with food until they had eaten themselves sick and then kill them all in their beds. And so Osmund only ate a little and pretended to eat and drink more, but actually passed his meat between his legs to the dogs under the table. And the rest of the Greenlanders were greatly undone by intoxicating drink, which Greenlanders are unaccustomed to.

Now all the men went to their benches for sleep, if they could indeed make it, so drunk were they, and Osmund went too, and pretended to sleep, but when all was quiet, he slipped out of his blankets, only bunching them up to look like a sleeping person, and he hid in a corner near the stacks of furs. Some while later, the door of the guest house opened quietly, and men entered, with Elias at their head. And as Elias was tiptoeing toward Oskar with his ax raised, Osmund sank far back into the dark, put a cup with a broken-out bottom to his mouth, and let out a great howl, using the broken cup to change and draw out the music so that it sounded like the wailing of a spirit. Elias hesitated, for he was somewhat afraid of spirits. The howling stopped. The Greenlanders, far gone in drink, only shifted in their sleep. Elias raised his ax again, and Osmund began to howl again, this time louder, as if he were calling across the fjord in the wind, so loud that he thought that his voice would give out, but indeed, he howled so loudly and so inhumanly long, that Elias was convinced that there was a spirit present in the room, and he dropped his ax and left.

In the morning, when Oskar woke up, Osmund related what had happened to him, and Oskar was much put out. That evening it was apparent to everyone that Elias hoped to try again, for he pressed food and drink upon the Greenlanders with unstinting generosity. But this time all of the Greenlanders did as Osmund had done, and only pretended to fall over in a stupor at the proper time. They went to their sleeping benches, and when all was quiet they moved off, and gathered in the shadows around the walls of the hall and waited. When Elias and his servants entered sometime later, they fell upon them and beat them, and Oskar, as a punishment, put a thong around Elias' neck and strung him up over the roof beam for a time, not killing him but hurting him very badly. And after this the Greenlanders were in possession of Elias' steading for the rest of the winter, and it happened that the next spring Oskar went looking for his relations in the western fjords of Iceland, for he was a rich man and a show-off, and he became acquainted with a wealthy widow who was a second cousin of his, and she persuaded him to stay with her in Iceland, and he did so. The others, including Osmund, took ship to Norway, where they sold their portion of the furs and found passage back to Greenland, and after these exploits, Osmund Thordarson was a rich man with a great reputation for cleverness, and it was true that he knew the laws very well, almost until the end of his life.

And when this tale was finished, the company had arrived at Gardar, where it looked as though the booths of the whole settlement were arrayed about the Thing field. The pile of weapons, for men lay down their weapons at the Thing to ensure that there will be no fighting, was large and impressive.

One of Eyvind's daughters, Anna, was pretty and well spoken, although slight. Eyvind found her a husband on the first day, and he was a man from Dyrnes, not rich but not poor. "Most important," said Eyvind, "not an Isafjord man," and Anna was happy enough, for this fellow, whose name was Ulf, was a young man to boot.

For many years now, the Thing judges had had little work to do, for the bishop, or Sira Jon, or Bjorn Einarsson, or the Greenlanders in their own districts had decided cases and dispensed punishments. But now it seemed to some powerful men in the largest districts that certain benefits of the Thing assemblies that had once gone unremarked upon, such as the opportunity to view prospective brides, or to trade goods, or to make plans for the seal hunts and the reindeer hunt, had come to be distinctly missed. Bjorn Bollason the new lawspeaker was one such, and he had gathered about himself a few other powerful folk who thought the same way, and who had sent messengers about to call people to the Thing. Outside of the booths of these men, tables of food were set up, and all who cared to were invited to partake, and usually while a man was eating, one of these men, perhaps even Bjorn Bollason himself, might begin speaking idly about this or that, but always ended up speaking about how the Greenlanders might dispose of their cases before the next bishop should arrive. And these men were strongly in favor of moving the Thing back to Brattahlid as in early days, and taking power out of the hands of the bishopric, at least until it should happen that another bishop should present himself. There was much talk then of Erik the Red and Leif the Lucky and other Greenlanders of the early days and their exploits, and also much talk of how heavily the tithe and the Peter's pence fell upon farmers these days, since the closing of the Northsetur. A man need only to look about himself at Gardar and see that the place was the richest steading in the settlement already, with the thickest grass and the most elaborate water system and the sleekest cattle and the most sheep and goats. And yet, said Bjorn Bollason, here was where a poor man was expected to come, rowing his little boat with difficulty against the storms of the fjord, risking his boat, if not his life, merely to bring more goods to the spot where the most goods in Greenland were already kept.

And, Bjorn Bollason or one of his friends went on, wasn't everyone nowadays a more or less poor man? The summer came later every year, more and more cows were carried out of the byre next to dead, the grass grew thinner, the hay crop smaller, the summer shorter every year, and then, in the fall, men went out again, in their small and ramshackle boats, and they caught the reindeer, and paid for them, with not only a tithe, but another fee as well. And at this point, Bjorn Bollason would fall silent, as if thinking, and then begin speaking again about something else, and the result was that there was a great deal of talk at this Thing about how hard conditions were and how magnificent Gardar was and how long it had been (fifteen summers now) since the death of Bishop Alf.

Some of this talk got back to Sira Pall Hallvardsson, and men watched how he took it, expecting him to blaze up and denounce the talkers, for indeed, someone must speak for the Lord, who is jealous of His rightful belongings. But Sira Pall Hallvardsson only smiled, as he usually did, and spoke politely to all men, and the Greenlanders were a little perplexed by this.

Six cases were decided by the Thing court, and of the thirteen justices that should have sat, ten were present, two having died in the previous year and one having fallen ill, and to fill out the court, Bjorn Bollason named two friends of his from Brattahlid and himself as judges, and in this way he broke with the traditional laws, which state that the lawspeaker shall have no vote on the court, but only sit as an adviser to it on the nature of the law, but Bjorn Bollason made himself head of the court, and made Isleif Isleifsson, who knew the law, the adviser, and so the law was changed. But there was little grumbling, as men were pleased enough to have the Thing busy again after so many years. Bjorn Bollason was a good-looking man and he had a loud, deep voice and a pleasing manner, for he spoke to everyone by name after he had met him one time, and asked after wives and children and servants as if he were an old acquaintance.

Of the six cases, two concerned killings, one concerned stranding rights over driftwood, one concerned a marriage annulment, and two concerned disputes over abandoned farmsteads, and all were decided fairly, in the eyes of most of the Greenlanders, but it was also noticed that Bjorn Bollason depended a great deal upon Isleif Isleifsson for the details of the law. Some folk said that yes, indeed, this was true, and regrettable, but then Isleif had been at Bjorn Bollason's steading only since Easter, and after another year, he could well have poured more of his knowledge into the neatly made, but apparently empty, vessel of Bjorn Bollason's head. In general, folk were well satisfied with what they found and what they themselves had to say about it.

It happened on the second day that Margret was sitting outside Eyvind's booth with Freydis after the morning meat, and a tall man with an equally tall son passed close to her, so close that she had to rearrange her robe so that it would not be stepped on, and the man had to excuse himself, and when she looked up, it seemed to her that she saw Gunnar Asgeirsson the man and Gunnar Asgeirsson the child. Now Gunnar said,

"Forgive us for stepping on you, old woman, but the ways between the booths are tight this year."

Margret nodded, and replied, "Folk have come from as far as Isafjord and Alptafjord. I had not thought there were any folk still living at Alptafjord, in fact."

Gunnar nodded, and urged his son before him, and Margret saw that he had not distinguished her, but the boy turned and looked at her in a quizzical fashion, with Birgitta's gaze in Gunnar's eye sockets. Now Freydis looked from him to her, and when Gunnar and Kollgrim had gone, she said, "It seems to me that a certain servingwoman is known by many folk."

Margret said, "A servingwoman often goes from steading to steading, that is true."

Freydis opened her mouth to ask another question, but then sighed and held her silence. Margret looked at her sharply. Finally, Freydis looked up and said in a quiet voice, "It seems to me that such will be my fate, to go as a servingmaid from steading to steading, and follow the children of other folk along the strand, calling to them not to tumble into the water."

"Indeed, though, your sister has found herself a healthy fellow and a pleasant farm to settle upon. Perhaps such will be your fate, as well."

"But she is the jewel of us all. Finna is humpbacked and knotty-fingered already, Brenna is sick with the coughing ill such as our mother had, and I am of a gloomy turn of mind, and it is clear to everyone that husbands do not care for gloomy wives."

"You are but fourteen winters old."

"Our mother used to tell our fortunes, and they were never good ones. Eyvind laughed about it, but it is true that she foretold her own death."

"I can foretell my own death as well, and so can you." But at this reply Freydis fell silent, though Margret prodded her gently, and would speak no more of these matters. She was, as she said, of a melancholic tendency, though birdlike in her movements, and deceptively quick to laugh. And now Eyvind came up to them and demanded his morning meat, and so ended their talk, but Margret was glad of it, such as it was, for it distracted her from the painful knowledge that Gunnar had failed even to recognize her.

Later that same day, when Margret was occupied with Finna in arranging Eyvind's booth so that certain holes between the reindeer hides would not be any larger than they had to be, two men came to the booth leading Isleif Isleifsson, and sat him on a pile of sheepskins beside the door, and Margret visited with him for a while, exchanging news of each other and of common acquaintances. In reference to his time with Gudrun and Ragnleif, Isleif said, "He that was last shall go first," with a sly smile, and "He that was lowest shall be lifted up," and though he laughed, Margret saw that he enjoyed his new state, for he asked her if she liked the stuff of his cloak, and Margret saw that, although it was of a sober hue, it was very thick and warm and finely woven. After this, he raised his feet, one at a time, and felt over his shoes with his fingertips, only so that he might appreciate again the softness of the leather, and then he let his fingers linger upon the weave of his stockings, and Margret saw that there was a figure in them, very neatly done. She smiled, but said soberly, "So it is that we are promised."

"It is true, though," said Sira Isleif, "that Gudrun gave me good gifts and handsome things to wear when the time came for me to leave. Those who do ill do not always intend it."

"And those who do good often do it for the eyes of others." And so they chatted, and Freydis looked on with undisguised interest, for Sira Isleif's identity was known to all, and it was easy to see that he spoke to Margret as to an old friend.

Sira Isleif had much to say of Bjorn Bollason's household. Bjorn Bollason's wife, Signy, was a very fine woman, who had previously been married to another man named Hrolf, who was the youngest son of a man named Hoskuld, who was the most important man in Dyrnes. Hrolf had been lost looking for some sheep in a great storm only one winter after he and Signy were married, and Signy had then married, at the advice of Hrolf's father, his foster son Bjorn Bollason, and Hoskuld had given as a dowry Hrolf's farm, but this farm was contracted to go through Signy to Hrolf's son, Hrolf, who was born only a little while after the death of his father, and who went to live with Hoskuld. Then Hoskuld advised Bjorn Bollason to take a boat and look about from fjord to fjord for goodly steadings that had newly fallen vacant. It was on the first of these trips that Bjorn Bollason saw that Ragnvald's steading at Solar Fell was deserted, and indeed, no skraelings were anywhere about there, and so Hoskuld claimed that giant steading as vacant, and Bjorn Bollason took the place over. All the folk from Dyrnes found Solar Fell much more comfortable than Dyrnes, and were intending to claim more farmsteads in the area, should they become vacant. And so Hoskuld, who was an ambitious man, had seen his ambitions realized, though in Bjorn, not in his own sons, and for that reason he preferred Bjorn Bollason to his own sons, and there was a touch of bitterness between them.

At any rate, Signy was as liberal and stately as ever the famous Marta Thordardottir had been, and as well dressed, and if anything more courteous, and to meet her a person would never think that she was from Dyrnes, but would assume that she had been raised in Brattahlid or Vatna Hverfi district. Between her and Bjorn Bollason, Isleif declared, was as deep an affection as you could care to see, and in the four years of their marriage they had produced four children, a girl, Sigrid, who was very bright and appealing, and three boys who were very manly little fellows, and played especially noisy and active games, and they were encouraged in this by their mother and father. In fact, Signy and Bjorn Bollason had this habit, that as soon as a child could talk, he was addressed with questions at his meat, questions about what he might do in such and such a case were he seal hunting or reindeer hunting or sailing to Markland or fighting Saracens in the Holy Land, and Bjorn Bollason judged their answers, and those who spoke foolishly were teased by the others. And in this way Sira Isleif passed the morning in Eyvind's booth, and Margret saw that he was much enamored of everything about the new lawspeaker's household.

On the fourth day of the Thing, Eyvind came to the booth in the afternoon, and declared in a loud voice that he had found yet another husband, this one for Brenna, and a man from Vatna Hverfi to boot, but when the man came with his relatives to see the bride and talk about the arrangements, they left again hurriedly without talking for very long. The young man was somewhat lame, but proud withal, and he looked at Brenna in a sneering manner. Margret saw that he was a nephew of Magnus Arnason of Nes, who accompanied him, and stood outside the booth while the negotiations, such as they were, went on. The Thing was nearly over, and Eyvind spent all of the last evening going from booth to booth and chatting about this and that, but the end of it was that Brenna and Finna did not find husbands after all, though Anna's wedding was set to take place in Isafjord some days before the reindeer hunt, and there was much to be done before it should take place. As they broke down their booth and prepared to leave, Eyvind declared that he had done a deal of work and gotten a fair return for his efforts, and he was very jovial, although his daughters were not so merry. Seeing this, he began to tease them until they went from frowning to laughing to weeping, and then he spoke soberly to them all, saying, "It is not the case that daughters float by magic spells from the steading of their father to the steadings of their husbands but by such effort as all must engage in, for a husband is a bird that must be snared by rich bait or by guile or by great labor, and the first of these is not something to be found at an Isafjord steading." And so Eyvind went about this job as he went about all jobs, Margret saw, by knowing the task for what it was and taking his loss at the beginning rather than being taken by it at the end.

As she was climbing the hill above Gardar, she saw Birgitta Lavransdottir. She saw that Birgitta saw her. Then Freydis came up to her and took her hand and they climbed over the ridge. When Margret looked back, Birgitta was already down beside the Einars Fjord jetty, loading Asgeir's old boat with their belongings. Margret could clearly make out the distinctive purplish color of the Gunnars Stead wadmal that they wore.

Now Birgitta, Gunnar, Kollgrim, Finn, and two other servingmen that Gunnar had taken on got into the boat they had brought from Lavrans Stead and rowed out into Einars Fjord. Birgitta seated herself in the boat so that she could gaze upon Kollgrim as he rowed, for he was a handsome boy, and she had lost none of her fondness for him, though it was true as everyone said that he had many faults. The only person about the steading that he did not tease relentlessly was Finn Thormodsson, and from time to time the beatings he gained from teasing Gunnar persuaded him to avoid his father for a bit, but he could not hold off longer than seven or ten days, and then Gunnar would once again find his horses hobbled together or his parchment marked upon with lines that mimicked writing but meant nothing or his neighbors put out because their cows had been driven into the shallows of the fjord. The only rest from these mischiefs happened when Finn took Kollgrim off with him, which he did much of the time. As yet no evil had resulted from these trips, though Gunnar predicted it and Birgitta feared it silently. They never asked Finn where he had gone, but only received the two when they returned and admired the game they had got.

It was the case that a rift had formed between Gunnar and Birgitta on account of the two children, Kollgrim and Johanna, for each parent was set upon the virtues of one child and the faults of the other. As for Birgitta, the names of Gunnhild, Astrid, and Maria were always in her mouth— Gunnhild had been the most beautiful, Astrid the most lively, and Maria the most affectionate of daughters, whereas Johanna was sober and staring and reserved, not ugly but not beautiful, either, and with the same uncanny radiance that Birgitta had always felt from her. It had happened at Yule time, when Johanna was five winters of age, that the famous first tooth loosened and fell out and Johanna carried it to Helga and showed it to her, and when Johanna then went off again, Birgitta, who was in the room, called Helga over to her and demanded the tooth. But she could not see anything in it. It appeared to be but a tooth. When she struck it, a fragment broke off, and there was nothing under the surface but more tooth, no squirming darkness of demons or worms. Even so, Birgitta took the tooth and buried it far from the house and the fields. She expected to find a change in Johanna, a lightening of sorts, as if a burden had left her, but nothing like this occurred, and Birgitta found herself turning from the child more than ever. When Birgitta chanced to see the child busy with her father or her sister, she saw that Johanna's manner was different than it was with her, but it pleased her no more, for the child seemed too quiet and attentive, and her eyes searched her father's face in a seductive way. Or so it seemed to Birgitta. At times she doubted herself and regretted the feelings she had conceived for this youngest daughter.

As for Gunnar, what he saw about Johanna was a desire to please those who would be pleased by her, and with this a naturally quiet temperament that shrank from loud words or anger such as Birgitta often showed toward her. Where Birgitta said she was sullen and stubborn, he said that she was daunted and afraid to speak or act. Husband and wife could not agree upon these things, and could not speak of the child without anger.

But such anger was nothing to what they brought to the subject of Kollgrim, who was certainly never daunted or afraid, but indeed seemed incapable of learning such things, for beatings and other punishments and indeed such ill rewards as he earned himself through his actions, as falling through the ice in the lake and nearly drowning, or being kicked by one of the horses so that his chest and cheek turned black and blue, all these went through the boy as if through a sieve, and soon enough he was back teasing the horses or trying his weight on the thinnest ice. The dogs would not go near him, so often had he blown in their nostrils or tied their back legs together or blindfolded them or induced them to eat something foul. But it was the case that he was always deeply remorseful, weeping and cajoling and vowing to avoid mischief, and when Birgitta looked at him, she saw his handsome face and his sincere remorse, and when Gunnar looked at him, he saw a deceitful surface that masked the corrupt depths. So it was that even when Kollgrim sat calmly before his trencher, relating with pleasure and charm his exploits with Finn or simpler events of the day, it seemed to Gunnar that his purpose was to gull everyone into such complacence as would leave the field for mischief wide open. In this way Gunnar saw he was truly repaid for the disappointment he had brought to Asgeir, and for the misjudgment he had shown in not sending the boy out as a foster son, for it was certain that he would have learned better manners at a steading where folk were unmoved by his looks and unafraid to beat him as much as he needed to be beaten. Instead, through laziness, Gunnar had entrusted the boy to Finn Thormodsson, and the outcome of this was still in the making, but it could not be good, for although Finn was a loyal and skillful servant, he was full of tricks and deceits, and was more likely to laugh at the boy than restrain him.

But every day, Birgitta saw signs of improvement in the boy, and the real beginnings of adulthood. And it soon came to be that Birgitta and Gunnar could not talk about the simplest thing without talking of these two children, even if neither name was actually spoken. Of Helga there is little to say; Helga was a good and virtuous child, attentive to her duties, courteous toward everyone, and devoted to Kollgrim.

Now they rowed swiftly along in the quiet water, and from time to time Birgitta looked at Kollgrim, and from time to time she looked at Gunnar, and after they had been rowing for a while, Birgitta spoke. She said, "It seems to me that the best course for Johanna will be to go out next spring, when she is of the proper age, to the steading of your cousin Thorkel Gellison, for he is a wealthy man and Jona Vigmundsdottir is a skilled housewife."

Gunnar replied, "The bird has not sung such a tune about her other nestlings."

"Folk say that it is better for a girl not to become too attached to her parents' steading, as Helga has. It will be with her as with Margret Asgeirsdottir."

And now Gunnar let go his oar and struck his wife a blow upon the cheek, and Birgitta fell against the gunwale of the boat, and seeing this, Kollgrim turned toward his father with a cry, and was only restrained from returning the blow by the actions of one of the menservants. These things set the boat to rocking so that much water came into it and drenched the packs lying on the bottom, and so all of the folk became quiet for a time, and the servant and Kollgrim exchanged places, and they rowed on in this way. And no more blows were exchanged, but when the party returned to Lavrans Stead, Birgitta moved her things to her father's bedcloset, and Gunnar and Birgitta had little to do with each other from this time forward for many years.

The winter that followed this great Thing was notable for bad weather— ice storms, followed by rainstorms followed by freezing weather, and the result was another serious hunger during Lent, and this time all over the settlement, not in isolated districts, as had been the case with the last hunger. And now folk remembered with disbelief the good luck of Bjorn Einarsson, that had been so great that it had radiated out from him, and from Kambstead Fjord to Hvalsey Fjord to Dyrnes and Brattahlid, so that the nearer folk were to him, the better their hay crop, the healthier their sheep and cattle, the more plentiful their stock of seaweed and bilberries. So, too, had the seal hunts and reindeer hunts been especially good in those years, and folk recalled how the seals had swarmed into Kambstead Fjord and even up onto the sands there, and the reindeer had come down from the north in herds and gathered near to Kambstead Fjord so that folk from those districts had not had to drag them far to get them home. Such was the talk that went back and forth during this famine, along with talk of the Northsetur, and the weather of earlier times, and the size of sheep in the days of Erik the Red and the quantity of seed that Thorleif had brought in his ship, and the good hay this seed had produced. And another thing folk remarked upon was the way in which, in these present days, especially good luck seemed to produce just enough to get through the winter on, while the usual run of luck produced less hunger or more at the end of the spring. Their fathers, folk recalled, had sometimes ended the winter with a small stack of hay left, a little mound outside the byre for the cows to chew over. At the end of recent winters it was the case that steadings that once had ten cows and five horses now had three of the one and one or two of the other. Steadings that had once had five cows had none. Folk had many more goats, and this was always considered a sign of bad times in Greenland.

Not so many folk had died, and it was said that those who died, died of fear, for when they saw their stores dwindling and their sheep starving, they were possessed to eat up everything they had, even if it made them sick, and then when they crept around to their neighbors, who had husbanded their provisions more carefully, there was little or none to share with them, and they were driven off, and some died and some did not, and at any rate these events caused bad blood in every district. And it caused also the abandonment of more farms, for indeed, this was the last thing that folk had to offer their neighbors in exchange for food and life, and though Sira Pall Hallvardsson and Sira Audun and Sira Isleif spoke against this practice, folk who had any surplus of food at all were not slow to accept such a trade. In this way, Vigdis of Gunnars Stead came into possession of two more large farms, and now, with Ketils Stead and Gunnars Stead, she was the most powerful farmer in Vatna Hverfi district, and Jon Andres, her son, was a man of many friends.

After this famine three years passed that were neither good nor bad, and during this time, the grandson of Ragnvald Einarsson, named Olaf Vebjarnarson, who had been pitched into the fjord when Ragnvald was running from the skraelings, was declared to be a saint on the evidence of three cures and a vision which was attested by Bjorn Bollason and his wife, who had lived at Solar Fell for five years now, and also on the strength of his martyrdom. A small shrine was built on the strand beside the spot where the child went into the water, and folk got into the habit of going there for cures and other intercessions, especially as it was not far from any district, and Bjorn Bollason and his folk were considered to be quite hospitable. The child was called St. Olaf the Greenlander and the water where he was drowned often gave off a holy glow. Many folk saw it. Folk discovered that he was most effective in problems of childbirth, and sufficient prayers to him could make a breech baby turn of itself and present its head, or slow gushing blood to a trickle. Some folk about Solar Fell who had lived there in the days of Ragnvald remembered that the baby's crying could be stilled by the sight of a crucifix, at which he would smile and gurgle with pleasure.

Sira Pall Hallvardsson did not know the rule about saints, and had little to say when he heard the news of the cures, and of the fact that folk had begun calling the child St. Olaf the Greenlander. When the new bishop arrived, Sira Pall remarked, he would look into the miracles and make a decision. Meanwhile, folk considered that if the lawspeaker himself referred to the child as St. Olaf, then others might do so.

It was the case, however, that St. Olaf the Greenlander had no effect on the weather, which was chill and damp and sunless every year, so that the hay crop was always poor. Cattle became fewer and fewer. Even at Gardar, only thirty cows stood through the winter in stalls built for eighty. And those cows that survived seemed not so sturdy nor so healthy as most cattle had once been. Now folk began paying attention to their sheep and goats, and taking the sort of pride in them that they had taken in their cows, and the news got about that the rams at Lavrans Stead in Hvalsey Fjord were especially large and potent, so that a ewe bred to one of these rams would almost always produce twins, and almost always both would survive. And so for a year or two folk got into the practice of bringing their ewes to Hvalsey Fjord just after Yule, when Birgitta preferred to breed her sheep, so that they would be born in the good weather, and Lavrans Stead prospered. When Johanna Gunnarsdottir went off to Hestur Stead in Vatna Hverfi to live with Thorkel Gellison and Jona Vigmunds- dottir, at ten winters of age, she took with her fine things in her chests, and when she went through these things, Jona Vigmundsdottir saw that her husband's cousin Gunnar was not such a man of ill luck as he was reputed to be.

Jona Vigmundsdottir had become a red-faced and loud woman with a hot temper but a kindly manner, and folk said that she was well matched with Thorkel Gellison, who was cooler and more calculating most of the time, but not unlike his wife in the way he welcomed folk to his steading and took pleasure in the roar of many voices about the place. If there were no visitors, Jona and Thorkel would gossip with servants. If the servants were working, the two would walk back and forth in front of the steading, looking out for travelers or itinerant servingfolk who might be going from steading to steading. Horse breeding and large fertile fields and access to both Vatna Hverfi district and Einars Fjord had made Thorkel a wealthy man. Thorkel prospered through these hard years, for indeed, in all times some folk prosper, even when most do not. These folk had grown sons living at home with their wives, and one of these wives had two infants, one of one winter in age, the other newly born. It was the duty of Johanna Gunnarsdottir to help care for these children, to follow the one about and carry the other, and to chew meat for the older one, as he did not yet have his teeth, and to look after their comfort in all ways.

It was the case that Johanna was not to go to Hvalsey Fjord even at Yuletide. Such visits, Birgitta said, had been confusing to Gunnhild when she made them. But the trip from Lavrans Stead to Hestur Stead was a short one, a hike through the valley that connected Hvalsey Fjord and Einars Fjord, then a crossing of Einars Fjord at its narrowest point, and it was easy both winter and summer, and so it happened that Gunnar found a great deal of business to do with Thorkel Gellison. One day when Gunnar had spent the night with Thorkel and was just getting up and preparing to return to Hvalsey Fjord, he went outside to wash in the washing vat and to see what the weather might be, and when he came out of the house he saw a group of men on horseback passing not far from the steading; indeed, they had just stopped to have a look at the horses in Thorkel's round horse paddock, and were setting off again. Gunnar recognized none of them. But then, as he was turning away, he saw that there was another rider a bit farther away. And then he saw that this rider was his own son Kollgrim.

Kollgrim was little practiced at riding and he sat the horse awkwardly. He rode up to Gunnar without hesitation and greeted him.

"Who are these men?" said Gunnar.

"There is Ofeig Thorkelsson," replied Kollgrim. "And another who

I believe is named Mar. The others are strangers to me." He spoke as if he had thought little of these men before speaking to Gunnar about them. Gunnar was much perplexed. He said, "Where is Finn, then?"

Kollgrim smiled and shrugged, saying, "After reindeer, I suppose. That was his intention."

"Who owns this horse, then?"

"A man to the north. But, indeed, it is a poor horse, not like Thorkel Gellison's horses at all." And before Gunnar could ask how the animal had come into Kollgrim's possession, the boy gave it a great kick and turned and galloped away. Now Gunnar went to the paddock himself, in search of a horse to borrow, but the paddock was full of mares with unweaned foals, and so he had to look farther afield, and the result was that when he had finally mounted, all of the riders, including Kollgrim, were nowhere to be seen. Gunnar rode a ways to the north and then to the south, for the fjord was behind him and a large lake before him. He went back to Hestur Stead, where Thorkel and Jona were sitting outside the steading, partaking of their morning meat. Gunnar went and sat beside them. He said, "What news do you have of your son Ofeig?"

"Little," said Thorkel, "and even that is unwelcome."

"Where does he stay, then?"

"He is fostered with Magnus Arnason, but it seems to me that he spends little time there. A group of Vatna Hverfi boys goes about with a certain someone. They do a little mischief, mostly among the serving-maids. In other times they would be taking ships to Norway and learning manners from strangers." Thorkel shrugged.

"In these times, from whom do they learn manners?"

Now Jona spoke up. "From Jon Andres Erlendsson, for he is the leader of the band. When one of their number is killed or outlawed through their mischief, that is when they will stop, and not before. Skeggi and Ingolf and Ogmund were not such as these are." These were her other sons. Gunnar got up and walked off before she could enter into a discussion of the childhoods of these three boys. Shortly he began his journey homeward, and of every person he met on the way, he inquired about Finn and Kollgrim, but the two had not been seen in many days. It had seemed to Gunnar that Finn's favorite hunting spots were to the north, past Dyrnes and almost to the now abandoned part of the settlement that had once been known as the middle settlement. In Einars Fjord and even in the wastelands just to the north of Vatna Hverfi there was little game to be had.

Some days passed until the return of Finn Thormodsson and Kollgrim Gunnarsson. They brought a great quantity of game with them, and

Kollgrim described without the least urging or hesitation the days of their trip, including a day when Finn rested at the steading of a friend and Kollgrim took one of the horses belonging to the steading and rode about Vatna Hverfi district, admiring the wealth of the grazing lands. Gunnar looked to Finn for confirmation of this tale. Finn smiled and nodded, and told of how fatigued he had been after chasing a whale that he had thought was going to strand itself among the inlets at the head of Einars Fjord, and then he had seen some reindeer, and so had been three days sleepless, and so on. Gunnar knew these things were not to be believed, but saw no way into these falsehoods, and so remained silent. Nor did he mention to anyone what he had seen at Hestur Stead.

On another visit, he asked Jona and Thorkel whether they had ever heard Ofeig speak of Kollgrim Gunnarsson, but they had not, and anyway were more interested in relating to Gunnar tales of the fondness that the infants showed for Johanna, for indeed, the older child preferred the girl to her own mother, and always called out for her when Johanna went out of the child's sight.

It must also be said that in these years after the lesser famine, Gunnar spent a great deal of time at his writing, summer and winter, and became more fluent, and one of the things he wrote about was Sira Jon, the mad priest who haunted Gardar. He set down the tales that folk told concerning the priest, but the truth of the case was difficult to discern, for Sira Pall Hallvardsson had drawn off from his old friends and associates, and now spoke to everyone only in the most formal and benign manner and disclosed nothing.

Now what is known as the great famine came on, and it did not come on unexpectedly, for most folk understood that life in Greenland had become more dangerous as the weather worsened and the numbers of folk on the farms dwindled, but it had always been the case that bad weather for cows was good weather for seals and reindeer. It happened, however, some eight summers after the departure of Bjorn Einarsson, that when the Greenlanders went out in the spring to herd the seals onto the beaches and kill them for the summer's and winter's food and oil there were no seals to be found, or only one or two where there had been scores and hundreds.

Of such an event as this there were a few tales from early times. In those times the result had been that most of the men of the settlement had spent most of the summer and part of the autumn in the north, and had brought back many walruses, and in the spring men had set out in ships for Iceland and brought back sheep and cows to replenish the flocks that had been eaten up during the winter. Such were the measures that those

Greenlanders had taken. But now the Northsetur was in the hands of the skraelings, even if the Greenlanders had had the boats to get there or a place to stop in the western settlement. And no ship had come to Greenland since the departure of Bjorn Einarsson. And some folk said that this would be a good time for Bjorn to return, or the bishop to come. Others planned for the autumn seal hunt and for a reindeer hunt on Hreiney, such as had not happened for many years. But there was little food for the summer, and Birgitta would say, as she served up the sourmilk, "Here is your cheese for St. Joseph's mass," or "Our Lenten fast will carry us straight to Heaven this year."

At the time for the Thing this year, which was the year of our Lord 1397, by the reckoning of Sira Audun at Gardar, Gunnar said to Helga that it was time for her to accompany him to the new assembly fields at Brattahlid, and Helga understood that the purpose of this was to find her a husband among the men of other districts, so she put together her best finery and braided her hair in an intricate manner, so that part of it spread golden and thick down her back and part covered the top of her head as a cap might. And on the day that Helga was to depart, Birgitta came to her and said, "It seems to me that you make your preparations with a cool hand, and are little eager for this journey."

"It is true that I have few desires one way or the other. It is many years since I have been taken to the Thing fields."

"Do you not think with pleasure on such a life as this is to open for you, of the wifely tasks you will have, among your own belongings? of your children?"

"No. I don't think upon it at all."

"Then such thoughts will take you unawares and lead you into danger, especially as you have an impulsive nature." But Helga turned away from these admonishments, and went off to the boat, where her father was awaiting her. Gunnar saw only that she looked very handsome and sturdy, and would attract a number of offers. He occupied his thoughts on the trip with questions of where he would like Helga to settle, and with what sort of folk. At Brattahlid he set up his booth in a prominent spot, so that folk would see Helga at her business many times each day. But the result was that Helga returned unbetrothed, for each time a man came to Gunnar and made an offer, Helga said only, "Let it be as you wish, Father," in a mild tone, with her eyes upon her shoes, and so it did not turn out as Gunnar wished at all.

At this Thing there was much talk of the failed seal hunt, and more talk of how successful the autumn hunt would be, and how many reindeer there must now be on Hreiney, after so many years—it would be five or six, since farmers of the settlement had received permission to hunt on the island. On the last day of the Thing a very peculiar event was witnessed by those few who lingered. One of the farmers who had land at Brattahlid was herding his sheep on the hillside above the Thing field, and a reindeer doe and her fawn ran among the sheep, scattering them. This was unusual, for reindeer were not so often seen among the farms of the Greenlanders, and were accustomed to stay in the wild districts. Now it happened that this farmer was not too far from his steading, and he sent his son into the steading for his bow and arrows, and before the deer could get out of range, he shot it with one of his bird arrows, but the arrow went into the doe's flank, and in great fear the beast ran down the hillside to the Thing field, where folk were taking down their booths. And when it ran among folk, others took out their weapons and tried to bring it down, so that soon it had three or four arrows sticking out of it, and one of these had gone deep into the chest, and blood poured forth from a heart wound. But the doe continued to run, as if its blood were being replenished by a magic spell, and it ran about the field, then up the hillside again, and then it disappeared, and the fawn with it, and no one had ever seen a deer show such strength before. Now the local farmers ran to get their dogs and track the beast, but it was never found, and the trail of blood ended in a thicket of willow scrub. And later folk remembered this deer, and saw that it was a sign of the future although at the time it seemed but a peculiar incident and was only remembered by the way.

A while after the Thing, around the feast of St. Christopher, there was another sign, and this came in the form of a dream to Petur the steward at Gardar. Petur had just eaten his morning meat with the others, and was walking across Gardar field toward the byre when he was overtaken by sleepiness and insisted upon lying down just where he stood, although men expostulated with him about such an odd course of action. He said, "No, I must sleep," and he lay down and slept. And this was his dream: A man was walking in a green field, and the grass of the field was thick and green and as high as the man's waist, and he was marveling at it in delight when a great wind blew up, a warm wind, as comes off the icecap in the spring, and the tall grass bent in the wind and as the wind got stronger, it lay flat, and the man lay down on the grass and covered his face. After a while the wind stopped, and the man sat up again, and the first thing he saw was that his clothing had been ripped to shreds by the wind, and the next thing he saw was that the field of grass had been covered over by gray sand and tiny sharp pebbles, so that it was nowhere to be seen, and the only bit of grass left in the whole field was the spot that he had covered with his body. All was desolation, and the man wept, and Petur the steward woke up weeping and at once told his dream. And then the men went on and did their work, but news of this dream went from farmstead to farmstead and was all over the settlement by the feast of St. Njot, and there was much discussion of what it meant, and whether it meant anything or not, for on the one hand there was no reason why a prophetic dream would come to Petur, who was not known to have second sight, but on the other hand, the way that sleep had overtaken him suddenly was known to be the way for such a thing. And soon it was time for the autumn seal hunt.

Now men from every farm came together at Herjolfsnes, and they had equipped themselves with every spear and every boat in the entire settlement, and, as always, the seals appeared to the south and the ocean was teeming with uncountable numbers of the animals, so that the boats could hardly be gotten among them. Now it happened that every boat exerted itself to the utmost, and many seals were driven upon shore and killed with clubs and spears, and this went on for six days, so that the seals were chased farther north than ever they had been before, well past the middle settlement, and men felt they had done well with the hunt. But when the carcases were counted up and distributed among the hunters, there were fewer than folk had expected as a return for their great efforts. Now there were some accusations of stealing and some fighting, but powerful men from Herjolfsnes and Brattahlid, such as Bjorn Bollason, instituted punishments for this. It seemed apparent to these men that for all the effort expended there had in fact been fewer boats and fewer hunters than ever before, and so fewer seals taken, and these seemed even fewer because when they were taken home and dried and put into the storehouses, the walls and floors there were bare, and not already partly filled with sealmeat and blubber from the spring hunt. And so men prepared for the reindeer hunt on Hreiney, and they were very hopeful, and all the churches and homesteads rang with prayers.

One of the boats that went to Hreiney was rowed by Jon Andres Erlendsson, Ofeig Thorkelsson, and their group of friends, and it happened that when they got to the island, they discovered Kollgrim Gunnarsson on the strand there. Now it was the case that Kollgrim had been following and teasing these men off and on for a number of years. Neither threats nor cajolery would keep him away from them for long. Once they had played a small trick upon him, stealing his clothing and setting him adrift in Einars Fjord in a tiny two-man boat, but this had only seemed to make him more anxious to be after them. From time to time Jon Andres was friendly toward him, and offered him food or spoke to him in a jocular fashion, hoping that he could then induce Kollgrim to leave him alone out of good feeling, but this method worked as little as any other. Twice Vigdis had had servants and dogs chase someone off the farmstead, and Jon Andres knew that this intruder was Kollgrim. Now the five men came upon the stand of Hreiney and saw Kollgrim there, standing alone and unarmed, and they decided to play another trick upon him, one that they had spoken about off and on since the previous summer. They pretended that they did not see him, and he pretended that he did not see them, but was instead awaiting friends. It was the case, however, that Kollgrim Gunnarsson had few friends other than Finn Thormodsson.

Presently, more boats arrived and were drawn up onto the strand, and the little bay filled up with armed men. Finn Thormodsson, wherever he had been, returned, and Kollgrim went over to him. He stayed with him all the rest of that morning. Now the Greenlanders split up into a number of bands and these set out to reconnoiter, with one band going off to inspect the old reindeer pits and the others going off in separate directions to find the largest groups of reindeer, and expecting not to have to go far. But such was not the case, for near the shore the reindeer were if anything rather sparse, and men began remembering how on Hreiney the deer tended to cluster here or there, anywhere but where they were then standing. It was a fact that forage on the island was poor, as poor as it was on any of the poorest farms in the eastern settlement. Now it was discovered that the pits were full of windblown sand, fuller than they had ever been, and unusable, and there was some grumbling about how Sira Jon and Sira Pall Hallvardsson had failed in their duty of maintaining the pits, but indeed, said folk from Gardar, how were they expected to do that and everything else too, for it was there as it was everywhere, too much land and too few hands. The great hopes of the Greenlanders began to be dashed, then, and some men sat down in discouragement and began to worry their food sacks.

But it happened that two groups, who had gone the farthest and ended up at the cliffs overlooking the wide western ocean, did find reindeer. Not teeming swarms, but plenty, if the hunters were canny and skilled, to feed the Greenlanders for the winter. And now the men, who had resigned themselves to finding nothing, jumped with a general shout and trekked to where the reindeer were, and the leaders of the hunt conferred as to the best method of killing quantities of the animals. Their considerations were these, that the deer had been hunted rather recently, and so would be wary of men, that the pits were no longer serviceable in any way, that the deer were on the other side of the island from the spot where in the past they had been herded into the water, that the cliffs were high and the water beneath them turbulent with underwater rocks, so that even if boats could get among them, were they herded off the cliff, the deer themselves would probably be much broken and damaged through the pounding of the surf. Now a party, which included Finn and Kollgrim, walked along the cliffs searching for another spot that was not too far from where the herds were which would offer at least some advantages.

It was the case that Finn knew this island of Hreiney rather well, in spite of the fact that hunters were prohibited from it without permission from the bishopric, and it was also the case that the taste of Hreiney meat was quite familiar to the mouths of the Lavrans Stead folk, although they did not perhaps know it, for the fact was that Gunnar never inquired too deeply into the sources of Finn's prizes. From his knowledge Finn saw two things, which he told in a low voice to Kollgrim, and one of these was that the best place on the north side of the island for herding the animals into the water was farther from the main herd than the Greenlanders would be able to take them, for reindeer are not like sheep, and can be held together only for a little ways, even with many dogs, especially if the herd is small. The other of these was that the herd itself would wander toward the spot during the night, perhaps, and the next day, for the grass there was better than it was elsewhere. But Finn was a servant and Kollgrim was a boy, and so they kept their mouths shut. Sometime later, after much arguing, the others came to the same conclusions, and all turned back to the main group of Greenlanders. And after this all the men and all the dogs retreated, so that the deer would not catch wind of them, and also so that the dogs would not catch wind of the deer and set up a clamor. All settled in to wait. Just after dusk, it began to rain, and it was a cold, wet, ocean rain, such as pierced the most tightly woven woolen clothing and left sheepskins soaking. Toward morning the deer began moving off as Finn had predicted, but in the rain they moved at a slow pace. Another night and another day passed, and all the men had eaten up their provisions, and the dogs were whining with hunger.

Now on the third morning, the sun rose upon the deer, and they were almost but not quite far enough toward the herding spot, and so those men who had boats took other men and went off to get the boats and bring them around to where the deer would go into the water. Those men who had dogs sat themselves down and resolved to wait, but soon the intelligence came that rather than moving toward the herding spot, the deer were moving away from it, to the south and inland, toward the hunters. And now the wind shifted, blowing the scent of the deer toward the dogs, and these beasts, which were numerous and hungry, set up a deafening howl. The deer began splitting up and running, and so the hunt began, although the lookout posted to watch for the boats coming around the island had given no signal yet. Men and dogs spread out in a wide semicircle that tightened as it moved toward the shore, scooping the deer before it, and, a piece of luck, panicking only a few of the deer into running straight ahead and escaping around the closing edge of the flank. Soon, too soon, the two flanks were at the strand, and it was time for the semicircle to flatten and push the deer into the water. But no boats were to be seen, so some men with spears, fearing to lose all of the effort, went among the deer with spears, killing a few and frightening the others, so that some of them broke past the rim of men and dogs and escaped. Now a great deal of shouting broke out among the Greenlanders, and men began to turn toward each other with their weapons raised, but then the lookout gave his signal, and the first boats appeared in the turbulent sea. The semicircle flattened quickly, and the deer began running into the ocean, the dogs at their heels.

The men in the boats rowed quickly into the herd and began laying about themselves with their spears. The trick was to thrust a spear into the chest of a deer, killing it with a single stroke, then to pull the deer close to the boat, using the spear, and grab the antlers, so that the beast could be lashed to the gunwale of the boat, but it happened that the sea was so rough from the rain of the previous two days that many beasts were lost. In addition to this, many spears were lost, and two boats, and two men were drowned, and when the day was over, it was seen that each farmstead represented would receive but three of the animals, and indeed, they were poor enough animals, for they had been grazing on skimpy forage for most of the summer.

On the fourth day, some men, led by Finn Thormodsson, set out from the main group of Greenlanders, and found a small group of reindeer, not more than two score, grazing in a blind culvert, and they ran them into a pocket made by three cliff walls, and took them all, even spindly, half-grown fawns. And this was the result of the reindeer hunt on Hreiney, great expense of effort for little reward, and folk began to talk about the deer that had run across the Gardar field on the last day of the Thing. It was also the case that not a few men sickened from the wet conditions of the hunt, and lay ill through part of the autumn work.

And this was the trick that Jon Andres Erlendsson and Ofeig Thorkelsson played on Kollgrim Gunnarsson on the last day of the hunt, when Finn was off with his band. They came upon him where he was sitting with the Lavrans Stead dogs, and seized him and carried him off away from the others to a spot overlooking the water, and there they took his hood and twisted it around so that his face was hidden, and they tied the shoulder pieces together so that it stayed this way. Then they ripped around the bottom of his robe and used this piece to tie his hands together behind him, and then they ripped around his robe again, so that his undergarments showed, and they used this piece to tie together his feet, and they tied it as well to the piece that bound his hands. And now they took him out in a boat that they found, for Jon Andres' boat was pulled up on the strand with the others, and they tipped him out of the boat and into the water, with the remark that perhaps this treatment would persuade him to leave them alone. After doing this, the men rowed back to where the others were, and declared that a certain man, of Hvalsey Fjord, had fallen into the water and needed help, and other men, good rowers in fast boats, went after Kollgrim, for it is the case that no man can survive for very long in the cold waters of Greenland. And Kollgrim was out of his senses, and was carried home in this fashion, and he remained insensible for many days, and only gradually returned to his old self in the course of the autumn. And in this way, Gunnar saw that the enmity between himself and the Ketils Stead folk was renewed, and he was wildly torn between anger at Jon Andres and Ofeig and anger at Kollgrim for provoking them, and he sat quietly at Lavrans Stead afterward and considered what sort of case he could make for the Thing.

In this year there was little festivity at Yule time, for folk were intent upon eking out what stores they had. It was a saying among the Greenlanders that folk who ate meat until the second Sunday of Lent would have cheese at Easter, but cheese on the second Sunday in Lent meant an Easter fast, and so the bits of meat were cut finer and finer to make them last. Finn Thormodsson and Gunnar, and Kollgrim, too, as the winter wore on, spent not a little time setting snares for ptarmigan, but this was the recourse for every farm, and the ptarmigan were not so plentiful as they might have been, or had been, in the days when Gunnar would get up in the morning to find a dozen birds hanging from the house eaves. And now folk talked of Petur the steward's dream and said that after such a sign, nothing would be enough, there could not be enough until God showed another sign that His curse was lifted.

It happened that after the fjords froze up and snow fell over the land, some folk got into the habit of making pilgrimages to the shrine of St. Olaf the Greenlander at Solar Fell, more than had been making these pilgrimages, and at the shrine, they would leave tiny trinkets in the form of whales carved from soapstone, for everyone longed for a stranded whale or two to take folk through the winter. Other folk began to go, sometimes, to Gardar for their pilgrimage and pray over the finger bone of St. Olaf, who was now called the Norwegian. Sira Pall Hallvardsson gave orders that a vat of broth with meat and fat in it should always be hot in the kitchen, and that each of these pilgrims should get a bowl of this food, and he also said mass if there were enough of them. At Solar Fell, folk were given bits of dried meat with their broth, but there was no mass to go to, as Sira Isleif had gone back to his brother's farm the previous winter. In addition to these pilgrimages, Sira Pall Hallvardsson said an extra mass at Gardar every day, solely to accumulate prayers for the relief of the Greenlanders, but each day passed as the days before it had, and there was no relief.

It was Sira Pall Hallvardsson's custom to go every day to the cell where Sira Jon spent his time and converse with the other priest. And he did this every day, no matter what else there was to be done, for it was not a duty to him, but a kind of fearful pleasure. Many times he would find Sira Jon sitting or squatting, with his eyes closed, and they would go on thus, in silence, for the whole period of the visit. Other times he would find the priest praying in wild loud tones, with greater vigor than Sira Pall Hallvardsson had ever brought to his prayers, and with great scowls or with tears coursing down his cheeks. Still other times, Sira Jon would be in a conversational humor and relate to him tales that he had been thinking on, and ask him for news of the outdoors, for it was the case that the mad priest never left his cell, out of dread, for he said that the low ceiling and tight walls contained him, and that in the open air he would surely burst. Once each year, toward the end of the summer, Sira Jon was obliged to bathe by force, and to be sewn into a new set of clothes, with the seams in the back where he could not reach them, and finely sewn of sturdy wadmal so that they could not be torn off, and sometimes in the course of this operation, he had to be knocked insensible so that it could proceed, for he longed with a madman's longing to be unclothed, and was always scheming to rid himself of his garments. Of his food he ate little, and in this autumn Sira Pall Hallvardsson began watching his trencher, and every day that he ate nothing, Sira Pall Hallvardsson was pleased, for he saw that a man could live on very little. And so the autumn passed at Gardar, and the Yule came on, and passed, as well, and the stream of pilgrims swelled a bit, to both Solar Fell and Gardar, and the broth at each place got a little thinner, and the dried meat at Solar Fell became a taste, no more, of cheese, and Signy went to her husband and declared that soon the pilgrims would be taking food out of the mouths of the servants and the family, there was so little, and at this news, Bjorn Bollason made his own pilgrimage to Gardar, and was sequestered with Pall Hallvardsson for an evening. And Bjorn Bollason said to Pall Hallvardsson, "It seems to me that such stores have accumulated at this bishopric as would carry us through the rest of the winter, and into the time of the seal hunt, for it is no secret that the Gardar storehouses are full, or nearly so."

"Folk think there is more than there is, or could be. And in addition to that, these tithes belong to the archbishop of Nidaros."

"And surely it would be the wish of the archbishop that the people be given alms in their time of need."

"Or perhaps it would be his wish that their alms be saved for later times, when conditions are even worse than they are now. At any rate, the archbishop has but a single known policy, and that is that his belongings be sent him as soon as possible, and saved for him until then."

"It seems to me cruel to sit upon all of these stores while folk are dying."

"Indeed, I have not heard that folk are dying now. It seems to me foolish to speak of our straits as desperate before they become so. A whale may strand in the south, or the reindeer may pass through, indeed, there are many ways the Lord might aid us, if He would, before we are reduced to stealing His belongings. Now is the time to pray, not to plunder His storehouses."

"The will of the Lord is a mystery even to you."

"But the will of the archbishop is not." And so Bjorn Bollason was balked, and returned to Solar Fell for a time.

It happened just before Lent that Sira Audun began one of his journeys to the south. He intended to go by stages to Herjolfsnes and then to return, saying Easter mass at Undir Hofdi church. He also intended to bring back with him his nephew, Eindridi, who had lost his wife and wished to be made a priest. Sira Audun had persuaded Pall Hallvardsson that Eindridi's knowledge of reading and writing outweighed his age (some twenty-six winters) and his knowledge of the wedded state. In addition to this, Eindridi had a son, Andres, a boy of some eight winters in age, and the boy, too, would be trained for the priesthood, Eindridi promised. Sira Audun went on skis with the servant Ingvald and they made quick time to Undir Hofdi church, where they settled themselves in and began receiving folk for prayers and absolution, and folk came in a stream far into the night, and some of these folk declared to the priest that they

little expected to live out the winter. Sira Audun was told that some folk
had died on two of the poorer farms, a man and his wife and their infant
son on one and two young men and their mother on the other, and these
were the first deaths in Vatna Hverfi district that were owing to this
hunger.

Now Sira Audun and the servingman made themselves beds in the
priest's house and went to sleep, and it happened in the night that thieves
came into the steading and stole much of Sira Audun's food that he had
brought with him from Gardar, and in the morning the priest and the
servingman had naught but two cheeses left over.

This morning was Sunday morning, and Sira Audun prepared to say
a mass, and the servingman Ingvald was to act as his assistant during the
mass. Many people now came to this mass, since after the death of Sira
Nikolaus, the services offered by Sira Audun were the only ones in the
district. And when the folk were assembled and sitting on the benches that
had been brought in, Sira Audun came before them and said nothing, and
sat himself down beside his servingman, and only stared ahead of himself
for a long while. Soon those gathered became restive and began talking
loudly among themselves, and finally one man named Axel, who was
known as a clownish fellow, shouted, "This priest must be dumb! Ho,
priest! Speak up! We can't hear you!" and Sira Audun stood up and turned
to face the assembly.

"Now!" he said in a great roar. "The Lord Jesus came among them,
and they stole His sustenance from Him, and took His shoes and left Him
without a coat, and then they turned upon Him and demanded, Why dost
Thou not bless us? And the Lord said to them, Why have ye taken My
things from me? And they said, Thou art God, Thou needst not the food
and clothing of men, but can conjure these things at will. But Jesus said,
Nay, ye are saved in Me only as I am a man, and when ye steal My shoes,
I cut My feet on the stones of the road, and when ye take My coat I shiver
in the cold and when ye eat up My food, I go hungry, and so My Father
appears to me in a dream, and He says, where are these things that Thou
must have to live? And I say that men have taken them from Me out of
their own greed, and have fought over them, so that the coat is torn and
the shoes are lost and the food is dropped in the dust, and My Father is
filled with wrath, and He says, what are these men, that they choose such
evil, why should they not be destroyed?" Sira Audun's voice rose. *"Why
should they not be destroyed!"* And then he spoke more quietly. "Ye are saved
when I am a brother to ye, and destroyed when ye deal with Me as an
enemy." And he sat down again and waited. Those present were much

taken aback by this speech, and made quiet, even though many suspected that it was a parable that Sira Audun himself had concocted. But even though Sira Audun glared out over the folk, no man stood up and admitted to the food stealing. After a while, Sira Audun got up and removed his vestments and left the church, and to Magnus Arnason of Nes, who was standing by the door, he declared that he would hold the service when the provisions for his trip were returned to him, and then he and the serving-man went into the priest's house and closed the door.

Now the people among the district searched among themselves for the perpetrators of the crime, and they found out one fellow named Vilhjalm, a poor man from the southern part of the district, and he admitted to having taken the things after his confession of the previous night, but the things had been shared out among the members of his family, and were now entirely eaten. At this, Vilhjalm was taken away by some of Magnus Arnason's servants and given a beating, and the folk of the district began to ask among themselves how they were going to make up the lost food, for everyone saw that Sira Audun was just beginning a long journey, and could hardly be expected to complete it on two cheeses. Even so, Magnus Arnason didn't have food to spare, and neither did Thorkel Gellison, and neither did any of the other big farmers of the district, for though they had more stores, they also had more mouths to feed. But now there came Vigdis, the mother of Jon Andres, walking in great state up the path from Gunnars Stead, and behind her were two servants, and each carried a large pack. Vigdis sailed past the assembled farmers and up to the door of the priest's steading, which opened before her, and a short while later, Sira Audun appeared, and he went into the church, donned his vestments, and conducted the mass, and Vigdis, who had not been at the earlier service, sat in the place of honor just in front of the priest. And so Vigdis was much praised by her neighbors for enabling the service to go on and the many confessions and prayers to be uttered and heard. Two days later, Sira Audun and his servingman set off for the south, and came to a nunnery, where they had no misadventures.

Even so, food was even scarcer in the south, and Sira Audun made presents of the food in one of his packs to all the nuns at the nunnery, who numbered seven, and when folk nearby learned that the nuns had some food, they came begging for a portion of it, and so the nuns gave it all away. Sira Audun said three masses there on Sunday, and two more on the days after, and at every mass, all prayed fervently for relief. The next day, Sira Audun made the short trip to Vagar Church, and there met his nephew Eindridi and the boy Andres.

And now it was the evening before the second Sunday in Lent, and Sira Audun prepared himself to receive the confessions of the folk around Vagar Church, but few came, and those who came seemed to drag themselves through the snow and they spoke in the faintest of voices, both women and men. Now Sira Audun turned to Eindridi, and asked if conditions were indeed so bad as this, that men could not bring themselves to church without risking death, and Eindridi said that conditions were actually worse, since many could not get out of their bedclosets to look into the bedclosets of their children or their parents, so weak were they. And so Sira Audun spoke a hurried mass in the morning, and then went around to the farms in the Vagar Church district, visiting folk, saying prayers, and doling out bits of food from the second pack Vigdis had given him. There would be plenty at Herjolfsnes, Sira Audun felt certain, and he gave with a liberal hand. Even so, some folk of the district had already died, and more were so far gone that bits of cheese or dried meat could do nothing for them but please the tongue. And so Sira Audun stayed for a longer time than he had expected in the district around Vagar Church, and on the last day there he went without food entirely, though he gave some to Ingvald. At last he set out for Herjolfsnes, and on the way there, he and his servingman spoke at length and without ceasing of meals they had eaten, and Sira Audun made up the following verse:

> *A stew of seal and hare, and a cup of milk*
> *And a morsel of cheese, some butter and dried sealmeat,*
> *My heart remembers every bite since my mother*
> *First chewed my meat for me.*

And so they came to Herjolfsnes, and as it happened, conditions were little better there than they had been elsewhere, but the wife there had put by a welcoming feast for the priest, for when he should get there, and Sira Audun and his servingman ate this with relish and thanks.

At Gardar, just after the departure of Sira Audun, Sira Pall Hallvardsson got up one morning and went outside to wash, as he always did, and there before him in the dark was an array of men, and at once he saw that they were armed. Bjorn Bollason, who carried a crossbow, stepped up to him, and said in a mild tone of voice, "We have come to help you assure the orderly distribution of the bishop's stores, for indeed, the Greenlanders are desperate for sustenance and neither God nor the bishop can continue to turn his face away."

Now it began to lighten, and Pall Hallvardsson saw about two score

men standing about in a semicircle, and all of these men were friends of
Bjorn Bollason, and powerful men, both of Brattahlid district and Dyrnes.
Pall Hallvardsson said, "Even so, the southern districts are not represented,
and the bishop must look equally upon everyone."

Bjorn Bollason smiled at the easy success of his plan, and then spoke
to certain of his men, who ran to the Gardar boats that were moored at
the Einars Fjord jetty. The next day, powerful men began appearing in
boats from every district, even Herjolfsnes district, and on that day, Pall
Hallvardsson had the stones that sealed up the storehouses taken down, and
the stores broken open, and it was the case that men trampled over the
wadmal and sheepskins to get at the stores of deer meat and seal meat, and
rendered blubber and dried mutton and dried beef and the many cheeses,
goat and sheep as well as cow cheeses. After the first storehouse was
emptied, the walls of the second were taken down on two sides, and that
one was emptied, as well, and in spite of Bjorn Bollason's promise, the
plundering of the storehouses was disorderly in the extreme, and indeed,
Bjorn Bollason himself was in the forefront of the raid, for this is what
Pall Hallvardsson considered it, although he made no attempt at defense,
and only stood aside as the stocks of ten years were taken out.

Bjorn Bollason and his men were much impressed with the abundance
of food at Gardar, and when it was all given out and taken away, Bjorn
Bollason came to Sira Pall Hallvardsson and said, "I expected to find a
mouthful for everyone and found instead a week of feasts. All your extra
prayers have done naught for the Greenlanders compared to these actions
of ours. Men go away thanking the benevolence of the bishop, for which
the bishop should be grateful."

Pall Hallvardsson replied only, "Time will show where gratitude
should lodge," and he turned away from Bjorn Bollason and went to his
chamber. The case was that he, too, had been much surprised by the
quantity of reserves, but indeed, after all these years of Sira Jon's madness,
he still hadn't solved the puzzle of the bookkeeping, and each winter the
time he spent huddled over those pages, either reading Sira Jon's hand or
making his own confusing and incomplete entries grew less and less. He
did not know as much about these things as he had at Hvalsey Fjord, when
at least he had looked daily into the two cupboards, and Sira Jon had
looked twice a year at his offerings. At Gardar he could not even frighten
himself with the thought of the coming bishop, or of a ship removing all
of the obligated stores to Nidaros, for indeed, after so many years, who
would know what was to be expected, or how much the tithes would
amount to? And so, perhaps, he had spent even less time over the books

in the previous winter than before. Perhaps he had spent no time at all, but only said to Olof and Petur and everyone else who came to him to do as they thought best, and use what they had to, and perhaps he had taken all of the tithes from all of the farms without looking at them very closely, or asking after the sheep and the seal hunt—those probing questions that Sira Jon had been so good at and that had made him detest the Greenlanders, who always seemed to be reserving something, even the smallest part of their due. Perhaps they were, perhaps they only appeared to be, as he himself had always told the other priest. But what man, who had not the eye of God, could see how much there was and how much was really owed? In the abbey where he had grown up, a score of monks had spent their days traveling about the abbey lands and reporting the activities of every peasant, every cow, every pig, so that when a peasant brought in his rent or his tithe, the abbot could say, "There is nothing here from that field of barley you planted at the edge of the forest," or, less often, "The illness of your wife brought hardship during the harvest, and you have paid too much here." Such was not the case in Greenland, where the priest knew nothing about a farmer's success except what the farmer himself told him. But indeed, all of this carelessness little mattered, as there had been so much of everything. Perhaps, Sira Pall Hallvardsson thought, it was not only uncounted, but also uncountable.

Sira Pall Hallvardsson sat in the high seat in the great hall and looked out into the dimly lit room, and saw this, that the Greenlanders would remember the prayers and masses he had said, and the broth he had given out and the meals he had given to the servants and such pilgrims as came by, and they would take them as deceptions, meant to hide a mountain of provisions and greed for hoarding them, and he wished, only for a moment, that there had been less abundance, or that it had been stored differently, or that men's eyes hadn't widened in disbelief at the sight.

He got up and went to the door of Sira Jon's room, and put his ear to it and listened. From inside he heard a scratching and swishing sound that he could not recognize, but when he pushed open the door, he saw the lunatic priest sitting quietly, as he always did, and awaiting him. Sira Jon, although just of an age with Sira Pall Hallvardsson, seemed to everyone to be older, for his beard and his hair were nearly all gray and his eyebrows grew in great gray tufts, like those of old men. He was squatting by the wall, with his hands in his sleeves, but now he presented his finger to be kissed, and Sira Pall Hallvardsson kissed it. Sira Jon peered at him, and then said, "I see that you will have to be bound today, for your mood is gloomy and inward. Such days are your worst."

"And your mood?"

"No mood has come to him today. He has eaten nothing in three days. He is especially good." Sira Jon always referred to his earthly corpus as if it were another man, unruly and capricious. Sira Pall Hallvardsson had seen him denounce this corpus in the roundest tones, vividly depicting the hellfire it was bent upon achieving.

"Surely he has had a drink of water?"

"The merest mouthful. And then he pissed it away at once."

"May I feel his arm?"

"His arm is indeed thin, but not too thin." Sira Jon's eyes widened, and he began to breathe heavily. "You may not feel it. It is not too thin. I am watching him closely." They fell silent. Sira Jon regained his composure, and after a bit said, "I see you have let these Greenlanders get by you. They are a devilish lot, indeed."

Sira Pall Hallvardsson smiled and said, "How have they gotten by me, then?"

"How should I know? There's no telling. You are a simple fellow. They play upon your sensibilities though they have none themselves."

"They are starving." This was the first Pall Hallvardsson had spoken of the famine to the other priest.

"If that were true, it would be good for them. But if they tell you of it, it can't be true."

"They creep into church and their arms and hands are like birch twigs lashed together, and also their faces are without flesh."

"These Greenlanders can do as they please with their flesh. It is not so long since I myself have seen them turn into devils and fetches. They may come to you all honey soft and full of prayers, but when they round the corner of the cathedral, those who crept along stand up straight and those who sucked in their cheeks let them out again. I have seen it enough. I don't have to be there to know it is happening. I am reminded of something that Bishop Alf saw when he was a boy in Stavanger district."

Pall Hallvardsson settled himself for the tale, as the fantastic adventures of Bishop Alf often formed a theme of Sira Jon's talk, even though Pall Hallvardsson happened to know that the former bishop had lived a life that was dry and bureaucratic in the extreme before coming to Greenland. But the mad priest kept silent, perhaps meditating upon his tale, but not telling it. He said no more, and Sira Pall Hallvardsson went off a while later.

The bishop's stores of food spread like a balm through the eastern settlement, from Isafjord to Herjolfsnes. Some folk spoke of the largest of the bishopric, but more folk talked of how Bjorn Bollason had looked on as the men brought out the stores, and how he had made certain that men from every district got a share equal to the numbers of folk they estimated still to be alive in that district, and when some men from his own district of Dyrnes had attempted to steal more for themselves, Bjorn Bollason himself had taken it from them and given it to the party from Hvalsey Fjord. At the last, when the food was loaded into the sledges and the skiers were about to set off, Bjorn Bollason had gone around to each sledge and greeted everyone by name, for he had a prodigious memory for names, and he had reminded everyone of the thanks that were due to God and the bishopric, for these provisions were the belongings of God Himself, and therefore especially wholesome, and this was generally considered a fine sentiment.

While Eyvind and the men from Isafjord were away at Gardar, Brenna Eyvindsdottir died in her bed of the coughing ill, and Freydis and Margret carried her corpus out of the steading and put it into a snowbank. Freydis was much cast down by this death, for it seemed to her that if Eyvind had gone away sooner, or returned more quickly, Brenna would have been saved, and it was in vain that Margret told her that Brenna had died of the sickness and not of the hunger. So it was that Freydis was very bitter toward Eyvind when he returned, and as bitter toward the provisions he brought with him, so that when they were put out upon the table and the family was ready to eat them, she swept them to the floor with her arm and began to scream.

It was the case that Eyvind had been on skis for three days since leaving Gardar, a trip which customarily went quickly in the winter. The parties from the north, weak from the famine, had encountered snow and bad weather, so that they had gotten lost between Brattahlid and Isafjord. Now, when Freydis began screeching, Eyvind grabbed her shoulders and shook her, and when she fell to the floor, he carried her out to the cowbyre, where the sheep were huddling in the warm dung, and he left her there, for he was much vexed at her. Afterward, he came in and sat down at his place and began to eat, and he made the others, Margret, Finna, and the two servingmen, eat as well, and as they were very hungry, they needed little encouragement. He said, "Freydis will soon come to herself and come scratching at the door." But the mealtime passed, and the folk went to their bedclosets, and Freydis did not come scratching at the door, so that Finna went to her father, and asked him to go out after the girl, but he would not, so much did he abominate the child's pride and willfulness. And so everyone, even Margret, who greatly feared the outcome of this fight, fell into a doze, as folk do when they have just eaten well for the first time in many days, and in the morning Freydis still had not come in, although the door to the steading was not barred in any way.

Now Margret got up and she saw that Eyvind was putting on his sheepskin, and he smiled at her, and said, "She would not be an Eyvindsdottir if her pride did not match mine, but I suspect that her remorse will match mine, as well," and he went out carrying some dried whalemeat and some bits of cheese, and he did not come in for a long while. Margret went about her tasks, and the others began to stir, and still Eyvind did not come in, and so Margret donned her cloak and went out into the yard. Eyvind and Freydis were not to be seen, although there was much crying of sheep from the cowbyre. Margret approached slowly. The door was ajar. She opened it a little more, and it seemed to her that some sights could not be prepared for and that this would be one of them. Inside the door, Eyvind squatted in the warm sheep dung. Above him, in the half light of the warm, turfed-up byre, Freydis hung by her neck from a beam, and she was dead. Now Eyvind began to cry out and weep with such violence as she had never seen before. He rent his clothing, and hammered his head against the stones of the byre, and the sheep ran about his legs and raised a great riot. He cried out that she was his favorite, his snow bunting, his darling, his baby, and Margret saw that he was afraid to touch the maiden's corpus. And at this sight, tears started from Margret's eyes for what she thought might be the first time in her life. Then the servingmen came out to begin their work, and Finna followed them, but none could get near Eyvind or Freydis, so wild was the father at the daughter's death.

Folk in Isafjord were not inclined to blame Eyvind for this mishap, but blamed Freydis herself for her melancholy and her high temper, both of which she was well known for. Some blamed the hunger, which maddened folk, or made fools of them. There was an old servingman at another Isafjord farm who had gone out not many days before and lost his way between the byre and the steading, a matter of some twenty paces, so that he had turned round and round and finally fallen in the snow insensible. And another Isafjord man had come upon his wife and beaten her, and his two children as well, so that they had nearly died. Folk in Isafjord were inclined to say that life in Isafjord was harder and more merciless than life elsewhere, and this seemed to Margret to be true. Even so, Eyvind greatly blamed himself, and had many spells of wild grief after the deaths of his daughters. Margret and Finna sat over their spinning and weaving, and each knew that the other was expecting the worst. The food from Gardar lasted through Easter, and then the grass greened, the lambs were born, and there was ewe's milk to drink.

Death had laid a heavy hand upon every district. Babies were still-born, mothers died with their infants at the breast, grandfathers went to their beds and failed to rise again, folk wandered away in search of food, and their families were too weak to go after them. Weakened servants lost their footing, fell, and were unable to rise again. Fires went out, and the effort to make them anew or go to the neighbors for more was beyond folk's strength, so they froze to death with food on the table, or more likely, gorged themselves with what they had as the cold overtook them. Around Easter, Sira Audun went from church to church with Eindridi and the boy Andres, and he said prayers of thanks, but in this year, no one rejoiced as they had after the last hunger, or after the vomiting ill. No sign had come to redeem the sign of the deer, or the sign of Petur's dream, Petur the Steward, God's Provisioner. The talk was all of how the following winter would be worse, not better.

Even so, there were those who, through witchcraft, perhaps, had not seemed to go without, but had seemed even to grow fat through the winter, as if feeding on the flesh of others. The most prominent of these was Vigdis of Gunnars Stead, whose gross flesh had diminished not one whit while her neighbors all dropped dead about her. Instead she waxed, red-cheeked and glossy-haired. Was not this suspicious as well, that her hair lay on her seventy-year-old head as dark as it had ever been? In addition, she had grown hard and changeable. Some days she would pet and tease Jon Andres with banter and affection, so that he could not dodge her, and he would go off with his friends to be away from her. Other days she would begin by stripping the bedclothes off the boy and then beating and cuffing him about the head and then serving him offal for his morning meat, and on these days she would follow him about with accusations and scolding, accusing him of hiding her belongings, or stealing them, or of killing the livestock or of feeding poison to the hunting dogs, or of breaking into her stores and giving them away. When she threw bedclothes out of his bedcloset, she always shouted after the servingwomen, demanding to know where he was hiding them. Nor could she remember things as she once had, but called her servants by other names, and even Jon Andres "Erlend," although he looked not at all as Erlend had looked, even in youth.

In this way, men knew that evil had come into Vigdis. More neighbors than one recalled what a gossip she had been. She was prideful and vain of her looks and her clothing. She had been covetous of Gunnars Stead, and had instigated Erlend into tricking Gunnar out of his farm. She had grieved little for her sons, and of her nursling, Ketil the Unlucky, she had even said, gazing upon his corpus, "Here is some trouble that won't worry us now." It is a fact that such sins as these attract demons, as rotting meat attracts dogs. Such were the tales that went around the neighborhood concerning Vigdis Markusdottir. Jon Andres removed to Ketils Stead with some of the younger servants, and Ofeig and Mar and the others of this band of men that had thrown Kollgrim Gunnarsson into the sea were always there with him.

Now it came time for the spring seal hunt, and this year, Gunnar Asgeirsson went along, and Kollgrim Gunnarsson did not, for the case was that the boy still had spells of insensibility and confusion from his dip into the icy water. When all the Greenlanders were gathered at Herjolfsnes and waiting for the seals to appear, Gunnar named witnesses and brought his case against Jon Andres Erlendsson, Ofeig Thorkelsson, and Mar Marsson in accordance with the proper procedures, and as the three young men were nearby, and all of the witnesses from both Hvalsey Fjord and Vatna Hverfi district, Jon Andres had to admit that he had been duly summoned. It turned out that one of Gunnar's allies against the three men was Thorkel Gellison, Ofeig's own father, and there was much talk about this.

After the summoning, men sat at Herjolfsnes for three days, awaiting the seals, and not a few grew discouraged, remembering the failure of the seals the previous year. But on the third day, the seals came as usual, perhaps not quite so numerous, but numerous enough. The men set off in their boats, and went among the pods of quarry, but indeed, though there were seals, they seemed enchanted, so elusive were they. They seemed to look upon the hunters with men's eyes, as if these seals, coming late, were not the usual seals of the spring, but were the souls of drowned men come to wreak their vengeance on the living. At any rate, the seals would not be driven upon the shore, and those few that were raced back to the water, eluding every kind of weapon. Spears thrust into their throats turned and slid harmlessly off their backs. Clubs brought down upon their heads bounced off the ice. Arrows went above them, or into the ice in front of them. The most able hunters, like Finn Thormodsson, had the same luck as the least experienced. And the seals swam fast, faster than a man in a boat could row, so that the men were exhausted and weakened at the end of each day, and the main body of seals was farther and farther away from them. The hunt lasted until they reached Kambstead Fjord, and then could go on no longer. The hunters had not the strength. In addition to this, three boats were smashed and lost, and countless spears and arrows. Two men were drowned when they tried to spear a seal from their boat.

It was also the case that Ofeig Thorkelsson kept his boat near Gunnar's and Finn's boat, and gazed upon them with a glowering eye, and in addition threatened them with his weapons in a peculiar way, making as if to aim his arrows at them, or the blows of his spear at their boat, when he could maneuver himself close enough. He was also full of taunts and curses, and these did not diminish when others were around, even when Thorkel was around, although they were directed only at Gunnar. On the first evening, when Ofeig would not go off, Gunnar called to him that he was prejudicing the case against himself by trying to provoke further conflict, but Ofeig was not silenced, and so Gunnar attempted to ignore him. The next day, Gunnar had Magnus Arnason, Ofeig's foster father, speak to Jon Andres Erlendsson, but if Jon Andres in turn made any attempt to control his friend, nothing was the result. Ofeig's taunts continued unabated. Now Thorkel himself went to his son, and was so angered by Ofeig's behavior that the two came to blows. Thorkel was a vigorous man for his age, but indeed, he was more than twice the age of Ofeig, and where Thorkel was wiry and not very tall, Ofeig was both tall and fat, but round and hard with big fists and frightening strength. Now Thorkel came at him with his hand raised, as a father comes at a child and chastises him, and Ofeig seemed not to know who was before him, but attacked his father as if attacking his bitterest enemy, pushing him down and kicking him and stomping him. And when Thorkel got to his feet, Ofeig lowered his head and ran at the older man, so that those standing around saw that Ofeig would not stop at killing his father. Four or five men now attacked Ofeig and held him, and he was so big and strong that this was no simple task. Thorkel was carried off senseless, but it turned out later that he had suffered no real injuries besides having his nose broken. Ofeig seemed not to know what he had done or who it was he had been fighting, but continued to rail against Gunnar Asgeirsson and interfere with his hunting. Now a few of the farmers considered that this spell Ofeig seemed to be under came from the enchanted seals, although there was no hint that he had eaten more of their meat than other men. A few others of the farmers declared that the charm went the contrary way, that the enmity of Gunnar and Jon Andres had driven off the wholesome seals and attracted these enchanted ones. When the hunt came to the islands at the mouth of Einars Fjord, Ofeig and his friends departed, but things were ruined anyway. With low spirits, men divided up the little meat that was obtained and returned to their steadings to wait for the Thing.

Now in this year, with provisions so low, and so much farm work lying upon the hands of those left to do it, there was some grumbling that the Thing had been moved back to Brattahlid, for Gardar was more centrally located, and easier for those from the south to get to. For this reason, the assembly was very poorly attended, and lasted only three days, instead of four. In addition to this, more than half of the judges from the southern districts had either died in the winter or were unable to attend, and there was continuous discussion about whether any cases decided would be legal. One case came up, the case of the Isafjord man who had beaten his wife and children, and this was decided by men from Dyrnes, Isafjord, and Brattahlid. After this case, not a few grumbled that they might as well have stayed home and decided the case amongst themselves. But in the midst of all this grumbling, Bjorn Bollason the lawspeaker walked forth among the booths, and greeted everyone, and asked how they did, and what was happening in their districts. He had many small discussions, and folk began recalling how he had gotten to the stores at Gardar, and saved the Greenlanders from starvation, and it was recalled that after all, Bjorn Bollason had had good reasons for moving the Thing back to Brattahlid, to the ancient fields of Erik the Red. And at the end of that day, which was the second, Bjorn Bollason established a new type of judge, to be known as an at-large judge, and to be appointed by the lawspeaker to sit in on cases when judges failed to come to the Thing, and these new judges were to be appointed from among the most prosperous farmers at the Thing who did not have cases pending, and they were to remain judges-at-large until they should have cases before the Thing, which would disqualify them for that year and two years after that. And even though most of the farmers had never heard of such a procedure, Sira Isleif reassured those who came to him that this was a legal procedure, considering the straits that the Greenlanders now found themselves in. And so Bjorn Bollason appointed six more judges, and they were all Brattahlid men, for Brattahlid men were the most prosperous in the absence of men from the south.

On the third day, Gunnar brought his case before these new judges. He called witnesses and described how his son Kollgrim, of some twenty winters of age now, and an able hunter, had been rendered periodically unsound of mind through a malicious trick played upon him by these three men, to wit, Jon Andres Erlendsson of Gunnars Stead in Vatna Hverfi district, Ofeig Thorkelsson of Hestur Stead in Vatna Hverfi district, and Mar Marsson of Vatna Stead, in the same district. And he told how these men had come upon his son where he was sitting beside his dogs, and had

torn his clothing and tied him so as to render him incapable of helping himself, and then forced him into a boat and rowed out a ways into
the western ocean, where they had thrown him in. And this had been at
the end of the autumn seal hunt, not long before the ice comes up from
the south, and so the water had been cold enough to render him insensible
within a very short time, and since then he had suffered many spells of
insensibility and foolishness, although these were fewer now than they had
been.

Could the boy feed himself, the judges said, could he dress himself,
and speak as usual, and do farm work and hunt. Yes, Gunnar answered,
he could do all these things most of the time, but even so, he was unlike
himself. He needed repeated instructions. His mind wandered, although
more on some days than on others. Where was he? The judges asked. In
Hvalsey Fjord, said Gunnar. And the judges conferred among themselves,
asking why Gunnar had left the boy at home if his injuries were the subject
of the case. Finally, they asked, what sentence against the three perpetrators
did Gunnar wish to receive? Lesser outlawry, said Gunnar, for the law
states that greater outlawry is not an appropriate punishment for such a
transgression.

Now it was Jon Andres' turn to defend himself, and folk spoke
together in low tones about Erlend Ketilsson, his father, who had been very
fond of bringing cases before the Thing, and who had known many of the
laws that even the lawspeaker had nearly forgotten. Jon Andres strode into
the circle where men were accustomed to speak of their cases and looked
about at the judges and at the other Greenlanders. He had Erlend's dark
coloring, but the open countenance of Vigdis, or even more, to those who
remembered her, of Thordis, Vigdis' daughter. He was by far the best-
looking of the Erlendssons, a sign, folk said to each other, that the cross
between the ill-tempered ram and the imperious ewe had not been such
a big mistake. He was as tall as Gunnar, who was among the tallest of the
Greenlanders, but broader, and by contrast not so angular or stiff seeming.
The eyes of the judges, and of the farmers standing around, fell upon him
with pleasure, for indeed, it was the case that these were northerners, men
not so familiar with the mischief Jon Andres, Ofeig, and their friends had
done about Vatna Hverfi district in the past few years. Jon Andres smiled,
and his smile was sudden and bright, like the smile of a young child. It
came and went, and it had this effect, that folk wished to see it again.
Gunnar was a well-known man, well known at least for his ill luck, and
not uncharming in his leisurely way, but it was the case that eyes and
thoughts that had drifted off to other things while he was talking now

turned alertly to the young man in the circle, and stayed there. Gunnar saw this even before Jon Andres began talking. And the six new judges, at least, were inexperienced enough to gaze upon the pleader, where older and wiser men would not do this, but would look away most of the time, and only listen closely to the words. Now Gunnar looked at Bjorn Bollason, and saw that Bjorn Bollason was impressed by the young man, and indeed, there was something about the one that was like the other. Gunnar smiled. It was easy to see that the case would not go as he wished.

Now Jon Andres began to speak. "Lords," he said to the judges, "and lawspeaker, it has not come to me before this to plead a case at the Thing. In Vatna Hverfi district, we talk among ourselves, and conflicts are resolved, and indeed, many of my neighbors must think this is enough, since they have not come to the Thing this year. It must be this way, that you will forgive me for speaking informally, as if we were just talking among ourselves, for that is how I am used to doing it, and the only way I know." His smiled flashed again. "This is a serious charge, that my companions and I willfully did injury to this boy, Kollgrim Gunnarsson, and it is made more serious by something else that I freely admit, namely the history of enmity between Kollgrim's family and my own. In fact, my mother lives at Gunnars Stead. I live, of course, at Ketils Stead, now, so you see, there is that flaw in Gunnar Asgeirsson's case, that he has summoned a man who does not exist, Jon Andres Erlendsson of Gunnars Stead. But even so, I am summoned, I understand the serious nature of the charge, and what's more, I freely admit to committing the act, and indeed, I am heartily sorry for the way things have turned out. Folk have said to me that Kollgrim was a good hunter and that he had other good qualities as well, but indeed, he is not dead, is he? He is not even here. Perhaps he is out hunting even now.

"I would wish that such enmity as exists between our families did not exist, but it does, and it is not my mother who made me know of it, but Kollgrim himself, who has for the past six summers and winters presented himself before me as an apparition might, saying nothing, offering nothing, doing little mischief, but some, nevertheless, such as tying together the tails of the cows or emptying the cistern that catches eave runoff at Gunnars Stead, or perhaps only lingering nearby, casting his gaze upon me as I went about my work, or following me and my friends as we rode out for visits among our neighbors. When this began, Kollgrim Gunnarsson was but a child. Even so, his attentions were a little tedious, and got more so as he grew older. And so we did these things—we asked him to go off, and he didn't hear us. We threatened him, but he paid no attention. We drove him off, but he came back. We ignored him, but he came closer, and teased us more. No place was free of him. As a good hunter, he was always away from Hvalsey Fjord, though what game there is in Vatna Hverfi I have yet to know. And so it happened that one day when we saw him, a devilish impulse really to drive him off, for good, came over us, and it was not just the three of us who are called in this case, but six of us, another small flaw in Gunnar Asgeirsson's case, that he has summoned only half of the perpetrators. Now they shall all stand forth, not only Ofeig Thorkelsson and Mar Marsson, but Einar Marsson and Andres Bjartsson and Halldor Bessason, and we all admit that each of us had a hand in this deed, and I may say for all of us, but especially for Ofeig and myself, that we had great regret of this, and of others of our deeds that we have done in our youth." Now the five young men, with Ofeig first, stepped into the circle and looked about, but furtively, as if truly ashamed. Even Ofeig had been pacified, and he stood as meekly as the others. Thorkel, standing not far off from Gunnar, colored and clenched his fists, and Gunnar saw this, and saw that Jon Andres saw it, too. And Jon Andres went on, "Now I will not say that our remorse was easily arrived at, for some of us were more angry than others, and are of a more naturally difficult nature. But, indeed, I speak for all, and I offer Gunnar Asgeirsson full self-judgment in this case, and also my apologies and those of my friends."

This statement was received with approval by the assembled farmers, and also by the judges, who saw with relief that they would not have to make a judgment in the difficult case. Now Gunnar walked off quickly with Thorkel, and returned to his booth, for it is the law in Greenland that pleaders who are given self-judgment have until the next meal to consider their demands, and the judges are not allowed to take their meat until the terms of the judgment have been proposed and accepted. At first, Gunnar was much pleased with the outcome, and declared that many goods as well as lesser outlawry could be exacted from the six of them, or they could be put to work as hunters for the Lavrans Stead folk, or he could demand some head of cattle. Thorkel said nothing, but only sat quietly in the booth for a while. At last he said to Gunnar, "Do you not see the trick he has played on us, and the eloquence with which he has gulled the judges? And even of those who know him and his band, only we were not taken in by his remorse and his charm." Gunnar saw at once that such was the case. He said, "Yes, my friend, the fact is that folk will speak harshly against us if we punish these men as they deserve. We will seem like fathers who return blows for their children's loving words. And indeed, talking of children, who should know better than I do that Kollgrim was not entirely guiltless in this affair? Hasn't that urge to send him off once and for all, that urge not to be teased, but to have some peace, come over me as well as it has over these young men? What allies do we have from Vatna Hverfi and Hvalsey Fjord who don't know Kollgrim and his ways, who haven't themselves untied the tails of their cows or found their cheese vats on the roof of the byre? No, we will get some hay of these boys, or a sheep or two, but Jon Andres will feel no sting of punishment or dishonor. Even those who dragged Kollgrim out of the water and carried him senseless to Lavrans Stead are more dazzled by what they see before them than by what they remember from half a year ago. But this is not the last of my relations with Ketils Stead, and it seems to me that it won't go even this well in the future." And so, just before the time for evening meat, Gunnar went before the judges and demanded half the game caught by the six men during the summer, until the time of the autumn seal hunt, to be brought to Lavrans Stead in Hvalsey Fjord in good condition, for the use of the family there. And then the judges went to their meat. The next day there were three more cases, and then the Thing broke up, and the tale that went back to every district was that Gunnar Asgeirsson had gotten little honor from his case, and folk who had not gone to the Thing were surprised by this, for they remembered the malice of Jon Andres and his friends, and the grievous injuries done to the boy.

During the summer, Jon Andres himself came to Lavrans Stead from time to time, bringing game, and it cannot be said that he brought very much, for these Vatna Hverfi men were not especially skilled with bow or spear or snare, nor did they know where the good hunting grounds were. In the middle of the summer, Jon Andres brought some ewes with lambs. These ewes were fat and big compared to Hvalsey Fjord sheep, but even so, when Jon Andres herded them among the rest of Birgitta's flock, he was full of praise for her sheep. The Lavrans Stead sheep, he said, were lovely sheep, perfectly formed, with thick, long, oily wool, and so forth. His own sheep were so obviously superior that his praise disconcerted Gunnar and made him suspicious. After that, Gunnar told Olaf to watch for the coming of the Vatna Hverfi man, as he himself didn't want to meet him again.

In this summer, no sign foretold the end of the famine. The sheep scattered far and wide into the mountains, looking for forage, but there was little to be found. The grass in the homefields greened late and grew slowly, for there was little sun. Folk began talking about how to catch hares and foxes and the little fish that swarmed in the fjords around the feast of St. Petur and St. Pall. Birgitta made her milk into cheese, and gave the family water to drink, but other wives made the other choice, to bring their families through the summer on milk and let the winter take care of itself. Men marveled at how ten cows could no longer get by on the land that had once supported nearly a hundred.

Now one day shortly after Jon Andres had brought the sheep to Hvalsey Fjord, Birgitta was sitting over her weaving and looking out the door of the steading at the water in the fjord, and she saw this sign: a boat rowed up to the jetty and two seals flopped out of it and began to climb the hillside, and as they neared the steading, they turned into men. Just then, Gunnar came from the direction of the dairy, and greeted them and talked to them. Soon they returned to their boat and rowed off to another steading, and Gunnar came with a smile into the steading. It was not the custom of Birgitta and Gunnar to speak much to one another, for they had been estranged many years, but now he told her that a whale had stranded at Herjolfsnes, a huge whale like a mountain of flesh, and that he and Kollgrim and Olaf would go off that day and get some meat. Recalling the sign she had seen, Birgitta cast her eyes down, and said, "It seems to me that this is not the boon that it appears to be." But Gunnar scowled at having his news greeted in such an ill-tempered manner and said nothing. Sometime later the men went off.

Toward evening, the rain stopped and the clouds rolled out to sea. The next day was the first bright clear day of the summer, and by noon the grass on the hillside was so dry that Birgitta and Helga brought the bedclothes out of the steading and spread them out, for they were damp and musty from the wet weather. After that they began emptying the clothing chests, and Helga went about her work happily, chatting of this and that, but Birgitta stepped heavily, and her spirits were not lifted, for it seemed to her that this heat boded no good. Nevertheless, all of the goods were dry and sweet-smelling by dusk, and Helga and Birgitta began to remake the beds. When she was just finishing, spreading the white bearskin over Gunnar's bedcloset, Birgitta was suddenly seized by a fit of weeping so that she could not stand, but fell on the floor beside the bedcloset. Helga, coming into the steading with an armload of clothes and unstitched wadmal, put down her bundle at the door and ran and lifted up her mother's head. Now Birgitta wept for a long while, and when she had subsided, she said to Helga, "It seemed to me when I put my hands into Gunnar's bearskin that I saw myself as a child in this very bedcloset, and my mother had not died yet, nor did I expect her to, but only expected that my infant pleasures should go on and on, and I remembered this one that I have not thought of in thirty-five or forty years, the feel of plaiting her hair, of lifting the heavy strands and twisting them into each other, not as I do now, without a thought, but as I did then, painstaking and diligent, because I wanted greatly to learn the patterns. And the weave of her dress and the brownish color of the wadmal, and also the slope of her shoulder and the look of her neck seemed to press upon me, and I seemed to hear the sound of her voice, for it was the case that she spoke in a round, low tone that is not as I speak, or as you speak, and so is lost. And it seemed to me that I was a dupe and a ninny as all children are, as I still am, going from day to day with schemes and prospects. It seems to me that we have come to the ending of the world, for in Greenland the world must end as it goes on, that is with hunger and storms and freezing, though elsewhere it may end in other ways." Now she looked into Helga's face, and she saw there fondness, but not understanding.

The next day shone clear and sunny, and the day after that and the day after that, and on the fifth day, Kollgrim, Olaf, and Gunnar returned from Herjolfsnes with the whalemeat in a net in the cold water beside the boat, and Birgitta hurried to dry it and to seethe it, for it is the case that whalemeat goes off more quickly than other kinds of meat, and then cannot be eaten without certainty of illness. Birgitta kept to herself; her spirits did not lift, and Gunnar blamed her greatly for this throughout the summer.

One day Finn and Kollgrim returned from a hunting trip with a pair of beautiful big seals, although the time of the seal hunt was over, and Finn admitted that he had received them from some skraelings at the mouth of Isafjord, in exchange for a set of cunningly made arrows of Finn's own design. Gunnar was pleased with the meat and hides, but indeed, the price was high, for a set of such arrows, made in pieces and fitted together so that they could break apart inside a bird and come out without tearing the flesh, took almost a whole winter to make. The skraelings, Finn said, had had many seals with them, and had been fat and well clothed besides, but of all Finn's gear, these arrows were the only things the demons cared to trade for, so it was these or nothing.

Now the autumn seal hunt came around, and after the men went off, Birgitta and Helga went to the storehouse to count up provisions for the winter so that Birgitta could estimate how many sheep would have to be slaughtered. The whalemeat had given them just enough relief, so that with the two seals traded from the skraelings, and a reasonable result from the autumn seal hunt, the folk at Lavrans Stead would come to Easter with cheese in their mouths and sheep in their byre, but Birgitta knew that this would not be the case with some of her neighbors. Now she went out and began to count the ewes and half-grown lambs, although in fact she counted these over and over as the year went by and always knew just how many she had and where they were. Even so, she went among them, and saw at once the larger Vatna Hverfi sheep, for these stood out among the others like large bits of meat in a stew. In addition to that, these sheep always nosed out the best swatches of grass and chased the others off. Now Birgitta called the shepherd to her and told him to cut out the larger sheep and take them to the farm of Hakon Haraldsson, which was not far off, and to present them to the young farmwife, whose name was Ragnhild, for she had two babies at home and expected a third before Yule, and would surely not get through the winter with her family and her flock together. Osvif went off, and Birgitta walked back and forth, watching the sheep and spinning. Helga came out to her and she said, "Now we have placed our trust in Heaven, and we must pray that the Lord will give back to us what we have freely given to others. It seems to me that sometimes in the past, Sira Pall Hallvardsson and Gunnar have spoken in the evenings of how Jehovah used to try the faith of the Jews through sundry hardships. Now we will try the mercy of the Lord."

"Sira Pall Hallvardsson would say that the Lord little likes to be tested."

"And I would say that the Greenlanders little like to be starved to death. What have we done to repent of, except give up all our goods, then all our lands, then all our children, then all our companionship?"

"Even so," said Helga, "Sira Pall Hallvardsson would say that we are steeped in sin, and can't repent enough or give up enough to whiten our souls."

"Nay, Helga." Birgitta smiled. "Sira Pall Hallvardsson would say no such thing, but Sira Jon would say it. Nevertheless, my intention is fixed, and soon Ragnhild will be thanking the mercy of the Lord, who moved my heart to send her these sheep. And so praise will rise up to Him who is fond of praise, but gives little as a return for it." At this Helga began to be uneasy, and Birgitta's smile grew broader, and after a moment, Birgitta said, "So that you may not fall into hearing such things, I think you might take a basket and gather seaweed by the shore. I will stay beside the sheep until Osvif returns." Helga went off, and Birgitta watched her, and it seemed to her that the girl's fate was not to die in the hunger, as she had been afraid of in the past year, but to live a longer and more peculiar life, for even just walking down to the strand, she seemed to be rushing toward something unseen, and it also seemed to Birgitta that soon it would be revealed to her what this was.

Some days later, the men returned from the seal hunt, and Birgitta saw that they had taken little. Gunnar declared that there were so few boats now, and so few experienced men, that the seals evaded them easily. In addition, some men who had gone to look over Hreiney had found nothing, no deer, little forage. That night, Finn fell to making another set of his bird arrows, for he was confident of encountering groups of skraelings later in the autumn. And so the days drew on and shortened, and at the end of the summer half year, most farmers slaughtered more than half of their sheep and some of their cows and goats, and folk from every farm went to Gardar and Solar Fell on pilgrimages and prayed for the souls of the Greenlanders, and for a big whale to strand at the mouth of every fjord.

Also in this autumn, Eyvind and Finna his daughter abandoned their farm in Isafjord, as did two other Isafjord farmers. Eyvind went to Dyrnes, to the steading of his daughter Anna, and Finna with him. It must be said that Eyvind's son-in-law was little pleased to see him, for his steading was a small one, and not much better off than Eyvind's had been, for that matter. In addition to this, Eyvind still suffered spells of wild melancholy, with much weeping that he could not restrain. Even so, Eyvind went to live there, and Finna as well, but Margret and the two servingmen had to find themselves other places, and it was also the case that things had been so bad at Eyvind's steading that all of the sheep had been eaten during the summer, and so Margret had only some pieces of weaving to offer to anyone who would take her in. In her years in Isafjord, she had never seen Sigurd Kolsson or Quimiak the father, although once she thought she saw one of his wives with another skraeling. For this reason, she did not mind going off to Dyrnes, for the skraelings were rather plentiful there, as well. Now that she was an old woman, the only longing that ever seized her was for the sight of this little boy. It seized her rarely but always with a breathless, smothering pinch, like the embrace of a polar bear, as she used to imagine it when she was a child and her uncle Hauk would tell her tales of the Northsetur. The loss of Sigurd was something she had not gotten over, and for this reason she had little hope for Eyvind, of whom she had grown so fond.

In Dyrnes, only one farmstead had room for her, and this was a medium-sized steading where the wife had four small children to care for and no servingmaid, and this woman, whose name was Freya, made Margret agree to give up half of her portion of meat to the children if the hunger should demand it, and to leave any time she was asked to, with no meat and no guarantee of another place, but only the pieces of weaving she had brought, or pieces like them, should they be used for clothing in the interim. Since the winter was drawing on, and Margret no longer cared to travel in the cold, she agreed to these terms, and did not blame Freya for them, for she saw that Freya was senseless with dread at the approach of death. The children sat about their mother and watched her closely, for they had caught her fear, and when she closed her eyes, or looked up, or changed her expresssion in any way, the oldest child would cry out, "What is it, mama!" and the next oldest would shudder and tremble, and the youngest would begin to cry, and so Freya would try to sit ever more still, or to send the children to the bedcloset, but they refused to be away from her. They awaited the coming of their father with dread, not because he was an unkindly man, but because he too was of a gloomy temperament, and came into the steading every time, from working or from hunting, with predictions of disaster on his lips.

In fact, Margret saw, they had done a good job of filling the storehouse over the summer, and had more stores than Eyvind had ever had, even in his better years. But Eyvind had been a sanguine fellow, and this was not the case with Freya and Gudleif, the husband. Each night they prayed fervently to be brought safely to morning, and each morning, they prayed fervently to be brought safely to evening. Margret found the steading oppressive. Gudleif's herdsman, his boy, and the other two servingmen stayed, by choice, in the byre with the sheep. Margret sometimes went to meet Finna and Eyvind for a little talk, but as the winter drew on, these meetings ended, for Finna suffered greatly from the joint ill, and could not walk in the least depth of snow, and Eyvind wished to stay with her.

Such games and pastimes as Margret was accustomed to in the winter, as she thought all Greenlanders were accustomed to, were wholly lacking at this gloomy steading. Gudleif carved no tops nor game counters for the children, nor did he tell tales to entertain them. No one gossiped about the neighbors or speculated about the ways of southern folk or folk in Jerusalem or life in Heaven, as Eyvind and his daughters had done. Freya sighed over her weaving and her spinning and her cooking equally, and both she and Gudleif measured out the children's portions of food with dour exactitude, telling them to be grateful for what they had, as if it were thin and ill-tasting, even when it was hearty and delicious, so that the children took no pleasure in their meals, but were careful to eat it all up. Sometimes visitors came, most often Gudleif's father and mother, who were both living, and not very old, and at these times, they, too, stared at the children's trenchers and spoke grimly of the coming winter, and Margret saw that such habits as these folk had fallen into had preceded the hungry times, and had been theirs always. Gudleif's father, whose name was Finnleif, spoke as if all of his direst predictions had now come to pass. In addition to this, he knew exactly what year it was, for he had always kept an accurate and detailed calendar. It would be 1399 at the new year. Did Margret think that this hunger came by chance in 1399? Nothing was by chance. Not many would make it to the new century, said Finnleif.

Dyrnes church was in a pleasant wide valley that went a good ways back into the mountains, and most of the farms were on an island across the sound from the church. The best land was around the church, and the Dyrnes priest had always been a rich man in the past, but now there was only Sira Audun who came four or five times a year, and so the Dyrnes farmers pastured their sheep on the church lands in the valley, and went back and forth to them across the sound, which was sometimes not without danger. Even so, the district had not the icy aspect of Isafjord, and the folk were somewhat more prosperous. They were all good oarsmen and boat-builders, and cared little for horses. Margret saw that they talked often among themselves of Bjorn Bollason the lawspeaker and his foster father Hoskuld, who were Dyrnes folk, and how important they had made themselves, in spite of the Brattahlid folk, and the Gardar folk, and the Vatna Hverfi folk; the conclusion of these discussions was often that Dyrnes folk might not be so prosperous as folk from certain other districts, but that the relative hardships of their lives made them more clever and observant. Concerning Margret, they were rather curious, unlike the Isa-fjorders, who often gave their opinions of things, but never asked questions. Gudleif's mother, whose name was Bryndis, was especially inquisitive, and wanted to know why Margret had been with Eyvind, and whether she had lived with him as a wife, and why she had not gone with him to his daughter's steading, was the daughter jealous? Here she looked briefly at Freya. And why had she offered herself to Freya with so few belongings? And where had she lived before she went to Isafjord, and where before that? And why had she never married and why did she not speak as a servingmaid, and how old was she, and if she was not so old in years, why was her hair so white and her skin so wrinkled, and most important, who were her family and where did they live? Asgeir had died many years before, Margret replied, seeking sheep in a January blizzard after losing part of his farm in a dispute with a neighbor, and then she got up and went to find the children. After the first or second visit, Margret made sure to be away in the dairy or the storehouse or at some intricate work when Bryndis came to visit.

Freya's mother and brother also came to visit, but they were very meek, and when the two sides of the family came at the same time, which happened often enough, Freya's mother and brother fell into the habit of handing around the refreshments as if they were servants, and also of receiving the opinions of Finnleif and Bryndis in silent agreement. Freya's mother never spoke to Margret at all, and didn't seem to know her name. Margret felt herself pleased enough with her position most of the time, though sometimes she envied the servingmen who slept among the sheep but at least had a little good fellowship. Now Yule came on, and Margret noticed that Freya would go to the storehouse every day with a little groan.

One day Margret was sitting and sewing sheepskins into sleeping sacks for the two younger children, for it was the case that these two, who slept with her, were restless and often kicked off their coverlets. Freya was at the loom, weaving wadmal, and Margret saw that her shuttle was going more and more slowly with each throw. The oldest child had stopped her spinning, and was looking on in speechless fear, but the others, who were under one of the coverlets in the bedcloset, had not noticed this. Now Freya dropped the shuttle and put her hand to her head, and at the sudden small noise, three heads poked out of the bedcloset, and in short order, every child was crying. Now Margret got up and found a bit of wadmal and she dipped it in a vat of rendered seal blubber. Then she helped Freya to her bedcloset, and spread the cloth over her forehead. There was a great clamor. Now Margret opened the door and looked out for Gudleif, but he was nowhere to be seen. After that she sat down with her sewing and told the following tale:

Many years ago, in Norway, before the time of Harald Finehair, when there were many kings in every district, there was a princess there, whose name was—now Margret looked at the second child and said "Thorunn," for the child's name was Thorunn and Margret could not remember the real name of the princess, it had been so many years since she had heard the tale. Little Thorunn smiled shyly. And she was a princess in Hordaland. She fell in love with a prince whose father lived in Hardanger, and they loved each other very much, and indeed, it was proper for them to marry, for their families were already related in small degree, but the father of this princess, who was a great Viking named Orm, had his heart set upon Princess Thorunn's marrying one of the men who was in his service, and he told her so. But Princess Thorunn was a true Viking princess, and she lifted her chin and said that she would not. Now Orm said to her that he would confine her in a dark tower, and he only meant to threaten her, for he loved her very much, but she only said, "You may do that if you must," in a cool voice, and so he grew angry and had a tower built of large red blocks, and turfed all around so that not a speck of light could get through, and inside he put Princess Thorunn and her serving-maid, and he gave the servingmaid a staff and he told her that when Princess Thorunn should change her mind, the servingmaid should hit the staff three times on the wooden floor of the tower, and then he would let them out, otherwise they would have to stay there for seven years, through Yule and Easter and the beautiful summer. But the servingmaid never rapped those three times, for indeed, it was nothing to Princess Thorunn to be true for seven years to her love.

Now the food began to run out, and so the princess knew that seven years was coming to an end, and she was glad enough of that in spite of her pride. But still no one came to get them, and Princess Thorunn turned to her maid and said, "Indeed, we shall die an unhappy death here if we do not help ourselves," and she took her spindle and began to scrape at the mortar around the red stones, and she scraped for a morning, and then the servingmaid scraped for the afternoon, and then the princess scraped during the evening, and after a while they got one stone out, and then two, and then three, and then the princess took her small knife, which had silver chasing all about the handle, and she began to cut away the turf, and this went on all the next day, until the light came in, and such was the effect of the light that although they were very tired and discouraged, their hearts rose and they redoubled their efforts, and the fresh air came in, and then a view of the blue sky with birds flying about, and the sight of the mountains, with dazzling snow on their peaks and glistening streams running down their flanks, and they worked harder, and soon they saw the green pastures, and they were very glad, but when the hole was big enough for the two girls to step out of, they were not so glad, for they saw no sheep or cattle or dairymaids about, and the castle was in ruins, and the horses had run off, and everything was waste, for one of Orm's enemies from Stavanger district had come and made war upon him. And so the two women had only the clothes that they stood up in, and they set out to find someone to take them in.

They went north and then east and then south, and nowhere could they find anyone who would take them in, for the land was in the grips of a great hunger. They ate all manner of poor food, such as grass and birch leaves by the side of the road, but at last they found a castle where the cook looked them up and down and said that they would do for scullery maids, since the king there was about the celebrate a wedding, and there would be many guests and many dishes to wash.

Now Margret could not remember what was supposed to happen next, and she thought of giving up the tale, but she saw that the four children were listening closely, and so she stood up and got herself a drink of water. Indeed, it was the tale of the tower that had always attracted her as a child, and she remembered now that her attention had always wandered during the rest. She took some sips of water, and the children looked at her expectantly. "Well," she said, and then from her bedcloset the voice of Freya said, "The bride. The bride was so ugly that she could not bear to look at herself in the mirror." And so Margret was reminded, and went on.

This was the very castle of the prince who had once loved the Princess Thorunn, but he thought she would be dead by now, and so he had let his father betroth him to another princess, from Germany, who was so ugly that she could not bear to look at herself in the mirror. She was very rich, but her father never let anyone see her, and so she came to Hardanger Fjord thickly veiled in silk veils. Now the wedding day arrived, and Thorunn, who was but a servingmaid, took the bride's morning meat up to her. The bride saw her and said, "Thorunn, you are a pretty maid indeed. This is my fear, that when we go in our procession to the church, the folk will laugh and throw things at me, for indeed, I am very ugly. I wish you to wear the bridal clothing and walk in my stead." But Thorunn said that this would be a sin, and she could not. Now the ugly princess grew very wrathful and swore that she would have Thorunn's head cut off if she did not obey her, and so Thorunn donned the wedding clothes and went down and took her place in the procession.

When the prince saw her, he was pleasantly surprised, and thought maybe his marriage wouldn't be so bad after all, because this German princess looked so very like his dear Thorunn. And so the procession began, and it was not simple as processions in Greenland are, for the church was very big, and the way was between two groups of folk who were all interested in the looks of the future queen, and everyone was dressed in colorful garments, and everything was very beautiful, but still the maid Thorunn's heart was heavy, and she said some verses. When she passed a birch tree, she said, "Little birch tree, little birch tree, what dost thou here alone? Once I ate thy leaves, unboiled and unroasted." And the prince looked at her, and said, "What?" and she said, "Nothing. I was only thinking of Princess Thorunn." And he was a little amazed, because no one had ever spoken of that princess in his hearing in seven years.

Now they came to a footbridge, and the maid was greatly afraid, and she said, "Footbridge, footbridge, break not beneath my step, I am the false bride, and I am heartily sorry for it." But when the prince asked her what she was saying, she only said, "Nothing. I was thinking of Princess Thorunn." Now they came to the church door, and the princess was nearly swooning in dread because of her falsity, and so she said, "Church door, church roof, break not asunder. I am the false bride, but I am heartily sorry for it." The prince said nothing, and they were married by the archbishop of Nidaros.

Now night came around, and the real princess came veiled into the prince's chamber, and when she took off her veils, he was much horrified, and he said, "You are not she whom I am married to."

"Indeed, I am your betrothed bride," said the princess.

"Then what was it that you said to the birch tree as we passed it this morning?"

"It is not for me to speak to a birch tree," said the princess. "I may be ugly, but I am a princess after all."

"Then how did you speak to the footbridge?"

"It seems to me that you are mad. I spoke to no footbridge."

"Then, indeed, what did you say to the church door and the church roof? If you cannot tell me, then you are not my wife."

Now the princess bethought herself, and said, "I must go and talk to my maid, for she keeps my thoughts for me." And she ran to the kitchen and found Thorunn and asked what she had said to the church door, and Thorunn told her, and she ran back to the prince and she said in a loud voice, "Church door, church roof, break not asunder. I am the false bride, but I am heartily sorry for it."

Now the prince leapt up and said, "Why did you say this? Indeed, you must tell me all, or I will have your head cut off." And the princess told about her fears, and said that she had sent the scullery maid in her stead. Now the prince insisted that she go get the scullery maid and bring her to him, and she ran down to the kitchen, but instead of taking the maid Thorunn up to the prince as she had been ordered, she began to denounce her, and shout for men to come and cut her head off. Thorunn ran into the courtyard and began to shout and yell, for she was not one to go meekly to such a death. The prince heard this yelling, and came out of his chamber, and saved the Princess Thorunn, and when things were quiet again, he said, "When we were going to the church, you spoke of Princess Thorunn. Have you news of her?" And she said, "Indeed, I am Princess Thorunn, though ill events have sent me penniless into the world." And the prince took her to his heart, and they lived happily at the castle, and the ugly princess went back to Germany, and married an ugly prince, who liked her very much, and they had seven ugly children, who were nevertheless very rich, and for the rest of their lives they were quite satisfied with themselves.

Now the children were smiling, and Freya sat up and said, "This was not the ending I had heard."

"But such an ending was typical of my nurse, named Ingrid, for she had much to say about the ways of folk who were not just like ourselves."

The children were pleased with this tale, but they did not ask for another, for they were not in the habit of asking for anything. However, the next day, the child Thorunn was sitting not far from Margret, and she said to her, "What is a king, then?" And Margret replied that a king was a great personage, so great that there were no kings in Greenland, but that if you thought of a body, then the king was like the head of the body. The child nodded and fell silent, but after this it happened not infrequently that Thorunn or Oddny, the oldest child, would come to Margret with a question: What color was the Princess Thorunn's hair, or what was the prince's name, or what was Germany, and Margret was careful to answer these questions in as serious a manner as that with which they were asked. Sometimes, they would talk of what the princess and the maid had done in the dark tower for seven years, how they had celebrated Yule and how they had lighted their work and what they had done when the fire went out, and what they had talked of. Other times, they tried to say just how ugly the ugly princess was, and Margret found a little pleasure in these conversations, although she saw that Freya was not pleased by them, but rather jealous. Gudleif knew nothing of these things. After Yule, Margret had to divide her meat and give half of it to the children, and conditions grew rather bad.

Now it was the case after Yule that Bjorn Bollason got on his skis and went to Gardar and asked Sira Pall Hallvardsson what was left in the storehouses, and Sira Pall Hallvardsson took him and showed him every storehouse and also the kitchen of the bishop's house, and Bjorn Bollason saw that there was nothing at all left, for he and his men had given everything away the year before, so confident had they been that another year of this sort could not happen. But this year the Greenlanders were in such straits that they remembered the previous year with envy.

Shortly after Yule, Finn Thormodsson left Lavrans Stead with his arrows, and went in search of skraelings. After some four days on skis, he found a large band of these demons, fat and warm and well fed, and offered them a set of arrows. They were much pleased with the arrows, and laughed heartily in amusement, the way they often do, and after a few moments, they brought out their own sets of the same sort of arrows, and Finn saw that the skraelings he had traded his arrows to in the summer had learned how to make their own, and taught everyone else the same trick, and so, although this band of skraelings was willing to take his arrows, they would only give him one small seal for them.

Indeed, those seals that the skraelings get in the winter, which can only be gotten by skraelings and never by men, are hard enough even for skraelings to get. Finn stayed with the skraelings for two days, for they are hospitable beings, and he watched two men hunting, and this is what they do. A man stands with a spear poised above his head, looking down at a seal hole in the ice, and he waits without moving or breathing for as much as a day or even two. The highest winds and the most blinding storms do not move him, for he is enchanted with a spell that turns him to stone. Now a seal comes to the hole to take air, and the spear flies downward, as if by magic, into the mouth and head of the seal, and then the same spear is used to pull the seal up through the ice, for somehow it catches in the seal's flesh. Finn greatly admired such skills, but it is like admiring the work of the Devil, for as soon as a man declares his faith in God, and puts himself in the hands of the Lord, then he loses the power to hunt in this skraeling way, for men must choose between this world and the next and not do as Esau the son of Isaac did when he sold his birthright for a bowl of broth.

It was the case in this year of the hunger, that the skraelings seemed everywhere fat and happy, and most folk considered that they were put before the Greenlanders as a test of their faith, and some folk were tested and did not endure, for there was a man in Kambstead Fjord who took his wife and child and went with the skraelings and afterwards was not seen for many years. His name was Osvif and his wife was named Marta and their son was named Jon, but sometime later it was heard that they had changed their names to skraeling names and that Osvif had taken a second wife, a skraeling woman with almost no hair on her head.

Now the time came for Sira Audun to set off on his yearly journey to the south, and some days before the journey, Sira Pall Hallvardsson came to him and asked him not to go, for there were not the provisions to support two men on such a journey, both Sira Audun and a servant. "Indeed," said Sira Pall Hallvardsson, "we have not enough for you to take with you by yourself to the southern part of Vatna Hverfi district. If you go among them with a little, it will not be enough to save anyone, and yet will look like a great deal to them, and if you go among them with nothing, they will feel obliged to support you out of their own stores."

"This may be so," replied Sira Audun, "but indeed, some of these folk haven't seen a priest or made confession or had the sacraments in a year, those whom I did not see in the autumn. It will be a great sin for them to be denied."

"It has always seemed to me that the Lord sees our condition better than the Church Fathers do, and that He is merciful to us in our transgressions, at least those such as this one."

"But folk will be looking for me, and will be cast down if I do not come."

Now Sira Pall Hallvardsson smiled and said, "These are the same folk whom you complain of and who complain of you. They do little enough to deserve you, that is what you have said to me privily in the past. A dispute in every parish between here and Herjolfsnes, and two disputes there, that is how Sira Audun makes his journey. This is what they say of you."

"Are you saying that men don't look for a little disputing to refresh a long winter? Greenlanders consider Christ to be a fighting man, and are disappointed if his representatives do not castigate them and quarrel with them a bit."

"Even so—" But Sira Pall Hallvardsson did not go on, for it seemed to him an impossibility that Sira Audun should make his journey, and he felt no need to say more. Nevertheless, some days hence, Sira Audun was not present for his daily meal. It was the case the folk at Gardar, as at all other steadings in Greenland, now ate one meal each day instead of two. After eating, Sira Pall Hallvardsson went to the other priest's chamber, and saw that, though as neat as possible, and even cozier and more well appointed than ever, the chamber was empty. He stepped back, and was about to close the door, but then was moved to go in and sit down upon Sira Audun's stool. There was no writing upon the table, and yet there might have been, so certain was Sira Pall Hallvardsson upon looking at the desk that Sira Audun had gone off to the south.

Even as Sira Pall Hallvardsson was sitting in Sira Audun's room, Sira Audun was out upon the frozen surface of Einars Fjord on his skis, and he was making excellent time, for he was burdened only with his vestments, and carried no packs of food. The weather was fine and clear and the ice of the fjord covered with a thick, smooth powdering of snow, so that his skis sank and slid with great swishes that carried him three or four steps at a time. His face was shrouded in a mask made of two thicknesses of wadmal, with only the tiniest slits for sight, to protect against snow-blindness. It seemed to Sira Audun that the past twenty years of his life collapsed into this one feeling, the feeling of setting out for the south in the middle of winter, on the Lord's work. Except that never before had he truly trusted the Lord, and gone forth alone, without the insurance of plenty of food and extra goods. Never before had he cast off his lower self in just this way, although he might have done it, it was so simple to do, any one of these twenty years. This time he felt such confidence in what was to come that if he could have skied faster, or cast off his skis and run toward it, or, perhaps, cast off his humanity and flown toward it as a bird does, he would have. At evening he made out the sand flats and the valley of the river that runs into the fjord near Undir Hofdi church, and soon he was standing in the church itself, lighting a little lamp.

The light flickered and spread around the small room, and shone upon the wooden countenance of the Lord hanging above the altar, and the Lord's face seemed to change expression as the light fell upon it, and to welcome Sira Audun to this cold and deserted church, and at that moment, Sira Audun knew that he had done the proper thing, no matter what the outcome of it might be, for it seemed to him that the Lord would have missed him, had he not come to Him. Sira Audun knelt on the cold floor and prayed a great prayer of love and pleasure, and after a little while the light in the church attracted the local folk, who had been looking for their priest, and waiting to confess to him. Sira Audun stood up and went to the confessional, and it seemed to him that he could have swooned from hunger as he stood, but that the Lord lifted him up and helped him to the booth. Now the folk began coming to him, and they were a sorry lot this year, even sorrier than the year before, and rather than confessing their sins, their talk wandered off to tales of the hunger and enumerations of who had died, and who would die soon, and pleas with Sira Audun, or with the Lord, to have some mercy on the Greenlanders. Sira Audun did not turn these digressions back to the proper channels, but only absolved these folk, and reassured them of Christ's mercy in such eloquent tones that they went off believing that he knew of something, some cache of food or some stranded whale that they did not know of.

These confessions went on most of the night. Last to come was Vigdis of Gunnars Stead. She made her confession in the usual way, and welcomed the priest, and when she was gone, Sira Audun came out of the booth and found a large cheese waiting for him, a thoroughly salty and savory goat's cheese, white and melting, the most delicious goat's cheese he had ever tasted. He cut it up and served bits of it for communion instead of the hard wafer made from dulse that the Greenlanders were accustomed to having. After the mass, he cut up the cheese into large pieces and passed them out to the poorest families, and when he went into the church, he saw that the Lord looked down on him with a flickering, secret glance of pleasure.

Just then there was a disturbance outside that rapidly spilled into the church through the open door. Sira Audun turned to acquaint himself with the source of some shouting, and saw a poor man, Thorstein Steinthorsson, who had already buried two of his children in the snow this winter, stumble backward through the door of the church, clutching his parcel of cheese to himself. He was followed by Ofeig Thorkelsson, who was shouting curses and grabbing for the cheese. Now Thorstein came against the stone wall of the church, where there was a soapstone carving of St. Jon the Baptist attached to the wall, and with his free hand, Thorstein grabbed this carving and pulled it off the wall and attempted to bring it down on Ofeig, but he was so weakened by hunger, and the carving was so heavy, that it fell from his hand and Ofeig bent to pick it up. But Sira Audun was there before him, and some of Ofeig's friends were on him just then, and pulling him back.

Sira Audun stepped up to Ofeig, with whom he was of a height, and slapped him hard across the face, saying, "Ofeig Thorkelsson, are you so sunk in sin that you would steal a man's sustenance, and kill him, too? What are you doing here? It cannot be that you have come to pray, as you have not taken confession in five or six winters, and your soul is even now in mortal danger." Ofeig showed no sign of having heard the priest, and his friends were about to drag him off when Sira Audun stopped them, for it seemed to him that if Ofeig could be brought before the sad and inspiring wooden countenance above the altar, he would be melted. He gestured to them to drop Ofeig's arms, and they did so reluctantly, for they were more used to his ways than the priest was. Now Sira Audun began to lead Ofeig toward the altar, and Ofeig followed with apparent docility. They came to the altar, and Sira Audun told Ofeig to get to his knees, and Ofeig did so. Then Sira Audun began to pray as follows, "Lord, fill this sinner not with fear but with joy, as You have filled me of late, for I was no better than he is, except through Your grace. Lord, it may be that his heart is so hard that he knows not that it exists, but You can find it and warm it. Lord, it may be that the demons who are as plentiful on the ground as mosquitoes in the summer have made a happy home in this man, but You can drive them out, and whiten his soul again. No man who breathes is lost to You, Lord. He has done evil, but if You come into him, he will repent, and sin no more."

Now Ofeig looked up and around. Those at the back of the church whispered expectantly. Sira Audun went on, "Lord, it has pleased You in Your mystery to make us look closely upon death, and yet some of us do not know what we see. Open our eyes, we pray to You." Just then Ofeig lifted his fist, and a sly smile flitted across his face. Suddenly, however, Ofeig was on his back on the ground, and Sira Audun was sitting on his chest. Ofeig was screaming in pain, for Sira Audun had butted his head into Ofeig's belly. Now Sira Audun's voice rose. "Lord, hear the demons screaming. How they hate to be driven off!" And he continued praying in a loud voice until Ofeig was silent, and then he stood up, and helped Ofeig to his feet. As Ofeig staggered off, Sira Audun said, "Go, then, and sin no more," but no one could say whether Ofeig heard him or not.

When the church was empty, Sira Audun knelt and thanked the Lord for filling him with such power against Ofeig's demons, and he prayed there for a while before coming out of the church and going about his business of visiting the farmsteads of the district.

This was a distressing business indeed, for at every farmstead he had to pronounce burial rites over one or two folk who had died, and give last rites to one or two others who seemed doomed. And it was also true that at every steading he was offered refreshment, even if it was only a few dried berries. At first he only said that he was not hungry, but he saw that folk were disappointed that he spurned what they had, and so he began telling them the truth, that the Lord had filled him with miraculous strength, and was feeding him some sort of invisible food that made him strong and able. And then he could induce the folk at the steadings to eat their own refreshments themselves.

Finally at the end of the second day, he came to Gunnars Stead, and he looked forward to seeing Vigdis after seeing her neighbors, for indeed, such sights as he had witnessed in Vatna Hverfi were wearing and fearsome, even to someone in such an exalted state as he was in. But Vigdis' mood had changed, or so the servants said who greeted him as he neared the steading. She was abusive and angry toward everyone, and rained curses down continually upon the heads of such absent folk as Erlend Ketilsson and Ketil the Unlucky and Gunnar Asgeirsson, as if the injuries that had been done to her had just taken place. It was best, the servants said, to wait her out, for her mood would change again in an evening, or a day. But Sira Audun was filled with the power of the Lord, and he went forth boldly toward the steading, and pushed open the door.

Inside, Vigdis stood with her clothing in disarray and her dark hair falling out of her headdress, arrested by the opening of the door in the midst of cutting some dried meat at the table. The room, in fact, as Sira Audun looked about, was full of food. Vats of sourmilk and whey-pickled pieces of sealmeat and blubber, rounds of cheese, hanging birds. And Vigdis was hugely fat, fatter than she had ever been, so that her breasts hung down to her waist and her chins hid her neck completely. Sira Audun saw at once that she had responded to the hunger of the settlement by consuming and consuming without cease. Even as he watched, she jammed some of the meat into her mouth and began to cut some more. But now she stopped doing this, and put down the knife and began yelling at him so that the food fell out of her mouth. "So even the priest is come to steal from me, eh! You had your cheese, and a fine cheese it was, the best on the place. But I see you are not satisfied and crave to eat me out of house and home! But indeed, I'll drive you off, I will. I'll have my servants chase you off with the dogs. They're hungry enough, I tell you, the dogs are!" She flourished the knife, which had been sharpened so many times that its blade was honed into a crescent moon shape. Sira Audun stepped forward, feeling the power of the Lord in his breast.

"The Lord steals nothing, but only gives grace and eternal life. Woman, your soul is in peril! You cut your path to Hell with your own knife, for indeed, gluttony is a mortal sin in good times, but in times such as these, such gluttony amounts to murder! Your neighbors are failing all about you for the want of a bit of meat or a dish of broth. Today I have spoken the burial service over seven children who died for lack of food, such a little food as would fill the mouth of a small child, such as fell out of your own mouth just now, it makes me weep to tell it, their little faces were so thin, all forehead, and their mothers wept over their graves in the snow so that they could not lift themselves up to go into the warmth of the steading."

Vigdis listened to this in silence, but indeed, when she was not talking, she seemed not to be attending at all, and when Sira Audun fell silent, she said, "I cannot sit up every night as hard as I try. Folk must sleep, and that's the truth, but some folk are not folk, and sleep nary a moment, but wait till you're gone and then take all the best bits. They think I can't see it, the devils, but a bite here and a bite there, all the best bites, and then the next best bites, the sweetest, tenderest morsels. They think I don't see, but I do. Sometimes I am only pretending to be asleep, and that's the truth. I see them go about, biting this and biting that even as it hangs!"

"Woman!" Sira Audun was shouting, as if Vigdis were hard of

hearing. "You must attend me! Satan awaits you, and the door is wide open, and your feet are steady on the path! You are old, and time is short. Satan himself is beginning to smile his knowing smile. But the Lord can cheat him at this late moment! Give up these demons!" He knelt down beside the door.

Vigdis went on, "Isn't that loathsome? It astonishes me what folk are brought to these days, but I know what I'm doing, and I see it all, indeed I do, and these folk shall be driven off by the dogs, and that's a fact, and for every bite they have taken, they shall be bitten about the flanks and nipped about the calves and they shall feel it, and that's the truth!"

"The Lord beseeches you, put off this burden of gluttony, give your food as alms to your neighbors. What rots in you shall nourish them! What turns to vermin in your hand becomes wholesome when your neighbors feed it to their starving children. Indeed, this may be the curse that brings the Lord's anger down upon us. What you give away shall be returned to you a thousandfold, when the reindeer run across your fields, and the seals teem in the waters of the fjord. It seems to me that you can do this for us all, if you turn away from sin as the Lord wishes you to!"

But Vigdis paid no attention, and fell to muttering and pulling at the meat on the table with her fingers. Sira Audun was panting, and he felt himself go limp, as if the power of the Lord had left him, and so he called out, "Lord, be with me, for I am in the presence of sin, and we sinners cry out to You to show us Your mercy!" But he was not strengthened, but instead, began to sway with dizziness and hunger, and also sickness at the odor of the food hanging about. He stood up with what felt like his last strength and went out of the steading, and sat down in the snow.

After a while, one of the servingmen approached him and sat down. He was a grizzled fellow named Gizur, and his hands were much bent with the joint ill. He sat down with a groan. He said, "So, priest, she was too much for you, eh? Well, you are not the first. She has been too much for every man, and that is a fact, I'm telling you. She is my second cousin, and that's a fact, and she is a rich woman and the mistress of the steading, and I spent my life sleeping in the cowbyre. Well, such a rise tells on a person, and it tells on her. She has her bad days."

"The steading is all hung about with food!"

"Oh, yes, that's her way. She has a magic touch with food, yes she does, like Jesus with his loaves and fishes, maybe. Never been a day without two meals at Ketils Stead, or at Gunnars Stead, since she's been here. Makes up for a lot of things, always has, though she doesn't lay the strap on us anymore, she's too old for that."

"Everyone in the district is dying of hunger!"

"Are they now? Well, I wouldn't know about that, and they don't know much about Gunnars Stead, and that's a fact. We keep to ourselves, and that's the way we always have done, and I expect that that's the best way for everyone." The old man put a crooked hand upon Sira Audun's arm. "That's the best way. Don't you think? But indeed, you are the priest, and you do look a little weak, and so let me go into the storeroom over here." Gizur crept back with a pair of cheeses and slipped them into Sira Audun's bag, and then he and another servant accompanied him to the boundary of the steading and pointed him toward Undir Hofdi church. He hadn't skied but a short ways, though, before he stopped and pulled the cheeses out of his bag, and indeed they were beautiful, and he could not resist pulling one of them apart and eating about a quarter of it.

Now Sira Audun had a poor night, for he could not forget how the Lord had left him just at the critical moment, and he spent much of the night in prayer and in examination of his soul for the sin that might have caused the Lord to give up on him or turn away. He could find nothing, everything. He took refuge in his usual prayers, and in the morning, felt somewhat better. In fact, it seemed to him that he was himself again, Sira Audun, the same man he had been all his life, self-satisfied, easily annoyed, content with his own schemes, and far from the Lord, farther than he had ever known himself to be. He divided the cheeses in a large number of segments, ate one with some water, and began to carry the others about the district, and when folk asked in wonder where he had gotten them, he told them simply and with humility, that he had called upon the Lord to bend the heart of Vigdis of Gunnars Stead, but the Lord had abandoned him. The next day he left for the south, and his trip was slow and difficult. He saw that his arms were visibly thinner, and his knees seemed to tremble with every stroke of the skis.

Folk in Vatna Hverfi district now began to talk about Sira Audun's three cheeses, the one he had given out at the church, and the two he had taken about to the farmsteads, and their talk first concerned how miraculously good these cheeses had been—soft, salty, free of mold, obviously made the previous summer, but then Vigdis had huge flocks of sheep and goats and some cows, for as sparse as the hay crop had been, Vigdis had more farms than just Gunnars Stead and Ketils Stead, and the men to care for them, didn't she? When this talk had been going on for a few days, for hungry folk chew over and over the news of food as if it were the choicest morsels, some men went to Gunnars Stead one night and looked about, in spite of the dogs, for one of the men knew spells, and cast a spell over the dogs so that they would not harry, or even bark. And these men saw that Vigdis had plenty of hay hidden at the end of the cowbyre, and also that the storehouse had food in it, although it was hard to tell how much. The cows in the dark byre felt warm and sleek to the touch. And the priest had said to Magnus Arnason himself that the steading was crammed with food. After a while Vigdis' dogs began to grow restive, and the men crept away.

Now it is the case that folk who have set themselves to look upon their deaths with resignation, and to anticipate the mercy of Heaven for themselves and their children are easily distracted by the knowledge of a store of food in the neighborhood, and their lot seems less bearable to them as they think upon these stores. So it was with Vigdis' neighbors. Folk recalled how fat she was, how proud, though only the daughter of a cowman, and how niggardly. Serving boys had been beaten for taking a bit of honey, and neighbors had been summoned before the Thing on suspicion of hay stealing or sheep stealing, when anyone could see that the hay had only been used up, and the sheep had only been lost in the hills above the steading. In addition to this, everyone in the district had received one of Vigdis' tongue-lashings, and in the time of Ketil the Unlucky, more than a few had had verses made against them, and been held up for ridicule. As folk talked about Vigdis' hoard of food, they began remembering these things, too, and, as it often happens, these injuries came upon them the more freshly for not having been thought of in many years.

Among those who talked about these things, Ofeig Thorkelsson and Mar Marsson were not the most backward, even in the presence of Jon Andres Erlendsson. Indeed, of late no one had suffered injuries from Vigdis as her son had, for the sight of him seemed to concentrate in her mind all the ills that had ever been done against her, and she was often moved to attack him and box his ears. Even so, Jon Andres never joined in the talk among his friends about his mother, and when Ofeig opened his mouth, Jon Andres would get up and go outside.

It was the case that the hunger was not so bad at Ketils Stead as it was at other steadings. For one thing, servingfolk at Gunnars Stead would send food to their relatives at Ketils Stead from time to time. For another, the Ketils Stead shepherd was a talented fellow, and had accumulated a large flock, so that in the autumn many sheep had been killed, and their meat dried for the winter and their heads singed into svid and their brains made into sausage and their feet boiled into broth. Even so, Jon Andres and his friends had little notion of household economy, and by Yule much of this food was eaten, or wasted, and Ofeig and Mar and the others were impatient at the prospect of shorter meals and eking things out as their neighbors did. Mar, in particular, could not stop talking of what there was to eat at Gunnars Stead, and urging Jon Andres to get some of it from his mother. But Jon Andres paid him no attention. After the argument at the church, Jon Andres had been avoiding his friends, and one evening he told Ofeig that it was tiresome to have these boys around him. "Indeed," he said, "they are not boys anymore, but men with no occupations and no inclination to return to the steadings of their fathers, where they might be made to do some work," and this was true. For some years, Jon Andres had fancied his band to be something on the order of a band of Vikings, Harald Finehair and his hirdmen was what they were called in the neighborhood, and Jon Andres did not mind this nickname, but after the conflict at the church he grew impatient, and spoke to his friends sharply if at all.

One day he came among them where they were lounging on the benches of the steading, and he said that it was his desire to send them away, back to their fathers, for the life he had been leading oppressed him, and he wished to change it. As a going away gift, he would give them each a suit of clothes, the horse that each had been riding, and some dried meat to take away with them to their fathers' steadings.

Ofeig Thorkelsson was not the only one of these men to be on bad terms with his father. Mar and Einar, who were brothers, had neither spoken to nor heard news of their father, who lived in the southern part of the district, since the summer, and they feared that he with much of his household had died in the hunger, for the steading was not a prosperous one. Even so, Jon Andres told them, they must find another place to live, for his intention was fixed, and he intended to be free of them by the evening, or at the latest, the next morning. Andres Bjartsson and Halldor Bessason now got up and began to gather their belongings together, and it seemed to Jon Andres that Halldor was actually relieved and pleased to go, while Andres was resigned, as he had had news of his father at Yule, and all had been well at his father's steading at that time.

Mar and Einar began to grumble. Jon Andres said, "After these years of friendship, it would not please me to throw you out, or for us to part with ill feelings. But it is the case that times are different now than they have been, and such bands as ours do not repay in good fellowship what they cost in wasted provisions and trouble with neighbors, for I will not hide from you the fact that folk in this district are angry at me for the mischief we all have done, and they speak against me, and declare that I have incited you. Arnkel Thorbergsson is especially angry at the seduction of his daughter and threatens action against me if he and she do not chance to starve before the Thing. But I knew nothing of this seduction until he told me of it." And Jon Andres glared at Einar Marsson, for he was to blame in this.

Ofeig settled back against the wall, and Jon Andres turned to him. "Do not think, Ofeig, that I exclude you from these arrangements. Although we have been companions since boyhood, your pranks no longer amuse me. I think it would be well for you to reform your character, and apply to your father for forgiveness, for after tonight you will get nothing more at Ketils Stead." He paused, then went on. "When I heard the priest pray over you not so long ago, my eyes were opened, though yours were not. It has seemed to me for these last days that I look damnation in the face and am too ignorant to recognize it, but if I did I would be a hundred times more terrified than I am now, and right now I am terrified enough." Jon Andres saw that Halldor was nodding a bit in his corner, as if he had had similar thoughts, and he went on, "Folk in the district will say that it was I who led you out of the proper ways, and indeed, I am willing to take this blame, if such a thing will recommend you to your fathers. When I look back, I see that I was full of seething resentments and longings that I couldn't speak of, they were so mixed together. But I see that you do not attend to anything I say, and so I will not go on, except to say that I expect you to attend to this, the necessity of being away from Ketils Stead by the morning light."

And for the rest of the day and evening, Jon Andres sat up and looked alertly about himself, for it seemed to him that Ofeig, and maybe Mar and Einar, would come at him and try to kill him, but they did not. They left quietly with Halldor and Andres, going on skis and leading their horses in a line behind them. After they left, Jon Andres slept, only with three servants standing guard over the steading, and when he woke up, he loitered about the steading rather aimlessly, wishing for companionship, for he had not been without some of these boys since he was twelve winters old.

After leaving Ketils Stead, Halldor and Andres parted from the other two, and took their horses and goods to the south, and what they found there was no better, but no worse, than what was to be found at any other steading in the district, namely that some folk had died and some had not, and there was little food to be had. Einar and Mar decided to go to the steading of their uncle, the brother of their mother, a man named Ari, and they parted from Ofeig and made their way to Yfirfoss Stead, where Ari lived, but they only stayed there two days, for Ari had nothing to give them. Ofeig made it his plan to linger about Undir Hofdi church, and to squat in the priest's house there, for he knew that Sira Audun would not be back for some weeks. It seemed to him that if Thorkel Gellison were to find him, he would kill him rather than take him in again.

Einar and Mar returned from Yfirfoss, and went to the steading of another uncle, this one the husband of their mother's sister, a man named Bengt, and they left this steading after four days. Then they went to the steading of a cousin, a man named Ingvald. Here they stayed for two days before leaving. At each of these steadings, the one thing they spoke of was how much food Vigdis of Gunnars Stead had stored everywhere on her farm, and it did not take long for this news to penetrate every steading in the district, and for men to begin to talk about what a crime it was for this old woman to have so much food all to herself. Sometime in their travels, Mar and Einar began to discuss a notion they had, of taking some of Vigdis' food and using it as a gift to win themselves a permanent place on some steading. In every case when they brought this up, as something that ought to be done, or could easily be done, one man or other on every steading looked at them with quickened interest.

Not long after leaving Ingvald's little steading, they ran into Ofeig, who told about staying at the priest's house at the church, and they came there and joined him. Ofeig had no food left, and Mar and Einar had just enough for a mouthful for everyone, and that night they began chatting again, as always, about Vigdis, and the next morning, all three of the men left the church house and went in different directions, and two days later, all three were back, and about twelve other men besides, and these men lingered about the church house all day, and then, in the evening, they departed in a band and directed themselves toward Gunnars Stead.

It was a saying among the Greenlanders, that "not every gobbet in the stew is mutton," and this was the case, also, with Ofeig's band of men. Some men will join any undertaking simply to see what might happen, others have vaguer motives even than this. They follow any movement, perhaps, simply because movement is of interest in the dead of winter. A few men, such as Bengt, the uncle of the Marssons, had heard of Vigdis' quantities of provisions and ached to see them, merely to see the truth of the tale. Mar and Einar thought of stealing a portion. Others, perhaps, thought of this, too, for more than a few of these folk were men with families and servants. One or two of these men bore recent grudges against Vigdis, or older enmity from the days of Erlend and his sons.

However their feelings stood when they left the priest's house, it is the truth that the quick walk through the snow in the frigid dark developed their appetites wonderfully, such appetites as men have who haven't been satisfied in two winters, or in the summer between them. They came to the steading as men come to a feast, or bears to their first kill of the spring. The farm buildings lay before them in the moonlight, as neatly turfed as in the days of Asgeir Gunnarsson or his father, for Vigdis liked things to be in good repair. The storehouse lay near the steading, and the cowbyre behind, with the sheep pens open to the south. Another cluster of buildings, which included a smithy and a bath house, lay off the path from the church, some ways in front of the steading, and here the band of men stopped and listened for the barking of the dogs. None came, for the dogs were in the chambers off the cowbyre with the cowmen, and the wind blew from them into the faces of the intruders. All was silent. Einar and Mar went to the storehouse and forced open the door.

The mixed odor of meat and whey rolled forth through the door like a blast of heat, inflaming Einar so that he stumbled into the storehouse and began reaching in the dark with his hands and grabbing anything he touched. There were sausages and joints of dried or smoked meat, rounds and loops of cheese hanging from thongs, lumps of butter stacked against the wall. Einar groaned so at the wealth of provisions that Mar and another man pushed him out of the way in the dark, and then stepped on him in their impatience to get inside. The doorway was low and narrow, as with all storehouses, and the men crowded around it, inhaling the rich odors.

It is the case that when folk come long distances for a feast, the wife and her servingwomen must feed them all as quickly as is seemly, for the longer they wait, the more quarrelsome they become, and the more they stare at the bowls and trenchers passed to their neighbors and the more they feel slighted at the size of their own portions. Now it happened that Einar's fall blocked the doorway of the storehouse, and in the darkness, men could not see how to lift him out of the way, or how to get around him, but they could hear Mar and the other man pulling things off the hooks and shelves, and indeed, they could hear the working of jaws and low grunts of pleasure, for it is with a man as with a dog—hungry ears are sharp ones. The men in the doorway began to shout at one another, and shove each other aside, and fear that other men were getting more to eat and to carry away than they themselves were. Now Ofeig said, "Nay, enough of this. There is more to be had in the steading." And he ran through the snow to the door of the steading, and with one heavy blow of his shoulder, he knocked it down.

At this, a dog began to bark, and soon some others, and men began to run from the storehouse to the steading. Inside the steading, Vigdis sat up in her bedcloset and held forth her seal oil lamp, and was heard to say,

"Now I see that Satan and his minions have come upon me at last." Two elderly servingmen came in from another chamber in the steading with raised staves, and a blow from one of these glanced off Ofeig's shoulder, angering him so that he turned and brought his great fist down on the fellow's neck. The man collapsed on the floor. Perhaps the band of men had intended to do no injury, only to take some food and leave, but after this blow, the doing of injury seemed a simple and natural thing, a thing that could not be avoided in the course of events. Other servants came running from the cowbyre, all old men, and they, too, carried staves, and shouted about the devil's work, and the dogs came with them, barking and howling at the top of their lungs, so that there was great confusion.

One man, named Thorvald, a friend of Bengt, who had once sat in Vigdis' place at the church, and thereafter was subjected to a humiliating scolding, pulled the woman from her bedcloset, so that she fell upon the floor, screaming and cursing. She slept naked, wrapped in furs for warmth, and the sight of her bare flesh was startling to Thorvald and Bengt and everyone present, for it glowed with fat. More than one man was inflamed by the contrast of this flesh with that of the wife he had just been with or the bones of the child he had recently buried, so that it was easy to land a kick upon the old woman, or slap her across her fat cheeks, or pinch her pendulous breasts until red circles stood out on the skin like burns. "Lord!" shouted Vigdis. "They bite me, they bite me to the bone. Their evil devours me!" And she screeched in pain even when no one was touching her. To stop the screeching, Ofeig kicked her hard in the jaw, and after this, she could not form words, but the screaming did not cease, and the men were stirred by it to actions they had not thought of before, and the joints of beef and reindeer meat that hung about the walls became weapons in their hands. Mar Marsson tipped over a small dish of honey, and the liquid seeped into the table, and he took the soapstone dish and brought it down on the head of one of Vigdis' servingmen, so that his skull was cracked and blood and brains spilled forth.

Ofeig and another man pulled Vigdis out from under the table, where she had rolled, and kicked and beat her with their fists until she fell silent. Now the other man stepped back, but Ofeig, seeing Vigdis' crescent-shaped knife upon the table, snatched it up, saying, "Let us gut this old bear and see what Christian children she has been feasting on," and he slit her from throat to belly, and opened the stomach, as a hunter would a reindeer, and those present saw that his eyes glowed with pleasure, and were not dull and dead as usual. It was not known, in the melee, just when Vigdis gave up her last breath, whether during the beating or not until she was disemboweled, for the wind makes noises leaving the corpus that are the noises of death, not life.

Now that Vigdis and two of her servants were dead and the other servants subdued, Ofeig's band fell to a great eating frenzy that lasted until daylight, and then, after retching, they fell about the steading and went to sleep. What greeted them when they woke up in the afternoon light was such a scene as they did not recognize or remember, and the events of the night before came back to them partially, if at all, as the fragments of dreams, or tales of other times. When Einar Marsson went out in the yard to retch again, he found Jon Andres Erlendsson and a band of some thirty men standing in a circle about the steading, and they were fully armed. Now Ofeig came out and saw the same thing, and he said, "Better we had killed all the servants, and that's a fact."

Ofeig turned and got inside the steading again, but Einar was dizzy from retching, and only stood looking at the band of avengers, until Jon Andres raised his hand, and another man, named Axel Josteinsson, who had a crossbow, let his arrow fly, and it lodged itself in Einar's breast, and he fell to the snow, gasping. The men inside the steading were without weapons, while Jon Andres' men had an assortment of weapons such as the Greenlanders could muster at this time, mainly axes and clubs and bows and arrows, including three old crossbows from the time of King Sverri, but no noble weapons such as men carried in former times, namely swords. Jon Andres shouted to the men inside the steading that they must send Ofeig forth to receive his punishment, but the only sign that these words were heard was this, that the door opened and the corpus of Vigdis' servant, Karl, was thrown out into the snow.

The inside of the steading was a great mess of blood and grease and vomit, and some of the men there thought that they would surely die of the stench, and they saw by the light of clear day that it was the stench of Hell placed before them. Some fell to praying and others to whimpering, and Ofeig did not mind these activities, but if any went near the door, Ofeig grabbed his arms and broke them or cast him back into the rear of the steading like so much whale meat, for Ofeig seemed to draw strength from the scene of his debauch, and new life, as well. He looked about himself with a pleased glow in his face. Once he picked up the corpus of Vigdis and rolled it into the bedcloset, and thereafter he threatened those who displeased him with being "locked in the old she-bear's embrace." And so it went on for some time, with only this change, that men's bowels tormented them increasingly, from the effects of the rich meats they had eaten in the night, and so they were forced to relieve themselves on the floor of the steading, since they were barred from leaving to find the privy, or even from going to other chambers in the steading. Ofeig knew that there were other ways out of the steading, more ways than he could stand guard over. Only Ofeig himself was free of these pains, and as he continued to eat, he laughed aloud at the groaning of the others.

Outside, the day drew on and Jon Andres began to feel impatient, and he and some of his friends spoke of burning Ofeig out of the steading, but the turf was fresh from the previous summer, and largely covered with snow. The steading itself was built more of stone than of wood, and the stones were set as tightly as any in Greenland, offering no entrance for a flaming arrow. A man could run to the door and pitch a torch dipped in seal oil into the steading, but Ofeig would see that and put it out before any damage was done. And so it seemed that the only course was to wait Ofeig out, but such a course angered Jon Andres so that he had great difficulty containing himself, and paced furiously back and forth before his men. His one consolation was that the light of the moon on the snow would prevent escape from any entrance to the steading, if his men were alert enough. Night drew on. Ten men went to sleep in the byre, where the cows, the last cows in Vatna Hverfi district, lowed in the peaceful darkness.

Inside the steading, night drew on as well, and men struggled against sleep so that they might watch Ofeig and escape when sleep overtook him, for indeed, Ofeig had found some ancient mead locked away in a deep cupboard and was partaking of it. Though he took it in great drafts, its only effect was to raise his spirits higher, so that he began looking about the room and shouting jests to the others, and once he lifted up a sturdy bench that was sitting against the wall and broke it over his leg. Such a devil seemed to be in him as was stronger than five men, or even ten.

And this is what some priests say that Satan is, a great mouth that sucks down all matter of beasts and men and carries them inside himself to the depths of Hell, where he shits them out, and it was the great sin of the Greenlanders that in the face of God's test of their faith, some of them made a lord of such a devil as Ofeig and were led by him into this Hellish steading, and Ofeig, like his master, stood by unsleeping to guard the door, and to prevent the escape of any of his hirdmen. Also like souls in Hell, these Greenlanders groaned at the agony of their guts, and dirtied themselves and repelled their fellows, so that no two of them could make a pact together and overthrow their master. They were sunk in fear.

Outside, the night grew lighter, and those who had been sleeping in the serene warmth of the byre roused themselves and came forth into the dawn. Jon Andres invited them to partake of the stores in the storehouse, and they did so with moderation, for great appetite is a ruse and a snare that betrays men into agony. After the men were fortified, they walked about the yard of the steading. They could hear the muffled shouts of those inside, as men can sometimes hear the muffled screams of demons imprisoned in stones. Jon Andres said, "Before long now they will come forth to their punishment," and he smiled a grim and angry smile, for indeed, his anger had not diminished since the day before. The sun rose over the snowy meadows and frozen lakes of Vatna Hverfi district.

Now toward noon the door to the steading opened and men began coming forth, staggering and shamefaced. Some fell in the snow and rolled about, while others only lay there as if swooning. Ofeig was not among them, and after all had come out, Jon Andres and three of his men ran into the steading, but indeed, Ofeig was nowhere to be found, in none of the many chambers, and the snow had been so beaten down by the tramping of Jon Andres' men that no tracks revealed the direction of his escape, if indeed, muttered some of the men, that direction had not been straight down, for it is well known that Satan cannot wait for some men, those whom he especially prizes, but he snatches them away in the midst of life.

Love

One day in the late winter, Thorkel Gellison and two of his servants came on skis to Hvalsey Fjord, and toward dark they banged on the doors of Lavrans Stead, but they had no answer. Thorkel and one of the servants looked through the sheep byre and saw that the sheep were in a poor state. Not only were they thin and weak, and a few dead, back in the corner, but they were also wandering at large around the byre and the steading, and could have, in a panic or in one of the strange notions that sheep take, wandered down to the fjord and drowned, or been lost in the rough hills above Hvalsey Fjord. It seemed to Thorkel that Gunnar and Birgitta must have abandoned the steading, and he was about to turn away and go off to some of their neighbors for news, when one of the servingmen put his shoulder to the door and it swung open. The inside of the steading was deeply cold, and Thorkel shrank from stepping through the doorway, but then he heard a low groan, and went in.

He found all of the Lavrans Stead folk except Finn lying in their bedclosets. Helga, Kollgrim, and two of the servingmaids lay in the bedcloset closest to the door, and it was Helga who had groaned. All of the four of these were able to open their eyes and speak. Kollgrim said, "Finn has returned," in a low voice. In the rear of the room, Gunnar lay face down under his bearskin, and he was asleep, or insensible. Beneath him, deep in the straw, was Birgitta. Thorkel thought that she was surely dead. In another bedcloset lay the shepherd and his boy, and when Thorkel approached them, the boy sat up and asked for food. In the farthest bedcloset from the door, Olaf Finnbogason lay dead of hunger. Thorkel saw that he had died a slender man. Thorkel said nothing of Olaf for the moment, and went back to the shepherd boy, who was peering around the door of his bedcloset. "Indeed," Thorkel told him, "I have cheese and dried meat, and Johannes here will cut some bits for you," and at these words, the shepherd, too, was able to raise himself. The other servingman from Hestur Stead set himself to starting a fire and lighting some lamps.

When the fire was started on the hearth, the servingman found a vat and made some broth out of the dried meat, for broth is the best food that folk can eat when they are close to death from hunger, as it is not overly rich for their bellies. The smell of the food aroused everyone but Gunnar and Birgitta, and, of course, Olaf. The story that Kollgrim and the shepherd told was just like every story in Greenland—the food had run out, Finn had gone off to snare partridges or find something else and had not yet returned. He had left four days before, perhaps five or six, but he had not been strong himself, and was likely dead. Two days ago they had taken to their beds, for keeping the fire was beyond their strength, and if Thorkel had not come, Lavrans Stead would have quickly become their tomb. Thorkel let everyone eat and talk in peace for a while before again approaching Gunnar's bedcloset, for he had some dread of this, and it seemed to him as he neared the moment of uncovering Gunnar's death that his cousin had been a great friend and ally to him for many years, and Asgeir before him, from the time when Thorkel himself was a young man. And it also seemed to him that each friend buried in a hunger time or a sickness time comes to a man as a fresh and painful injury.

But it happened that Gunnar was able to rouse, though with difficulty, and Thorkel was able to get some broth between his lips. More than this, the corpus of Birgitta was no corpus, but warm and living, barely living. Her eyes flickered and her lips moved when Thorkel brought her up out of the straw, and she, too, was able to swallow some broth. And so it was that most of the Lavrans Stead folk were saved toward the end of the great hunger by the good luck of Thorkel Gellison, although Finn Thormodsson never returned and was never found, and he, like Olaf, was a great loss to the household. Olaf was buried in the little churchyard at St. Birgitta's church.

By the third day, Gunnar was able to sit up and hear the news of Vatna Hverfi, and Thorkel told him of the two great events, the murder at Gunnars Stead and the death of Sira Audun between Petursvik and Herjolfsnes. Thorkel was extremely bitter about Ofeig, and wondered aloud how such a devil had come into his family, and said that he and his wife Jona had had many words about the parentage of the boy, so that things were sour between them. He had gone to Jon Andres Erlendsson himself and given the young man self-judgment, and Jon Andres had not demanded Hestur Stead, as in law he could have, but had only exacted the promise of a pair of good horses of his own choosing, not, he said, because he held Vigdis' death to be a small matter, but because he wished to exact his payment from Ofeig himself, for he did not concur that Ofeig had been stolen away by his infernal master, and was certain that the fellow would be found soon enough.

In addition to this, Jon Andres had declared his resolution to relinquish Gunnars Stead and have the steading found abandoned in law, for it was a steading full of ill luck. He told Thorkel that he doubted anyone would live there now, or even farm the fields, for fear of Vigdis' spirit. Talk was, however, that Bjorn Bollason the lawspeaker had no aversions to possible spirits, and that he and Hoskuld his sponsor had already prepared to take the steading over. To this news Gunnar made no response.

Concerning Sira Audun there was this to say, that he had lived on air for four weeks, and just before leaving Petursvik on his skis, he had turned down some broth that one of the women there made for him, saying that he had his own food. But no food was found with the corpus, and his muscles had been so wasted that his knees and elbows were the biggest things about him. Even so, he had died smiling, with his eyes open so that they could not be closed.

Now Gunnar asked, how was it that Thorkel had had food to bring them, were conditions so much better in Vatna Hverfi, so that the Lavrans Stead folk could count on seeing Johanna Gunnarsdottir again? For they had given up that hope with all others. Thorkel said that conditions had not been at all favorable, until the storehouses at Gunnars Stead were opened, and it was seen that Vigdis had been hoarding food for ten summers or more—so long that certain things had turned to dust, but the rest was taken about to all the local farmsteads, and that, plus their own stores, would carry the district through Easter.

And on the next day, Birgitta awakened, and sat up, and the news was told to her, and she listened carefully, and then she said, "There is always a jest to be played upon the Greenlanders." And now the hunger ended, for two whales stranded, one at Kambstead Fjord and one at Siglufjord, and after that the snow melted and the grass greened and the ice broke up and was blown out of the fjords, and one day in the late spring, folk got up and went outside to find swarms of reindeer running across their farms, reindeer in such numbers as the Greenlanders had never seen before, and only heard of in tales of the western settlement. Sira Pall Hallvardsson prayed on his knees in the Cathedral of St. Nikolaus for three days without sleeping, in thanks for the bounty of the Lord.

Sira Pall Hallvardsson was much cast down at the death of Sira Audun, more cast down than he considered proper, for such grief as he felt attested to his regard for himself rather than for the soul of Sira Audun. Every day, a great longing came upon him to go into Sira Audun's chamber, such a longing as he had once felt for other sinful acts, as he had once felt for the presence of Gunnhild Gunnarsdottir, in fact. It could not be said that the two priests had become knowingly intimate. They had never spoken with the frankness that Pall Hallvardsson and Jon spoke with, and Sira Audun had retained his habit of brusque impatience. It had been his way, for example, to open his chamber door just a crack when anyone knocked upon it, and peep out. Although there were times when he stepped back and invited Pall Hallvardsson in, there were as many times when he did not, and Pall Hallvardsson was left standing in the passage. These were the times, he said, when he was working at his writing. This may have indeed been true, but of that activity Sira Pall Hallvardsson knew nothing. The verses and prayers that came of this work Sira Pall Hallvardsson did admire, as far as he was able. He detected in them the same brusque impatience, though it was concealed in "ironia" typical of the Greenlanders. What Sira Pall Hallvardsson knew and remembered of Sira Audun, even after many years of acquaintance, did not add up to the desolation he felt now at the other priest's passing, and Sira Pall Hallvardsson feared the strength of his sorrow. It was common knowledge that such griefs could open one to madness.

It was Eindridi Andresson, Sira Audun's nephew, who wanted to have the dead priest's chamber for his own, and his arguments were not unpersuasive. We should not shrink, he said, from accepting the ways of the Lord, and Pall Hallvardsson knew that when Eindridi looked at him, he saw that he, Pall Hallvardsson, did shrink. And thought less of him for it. But Pall Hallvardsson, on his side, considered Eindridi to be one of those hard-bitten, practical men from the south, whose difficult lives have driven out all softness. On adopting their new life at Gardar, for instance, Eindridi and Andres, his son, had become as distant as any newly acquainted students might have been, and had maintained this distance for the year since their advent. Eindridi said that it was better for the boy to put off his earthly father, so that he could the more readily take his Heavenly Father into his heart, and go to Him with greater eagerness when the time should come. In Greenland, said Eindridi, the time must come soon, or even sooner. In the early days, when the boy came to his father with complaints or griefs, Eindridi was cold and firm about sending him off to pray, and laid no comforting hand upon him, nor said a kind word. Now the boy, who was some nine winters old, was as cool as his father, and as ready to bid others to pray.

At their learning, they were apt and diligent, as might befit kin of Sira Audun, and Andres was especially quick, but both of them preferred never to ask a question, and to be found mistaken was a great shame to them. It fell to Pall Hallvardsson to teach them as best he could, but he found this a peculiarly unpleasant duty, and shrank from that, too, and saw that Eindridi noticed his shrinking. In short, there was no satisfaction to be gained from these two, and, as a sort of evil jest, Eindridi looked rather like Sira Audun in certain moments, usually those moments when he was being most unpleasant.

The case was that most things about Gardar were not so congenial as they had once been, for the hunger had struck there with the same force as it had all over Greenland, and Olaf was dead, and Petur the Steward, and all of those with whom Sira Pall Hallvardsson had felt affinity. In addition to this, folk said that he did not know how to order things so that folk were trained to take up these places, and he had to admit that this was true. Concerning this difficulty, he had but one recourse, and that was prayer, but as yet the Lord had not favored him with new knowledge, and the cook's attempts remained bad, so that the servants made bitter remarks to his face about ill rewards for great labor.

Sira Pall Hallvardsson could not tell if the other priest was still mad. It seemed to him at times that Sira Jon had traded a set of uncongenial habits for a set of congenial ones. Certainly now and for the last eight years he had done just as he pleased. He had stayed by himself in the smallest chamber he could find, sometimes crying out for a smaller one. The door to his chamber was unbarred and occasionally fell open, unnoticed by the man within. He had ceased having any intercourse at all with Greenlanders, and was relieved thereby of resentment, or even, perhaps, knowledge of them. He spent his days in dialogues with the Lord, or with himself, or, from time to time, with Sira Pall Hallvardsson. Sira Pall Hallvardsson had heard of hermits who went into the deserts to do the same thing, and anchoresses who were walled into tiny cells hard by convents that were not unlike Sira Jon's cell. Such practices were not exactly the fashion they once had been. Certain thinkers Sira Pall Hallvardsson knew of spoke against them now that working in the world was considered the better way, but every bridle does not suit every horse, that was what the Greenlanders would say.

Sira Jon had survived the hunger very well, if it could be said that he had noticed it at all. The poor life that he led told on him greatly, though, and he was much bent with the joint ill. When he closed his hands, the fingers did not meet well enough to grasp a spoon, and from pain he could not lift anything heavier than a bit of cheese. Sira Pall Hallvardsson himself fed the other priest, and saw that he was offered his share of whatever there was to be eaten, though he might not eat it. The cook was from Brattahlid district. She had never seen or spoken to Sira Jon, and knew him only as "the mad one." Even so, Sira Jon was the only one of the steading who did not complain of her cooking. When Sira Pall Hallvardsson carried his trencher to him, as he was doing now, he knew that it would be welcomed with the same indifference as it had always been welcomed.

Sira Jon was huddled beside the wall. At the sound of the tray being set upon the floor, he held out his finger to be kissed, but did not turn around or look at Sira Pall Hallvardsson. Sira Pall Hallvardsson knelt with difficulty and kissed the finger, then sat upon his knees and waited for the other to speak. Sira Jon was so bent and thin and had such little color in his skin or hair that if the Greenlanders should see him they would surely suspect that he was another man from the one that they remembered. They would recognize the passage of haughty looks over his countenance, however, and that this was the bishop's nephew would finally be as unmistakable to them as it was to Sira Pall Hallvardsson, orphan boy and descendant of Flemish merchants.

After a while, Sira Jon said, "What lies they tell."

Sira Pall waited. He knew that no reply was expected of him as yet.

Sira Jon cast a furtive glance at the food tray, then said, "It was all for the sake of that oaf. Perhaps he is dead now, perhaps they all are. They take the beasts into their houses and regard them with the fondness that other folk reserve for their children, but this is because they are themselves half beasts."

Still Sira Pall Hallvardsson did not speak. Partly, he was not sure of what Sira Jon was referring to, if it was actually any knowledge common to them both, and partly he desired to wait out the usual references to beasts and animals that the old priest chattered about when he first looked at his food. He had been trained to eat a little, calmly, by years of force feeding, as he had been trained to cover his nakedness by years of enforced bathing and dressing, so that now in these things he was docile if contemptuous.

"Indeed, this everlasting flesh that we must chew upon and choke down, without bread or wine, it seems to bring the nature of beasts into a man through his mouth. And what was it you brought to me a while ago, that tasted of rot and salt at the same time? What was it?"

"Sira Jon, you know that this was whalemeat, and men were glad of it."

"Fish they call it, for the sake of the fast, but it tastes like no fish that ever swam, and it is red flesh, as red as the flesh of an old bull. Do you not long for a cabbage? It seems to me that if I could have a bit of cabbage, I would be right again. A bit of cabbage and a loaf of bread to break my thirty-year fast. Is it thirty years?"

"Thirty-one, by my reckoning. You seem pensive today. We do not often speak of such things."

"Perhaps I am about to die. It often seems to me that when I get into an easy state of mind, that this is a sign that I am about to die. But each time I am disappointed. It is a sin to serve watered milk and seaweed for the sacrament."

"The Lord sees what we are reduced to."

"It is true that you have always been confident about what the Lord sees. Did you know that I spent the happiest day of my life in Greenland? I thought you would be surprised to hear it, but I often meditate upon it. Not upon what they told me, for that was a ruse and a trick that they concocted to further their own schemes, but upon how it came into me, the knowledge of what they were saying."

"Will you tell me the tale of this day?"

"I need not tell you the tale, as you yourself were there and colluded with them."

"Then tell me what I do not know of these things."

"Perhaps I will." He glanced at the tray again, and pulled it toward him. It contained a small bowl of sourmilk and a small bowl of broth that was especially foul from being burnt by the cook. He motioned Pall Hallvardsson to give him a taste of the broth and then of the sourmilk, and the broth was not so foul that he did not eat it up. As careful as Sira Pall Hallvardsson tried to be, some of the broth spilled into the other priest's beard, but the sourmilk clung to the spoon better. When he had eaten the small amount served to him he turned away and did not ask for more. He said, "You know that the bishop was a great traveler in his youth, always upon the roads, thinking nothing of a night under the sky, so assured was he of the Lord's care. It so happened that when I came to him from my mother's house in Stavanger district, and I was some fourteen winters in age, after I had been with him for a month or two, he sent me over the mountains to the next fjord carrying a message. The way was through thick woods and I lost myself for a while, so that I did not arrive at the steading I was seeking until well past dusk, but I had no ill adventures. Even so, when it came time to return to my uncle the next morning, I was so seized by fear that I would not leave without an escort.

My horse could have smelt the way home of himself, but it was not of getting lost that I was afraid. I was simply afraid, and the next time I was given a commission that involved being sent away, I fell down in a swoon. My uncle was much displeased with me, and with his sister for being so soft with me. He chastised me, and told me that I would be of little use to him if I couldn't even carry a message, and he had me beaten every time I swooned at a new commission, but he could not induce me to leave him, and I stayed beside him from that day forward, and soon enough he left off, for isn't it the case that the child must always endure, if he is stubborn enough?

"And so it happened that from that time on, until we came to Greenland and after, I had never been apart from my uncle, farther than the distance from one end of a farm field to another. When he delegated you and Petur to go about from church to church, it was partly because he knew that I simply could not do it. But then that low fellow, Olaf Finnbogason, was recalled from where they had been hiding him in Vatna Hverfi district, and he told his lying tale of being betrothed to that whore, and without blinking an eye, my uncle sent us off to find out the rights of it. He saw, indeed, with his penetrating sight, that I was terrified, and while you went off to order the boat, he came up to me and ordered me to subdue my terror, under threat of being banished to Herjolfsnes, and his cruelty was the hardness and wisdom of the Lord who sees what is needful. I remember that we set out, and I sat behind you in the bow of the boat. We set a pace rowing the boat so that it seemed to fly through the water of its own and we talked of this and that. Although it was autumn, we were warm from the exercise, and much stimulated. Nothing frightened me at all—not the icebergs in the fjord—remember how we pushed them off with our oars—nor a gusting wind that raised whitecaps in the water; not even being apart from my uncle frightened me. When we got there, we leapt out of the boat and dragged it up on the strand without a pause in our discussion, and then that old woman, who was Sira Nikolaus' concubine, met us and asked what we might like for our evening meat, and we told her, and then we nearly ran over the hills to Gunnars Stead, talking all the way. I had never expected such a feeling of liberty and animal pleasure. No thread drew me back toward Gardar. Perhaps I thought of my uncle twice.

"And then they greeted us with that tale, the tale of the Virgin and Child walking upon the grass. I see now that it was a concocted story, meant to distract us from our purpose, but it seemed so simple and marvelous then, that the Child should be robust and playful, and clothed only in a white shirt, and that the Mother should take such delight in Him, and that They should laugh together among the flowers. It seemed to me that all my doubts, about going off from my uncle, about the Greenlanders, whatever my doubts might have been at the time, the foolish doubts of a young man about the nature of worldly things, let us say, all of these were answered, and what this girl said she had seen, it entered my own mind as an indelible vision of joy, as if I had seen it myself. And then, when I was sufficiently transported, our business was conducted to their satisfaction, and we departed, once again nearly running, hungry as we could be, so that we ate up the food at Undir Hofdi church with relish, and then dragged the boat down to the water and threw ourselves into it, and came, in the dark, back to Gardar, where the bishop was already asleep, and when I slept myself, which was almost instantly, I dreamt over and over of the Two, strolling on the grass, and when the bell rang for vespers, I went to my prayers as to the greatest joy, without a jot of fatigue or pride or dutifulness. I was as if subdued to a jelly, and the love of God rose off me like an odor." He smiled. "These are the things I think on of late, although as always, these thoughts will leave me, and others will come in that are not so pleasant. My mind is like a room where the door swings free in the breeze, and many visitors come and go and stay and vanish as they will."

It seemed to Sira Pall Hallvardsson as he went away to other duties that Sira Jon must die now, in such a state of peace, but he had no faith of this outcome. He himself had never felt such pleasure as the other priest described, but he did not envy it. He saw that he was a man made for this world. It was true that he had never solaced himself with images of Heaven, nor frightened himself with images of Hell. Even as a boy in his monastery, his attention had wandered during the course of such catalogs, and he had never convincingly made a sermon about any world beside the one he was right just then standing in. Such thoughts cast him down, for it is the duty of priests to cause men to think upon their eternal deserts. He came into the great Gardar hall and found Bjorn Bollason the lawspeaker and most of his household loitering about. He saw that among them was the old woman Margret Asgeirsdottir.

The folk who lived at Solar Fell had gotten into the habit of wearing amulets around their necks that looked like small faces and were carved of bone. These white bits had "O.G.N.S." incised into their obverse sides, which meant "Olaf the Greenlander preserves us." Bjorn Bollason's wife, Signy, and his daughter, Sigrid, wore amulets that were very large, strung about their necks on intricately woven ribbons. Sira Pall Hallvardsson considered that they were ostentatious as well as against church teaching, but he had never said anything about it, and he did not say anything now. Bjorn Bollason came up to him as soon as he saw him, and inquired after his health in a friendly way, then brought Signy and Sigrid forward, and they knelt and kissed his finger, and then the boys bowed and spoke to him respectfully. The lawspeaker and some servants had skied over to Gardar once before since the stranding of the whales, and so Sira Pall Hallvardsson knew the news from there, about how stores had just begun to run out when the whales were discovered, and so everyone, even old Hoskuld, even the least regarded of the servants, had survived the hunger. But no one was fat, Pall Hallvardsson could see that. Everyone looked just as he or she should. Pall Hallvardsson buried his suspicions and walked toward the high seat. He disliked sitting in the high seat unless he was entertaining Bjorn Bollason in some way.

Bjorn Bollason followed him, saying, "You see we have with us your old friend Margret Asgeirsdottir. We think very highly of her. Sigrid is especially fond of her. She is a very courteous person, and it is hard to believe she has lived in such places as she has lived for so many years. You will certainly want to speak with her later on."

"I was hoping for an occasion."

"Now that we have her to stay with us, for that is what we think of her, that she is our guest, though she came seeking work as a servant, and she won't let a day go by without turning her hand to some sort of cooking or weaving, I greatly regret the death of Sira Isleif, for they, too, were friends, and could have had some pleasant talks beside our fire."

"Yes, I'm sure——"

"Which is not to say that she chatters on and on. She is much too courteous for that, but only speaks when she must, and Sigrid takes her for a model in all of these things."

"But this can't be the business which has brought you with all your train to Gardar?"

"No, indeed, but it is partly a pleasure trip, partly a pilgrimage to the relics you have here, and partly for doing business, and of that I will say at once, that if you are planning a feast of thanksgiving here, it seems to Hoskuld, Signy, and myself a happy thought that the feast should take place at Solar Fell rather than at Gardar, in the field above our shrine to St. Olaf the Greenlander there. For it is to him that we attribute the salvation of the Greenlanders."

Now Sira Pall Hallvardsson sent up a little prayer for the courage to contradict Bjorn Bollason, and speak the truth about "St. Olaf the

Greenlander," that he could not be called a saint until his case had been argued in Rome, and many uncontested miracles had been observed as his doing. In addition to this, it was a great sin for someone to ride the "sainthood" of this unfortunate child as a horse that would carry him where he wished to go in the world. But even as his temper rose, a countervailing pity for Bjorn Bollason's tiny battle against the limits of the world he lived in filled Pall Hallvardsson's breast, and he looked across the room at the well-dressed and haughty pride of Signy and her daughter, such a small flickering lamp sending out a single ray into the darkness of the western ocean. Their careful robes and their headdresses, which many women had given up now, made him feel as far from Europe as he had ever felt in his life, farther, perhaps, than it was possible to be from Europe, measured in mere travel. And so, once again, he did not speak. He had not thought to have a celebration, anyway. Bjorn Bollason's plans seemed as good as any. He shrugged and nodded, and Bjorn Bollason smiled with pleasure. Pall Hallvardsson said, "Surely you have had a difficult trip, at least difficult enough to warrant a little refreshment?" and he called in Andres Eindridason, and told him to order some refreshments from the cook, something like sourmilk, that did not have to go over the fire. Then he confided to Bjorn Bollason that the cooking had fallen to such a low state that the servants were loud in their complaints.

After this food, the folk from Solar Fell went into the cathedral and prayed there. Though they did not have a regular mass, Eindridi Andresson was pleased to lead them in a Te Deum and other responsive thanksgiving prayers. Eindridi admired Bjorn Bollason and Bjorn Bollason was much pleased with Eindridi. These prayers went on for a long time, for Signy was a great one for praying, and so it was not until dusk and time for departure that Pall Hallvardsson was able to speak to Margret Asgeirsdottir. He asked if he could walk with her over the hill to the Eriks Fjord jetty, and speak with her on the way, and this is what they did, so as not to delay Bjorn Bollason and risk having him and his whole party spend the night at Gardar.

"So you have found a good place," he said, when the group had stretched out and left them alone.

"It seemed to me at the time that I had found the only place in all of the north where there was an extra bit of food for an extra mouth. Such trials as folk endured in Dyrnes I hope never to witness again. When I went to my previous place, I agreed never to take food from the mouths of the children, but as Lent went on, I began to dream that I could feed them with my own flesh. Such a happy course of action was not available to me, though, and I had to leave them. Even so, the two little ones died and their mother, who is Freya, the wife of Gudleif Finnleifsson, is much cast down, almost to madness, it is said. And others have died, as well, Finna Eyvindsdottir, and many more. None at Solar Fell, though the broth was thin enough at the end. It must be said that Bjorn Bollason and Signy did all that was within their duty, and maybe all that was within their power. They welcomed me with smiles, though I brought nothing for my service besides a piece of cloth."

"It is true that they are generous folk, and the rewards that they hope to receive are only such as men should give to anyone who benefits them."

"Another thing seems to me to be true about Signy, although of Bjorn Bollason I know little, and that is that whatever rewards she gets, she is happy enough with them, and she is not jealous of those she does not get. Still—"

"Still what?"

"They make much of me, and it is uncomfortable to be with them. They would like to be made much of, themselves, and so they think that this is everyone's desire." She walked along for a while, and Pall Hallvardsson was hard put to stay with her, for she still walked with a free, swinging stride and a straight back. The joint ill, he could see, had not touched her. She said, "I hope that I will be forgiven for such unreasonable complaints. Truly, when I came scratching at the steading for a place, Signy herself welcomed me in and begged me to sit on the bench and offered me dry socks and asked me no questions until I had slept."

"I wish you had come to Gardar."

"I heard of Olaf and Petur, as well. You are hard put without Olaf, I suspect."

"It seems to me that I am as a man who is walking down the road and hears the footsteps of robbers behind him. He fears to look or to stop, and only thanks the Lord that they aren't upon him yet."

She glanced at him briefly, and then away, her face white in the deepening twilight. He said, "The folk at Lavrans Stead are well, although it was a close thing with Birgitta, or so Thorkel Gellison says. Olaf has died." Margret nodded. Now they came to the top of the hill that overlooks Eriks Fjord, and Pall Hallvardsson stopped and gave Margret his hand. At the bottom of the hill, the younger folk were pushing the boat off the strand, and behind them, Signy was calling out names and admonishments to make haste. Margret said, "I think often of Olaf these days. It was a great sin that we always used Olaf as a tool, and overlooked him when it suited our pleasure to do so. I wish he were here to replace Petur, and to care for the Gardar cows." She turned away and began down the slope, then turned back and called, "There is a lovely valley behind Solar Fell that they say is abundant with both northern and southern sorts of herbs. I will bring some in the summer for the Gardar stores!" She waved, then walked and trotted down the slope. Bjorn Bollason himself helped her into the boat, with that smile of his. Pall Hallvardsson saw that he wouldn't get to the escarpment above Gardar before dark.

It seemed to Margret that Solar Fell was to be her final home, and that her final trial was to be watched and imitated without cease by Sigrid and even Signy herself, who had a habit of glancing at Margret as she worked, and then cocking her head or fixing her hand so that it imitated a gesture that Margret might be making. She was always admonishing Sigrid, by pokes and nods in Margret's direction, to stand up proudly. This attention discomfited her for more reasons than one. It seemed to Margret that no Greenlander could be without knowledge of her adultery with Skuli the Norwegian, but indeed, Signy had been but a child of fourteen in those times, and Bjorn Bollason himself only nine. Hoskuld would have been at the Thing where Gunnar tricked Kollbein Sigurdsson out of his judgment, but even Hoskuld seemed not to remember or to recognize her. Perhaps it was only that he was an old man and had his own ancient quarrels to ruminate upon. Or perhaps folk didn't care about such things as they once had. Bjorn Bollason and Signy, for example, had a number of friends in both Brattahlid and Dyrnes who had left their families during one year of the hunger or another and gone to live with mates before the wedding. And most folk, it was said, were too poor for weddings now, anyway. Too poor to send for the priest, too poor to give a feast, too poor to carry gifts to the bridal couple, too poor to leave off the farm work for such pleasures. And even if there were no weddings, there had to be children, didn't there? Of all folk, children had suffered and dwindled the most during the hunger. Perhaps, Margret thought as they rowed the short trip across the fjord to Solar Fell, folk hadn't cared much then. Perhaps only she and Gunnar had cared so much.

Always, when they came up the slope toward the steading, the Solar Fell folk stopped at the shrine of St. Olaf and said a prayer to him, or looked for evidence of a miracle, and it was Margret's habit to linger behind so that her failure to do this wouldn't be noticed. This time, however, even in the dark, Sigrid did notice, and came up to her and took her hand, saying, "Do you not love St. Olaf for his innocence?"

"He was surely a good little boy, and much loved by his family, but I do not know the truth about his holy nature."

"But my father says that he has saved us from the hunger, and that it was our great good fortune to live so close to the shrine."

"I would not contradict him, if Sira Pall Hallvardsson does not."

Now Sigrid fell silent but continued to hold Margret's hand as they entered the steading. She was a handsome child, with surprising dark hair and bright blue eyes, for indeed, it was said that some Irishmen had come with a boat of Icelanders to Greenland in the time of King Sverri and left their mark on the lineage of a few Dyrnes families. At any rate, both Bjorn Bollason and Signy thought a great deal of the girl, more perhaps, than they thought of any one of their four sons, although Bjorn Bollason always brought the boys forward as a group and bade them to plant their feet just so and straighten their shoulders and look folk in the eye, and on and on. The regard of the parents had not spoiled Sigrid's temperament, though, and she had the open manner of one who thought well of herself but knew that pride was a sin.

Margret's principal task at Solar Fell was to weave fine wadmal for Sigrid's dowry, as the girl was now some sixteen winters old and expected to be married within the next four or five winters. This weaving was a pleasure to Margret, for the Solar Fell steading was one of the finest sheep-raising places in Greenland, with wide, moist, south-sloping pastures for growing hay, rising to tarn-filled highlands for the summer grazing. The wool of the sheep was long and soft, with much distinction between the silky outer coat and the woolly undercoat. If she spun her thread from only the outer wool, the cloth she wove was thin and liquid, and nicely showed off her patterns. If she spun the two together, the wadmal was thick but light and springy to the touch. Signy was full of praise for her work, and greedy for it, so that she left off drawing her away from it. Throwing the shuttle and devising the weaves reminded her of Kristin and Marta and Ingrid and the others who had taught her to weave and were all now dead, of old age or sickness, and they in turn reminded her of Asta and Hauk Gunnarsson and Asgeir and Skuli and Jonas and Olaf and Gunnar as a child, and she sat at her loom, deep in thought, day after day. This lengthy reflection was another thing that made her feel that Solar Fell was to be her last home, and that this year, or the next year, or the year after that was to be her last.

Now it happened that the dreaded turn of the century came around and passed, and another three years as well, and although Finnleif Thorolfsson's prophecy about the fewness of those that would be there to greet the new age was borne out, folk considered that there were not so few as to be a sign of anything. Hunger and disease had come and gone before, and now that the great hunger was over, men saw that such things happen in the natural round of events, for the world is by nature fallen from Paradise, and the Lord has made no promises about repairing it for the pleasure of men, but asks men to use the world as a tool for repairing their own souls.

There were many abandoned steadings, and the greatest of these was Gunnars Stead, but there were other good steadings, as well, in Brattahlid and the southern part of Vatna Hverfi district. Any man in Isafjord could have himself a new steading, but there were no men left in Isafjord, and the place was abandoned to the skraelings.

Now it seemed to folk that they had learned something new. It seemed to some that they had learned of the importance of the appearances of things, that, for instance, a few articles of clothing nicely made and painstakingly decorated gave more pleasure than many plain robes, or a small quantity of food eaten slowly, using the spoon even for the bits a man might have picked up with his fingers before, lasted as long and filled one up almost as well as a large quantity. It seemed to others that they had learned how appearances were unimportant, for death came to all men, whatever they were wearing and wherever they slept, whether in the steading or in the byre, and a strong sturdy boy infant was a marvel whether the priest had had anything to do with his parents or not. Still others reflected on how quickly the food could be snatched from a man's table, or the child from a woman's breast, or the wife from a man's bedcloset, that no strength of grasp could hold these goods in place. And others remarked to themselves how sweet these goods were, in spite of that, and saw that the pleasure lost in every moment is pleasure lost forever. Some folk learned the nature of God, that He was merciful, having spared a husband or some cattle, that He was strict, having meted out hard punishment for small sins, that He was attentive, having sent signs of the hunger beforehand, that He was just, having sent the hunger in the first place, or having sent the whales and the teeming reindeer in the end. Some folk learned that He was to be found in the world—in the richness of the grass and the pearly beauty of the Heavens, and others learned that He could not be found in the world, for the world is always wanting, and God is completion. Some declared that they had learned that a man's luck and his might are his only god, as folk once thought in the ancient days. Was Erik the Red so unfortunate a fellow, or the men with him who never accepted the teachings of the church about the White Christ? Old tales did not say that they had done so poorly as the Greenlanders were doing now, although churches and shrines stood in their land, and folk paid for them and prayed in them. Some said, as did Birgitta of Lavrans Stead, that there was always a joke to be played upon the Greenlanders.

Gunnars Stead stood empty for these three years, and every year, Thorkel Gellison came to Gunnar and attempted to persuade him to return to the steading, but every year Gunnar shrugged and declared that he had not thought about it. In fact, however, he knew that Birgitta was much opposed to such a move, and though he longed for it himself, he hesitated to force it upon her. The case was that her strength and her spirits did not seem to recover from the hunger as those of the others did. She could barely tolerate the light and the play of breezes outside the steading, and so she stayed within her bedcloset most of the time, and her limbs never regained the plumpness they had had, nor the strength. Nevertheless, she made room in her bedcloset for Gunnar now, and greeted him pleasantly each night, with caresses and questions about his activities. As she had once held and gazed upon the hands of her babies, or their toes or their knees, now she was pleased by Gunnar's strength and firmness of flesh, and especially at the warmth he radiated, which was the warmth that had kept Death off her when he came seeking her at the end of the hunger. It seemed to her that she had seen him himself, and he had not been a large man with a white face, dressed in black, as the tapestries in the cathedral showed him to be, but instead Death was a white, shaggy, bearlike fellow with huge hands like paws and nails like curved claws that raked away one's garments, one's skin, one's life. In fact, it seemed to Birgitta that, like others, she too had learned something, and that was that the Greenland wastes was where Death had his home, and he was the more ready to come among the Greenlanders because of proximity. The image of his claws reaching around Gunnar, groping after her, was one that she could not escape, and it did not seem to her that such a beast would be gathering her into the pleasant home of her eternal life, as priests said. Besides, the new priest, Eindridi Andresson, who came to St. Birgitta's at the prescribed times and was rumored to be a nephew of Sira Audun, said that Hell was seven times bigger than Heaven, because for every soul that God took to himself, the Devil took seven. He also said of himself that it was his intention to harry the Greenlanders into the knowledge of God, not to cajole them into it. God was not as a mother, who holds out a bit of chewed meat so that the baby will toddle away from the open fire, but as a father, who chastens the child with blows so that it will know that the fire is painful. Eindridi Andresson was not a comforting priest, but most folk said that they had been comforted too long, lulled into sin, perhaps, which was why they had been punished. Others did not agree with this view.

It was Helga who took up her mother's interests in the sheep, for she was not unlike Birgitta in her ways, although she was much more like Gunnar in her looks. In addition to this, Johanna returned from Hestur Stead, and most of the inside work fell to her. It had been Gunnar's hope that Johanna and Helga would be friends and companions to each other, but they diverged so in temperament and interests that it was almost as though they were unrelated to one another. They did not even know enough of each other to quarrel, but were entirely indifferent.

Indeed, Gunnar, who had gotten quite used to Helga's ways about the steading, which were like Birgitta's, hardly knew what to do with Johanna, who went about behind him, picking up his tools and arranging them, picking up his socks and folding them together, putting everything out of the way before it was even in the way. After his meals, she whisked away the trencher or the bowl before he had pushed it from him, and he often had the feeling that there might be something left in it, although if he asked for it back, there never was. These were Jona's ways, for Jona had a great reputation as a neat and tidy wife.

Johanna was still of an observing turn of mind, and Gunnar often found her gazing at him. Nor did she look away confused when he met her gaze, but only smiled and went about her business as if she'd done with looking at him. She was impartial about this steady, inquisitive gaze, bestowing it upon everyone, Kollgrim, Helga, Gunnar, the shepherds, the sheep, visitors, neighbors, the water of the fjord, the sky, the grass, the drying racks with their burden of reindeer meat and whale meat. She gazed at Gunnar's writing so fixedly that he thought she must have learned to read, although the folk at Hestur Stead were not the reading sort. He asked her if she understood what the writing said. She smiled and shook her head, and said only that the patterns of the strokes set her to thinking. Gunnar read aloud what he had written:

"In these years, the farmers of Herjolfsnes were cut off more and more from the rest of the Greenlanders, but Snaebjorn Bjarnarson and the other principal landowners of the district refused to abandon their steadings and take up available steadings farther to the north."

"You are writing of the Greenlanders, then," said Johanna. "It seemed to me that you would be putting down tales such as those you relate to us in the evenings."

"I would not be sorry to do that, but indeed, the pen goes so slowly that as I make the words, first I lose the thread of the tale, and then I lose the pleasure of the telling. Those tales are meant for speaking, perhaps, while these duller things are meant for writing down."

"This must be like making cheese. What is made in a day is eaten in a moment."

Such observations Gunnar found congenial and even amusing, but only he knew how to listen for them. Most often, when Johanna said something of this sort, Helga and Kollgrim, when he was about, looked puzzled and said nothing. Kollgrim had taken Finn's place as the household's representative to the year's hunts, and in addition to this, he often went off by himself, after birds or hares or foxes, and his skills were good enough. Folk praised them and said that Kollgrim had recovered well from both his dunking and his peculiar nature as a child. Even so, Gunnar saw that confusion still sometimes overtook him, from his dunking, and an imp still looked out of his eyes once in a while, as if calculating the possibilities for mischief. Whatever Kollgrim had learned, though, and however they depended upon him for game and whalemeat, it was obvious to Gunnar that he was not yet the hunter that Hauk Gunnarsson had been, or Finn Thormodsson. No Greenlander was, anymore, just as no Greenlander had the wit to write down the tales folk knew, as they had once written down the tale of Atli, in verse, or the tale of Einar Sokkason and Bishop Arnald. When he suggested these things, Helga and Kollgrim smiled as if he were only an old man taking all virtue for the folk of his youth, but Birgitta knew that he was not mistaken, and said further that it was well for the Greenlanders that they knew not fully how things had declined for them since the days of their great-grandfathers, when men had had time enough and pleasure enough to build such a church as St. Birgitta's, for example, with its arched window and fine glass brought from Bergen.

It was difficult not to be fond of Helga and not to enjoy her company, for she was affectionate and merry, and stubborn on only one subject, and that was the subject of marriage. Each year Gunnar took her to the Thing, and each year it was as if she had become a different person. She kept her eyes cast down, and spoke soberly and obediently to him in every particular. He went out among the other booths and sought for likely husbands, and when he saw a man who was well enough looking and found out about him that he had a good farm and some cows left and a boat, he would bring the fellow and his kinsmen back to his booth. There he would find Helga going solemnly about her business, and he would introduce the fellow, and Helga would raise her eyes to his face, and look at him squarely for a long moment—and then she would lower her eyes and say for the tenth or the hundredth time that she would do as he wished. And then he would look at the fellow again, and the fellow himself would be as if transformed. Gunnar would notice that he was slope-shouldered, or had a squint in one eye, or that even if he was prepossessing enough, his nearest kinsmen looked low and cruel, or simpleminded. And so he would make excuses for her and she would go unmarried for another year. She was twenty-seven winters old, seven or eight winters older than most newly married women, older than Margret when she married Olaf. A dangerous age, Birgitta dared to say. These days Birgitta dared to say many things, and Gunnar cared little, for he was much pleased to have saved her, and it seemed to him that nothing could ever again rob him of that pleasure. They were old folk now, and ready to die, he told her. None too soon, was what she replied. But she did not mean what she said, and wanted with all her heart to hide from the furry claws of Death for as long as possible. At any rate, while all about them, folk of every age were rushing to replace their lost mates or lost children, whether the priest was called in or not, Helga turned a cool eye on all such proceedings.

Now it happened one day that Kollgrim intended to snare ptarmigan in the hills above Vatna Hverfi, and he came to Helga and asked if she wished to go along with him, for he had something to show her. Occasionally she did go with him, for she had delicate fingers and was good at tying snares, and the two of them, not so far apart in age, were good friends. She agreed to go, and they set out early the next morning, hiking through the valley that opened upon Einars Fjord across from Hestur Stead, then getting into the boat that Kollgrim kept moored there, and rowing to the sand flats around Undir Hofdi church. Here they got out and pulled the boat onto the strand. Helga could not remember anything of Vatna Hverfi district, and she was much delighted by its pleasant aspect, for the land there is greener than elsewhere in Greenland, and the meadows and fields wider and more fertile. They went into the mountains above the church and snared many birds, and after a while the dusk came on, and Kollgrim led Helga down past the church and around the hillside to Gunnars Stead.

The steading was still in good repair, for Vigdis had reset the turves in the summer before her death. Kollgrim pushed open the door, and they entered the large and comfortable main room of the steading. Helga asked where they were. "It is an abandoned farm. I will tell you about it in the morning, when I am not so fatigued." At this, he climbed into one of the bedclosets, and Helga climbed in after him, and they lay all night. Helga went quickly to sleep, and woke up only once during the night, but she did notice when she awakened that Kollgrim, for all that he complained of fatigue, was restless and lay with his eyes open. Then she went back to sleep. In the morning, she roasted two of the ptarmigan over a fire he made in the hearth, and commented upon how comfortable the steading was, and how little the hearth smoked. Now Kollgrim said, "This steading is our steading, and only the obstinacy of our father prevents us from laying claim to it. He may indeed wish to keep Birgitta at Lavrans Stead where she is happy recalling her mother and father, but we could live here as brother and sister, as our father and our father's sister did many years ago."

"Have you spoken to him of this?"

"I wished to see if we could sleep here comfortably first."

"It seemed to me that I slept here more comfortably than you did last night."

"You heard nothing then? Felt nothing?"

"Nay. I slept very well."

"Then it may be that Vigdis is elsewhere, or that her ghost has not laid claim to the steading, for it was here that she was murdered by Ofeig."

"You have done me an ill turn to bring my soul into such danger," said Helga.

"But it has not turned out to be dangerous. In addition to that, I have slept here seven times now, and have never heard a sound nor felt a thing. Anyway, they say that her son had priests in the place shortly afterward, and that they have purged the spirits." And so they looked about the steading, at the buildings and the furniture and the stalls of the byre, and they saw that all of these things were much finer and more conveniently made than they were at Lavrans Stead, and Kollgrim saw that the greed for such a life as one might live on such a fine steading was rising in Helga as it had risen in him. Helga found herself reluctant to leave, although the day was drawing on. They were standing in the byre remarking at the numbers of cows that had once been wintered there, when a figure appeared in the doorway, and startled them.

Kollgrim glanced up, and then glanced away, and stood as still as a post. Helga put her hand upon his shoulder, and felt that it was trembling, but then he shook her off and seemed to come to himself. He called out, "We are but looking over the abandoned steading. We have stolen nothing and mean no harm." The figure stepped out of the doorway and disappeared, and Helga said, "I do fear to go out and gaze upon this spirit. They say that such things are so horrible that they enter one's dreams forever afterward."

"Nay, it is no spirit, but it is an enemy nonetheless. It is Jon Andres Erlendsson. We must not skulk about, but must go forth boldly if we intend to be his neighbors."

"Perhaps such enmity is good reason for not being neighbors. If he strikes such confusion and fear into you—"

Kollgrim flared up. "Speak not of that again! Jon Andres Erlendsson is but a man, and neither as tall nor as broad as I am. Without Ofeig and his other accomplices he is nothing."

"Then what is stopping us from going out?"

"Nothing." But still he waited a moment before taking her hand and pulling her toward the entrance.

Jon Andres was sitting on the slope in front of the byre with his back to them, watching his horse crop the grass in the homefield a little ways off. He turned and looked upon them, and Helga, like everyone who had ever seen him, noticed his handsome looks and graceful manner. He said, "I was passing and I saw your belongings in front of the house. The steading is indeed abandoned, and therefore no more a concern of mine, but I do not wish its furnishings to be destroyed or stolen. You may look about as you wish."

Helga replied, "I am Helga Gunnarsdottir, and although I was born here, it is entirely new to me, and of great interest."

"I know who you are. I saw you from afar when I was carrying game and sheep to your father's steading some years ago."

Kollgrim flushed angrily and gripped Helga's hand so that it hurt, but said nothing. Helga said, "We had intended to make our way back to Lavrans Stead this evening, and as it is a long journey, we had better be off."

"Will you take meat with me at Ketils Stead? It is not far."

Now Kollgrim was gripping her hand so tightly that it was only with difficulty that she didn't cry out. "Nay," she said, "we must not take the time, but you are kind to invite us." Jon Andres nodded his head, and called his horse to him and mounted the beast. Only when he had ridden off did Kollgrim relax his grip. Helga turned upon him. "Now you have nearly broken my hand!" she exclaimed angrily. "And met his courtesy with rude silence! If you are so tall and so broad and so unafraid, then why have you let a woman speak for you?"

But Kollgrim, too, was angry. "I see that your eyes leapt to his quick enough, and your cheeks flushed when you talked to him! He is my bitter enemy, and he paid a compensation that was insultingly low for the injury he did to me!"

"It is you who has brought me here! If he is your bitter enemy, then it were best that you did not live cheek by jowl with him. But I can see in your eyes that such proximity is part of the attraction of this steading for you! Always it has been the case that you cannot bear not to look upon the trouble that you could avoid if you would. You would rather tease it toward you. I will not help you persuade father to claim this steading."

"Will you talk against me?"

She had never denied him anything, since she was but a toddling child and he cradled among the furs of their mother's bedcloset. They walked to the boat, and pushed it off the strand and got in. He rowed with great energy and a practiced, easy motion. She looked upon him, and finally said, "Nay, I will not talk against you, but I will pray against you."

Kollgrim smiled.

Against this scheme, Gunnar raised many unanswerable objections. There were neither servants nor sheep to spare for another steading. Kollgrim's services in getting game for the table could not be spared. Helga's services in looking after the sheep and the dairy could not be spared. It was not seemly for an unmarried woman to go off before marriage and live by herself, as she would often be living if Kollgrim was out hunting. The steading itself bore a burden of ill fame and ill luck. They would do better for themselves if they stayed away from it, and left it to Bjorn Bollason the lawspeaker, although rumors of Bjorn Bollason's interest in the steading had died down. Steadings were being abandoned in Hvalsey Fjord, if Kollgrim was so intent upon raising sheep. But Kollgrim was not intent upon raising sheep, only upon having this particular steading. And on this point Gunnar grew the most irate, and accused Kollgrim of always having been dissatisfied with Lavrans Stead and the life there. After these arguments, there was a long period of bitterness between father and son, for Kollgrim was loud in his complaints of Gunnar's injustice. Helga put away any expectation of removing to the other steading, although with difficulty. Every arrangement at Lavrans Stead now seemed poor and inconvenient.

One day it happened that Thorkel Gellison appeared with two of his servingmen, saying that his wife Jona was ill, and wished to have Johanna with her for a few days, but after Thorkel and Gunnar had talked for a while, it came out that Jona was not very unwell, and still perfectly capable of getting about the steading and doing her work. In fact, she had been more ill earlier in the summer, and had not thought to call upon Johanna. Now Gunnar wished to know the real purpose of Thorkel's visit, and Thorkel admitted that he intended to persuade Gunnar to allow Kollgrim, at least, if not Kollgrim and Helga, to take over the abandoned steading, for, he said, Kollgrim was a much steadier fellow than he had once been, and he needed but some additional cares to mold him into a proper man.

Such an effect had taken place with Gunnar himself, in the year of the vomiting ill, and Kollgrim was already five or six winters older than Gunnar had been then. The boy, folk said, lived too close to his mother and his father, and they watched over him, folk also said, as if he were a child. In addition to this, many folk in Vatna Hverfi district would be relieved at the occupation of the steading, especially by Vatna Hverfi folk and not by strangers from the north. Folk who knew Bjorn Bollason and Signy considered them well enough, and Bjorn Bollason seemed to be enterprising as lawspeaker, whether or not he actually knew all of the laws, but he and Signy were alert and pushing in that northern way, not so pleasant to be with, and yet always offering this and that or making invitations. And the fact was that they would think so well of themselves if they got into Gunnars Stead that they would be unbearable. Now Gunnar laughed and said that they did not think of such things in an out-of-the way place like Hvalsey Fjord, and Thorkel laughed in return and said that the Hvalsey Fjorders had always been proud of their humility, and that was a fact, and the conversation died.

The case was, that Gunnar was much angered at Kollgrim for putting his scheme to Thorkel, but in this as in all things, he thought, Kollgrim had gotten the better of him, for he owed such a debt to Thorkel that he could never simply dismiss any of Thorkel's wishes, and besides that, Thorkel was a much older man, now, and Gunnar looked forward to his death with dread. Even so, he considered that Kollgrim showed little wisdom in this plan, whether or not he felt much antagonism toward Jon Andres Erlendsson, and it was hard to know Kollgrim's real feelings on this score. On the one hand, a man could live with neighbors who were enemies. Many had, and through such generations as had lived in Greenland, every family had fought with their neighbors, and even killed their neighbors at one time or another. In addition to this, Ofeig and the other members of the band of mischief-makers had gone off long ago, and in fact it was not known exactly where Ofeig was. Some folk said he had taken up residence as an outlaw in some of the abandoned farmsteads in Alptafjord. On the other hand, however, Kollgrim flew to trouble as sparks fly upward, and Gunnar had little faith in the effect of new cares upon him. There was a difference between going off to live with an indulgent older sister and in taking a childish and dependent wife onto a farmstead where there was already such a husbandman as Olaf had been and such a housekeeper as Margret had been. Even so, Gunnar did not know how to stand against Thorkel, except by saying that he could not divide his flock or his servingfolk, and that Gunnars Stead was much too big to be taken on by two such as Kollgrim and Helga. And Thorkel said no more, except that if a way was found around these difficulties, he himself would send a pair of horses over to the steading. Now discussion of this scheme ended, and Kollgrim seemed to be reconciled to his father, and the autumn came on. Kollgrim went on the seal hunt, and brought back a great deal of meat, and things were quiet for the winter. Gunnar suspected, though, that he had not heard the last of proposals concerning Gunnars Stead and he looked forward to the spring with some misgiving.

At Easter, one of Gunnar's neighbors, an old man named Thorolf, with two daughters and three sons, came to Gunnar and said that he intended to go away from his steading and seek service, for his oldest son wished to take over the steading. But the steading was much shrunk, and could not support as many folk as it had. Therefore, he himself was seeking service, and one of his sons and both of his daughters as well, and Gunnar took them on, with a great sinking of his heart.

Now, shortly after this, at about the time when the ice was breaking up and blowing out of the fjords, another neighbor of Gunnar's came to Lavrans Stead. This was Hakon Haraldsson, and he was driving before him some twenty ewes and lambs, all fine beasts, and he left them in the care of his small son, to mill about in front of the steading while he sought out Gunnar. "Now, neighbor," he said, "I have come to pay my debt to you and Birgitta Lavransdottir. I bring back such beasts as you and she once sent to my steading, when we were in poor straits and looked forward only to a slow and painful death. But now things have changed, and we have many fine beasts, and not enough pasturage for them all, and so you must take them, and not turn them down as you did two summers ago." And Hakon was very proud of the beasts, and of the largess he showed in making his gift, and Gunnar could not therefore turn it down, but his heart sank again. And so it was that Kollgrim and Helga were allowed to carry out their scheme, and claim as abandoned the ancient farm of Gunnars Stead in Vatna Hverfi district.

Now it happened that on the night before they were to take their sheep and their furnishings in the big boat around the point of Hvalsey Fjord and up Einars Fjord, just as Birgitta and Gunnar had done some thirty-three summers before, Helga stayed up praying for the whole night, for she could in no way cause sleep to come to her, but she did not know whether she was praying for the move or against it, so confused did she find herself. She had dutifully fulfilled both of her promises to Kollgrim for many months. She had spoken not a word against his scheme, although she saw that Gunnar wished her to, but she had prayed against it, or else for a sign that it was opportune, every night. There was none, except, perhaps, for the fact that it went forward in such a way, with old Thorolf coming to them at Easter of his own will, and then with Hakon bringing the sheep of his own will, that the signs seemed to be for it. Against this, however, was Kollgrim's manner, for there was no doubt that he was greatly agitated, and thought less of the steading that he was to take over than of the neighbor he was to live beside.

In her heart, Helga, too, thought often of Jon Andres Erlendsson, for the sight of him was uniquely pleasing to her, and she could not square this with what she had heard of his evil nature. She remembered how folk speak of the way that the Devil comes smiling among folk, but such a smile as Jon Andres' smile was not what she had pictured all her life as the Devil's smile. Now on the night before her departure, she went to Gunnar and she said, "I am much afraid of our neighbor."

"It is unlikely that he will harm you, now that he has given up his riotous companions. It may be that you will not see him from season to season, if you keep to your own steading and attend to your tasks. The farms are not so close that you must look into one another's byres," replied Gunnar. Behind him, Birgitta rustled about in her bedcloset.

"I had not thought that he would come to Gunnars Stead and harm us. But I am afraid of his nearness. I am sure that I will walk upon that part of our steading that lies by his with trembling."

Now Gunnar chuckled shortly. "Indeed, my Helga, he is but a man. There is no tale that he has to do with witchcraft. If you are willing to go into the air of that unlucky steading, then you may certainly endure whatever emanations float from Ketils Stead. My fear is that Kollgrim will look and look for enmity from that quarter, and find it soon enough. There is your danger, and you may tell me from your friendship with your brother whether you think my fear is well founded."

Now the memory of Kollgrim's grip upon her hand rose in Helga's mind, and she was on the point of relating the incident, when Kollgrim himself pushed open the door of the steading and came into the room. He entered with much self-importance, his shoulders square and his back straight, and he addressed Gunnar about the new servant, Thorolf Bessason, in a calm and manly fashion, without any of the resentful manner that had tinged his demeanor toward Gunnar for as long as Helga had known him. When he went out again, Helga was silent. It is often said that strangers see more in a man than his family does, and many Greenlanders once went

off to other lands and made much of themselves, and so Helga thought of
Thorkel and the portent of Hakon's sheep, and returned to her chamber
without encouraging Gunnar's doubts.

Later, when Gunnar climbed into the bedcloset, Birgitta said, "Their
fates are their own, as Gunnhild's, Astrid's, and Maria's were. It seemed to
me once that I saw early deaths for them, but they are grown and strong,
and have survived what others have not survived. Perhaps what I saw was
as false a promise as the vision of the Virgin and Child I had. At any rate,
I have no uneasiness about them, although I thought that I would." And
Gunnar was comforted by this news. The morning dawned clear and calm,
and Kollgrim, Helga, Thorolf, and his daughter Elisabet set out in the large
Lavrans Stead boat with twelve ewes and their lambs.

There was a man in Brattahlid district, who claimed the lineage of
Erik the Red, through Erik's son Thorstein and a concubine named Thorunn. This man did not have his own farmstead until after the hunger, but
lived as a servant to Ragnleif Isleifsson, and he was known as a bombastic
sort of fellow. He had no wife, and his name was Larus Thorvaldsson. After
the hunger, Larus, who was not a bad husbandman for all his unpleasant
manner, claimed a small farmstead and also offered himself in marriage to
a widow named Ashild who had one child and some livestock. One day
during the same summer that Kollgrim moved to Gunnars Stead, Larus
Thorvaldsson came to Ragnleif's steading on a visit, and began to talk a
great deal about the desires and strictures of God Himself. Larus declared
that God had presented Himself at Larus Stead three nights running, around
the time of Easter, and had spoken clearly to him about many matters. One
of these was that the old priest who was kept at Gardar was the Devil
himself, and that the servants and the other priests there did him homage.
Folk laughed at this news, but listened more carefully to other things,
namely that in three years, a ship would land in Greenland, and it would
carry many Icelanders, and also that God had reviled both the Roman pope
and the French pope, and had not allowed anyone into Heaven who had
died since the beginning of the schism, for the real pope hid himself in
Jerusalem, and would soon burst forth with such a light that it would be
visible and known even to the Greenlanders. He said much more in this
vein, and some folk laughed at him and some folk did not. After a few
days at Ragnleif's steading he went home again. Even so, he was much
talked of in Brattahlid through the summer.

It was the duty and right of every steading to send a man, at least,
with arrows, or some other weapons, to the spring and autumn seal hunts,
and those steadings with serviceable boats were required to send these also.

Such was a new law made by the Thing shortly after the passing of the hunger. What once had been custom was now compulsion, for there were few men in Greenland and fewer boats, and every one was needed if folk were to have enough meat for the winter. This autumn was the first Larus Thorvaldsson spent on his own steading, and as he was the only man there, he was the one who had to attend the hunt, although he had never done so before. It happened that Larus made of this hunt an opportunity to expound upon the views of God about the ways of the Greenlanders, and their futures. It was not, Larus said, that the popes of Rome and Avignon could not or would not approve a new bishop for the see of Gardar, or even that the archbishop of Nidaros was negligent, but that the church itself was being overthrown in Europe, even as the Greenlanders were now speaking of it, and priests and nuns and bishops and archbishops were being tossed out of their pits of corruption and dispossessed of their sinful wealth. When the ship that was coming should arrive, it would carry the tidings of a new age. No priests would stand between the pope of Jerusalem and the faithful folk. God would give up Latin and speak in the tongue of the people. Each man would give himself and his family the meat of communion. So Larus spoke, wandering among the seal hunters as they sat about each evening after their work, and although it is not the way of Greenlanders to allow fear much entrance, some shifted in their seats and looked about themselves, for they were afraid.

Larus Thorvaldsson could not be moved from his tale that God had come onto his steading and spoken to him. He had sat upon the bench with Larus and Ashild and little Tota and partaken of their sourmilk and their new goat cheese. He had filled Larus' bedcloset with light. He had turned rotten meat back to fresh, folk could come back to his steading and see the meat itself. He had spoken in a low, golden tone. When Larus had asked Him why He had come to him, Larus, and not to someone else, He had laughed and said that Larus was as good as anyone else, was he not? All souls look the same to God, who sees not the carapace of self men wear in the world. And although some folk quizzed Larus on these particulars, saying that he was known as a great liar, he was firm in his relation of them, and even folk from Brattahlid, who were the most inclined to laugh, held their peace. Later in the fall, long after the seal hunt, three servingmen came to Larus Stead and summoned Larus, Ashild, and Tota to Solar Fell, for Bjorn Bollason, who had not himself participated in the seal hunt but sent some of his servingmen, was very curious about the tales Larus had to tell.

Now Larus was brought into the steading and put into a small chamber and left there. Ashild and Tota were given a bite to eat, and put into another small chamber with a little lamp for light and heat. After some time, Sira Eindridi Andresson, the hardest man that Gardar had to offer these days, came in to Larus, and spoke to him, and elicited his story from him, and then declared that such tales were heretical lies, and described in colorful terms the fate of souls convicted of heresy, how they would be ground into small bits and rendered in the fires of hell and pierced and poked and sliced and mashed, for as long as all eternity, which was so long that all the generations of men since the time of Erik the Red were as an eyeblink in a whole life. But Larus, although he wept and cried out, did not depart from his tale.

Now Larus was taken into the greatest chamber in the steading, and Bjorn Bollason the lawspeaker was seated in the high seat, with Sira Eindridi beside him, and Bjorn Bollason himself commenced to question Larus, and to tell him what the law requires of men who perjure themselves about the Lord. It requires their property, down to the last rag upon their backs, the last broken spoon in their pockets. It requires that they be outlawed, and sent to the ice and the barrens above the settlement. It requires that their steadings be burnt up, so that no one else will go into that evil place. It requires that salt water be hauled up from the fjord and dumped upon their homefield. It requires that their wives take other husbands and their children assume the names of bastards. Now Larus begged that these punishments not be brought to bear upon him, for it was not his desire or doing that the Lord should appear to him and tell him anything, "For," he said, "when great folk tell you anything, they blame you for it afterwards."

Now Ashild was brought forth, and she, too, was told what the law requires of heretical liars, and she too was reduced to begging for Larus' life. But, indeed, she was not moved from her tale that she had dipped up sourmilk for the Lord Himself twice a day for three days, and that she had washed His spoon and put it away in His spoon case, and a plain spoon it was, simple horn, like anyone's spoon.

Now little Tota, who was five winters old, was brought forth and made to sit down upon the bench, and she was asked what the visitor had done when He was among them, and she said that He had taken her upon His knee and also that He had turned the meat she didn't like back to good again. After this, the three were taken again to their two chambers, and Bjorn Bollason and Sira Eindridi conferred.

Now it was the case that Bjorn Bollason regretted the death of Sira Isleif, for although he had spoken to Larus with great force, he was not really certain what the law was in these matters, and how far he should carry out the threats he had made against a fellow who was so firm in his convictions. The fact was that Bjorn Bollason was somewhat reluctant to punish Larus, and wished that he had not brought the man to Solar Fell, but had ignored the predictions. Sira Eindridi said that the fellow might be tortured and made to confess that he was telling lies, but of course this had to be done by Bjorn Bollason rather than by Gardar, for the Church does not engage in torture of the souls in her keeping. Now Bjorn Bollason bethought himself, and tried to remember as much as possible of the laws, and after a while he said that it seemed to him that the Thing itself had never ordered torture of anyone, but that folk who were to be tortured had been in the hands of the king of Norway's representative. Sigurd Kollbeinsson, it was said, had had a fellow tortured. Some hot irons were applied to the palms of his hands, he thought. He could not remember the nature of the crime. Of course, both he and Sira Eindridi were but children in the days of Sigurd Kollbeinsson. Now Bjorn Bollason called one of his sons to him, and told him to beg a conference with his foster father, Hoskuld.

Hoskuld came to the men with difficulty, for he was much afflicted with the joint ill. He had little to say of Larus, except that the fellow was a nuisance. He could not remember anything about torture in the time of Sigurd Kollbeinsson. Then he began to complain of pains in his hips from sitting, and he was led away to his bedcloset. Bjorn Bollason and Eindridi sat in thought for a while, then Bjorn Bollason suggested that if they chose to torture the man, then they must torture the woman and the child as well, since both of them held tightly to their stories. Now Bjorn Bollason said that such wild fellows as this Larus, and also Ofeig Thorkelsson of Vatna Hverfi, seemed to be about more than they once were, and the men fell silent again. After this, Sira Eindridi suggested that they pray over the problem for a while, and they did so, until it was almost dusk, and time for the evening meat, but Bjorn Bollason would not allow anyone in the steading to eat until a decision was reached, as at the Thing.

At last, Larus was brought forth and made to stand before Bjorn Bollason the lawspeaker and Sira Eindridi. The woman and the child sat nearby, staring into Bjorn Bollason's face and then into Larus' face and they were greatly afraid. Bjorn Bollason drew himself up to his most imposing height, and said, "Larus Thorvaldsson, the case is that our settlement has had the misfortune to lose for a time the arm of the king, whose duty it would be to ascertain the truth of your tales through forcible means, for it may be that you are an obdurate liar whose soul must be vigorously cleansed. The Devil clings fast to those he has captured. It may be, however, that an angel of the Lord has truly visited you, as the Angel Gabriel appeared to Our Lady, and twice to Daniel as well. The souls of the Greenlanders are as close to the Lord as souls anywhere, and the Lord may walk among us if He should choose to. For this reason, we intend to allow you to go back to your steading with your wife and your wife's child." Now Bjorn Bollason looked upon Larus with a lowering gaze, and went on, "But we must command you to abjure from telling these tales for three winters, until it happens that the ship you foretell comes or does not come. If, indeed, it does not come, then you will be stripped of your property and your life and any mercy the Church might have upon your soul." And so Larus was released and sent home, and without being fed, although Signy gave the wife some bits of cheese for the journey. And Bjorn Bollason said to Sira Eindridi that certainly that would be the end of Larus Thorvaldsson, and they had not done badly with him, all things considered. The next day Sira Eindridi went back to Gardar and reported to Sira Pall Hallvardsson everything that had taken place, and Sira Pall Hallvardsson did not agree that they had seen the last of Larus Thorvaldsson, "but," he said, "events will take their course, as always in Greenland."

After the affair of Larus Thorvaldsson was past, Bjorn Bollason grew more cheerful, and so did the rest of the folk at Solar Fell. Margret had noticed that folk at Solar Fell were almost always cheerful, for, indeed, almost everything went their way, so that they expected to prosper, and their expectations were usually borne out. By this time, Margret had woven a great many pieces of cloth for Sigrid Bjornsdottir, but the case was that no man could be found to marry her, her kin were so prosperous and she herself was so pleasant and handsome. Such young men as were left on the best farms were not so good-looking as they might be, and in many cases were ill taught, so that Sigrid shamed them with the quickness of her wit and the breadth of her knowledge. Twice Bjorn Bollason took his boat and went to Herjolfsnes, for the family there was prosperous and proud, but the oldest son there was a mere twelve winters old, fully six winters younger than Sigrid. Sigrid herself was not so eager to go off to Herjolfsnes, for folk didn't hear from Herjolfsnes from one season to the next, and she was greatly fond of her father and mother and brothers, and her petted position among them.

Now it happened that one day in the autumn, after the questioning of Larus Thorvaldsson, but before Eriks Fjord had iced over, the folk of the steading were down upon the strand, gathering seaweed for winter fodder, when a man in a small boat rowed past, and in the boat lay the pelts of some blue foxes. Sigrid could see them from the height of the strand, and she called out to the fellow to draw up to the shore. Seeing her fine clothing and friendly smile, the owner of the boat pulled around and called out to her, "Do you have something for me, then?"

"Nay." Sigrid laughed. "It is you that has something for me!"

The man got out of his boat. "And what might that be, then?"

"Your foxskins. They are the most beautiful foxskins I have ever seen, not black, not blue, not white, but all of these. I could make a flattering hood of them."

"For whom?"

"Why, myself of course."

"They are indeed very fine skins, for they come from the glacier east of Brattahlid, and that is where the finest foxes in the eastern settlement are to be found. I had thought to give them to my sister, but it may be that you have something to trade for them."

"Indeed, I have nothing to trade," said Sigrid, laughing merrily. "I thought that you might give them to me."

Now the hunter himself smiled at the absurdity of this notion. "Why might I give them to you, for no return, then?"

"For these reasons," said Sigrid. "Because I want them and because it is the case that folk often enjoy giving me things. It is something that I have noticed. But if you do not give them to me, they are still beautiful, and I am pleased to have seen them and to have spoken to you, as well, for I don't often meet strangers."

"I am Kollgrim Gunnarsson, and, as this is Solar Fell, it seems to me that you must be Sigrid, the daughter of the lawspeaker."

"I am indeed."

"You live a grand life here."

"Do we?"

"Folk say so."

"It seems to me that folk live grander lives in Vatna Hverfi district, for I have heard that the pastures there are wide and fertile, and that the sheep are twice the size of other folk's sheep, and that folk there wear colored clothing every day." She laughed again, and Kollgrim saw that she was teasing him. He said, "When I go back there, I shall look about me and see if this is the case." Now he turned and went down the strand toward his boat, and Sigrid called out cheerfully, "You will not give me your furs, then?"

Kollgrim turned around. "Nay, I will not, for these are promised to my sister, who will also look well in them. But if I come by here again with similar furs, or even better ones, whiter as the winter draws on, and you have something to trade for them, some little thing, then I will give you as many as you care to have."

"I will look for you!" called Sigrid. Then she walked up the strand and joined her brothers, and told them of her encounter, and her brothers said that this was a great promise indeed, for Kollgrim Gunnarsson was well known as a hunter, and in addition, he was the nephew of Margret Asgeirsdottir herself. After this, Sigrid pondered what small thing she might give Kollgrim in return for the furs. Neither Signy nor Bjorn Bollason spoke a word against this transaction, for both Signy and Bjorn Bollason always looked for the best from every occasion.

At Gunnars Stead, the winter was early but mild and snowy, and, as there were no sheep to be slaughtered, only the twelve that had to be gotten through the winter on the little hay they had been able to cut from the homefield, circumstances were narrow, although not gloomy. The steading itself and the hills above it, between Gunnars Stead and the fjord, seemed to be overrun with hares, which Helga seethed and roasted and seethed and roasted again. It was not whalemeat, at least, the winter staple of Hvalsey Fjord, and it seemed to Helga that she would not soon get tired of this meat, partaking as it did of her new life on this fine steading, where the bedclosets were neatly carved with the figures of birds and bears and foxes and men and women and children, where the storehouse had wooden planks as shelves, planks cut from the timbers once carried from Markland, where the sheep byre faced south and the cowbyre was as tight as the steading and the bath house had a convenient little stream running through it.

The ill deeds done in the steading seemed to her to have departed with the men and women who did them, and to have left none of their spirit behind, but she did seem to sense the spirit of other doings, of her mother's sight of the Virgin and Child walking in the homefield, of the birth of herself and her sister Gunnhild, whom she remembered with affection, of, perhaps, the love between Margret Asgeirsdottir and the Norwegian, which she knew about well enough, from the gossip of Jona, Thorkel Gellison's wife. Jona made the Norwegian out to have been a handsome and personable man, very quick with his hands, and as brave as anyone when the time for his deathblow came. It was a pity, Jona said, that Margret had been tricked into marrying Olaf, and that was a fact, for Olaf was more like a farm beast than a man, and always had been. Helga had grown up with Olaf, with his smell and his coarse manner, and she had not thought much of it when he died at last, after years of complaints. That

Gunnar had himself killed the Norwegian made both the Norwegian and Gunnar glitter in Helga's imagination, as the folk in Gunnar's tales always glittered in her dreams after an evening of stories. She could not remember when any of these folk, Margret, tall and beautiful and as pale-haired as Gunnhild had been, and Skuli, broad-shouldered and handsome and a member of Queen Margarethe's court, had ever been spoken of at Lavrans Stead, but that didn't mean that she did not consider them in her heart. Other folk were ready enough to talk about them.

As for Kollgrim, she got along well enough with him these days. When he came home from his trips away hunting, he was eager to chatter about this and that, what he had seen, whose steadings looked trim and prosperous, whose did not, what stratagems he had used to get these birds, and how those foxes had nearly escaped, how he had a new idea for a sort of trap that would hold the foxes better without doing so much damage to their pelts. When he came home and said that he had had conversation with Sigrid Bjornsdottir, she did not think much of the news, since he was ready to have conversation with anyone he might meet, and, like most of those who hunted a great deal, he knew a bit of the skraeling tongue, and even had conversation with them. Anyway, she heard little of his talk, so taken was she with the foxskins he brought her. That very evening she set about scraping and softening them so that she could make herself a hood for Yule, for Thorkel Gellison had sent out messengers announcing a great Yule feast to be held at Hestur Stead, and Helga and Kollgrim were to be guests of honor. The servingmaid, Elisabet Thorolfsdottir, said that she had never seen such skins, of such an unusual color, and it seemed to Helga that everyone would admire her and that therefore she would have great pleasure at the feast.

Of Jon Andres Erlendsson they had seen nothing since coming to Gunnars Stead, and Helga's fears of him were eased as she became accustomed to the proximity of Ketils Stead. One day shortly after the first snowfall, however, she went out in the morning to look after the sheep, and saw that a strange horse, a very fine beast, was standing with the two horses Thorkel Gellison had given them. It was black, with white on its face, and rather taller than her two. When she had seen to the sheep, she went back inside and found Thorolf at his morning meat and said, "Thorolf, there is a strange horse in the field with our two. When you are finished eating, you must catch it and lead it around the hillside to Ketils Stead, and give it right into the hand of Jon Andres Erlendsson, and say that the folk at Gunnars Stead are returning their stray horse as quickly as can be done, and that they send their neighborly regards." In this way she hoped to avoid any appearance of unfriendship between the two steadings, and also to banish the new horse as quickly as possible.

At mid-day, Thorolf returned, and Helga, who had been watching for him, accosted him at once and said, "Have you given the horse right into the hands of the master of the steading?"

"Yes."

"And what was his reply?"

"He said, 'Thank you. What is your name, then?' and I said, 'Thorolf Bessason of Hvalsey Fjord.'"

"And what did he say to that?"

"He said, 'Good-bye.'"

"That was all?"

"Yes, indeed."

"And you are sure that it was the master you spoke to?"

"One of the servingmen told me that it was, when I wouldn't give the horse to him."

"And that was all he said?"

"Yes."

Helga turned away, and knew not what to think, either of Jon Andres Erlendsson, or of herself.

Now the time for Thorkel's feast drew on, and Johanna Gunnarsdottir went off on skis from Lavrans Stead, to carry some cheeses Birgitta had made and to offer Jona her services with the preparations, and Gunnar accompanied her. When he got to Hestur Stead, Gunnar saw that the preparations were going forward with great dispatch, for there were others from other steadings who had come to help as well. Jona expected to seat fourscore folk and more, if children and servants were counted. No one had held such a feast in Greenland since the time of Bjorn Einarsson Jorsalfari. Jona was in a great tizzy of business, and very pleased with herself, but Gunnar saw that Thorkel was somewhat cast down, and said to him, "Some folk about Hestur Stead seem not so high spirited as others."

Now Thorkel replied, "Some folk have ill tidings to consider."

They sat silently for a while. Then Thorkel said, "My wife's brother, Hrolf, has recently spoken with Ofeig, but he has told no one of this, not even his own wife. Ofeig proposes to live at Hrolf's steading with him, whether or not he is wanted. Either that or Hrolf must find him an abandoned steading, and furnish him with meat and other sustenance for the winter."

"I thought Ofeig was content in Alptafjord. An action of outlawry must be brought against him."

"Whether he is made an outlaw or not, he is no longer content to live as an outlaw."

"If he is made an outlaw, then he must live as an outlaw, for if he comes into the districts of men, they may kill him with impunity."

"They may, but can they? What weapons do the Greenlanders have now against such a bear as Ofeig? It is as it was twenty winters ago, when Ofeig was a child. He could not be chastised, and defied beatings, so that folk were tempted to beat him harder and harder, to make sure that the blows were felt. We prevented his mischief only by the harshest measures, and only as long as our strength was greater than his."

"At any rate an action must be brought, and you must persuade the master of Ketils Stead to bring it, and you must find someone to take Ofeig's behalf so that everything is according to law. After that a way will be found to stem the child's mischief."

"It may be as you state, and it may be that Jon Andres Erlendsson will summon witnesses against Ofeig, although he hasn't before this, and it may be that the relatives of Einar Marsson will not insist upon damages from Jon Andres Erlendsson, but a half a year lies before us until the time of the Thing, and Ofeig will not sit quietly for us, nor go where we wish him to go. Indeed, it seems to me that he can be counted on to make a great deal of noise and go where he is least wanted."

"If we are defeated before he comes among us, then we might as well abandon all to him, and go ourselves into the wastelands as outlaws."

"The fact is, that I am an old man and he has indeed defeated me. He has risen up among my sons like a polar bear grazing with sheep. The shepherd knows he should stay, but longs to run back to the steading."

"Even so, you will have many prosperous farmers here for the Yule feast, and more than a few of them can lead Jon Andres Erlendsson into talk of Vigdis and Ofeig. Erlend was a litigious man, and Vigdis knew more law than any woman. If the son is scratched, he must bleed the father's blood."

"Is it in such a way that folk condemn me, when they speak of Ofeig?" said Thorkel Gellison. Now Gunnar left on skis for Lavrans Stead, and Thorkel went to find Hrolf, and he sent with Hrolf some extra provisions to be given to Ofeig, for Hrolf was not a prosperous man, nor was he especially stout or skilled at fighting.

At Lavrans Stead, Gunnar set about trying to persuade Birgitta to go with himself and Johanna to the Yule feast. When she said that she was too weak, he promised that they would pull her on a sledge. When she said that she was more comfortable at home, he said that such comfort would be her death. When she said that her presence or absence were of no concern to anyone, he said that Jona and all of her helpers had wished to have Birgitta among them. When she said that her robes were old and ill kept, and not very festive, he said that such was the case with all the Greenlanders these days, and perhaps he would set about weaving her a piece of wadmal himself. The skill had not left him. From these replies, Birgitta saw that Gunnar was determined for her to accompany him to the feast, and she made up her mind that she must go, elsewise he would not leave her alone.

After this, she crept about, looking into chests and pulling out gowns and carrying them into the light. Once she said to him, "It is easier to be an old woman in the darkness of one's bedcloset than in the light of many stares. Folk will look at me and say that Kollgrim is my grandson and that you are my son. How did I become so little and bent? I dare not look into the rainbarrel. When I have braided my hair, you must say if it is neat or not, for old people must look trim and thorough, or folk will say that they can no longer care for themselves."

Once she had found a decent robe to wear, and had decorated it with a bit of colored tablet weaving about the hem and the sleeves, then she began asking Gunnar what Jona and the others had been preparing for the feast, what stews and pickles, for example? And after he told her what he had seen, which was not much, she went into the storehouse and found some birds that Kollgrim had snared for her, and some seal fat, and some thyme and bilberries and other herbs that grew about Hvalsey Fjord, and she seethed the birds until the meat fell from the bones, then rendered the seal fat and mixed it with the fat from the birds, and then lay down the meat and the fat and the herbs in layers in a vat, and masked all with more fat, and decorated the top with a design of white cheese, cut finely and laid into the cold dark fat so as to look like a bird in flight. The dish was very pretty, and Birgitta was pleased with it, so pleased that she went out into the storehouse for a morning and sat among the stores, counting out what would get them through the winter. In the days after that, there were things to clean and arrange so that she stayed out of the bedcloset most of the day every day.

Now Yule and the time for the feast were come around, and Gunnar and Birgitta made ready to go to Hestur Stead. Birgitta was still too weak to go under her own power, and so Gunnar and two servants were to pull her on a sledge, and they considered that this would be light enough work, for the snow was crusty and slick. Birgitta thought that she might be able to skate across the fjord herself, for that is little work and much pleasure.

A horse-drawn sledge would meet them at the landing and carry Birgitta to Hestur Stead. And so it was that all the arrangements were made, and the clothing set out and the dishes Birgitta had made and also her gift for Jona, which was a length of striped wadmal, green and white, which Thorolf's second daughter, Thurid, had woven during the autumn. But it happened that early the day before they were to leave, Birgitta crept into her bedcloset and hid there for the rest of the day, until Gunnar joined her after his evening meat. He saw that she was much cast down, more so than he had seen her even in the early autumn, and he said, "My wife, we have made good arrangements for the days to come, and I am eager for the morning."

"I have counted the days since I first got up and went about looking for something to put on, and it has been ten days. In fewer than half of that number, the feast will be finished and we will have returned to Lavrans Stead with nothing to anticipate besides another starving Lent. It seems to me that for the last ten days I have been like a person creeping over the fjord in early winter, when the ice is clear and thin and the water below is black. Only a fool would set out on such a journey."

"It is always fools who set out on journeys. It is always fools who set out on any endeavor. But fools do seem to me bold in their foolish laughter, and courageous in the way that they look out for pleasure. My wife, lately I have been remembering when I took you from this steading to Gunnars Stead, and how readily you set out, and how you took things in hand there, although you were but a child, and how you got me out of my bed when I had been lying motionless underneath this bearskin here for winter after winter. It grieves me that I cannot do the same for you."

"That girl seems like one of my daughters to me. When I think of her, I confuse her with Astrid or Maria. She was not so little as I am, nor so afraid of the bear. I remember that my father had a bear once, before I was born. He kept it in the cowbyre here, and the cows stayed in the sheep byre through the winter, and the sheep wandered about the place. It was said that he lost more than half of his cows for that bear, and folk considered him a foolish man. I dream often that that bear is still in the cowbyre, and that my father is a young man who goes to look at the bear over and over, and cannot get enough of looking at it. Our cowman, Ivar, had a great piece of flesh taken out of his arm by that bear. I do not want to go to Hestur Stead."

"Even so, you must go."

"You cannot pull me out of the water should the ice break."

"The ice in the fjord is thick and white and covered with snow, and the sun sparkles on it."

"You have not understood me."

"I have indeed understood you. Is it the case that you regard me as a woman is supposed to regard her husband, with respect and trust?"

"Yes," said Birgitta. "It is the case."

"Then I will take you over the fjord in my own arms, and we will be as fools, laughing and looking out for pleasure, eager to see our daughters and our son, and our cousin Thorkel and our other friends as well, eager to tell tales and to hear the news from every district. You must feign this, no matter how you feel. Will you promise it?"

"Yes," said Birgitta. And that night a dream came to her of Margret Asgeirsdottir as a young woman, tall and beautiful, leaning toward her as she sat in her bedcloset, offering some broth, and the broth seemed to go between her lips and warm her throat and her chest and her belly, so that she could not get enough of this salty and delicious broth, and when she asked for more, Margret smiled, and Birgitta awoke and it seemed to her that she was remembering for the first time in many years Margret Asgeirs-dottir's rare and radiant smile. This seemed to her a good sign, and when Gunnar awakened she told him of the dream, and then it was time to go off.

At this same time, folk from Brattahlid and Solar Fell were waking up at Gardar, where they had stayed for the night, and making ready to go on skis to Vatna Hverfi district. Sira Pall Hallvardsson was leaving final instructions with the new steward, Haflidi, and the cook Bjorn Bollason the lawspeaker had sent him. Sira Eindridi and his son Andres were bringing the packs of vestments and provisions and gifts that they would carry on their backs out into the moonlight, and looking them over to see if anything had been forgotten.

At Ketils Stead, Jon Andres Erlendsson was folding together some sheepskins that comprised his gift for Jona, and one of his serving boys ran up to him and said, "Now they are just leaving, and it is only the master and the sister. The servants are staying behind." He had been watching at Gunnars Stead, where neither Kollgrim nor Helga had seen him.

Helga was wearing a thick white cloak with finely woven purplish trim, and a striking hood of blue fox furs that was drawn tight about her face, and then fell over her cloak nearly to her waist. In his pack Kollgrim carried a dozen more fox furs, these nearly white with just a tinge to them of blue the color of twilight. Sigrid Bjornsdottir, he knew, would be at the feast.

Helga carried her skates, for the most direct route from Gunnarstead to Hestur Stead lay partly across the ice of two Vatna Hverfi lakes. Now it happened that the sun rose, and Helga sat herself beside the ice of Antler Lake. Kollgrim was not far off from her, standing on the ice of the lake and looking across it for telltale dark areas in the snow that would indicate weak or melting ice. Kollgrim shouted to her that the ice looked safe to him, and Helga began to tie on her skates with some relief, for the other route to Hestur Stead, which lay over some hills, was much harder in the winter, without horses, than it was in the summer. Just then it happened that she saw a figure nearby, in the corner of her eye, just where the Devil appears, and at first she was afraid to look, because she feared that the figure might disappear, and then she would know that it was the Devil she had seen, but just then Kollgrim cursed and exclaimed, and Helga looked up, and she saw that the figure was not the Devil himself, but Jon Andres Erlendsson. Kollgrim said, "It cannot be that he, too, is going to Thorkel's feast."

"It seems to me that Thorkel would hardly have a feast and fail to invite the greatest farmer in the district. Especially since folk would say that such an oversight was a sign of enmity."

"But—"

"Indeed, my brother, you must turn away from him, and act as if you have not seen him. I am finished, and we must make our way across the lake." He stepped over to her and lifted her to her feet, and they began across the lake without saying anything more, but it seemed to Helga that the other man was coming closer and closer to them, that she could feel degrees of heat as he approached, indeed, that she could feel the ice under her feet tremble when he stepped onto it with his servingman. She thought of how she would greet him, as if in surprise, or perhaps more coolly and distantly than that, knowing that he knew that she had seen him. It seemed an impossible thing to be cordial to him, and yet when she stumbled and Kollgrim took her elbow to steady her, she could feel in Kollgrim's hard, trembling grip that he was much angered, and so at once it seemed to her that it was an impossible thing not to be cordial to him. She wrenched her elbow from Kollgrim's grip, and they skated onwards, somewhat farther apart. Helga saw that Kollgrim was looking at her, and so she dared not glance back to see where Jon Andres Erlendsson might be. She promised herself that she would see him at the feast.

And indeed she did, for Thorkel made much of him, and he was everywhere in evidence. Even though it was clear to everyone that Thorkel's regard was partly for the sake of separating himself from Ofeig, it was also the case that Jon Andres Erlendsson was a personable man, and charming even to folk who should have known better, who had suffered from his mischief or lost cases to Erlend's and Vigdis' tricky legal maneuvers. Kollgrim said, "How the Devil has the trick of making himself attractive to folk." It was not a trick that Kollgrim himself had, Helga well knew. "Even so," she replied, "it would be well for you to dissemble your curiosity before our father, for he is looking for a reason to bring us back to Hvalsey Fjord, and I can see him approaching now." But indeed, dissembling was no trick of Kollgrim's either, and the agitation of his spirit was as visible to Gunnar and Birgitta as it was to Helga.

Now Birgitta greeted her children joyfully, and pinched their arms, as mothers do in the winter, to see if they have any flesh, and looked into their faces, and she gazed first upon Kollgrim and then upon Helga as if she could not look at them enough. "Indeed," she said, "I would not have other folk overhear me say this, but truly I had forgotten how they glitter, these children of the Asgeir lineage. I have to beat back my pride as folk beat back their hungry dogs with a stick."

Now the party from Gardar and Solar Fell came in. Bjorn Bollason went about and began greeting everyone, and there was not a name that he did not know, nor a face that he did not remember. After him came Signy, and after her came Sigrid, and the two of them were dressed very richly, in shades of green wadmal much decorated with white and blue tablet weaving. Sigrid's dark hair fell in luxuriant curls almost to her waist, and her face was full of merry eagerness. Helga saw Jon Andres Erlendsson pause in his talk to look at her, and indeed, they were two of a kind, two dark heads in a room of pale folk, and one could not help staring after them. Jona came forward and led the two Solar Fell women to the upper bench of the main room, and offered them some refreshment after their journey, and she also led Sira Pall Hallvardsson to the high seat, and gave him some refreshment, also.

Hestur Stead was a large steading, with fourteen large rooms and many more smaller ones, and of these, some five or six had been put up by Thorkel himself, as his horsebreeding prospered. By dusk, it seemed to Helga that there were folk in every room, more folk than she had ever seen gathered in one place, and more folk than could sit at benches in the hall of the house, and so benches and tables had been set up in four of the rooms, and Helga was to sit in the high seat of one of the rooms, Kollgrim in another, Bjorn Bollason in a third, and Thorkel himself in a fourth. It was not a usual thing for a woman to sit in the high seat, and concerning this, Helga was a little shy, but Thorkel would not let her forgo it, and said, "The Greenlanders pay little attention to custom any longer." Still Helga hesitated, but then Thorkel said, "It is my wish, but you may have Gunnar beside you if you care to," and so they sat in this fashion, and had an opportunity to converse apart from Birgitta and Kollgrim.

After they had eaten a little and exchanged news of the servants and the livestock and the neighbors, Gunnar said, "What ill luck have you encountered at that steading?"

"Indeed, my father," answered Helga, putting down her spoon, "there is no sign of Vigdis or either of her servants who were killed, nor, in the hills, is there any sign of others who have been killed on the place. Things are as calm as if nothing has happened there. In fact, it seems to me that the air about the steading is fresh and warm and pleasant."

"You think that because you have lived in Hvalsey Fjord, where the wind blows from the open sea."

"No doubt you are right in this, Father, but even so, our move has brought me much pleasure, and only the grief of longing for my mother and father, and wondering how they are getting from day to day."

"And your brother? What has the move brought him?"

"He brings home a great deal of game, and is very industrious about the steading."

"And is he, too, a calm spirit about the place?"

"One might say that in general he is. Once or twice he has fallen into his old state of dismay and confusion and weeping, but he is open and generous with us, and wishes to be good to us." Helga looked down and said in a low, but brave tone, "It seems to me that these states are fewer because we do not search his face and his doings thinking that we might find something wrong with him."

Gunnar smiled. "It may be that you can reprove my vigilance. Birgitta does so often enough. Does he hang about Ketils Stead, then?"

"Nay, Father, he avoids the place, and avoids the man."

"Is this a better sign? I am not so sure. It shows what he is thinking of."

"It shows that he is thinking of himself, as well, and guarding his behavior."

"My daughter, do you think that I can still govern the man or the steading? The arrow is shot. If it should land ill, then it is best to know about it."

"It has not landed ill, Father. We are well, and fed, and very self-satisfied at Gunnars Stead." Helga smiled at Gunnar, who smiled back. "I am telling you the truth. And you must tell me the truth, also, about my mother."

"It may be that she longs for you and Kollgrim. It seems to me that she is much afraid, but not more afraid than she has been since the end of the hunger. At least she came to this feast, and folk are making much of her." Now the two were served more meat, and each, out of courtesy, turned and spoke to the others they were sitting beside.

Some time later the eating was finished, and folk began to take down the benches and tables and go from room to room, speaking with praise of the food. Kollgrim did not move from his high seat, but only gave up his trencher to one of the servingwomen and sat with Birgitta, looking out over the folk who had eaten in their room. Now he moved his hand along the bench and put it over the hand of his mother. Birgitta said, "You have a great reputation as a hunter. Praise of your skill has come to us from three separate quarters this fall."

"This is how we see that the skills of the Greenlanders have fallen off in late years. I know that I learned but a portion of what Finn had to teach. Game has been plentiful, and my skills appear greater than they are. I spy on the skraelings, as Finn did. They have many tricks."

"Devilish tricks, folk say."

"That's what I think when I cannot mimic them."

"You got beautiful foxskins for Helga. Her hood catches all eyes."

"I have others that I would like to give you, my mother. They are the purest white, with only a shading of blue."

"Nay, white foxes are too bright for old women. Folk would speak ill of me."

"Let me show them to you. I have them with me."

"Kollgrim, it is painful to desire what one cannot have. Promise me some suitable sealskins or even some dark foxes next summer."

Kollgrim squeezed her hand. Birgitta went on, "Now it seems to me that folk are wandering from room to room, and they must wonder why we continue to sit here, gossiping between ourselves and avoiding our neighbors."

"Must they? It seems to me that folk care little about what one does, one way or another."

"And yet everyone has always had an opinion of you, Kollgrim, and I am not rebuking you when I advise you to think of this. It pleases me to hear praise of you."

"After years of blame?" Kollgrim laughed. "Perhaps I wish only that folk did not care one way or another. There are my father and Johanna, and they are looking for you." Kollgrim gestured across the room, and Gunnar approached.

It was one fault of Hestur Stead that the builders had not had much notion of the flow of air through the rooms, so that after many folk and much food and many seal oil lamps, the steading became close and smoky, and folk began going outside into the snow for fresh air. The sky was clear and starry, and the crusty snow cast the starlight back into the air, so that much could be seen, although the moon was but a slim crescent. Folk spoke to each other about how pleasant it would be to take their skates out on the fjord, or to find sealskins to slide upon down the crusty, slippery hills above the steading, and a leader in this merriment was Sigrid Bjornsdottir. Thorkel, who saw that his feast was going well, fell in with these plans at once, and went to his storerooms and found eight or ten sealskins and some old skates for folk who had not brought their own. Soon there were races and other games, and much laughter and shouting, so that those left inside were moved to put on their cloaks and come out and sit on the hillside in the starlight, talking and watching those who joined in the games. The air was still and not especially cold.

Now Johanna came to Helga and begged to borrow her skates, for she had been inside all day helping with the feast and, she said, her bones ached for some activity, and so Helga gave them to her sister, but with a twinge of regret, for she saw that Jon Andres Erlendsson and Kollgrim and all of the younger folk were out on the ice, and only the older folk were sitting about. Even so, she sat down between Gunnar and Birgitta and put her arms through theirs. Helga listened as Gunnar and his neighbors spoke of this and that, and it must have been that she dozed, for when she awakened, she saw that folk had gone to their beds, and she was alone, leaning against the turf of the steading, wrapped in a warm robe made of reindeer furs that she did not recognize.

The moon had declined, and now cast the shadow of the steading in front of her, causing the ice of the fjord to gleam with pale brightness. Where the skaters had swept it clean, the light caught in the cuts that they had made with their skates. Helga stretched her legs before her and began to massage the stiffness out of them, when two figures stepped around the corner of the steading. The moonshine revealed them to be Kollgrim and Sigrid Bjornsdottir.

"My brother!" said Helga. "Please——" But the two did not hear her or turn in her direction, although she could hear them well enough. "Nay, Kollgrim Gunnarsson," exclaimed Sigrid, laughing, "if there are to be but six, then I will have none at all, for my heart is set upon a hood like your sister's, and I can see that such a hood would take ten or more." She paused and then went on, "You can see how I have kept my promise. I would not give a cheese in trade, or some dried meat. I have brought along my own scissors, which were made in England and given to my foster grand-mother in the time of Thorleif's ship, and they have damascening all along the blades here. You can see it in the light."

Now she held up what was in her hand, and Kollgrim laughed. "Indeed, what would I do with your scissors?"

"I care not. You may give them to your sister or melt them down, for the handles are pure silver. But I will have the furs you promised me."

"And what will you cut your thread with, if you have no scissors?"

"I will bite it, as the skraeling women do. Besides this, do you think that the household of the lawspeaker is so poor that it has but a single pair of scissors?" Her voice seemed to Helga to flow out into the moonlight in cascading ripples. Kollgrim backed away, laughing, and Sigrid pursued him. Helga saw at once that the lawspeaker's daughter was intent upon him, although he himself did not see this. He stumbled in the snow and threw up his hands, laughing. "Take them all, then," he said. "I have twelve or thirteen in my pack. I would not have you think that I intended to shortchange you, rather to give more in this bargain than I thought I would receive. Truly, folk say of you that you are a persistent child!"

"Do they say I am a child then?"

"Indeed, I know not what they say, for I am not in everyone's confidence, but if they do not say this, then they should, for I have not met another like you for relentlessness."

"Then we have made a bargain, and we must act on it now, while it is fresh." She pressed the scissors into his hand. "Now they are yours. I would not touch them again." Her hand fell upon his sleeve, and grasped it tightly, and after that the two went off. A little while later, Helga stood up and shook out her dress, and Gunnar came around the corner of the steading. "You have awakened, then," he said. "Your mother has just been spreading some furs in Johanna's bedcloset for you. I thought I would have to carry you there, as I used to when you were a child. Johanna is already asleep." And he told her what feats of skating and storytelling she had missed, but she told him nothing of Kollgrim and Sigrid Bjornsdottir. During the next day, she could think of little except the desire in Sigrid Bjornsdottir's gaze, and the power of her grip when she laid her hand on Kollgrim's sleeve, and these thoughts shamed her when Jon Andres

Erlendsson was about, and so she avoided him for as long as the feast lasted, which was until the morning of the third day.

At Gunnars Stead it was apparent to Helga that Kollgrim cared little for the scissors, for he left them about thoughtlessly, and finally threw them into one of the chests as if they were in his way. This seemed to Helga a shame upon Sigrid Bjornsdottir, although only Helga knew of it. After the feast, Kollgrim went hunting a great deal, for hares and ptarmigan to put upon the table. He was out almost every day and many nights as well. He began going sometimes to the bedcloset of Elisabet Thorolfsdottir, and the servingmaid had the effect upon him of making him very gay.

One day in Lent, a servingman from Ketils Stead carried some cheeses over to Gunnars Stead and gave them to Helga, saying that Helga's and Kollgrim's late coming would have robbed them of the summer's milk. The fellow was ill at ease, and not very well schooled in the proper phrases. Helga thanked him and he went off. Now Helga sat down in the steading by herself and gazed upon the cheeses. They were misshapen and Birgitta would have thought them very badly made. Helga looked at them for a long time, as if they were an omen whose meaning she could divine.

When Bjorn Bollason and his family returned to Solar Fell, Sigrid went at once to Margret Asgeirsdottir, who had stayed home from the feast, and showed her the foxskins, and she said, "These were gotten for me by Kollgrim Gunnarsson, your nephew, who seems to me a fine fellow, with a great steading and the reputation for many skills. His father is a man who is said to read and write as a priest does, his sister is married to the foster son of the greatest man who ever came to Greenland, and his other sister is a handsome and well-dressed woman with no reputation for peevishness. It seems to me that such a man would be proper for me, more proper than any lad from Herjolfsnes could be."

The next day, when the two were at their sewing, and Sigrid brought these things up again, Margret said, "Is it not better that you should speak to Bjorn Bollason of this matter? He has more of worth to say to you about it than I do, and also more to say to those you think upon, for indeed, I cannot help you there."

"My father cares little to hear of how this Kollgrim's eyes twinkle, or how he laughs aloud when I laugh, or how tall he is, or how quick he is at untying the knots of his pack. My father would wish me to say that Kollgrim Gunnarsson goes about as other men do, only with more weight." She laughed merrily. "But indeed, he is not as other men, and they would rather be apart from him and he from them."

"It seems to me, my Sigrid, that your days will be happiest if you find yourself some prosperous, sanguine, and energetic fellow with wide fields and plenty of livestock, as well as many friends who think well of him."

"What Greenlanders are there these days who could be so described? None that my father has found, other than himself. Even my brothers seem to stand gaping in the presence of Bjorn Bollason, and there is more to them than most other folk. This Kollgrim stands apart from the rest of the Greenlanders, as you yourself do. You are an old woman, but you stand as straight and move as quickly as a girl. Gunnar Asgeirsson looks to be his own wife's son, and his own son's brother."

"But things in the world do not look as they are. Nor does the unreliable husband look anything like the handsome suitor, though they be the same man." Now Sigrid Bjornsdottir laid her sewing in her lap and looked at Margret with her lips tightly closed, and Margret saw that the girl's purpose was fixed. She said, "We Gunnars Stead folk are an unlucky lineage."

Sigrid tossed her curls and laughed. "And we Solar Fell folk are as lucky as can be." And that was all they spoke of the matter for the time. Sigrid made herself a very long hood that came down around her shoulders and dangled in the back almost to the hem of her dress, and this hood was neatly sewn, so that the bluish color in the foxskins formed a pattern of chevrons over Sigrid's shoulders and about her face, and was flattering to her.

Now the spring came on, and the ice broke up in the fjords, and the time for the seal hunt came around, and at the seal hunt, Larus the Prophet, as folk called him, sneeringly, declared in the hearing of many men that a dream had come to him in which St. Nikolaus himself declared that Bjorn Bollason the lawspeaker was to be made king of Greenland, for the king of Norway, St. Nikolaus said, had been consumed in a great fire, with all his offspring. He was to be crowned with a crown carved of walrus ivory and anointed by the new bishop, the episcopal representative of the pope of Jerusalem, who would shortly appear on the long-awaited ship. Men considered Larus the Prophet a peculiar fellow indeed, for he would not leave off these speeches, although he was threatened and then beaten for them, but he only took a breath and started in anew, and he always had something more to say. The seal hunt was not so successful as it had been in recent years, and men were angered and disturbed by this, and blamed it upon the ravings of Larus.

After the seal hunt, these things were reported to Bjorn Bollason, and he went to Gardar and spoke at length with Sira Eindridi Andresson, his friend, but afterwards he had little to say about the matter, perhaps because he had come off so ill in the earlier encounter with Larus. At any rate, nothing prevented Larus from speaking, now, and he spread his tales about the Brattahlid district all during the summer. The ship, he predicted, would arrive in one summer, and it would carry both men and women, numbering thirty together.

Also in this summer, Eyvind Eyvindsson fell and broke his leg in the hills above the church at Dyrnes, and was out among the hills for three days, and died of exposure to the weather. When news of this was brought to Margret from Anna Eyvindsdottir, she was much cast down, for Eyvind was in the habit of visiting her at Solar Fell when he could. His shoulders and hands had been much twisted with the joint ill, but he was still a wild man, disdaining his pain and his disabilities, and full of a great deal of talk. It seemed to Margret that he had been much overlooked by everyone, including, perhaps, herself. And now the Thing came on, and the folk at Solar Fell prepared to make a great display there.

In this year, Gunnar carried with him to the Thing fields at Brattahlid a new booth, for his white reindeer skins had fallen into rags, although he had looked after them carefully. His new set of reindeer skins was pieced together with wadmal, and the booth was not so nice as Gunnar had hoped it to be. Indeed, however, when he looked about, he saw that with the Greenlanders' booths it was as it was with their clothing—most folk could not furnish themselves as they once had, but made do with a bit of trim here and a bit of color there. Now as Gunnar was arranging his provisions inside the booth, Thorkel Gellison came to him with one of his sons. When Gunnar turned to greet his cousin, he saw that Thorkel's face was gray, and he was much aged, even since the Yuletide feast. Gunnar said, "You do not have good news for me, I can see that."

"Nay," said Thorkel, "but it is no worse than news I have brought you before this, since that has been as bad as can be."

"Ofeig has come among the Vatna Hverfi folk, then. If he has done ill to Helga, you must tell me straight out."

"Nay. He is closer to Hestur Stead. He has forced a man to take him in and feed him. Do you recall Arnkel Thorgrimsson and his wife, Alfdis? Little good will come of his visit there."

"I have seen these folk."

"They have nothing to defend themselves against such a fellow as Ofeig. He has his way with the wife, for one thing. And the neighbors are small folk, who can do nothing."

"Have you this news from Arnkel himself?"

"Nay, from his cousin, who sent his servingman there a while ago. His news was that they were putting a good face on things, out of fear. This cousin is himself afraid to go near the steading."

"I have told you before that Ofeig must be outlawed by some means or another, and indeed, it should be quick enough work. I must say, with all respect and affection, that you have been remiss in not getting an action brought by Jon Andres Erlendsson. He wishes to be a respected fellow, folk say."

"I have spoken to him, but he sees Ofeig differently. He is reluctant. He has no answer other than that he can't bring an action, although he is courteous enough about it."

"Then many farmers must go to him at the Thing, and he must be shown how a worthy man does his business, and acquits himself with his neighbors. I shall not go with you, but I will speak to others. You must go to Bjorn Bollason and to Ragnleif Isleifsson, who is the most prominent farmer in Brattahlid." And so they set about finding support, and this took most of the first day.

This support was not as easy to find as Gunnar considered it would be, for it is the case that however apparent an evil is, men are reluctant to take it upon themselves to rectify it, and many obstacles stand in the way of action, and the greatest obstacle is this, that men do not care to do what they are not in the habit of doing. Twelve men went with Thorkel to Jon Andres Erlendsson on the morning of the second day, and these were the men: Bolli Bjornsson, the eldest son of the lawspeaker, who had recently taken over Hoskuld's steading in Dyrnes; Arni Magnusson, a prosperous farmer in Vatna Hverfi district and Thorkel's friend and neighbor; Ozur Osmundsson, the stepson of Ragnleif Isleifsson and the son of Osmund Thordarson, the former lawspeaker; Ragnleif himself, although he was old and bent with the joint ill; Bardi Helgason, a neighbor of Arnkel; his brother, Eyolf Helgason; Thorkel's own son, Skeggi; and Jona's brother, Hrolf. Four men from Hvalsey Fjord went as well, including Hakon Haraldsson, Gunnar's near neighbor.

Jon Andres Erlendsson's booth was a large and commodious one, and he invited all of the men inside and offered them refreshment. When they declined this, he said, "It must be the case that you have come to speak with me about Ofeig, for indeed, that is the only thing Thorkel ever wishes to speak to me about." He smiled.

Ragnleif Isleifsson said, "It is true that Ofeig forms part of our concern, but we have more general things to say. A man who won't defend himself when injury is done to him shows that he thinks little of himself."

"I do not think little of myself, nor indeed, of my mother, but it seems to me that I am much to blame in her death."

"You were prepared to take Ofeig or even to kill him when you stood your men about Gunnars Stead and Einar Marsson was killed."

"In the heat of events, men are often prepared to do what they later regret doing. I regret the death of Einar, who was my companion and friend. I regret a great deal of mischief that I was a part of for many years, although it seemed a pleasure at the time. I regret that folk have been injured at my hands and the hands of my friends. I have put aside the doing of mischief now."

"Now Ofeig has come among these other folk, who can ill afford him, and folk say he abuses them, and has his way with the wife."

"Perhaps this is the case, and perhaps it is not. It seems to me that Ofeig is ill-bred and ill-mannered, and it is also the case that he has to live somehow. Perhaps his father would care to take him in, or to find him an abandoned steading in the neighborhood. It does not seem to me that the case is so severe as you make it out to be. I do not see what will make me agree to summon Ofeig and bring an action against him. My father was a litigious man, and got little but ill feeling from it. It seems to me that cases at the Thing end in fighting and killing sooner or later, and always have."

Now Ragnleif said, "There was a time when the king's ombudsman would have taken care of these matters, but now we must rely upon the will of folk themselves."

Jon Andres replied, "I see these things differently than you," and Bolli Bjornsson colored in anger, and said, "There is no room in these things for each man to see them in his own way. Sira Pall Hallvardsson would say that the Greenlanders are too wayward for their own good."

Now Thorkel said, "It seems to me that the result of these discussions and hesitations will be very ill, and we will look back upon them with regret. But I see that the master of Ketils Stead thinks himself a great fellow, and is proud of his opinions. Nothing we can say will move him." Now the men stood up and went out of Jon Andres' booth, and they spoke of whether Ofeig might be dealt with if a case were not proved against him, but everyone was reluctant to take this course, or, at least, to have others know that he wished to take this course.

Thorkel went back to Gunnar's booth and reported that the fox had turned into a lamb, and that he half expected to see a halo form over the fellow's head, or one of those amulets with O.G.N.S. to appear around his neck. "In short," he said, "someone living at Ketils Stead has refused to summon a case, and soon we may anticipate wine grapes growing at Gardar." He was much put out. And after he left, a surprising thing happened, and that was that Jon Andres Erlendsson appeared at Gunnar's booth with some men that he knew, all prosperous farmers from Vatna Hverfi district, and he asked for Helga Gunnarsdottir in marriage.

Now Gunnar invited the men inside his booth and asked them to sit down, and the men, who numbered seven, with Jon Andres, were all men Gunnar had known in Vatna Hverfi district, or else the sons of these men. They were men whose envy of Asgeir had turned into pleasure at the trick that had done Gunnar out of his steading, or so it seemed to Gunnar. Although they sat about smiling, as folk do when there is talk of marriage, their smiles seemed evil and false to Gunnar, and aroused in him a painful sense of shame that he had not especially felt since his removal to Hvalsey Fjord. These were men who had amused themselves by repeating the verses of Ketil the Unlucky against Margret Asgeirsdottir, who had clung tight to Erlend Ketilsson in every case against Gunnar, who had gossiped about the Gunnars Stead folk whenever they could. Now one of them said to Gunnar, "My friend, it is not usual for a man to remain silent when the master of such a steading as Ketils Stead, and all the steadings that go together with it, makes such a proposal."

Gunnar said, "Indeed, I must hold on to my thoughts if I am to make something of them. I had no notion of this."

"But the maiden is well past the ideal marriage age. How many different thoughts can there be of such a case?"

Now Jon Andres Erlendsson said, "A man must come to a reply in his own way, and it seems to me wise to let him do so, rather than to distract him and tempt his annoyance." And so everyone sat about for a little while longer. Gunnar looked at the fellow, and he saw that he had not lost this quality that he had had earlier, when defending himself in the action of Kollgrim's dunking, a quality of smoothness and charm that had to be likened to something bright—a fire, or a star. If Helga's gaze were to reveal something unsightly about him, Gunnar could not imagine what it would be. And his friends looked to him in all things, it was easy to see that. Gunnar looked away from him, and reminded himself of the injuries done to him and his father by this man and Erlend, and even Ketil, if old stories were to be believed. Jon Andres said, "Old man, you are scowling, and thinking of what has gone before, but it seems to me that these things may be laid to rest now, for I am heartily sorry for my father's sins and my own." The other men smiled and nodded in approval at this speech.

"Nay," said Gunnar, "I am thinking of what is to come, for business remains unfinished that endangers many folk, and it seems to me a sign of unwisdom to let it linger."

"I have spoken about Ofeig many times, until I am asleep with the tedium of it." And in spite of himself, he flushed in anger, although he spoke mildly, and at the sight of this anger, Gunnar, too, grew angry, and turned away from the men, saying, "I am accustomed to referring such matters to the woman herself, but in this case, I have no hesitation in declining the offer." And so the men got up and went off, and news of this offer and its result went about the Thing. In this, folk said, Gunnar showed himself to be the unlucky fellow he had always been. And that evening, the Thing broke up and folk returned to their own districts.

Later in the summer it happened that Kollgrim was hunting with some men, and they began to twit him with the failure of Helga's marriage offer, and Kollgrim said, "A maiden is unlucky to marry out of a good steading and into a poor one," but in fact he knew nothing of this offer. The others laughed, and one of them said, "Now that is the first time Ketils Stead has been called a poor steading that I've heard." Kollgrim said nothing in answer to this, and soon the men divvied up the game they had gotten, and went back to their steadings. When he got to Gunnars Stead, Kollgrim was silent and gloomy, and did not greet Helga with his usual affection. Helga set before him for his meat a bowl of rich broth, but after a few bites, he pushed it from him, spilling some on the eating board. Now Helga sat down beside him on the bench and put her fingers lightly into his hair. She said, "It seems to me that you are downcast, my brother, but things have gone especially well for us this summer. Our father can have no complaints about how we get on here."

"I am not thinking of our father."

"Perhaps you are thinking of our mother. She—"

"Nay, I am not thinking of our mother." Now Kollgrim got up and walked out of the steading, and when Helga went after him a little while later, she saw that he was standing out by the homefield fence, gazing off into the distance. She began to be afraid that they must prepare for one of his spells of confusion and grief, and she made such prayers as she always did during these spells, that he would return to himself, that he would hurt no one, and especially not himself, in his grief, that she would have the strength to endure if things went on for a long time. Now she went to the dairy, and called for Elisabet Thorolfsdottir, and said, "It seems to me that our Kollgrim is discontented by this trip he has come back from. We must not be afraid, but must deal with him strongly if we have to. You should go to your bedcloset and shake out the clothes, and carry some soothing herbs in there, and also comb your hair and put on a bit of decoration. Perhaps such things will distract him."

Now Elisabet did what Helga had asked her to do, and she looked very pretty, Helga thought, so Helga gave her a trencher with some pieces of dried meat on it, and sent her out to where Kollgrim was standing, but he declined the food, and seemed not to see the loveliness of the girl, and Helga grew more fearful. Sometime after this, Helga and Elisabet and the servingmen went to the bedclosets, and Helga lay awake for a long time, but she never heard Kollgrim come into the steading, and so she dropped off to sleep. Now this state went on for two more days, but did not change to such weeping as Helga expected, and on the third day, at his morning meat, Kollgrim looked up at Helga from where he was sitting at the table, and said, "The farmer at Ketils Stead has made an offer of marriage for you to our father." And he looked at her closely, and Helga dropped the spoon she was holding. Kollgrim went on, "It seems to me that you will allow yourself to be stolen away by him, although things at that steading can't be better for you than things here. But women are deceptive and weak, and we are mistaken to place our trust in them."

Helga replied, "This offer means nothing to me, and this is the first time I have heard of it. If our father turned it down, then you have little to concern yourself with, it seems to me."

"Then you have not been holding conversations with the fellow when I am gone off on hunting trips?"

"When you are off on hunting trips, there is little time for conversation even with the servants."

"But you think of the fellow enough."

"Nay, Kollgrim, you misjudge me severely."

"You would like to be married, I'm sure, tupping and rutting, as the mares do."

Helga fell silent, astonished, for Kollgrim had never made such a speech to her before, and she had no breath to speak. He said, "You see, I have spoken what is in your mind. You are not as deceptive as you may try to be."

"My Kollgrim, I am little used to such cruelties as these from you."

"But you think of leaving me."

"For ten summers, my father has thought of taking me to the Thing and finding me a husband. A woman must always think of leaving her home."

"I see that you try to deflect me with quibbling, but if you are my friend, then you will say what has been in your mind."

"Nay, Kollgrim, I will not say anything more to you." And after this, for six days, Helga would have no conversation with her brother. On the seventh day it happened that a storm came up and blew some meat drying racks down, and all the folk of the steading went out and began to work at setting them up again, and during this work, Helga and Kollgrim exchanged some words, so that Helga was sorry for her hardheartedness, and said, "Every day that I have no talk with you, my brother, is a sorry day for me."

"Say what you have been thinking, then, and admit what encouragement you have given the master of Ketils Stead." And Helga saw that his anger at her was undiminished, and she closed her lips tight. A day or so later, Kollgrim went off again, as the time was at hand for the autumn seal hunt. And now, while she was busy cleaning and preparing the storerooms for the meat and blubber Kollgrim would bring home, thoughts of Jon Andres Erlendsson did come to her, so thick that she could not keep them off. She could remember his looks exactly, although it was the case that she had seen him only a few times, and for the most recent of those times, she had been afraid to look at him, but she must have seen him somehow, because she remembered his long red cloak, and the pattern that ran up the side of his boots. She remembered his face, which was thinner and more pointed than the faces in her family, and broadened at the top to a wide, smooth forehead topped by luxuriant curly dark hair. When he was serious, his face had one shape, and was all forehead, but when he smiled suddenly, his face changed to a balanced whole, for his smile was wide and white. That she remembered these particulars so clearly magnified the sting of Kollgrim's wrath, and made her ashamed. She was greatly unhappy for the entire duration of the seal hunt, and for the first time in her life found her work so taxing that she was tempted to slight it. Elisabet Thorolfsdottir, too, seemed cast down, for Kollgrim had treated her angrily two or three times before his departure. The days were very long.

The seal hunt was successful, but uncomfortable, for heavy rains fell every day, and as a result of this, men grew angry with one another. A second annoyance was the presence of Larus the Prophet. It seemed that nothing would stop his mouth now, and the hostility of men only goaded him onward, for, he said, it was the case with our Lord Jesus Christ that His very goodness drove men to injure Him, and the extent of His injuries was a sign of the extent of His goodness. Though Bjorn Bollason was present on the hunt, he stayed far from Larus and Larus stayed far from him, although the lawspeaker's name and his destiny as the king of Greenland was always in the man's mouth. These were some of his prophecies: That folk on the ship bearing the bishop and the thirty Icelanders would seek out and destroy a devil who lived among the Greenlanders, who looked like one of them, but perverted them into evil ways. This man would die through burning at the stake, a punishment that had not been carried out in Greenland since the days of King Sverri. That the women on the ship would be of supernatural beauty and holiness, and they would themselves lead the Greenlanders into holiness. That letters carried by the bishop from the pope of Jerusalem would be written in gold upon scrolls of scarlet parchment, and they would be written so that every man could read them, not only those few who had had the teaching of reading and the practice of it. These tidings, Larus said, had been brought to him by a certain saint, Saint Catherine of Xanderberg, who appeared to him spinning around on a great wheel of light, one summer night, after his evening meat. Most folk had heard nothing of this saint, and many said that the words of women saints were unreliable, but others were impressed by the growing volume of particulars that Larus had to relate. It seemed to many lesser folk that Larus was keeping great company indeed. There would not be another such seal hunt as they were then engaged upon before the coming of the ship, said Larus.

Gunnar, too, went upon this seal hunt, and it was his plan to lend his boat to some other men from Hvalsey Fjord, and go in Kollgrim's boat with him. It seemed to Gunnar that the rain had made Kollgrim very annoyed, for he spoke little, and then only sharply. Folk considered that this was one of Gunnar's unlucky qualities as a father, that he endured the anger of his son without correcting him, and always had. Gunnar was little experienced at seal hunting, for a man of his age, but the law was that every farmstead must participate, and Kollgrim now had his own steading. Kollgrim snorted a great deal at Gunnar's incompetence, and cried out that his father was a fool when Gunnar allowed one of Kollgrim's spears to get away from him and be lost. Gunnar said little at the time, but at the evening meat, he took Kollgrim's elbow, and pulled him apart from the rest. He was still a strong man, unafflicted by the joint ill, and half a head taller than his son. He said, "Folk have taken pleasure in speaking ill of us for many years, and they have many opinions concerning my failures in guiding you to manhood. But now I see that folk are annoyed with us for carrying our disagreements into their work. This is what I advise you, my son, that you hold yourself in for the duration of the hunt, and then if you must fight me, we will see to it that you have your chance. But now we are raising talk and more talk that is little to our credit." And he held Kollgrim's elbow so tightly that Kollgrim was hard put not to cry out in pain. He said, "It seems to me that you will finally give my sister to our enemy."

"I have turned down the offer, almost without thinking about it. And I have no regrets for doing it."

"Even so, your mind will change, no matter how I feel about it, for you have always sought to thwart me."

"Nay, my Kollgrim, I have sought to make my way about you with as little disturbance as possible. When you are less overwrought, you will think better of these things."

"Why is it that my sister's marriage plans must become the topic of general talk before I hear of them?"

"Were you present at the Thing when the offer was made? Have I seen you since then? You do not bang down the door to our steading with your habitual visits."

"Men laughed at my ignorance and shamed me."

"That is the occupation of the Greenlanders, to laugh at one another and then fight about it."

"My sister is well suited to my steading, and she is happy there."

"Nevertheless, if I receive a suitable offer, I will do as I am accustomed to do, and ask her what her wishes are." At this they went back to their meat, and there was ill feeling between them, but it was not so apparent to the rest of the hunters.

Now the autumn drew on, and folk went about their work, and although affairs between Kollgrim and Helga were not as pleasant as they had been, they were able to speak to one another with courtesy, at least in front of the servingfolk. One day sometime after the first snowfall, when the snow was hard and crusty on the ground, Helga discovered that she was missing a pair of fine sheep from the fold, and she feared that they had been lost. As Kollgrim was away, snaring ptarmigan, she took Elisabet Thorolfsdottir, of whom she was very fond, and went on skis up into the hills. It was a bright day, cold and still, and Helga was pleased with the change from the inside of the steading, which was close and smoky from the burning of lamps. It seemed to her also that Elisabet Thorolfsdottir was of a mild but melancholy disposition, and much in need of strengthening, and she wished to speak to her, and elicit her replies. Nowhere was there any sign of the sheep, and Helga began to fear that they had been stolen, and to regret it, for they were fine ewes, large and healthy. After they had been searching for a while, Helga stopped and took out her food sack, and spread her cloak upon the snow. The sun on the snow was warm and bright, and she sat in her gown and shawl. Elisabet set out the food between them, and began to chat of the weaving pattern she had been busy with the day before. "It seems to me that it will never come out right," she said, "for no matter how diligently I count, I find extra threads waiting for me at the end of the throw. Even so, my mother's sister in Hvalsey Fjord has a gown of the stuff, and it hangs very full. When she dons it, she looks rich and imposing, even though the dye stuffs they use there are dull as can be, all browns and dirty greens. I wonder that she has eyes in her head." She let out a large sigh and picked up her trencher of dried reindeer meat.

Helga said, "It would please me to find a good red somewhere about, but Gunnars Stead folk have never worn red. My mother says that such things are for Brattahlid folk, who care little who sees them going about their business."

"There were some folk in Hvalsey Fjord who had a nice blue color, but it was almost not worth their trouble, for it took so much extra work. Folk said they got it from sea shells. Still, sometimes I long for a nice blue. Such a color goes well with fair hair such as yours and mine."

Now Helga said, "Do you think of other folk in other places, who wear bright clothing every day? I think of my sister Gunnhild, who went off with Bjorn Einarsson and his foster son Einar. The dress they gave her for her departure was as yellow as buttercups."

"Why should folk in other places have brighter clothing than Greenlanders? I have not heard of this before. Do you think that she wears it every day?"

"Sometimes she wears purple, sometimes green, sometimes blue the color of the day sky, sometimes blue the color of the night sky, sometimes red or yellow or gold, and sometimes her robe is full of all of these colors at once. That is how she appears to me in dreams."

"Such things are said about Our Lady."

Now Helga picked up her meat, full of thoughts of Gunnhild, and she was so engaged with them that she failed to notice the approach of some other skiers, until they were right beside her. She caught her breath suddenly in surprise, and she knew that the presence behind her was Jon Andres Erlendsson a moment before she looked up at him.

He said, "It pleases me little to see you take your rest upon the hillside, here, and for this reason—folk say that Ofeig has come among us."

"We are seeking after sheep that are lost from our fold," said Helga.

"You will not find them among the hills," said Jon Andres. Helga saw that he carried weapons, a short ax, a crossbow, and a small knife. Two of his men had clubs and one had another ax. When she looked at him, she saw, with relief, that he was disinclined to look at her. His cheeks above his beard were red from the glare off the snow. She put her palms to her own cheeks. She said, "Ofeig Thorkelsson was in the southern part of the district."

"He is no longer there, though he has left tokens of his stay." And he spoke in such a dark tone, that Helga was not a little afraid to ask what these might be. Jon Andres looked at her. She said, "Tokens?"

"The corpus of Arnkel Thorgrimsson, lying upon the corpus of his wife Alfdis, in an obscene posture, for that is Ofeig's pleasure, not only to kill, but to desecrate, as well." His eyes held hers, until she could no longer look at him, and in spite of her fear and confusion about Ofeig, she saw the shape and color of his eyes so clearly that later she could not put them them out of her thoughts. He lifted her to her feet, and shook out her cloak for her, and then the men went with her to Gunnars Stead, and Jon Andres spoke to the servingmen, and left one of his own men there, to stay until Kollgrim should return.

It was the case with Kollgrim that he went out with his weapons, on skis or in his boat, and each day it seemed to him that he should go farther, for he was the sort of man of whom it is said that he is led by the eyes, not the wits. So it was that he never told Helga when to expect his return, for he himself knew not when to expect it. Now it happened that he went on his skis here and there about Einars Fjord, in the hills that rise above Gardar, where men have no steadings. He snared many ptarmigan, and carried them in a large leather sack. He was much distracted by thoughts of Helga as the wife of his enemy, and these thoughts lured evil to him, for as he was making his way along a bluff above Eriks Fjord, he slipped, and in preserving himself from a long fall, he lost his sack with all of his prizes. Much custom of skiing made him nimble enough not to lose his footing, but indeed, the slope was a steep one, and Kollgrim saw the sack break as it rolled down, and birds spun and flew outward, as if still alive. "Now," he said aloud, "news of this event would ill please my mother, it seems to me, for she would see in it an omen of what is to be lost, and so it appears to me, as well." Now he made his way along the top of the bluff, and toward dusk, he skied down into the dale that formed the northern district of the bishop's holdings at Gardar, and he stayed that night in a sheepherders hut there.

The next day was bright and filled with sunshine, and so Kollgrim donned his dark hood, with only slits for sight, to protect from snow blindness, and he made his way on skis across Eriks Fjord. It seemed to him that he would find more birds more quickly in the hills between Eriks Fjord and Isafjord, and make the longer trek worth the trouble. Men had already made tracks between the Gardar peninsula and the Solar Fell landing, and he skied in them.

It happened that there was a witness to his approach to Solar Fell, and this was Sigrid Bjornsdottir. Although his face was covered with his snow hood, Sigrid knew his figure, and went to her chest, and donned the hood of foxskins that she had made for herself. After that, she went to the storehouse and chose the choicest morsels of food that she could find, and she laid them in a silver plate. Now she went out again, and looked down upon the fjord, and saw that he was getting closer, and she stood silently, awaiting his coming. She saw that he looked about, and then that he looked up, so that his gaze must fall upon her, but in his movement and in his posture, nothing was registered of shock or interest. He only kept coming onward. Now Sigrid turned to the steading, and carried the plate inside. A servingwoman was standing beside the fire, and Sigrid said to her, "There is a man coming across the fjord. He will be looking for refreshment. He may regale himself with these bits, if you don your cloak and take them to him." And she went to her bedcloset and lay there in her cloak and hood.

It is the case that Solar Fell lies in a less foggy district than other parts of Greenland, and for this reason is named after the sun. The land there has a southern slope and a friendly aspect, and the steading has always been desirable. It seemed so to Kollgrim as he approached it on his skis. Sheep decorated the hillsides, and their thin cries made welcome music in the crystalline air. Now it seemed to Kollgrim that he was voraciously hungry, for he had had nothing to sup upon after losing his sack of game, and even as he was thinking of this, he saw a woman pass the little shrine to St. Olaf the Greenlander, and begin to descend to the strand. He followed the ski tracks until he met her, and, as if she were an angel, she carried a dazzling silver plate, and upon the plate were such bites of ewe cheese, and stewed meat, and roast meat with butter, and goat cheese as men are not often allowed in the fallen world, or so it seemed to Kollgrim. And this, too, appeared to him as a sign, and so he said only that the giver of these gifts must be thanked, and he went into his pocket and he pulled forth a walrus tooth that had been carved to look as a whale looks, rounded and slick, and he set it upon the plate, and turned his skis and went on. Four days later, he returned to Vatna Hverfi district and found one of Jon Andres Erlendsson's men fixed at Gunnars Stead. This was the case with Ofeig, that men did not see him, but saw the evidence of his presence, from Yule, through Lent, and into the spring. Some folk, hearing of his work with Arnkel, sought to propitiate him by leaving out such articles as they could spare—some shoes or woven stockings or a hood to distract him from the sheep byre. Other folk sat alert, day and night, watching over their steadings and waiting for his coming. Still other folk said this, that he would come for them or not, such a thing was in the hands of the Lord, and it ill behooved men to anticipate the ways of the Lord. He was the tallest man in Greenland, it was said, and as round as two men. His feet were reputed to be so large that he could walk across crusty snow without breaking through, but with all his size, he was a light-footed fellow, and could enter a steading or leave it without the sleeping folk knowing of it. He was not to be seen, although some men looked for him diligently. This was taken as a manifestation of Ofeig Thorkelsson's devilish nature, and some folk, mindful of the words of Larus the Prophet, declared that the folk on the ship that would soon arrive would see Ofeig without the cover of invisibility that hid him from other folk, and they would rid the Greenlanders of his burden. Larus, himself, however, spoke nothing about Ofeig, neither at Yule, nor through Lent, when he went about to various farms on skis and related what he had learned in the autumn from St. Olaf the Norwegian, who, as all men know, was a renowned warrior, and fought a man who resisted Christ and dealt him his death blow with a great crucifix, although the man carried a sword and an ax.

Toward Easter, the spring came on early, and the winds off the glacier started up, and soon the ice in the fjords broke into pieces and was blown out into the ocean, and at Easter, Bjorn Bollason declared that he had accepted a betrothal offer from Ari Snaebjornsson of Herjolfsnes, for a marriage between Sigrid and Ari's eldest son, Njal, with this provision, that the couple would have a large farm in the north, to be given them by Hoskuld, Bjorn's foster father, and they would live at this steading for part of each year, and they would have enough servingfolk to do the work on both steadings. And at this news, Sigrid swooned away at her place beside the table, and when she was revived, she lost herself in a flood of weeping.

Bjorn said, "It is the case, right enough, that Njal is but a boy, some fourteen winters old, but he is well grown, already half a head taller than the bride. The Herjolfsnes folk are said to fill out late, but indeed, they are sturdy men." But as he said this, he looked about the gathering as if disconcerted. Now Signy, his wife, went to Sigrid, and commanded that she stop weeping, for such a course showed that she had not been married soon enough, and fixed her, Signy, in her resolution to see that the marriage should take place as soon as possible. But indeed, Sigrid could not stop weeping or laughing, and no amount of shaking or remonstrance would remove the fit from her. She was carried into her bedcloset and left there to find herself, and later in the evening, she began letting out terrible screams, as if being pinched by red hot pincers, or bitten by devils. Bjorn Bollason was much distraught, and refused the advice of both Signy and Hoskuld that the maiden must be beaten into silence.

Now the time for sleeping came on, and Margret Asgeirsdottir donned her sleeping gown and went to the bedcloset that she usually shared with Sigrid, where Sigrid had fallen into croaking moans, and she climbed into the bedcloset and took the girl onto her lap. She said, "My Sigrid, I will tell you a tale now, if you quiet yourself, and if you make up your mind to listen to hard words, although you are not in the practice of hearing them."

"I have heard hard words tonight, have I not?" said Sigrid.

"None harder than other girls hear. Perhaps less hard, for your father has made it his purpose to satisfy your wish to be near Solar Fell." Sigrid lay silently. Margret went on, "This tale that I have to tell takes place in the time of King Sverri, for folk in Greenland were very prosperous then, and thought nothing of getting whatever fine things they wished for from Norway or Iceland or England or even France. Bits of lace and a pattern or two from France were not unknown at that time, and the folk at Herjolfsnes always had what there was to be had, for they are great seafarers, and a good folk to live among. The fortunes of the Greenlanders are not always the same as the fortunes of Herjolfsnes folk, and that is the truth. Anyway, at the time of this tale, there was a young girl in the Vatna Hverfi district, who was without a mother, for her mother had died in birth with the girl's brother. This girl's name was Marta, let us say, and she was much accustomed to having things her own way. She had the raising of her brother all to herself, for her father was not much interested in the boy. It was her pleasure to watch this child, and draw his gaze to herself, and then arouse his smile, and this pleasure never ceased for her, nor grew empty, not when he was a baby nor when he was a child, nor when he was a young man. Folk in the district declared that he was the loveliest child that they had ever known, and folk often say this, but it seemed to Marta that they meant it in the case of this child, who was named Gudmund. Another pleasure that she had, from her earliest years, was in feeling the weight of this child on her back, for she would carry him about in a sling, out into the hills, or up along the fjord. It so happened that the child spent so much time with Marta that he was disinclined to go among the men of the farm, and do the work he was born to do, for no Greenlander has ever been so prosperous that he was able to give over working his steading with his own hands. But this Gudmund was a great disappointment, for he detested any kind of work, and cared only to be with Marta. He was a great disappointment to everyone but Marta herself, for her longing to be with him, to listen to his prattle and feed him and draw his smile to her face never was still, and never was satisfied. He grew into a handsome wastrel, not unkind or unloving, but worthless. Even so, Marta doted upon him, and so did their old nurse, who died about this time.

"Now it happened that the father died, and through some mischance, part of the farm was lost—not the best part but the most gratifying part, the part that set the steading apart from the steadings of the neighbors, and formed the pride of the farmers there for many generations. Now Gudmund was the master of the farm, but he had little skill and less interest in the place, and the only way the work got done was through a foster son, a low fellow who was especially dear, but also especially repugnant to Marta. His name was Odd. He had lived upon the farm for many years, and always it had been the case that when Odd came into a room, Marta felt the wish to go out of the room. This repugnance was something that Marta prayed over and castigated herself for daily, for it had only to do with low, physical things, and the priests tell us that these things are like the clothes we put on for the duration of our lives, and when we lie down in death, we will take them off again, and all our souls will be indistinguishable. This truth was what Marta made herself ponder when Odd was in the room, but it had little effect, for he seemed to fill the space with his odors and breathings, and she seemed to herself to be choking.

"Now one day Gudmund got up out of his bed, and donned his clothing, and announced that he was going to the Thing, for that was the duty of men. And when he went off in his old boat, with his father's booth, he gave Marta a smile of such dazzling love and care that she saw herself and him living quietly on their steading, poor as it was, for the rest of their lives, and such a thing seemed enough, seemed to fill her completely. But the case was that he returned from the Thing with the news that he was betrothed, that the wedding would take place in the autumn.

"Now it seemed to Marta that she was filled with a vapor, such a smoke as folk have in their steadings toward the end of winter, that is the accretion of all the fires that have been made over the winter, and all the

food that has been cooked, and all the breaths that have been taken. This
vapor filled her and surrounded her, so that it fogged her thoughts and
slowed her actions, and separated her from Gudmund, and it seemed to her
that the last thing she had seen clearly was that departing smile, as transpar-
ent as the water in some of the high tarns above Solar Fell. Now the
autumn came on, and Gudmund went to be married, and returned to Vatna
Hverfi district with a woman who was but a child, little and thin, and
without skills, but withal very opinionated and clear sighted, and Marta
did not tell the girl that she must go into her husband's bedcloset as his
wife, but kept the girl in ignorance, and slept with her in her own
bedcloset, and also during the day used up the girl's time with this task
and that, so that the husband and wife had little talk with each other. But
this was true also, that Gudmund was much confused by his new respon-
sibilities, and only Odd kept the farm going, and one day when Odd was
called away, Marta saw that they would all die. On that day when Odd
was called away, Marta went out into the hills to look for plants, as she
always did, and she fell down in sleep and had a little dream, and the dream
was of two things, that is, that a great polar bear skin was lying across her
and preventing her from breathing, but at the same time, she was being
fed delicious morsels of reindeer meat, and also the sweetest bilberries. And
this dream meant that it was for her to marry Odd, and keep him on the
farm, so that Gudmund might live as he wished, for it was Marta's only
desire that Gudmund would have things as he wished them. A few days
later, when it seemed that Odd might come back if Marta would agree
to marry him, then Marta agreed without an eyeblink, and her intention
was to save Gudmund, but also to hurt him. And so she and Odd were
married. It was the case that they lived without disagreement for a number
of years.

"Now it happened that a ship came from Norway, carrying some
men who were sent by the king, Sverri that was, to take care of royal
business in Greenland, and on this ship was a man who had been in
Greenland before, and who had befriended Marta's father, and this was the
first thing that recommended him to her. His name was Sigurd. Sigurd
looked not at all like a Greenlander, for he wore bright clothing, and
walked about as if he wished to, rather than because he had work to do.
About all of his actions and ways there was something added, something
that was given away without thought. Greenlanders considered him careless, for Greenlanders are a very conserving folk, who stick tightly to what
they have, whether words or sheep or turves about the steadings. Nevertheless, he was a popular man, and soon got into the habit of making visits

all about most of the districts, and he was welcome wherever he came. He came often to Marta's steading, and when he was there, Marta felt this vapor go out of her, and drift away from her, and she determined not to think of anything at all except how to be near him, and to talk with him, and to draw his smile to her, as she had once drawn Gudmund's smile to her, and her will was met and matched by his, and they fell into sin without remorse. The short result of these things was that Gudmund and Odd did as they must have done, and killed Sigurd where he stood weaponless, and the long result of this was that Marta was bereft of her Gudmund for the rest of her life.

"Now these are the hard words that I must say to you: The Lord in Heaven lays out His punishments in a great array for women who follow their own will. If they will themselves to marry in deceit, then their punishment is always to be smothered and crushed by the presence of the unloved husband, whose every innocent action seems monstrous and repellent, who cannot sit at his meat without bringing vomit into the wife's mouth, or, worse, bitter reproaches. And swallowing back the one is not less difficult than swallowing back the other. If, however, women will themselves to have whom they desire in their weakness, the punishment is even greater, for everything is lost—the lover, the comforts of the family, the issue of the union, if there be one, and the woman is rubbed down to a stone, and is certain of eternal damnation in addition to this. Thus it is that I say to you, Sigrid, that you must have no desires and no will, for they cannot go against the desires of the Lord. The grief that lies in the heart is never emptied out, but is always fresh and bitter, and the very sights that once call forth joy turn upon themselves and then call forth torment."

Now Sigrid lay silent for a long time, but Margret saw that she was awake, although from the other bedclosets came the snores and shufflings of sleep. After a long while, she said in a croak, "It seems to me that I must have him."

Margret smiled, and said, "It is not a bad thing. The Herjolfsnes folk are said to be——"

"Not this child from Herjolfsnes, but Kollgrim Gunnarsson."

"Is it the case that you heard nothing that I have told you?"

"But the flaw in your story is this, that Sigurd came too late. If Marta had married him instead of this low fellow, there would have been no punishments."

"Nay, it is the will itself that leads a woman into sin."

"Nay, it is not, it is that men and women work their will without thought or plan." And it seemed to Margret that this was spoken from the mouth of Bjorn Bollason himself. And she took Sigrid in her arms, and lay with her until she slept, but Margret did not sleep.

It happened that when Kollgrim had returned to Gunnars Stead and found one of Jon Andres Erlendsson's men sitting at his table and eating up the game he had caught, he was extremely wrathful, and he sent him off with dire threats. Early in the spring, Jon Andres Erlendsson himself came to Gunnars Stead, and he came on foot and without arms, wearing only a thin gown and no hood, so that it would appear that he had nowhere to conceal even the smallest knife. And Jon Andres boldly walked up to Kollgrim, without waiting to be beckoned, and he said, "Kollgrim Gunnarsson, you may wish to kill me, and for this you may have good enough reason, or you may not. It seems to me that mischief is not always unprovoked, and when our case was argued at the Thing, other men agreed with me."

Kollgrim stared at the other man, and then said, "So you made them think, for you have a trick of speaking, just as now you have a trick of looking helpless, but not being so."

"Indeed, you are a skilled man with weapons, and you have some axes at hand. I will neither run, nor lift my arm against you."

"Why do you tease me and provoke me in this fashion?"

"Such is not my intention." Jon Andres Erlendsson spoke mildly.

"Then speak your intention out as a man should and be gone from this steading."

"It is my intention that the history of enmity that lies between these two steadings be broken up as the ice in the fjord is broken up in the spring, and blown out to sea. I give it to you to decide how this shall come to pass."

"Nay, indeed, this is the greatest trick of all, for soon enough you will ask again for the hand of my sister, and she will be stolen from me."

"Indeed, that is my plan for the Thing assembly this year, I will not deceive you in this. But men may not look to their sisters to keep house for them all their lives. Is it not better for a sister to marry around the hill than to go off to another district?"

"She is well fed here, and has plenty of work to keep her out of trouble."

"This may be, and yet I will not stint my effort to remove her from you. We may be friends even so. A wife's brother does as well in a fight as a brother, and you and I have no brothers."

"What fights could the two of us share in?"

"It is not unknown to you that Ofeig is about."

Kollgrim's face darkened. Jon Andres went on, "It seems to me that the tangle of injuries between us is so snarled that every word does damage, whether or not damage is intended. But even so, I am persuaded now that Ofeig means to do ill in the district, and he is more than one man in his strength and cunning."

"Folk in other districts say he is a devil among us."

"Folk have often said that there is a devil in him. But he may be hunted down as bears are hunted down."

Kollgrim smiled. "Bears are no longer hunted down, are they? So far have the Greenlanders fallen that their bearskin bedclothes are rat-eaten and thin. I have never killed a bear, although my father's uncle killed many."

"But we may kill this bear, if we put off our animosity."

"You are too sanguine about both, it seems to me, but I will not kill you today, as you are unarmed." And Kollgrim turned away and went into the steading, and it was the case that he did put off his feud with the other man, although it was with a taste of great bitterness in his mouth that he did so. And during the spring, the men of Vatna Hverfi looked about the district for Ofeig. It appeared that he had stayed for some time in the priest's house at Undir Hofdi church and left that place in disarray, but no men saw him there. Jon Andres hesitated to kill him before he was outlawed at the Thing. Jon Andres had no meetings with Helga, but through the spring when Kollgrim went off hunting or snaring birds, two of Jon Andres' armed men went to live at Gunnars Stead, and they were rough but polite, and helped around the steading with the lambing and the early spring manure spreading. Now the time for the Thing came on.

This was the summer of 1406, as men reckoned with their stick calendars, and of all of these, that of Finnleif Gudleifsson was the most accurate, and so men remarked among themselves that it had been eight years since the great hunger, and Greenland was full of the sound of children's voices, but it seemed to folk that they could not hear these voices without sadness and fear, for men never know when the heavy hand of the Lord will fall upon them, for the Lord chooses which sins He will punish, and which He will not, and it is His power to know better than men do what pleases Him. Even so, it seemed to the Greenlanders that their children were a great treasure to them, and that they could not have enough of this treasure. In some steadings four or more children followed upon one another year by year, and the wife and all the servingwomen were round with more.

At this Thing, Bjorn Bollason the lawspeaker said all the laws that he could remember in one day, although it had always taken three days in the time of Osmund Thordarson. After that, cases were conducted, and Ofeig Thorkelsson was outlawed, with only a formal defense by his mother's brother Hrolf. Men got together from every district, and the priest Eindridi Andresson with them, the men to discuss how the outlaw might be captured and killed, and the priest to say what would be done if Ofeig was indeed a devil. This priest was a hard and outspoken man, but he was not Sira Audun, and folk recalled with wonder how Sira Audun had knocked Ofeig down and sat upon his chest, praying loudly to the Lord. Sira Eindridi would be hard put to do such a thing, folk said.

Also at this Thing, Jon Andres Erlendsson asked again for the hand of Helga Gunnarsdottir, and Gunnar Asgeirsson did as folk said he should have done the year before, and consented to the marriage. Kollgrim Gunnarsson went about the assembly field at Brattahlid looking dark and ill-tempered, but indeed, he said nothing and threatened no one. And on the last day of the Thing, a peculiar affair took place, and it went as follows.

Bjorn Bollason had a large new booth, as befitted the lawspeaker, and his wife Signy and his daughter Sigrid arranged it attractively, and were hospitable about serving food to folk who were nearby, and so it was that not a few folk made it their business to be nearby. But among these, there was never anyone from Hvalsey Fjord, for the Hvalsey Fjorders were not especially interesting to the folk from Solar Fell, nor interested in them. But now every time anyone went into the booth, Bjorn Bollason asked after some of the Hvalsey Fjord folk, and about every fourth time he brought up the name of Gunnar Asgeirsson: was Gunnar at the Thing; where was his booth; had he brought any of his folk with him; did Kollgrim Gunnarsson come with him or have a booth of his own; were the father and son on good terms, or were they estranged, as some folk said; was it true that the daughter had been betrothed to a family enemy, and at this very Thing, did Gunnars Stead belong to Gunnar or to Kollgrim; what sort of steading was it, as prosperous as it had once been, or fallen off; was it intact, with two large fields, or had it only the one; what would happen concerning these matters when the marriage took place between Helga and Jon Andres? In short, Bjorn Bollason's curiosity about Gunnar's affairs could not be satisfied, and news of this got back to Gunnar, who sat outside his booth and smiled to himself, for he thought that surely Bjorn was thinking to make an offer for Johanna on behalf of one of his sons, and though folk said that the sons were all but indistinguishable from each other, Gunnar thought it would be a good household for Johanna, and he recollected that as matters had turned out, he had not done badly for his daughters after all. But although many folk reported to Gunnar that his name was always in the lawspeaker's mouth, the lawspeaker himself never appeared, and so Gunnar began to get annoyed, and decided to strike his booth and pack up a little early—on the morning of the fourth day rather than toward evening. And so he was packing his furnishings when a boy who must have been one of the sons came up to him and said in a polite but authoritative way, "Gunnar Asgeirsson, Bjorn Bollason the lawspeaker wishes to see you privily in his booth." Such was not the courteous procedure for betrothal, so Gunnar took his time in finishing his task and arranging his clothing and walking over to the lawspeaker's booth.

The lawspeaker had grown heavy in the years since the great hunger, for indeed, there was no stint of provisions at Solar Fell. He was also finely dressed, and the weaving of the stuff of his robe attracted Gunnar's gaze with its softness and the complexity of the pattern. It was not dyed at all, for the lawspeaker was known to affect clothing that was as white as possible. As soon as Gunnar entered the booth, Bjorn bustled about to put him in the high seat and find him refreshment. Then he turned to everyone else in the booth and sent them away, even Signy, his wife, and Bolli, his eldest son. It seemed to Gunnar that he might be a little offended, if the procedure weren't so unusual. Now Gunnar sat with his bowl of sourmilk, and Bjorn watched him taste it, and nodded, smiling, as if he wished Gunnar to appreciate especially its smoothness and thickness. Gunnar said nothing and looked boldly about. The booth was a rich one, made partly of reindeer skins and partly of foxskins, with decorated wadmal hung about inside. Finally, Bjorn began in this way: "It seems to me that the marriages of one's children turn out to call for more care and effort than they should. Why is it that they can't simply be matched up as a father sees that they should be? Instead of this, there is much exertion of will and a great deal of noise about the steading."

"No father would disagree with what you say."

"And yet, two of your daughters have made great matches."

"Folk say so."

"It seems to me that it must be different for you than it is for me, as you have many daughters and I have many sons. Sons are said to be more rowdy and troublesome, but all of my four sons give me less grief than my one daughter."

Gunnar smiled. "Folk would say the same of my one son. Folk would say that trouble is in his nature."

"Indeed, I am not a little sorry to hear these words of you, for my troublesome daughter has set her heart upon your troublesome son, and is fixed in her resolution to be married into Gunnars Stead."

"I had not thought that Kollgrim would ever be wed."

"He is a handsome and skilled fellow, the best man for hunting of all the Greenlanders, folk say."

"Even so, he is like my father's brother, Hauk Gunnarsson. He has not the faculty for living with a wife. The concerns of women are so remote from him, that he thinks not of them. It seems to me that it would surprise him to know that such concerns exist." Gunnar fell silent, in thought, then went on, "But perhaps I am speaking of my uncle and not of my son, for Kollgrim is greatly attached to his sister, and grieves at her marriage more than a brother should."

"Does he treat her well or ill?"

"Well, she says, but she has devoted herself to him since he was an infant swaddled in the bedcloset."

"But now she is going off."

"Sisters go off, in the course of events." Now the two men fell silent and looked carefully at each other. After a bit of time, Bjorn Bollason said, "Folk must have told you the whereabouts of Margret Asgeirsdottir."

Gunnar colored. "Folk know better than to tell me of her."

"Even so, should anything come of this talk we are having——"

"It seems to me better for your daughter that nothing come of it. Many years ago, Kollgrim was dunked into the ocean as a trick. The event has left its marks. It is not for the carefully raised only daughter of the lawspeaker to take this upon herself. When I have seen her about, for example at Thorkel Gellison's feast, I have seen that she is a merry one, very pert and full of talk. It seems to me that Kollgrim would confuse her, and also that she would confuse him."

Now Bjorn Bollason sat long in thought, and Gunnar could see that he was discontented with the outcome of this talk. At last he said, "But is it not better to let them discover their own foolishness in their own way?"

"But Kollgrim has never spoken of Sigrid Bjornsdottir. And my Helga tells me that a servingmaid at Gunnars Stead is with child. These things do not seem auspicious to me. Kollgrim is nearly thirty winters of age. I favor early marriage, as I was myself but nineteen and my Birgitta but fourteen when I gained her at the Thing from Lavrans Kollgrimsson."

"I will tell her it cannot be, then." And he smiled sheepishly, and Gunnar envied him not at all for carrying this news. Then Bjorn said, "But let it be that we part as friends, for you have done your best to save my folk from injury. If trouble should arise for you, from whatever quarter, you may say that the lawspeaker is as a brother to you, and will help you in every way."

"Folk say that I am an unlucky fellow, and so I pray that you will not live to regret such liberal words." And the two men stood up, and parted, and it seemed to them that they had decided the outcome of the matter, and they were both much satisfied.

Now it also happened on the last day of the Thing that Kollgrim was standing outside his booth, and he had just finished washing himself in a basin of water, when Sigrid Bjornsdottir ambled past. She was dressed very richly, and Kollgrim saw that she had made a fine hood for herself out of the foxskins he had given her. She passed him without looking up or speaking, and he let her go for a bit, until she was well past him. Then he called out, "Indeed, Sigrid Bjornsdottir, it would befit you to thank me for those foxskins you are so vain of."

She spoke without turning around. "Have I not made my trade, and paid their full worth? Can there be more that you want from me?"

Now Kollgrim went after her, and stepped in front of her, and said, "You have a merry smile. A sight of that would be good thanks, except that perhaps it is the case that I would wish for more payments after I had the one."

Sigrid laughed. Kollgrim said, "Indeed, I do wish for more."

"Men are not to wish for such things. It is discourteous."

Now Kollgrim laughed. "I am a Hvalsey Fjorder. It is not for me to know what is discourteous, as the daughter of the lawspeaker herself does."

"Folk say you are a Vatna Hverfi man, though."

"And folk say that you are living at Solar Fell, but I happen to know that you were born elsewhere, in Dyrnes."

"We share something then." She smiled brightly, and Kollgrim looked her up and down. She was much unlike Helga, small and trim and lively, with those curls spilling out of her hood and falling about her face. He said, "It seems to me that we might share more things, if events turned out a certain way."

"Even so, folk know nothing of what is to come. At any rate, the Thing is breaking up today, and when our servants have our booth down, then we must depart. But indeed, it is a large booth, and my father has brought along many furnishings. Of course, also there are not a few servants." After saying this, Sigrid began to walk up the hillside, and Kollgrim followed her, and they had more conversation. At the top of the hill, Kollgrim turned off, and went to Gunnar's booth, which was nearby. Gunnar was beginning to separate the reindeer skins from one another, when Kollgrim entered the booth. He said, "My father, I will not mince words with you. It is my intention to wed Sigrid Bjornsdottir of Solar Fell," and this speech was so unexpected to Gunnar, that he let out a great noise that was half a gasp and half a groan. Now Kollgrim went on, and said, "I see that it is your wish to thwart me in this matter, too."

"It seems to me an ill-omened match, especially as we hear from Helga that Elisabet Thorolfsdottir is with child. A wife and a concubine on the same steading always bring trouble, and the sons know not how they stand with one another."

"Elisabet Thorolfsdottir may return to Lavrans Stead. Whatever the outcome of the birth, there will be room for the child on one steading or the other. But it is not for a servingmaid to stand in the way of a good match. Helga is leaving me, and it pleases me to have a woman about the place."

"Sigrid Bjornsdottir seems more like a girl to me."

"She is a good many winters older than Birgitta Lavransdottir was when you brought her to Gunnars Stead. Solar Fell is a well-arranged steading. I doubt that her training has been lacking."

"Even so, the folk at Solar Fell are used to good fortune, and none more so than the only daughter. I am not sanguine." Now Gunnar looked closely at Kollgrim, and said, "But nevertheless, my Kollgrim, I will not stand in the way of this betrothal, for your fate is your own, as is the case with all men, despite the views of their fathers. Perhaps if I support you in this, you will see that I am your friend."

"My mother will be pleased with the news."

"Pleased enough. More pleased if you should come to Lavrans Stead and tell it to her yourself."

"Now you must find Thorkel and Arni Magnusson and go with me to the lawspeaker's booth. It seems to me that we won't be disappointed in our reception." And they went off. After the betrothal was agreed upon, the Thing broke up, and folk went back to their own districts with much to talk about. Gunnar saw that Bjorn Bollason was indeed an easygoing fellow, for he made not the smallest objection to Sigrid's plans. And he saw that he himself was as easygoing as Bjorn Bollason, although perhaps not as sanguine.

After the Thing it was decided that the wedding between Jon Andres Erlendsson and Helga Gunnarsdottir would take place just before the autumn seal hunt, that is, on the feast of St. Bartholomew, or as close to that as those with calendars might agree upon. And now Birgitta came out of her bedcloset, and went alone with many of her belongings to Gunnars Stead, so that she could oversee the preparations. The wedding itself was to take place at Ketils Stead, for it is not considered seemly for a bride to be married out of her own steading, unless she be widowed. And so it was the case that Birgitta was often thrown into the company of Jon Andres Erlendsson, and at first these meetings disquieted her very much, for she was reminded of the summer of her pregnancy with Gunnhild, when it seemed to her that Vigdis was casting the evil eye upon her. Although folk said that it was remarkable (or worse) how little Jon Andres looked and acted like his parents, nevertheless, Birgitta saw his mother's eyes staring out at her from under the dark eyebrows, and was hard put to keep up the talk. But he was devilishly thoughtful of her, and always sent one of his fine horses for her to ride upon, with a handsome servingman to lead it, or else he came himself to Gunnars Stead, and they spoke at length of cheeses and dried meat and stews and roast ptarmigan, as well as tapestries that could be repaired, and benches and tables and the names of guests.

It seemed to her that the outbuildings of Gunnars Stead rested as peacefully in the wide sunny fields as icebergs floating in the blue fjord in midsummer. She said to Helga, "I have forgotten the pleasant aspect of this steading. The wind never blows here, more than to ruffle the outer hairs of the sheep. Ketils Stead has not such a favorable look about it."

"It seems favorable enough to me. This will be good for Sigrid Bjornsdottir. She is accustomed to agreeable surroundings."

"The servants there are well meaning, but ill-trained."

"If they are well meaning, then they may be well trained."

"Helga, have you no fears, then? Every bride goes to her husband as to a great enigma, hoping that not too much that is ill will be revealed, but in this case, it seems to me the enigma is insoluble, and that, every day, Jon Andres Erlendsson will be a great source of surprise to you."

"I have no fears." And Birgitta saw that this was the case. But it seemed to her anyway that Helga was doomed, and this came to her as a great certainty, but she drew from her certainty a special calm and saw that it is fruitless to argue with maidens about the husbands they choose.

Now the time of the wedding drew near, and Gunnar and Johanna and many of the servingfolk from Lavrans Stead put aside their work at that steading, and came to Vatna Hverfi, although Gunnar stayed far from Gunnars Stead. The weather continued warm and calm. Sira Pall Hallvardsson came to Undir Hofdi church, and opened up the priest's house and lived there for three weeks, and each week he held the services and called the banns. The priest's house was in great disarray, but Ofeig had apparently gone off to the south to some other district, for he was nowhere in Vatna Hverfi district all during the summer. Sira Pall Hallvardsson was so old now that he walked with a crutch, but folk still liked him better than Sira Eindridi Andresson, or the boy priest, Sira Andres Eindridason, who seemed to know little, and yet think quite well of himself. Of Sira Jon, who was still alive, no one spoke. No one even recalled him, except to say among themselves that once there had been a mad priest at Gardar, whose arms had swiveled in their sockets at the onset of his madness.

Now it happened that on the day before the wedding was to take place, a great ship sailed up Einars Fjord, and it was full of Icelanders, thirty-two of them, both men and women, and the case was that this ship was traveling to Iceland from Norway, and was blown off course, and the people on the ship were suffering greatly from hunger and exposure, for it was late in the season to be coming to Greenland, and the ice had already begun to float up from Cap Farvel and gather at the mouths of the fjords. When they heard this news, folk remarked that Larus the Prophet had indeed been right in his prophesying. And so it was that these thirty-two Icelanders, or at least those who had the strength for it, were invited to come to the wedding at Ketils Stead, and they brought a great deal of news and some good gifts, namely four chased silver goblets, a neatly carved ivory crucifix, and twelve of the new coins of Queen Margarethe, which were shiny silver crowns, beautiful but not so heavy as the old coins from the time of King Sverri.

One item of news was that the antipope still held court for the French in Avignon. Another bit was that Queen Margarethe had brought about the union of Norway, Sweden, and Denmark under one house, not only through fighting, but also through marrying and making treaties, and there were Germans and Danes overrunning everything in the north—no northern men did anything but sit at their farms, plotting against the queen, but indeed, the farms were so emptied out from the Great Death, that all these men could do was plot, for there were no armies to be made—all the peasants were in the fields, tilling, sowing, and reaping as hard as they could—and asking high wages to do it. What about the pope of Jerusalem, said the Greenlanders. The Icelanders greeted this with perplexity—were not two popes sufficient? But indeed, there had been a great conqueror in the east, by the name of Timur the Ferocious. After putting great cities to the sword, cities such as Damascus, where St. Paul received the Lord, and Baghdad, this demon would hitch a hundred beautiful maidens to his golden chariot and whip the clothing off them so that they pulled him until they dropped dead. And this was the least of the horrors he perpetrated. But there was no pope in Jerusalem. And folk said that this Timur had himself died not so long ago. It seemed a great thing to Jon Andres Erlendsson to have these Icelanders at his wedding, a good sign of what was to come. He set their gifts right beside those he had given Helga and those she had given to him.

Now the time came for the procession to the church, and Helga was brought out of one of the smaller rooms of the steading, and she wore only this, a simple robe of rich weaving, of a green color, decorated with white tablet weaving, and also a silver circlet around her head that was the bridal crown in the Ketils Stead lineage, and Gunnar held her by the arm, and when they came near to Jon Andres Erlendsson, he felt her jerk away from him, but not meaning to, only called out of herself by the presence of the husband she was about to take, and this movement of hers filled Gunnar with pleasure. Now the bride and groom went up beside one another, and began to walk through the valley to the church, and all the folk who had been invited to the feast walked behind them. The air was still and the sun shone brightly on the late summer green of the fields, and as Gunnar watched the backs of these two heads, his daughter and his former enemy, it seemed to him that he had shed the capacity of enmity itself, that he was preserved forevermore from acts of revenge. The groom turned his curly head and smiled upon the bride, who turned and smiled back at him, and Gunnar whispered to Birgitta, "This cub cannot be of the Ketils Stead lineage, but must be of the angels, for he has cast away the Greenlander's greatest pleasure, which is doing injury to those who have injured you."

Birgitta leaned toward him and cupped her ear, and he only said, "All signs seem favorable to me." And soon the bridal couple were at the church door, where they knelt and received Sira Pall Hallvardsson's blessing, then went inside for the mass and the wedding service. Jon Andres' servants had decorated the church with branches of birch and willow scrub, and many seal oil lamps burnt brightly about the walls. Afterward they returned for the feast, and folk marveled at the variety of viands, more at one time than most folk might see in a year, and this was the doing of Birgitta Lavransdottir, old and bent as she was. The feast went on for two days after the bedding of the bride, and then the time for the autumn seal hunt drew on, and the feast formed the substance of much of the talk on the seal hunt, the feast and the coming of the Icelanders, whom everyone wanted to catch sight of and hear about.

The leader of this ship was a man named Snorri Torfason, and he was a slight man compared to the Greenlanders, wiry and nearly bald, although folk said that he was but a young man, only thirty-five winters in age. He was quiet-spoken, almost sullen, folk said, but his ship was large and well fitted out. Those he had with him paid attention when he spoke, and looked to him in all things. There were six women on the ship, two of them sisters, and these were quite imposing women. Their names were Thorunn and Steinunn, and they were the daughters of a man prominent back in Iceland, whose name was Hrafn. They were married to a pair of cousins. Thorunn was married to Onund Sigmundsson, who was Snorri's special companion, and of the two women, Thorunn was the more out-spoken and richly dressed. Steinunn was married to Thorgrim Solvason, who was a young man of looks and promise. All the Greenlanders were impressed by him. This Steinunn was more reserved than her sister, and always stood a little behind the other Icelanders. She was broad-shouldered and full-breasted, and altogether a fine-looking woman. There were, how-ever, no unmarried women or nuns on the ship, as Larus had prophesied, and it did not seem to the Greenlanders that these six women would be leading them into the ways of holiness any time soon.

Bjorn Bollason was much impressed with these Icelanders, and brought Snorri and some of the others to live with him at Solar Fell, where he showed them the shrine of St. Olaf the Greenlander, and told them the story of Ragnvald and the martyrdom of St. Olaf. Other Icelanders lived about the eastern settlement, some at Gardar, a few at Brattahlid, one with Thorkel Gellison. A few of the sailors took over two adjoining abandoned steadings in Vatna Hverfi district, and the Greenlanders gave them some sheep and some reindeer meat. Now the time of the seal hunt and the reindeer hunt passed, and autumn came on, and farmers began slaughtering their sheep for the winter. One day after the ground and the fjords had frozen, but before the deep snows, Gunnar went on foot and on skates up to Gardar, where he sought out conversation with Sira Pall Hallvardsson, and instead found Bjorn Bollason, and his family, and the Icelanders visiting and praying.

Now Gunnar came into the bishop's house, and there he saw Sigrid Bjornsdottir and spoke kindly to her and embraced her, for the wedding between her and Kollgrim had been set for Yule, and preparations were beginning, and it seemed to Gunnar that it might be a favorable thing after all, for indeed, the girl was pretty and neat, and everything she turned her hand to was well done. In addition to this, she spoke such merry and witty sayings, one after another, that Gunnar was quite taken with her. He said, "How seems my Kollgrim, then?"

"He seems as always, quiet and reserved, and much turned in upon himself, but it seems to me that he is pleased with things as they stand."

"I am not your father, Sigrid, but soon I will have such a fondness for you as a father has. With this in mind, I pray that you will be generous to my boy, for he knows not what he does, although his heart is warm, and his intentions are noble ones. It seems to me that he loves you as a man should love his wife, but you must teach him how to know it and let you know it."

"That does not daunt me." And Gunnar smiled at the fearlessness of women. Now he went to seek Snorri Torfason, and found him eating from a bowl of sourmilk. Bjorn and the others had gone into the cathedral. Snorri put down his spoon, and greeted Gunnar in a friendly fashion, and Gunnar told him to go on eating. "For I disturb you only on the chance that you may have news of folk that are dear to us, that is Bjorn Einarsson Jorsalfari, or his foster son Einar, who is married to my daughter Gunnhild."

"These are Borgarfjord folk, and not well known to me, for we are from the south of Iceland, near Hlidarendi, but indeed, who has not spoken in his time with envy of Bjorn Einarsson Jorsalfari, who is a man of great luck."

"Is Bjorn still living then? For he has not been heard from in these seventeen winters, since my daughter went away a child, and unmarried at that, for she was but fifteen winters old."

"It seems to me that Bjorn is not still living, but indeed, I have not been in Iceland for four winters myself, but have been living in Sunnfjord. Of Einar, I know nothing, but it may be that others of the ship's folk will know something, as a few of them are from the western districts near Borgarfjord."

"I hope to hear good news of Gunnhild, but every father must resolve to hear of the evils of childbirth, and so I am ready for that, too. But even with all of this, I am pleased that she finds herself in Iceland, as the affairs of the Greenlanders have gone so ill in late years."

Now Snorri sat up and grunted, and looked Gunnar up and down. "It seems to me," he said, "that the Greenlanders do quite well for themselves. The country is so rich in game that seals and reindeer hang drying about every steading, and the sheep are plentiful and free of plagues."

"We have few cows, anymore, though, and few horses enough. Our hillsides are overrun with goats. Not many folk cherish their goats."

"Even so, the Lord saves special punishments for the Icelanders, it seems to me. This girl, Steinunn, and her sister, Thorunn, whom we have with us—their steading was destroyed sixteen winters ago, and they were saved only because they were infants being fostered out at another steading."

"How destroyed?"

"Such explosions at Hekla the volcano as sounded even in the farthest districts of the westfjords, and these were accompanied by hellfire shooting into the heavens, not only from the top of the mountain, but also from the surrounding forests, where the trees were seared as they stood, and this went on for two days and nights, and was followed by two days as black as midnight, and the air so thick with ash that folk considered that the earth had risen of itself and covered them. After this subsided, folk saw that a great avalanche had covered the entire steading of Langahlid, and scores of folk came out to look for Hrafn Bodulfsson but nothing of him was found, although the wife was uncovered and given burial. Some serving-folk were found dead in the byre, too. These girls, Steinunn and Thorunn, were with their mother's mother at another steading."

"This is special punishment indeed, but even so, the Icelanders have ships, and go off to Norway and Germany for goods. The Greenlanders sit idly in their steadings and hope for life or death, whichever seems to them the most desirable at the time."

"Do the Norwegians have much for us Icelanders? Folk differ in their views on this. Most folk say that the Germans have stolen it all. They are an evil folk, but much preferred by the queen even so. At any rate, a dozen ships in the harbor cannot replace all of the lost cattle, or the sheep, or the grazing lands, or the steadings. And when these ships come, they bring goods, but, indeed, they also take away the queen's impositions of tax. Men are better left to themselves. That is my opinion."

"You have a bishop, the folk are blessed and married and buried, and prevented from falling away from the Lord through ignorance."

"You may say so."

"Indeed, we Greenlanders have had no bishop in nearly thirty winters, and of our old priests, the best educated one wastes away as a madman in a tiny chamber here at Gardar."

"We have had bishops, indeed, but they have been fighting men or fools. We are better without them. Folk do not want to hear the Lord speaking through such fellows. And here is another thing. I have heard this summer from ships at Bergen that the Great Death has swept through the Icelanders, and many folk have been taken, although there has been no recent rising of this black miasma elsewhere, not in Norway or in Germany or even in England, where the venality of the folk makes them especially susceptible to this evil."

And to these speeches Gunnar had no reply except the usual remark that the priests say that the people can bear their burdens well enough, and to this Snorri grunted, and then he went back to his morning meat, and Gunnar went out of the bishop's house.

Now the winter came on, and folk were making their preparations, and it happened that some svid was stolen from a steading in Vatna Hverfi district, and after that some reindeer meat and some sealmeat, and from this, folk knew that Ofeig had returned to the district. Now men came together, and they agreed that any outlaw could be captured and killed, if his pursuers were sufficiently determined, and so Jon Andres Erlendsson, Arni Magnusson, and Hrolf, the brother-in-law of Thorkel Gellison, made it their purpose to find Ofeig and kill him. Sometimes Kollgrim Gunnarsson joined them, and he was especially valuable in his knowledge of signs and spoors, and folk say that this is a God-given boon that all men may not have, however attentive they are.

In this winter, there were three occasions when Ofeig was seen, and two when it seemed to Jon Andres that they might catch him. The first of these happened shortly after the first winter nights. Early one morning, long before sunrise, Jon Andres was lying with Helga in their bedcloset, when a boy came into the steading, and declared that there was a bear in the byre at Mosfell Stead, and that the farm folk had risen up upon realizing that Ofeig was in the byre and set boulders by the door, but indeed, there were some sheep and goats and other goods in the byre, and if Ofeig were to wake up, then surely he would kill these. Now Jon Andres leaped from his bed, and found his ax and his crossbow, and gathered his men, and they went on horseback over the frozen ground to this steading, which was not as nearby as Jon Andres might have wished it to be.

Mosfell Stead sat on a neck of land between two ponds that flowed out of Broad Lake, which was the second lake of Vatna Hverfi district. The steading sat on a hill looking down upon the lake, and the byre sat lower, so that from the steading, the turves over its roof seemed to blend into the hillside. The farmer on the steading was a woman who had three sons, but whose husband had died in the hunger, and it was this woman, whose name was Ulfhild, who had thought of rolling the stones against the byre door. When Jon Andres and his men rode up to the steading, Ulfhild and her sons and their children were standing in front of the steading and looking down at the byre, and the bleats of sheep and the cries

of goats were coming from the byre, but muffled by the turves. Ulfhild
said to Jon Andres, "Now, my man, you must kill this devil, for a poor
woman loves her sheep more than she loves her children, for the one puts
food in her mouth, and the other takes it out, and I can tell the voices of
my beauties as they cry out below."

But the eldest son was discontented with this, and fell to bickering,
saying that the whereabouts of Ofeig Thorkelsson was no business of theirs,
and that they were better to have let the fellow sleep out his fill and rise
up and go off.

Ulfhild tightened her lips. "And who is to say, my fool, that he
would not have gone off up the hill to our steading and rummaged about
there? It seems to me that you think of nothing, and had better close your
mouth than open it." And Jon Andres and his men dismounted and tethered
their horses to the birch scrub that stood about the steading.

Jon Andres went down the hill to the door of the byre and shouted,
"Folk say that bears have returned to Greenland." There was no reply.
Now Jon Andres went on, "Folk say that in former days, it took ten men
to capture a bear, but only six to kill it. We have ten men here, and would
hate to use only six of them, for all are ready for a fight." Still there was
no sound of human words, only the crying of beasts. But suddenly there
was a great crash against the door, and the door shook with it. There was
another crash, and the door shook again, and Jon Andres stepped back, and
gestured to two of his men to come up to him, and this was their plan,
that they would quickly and silently roll back the stones, so that Ofeig
would crash out of the door and fall forward at their feet, and then they
and the others would use their weapons against him, and capture him or
kill him. The other seven men gathered in a tight circle some paces below
the door, and the first three began to roll back the stones, but it happened
that as one of the men was pushing on his stone, quite a large one, Ofeig
crashed against the door, which slammed into this fellow and knocked him
down, then broke, and fell somewhat open. Instead of tumbling at their
feet, Ofeig leaped out of the byre and jumped over the fallen man, and
began to run down the hillside, and when he came to the circle of men,
he dived and rolled through them, then regained his feet and ran down
the hillside. A horse was grazing at the bottom of the hillside, the widow's
only horse, and Ofeig jumped on this and began to beat it, and by the time
Jon Andres and his men had climbed the hill to their tethered horses and
mounted them, he was far away across the lake, and though they pursued
him, they did not catch sight of him again.

When they returned to the steading later in the day, they saw that the partitions in the byre were knocked down and that some sheep had their necks broken. In addition to this, the horse was lost, and so Ulfhild said, "It seems to me that you men are of little use in this." Jon Andres promised her two sheep and another horse, and they returned to Ketils Stead, and sat there quietly for a while.

It was the case that Helga went every day from Ketils Stead around the hillside to Gunnars Stead, and she prepared a meal for Kollgrim and set it out for him. It was also the case that she talked every day with Elisabet Thorolfsdottir, who was growing rounder and rounder with Kollgrim's child, and this child was expected to be born before Yule. Helga wished Elisabet to return to Lavrans Stead, or at least to remove to Ketils Stead before the confinement and the arrival of Sigrid Bjornsdottir after the wedding. But Elisabet Thorolfsdottir would have nothing of this, and whenever Helga spoke to her of it, she would sit patting her great belly and weeping. She wept shamelessly and without cease, soaking the front of her robe with tears, but this weeping seemed not to relieve her at all, nor to give her any strength to get up and move about the steading, even to prepare food or make a fire. In fact, the weeping had no strength, but rolled out of the girl as water rolls out of the mouth of a stream into the fjord. Helga was by turns sorrowful, angry, and amused, but nothing that Helga said or did had any effect on this weeping at all. Kollgrim came and went. He was tender and friendly toward Helga, more so than he had been in a year, and he paid no heed at all to Elisabet Thorolfsdottir.

This grieving cast a pall over Helga's spirits, so that she especially dreaded to see Jon Andres go off on one of his expeditions after Ofeig, and the whole time that he was gone she dreaded his return, for it seemed certain to her that he would come back to the steading injured or killed, as Greenlanders often do. Toward Yule it happened that Ofeig was seen again, this time at Undir Hofdi church, in the priest's house, and all the men at both Ketils Stead and Gunnars Stead, plus some others from nearby, went off in the middle of the night to capture him. Helga had to get up with them, and bring bowls of sourmilk around to the men, to her brother and her husband. They stood talking in the moonlight, their weapons in the snow at their feet, one tall, straight, and blond, so turned in upon himself that he did not raise his eyes from his feet, even when he was giving orders about the arrangements of things. The other, as tall, was supple and dark, and his eyes ranged over the horizon, over the other men, over Kollgrim himself, always taking measure, comparing one thing to another. When Helga handed him his bowl of sourmilk, these eyes fell upon her,

and regarded her with pleasure, and this look, at such a time, seared her
to her boots, but she only smiled in return and cast her own eyes down,
as priests always say that it is good for a woman to do. Now the men
mounted their horses, and rode off.

The first snowfalls of the season covered the ground with thick
powder, and the horses kicked up great plumes of white in the moonlight
as they trotted and galloped toward Undir Hofdi church. After no long
time, both horses and men were silvery white from hood to hoof. The
scheme was this, that they would arrive at the priest's house and surround
it, but do nothing, and make no sound, only wait for Ofeig to arise and
go outside to relieve himself in the snow, and then some men would close
upon him with their axes. Should he escape these men, others would attack
him with their crossbows as he was running off. No unarmed man would
get near him, for such an unlucky fellow would surely gain his death, so
strong was Ofeig known to be.

They came up to the dark bulk of the church in the moonlight, and
they dismounted their horses and led them into the church, so that any
noises the beasts might make would be muffled by the turfing around those
walls. The steading was dark and silent. Kollgrim estimated that it was still
some time until dawn, for the days were nearly their shortest now. The
men sat down in the snow with their cloaks and furs about them, and they
watched for the door of the steading to open. Kollgrim had forbidden any
talking at all.

Jon Andres sat cross-legged, warm inside his furs, and set himself to
watch the door to the steading. Kollgrim was beside him to the left, and
a servingman, Karl, who was especially good with a crossbow, beside him
to the right. He looked over the heads of all the men, and back at the door
to the steading, and he wondered if Ofeig was indeed inside, or if they
were, with great effort, silently waiting out silence while Ofeig slipped
away to another steading, to steal more food or kill more sheep. Folk in
the district now habitually referred to Ofeig as "that devil," and more than
a few looked to the Icelanders to do something about him, according to
the predictions of the fellow Larus. It had been so long since Jon Andres
himself had seen Ofeig, that when he heard of the deaths of the fellow
Arnkel and his wife Alfdis, he, too, had seen something devilish in it. Now,
however, it was not Ofeig's devilishness that made Jon Andres want to kill
him, but the knowledge that Ofeig was a man like any other. If anything
had brought this knowledge to Jon Andres, it was the sight of the fellow
running and rolling down the long hillside at Mosfell, in clothes that were
ill-fitting and too small, boots that were mismatched, a threadbare cloak.

And he had Ofeig's face and hands and manner. He was Ofeig, whatever corruption seethed within.

Now it seemed to Jon Andres that much time had passed since they had sat down, although the sky was no lighter, even to the east, and he was still warm in his furs. He looked over the other men. They sat as if cursed with spells, such spells as the skraelings know, that make a man motionless for days at a seal hole in the ice. Only Kollgrim had changed position, although soundlessly, without even a rustle of clothing. He was looking toward the church, and when Jon Andres followed his gaze, he, too, began to hear an intermittent noise, as if one of the horses had broken loose, and was moving among the others. Kollgrim turned and caught his eye, cocked his head, and shrugged. Jon Andres was relieved. The noise was indeed a small one, and would be doubly muffled to Ofeig's ears, inside the turves of the priest's house. Kollgrim turned back to the door of the steading, and watched intently. He had a predator's concentration, or a skraeling's. Jon Andres did not know what to make of his wife's brother, only that Kollgrim had not put aside the enmity between them, except for appearance. He would not, Jon Andres thought, ever put it aside, though he might save Jon Andres' life, or Jon Andres might save his. It seemed to him that unfriendliness formed the other man's backbone, unfriendliness and melancholia. And it was also the case that however much Jon Andres disapproved of this trait among the Greenlanders, he loved rather than hated Kollgrim for it. Helga had nothing to say to this. Her devotion to Kollgrim was a habit with her.

But still the darkness did not lighten, and no movement relieved the scene, and now Jon Andres himself felt the spell descend over him, yet he dared not move or change position, for he had not the talent of soundless movement. A strong memory came to him, of Ofeig as a child, when he sometimes came to Ketils Stead with Magnus Arnason, his foster father, the memory of Ofeig sitting over his trencher, and dipping his spoon into his broth, for he did it always in this wise, he would press the bowl of the spoon ever so slowly into the steaming liquid, as if protracting the pleasure of its filling, as if every mouthful was almost unbearably delicious, and Jon Andres, to whom meat was indifferent, watched every spoonful that went into Ofeig's mouth as closely as Ofeig did. Now, in the darkness, staring at the door of the steading, Jon Andres half expected it to open and disclose Ofeig the child, his spoon in his fist. And it seemed to him that the spell covered him more deeply, and only the alertness of Kollgrim offered hope for release from it. He grew afraid, although he was not by nature a fearful man.

Now Jon Andres lifted his eyes from the door of the steading, and even the movement of his eyes seemed to him to make a noise. He looked past the church to the fjord, icebound, beyond, and the black bulk of the mountains beyond that. It seemed to him that if he were to turn his head, and look back toward Ketils Stead, he would see Helga there, that he would see her turn her serious face toward him, as she did mornings, lifting her lids slowly and gazing candidly upon him. He had never thought of marrying before seeing Helga, and after seeing her, had never thought of marrying anyone else. This was another reason to kill Ofeig, for Ofeig hated him, and was clever enough to understand the most terrifying way to injure him. He did not turn his head, but he did lower his gaze again, just as Kollgrim made a sudden movement. The door to the steading was open, and Ofeig was lowering his head to step outside when he caught sight of the white figures in the white snow. He let out a great roar, and they were on their feet. Now all stood for a moment, gazing upon one another, except Karl, who let fly one of his arrows. It lodged in the turf beside the door.

Ofeig turned and began to run toward two Gunnars Stead serving-men who held the flank not far from Kollgrim. These fellows, Jon Andres knew, were little more than boys, although one of them had a good ax. Ofeig raised his arms, still roaring, and threw himself toward them. Koll-grim nocked one of his bird arrows. The boys stood their ground at first, then one of them stumbled backward, and Ofeig was upon him, felling him with one blow of his own ax. The arrow flew, and went short. Another of Karl's arrows flew, and lodged in the snow. Jon Andres ran around Kollgrim, and it seemed to him that Ofeig was nearly in his grasp. If he were only to run a bit faster or reach out more readily, he would put his hands upon the fellow. But he could not, and he began to shout, "Ofeig! Ofeig! Ofeig!" a command, a plea, an echo of childhood games. Ofeig glanced around once, perhaps at the sound of his voice, and one of Kollgrim's arrows lodged in his shoulder. Still running, Ofeig reached for it and ripped it out of the flesh and threw it down. Now he roared again, and raced ahead, toward the fjord, the river, and the mountains. They could not catch him, and by daylight he was gone. They went back to the church and gathered up the corpus of the Gunnars Stead boy and got their horses out of the church, and they were much cast down by these events.

A few days later, Helga returned to Ketils Stead from Gunnars Stead with the news that the wedding between Kollgrim and Sigrid had been put off until Easter for some reasons that both bride and groom agreed to, namely that Gunnars Stead was not ready to receive the bride (Elisabet

Thorolfsdottir was still there) and Solar Fell was not ready to give her up. Such things were not unusual, and Helga thought nothing of the postponement, except that she was much angered with Elisabet Thorolfsdottir, and did not know what to do with her. Just before Yule, she gave birth to a boy child, but she showed little interest in it, and did not even care to give it suck, when her breasts were flowing with milk and soaking her robe to the waist. The child was named Egil.

At the Yuletide feasts, at Gardar and Solar Fell, as well as in Brattahlid and at Arni Magnusson's steading in Vatna Hverfi, the Icelanders were much in evidence, for it was the case that they had a great deal of news to tell over and over. It was also the case that a few of them knew how to tell long tales such as was the fashion to tell in Iceland. These were in rollicking, rhyming verse, and sometimes they were spoken, but often they were sung, and the women—Steinunn, her sister, and the others— were fond of dancing to them. The Greenlanders thought this a great entertainment. One of these rhymers was a man named Thorstein Olafsson, and he was a cousin of Snorri the ship's master, from the southeast of Iceland, and he was said to have a large steading there, with fifty cows and hundreds of sheep, which he shared with his brother. He was about twenty-five winters of age, and he had a great, rolling voice which he used to good effect when telling his rhymes. He also had this faculty, that he could make up verses at the moment, about such things as the evening meat or the look of the clouds above the fjord, and he could make these verses either in the old style or the new style, tight, as folk said, or slack. The Greenlanders thought well of him, and he stayed with the priests at Gardar, although there was much going back and forth between Gardar and Solar Fell all winter long.

Snorri the ship's master and Bjorn Bollason the lawspeaker became good friends in this winter, and it was agreed between them that Bolli Bjornsson would go off with the Icelanders when they should depart, although when this might be, Snorri was not especially ready to decide. He was happy enough in Greenland, he said, especially as he knew not what he would find when he should return to his steading. The tales of the Great Death in Iceland were grim ones, that was a fact. He supposed that it was to be expected that the Greenlanders would be eager for news of elsewhere, but such news as Snorri brought with him he would not be eager to hear, if he were the Greenlanders, for it was all bad. For Snorri this winter, it was sufficient to go from bedcloset to table to the southern slope that lay before the steading and back to the bedcloset, where he lay under the furs and called out to such folk as were about to come and talk to him. The

Greenlanders considered this peculiar behavior for such a well-thought-of ship's master, but Thorstein Olafsson only laughed and said that this was Snorri's nature—he didn't know what to do with himself on land, which was why he left his steading to his wife. Thorstein said that she was glad to have him off, since he never turned a hand to a lick of work. But indeed, he was a good ship's master, and had never lost any cargo, much less any folk, or a ship itself. On a ship he was as light and active as a goat, running here and there, seeing trouble before it appeared. Folk were glad to travel with him, if they must travel.

Bjorn Bollason did not seem to care that Snorri had supplanted him as the center of the household at Solar Fell. He spent enough time sitting in the doorway of the bedcloset himself, asking about this and that—what folk did in Norway and Iceland mostly. Snorri was especially fond of Sigrid, for the sake of her jests and merriment, and she got into the habit of sitting nearby every day, and he would tease her in this wise:

"It seems to me that you will make a poor enough wife."

"Nay, indeed, I will make a good wife, a wife such as many men want but not all men deserve."

"And what sort of wives do most men deserve?"

"Little meek things, who serve up the sourmilk with a spoon and a wince."

"It is true that a wife must cast her eyes down before her husband."

"As men cast their eyes down before the face of God. Yes, folk say this, but wives who cast their eyes on the floor see nothing but their own feet."

"And what sort of wives do most men want?"

"Someone who will tell them what they might do, but not what they must do."

"And what sort of husbands do most women want?"

"Someone to tell them what they must do, but let them do as they please anyway."

"Indeed, you will make a poor wife."

"Nay, my betrothed is a great hunter and a bold man. He will have pleasure upon coming home to me, and I will have pleasure arranging his affairs for him."

"What else is there to know about him?"

"He is a handsome fellow. He is the brother's son of Margret Asgeirs-dottir, whom you know."

"This old woman who speaks little?"

"She speaks when she has something of worth to say, or someone of worth to say it to."

"You are marrying the brother's son of a servingmaid?"

Now Sigrid colored, and fell silent, and Snorri could see that she was annoyed with him. She said, "Strangers bring news from afar, but they know nothing of the news at home. You have been to Vatna Hverfi district, so you must know that it is the richest of all the districts, and my Kollgrim has possession of one of the greatest steadings there, and his sister is married to the man with the greatest steading and the most other holdings. Margret Asgeirsdottir's tale is her own, and you would be a lucky man if she told it to you, for she has never told it to anyone." She paused, and then said, "She goes as a servingmaid of her own accord, but my father and mother consider her a guest, and the weaving she does for us in the nature of gifts to us."

Snorri smiled teasingly, and said, "There is no place for anger in a good wife."

"Then indeed, there is no place for honor or virtue, it seems to me. I am tired of this talk, and have many things to do." And so she got up, but the next day she came back, for Snorri was not an ill-tempered man, and his teasing was pleasant to her. After this talk, though, Snorri endeavored to have talk with Margret Asgeirsdottir, but she had nothing to say to him, no matter what he might say to her.

Another one who liked to talk to Sigrid Bjornsdottir was Thorstein Olafsson, and whenever he came over from Gardar, he made it a point to waylay her and amuse her with new verses that he had made, and it happened that one day when he appeared on skis with some other folk from Gardar, she went up to him and said as follows:

> *Folk who pay for meat with song*
> *Must chew for a moment, and sing all evening long.*

Thorstein was much pleased with this, and said as follows:

> *But they may look while they sing*
> *Across the room, at smiles blossoming.*

From time to time Kollgrim came to Solar Fell on his skis, bringing game for meat or furs, and he, too, was much drawn to the Icelanders. Although he said little to them, he watched them so that he made them uncomfortable. One day Snorri said to Sigrid, "Your betrothed has more eyes than tongue."

"That is a virtue in most folk, to look about but to keep foolishness to oneself. You may see the results of his ways in the furs he brings me and the broth you are supping so eagerly."

"This fellow seems to me the perfect Greenlander, half man and half bear."

"I see nothing of that in him."

"He looks at folk as if he were about to eat them up."

"And others look at folk as if they wished them to do their business for them. My Kollgrim will eat no one up, but other folk will succeed in having their work done for them."

"This sharpness ill behooves a good wife."

"As you have not seen your own wife in five winters, it may be that you have forgotten what behooves a good wife. But surely she has not, as she has carried on your business without you." And so their conversations went on, and Snorri spoke highly of Sigrid to Bjorn Bollason, but never to Sigrid herself, and Sigrid went to Snorri's bedcloset every day, but only as if she could not avoid it. Even so, the Icelanders continued to make little of Kollgrim, and said among themselves that the merry maiden was thrown away on such a sour fellow. And seeing Kollgrim, and his quiet ways, Thorstein Olafsson felt emboldened to talk with Sigrid more and more and beguile her with rhymes, many of which were about herself, and all of which made her laugh.

It was also the case that Kollgrim befriended his father's sister, and sometimes sat near her while she was weaving and spun bits of wool for her, for he, like Gunnar, had this knack, but they hardly ever exchanged words, and never spoke of Gunnar. It seemed to Margret Asgeirsdottir from time to time that it was Gunnar himself sitting beside her, but most times it did not seem like this. One day it happened that she was sitting at her weaving when Kollgrim appeared with a dozen hares, and then he sat down near Margret and looked at her work without speaking. Sigrid was away from the steading. Margret threw her shuttle quickly and rhythmically, hardly pausing to count her threads. She was weaving wadmal for one of Sigrid's shifts, and it was the purplish color that folk from Gunnars Stead were known by. A little time passed, then Margret said, "It seems to me, my Kollgrim, that we are dead sticks among this chattering flock at Solar Fell."

"These Icelanders make a great deal of noise."

Now they sat silently again, listening to the click of the shuttle. Then Margret said, "But those who chatter are always apprehensive of those who say nothing."

"They may be. I have thought little of this."

"Asgeir Gunnarsson used to say of Hauk, his brother, that he could make killing the fiercest bear sound like a day at the butter churn."

"Some don't have the trick of storytelling."

Now Margret turned from the loom and looked Kollgrim straight in the eye, and she saw that he saw her and was listening to her, and she said in a low voice, "But some do." And they were silent again for a space. Then she said, "It is not such a good usage to seek the waste places all the time."

"There must be meat on the table."

"And herbs and greens. But there must be folk in the steading as well. My father's brother took no wife, and no wife brought him sorrow and he brought sorrow to no wife."

"It is hard for a man with fixed habits to hear such things. I am accustomed to my sister Helga, and now she has been stolen from me, and all that folk do about it is to shrug their shoulders and say that that is the purpose of sisters, to go elsewhere."

"She has not gone far."

"Far enough. She thinks little of me anymore. Her heart is full of him."

"You speak like a child, my Kollgrim." But she said this in such a kindly, low voice that he did not take offense, and only sat quietly as she turned back to the shuttle. Just after this, Sigrid came into the steading, and her eyes fell upon the two sitting together, and she was much pleased. Toward Kollgrim, she was never sharp, for she was a little afraid of him. Now she came up to him and said, "My Kollgrim, you look in need of refreshment," and he put his hand lightly on her sleeve, for truly she was a pretty bird, and it raised his spirits somewhat to gaze upon her. She turned away, and bustled about the steading, and soon there was food before him, and she gazed upon him while he ate it.

One day when Helga was at Gunnars Stead with Elisabet Thorolfs-dottir and the child Egil, Kollgrim came into the steading, although he was not expected for two or three more days. He laid down his weapons and threw off his furs and sat without speaking at the table. Elisabet Thorolfsdottir was also sitting at the table, holding the child far too loosely in her arms, it seemed to Helga. Egil was not crying. He had his mother's listless way about him. "Welcome back, my Kollgrim," said Helga. "You have cut short your trip." She set a bowl in front of him, full of the sourmilk she had been dishing up for herself.

"It seemed to me that I wanted to see this boy here." He reached over and took Egil into his own hands and gazed upon him.

"He is a handsome child," offered Helga. "Not so many infants his age have such hair on their heads."

Kollgrim said nothing for a while, only looked at the child, but then he said, "It seems to me that he has the look of death on him, like an early lamb." He took the boy's fingers and bent them over his forefinger with his thumb. They were long, thin, and bluish. "All the parts are here, but little is holding them together."

The boy had looked this way to Helga, too, but she said, "Indeed, you are seeking after evil, and I pray that you find it not. The boy lives and breathes, and it is not for us to look into his fate."

"I may look into my fate, though, and I see that Elisabet Thorolfsdottir and Egil Kollgrimsson are my fate, and not the chattering birds of Solar Fell, and that is fine with me." And this is how Helga learned that the betrothal between Kollgrim Gunnarsson and Sigrid Bjornsdottir was broken off. Gossip did not tell who or what had sparked the parting, for neither Sigrid nor Kollgrim remarked on this subject to anyone. The two kept apart, as was proper, but each seemed little grieved to those about them, and one day Bjorn Bollason met Gunnar Asgeirsson at Gardar, where Sira Pall Hallvardsson was holding his Easter feast, and he said to him, "Things have turned out well for us."

"It seems that this is the case. But with Kollgrim, nothing has ever gone so smoothly as this."

"Nor with my Sigrid, but it may be that they see with the eyes of men and women now, instead of with the eyes of willful children. I am sanguine for now."

"Indeed, lawspeaker, you are sanguine always." And so Gunnar's friendship with Bjorn remained firm and untested.

Now folk sat quietly at their steadings through the summer, and it was not such a prosperous summer as many had been recently. It was the case that folk expected the Icelanders to make much of Larus the Prophet, or at least expected him to make much of them, but in this summer, he began talking of other things besides the ship and the pope of Jerusalem. In this case, he said, his informant was the Virgin Herself, who had come to him three nights running and given him suck from Her breasts, and these were full of milk that tasted like the sweetest honey and ran like water into the fjord. And this was also the case, that it seemed to him that She had taken him onto Her belly like a newborn baby, and cradled him there. And this is what She told him, that a great devil lived among the Greenlanders, someone who walked as a man but had the parts of a woman as well, and the feet of a bear. This devil, She said, was seducing folk away from goodness and no man had any resources against him. If he gave you food, the food would poison you and turn your thoughts to evil. If he spoke to you, his words would enter your ears and buzz around your head like bees and spiders. If he gave you water, the water would be as fire, burning the Godliness out of you. If he turned his hand to your homefield or your sheep, then his touch would corrupt them until the coming of the Lord as is written. Simple clods of dirt would turn into teeming corruption, worms would crawl out of the nostrils of the sheep, meat from these animals would turn rotten in the mouth, milk would sour, but give off the odor of death, not of sourmilk. The Virgin's eyes, Larus said, had been spinning circles of icy blue and Her embrace as tight as the clasp of a walrus, that crushes the life out of men.

Now it was the case that Larus had developed a certain following, mostly of women, it is true, and these women came to Larus Stead and sat about with Ashild and little Tota, and they listened to Larus embroider upon his tales, and at first they did nothing that might be called worship, for they were fearful of such a sin as kneeling outside church. Truly enough, they had knelt many days of their lives to say Hail Marys or Our Fathers, or such other prayers as the priests instructed them in, but now the thought of kneeling at Larus Stead, with their ears full of Larus' visions, rather frightened them, and yet none of these women, or the few men who came with them, could make herself stay away. Ashild was a model for them, and little Tota, too, the one an innocent child who carried her trencher to her stepfather and bowed before him, the other a very figure of goodness, who served Larus, but seemed to direct him, too. "Let us have our refreshment now," she would say, or "Larus must rest in his bedcloset for a while." Larus said that the Lord and his saints had given her the perfect wifely temperament, for they had drained all discontent from her, but also all fear.

And so it happened somehow, through the winters, when the priests were snug at Gardar, that some of the Larus Stead neighbors got in the habit of going to Larus Stead at special times, when there would be meat on the table, set at twelve places, and Larus would wear a special robe that one of the women had woven for him, and folk would sit at the table and partake of the dried sealmeat and the broth, and Larus would speak of one of his visions—never more than a part of one really, but each in order, from the first to the last. At another time during the meal, he would speak of the persecutions of the Greenlanders, of his trial and victory at the hands of Bjorn Bollason and Eindridi Andresson, of the taunts of the farmers at the seal hunts, of how he was received in this great steading and that one.

Now when the Easter of 1407 came, and there was a priest in Thjodhilds church, it seemed to some of these folk that they had sinned and betrayed the Lord, for they shifted in their seats and their blood thrilled in their veins during Eindridi Andresson's service, and some of these folk swore to themselves that they would stay apart from Larus. Others, however, saw the deficiencies in Sira Eindridi's service, how he mumbled the Latin through not knowing it very well, and how he even skipped bits of the service that they thought they remembered, and how he tried to make up for these things by intoning a long sermon full of dire threats and harsh words. These folk thought fondly of the simple meals at Larus Stead, and the supple way that Larus told his tales, as a grandmother may tell a tale that everyone knows already, in her own voice, but also in the voices of many who have come before. What talent had Larus had for such things when he was a servant at Brattahlid? None to speak of. Was not this itself evidence that the saints and the Lord and the Virgin were indeed talking to him, as he said they were? At any rate, after Easter, some of the women fell away, and did not come back to Larus Stead, but others came as often as they could, and brought other folk, kinfolk and neighbors, with them. It happened that Gudrun, the wife of Ragnleif Isleifsson, and the former wife of Osmund Thordarson, looked in one day, and though she did not stay long, Larus told Ashild that this was a great victory for them, and Ashild agreed.

News of these doings came to Bjorn Bollason, for indeed, Larus Stead was not so far from Solar Fell, and Bjorn Bollason did not know what to think, and he spoke about them to the Icelanders, telling Snorri how Larus had predicted the coming of the ship over and over, although other details of the predictions had been false ones. But still, he had seen the ship, and the women upon it, and Bjorn was perplexed by the mixture of truth and error. And so Snorri sat up in the bedcloset, and put his trencher of meat away from him, and he told Bjorn the following tale:

Once when Snorri was a young man on his uncle's ship, carrying dried cod to England, it happened that the ship was blown off course in the passage between England and France, and a great storm came up, and they took refuge in a certain town of France that was named Calais, and this was a great shipping town, but also a great warring town, sometimes English and sometimes French, so that the folk there spoke the language of France equally with the language of England. It was not a place such as Snorri cared for—cramped and full of rough folk. Now it happened that although the cargo of the ship had been saved, the ship itself needed some repairs, and so Snorri and his mates stayed in Calais for some weeks, lamenting all the time the passage of good sailing weather and the coming of winter, for they cared little for the idea of staying in Calais until spring.

Now it happened that one day Snorri and another young man were out upon the streets of the town, and they saw folk streaming toward a large square, and so they were taken up in the stream, and soon they came to a place where a scaffolding had been set up, and many folk were milling about and eating and drinking flagons of ale or wine. Pretty soon, a certain priest climbed the scaffolding, a great tall fellow with long arms and a big head, and he began to harangue the crowd with strange tales about the Devil, and the Lord, and the coming of the end of the world. His voice seemed to Snorri to rise like a great wind, and pass through the crowd, bending them in this direction and that, until men did not know what they were doing or where they were going, and only pressed in upon the scaffolding that held the priest, so that some folk fell to the pavement and could not get up, but were crushed beneath the feet of the others. And this also happened, that the fellow's voice seemed to get louder and louder, without strain, and folk gave over talking and eating and drinking, and only listened, and Snorri and his companion as well. Folk began to weep, and not just women, of which there were many. And soon after they began to weep, they began to wail, and even to scream, so that the square was full of a great noise. But this was also the case, that the priest got louder and louder, and Snorri heard every word that he said, and the reason for this seemed to be that he was speaking directly to Snorri himself, as if into his very ear. Now Snorri could not say how long this preaching went on.

The afternoon seemed as if it would never end, but suddenly another thing happened, and this was that some men on horseback, some magistrates and knights, rode into the crowd, and got up on the scaffolding, and pulled the priest down, so that he disappeared among the horses and the milling folk. But even though he could not be seen, he seemed to raise his voice, calling out to the Lord for help, and this came into every man's ear, as the sermon had done, and the crowd began to press upon the magistrates, and fighting broke out, so that other men on horses, who were lingering by the side of the crowd, galloped among folk, wielding their weapons, and folk fell under the hooves of the horses, but other folk took out their knives and severed the tendons of the horses, so that they fell to the cobblestones, and then these folk fell upon the riders and beat them.

Snorri and his companion spoke between themselves, and agreed that these French-Englishmen were of an especially volatile temperament, for indeed, the preaching had inflamed them mightily. The two Icelanders tried to make their way out of the crowd. Numerous blows fell upon them, but at random, and they came to the edge of the square. Now great bells had begun to ring all over the town, making a resounding clamor, and more men on horseback galloped to the scene, and others came as well, on foot, and the result was that by nightfall, many folk lay injured and even dead in the square, and a proclamation was made in the town that those in the square whose dress told them to be of low estate could not be touched, even out of Christian mercy, whether for burial, or sacraments, or healing. And the racket of the bells went on all through the night, and in the morning, it was proclaimed that this priest, who was himself a devil in disguise, had been tortured and executed at the hands of the magistrates, and that the folk need not fear him any longer. And then the ban was lifted on attending to the folk in the square, and these men and women and children were carried off to their homes or their graves, as was necessary.

Now after this event, there was a great discussion of the nature of this priest—where had he come from, how had the scaffolding gotten into the square, how was it that his voice grew louder and softer at the same time, so that it rose above the noise of the crowd and yet seemed to whisper into your ear, what was the truth and what was the sin in those words he had said, how long had he preached—all afternoon, only a short while. And no one agreed on any of these questions. Some priests said that this fellow was a true prophet, from Paris, and others said he was a devil, with no earthly home, and some said that men had built the scaffolding in the night and others said that devils had carried it there, and others said that angels had carried it there, and some said that those who died in the square were martyrs and others said that they were damned sinners, and there was no authority who could persuade all the town of any one view. Then it came time for the Icelanders to leave, and Snorri was glad enough to go, but since then he had been turning this scene over in his mind sometimes, and it seemed to him that the truth of it was that the preaching, whether true or false, had inflamed the folk, and brought about great evil. Any Icelander knows of the evils in the world, especially of those that no man can help—such as cattle diseases and volcanic eruptions and the coming of the Great Death—but this was an evil that men rushed to, not one that came to them.

Now Bjorn Bollason looked at Snorri in silence and then he said, "It seems to you that this fellow Larus will bring about such an evil?"

Snorri shrugged.

"We have tried to stop his preaching before, myself and Sira Eindridi. But it seems to me that our efforts only gave him strength."

"You may kill the fellow."

"I have thought of that."

"But it happened in Iceland that Abbot Thorlak, of Thykkvabaer, was driven off, and though he was a bad man, folk venerated him after he was beaten, and he lived out the last two winters of his life in great respect. It seems to me that the evil has begun here with this fellow Larus, and that events will take their course, as always." And indeed Bjorn Bollason nodded, for he had no notion of what to do.

Now the time for the autumn seal hunt came on, and some of the Icelanders asked if they might go along to help or watch, and Bjorn Bollason sent some in his large boat, and he persuaded another farmer, in Brattahlid, to let some go along in his boat. There was grumbling among the Greenlanders that these folk would cause inconvenience at the best, and ill luck at the worst, but indeed, as folk said, "The lawspeaker would sell his head to become an Icelander. His eyes and ears are already theirs." And this witticism went about, and the Greenlanders were much pleased with it. Two of the Icelanders turned out to be of some use on the hunt— Thorgrim Solvason, husband of Steinunn, and the taleteller Thorstein Olafsson. Thorgim carried a great ax with a sharpened steel head, and felled many seals with it, and Thorstein carried a sword. These two Icelanders thought that this was the best hunting they had ever seen. The other Icelanders, however, had not the stomach for the killing and the blood, and were mostly good only for rowing in calm water.

It also happened on this hunt that Kollgrim Gunnarsson did a great deed, and prevented a man from his district, whose boat capsized and went under the waves, from drowning, or even getting more than his legs wet, for Kollgrim saw the danger he was in from the seething pod of seals, and maneuvered his boat near to the fellow, and so when the other boat began to turn over, Kollgrim leapt forward and grabbed this man under the arms, and dragged him into his boat, which might have capsized it, except that Kollgrim was known to have uncanny balance. Men made much of this, but Kollgrim only said that he regretted the lines and spears and oars that were lost, and the boat, too, for it was waterlogged, and could not be saved.

After the seal hunt, the autumn came on, and slaughtering of sheep, and Sira Pall Hallvardsson sent about messengers, calling folk to a great feast, in honor of St. Michael the Archangel, although some time after that feast day actually takes place. All the Greenlanders knew that the Icelanders would be there, and that they would have a great many tales and rhymes to tell, and so, although they feigned inconvenience at the trek, especially in the autumn, before the fjords were certain to be frozen, all made great efforts to get there, and those who were bedridden or otherwise incapable, called their folk together and pledged them to commit to memory as much as they could of these outlandish rhymes they were to hear.

Jon Andres, Helga, Kollgrim, Elisabet, and Egil also intended to go to this feast, although Helga was very far gone with her first child. One day while Helga was standing about the fire on which the servingmen had seared the sheeps' heads for svid, and she was stirring up the bits of wood, so that the ashes could burn all the way down for soapmaking, it came to her that she must go around the hill to Gunnars Stead, although it also seemed to her that this would be a great labor for her, as her ankles and legs were much swollen with the humors of the coming child. Still, she could not put this thought of seeing Kollgrim off from her mind, and so she called a servingman to her, and sent him to find Jon Andres, who was about the farm buildings somewhere. But the servingman returned to say that Jon Andres had gone off after some horses that were hobbled in the hills above Undir Hofdi church, and could not be found, and then Helga was tempted to send the servingman to Kollgrim, and she began to give him the message, that the knowledge had come to her that he must not go to the Gardar feast. She saw at once that the message did not fit the man, and when he repeated it back to her, she saw that it was unconvincing in his mouth, and would have no effect on Kollgrim—indeed, he would not even remember it as soon as the man was departed, and so she took a few steps away from the fire, thinking that she might go off to Gunnars Stead herself after all, but these few steps gave her such burning pains in the tops of her legs, that she sat down upon the ground, and sent the servingman off after all. And this seemed to be the case to Helga, that her own child would bring about the death of her brother. And this was something else that she thought, that folk had been expecting Kollgrim's death through misadventure for the whole of his life, and he was still walking about. So it happened that the message was given, but not heard, and all of the Ketils Stead folk and the Gunnars Stead folk went together in the large Gunnars Stead boat to Gardar, and it was so late in the season that two servingmen had to push off the ice floes with ax handles.

Sira Pall Hallvardsson was much bent with the joint ill and went about on two sticks. His knees and hips were much misshapen, and he was unable to kneel at prayer, but indeed, he said to Gunnar, if the Lord has no eyes in his head to see the burdens of his folk, then no one has such eyes. Whatever men see, the Lord sees with infinitely greater clarity. Sira Jon, he said, was indeed still alive, and he asked Gunnar please to come into the man's chamber and speak to him, for it was the case that Jon spoke of Gunnar from time to time. "My friend," said Sira Pall, "it may not soothe his spirits to see you, but it will help his eternal soul." And Gunnar followed Sira Pall Hallvardsson to the other priest's chamber with some trepidation.

Sira Jon was as small as a handful of twigs lashed together, and he lay covered with a piece of wadmal on a pallet of woven rushes. The room was close and damp, small enough so that the breathings of the man warmed it. Gunnar stood hunched beneath the low ceiling. Sira Jon's hands lay upon the coverlet. The fingers were so afflicted with the joint ill that they were turned back upon themselves, and the flesh of the man's arms had wasted away to bone. Sira Pall Hallvardsson said, "My brother, here is a soul who seeks comfort from you."

"He is a Greenlander, I see by his brawn." He spoke with bitterness.

Gunnar looked at Sira Pall Hallvardsson, and then at Sira Jon, and said, "All men seek the Lord's forgiveness for their sins. I, as well."

"It may be that the Lord forgives them, it may be that He does not. Such things are not for a priest to know, that is the substance of the tale I have to tell. Seek nothing from me, Gunnar Asgeirsson."

"Indeed, I know not what I seek, except a kindness between men."

"The Lord cares nothing for the kindness of men."

"But men care for it."

"I care not for it. You and your sister were as ripe figs, swollen with pride in your beauty and the sweetness of your wayward natures."

"I remember this not."

"It was the case that the vision came to your wife, the vision of the Virgin and the Child, and in your carelessness you deserved it not."

"Indeed, Sira Jon, I saw it not, for I was sleeping. Only the girl saw it. You must forgive her, my Birgitta, for she has suffered from her visions, and never gained pleasure from them."

"Greenlanders know little of suffering."

"It seems to me that each man knows the suffering of others through the suffering he feels. If you say to me that Greenlanders know little of suffering, then I must reply that it is you who know little of suffering."

"You Greenlanders have always held my office in small respect. I am not surprised to hear such speeches from you."

All of this time, Sira Pall Hallvardsson had been leaning himself partly against the wall and partly against his two sticks. Now he stumbled, and Gunnar reached out and lifted him up, and then said, "It seems to me that we are old men wrangling as young men. On the day of my Helga's wedding I gave up the Greenlander's pastime of cherishing enmity. I seek the forgiveness of the Lord and the kindness of men from you, Sira Jon."

"Nay, Gunnar Asgeirsson, these goods are not mine to give you. Look elsewhere than in this coffin. Be off now, for I care not to have you stooping about here any longer." And he closed his eyes. Gunnar helped Sira Pall Hallvardsson through the door and followed him into the passage. Sira Pall Hallvardsson smiled sadly into Gunnar's face, and said, "Here is the brother who was given to me. His flesh is as well known to me as my own, his words pour into my ears. I am his priest, his nurse, and his only companion, for the others about the place fear him. He nears death, and I can give him nothing for the journey."

"Thus it is that I think of my son, Kollgrim. It seems to me that there are men whose way through life is so lonely that they shun the Grace of God itself."

"Every man may be saved in the last moment of his life."

"Do all men wish to be?"

"It is said that they do."

"Then it must be the case. We are old men who will soon know for ourselves."

"Sira Audun made a prayer for me once, to tease me with it. It goes, 'Our Lord, this is I, Pall Hallvardsson, far out on the western ocean. I am the priest in this place who thinks well of You.' "

Gunnar laughed. Sira Pall Hallvardsson said, "This is my daily prayer." And they walked out of the hall and into the field, where many folk were milling about and exchanging news of the autumn.

Birgitta was sitting on the hillside, between Helga and Kollgrim, and she had her arms through theirs. Below her on the hillside sat Elisabet Thorolfsdottir, with little Egil at the breast, and though Birgitta clung tightly to Helga and Kollgrim, it was Elisabet that she was speaking to. She said, "My girl, you must sit up and hold the boy up, and let him suck the teat far into his little mouth, and then, indeed, he will not be able to bite you. But he is too young yet even to have his meat chewed for him."

Elisabet murmured, "Yes, well," in a low voice, but the child shifted and fell away from the teat again, and the mother made no effort to lift him. He began to whimper. Birgitta said again, still with patience, "Indeed, girl, your child is hungry and desires suck. Does this not give your ears pain to hear his cries?" And Elisabet remembered herself and sat up straighter on the hillside. Birgitta turned to Helga and said, so that Kollgrim could hear, "This child is as small as a puppy and prattles not, though he has lived most of a winter and a summer."

"Yes, my mother," said Helga.

"Every one of my children was standing and looking about after such a time as has passed with this one. My boy Kollgrim was already walking out of the steading. These are a poor stock, this lineage of Thorolf. Their blood is thinned by too much fish, it seems to me. They are like priests. Thorolf is willing about the steading, but indeed, at times in the winter he cannot lift himself out of the bedcloset. The son will be as bad when he has gotten on a few years. Have you hope for this child, Helga?"

"I hope in the morning that I will see him in the evening, and I hope in the evening that I will see him in the morning, and my hopes are always fulfilled."

"But soon you will have your own child, and have to give over your visits to this one."

"We may yet persuade Elisabet to bring the child to Ketils Stead. But, indeed, it is a hard thing to move her. Jon Andres declares that she looks like a bird but is as heavy as a whale."

Now Kollgrim said, "Things are not ill for her at Gunnars Stead. There is plenty of food about the place, and warm furs in the bedclosets." And after this, Birgitta and Helga gave over their talk of Elisabet and the child. Now a procession of finely dressed folk came down the hillside, and the group was comprised of Sigrid Bjornsdottir and some other Solar Fell folk and some Icelanders, including Thorstein the rhymer, Thorgrim, his wife Steinunn, her sister Thorunn, Snorri the ship's master, and some other folk. All the Greenlanders turned their heads to gaze upon these newcomers, and Kollgrim gazed upon them, too, Helga saw, as if his eyes were starting out of his head, and Helga had not known that he cared so much for Sigrid. She grew frightened, and gripped her mother's arm tightly. Now the group passed where they were sitting, and Sigrid's gaze fell first upon Helga and then upon Kollgrim, and she smiled, but as much in embarrassment as in pleasure. Helga saw that her eyes searched Kollgrim's face for a moment before dropping to the grass. Helga turned and looked at Kollgrim. He looked at Sigrid not at all, but at someone else in the group. Helga could not discover who this might be, for all were bunched together and talking merrily. Sigrid joined them with hardly a hesitation, only the hesitation of her fleeting look at Kollgrim, then at Elisabet Thorolfsdottir, then at the child. The procession passed on. Now Helga looked at her mother, and Birgitta looked as well at her daughter, and it seemed to Helga that some knowledge passed between them, and Helga was much afraid, for Birgitta had a great reputation for sight.

It was the case with this Gardar feast that there were actually two days of eating, as well as four services, for indeed, if many men were to make their way to St. Nikolaus Cathedral, then they must gorge themselves on liturgy and prayer, for they would see little enough of it through the winter, in spite of the efforts of Sira Eindridi and Sira Andres. The cathedral was always full of folk, for folk like to pray in the presence of a relic, though it be only the last finger bone of the least finger. Many offerings were left to this St. Olaf the Norwegian, and folk felt better for it. Larus the Prophet himself spent a deal of time kneeling before the reliquary, and folk remarked at the stillness of his posture and the length of his prayer. Ashild stood nearby, with little Tota, watching him, and when he was finished, she helped him to his feet, and he staggered away leaning upon her shoulder.

Now folk were called into the cathedral for the first service, and they packed in so tightly that they sat upon one another on the benches, and although there was no fire, there was sufficient warmth. Sira Eindridi pronounced the mass, and it seemed to some folk that he filled out the parts he didn't know with bits of prayers that he remembered from elsewhere, or had made up. As usual, he gave a great long sermon, full of damnation and sorrow, and dire predictions of Hell, where, he said, fire burned like ice, and damned souls eked a bit of rotten cheese out for eternity and their bellies were never full, and always raging with the stomach ill, so that they covered themselves with shit, and suchlike predictions, and during this sermon, as usual, folk began to talk quietly among themselves, which drove the priest to an even greater pitch of anger, so that his face grew as red as ash berries and he had to stop speaking for gales of breath that shook him. But now came the communion time in the service, and men fell quiet and attended to their prayers.

It happened that Sira Eindridi's sermon went on so long, and the cathedral was so close with folk that some of them had to go out into the air toward the end of the service, and one of these was Steinunn Hrafnsdottir, the Icelandic woman. She slipped away from the side of her sister Thorunn, and when she stepped onto the grass, she saw that the fjord below the cathedral was lit by the red and white glow of the setting sun, and so she thought to stroll down beside the landing place, where all the boats were drawn up on the strand. Her sister Thorunn was somewhat afraid of the Greenlanders, and disliked to walk among them alone, but Steinunn could not see this. These folk had rather poor manners, and were inclined to stare, and knew not how to speak with the proper forms, but in Steinunn's view, they were no worse than some Icelanders who lived in remote districts. The field before the cathedral sloped gently downward, and Steinunn took some deep breaths of the chilly air. She was not a little pleased to be by herself, for indeed, Thorgrim, her husband, was a hovering, attentive fellow, and his hands were always upon her. Now she walked among the little boats and marveled at them, for they were patched together any old way, out of scraps and pieces of planking, and they stank strongly of seal oil. All of Greenland stank strongly of seal oil, Steinunn had discovered. Even so, she had no longing to return to Iceland, but rather a horror of it, although Thorgrim was a powerful man there. It seemed to her that Thorgrim would do well to settle in Greenland, since he had not chosen to settle in Norway. It was said among the Greenlanders that there were many good abandoned farms, and it would not be so hard, after all, to go off to Iceland or Norway for a cargo of sheep and cows. Snorri's ship was big enough for that. Whatever Thorgrim chose to do, it seemed to Steinunn that she could not go back to Iceland, for indeed, everyone there, it was said, had died. The thought made her heart flutter, and she put her hand to her breast and stopped walking to catch her breath.

Now, in Greenland, she saw what a mistake she had made in accepting Thorgrim, a failing of will that she had expected to regret at the time, and did regret now. But her days among the Norwegians had been unhappy ones, and the only Norwegian farmer who had made an offer for her hand was a fellow with a great goiter at his neck, and although he was wealthy and powerful, she saw at once that he had never had a chance among the Norwegian girls, but had thought so little of her that he had been confident of her acceptance. A woman who had lands in Iceland, especially lands partly covered with smoking lava, was not such a prize to a Norwegian. Even if her father had been lawspeaker, her father was dead now, and his death in a volcanic avalanche so peculiar as to put folk off, unless they were Icelandic.

Thorgrim was fair enough, and it had been a great pleasure to Steinunn to speak to him of things they both knew. It seemed to her that her melancholia lifted when he was about, or else she made it lift for his sake. It lifted little now, except when she raised her eyes to the mountains of Greenland and reflected that none of them were volcanoes, that their shapes and their quiescence were changeless and eternal. The winter would pass, and the summer would come on, and Snorri would make up his mind to go off to Iceland and see what his wife had done with his farms over the years.

The sun had set, and twilight deepened over Gardar field. Only the snowy tips of the mountains cast any light back to the sky. Steinunn turned away from the boats, and began the climb back up the hillside, and she was so sunk in thoughts that she nearly stumbled over a man who was kneeling in her path between two of the boats. He leapt up and caught her, so that she did not fall, and she saw that it was the tall fellow who had been betrothed to the girl Sigrid, but she could not recall his name. She had seen him only once or twice. "Indeed," she said, "the darkness makes me careless," and it seemed to her that though she spoke of the lack of light, she was referring to her thoughts, and this fetched from her a deep and melancholy sigh.

"You have strayed from the flock gathered to hear the priest."

"And you, as well."

"Priestly talk does not much interest me."

"This Sira Eindridi likes to attract attention."

"That may be. I know nothing about it."

"Then why have you come to the feasting?"

"I heard there would be Icelandic tales. I thought they would beguile the mother of my son."

"Why does she need to be beguiled?"

"Because she is a woman, it seems to me. I know not what she is determined upon, whether life or death. Tales are entertaining to most folk. Perhaps they will draw off her thoughts from whatever they linger over now. Why have you strayed from the flock?"

"I grew breathless among them."

"I have seen you before. Among the chatterers, you have the least to say."

"Is that the case?"

"It seems so to me."

Now they fell silent, and he took her hand and placed it through his arm, and led her among the boats to a space above them, where she would have clear walking back to the cathedral, but as they stood in this space, she did not want to give up his arm, nor did he give up her hand. They stood silently for some little while, neither looking at one another nor looking away from one another, and it seemed to Steinunn that her earlier disquiet was stilled by the fellow's presence. Now he released her, and put his hand lightly on her shoulder, and pushed her away from him, and she began up the hillside, and he went back to the strand, and continued with whatever he had been doing. When she got to the cathedral, Steinunn recollected the fellow's name, Kollgrim Gunnarsson, a great object of joking among the Icelanders for his betrothal to Sigrid Bjornsdottir.

Now the time came for the first evening's feast, and all the folk poured into the great hall of the bishop's house, and sat themselves at the benches, and the women and servingmaids went about with bowls of ptarmigan stewed with seal flipper and seasoned with thyme, and this was considered a good dish, even among the Icelanders. After this came bowls of sourmilk, thick and cold, sweetened with bilberries, and these had been gathered for the feast over three separate days in the hills between Gardar and Hvalsey Fjord, and they were fat and juicy. After this came svid and also roast mutton, and this mutton was a little tough and overgrown, but savory all the same, and folk considered that they had done well to make their way to the Gardar feast. Now there was another dish, and this was dried capelin with sour butter, and this is a dish that Greenlanders are very fond of, for the little fish snap and crackle between the teeth and the butter makes the lips pucker. The Icelanders were not especially taken with this dish. Now was the moment in the feast when folk begin to push themselves away from the table, but even so, look around a bit for just a single last thing to taste before they finish. And so the women and servingmaids came about with something most folk had never tasted before, and this was angelica stalks seethed in honey, and this was so delicious and sweet that folk's teeth ached with the pleasure of it.

After this, the tables were taken away, and folk pushed the benches back, and the Icelanders began their entertainments, and it was the case that the Icelanders had been among the Greenlanders for a year, long enough for some of the Greenlanders, but especially the Solar Fell folk, to learn steps and words to a few of the rhyming songs, and so eight women, including Sigrid Bjornsdottir, and eight men stood up and made the figures while Thorstein Olafsson shouted out the song. And this was a song, an outlandish rhyme about a fellow named Troilus, who was a hero of early times, and his concubine, named Criseda, who sinned and was greatly punished for her sin. Some time passed, through the telling of other, less scandalous tales, and folk were called again into the cathedral for the second service. The first to enter the church discovered Larus the Prophet there, on his face on the stones before the crucifix, and he had to be lifted up and carried out, for he seemed insensible, and after folk spoke among themselves, it was revealed that Larus had not partaken of the feasting, but had spent the entire time at prayer in the cathedral, with Ashild and little Tota nearby. These two fell asleep, and had to be roused for the service.

This service was given by Sira Andres, who was but seventeen winters of age, and although his ways were more congenial than those of his father, he knew even less of the mass, and mumbled a great deal more. He, too, liked to make his sermons on the subject of the wages of sin, but the wages he predicted were less dire than those of Sira Eindridi, and sometimes he got lost in his text, which afforded folk a small degree of relief. This service was shorter than the earlier one, and after it, folk went to their booths and their chambers to sleep.

Now it was the case that Sira Pall Hallvardsson was to say both masses on the second day of the feast, and folk were pleased with this, because he knew all the prayers in the right order, and never mumbled, and the communion he gave was considered to be holier than the communion given by the other two, and so all of the second day there was a great deal of shriving going on, and many folk were in and out of the cathedral all day long. The first of these, who came into the darkened church long before dawn, discovered Larus the Prophet before the Crucifix, and he stayed there all day, prayers on his lips, but he was not shriven.

On this day there was a morning service, followed by a daylight feast, to be followed by an early evening service, and then folk who lived nearby would go off, and in the morning the rest of the folk would go off. It happened before the morning service that the Icelandic woman Steinunn Hrafnsdottir went out of Gardar hall and began wandering about below the buildings, not far from where the boats were drawn up on the strand, and her husband, Thorgrim Solvason, went out after her, and when he caught up with her, they fell into conversation. Thorgrim said, "My Steinunn, your sister requires your presence, for indeed, she needs you to arrange her headdress for her."

"She has arranged her headdress for many mornings before this one without my help."

"Even so, she asks after you. And this is true, as well, that it is not seemly for you to walk about like this, for there are many folk at this feast who are unknown to us."

"You and Thorunn think too ill of these Greenlanders."

"They are rough folk."

"Nay, they are ill-looking, and dress oddly, in furs and such, but they are no rougher than any other folk we might know, in Norway or in Iceland."

"How have you knowledge of this?"

Now she cocked her head and looked him in the eye. "My Thorgrim, I, too, have lived in Greenland for a year, and I, too, have spoken with Bjorn Bollason and his sons and other such folk as are about Solar Fell. May I not make up my own mind on this score?"

"It seems to me that a woman must be guided by her husband and her sister in such things."

"Thorunn is three winters younger than I am."

"But she is of a different and more cautious nature. She saw that you slipped out of the service last night and how long you absented yourself."

"Indeed, the place was very close."

"If you had found me, I would have taken you out, and we could have strolled about together, as a husband and wife should do."

"We may do that now, my Thorgrim." And so they did so, down the hill and back up it, and soon enough it was time for the service, and they went into the cathedral and found places to sit.

Now Sira Pall Hallvardsson began to pray, and then he gave a sermon of thanksgiving for the bounty of the Lord in all things, and these were some of the things he spoke of: the children of the Greenlanders, whose faces shine about every farmstead like purple stonebreak at the feast of St. Jon the Baptist, the houses of the Greenlanders, so thickly turfed that two or three seal oil lamps keep them warm in the winter; the reindeer, who give fur and flesh and bone; the seals, who give fat and fur and flesh; the winter, which gives rest; and the summer, which gives work and sunlight; the yearly round of planting and hunting and milking and harvesting and hunting again, from Yule that reminds men of birth into the world, to Easter, that reminds men of rebirth into Heaven, to the feast of all the saints, which reminds men of how to get from one to the other. And folk were much lulled by this talk, and regretted that it ended quickly, for indeed, Sira Pall Hallvardsson could not stand for a long sermon, and especially two in one day. After the service was over, folk walked out into the light. It had snowed above Gardar in the night, but the south slope of the hillside was warm and pleasant in the morning sun. And now folk talked of the coming winter, and all were sanguine about their stores of food and the health of their flocks, and some folk, who had had to do with the Icelanders, reflected among themselves that these foreign folk would do well to keep their ship in Greenland and take over some of the abandoned farmsteads that lay about in every district. Were conditions not as they had been in the days of Erik the Red, with much good land lying about for the taking? The answer was that conditions were better, for the land was improved already, with houses and byres more suited to the weather than the old sorts that Erik and his fellows had built, with their long halls and greedy great fires. Such was the gist of the Greenlanders' talk as they went in to the second feast. They were much pleased with themselves.

Toward dusk Sira Pall began upon the second service, and he spoke the prayers in a low sonorous voice that was pleasant to hear. The cathedral was as full of folk as it had been for the first service, for, indeed, even those from the farthest districts were loath to miss any of Sira Pall Hallvardsson's service, for he was an old man, and who was to say that he would survive the winter? Not everyone did.

It happened as he was finishing the Kyrie that Larus the Prophet spoke up and said in a loud voice, in Norse, "The Lord is with me! Hear me speak!" and a farmer who lived in his district, standing near him, said, "Indeed, Larus, you speak out of turn. Now it is time to hear the priest speak." Some other men put their hands on Larus' shoulders, but he shook them off. "Nay," he cried, "the Word of the True Lord is never out of turn, but calls out from the mouths of babes, or from the wind that howls in the mountains, if it must. Here is what I say to you: Rome has abandoned you! The pope thinks of you not! The archbishop of Nidaros sleeps peacefully every night, untroubled by the knowledge of your long-ings! Those who guide your souls care not whether you fall into sin daily, or hourly, or moment by moment! They spend not a crown nor do they lift a finger to help you toward your salvation. They think more of their underlinen than they do of your souls! They have forbidden you to save yourselves, and now they refuse to save you! Have you wafers? Have you wine? Do you think that the blood of the Lord was water and His flesh was seaweed? It is not written so. Indeed, Greenlanders, you are cursed, not blessed, however you fill your bellies, because the path to salvation is closed to you. Perhaps the Lord Himself speaks to the archbishop of Nidaros, and bids him in his ear to send the Greenlanders a ship, and some priests that have been duly consecrated, not like these false Greenlanders who call themselves Sira, but have never been ordained, but the archbishop of Nidaros stops his ears. He hears not the word of the Lord, nor does he hear the cries of the Greenlanders for salvation. All these folk that have died here, these wives and husbands and mothers and fathers and brothers and sisters who have died of the vomiting ill and the stomach ill and through mischance and starvation and freezing to death and drowning, think you that they have made their way to Heaven? Think you that they sit at the feet of the Lord, and listen each day to the singing of angels?

Nay, 'tis not so. They burn in Hell, for they are unshriven of their sins, they are not in communion with the Lord, they are the abandoned of the earth, and Jesus Himself hears not their cries. This is what I say to you!" And after he had spoken, Larus looked about himself, and the Greenlanders were hard put for words, for no man had the knowledge in him to deny what Larus had said.

Now Sira Pall Hallvardsson resumed the service where he had left off, as if Larus had not spoken, but almost at once, the loud chattering of the Greenlanders interrupted his prayers, so that he had to raise his voice to make himself heard, and now the Greenlanders subsided, and Sira Pall Hallvardsson made his way through the service to the sermon, and then folk sat up and looked at him, for they were curious to see if he would address Larus, and how he would do so. And this is what he said: "It happened one day that the Lord Jesus Christ did go into a town in the east by the name of Bethany, and He spent the night there with some very poor folk, so that when He arose in the morning, He saw that they had but a single loaf of bread among them, although there were seven of them, and so He said that He hungered not, and He bid them farewell, but indeed, He was a man like all men, and He hungered greatly for His morning meat. There was a fig tree by the side of the road, and though it was covered with leaves and blossoms, even so, no man could find a single fig upon it, and with the wrath that comes to all men when they have hungered and been denied, the Lord Jesus Christ, in His manly nature, said to the tree, 'Ye be cursed henceforward, and neither will ye send forth leaves, nor blossoms, nor fruit ever again,' and at once the tree withered and died, even before the very eyes of the folk standing about.

"Now these folk marveled among themselves at the tree, and were greatly surprised, but our Lord Jesus Christ thought little of their amazement, and this is what He said to them, and He was greatly wrathful, 'In sooth, I say to you that if ye have faith and doubt not, ye shall not only do this which is done to the fig tree, but this also: if you say to the mountain that looms above you, blocking the sunlight, Be thou removed and be thou cast into the sea that swirls at the foot of the homefield, this too shall be done. For this is the truth that I say to you, and you must listen with your ears and your heart, whatsoever you shall ask in prayer, believing, you shall receive it, for I am listening to you, and I am the Lord God who is powerful over all.' " And now Sira Pall stepped back to the altar, and continued with the service, and gave communion to all who stepped forward to receive it, but even so, men considered that Larus had not been well answered, and they were much cast down. It was the case, after all, that Sira Pall had not dared to gaze up to the mountain and order it into the sea, had he?

Now the winter came on, and the weather was bad from the beginning, warm and rainy, or dry and windy, so that sand came into the byres even after they were closed up with stones, and the turves about the steadings grew sodden with wet, and then crumbled away in the wind, but little snow or still weather came into any district, and it remained this way through Yule. It also happened that not so long after these happenings at Gardar, a child was born to Helga Gunnarsdottir at Ketils Stead, and this child was a girl, who was named Gunnhild, but Helga did not recover from this confinement as quickly as she might have, and was still in her bedcloset at Yule, greatly weakened. It also happened that the child Egil Kollgrimsson suffered a great mischance, for as he was sleeping by the side of his mother in her bedcloset, while Kollgrim was away hunting, Elisabet Thorolfsdottir rolled upon him in her sleep, and smothered him, and he was found lifeless in the morning, and Helga was much cast down by this news, as well.

This was the second winter that the Icelanders stayed at Solar Fell, Thorgrim and Steinunn as well as Snorri and Thorunn and her husband, and in this winter the Icelanders began to talk among themselves of returning to Iceland, but Snorri the shipmaster was disinclined to hurry his decision. Conditions were pleasant enough among the Greenlanders, and conditions in Iceland were unknown, but reputed to be ill. Snorri sought out Bjorn Bollason, but Bjorn Bollason's eagerness for the company of the Icelanders was unstinting. The ship was not in such good repair, and Snorri was disinclined to make the effort to repair it. In short, the winter weather was not so ill as to drive Snorri away, and so those who were more eager to go, as Thorgrim was, mumbled their discontent into their beards.

Steinunn shared Snorri's disinclination, and was pleased enough with the way he put Thorgrim and the others off, but she was pleased with little else, and the howling of the dry wind about the corners of the steading grew tedious to her. She could not sit at her weaving or subdue her hands to spinning, but wrung them together repeatedly, so that Thorgrim was always looking at her, as if to probe her temper. Indeed, had he asked her, she would not have known what to say, except that the blackest melancholy was upon her, but a melancholy so irritating that she could neither sit nor sleep nor take pleasure in her meat. It happened that Thorunn grew much annoyed with her, and so enmity between the two sisters was added to the discontent of the Icelanders, and the folk at Solar Fell were somewhat less merry than they had been the previous winter.

Now it happened that Signy, Bjorn's wife, came to Thorunn one day and said the following, "Thorunn Hrafnsdottir, you have been a good friend to me in your time among the Greenlanders."

Thorunn smiled. "Whoever is not a good friend to such a generous hostess is ill-mannered indeed, but aside from this, it seems to me that we see alike in some matters, and that our talk has been pleasant to both of us."

"So it seems to me as well. But now there must be unpleasant talk." And she fell silent, for, as folk said, Signy of Solar Fell preferred starvation to unpleasant talk.

"You may say what you wish to say to me, my Signy, and it will not diminish our friendship."

"It is the case in Greenland that winters are very long, and steadings are very close, and folk bump elbows even on the largest holdings, like Solar Fell."

"This is the case throughout the north." Thorunn smiled. "Greenlanders think they are alone in their hardships, I have discovered."

"Perhaps so. I cannot judge this. But it seems to me that the darkness of your sister's spirits casts itself over all, Icelanders and Greenlanders alike, and Yule is hardly past. Greenlanders do not consider the winter to be over until the cows are carried out of the byre after Easter."

"It is true that my sister is not of a sanguine nature, and in the past she has been given to these sulks."

"She, and Thorgrim, too, should he wish, might go to Gardar and stay among the priests. Sira Pall is much loved among the Greenlanders, and Sira Eindridi is a brisk fellow. But indeed, it seems to me that I am being inhospitable, and my own words shame me."

"Folk who stay with others for over a year must live on other terms than mere hospitality, and it seems to me that such a removal would please her, or if not, please us and do her good." And now the two women saw that they were agreed on this score, and smiled together and planned how to approach the subject with Thorgrim.

And so it happened that Steinunn Hrafnsdottir was removed to Gardar, and Thorgrim with her, except that after a few days, Thorgrim found the spot gloomy and dull, compared to Solar Fell. All the Icelanders who had been staying there in the previous winter had gone to other steadings, there was little to do, and the cooking was rather ill. After Thorgrim returned to Solar Fell, Steinunn persuaded Sira Eindridi to give her an outside chamber, one not far from the doorway to the homefield and to the cathedral, for Steinunn declared that she wished to go freely to her prayers without disturbing the life of the priest's house, and so she did, and she prayed a great deal, and also walked about a great deal for there was little snow. After this, Sira Eindridi went off to the south with Sira Andres, for the beginning of Lent was near at hand.

And so it happened one day that Steinunn Hrafnsdottir saw Kollgrim Gunnarsson carrying a string of furs down from the hills above Gardar, and after that she began meeting him from time to time, and these meetings left her spirits in a state of peacefulness, more than they were after prayer. And she and he went on like this for a short time, and their meetings were pleasing to both of them, so that they began to be careless about who might see them, for indeed, as Steinunn declared, they exchanged but talk, and the gestures it is proper for a man to show a woman, namely to help her over rocks and rills and up and down hillsides, if she is walking about, or to help her to her feet, if she is sitting and wishes to stand up.

After some days, it seemed to Steinunn Hrafnsdottir that she had conceived a great passion for Kollgrim Gunnarsson that he did not return, though indeed, he sought her out with as much frequency as possible, but even so, his ways were so reserved and self-contained that it seemed to her that he left her presence each time with hardly a regret or a thought of her, while thoughts of him ate her up, and gave her no relief until she saw him again. He was in her mind so constantly that she hardly knew how he looked, but only that he stood over her, and that his presence was as a balm and as a sting at the same time. Now it happened for some two days that she poured herself into her prayers, and went only from her room to the cathedral, where she lay on the stones in front of the crucifix, and begged the Lord for relief from her longings, but indeed, she avoided all the priests, and did not confess her sin, for it was the case that she did not yet wish to give it up, in spite of her prayers. It is truly said that the Lord hears many things that are not meant for His ears.

During these two days, Kollgrim Gunnarsson went away from Gardar, to Vatna Hverfi district, where he sat about Ketils Stead, but he had little to say to Jon Andres, or to Helga, and looked hardly at all at Gunnhild, although she was a comely babe, and lively and full of smiles. And Helga saw him go off without thinking much of his visit, except that he must be full of sorrow at the death of Egil Kollgrimsson. Kollgrim went back to Gardar, and it happened that he met Steinunn Hrafnsdottir at the cathedral door, as she was going back to her room, and he took her in his arms and embraced her tightly, and it seemed to her that her prayers had been answered, and that her longings were stilled forever.

Now it happened some days later that Thorstein Olafsson the taleteller and another Icelander by the name of Bork, as well as some servants belonging to Magnus Arnason, came on skis to Gardar to have talk with Sira Pall Hallvardsson, and also to carry back to Magnus' steading some belongings of Thorstein's and Bork's that they had left behind. There was now just enough snow on the ground for this skiing, but the going was difficult, and took longer than Thorstein and Bork had expected, and so when they arrived, late in the evening, they were hungry and full of annoyance.

The servants at Gardar had gone off to their bedclosets, and Thorstein and Bork, who was a loud, unrestrained fellow, began walking about the cathedral and the residence, shouting and beating upon the doors, until one of the servingmen got up and let them in. Then it was the case that they demanded food, and so the cook, a woman named Una, got up and began to put some things together. While she was doing this, Thorstein went out of the priest's house to relieve himself in the privy, and it happened that he went out by the door nearest the chamber occupied by Steinunn Hrafnsdottir, and he heard noises coming from this chamber, namely the cries and moanings of a woman, and he paused and listened for a moment through the door. Then he went outside and did his business, and returned. The sounds had died down, and he thought not of them for a while. After eating, he and Bork and Magnus Arnason's servants went off to their rest, and all awakened late in the morning, after the day's work had already begun.

Bork and Thorstein were not anxious to begin the return journey to Vatna Hverfi district, simply because the skiing was so ill, and so they walked about the Gardar fields after they had their morning meat, putting off their errands, and chatting about this and that. Now it was the case that they saw a man down the hillside, dressed in thick furs, doing something among the boats that had been drawn up on the strand and turned over for the winter, and Thorstein saw that this man was Kollgrim Gunnarsson, and so he watched him closely, for it was the case that Thorstein thought highly of Sigrid Bjornsdottir, and often wondered to himself about this fellow Kollgrim, whom the girl had been all set to marry before he, Thorstein, came along.

The fact was that Thorstein didn't think much of Kollgrim. He was tall enough and well-enough looking, but he had none of the talents that please folk when they are sitting about the steading in the winter, and so was fairly useless, it seemed to Thorstein, but it was also the case that he drew folk's eyes, and caused them to consider him when they would rather consider something more pleasant, and so Thorstein looked upon Kollgrim,

and considered him, when he would rather have been considering something else. It came to him to wonder, in fact, whether the fellow had
tupped the young heifer in the course of their betrothal, for Sigrid, as all
folk knew, was allowed a great deal of freedom in her coming and going,
and in every other way, as well, and so such a thing was certainly possible.
Once this thought had come to Thorstein, he could not get it out of his
mind, and he stared at Kollgrim until Bork shook him and led him off.

Now the day went on, and Steinunn Hrafnsdottir came out of her
room and went into the great hall of the residence, and there she encountered Thorstein Olafsson, who was continuing to put off his departure, and
he was as surprised to see her as she was to see him, for he had not known
that she was at Gardar. She greeted him kindly, and stepped forward and
took his hand, but he saw that she reddened to the roots of her hair, and
cast her eyes about as much as she looked upon him, and the thought of
Kollgrim Gunnarsson tupping Sigrid Bjornsdottir came into his mind, and
after he had had a few moments of talk with Steinunn, and she had gone
off to do some weaving, he went to Bork, and declared that they would
stay another night, and leave early the next morning.

Now Steinunn sat at her weaving, and she could hardly lift her hands
to grasp the shuttle, for she saw that the presence of Thorstein Olafsson
must put off any meetings with Kollgrim, but indeed, it seemed to her that
these meetings were so necessary to her peace of mind that to put them
off would be insupportable, and as she thought of these things, her longings, which had been quiet enough before seeing Thorstein, rose up and
battered her, so that it was not enough to meet him later in the afternoon,
as she had planned, but she must see him right now, and speak to him, and
touch his sleeve, his arm, lay her head upon his breast, entwine her fingers
with his. And she put her hands down and grasped her bench to prevent
herself from rising up and running to where she knew he was, which was
down by the strand, sorting his snares. And so she sat, gripping her bench
and staring at the unfinished weaving in the great Gardar loom.

Now it came to her that Thorstein had seen the mark of sin upon
her, for it is said that this is readily visible to men of astute vision, and
certainly Thorstein had that reputation, and now Steinunn became curious
to know what she looked like, and she looked down at her robe, and saw
that it lay smoothly across her belly and breasts. And she felt her headdress,
and felt that it was neatly arranged, and she was somewhat relieved, and
grew convinced that all things could be hidden within, at least from the
sight of men. Was not Thorgrim assured of her pleasure in his caresses, even
though she took none? But now she recalled how her face had grown hot

when first she laid her eyes upon Thorstein, and how her hand had trembled, just a bit, when she put it into his, and how she had looked about the Gardar hall rather than into his face, and it was hard to know what he would make, if anything, of these signs, or indeed, what the servants, who knew him from the previous winter, would say to him. Now her flesh chilled and hardened at this thought, and her breath left her, for she had been careless about the servingfolk, and at Gardar they were everywhere. She had been careless of everything, in fact, except of seeing Kollgrim, for he had filled her mind and driven out all other thoughts. It seemed to her that he could save her from these consequences that she was turning over in her mind, and the urge to run to where he was was nearly uncontrollable, but then it seemed to her that nothing could save her from them, and she sat still on her bench.

It happened then that Sira Pall Hallvardsson came into the hall and asked Steinunn if she was warm enough, for she appeared to be blanched with the cold, and she said, "I was occupied with my thoughts, and I did not notice the cold, but now that you speak of it, it seems to me that I am chilled to the bone."

He took off his cloak, which was of sealskin, and placed it around her, and as he did this, she began to shiver under his touch. He sat down beside her on the weaving bench and smiled upon her, and she clutched the sealskin cloak about her shoulders, but indeed, it seemed to her that she was chilled, not with the Greenland winter that folk made so much of, but with the frost of sin, and this cold sat in her bones and floated out of her and chilled the room, the hall, the world itself. Sira Pall Hallvardsson's kindly smile offered to warm her as the sun warms the green hillside, and news of her sin came into her mouth. She saw that prayers had been no relief, but instead had brought her to thinking upon her desires without ceasing. It seemed to her a clear and simple act, to confess that she was an adulteress, and ask forgiveness, and abase herself before the priest, the Lord, the Icelanders, and the Greenlanders. Such words as she needed were simply formed, and he was waiting for them, rubbing his knee with his hand, as she had noticed he often did, his old head, nearly bald, cocked quizzically. Such tidings as she had to tell him he made seem like a gift that he longed to receive. Surely it was a gift that she longed to give. She touched his hand, the one that was rubbing his knee, with her finger, and turned her eyes to his, but at the end, she could not divide herself from Kollgrim. Were she to speak these words that hung on her lips, it came to her that she would never see nor speak to Kollgrim again, not feel his presence nor move under the touch of his hand nor know the weight of his gaze. Most of all, he would never again carry to her the peace of mind that she craved, and that he never failed to give her. And so it happened that she swallowed her words, put her hand in her lap, and smiled as women do when they are open and free of deceit. Sira Pall sat with her in silence for some little while, then a servingmaid came to him with a message from the cook, about meat for Sira Jon, and he went off. And so it was that all was lost.

Now Thorstein went to one of the servingmaids, with whom he had been friendly in the previous winter, and he asked her where the woman Steinunn might have her chamber, and the servingmaid pointed out the chamber where Thorstein had listened at the door the previous evening, and now Thorstein said, "And where does the Vatna Hverfi fellow, Kollgrim Gunnarsson, have his chamber?" And the girl glanced up at him, and smiled slightly, and said, "Nay, sir, Kollgrim has no chamber here," and from this Thorstein knew all he needed to know, and toward dusk he went up the hillside, taking Bork with him, and it was his plan to find Thorgrim Solvason and Snorri Torfason and bring them back with him to Gardar.

Also toward dusk, Kollgrim Gunnarsson went away from Gardar in another direction, around the bottom of the fjord and up the side of the big mountain, called Bishops Fell, that stands above Gardar to the east. He was intending to lay some snares for ptarmigan, and gather them up the next morning, and take them, with some other meat, to Gunnars Stead, for he rather feared for Elisabet Thorolfsdottir. It happened, however, that as Kollgrim climbed the mountain, he was overtaken with a great fatigue, and the desire to lie down and sleep possessed him, and so he did so, and he dreamed the following dream:

A man was sitting beside a small booth that had been pitched in a great icefield, and he had with him some weapons—two or three fine spears and a bow with some bird arrows. He also had an ax, but this ax was in poor shape, with the handle broken and the blade almost rusted away. The man sat very still, and looked off into the whiteness, and he did not wear a hood against snow blindness. Now it happened in Kollgrim's dream that a group of seals came out of the water, and began moving toward the man with that great swishing and flapping noise that seals make, and that reverberates across the ice. The man sat up straight and brought his weapons near to his hands, for he intended to kill some seals for winter meat. The seals came closer and closer, in a great group, many at the front and many more behind, and the man thought how easy it would be to kill any number he cared to have, and he was very pleased with himself. The seals drew closer. As they neared him, and he saw their faces, the man saw that the seals had the smiles of men, and that they were not seals, but the souls

of drowned men, and the man knew that it was great ill luck to kill any
such seals, and so he put his weapons away from him, and vowed to do
no harm. But still the seals came on, and drew closer to him, and did not
swerve to avoid him, so he stood up and waved his arms at them, and now
the dream changed, and the man was underneath the seals, and they were
eating the flesh off his bones, though his arms and legs still flailed about,
showing that the life was still in him. And after this dream, Kollgrim
awakened, and looked about, and saw that it was completely dark, except
for the light of the stars in the arctic sky, and he thought to set his snares,
as he had planned, for as a rule, he thought little of dreams. But after such
a dream, the taking of game seemed distasteful to him, and so he turned
down the mountain, and sought the chamber of Steinunn Hrafnsdottir, and
she was much gratified to receive him.

Always it was a pleasure to Steinunn simply to sit in the presence of
Kollgrim Gunnarsson, for silence seemed to be his natural state, and this
silence flowed over her like a balm, especially after the sting of desire had
been eased. But on this evening, there was another quality to the silence,
the quality of something withheld rather than of everything given, and
Steinunn found herself fidgeting after him—touching his arm more than
she meant to, or putting her hand in his hair, as if to draw his attention
toward her, when she had never had to make this gesture before, and she
was much cast down by this, for she saw that in the space of the day, what
she had sought to keep for herself through sin and deceit had been lost
anyway, and she went off from him, and sat by herself on the edge of the
bedcloset, and he did not follow her, but sat abstracted and deep in thought.
Now she put off her shoes and pulled on her bed socks, and climbed into
the bedcloset, and lay there without speaking for a long while, and it
happened that the small seal oil lamp that had been illuminating the
chamber went out, and the chamber grew dark.

Sometime after this, Steinunn heard Kollgrim stand up from his stool,
and begin to remove his shirt and reindeer hide boots. Then she heard his
footsteps approach across the stones and the rushes of the floor, and then
she sensed his presence, and felt his hand in the straw, and then upon her,
upon her shoulder, and as he climbed into the bedcloset with her, he said,
"My Steinunn, I have had a dream, and I wish for you to interpret it for
me, for I know little of such things," and he told her the dream that had
come to him on the mountainside, and she lay for a long while after that,
turning the dream over in her mind, and finally she said, "My Kollgrim,
it seems to me that this dream predicts your death, and that these creatures
were not seals with the smiles of men, but men with the shapes of seals.

It is not in the wastelands that you will find your death, but among men, and it also seems to me that you should go in haste right now, and leave this chamber and this steading, and seek Gunnars Stead. That is how I interpret your dream." But Kollgrim made no reply, nor did he release the woman that he held in his arms, but instead gripped her more tightly and she him, and they lay there in perfect silence for most of the night.

It happened that the sounds of newcomers came to the ears of Kollgrim Gunnarsson as the snufflings of hares in the snow would come to him, noises that would go unheard by others, and so he kissed Steinunn Hrafnsdottir upon the lips, and slipped out of the bedcloset and put on his long shirt, then he took up his weapons and sat down on the stool that was in the room. There was no light, only the clamor of men approaching, and then of the door being beaten upon, and falling inward with a crash. Light came into the room, and the faces of the Icelanders, eager to see what could be seen, and they saw that Kollgrim was fully armed and ready, with a sharp ax and a dagger. His bow and sets of arrows, for birds and hares and foxes, lay behind him with some spears.

Thorstein carried a sword and Thorgrim his ax. They stopped and looked about the room, and at length, Thorgrim said, "Where is the whore?"

"Steinunn Hrafnsdottir lies in the bedcloset."

"It is permitted in law," said Bjorn Bollason, "for the husband to kill you, Kollgrim Gunnarsson."

"He may try to do it," said Kollgrim. "It is not written in the law, I'll warrant, that I may not try to kill him, as well. My father's uncle, Hauk Gunnarsson, was a great bear killer in the Northsetur, it is said. A man is smaller than a bear. I have never killed a man before, but I am ready to do it."

"There are six of us," said Bjorn Bollason.

"But you are my father's sworn friend," said Kollgrim. "I do not think that you or most of these folk have the stomach to do it, and I do not think the others have the prowess to escape unscathed. Thorgrim Solvason, you should have asked yourself whether being cuckolded was preferable to being killed. Many folk consider that it is." He picked up his ax. "At any rate, Bolli should be off to fetch the priest, for some of us need to be shriven now, and no man can say who that might be." Bolli looked to Bjorn, but Bjorn looked not at him, for indeed, as always, he did not quite know what to do. Now Snorri the shipmaster spoke up. "Not every plan goes aright the first time, and this plan seems to me doomed. Our blood is not so hot as it was in the passage, and men need hot blood for fighting. But there are ways, when blood has cooled, for punishing those who sin without care. It seems to me that for now it is best to take the woman to her sister and let the cock go off to his own coop. But these doings are not finished as yet." And so, while Kollgrim sat upon the stool, Thorgrim and Bork went to the bedcloset, and brought forth Steinunn Hrafnsdottir, who was pliant, but nearly insensible, and could not stand or sit, and had to be carried off in the arms of her husband; indeed, she could not even hold her arms around his neck. After these folk left, Kollgrim went off on his skis to Vatna Hverfi district, and stayed there for the rest of the winter, until nearly Easter.

It seemed to Thorunn Hrafnsdottir that her sister had been bewitched, for she could neither speak nor lift her hands, but only lay in her bedcloset with her eyes half closed. The broth that was spooned between her lips ran out the sides of her mouth. If she was pinched or slapped, she winced not, nor showed any pain. Neither Thorunn nor Signy had ever seen such a thing, except that Thorunn had heard of a child in Hordaland and another man in Borgarfjord in Iceland, who had had these spells put over them by witches, and they spoke frequently of such things—for indeed, said Thorunn, the priests in Norway were much concerned with witches and sorcery and devilish practices. Through talking, Signy and Thorunn became convinced that Steinunn had been bewitched, for otherwise her actions were unaccountable, they agreed. Thorstein half agreed with them, as well, for he had gone about among the Norwegians for a number of winters, and had himself heard numerous tales of these sorts of practices, done in secret. Besides, he told the women, how else would such a fellow as Kollgrim Gunnarsson make himself attractive to a woman such as Steinunn, whose husband was a respectable man, handsome and personable and talkative, as well as prosperous and well-mannered? Now Signy took issue with this, and maintained that Kollgrim was a fine Greenlandic man, with a good farmstead and many skills, but the others dismissed her opinion, for indeed, she had been in favor of Sigrid's marriage to the fellow, had she not? Sigrid herself had been sent with Margret Asgeirsdottir to Dyrnes, to her uncle's steading, along with the two younger boys, so that the sight of Steinunn Hrafnsdottir would not weigh upon their spirits too much.

As for Thorgrim, he did not know what to make of these events, for his wife Steinunn seemed to him to have had no complaints. Indeed, she had always smiled upon him, and held her hand out to him, and served him as a wife should do. All features of her behavior seemed unaccountable to him. He could not remember that she had ever looked upon this

Greenlandic fellow throughout the time when he had been about Solar
Fell, nor had she ever spoken to him. Thorgrim could not see what the
fellow had done to draw her eyes to him, and when Thorstein mentioned
that there were such spells, it seemed to Thorgrim that this was the only
possibility for explaining what she had become. In fact, it seemed to
Thorgrim that there must have been two spells, one to draw her eyes and
affections to the fellow, and another to render her numb as a stone, as she
was now. That, it seemed to Thorgrim, was what the fellow had been
doing before he sat upon the stool, bewitching Steinunn so that she would
never be as she had been before. Thorgrim was much cast down, and sought
out Thorstein's company day and night, for Thorstein was rather older and
more experienced than Thorgrim.

Now Snorri and Thorstein and Bjorn Bollason sat with their heads
together, preparing to summon a case against Kollgrim before the Thing,
and they had strong disagreements about the nature of the case, for Thorstein and Snorri wanted to have the man convicted of witchcraft as well
as adultery, because for the one, the penalty was lesser outlawry, which
would be no punishment at all for Kollgrim Gunnarsson, as accustomed
as he was to the wastelands, but the penalty for the other was death by
burning, at least in Iceland and Norway. Bjorn Bollason did not know
what the penalty was in Greenland, as there had never been such a case that
he had heard of. To this, Snorri and Thorstein made the answer that the
laws of one northern place were much the same as the laws of another,
since the king was the head of all. Bjorn Bollason cited certain laws that
were held among the Greenlanders, especially about trade, that went
against the king's laws, but indeed, the three did not know, for a long time,
how to agree on this question, and so they argued about it every day, and
there was no improvement in the condition of Steinunn Hrafnsdottir, and
it seemed as though she would die.

Now it happened that shortly after Kollgrim returned to Gunnars
Stead, Helga went around the mountain, carrying little Gunnhild, and she
was much afraid of what she would find at her brother's steading, for she
had not been there in a long while, since before the death of Egil
Kollgrimsson. But when Helga pushed open the door to the steading, she
grew sanguine, for things about the rooms were neat and well arranged,
more so than they had been in many seasons. A fire was laid and a bird
was roasting on a spit above the fire, and Helga turned the spit, then went
out again. Elisabet Thorolfsdottir was in the storehouse when Helga found
her, cutting pieces of some cheese that Helga had made for the Gunnars
Stead folk the previous summer. Helga saw that there were four large

rounds of cheese left, a fair number for so late in the winter, and she said, "My girl, you have been a thrifty housewife, to have so many whole cheeses these days. We will be coming to you with our hands out before Easter." But Elisabet did not look around or smile. Helga stepped closer. "Has Kollgrim returned, then?"

"He has. He has returned from another bed, that is what he has done."

Helga laughed aloud at the absurdity of such a thought, and Elisabet Thorolfsdottir looked up at her bitterly. "You may laugh if you please, but he has been discovered with the Icelandic woman, Steinunn Hrafnsdottir, and only just escaped being killed by some Icelanders. It seems to me that he should have been killed by them. It is a thought I think on every moment of the day, because it gives me such pleasure. As poor as my father Thorolf's steading was, and as meager the meat, I regret the day he went off to Gunnar Asgeirsson, for on that day it seems to me I was destroyed."

Helga had no answer to this, but only hugged her child tightly to her breast, and stared at the servingmaid, who stared back at her. At last, Helga whispered, "Is my brother nearby?"

"He may be in the byre doing something. I know not. He seeks my bedcloset at night, not to come into it with me, but to speak of my Egil. He draws news of the boy out of me, and it seems to me that with his questions he stabs me with a dagger, and with my answers, he pulls the dagger out of me, and yet I can't turn him away, for indeed, Helga Gunnarsdottir, he is in great torment." And Helga saw that the other woman's eyes filled with tears.

Now Helga was much afraid to discover her brother, and it seemed to her that she could go off to Ketils Stead and send Jon Andres in her place, but as she stood still, making up her mind what to do, Kollgrim appeared at her back, and said, "My sister, you have come a long way to find little."

She turned and said, in a low voice, and all the time holding the infant tightly against her, "My Kollgrim, what do I find here?"

"Mortal folk, preparing to seek their fate."

"What trouble have you made for yourself?"

"Some men are angry with me. I care not about that. But I am parted from my soul, and so there is little left of me to entertain you here."

"Is it true that you have been with one of the Icelandic women? If you keep apart from her, it is not such a great crime. They will be unable to kill you, and the penalty in law must be small these days, for the ways of folk are looser than they once were. I cannot see how this could be such a great trouble, and yet . . ."

"And yet, indeed. Gunnars Stead seems to me to have been transported northward by devils, so dark is it about the place." He smiled. "Take your child away, my Helga. Here is the last thing I will say to you: all of my life, I have sought to take everything from you, to have you to myself, for I thought this was my due, and whenever you turned away from me, even to fetch me something, I hated you for it, and wanted more of you. Oh, my Helga, I am heartily sorry for this, and I beg your forgiveness, and as much as I always desired you, so much do I now desire you to stay away, and not be drawn to me or to this trouble, neither you nor your husband, nor our father, and so you must go off with the child, and say nothing to Jon Andres, and send no messages to our father, who has been trying to save me from my fate for my whole life. You must make me this vow."

"How can I?"

"You must, or I will take you by the arm and not let you go until you do, as I did once before."

"I will say nothing, but I will pray, as I did once before."

"And it will have the same result as it had once before, I trust. Now be off." And Helga turned and went off, and for two days she kept her vow not to speak of this matter to Jon Andres, but after that he came to her, with news of his own that he had heard from other folk, and she answered the questions he asked her.

Now Easter came on, and Bjorn Bollason had agreed with the Icelanders that if Steinunn Hrafnsdottir made no change in her insensible condition by Easter, then he would summon the case as seduction by witchcraft, and as Easter approached, and the woman sank deeper and deeper, he sent for Sira Eindridi, for he wanted to speak to the priest about witchcraft, and Sira Eindridi came as fast as he could on skis, although he had other duties to attend to. Bjorn was sitting at his evening meat when a servingman came into the steading with news that Sira Eindridi and another man were approaching, and Bjorn jumped up and went out of the door to the steading, feeling the eyes of the Icelanders upon his back. Now he went down the slope, and met Sira Eindridi below the shrine to St. Olaf the Greenlander, and before the priest even had his skis off, Bjorn was walking back and forth in perplexity, pouring out the tale of Steinunn Hrafnsdottir. "Indeed," he said, "with Sigrid, and now Steinunn, it seems to me that these women are unaccountable. As soon as they grasp a man, they cease to want him, but want another."

"Desires flow through them like the breezes, that is all we know about them," said Eindridi.

"Now Snorri and Thorstein have been convinced by Thorunn Hrafnsdottir that the fellow used witchcraft to win her sister, and they say they have seen such things many times before. Indeed, they are common as flies in Norway and other places like that."

"Such a thing would not surprise me. The Devil works among us, and he has his agents. This fellow Kollgrim spends all his time in the waste districts, where the Devil holds sway. And he goes there alone, not with other men. How hard would it be for the Devil to come to him and speak privily into his ear? How hard would it be for the Devil to take the shape of a hare or a fox or a seal, and speak unto him, and tempt him? And how hard would it be for such a man to resist? The Gunnars Stead folk have always been wayward, even for Greenlanders. Does this woman Margret Asgeirsdottir take communion or confess herself? Nay, she keeps her own counsel, does she not?"

"You speak as hardly as the Icelanders."

"We have known each other for many winters, Bjorn Bollason, and surely by this time you know that I speak my mind. Sira Pall Hallvardsson has done the Greenlanders an ill service by being so weak and kindly. They think that sin is a little thing, and that the Lord is their mother, who pats them on the head and sends them off to find another pleasure when they have destroyed their own playthings."

"Even so, what are the laws about witchcraft? Know you those of the Church? I'll warrant you are as ignorant of them as I am"

"What we don't know of the letter, we know of the spirit. This Snorri is full of notice. I suspect that he knows more than he tells of such things. And the laws of most places are the same in regard to most grave crimes."

"That is what the Icelanders say."

"If there is a devil among us, then it is a greater sin to let him go free than to punish a guiltless man, for as soon as a guiltless man receives his death, he is forgiven in the eyes of the Lord, and welcomed all the more fervently into Heaven for the injustice of his punishment. But a devil who goes free turns others away from the Lord, and brings them into the kingdom of Satan, does he not?"

And Bjorn had no answer for this, and it seemed to him right and proper that in this circumstance, he should give his judgment over to Sira Eindridi, who, as a priest, would know more of such things.

In Hvalsey Fjord, the winter weather was somewhat colder and snowier than it was in districts farther inland, and it seemed to Gunnar that he and his household folk had a difficult time of it this year, for indeed, he saw that everyone was old now, and more or less afflicted with the joint ill, or other ills. Only Johanna and Thorolf's son Egil could not be called elderly, but Johanna was getting past the marriageable age without suitable offer, and Gunnar was getting past the age of having the vigor to go to every Thing and negotiate a match for her. The fact was that her virtues were those that become known after long acquaintance—at first she might seem to a shallow young man rather forbidding and unpretty, for though she had the Gunnars Stead features, they were not softened by anything from Birgitta, and in repose, her face seemed to be carved from stone. That out of this stone mouth often came remarks of such pungency that Gunnar was delighted for days was not a marketable quality in a wife. In addition to this, she seemed pleased enough with her condition, and, like Helga before her, considered finding a match more of a duty than a pleasure. Gunnar was nearly decided not to go to the Thing this year, although he had never missed the assembly in his adult life, even when most farmers of the settlement were keeping away.

But it was the case that Birgitta would not be capable of making the trip, and Gunnar did not care to go away from her. These days she was much afflicted by the joint ill, in her fingers, and her shoulders, and her hips, so that there was little she could bear to do for the pain of it. The dampness of the winter helped her not, but instead increased her pain and the red swelling of her finger joints so that Gunnar had to take her hands in his and rub them gently for long periods of time, and also to feed her, and carry her about, for it was the case that he was hardly afflicted with the joint ill at all, and stood as straight as a young man. It was also the case that as he stayed with her and carried her about, he tried to convince her to remove with him to Gunnars Stead, where she could be with Kollgrim and the girl, Elisabet, who certainly needed guidance, and also near Helga, and also out of the dampness of Hvalsey Fjord, but she was unaccountably stubborn in her opposition to this notion. Her only argument against it was her age—she was too old and close to death for a new life, she would miss the scenes of her childhood, Gunnars Stead had always been too grand for her. She even told Gunnar that her reasons were paltry ones in her own eyes, but her disinclination was firm for all that. It could not be done.

And so it became a game between them. If he beat her at chess in the evening, then they would go off to Gunnars Stead the next day. If a spoon dropped to the floor, and landed bowl upward, they would stay at Lavrans Stead, but if it landed bowl downward, they would go off to Gunnars Stead. If a black lamb was born, they would go, a white lamb kept them where they were. If Birgitta could guess the answer to a riddle Gunnar made up, then they would stay, if not, they would go. One day Gunnar said to Birgitta, "It did not seem to me before that the world was so full of signs."

"It seems to me the case that all these signs point in one direction only."

"What is that?"

"That Gunnar and Birgitta are elderly, doting folk, who must fill up their time in some wise." But she smiled, then, and said, "Here is a fellow coming on skis. My eyes are still sharp enough to see whoever comes before he knows he is coming. If it is a stranger, then we will stay here, and if it is a friend, we will go off to Gunnars Stead."

"Agreed, then." And they watched the skier for a long while, and then Gunnar got up from where he was sitting, and went to greet the fellow, and saw that it was Jon Andres Erlendsson, and he knew that the news would be ill.

Jon Andres greeted his wife's mother with a great smile, and an affectionate embrace, and then sat down beside her and spoke at length of the child Gunnhild, how large and active she was, and how fondly Helga cared for her, and how plentiful Helga's milk was, so that she had enough for two, if there had been twins, and indeed, such a case might turn out, for she was with child again, she had felt it quicken some days hence, and expected the birth in the autumn again, a good time for another birth, and she thought herself much stronger for this one, and everyone about Ketils Stead was sanguine. Now Birgitta said to him, "Even so, Jon Andres, I see in your countenance that this good news is not the news you are bringing to us."

"Indeed, there is a matter that I might consult Gunnar upon."

Birgitta looked at him sharply. "This is not so small a matter as you are making it out to be."

"I know not what to make of it, myself." And now Jon Andres sat silently, for he knew not how to speak of Kollgrim to his mother, and he hoped that Gunnar would take her off. But it did not appear to occur to Gunnar to do such a thing, for Gunnar was staring off toward the ice in the fjord. Birgitta followed his gaze for a moment, down the slope to the strand and the foggy blankness of the ice sheet, and then she said, "My boy, I have seen all of these things long before this. When Johanna was within me, I looked across the strand, just at the place where we are looking now, and I saw all of my five children vanish before my eyes, and now I see from your coming that the fate I thought to avert will come to pass."

Still Gunnar was silent, and so Birgitta said, "My boy, you must speak what you know. No man reports that his wife is well when she isn't, and so the trouble must be from Kollgrim."

"He has been with this Icelandic woman, Steinunn Hrafnsdottir, when she was staying apart from her husband at the cathedral, and they have been discovered. Now these folk are preparing a case against him, but I have been unable to learn the nature of the case. It does not seem to me that they will settle for lesser outlawry, or anything less than death, if they can get it."

Now Gunnar spoke. "Is Bjorn Bollason the lawspeaker in on this case?"

"The husband and the shipmaster were staying at Solar Fell, and now some other Icelanders are there as well. The woman and her sister are there, too."

"Bjorn Bollason is my sworn friend. It seems to me that we may rely upon him."

"If we may get him apart from the Icelanders long enough to confer with him, this may be the case. But the tale is that he clings to them even more tightly than before."

"That may be appearance. A Greenlander must know where he is living, mustn't he? And what of Kollgrim? Does he attend to the gravity of this pinch?"

"Helga says that he thinks only of the woman, and cares not what happens to him."

Now Gunnar looked at the other man, and said, "But it seems to me that little can happen to him, for folk do not think so much of this sin as they once did, and if the Icelanders have not killed him before this, they will not get at him now. Even if he is outlawed and must go into the waste districts for a while, what of it? His real home lies there, anyway."

"Even so, and knowing all of this, Helga is much cast down about him. The case does not fit the facts, it seems to me. We must go about to our friends and neighbors, and prepare them for this case, for it seems to me that the Icelanders have a plan. Perhaps there will be a fight at the Thing, for they are well armed, with iron weapons, and Icelanders always resort to fighting if they can, especially if they have some advantage, like these weapons."

"That is their reputation. When you were a child, some Icelanders were in Greenland with a damaged ship, and they fought with the Greenlanders for two winters about driftage rights, and in the end they burnt the ship to the waterline rather than leave it to the Greenlanders without sufficient payment. They are a hard folk."

"Then we must meet their hardness with our own." But the fact was that neither man knew just how this might be done.

Now Bjorn Bollason and Bolli Bjornsson began going about on skis every day to farms in Brattahlid district, where Bjorn had many friends, but Gunnar Asgeirsson and Jon Andres Erlendsson were not so well known, and at every farmstead, Bjorn Bollason gave gifts, and enlisted the friendship of everyone, and all remembered how he had distributed food during the great hunger, and how he had kept the Thing together when most of the judges had died off, and all of the farmers swore their friendship to him, without, however, knowing the nature of the case that was being prepared, for Thorstein and Snorri had insisted upon the secrecy of this. This also happened, that Bork and Thorstein went back to Nes in the southern part of Vatna Hverfi district, where they had been staying and talked privily among the other Icelanders there, but because this was Jon Andres Erlendsson's and Kollgrim Gunnarsson's district, the Icelanders spoke not to their hosts concerning these matters, but hung together and kept their peace.

Gunnar now went to his cousin Thorkel, and he explained the case to him, and Thorkel was as sanguine as could be. Indeed, no man that Gunnar or Jon Andres spoke to about the case could understand how things could go badly for Kollgrim. The greatest penalty for such a crime was lesser outlawry, and he had, after all, gone with an Icelandic woman, not a Greenlandic one. None of the judges were related to the woman, were they? And she had gone off from her husband to live by herself with the priests, had she not? Does a man, seeing a trinket lying before him in the grass, fail to pick it up? And so Gunnar and Jon Andres went about Vatna Hverfi district, both the northern and the southern parts, and they garnered a great deal of support, and in every farmstead they told what they suspected, that the Icelanders would try to break up the Thing through fighting, and men vowed to carry what weapons they had to the assembly fields, spears and bows and arrows and bone axes and such. And after going about Vatna Hverfi district, Jon Andres went farther south, to where he had other farms, and he found what support he could find there, and Gunnar went about Hvalsey Fjord and over the hills to Kambstead Fjord. Still it was the case that the Icelanders did not summon Kollgrim, and though all folk knew that the case was pending, there was no common talk of it, nor any talk of the woman, only enough to say that she was ill, and had been since early in Lent.

Now Larus the Prophet began going about, as the spring came on, with news of more visions, this time from the angel Gabriel, who, he said, had called him by the most endearing names, for example, my child, and my brother, and my boy, and who had been clothed in his angelic robes, which could not be seen as much as they could be felt, for it seemed to Larus that his fingers became as eyes and his eyes became as fingers, this was how he saw the angelic robes, the halo, and the great wings, which opened out like the wings of an eagle diving for a strike, and each feather was barbed with light. That, said Larus, was the angel Gabriel, and here was his news, that a new age was at hand, and the sign of this new age would be the taking of a certain devil who had long lived among the Greenlanders, and folk, especially those of the southern parts, knew this to be Ofeig Thorkelsson, for his sins and depredations grew season by season, and the folk of the south felt much oppressed by them. When this fellow was taken, the angel Gabriel said, the sign of the new age would be that men would bring bits of wood and planking and furniture and they would comb the beaches and gather up every burnable thing they could find, and they would build a great pyre, and the fellow would be tied to the pyre and burnt up, and the Devil would take the fellow's soul for his own, and all other men would be saved. But men, the angel said, must deprive themselves and their own families of light and heat in order to make up this pyre, or otherwise they would not be saved, and these were the rewards that they would find after the burning was completed: a ship would come, ornately carved, painted, and decorated with purple, and on it would be the longed-for bishop, a young man in purple robes, with half a dozen trained priests, who would, right there upon the strand, go among the Greenlanders and shrive them and give them the true wafer of wheat and the true drink of wine made from grapes. These folk would bring news that the two popes had died off, and a single pope, the pope of Jerusalem, had risen up and returned his church to holiness, and they would also bring new furnishings for the cathedral—tapestries of silk sewn with golden thread, ewers and chalices of gold chased in silver, altar cloths from far to the east, also made of silk, new glass, of many colors, for the cathedral window, and another set of bells, so that the ears of the Greenlanders would thrill to the rising and falling tones of many bells, not just the booming of the one that hung in the belfry now. This would also be the case, that the new bishop would recognize the holiness of Larus himself, and establish a house for him, where he and his neighbors could have their simple meetings. Such were Larus' predictions, and for lack of anything better to do, most people talked of them, as they had of his other predictions. He went from farm to farm, and there was always something special to eat for him, and something for him to take home to Ashild and little Tota.

The spring weather was of a piece with the winter weather, that is, there was much wind and little rain, and sand got in everywhere, and folk were not hopeful for the summer season, for such winds as these carry off the moisture in the grass, and only those steadings with large systems of streams and canals manage to get by with hay for the winter. Even so, the seal hunt was a prosperous one, with many large and small seals for every steading. And after the seal hunt, Thorgrim Solvason brought his case against Kollgrim Gunnarsson, and named his witnesses, and declared that this case would be tried at the Thing. And still Gunnar Asgeirsson had been unable to talk privily with Bjorn Bollason, but at any rate, he was rather sanguine about the case, and considered that unless the Icelanders killed Kollgrim at the Thing, through a pitched battle, the penalty would be one of lesser outlawry, next to nothing for such a man as Kollgrim.

Gunnar and Jon Andres quietly made their plans to defend themselves in a pitched battle, and those were these, that they and the Thorkelssons and some other men from Vatna Hverfi district would arrive at the assembly fields early in the day, and lay down such weapons as they usually had with them, as by law men must do at the beginning of every Thing, but they would keep other weapons with them in their booths. Their booths they would set up on the high ground above the spot where the law courts normally were held, four or five booths in a row across the hill, and men would always be in these booths, so that when the Icelanders should begin disrupting the court and fighting, these men could quickly run down the hill and fall upon them with such weapons as they had.

Some time before the Thing, Jon Andres and Gunnar went to Gunnars Stead, to explain these precautions to Kollgrim, and also to enlist him in his own case, for he had said nothing all spring about his plans for the Thing. It was the law that every accused man had to be present to hear the case against him, and also to hear his defense, if he chose not to make it himself. Gunnar went first to Ketils Stead and spent the night there, and had talk with both Helga and Jon Andres about Kollgrim, but neither of them could surmise how he would receive the plans, for Helga said that he was much confused, it seemed to her, as he had often been years before, after his dunking. If he spoke, she said, he spoke only of his fate and his mortality. Elisabet Thorolfsdottir was no help to him, Helga said, because she was very angry against him for going with the Icelandic woman, and could not swallow the bitter words that came into her mouth. Even so, Kollgrim stayed about the place, and heard the girl out, and seemed not to care what was being said.

It was the case that Gunnar had not actually visited Gunnars Stead since removing himself to Lavrans Stead—that is, for the entire life of Kollgrim Gunnarsson, some thirty winters—and when he and Jon Andres and the servingmen came on their horses around the hillside, and the broad fields of Gunnars Stead with their peaceful buildings lay spread before him, he stopped and gazed and knew not what to say, for indeed, the steading had a wide and pleasant aspect. The blue of the sky was cast back by the blue of the lakes that dotted the fields, and the ancient water system ran through the thick grass, glinting here and there. The great hillside where he had gone to gather blueberries with Margret, and where he had later gone to kill Skuli Gudmundsson, rose, pale and serene, off to the west, and the sun shone upon it. Now he gave his horse a little kick, and the animal trotted into the scene that Gunnar had just been gazing upon, and it seemed to him that he was indeed an unlucky man, but that his ill luck had always taken this lovely shape, so that as it destroyed him, still he clutched it to his breast.

Kollgrim took no interest in their plans for his defense, and they got little satisfaction from him, and so, though they lingered through the day, at last, toward evening, all agreed that there was no more to be said on this subject. Gunnar and Jon Andres returned to Ketils Stead for the night. And now, after their evening meat, when Helga and the child Gunnhild had gone to their bedcloset, and all of the servants as well, Gunnar and Jon Andres sat on the slope that looked from the steading down toward the water of the lake.

Gunnar said, "It seems to me that I have never told you a tale, although it is my habit to tell such tales as I know."

Jon Andres looked at him with some pleasure, and said, "It would please me to hear such a tale as you might have told my Helga when she was a child."

"I will tell this one, then. It is said by folk that some seventy-five winters ago, when my father Asgeir was a boy and folk still lived on the farmsteads of the western settlement, there was a certain man there named Kari, who went out one spring and slew a great she-bear, the greatest that was ever taken in Greenland. This bear was some ten ells from nose to tail and stood on her hind legs as tall as two men. But her cub, which Kari saw after he had made the kill, was as tiny as a puppy, and so Kari, who was a softhearted fellow after all, forbore to kill it, and took it home with him. But instead of putting it in the byre, he brought it into the steading. Now Kari's wife, whose name was Hjordis, had a new baby at the breast, and Kari gave her the following choice, she could either suckle the bear and the child together, or she could milk herself and and feed the bear through an eagle's quill, as folk do when a child is unable to suck. This woman Hjordis was a lazy and not very particular sort of person, and so she chose to suckle the bear and the child together."

Gunnar's voice was nearly a whisper, as if he were speaking to children huddled together in the bedcloset, and Jon Andres moved closer and closed his eyes, for indeed, he had had a fondness for tales as a boy, though gossip had been more the rule with Vigdis and Erlend than tales had been.

"Now the baby and the bear grew apace, and each looked at the other while they were suckling, and each thought that the other was his brother, or himself, and the two began to chatter to each other, bear and boy. Kari was rather pleased with this, and Hjordis, too, but the priest of the parish was less pleased, for men must look upward to the angels, rather than downward to the beasts. Even so, Kari and Hjordis paid little attention to the priest. They named the bear Bjorn, and the boy's name was Ulf. It happened that after the bear came, Hjordis had no more children, and so they looked upon these two as their children.

"The boy, as it turned out, was not so handsome, for he had a squint and a humped back. But the bear was a beautiful bear, with long, soft, white fur that glowed in the light and the dark, and he had a shiny black nose and large, shiny brown eyes, and they were not the eyes of a wild beast, which communicate nothing to men, for there is a veil between them that God Himself put there. Bjorn's eyes were the eyes of a dog or a horse when such a beast looks longingly at a man and seems about to speak.

"Now, when the bear was four or five winters old, which is about full-grown for a bear, Kari bethought himself, and said to Hjordis, 'It seems to me that we cannot keep our Bjorn with us much longer, for he is too big for his bedcloset, and he eats up all of our meat, and he is no longer content to sit upon the bench for his meals. It seems to me that he must go into the wastelands and live as other bears do, although indeed he is the smallest bear I have ever seen.' And so, Kari's heart was moved again to pity, at the thought of his little Bjorn out in the wastelands. They did nothing and did not speak of sending him away for another few winters.

"At last, when the little bear was some ten winters old, Kari made up his mind, and he put on his skis and took little Bjorn by the paw, and went with him into the wastelands. They spent the night in a shelter that men of the west had built for their hunting trips, and in the morning, Kari divided his meat with the bear and said, 'Now, my Bjorn, we must part, and you must go as a bear, and I must go as a man.' And he put his hands into the bear's thick fur and looked with longing into his eyes, for Kari, as I have said, was a softhearted fellow, and very fond of his bear son. And the bear looked with longing back at Kari. But after that, he went down on all fours and trotted away into the mountains. When Kari got back to his steading, Hjordis declared that Ulf was nowhere to be found, and though they looked everywhere for him, and had the neighbors in, searching, they did not find him, and they were much cast down, for where they had had two children, now they had none. And so they went through the winter.

"In the spring Kari could stand it no longer, and he went back to the wastelands where he had left Bjorn and began to shout for the bear. He stayed there for three days, shouting and looking about, and he saw that nothing was to come of his trip, and he was about to leave, when he heard his name on the breeze, 'Kari! Kari!' Just then, a white bear of enormous size appeared nearby, and Kari saw that it was Bjorn, only he had grown into a real bear during his winter in the wastelands. And Bjorn looked at Kari, and he opened his mouth, and he said, 'Greetings, Kari,' in a growling and bearlike, but friendly, voice. And Kari exclaimed, 'My son! My son! We long for you every day. Please return to us as our Bjorn again!' But Bjorn was a grown male bear, who had swiped fish from the ocean and wandered far and wide and known grown she-bears in the winter. He had little interest in sitting on a bench or sleeping in a bedcloset any longer. It seemed to him, however, that he would like to learn one thing, and so he said to Kari, 'I will come with you if you promise to get the priest to teach me how to read.' And Kari, who wanted nothing more than to have his Bjorn back again, made this promise.

"But indeed, this was a hard promise to keep, for the priest was a stubborn fellow, and Kari knew that the man had never countenanced raising the bear, and that he would consider the bear's talking a devilish thing, and so Hjordis made the bear a large robe with a close-fitting hood, and when the bear put it on, all that could be seen were his beautiful brown eyes. Now Kari went to the priest and said, 'My son has returned to us a changed fellow, for he has been among the folk of the eastern settlement, at Herjolfsnes. But though he has many strange ideas, he would like to be taught to read, and so we beg you to do this for him, for no one knows what his fate will be.' And so, out of pity for Ulf and also because Kari gave him many fine gifts, the priest came with his books and taught the bear to read, and he said to Kari, 'Your son has a very strange voice. It is almost a growl, although not unpleasant.' And Kari said, 'Did you not know? Such is the tone of voice that they cultivate at Herjolfsnes.'

"Every night that this was going on the bear asked for a great deal of meat, so that all the seals that Kari got on the seal hunt were eaten up by the middle of the summer. Then, one day, he said, 'Indeed, my father, your bedcloset where you sleep with my mother is larger than mine, and I would like to stretch out. I fear that if you don't give me your bedcloset, I will have to go off to the mountains, for life in a steading is very cramped, isn't it?'

"But his fur was so soft, and his eyes were so beautiful, and he was so heavy and bearlike, yet withal so graceful that Kari couldn't endure to give him up, and so he and Hjordis went out of their bedcloset and Bjorn went into it, and he lay there, sometimes all day, reading what books could be had for him.

"Now it happened that one night Kari saw Bjorn roll out of his bedcloset and leave the steading, and Kari followed him. The bear went out to the sheepfold in the moonlight, and he climbed up upon the wall. The sheep, being used to the smell of bear, both of Bjorn and of Kari, whose hands smelled of bear after he had been with Bjorn, were not alarmed, and only went on sleeping or grazing, but Bjorn reached down, as bears do with fish, and swept one into his arms, and broke its neck with his teeth, and ripped it open and ate it. Then he went back into the steading.

"In the morning, Kari came to Bjorn and said, 'My Bjorn, there is the carcase of a sheep outside the door, one of my best ewes. Know you of this?'

" 'Yes, indeed,' said the bear. 'This ewe was a tasty morsel for me when I awoke hungry in the middle of the night.'

" 'But Bjorn,' said Kari, 'you must not eat up my ewes, for they are my wealth and my security.'

"And the bear looked at him for a long time, and he looked at him with the eyes of a wild beast, and finally he said, "But indeed, my father, I was hungry.' That was all they spoke about it, but the next morning, Kari found another carcase outside the door, and said to the bear, 'Bjorn, we have spoken of this before. I am seriously displeased.' And Bjorn said, 'Indeed, Father, I was hungry.' And this went on for three more days. Finally, Kari told Bjorn that he must under no circumstances dare to eat another of the ewes, but Bjorn only said to him, 'Does it not say in old books, Father, that those who are hungry must be fed?' Now Kari did not know how to reply to this, for he knew nothing of old books.

"That afternoon he loaded himself up with gifts and valuables and he went to the priest and he gave him the gifts and told him the truth of the case, and they put their heads together for most of the afternoon. And after Kari had spoken to the priest, he saw that things could not be as he had hoped them to be, for a bear cannot talk or read his way into knowing what is right for men and what is wrong for them. He will be a bear in the wastelands or he will be a bear in the steading. In any case, he will always be a bear. When Kari returned from the priest's house, he saw that three more of his best ewes had been killed and eaten, and he was very angry, but when he got into the steading and saw the handsome white bear, with his soft fur and beautiful brown eyes, he said nothing.

"Hjordis and Kari and Bjorn now sat down at their evening meat, and Kari looked about his steading. There was nothing upon the shelves that went around the walls except two small seal oil lamps, although Kari had once been a prosperous man, one of the richest in the western settlement. The priest had everything now, all the tapestries and the cloths with their borders of tablet weaving, and the chess set carved from walrus tusk, and the silver cups from England, and all the other bits and pieces that Kari had once had about him. The three ate from their trenchers—some pieces of dried reindeer meat and some sourmilk and some dried sealmeat with butter spread upon it, and pretty soon Bjorn began to look about, for he was still hungry, but there was nothing left in the house, and only some old, tough, and meatless ewes out in the sheepfold, and still Bjorn looked about, for the meat they had eaten only whetted his appetite. Kari was finished with his meat, also, and so he had none to offer his bear son, but Hjordis pushed what was left of hers over to him, and he ate that, but still he was hungry, more hungry, it seemed to Kari, and the man looked into the bear's beautiful brown eyes, and the bear looked into his, and he saw in the bear's eyes only hunger, and he remembered how the bear had said, "Indeed, Father, I was hungry," with such animal innocence, and his heart melted for the bear, as always, and now he pulled back the sleeve of his robe, and he held his arm out to the bear, and the bear took it into his great paws, and closed his claws around it, and with a great crunching of bone, he took a bite, and Kari was surprised to discover both the pain and the pleasure of it. But even so, he knew that the bear would never be satisfied with only an arm, but must, in the end, eat him up."

Now Gunnar fell silent, and Jon Andres gazed upon him, and at length Gunnar said, "When I used to tell this story to Helga, it ended differently than this, but indeed, I am growing old, and cannot bring that ending to mind." After this, they went to their bedclosets, and early the following morning, Gunnar went off to Hvalsey Fjord, and stayed quietly there until it was time for the Thing.

Now Jon Andres and Gunnar and their friends did as they had planned, and carried their booths to the Thing field at Brattahlid, and also all of the weapons they could find, and they came early, and set their booths up near the top of the hillside, above the spot where the judges would meet and hear the cases, and they sat quietly in their booths for two days, while the judges heard some cases about sheep stealing and killings in Herjolfsnes. Bjorn Bollason stayed far away from Gunnar, and said little to anyone who was associated with him, and made it appear as if he had a great deal of business, and had to run from place to place day and night. Kollgrim stayed quietly in Gunnar's booth for the whole time. He brought no weapons to the Thing. Birgitta stayed home, for indeed, Gunnar did not want her to see what might happen. Helga stayed at Ketils Stead with Gunnhild.

Late on the second day of the Thing, the Icelanders appeared with Bolli Bjornsson and the other three Bjornssons, and they marched straight up the hill in force, for there were twenty-four of them, and they made an imposing company. They laid their weapons down at the agreed-upon spot, and folk got a good look at what they had, including four swords, some daggers, and lots of axes. Now Thorgrim stepped up into the circle where the judges were sitting, and this is what he said: "I name my case against Kollgrim Gunnarsson of Gunnars Stead in Vatna Hverfi district, for this man has done me grievous injury through my wife, and this injury has two parts, which are these. The first part is that he has seduced her affections away from me, although for our entire married life before this, which amounted to some two years, she was faithful and attentive to me, and treated me as the best wives treat their husbands, that is, they do not turn aside from serving them and they make their husbands' concerns their own. And as witnesses to this behavior, I call my fellows Snorri Torfason and Thorstein Olafsson and Bork Snaebjornsson, who were with me when I offered for the lady's hand, and when we made our marriage together. And I also say this, that I have treated the lady in all ways as fitting, giving her good clothing and other articles of value, and never beating her or showing her more anger than a man must show his wife to assure her good behavior." Now he stopped and looked around, and took some deep breaths, for he had never made such a case as this before, but it is the law that the injured husband must make his own case at the Thing. He went on:

"Now it is the case, and I name the same witnesses to attest to this, that the fellow Kollgrim Gunnarsson was once a frequent visitor to the

steading called Solar Fell, where he was betrothed to the daughter of the
house, whose name is Sigrid Bjornsdottir, and at that time, the woman
Steinunn Hrafnsdottir, who is my wife, never once looked at or engaged
in conversation with this man, and otherwise showed no knowledge of his
presence, and this was true for the entire winter that she lived at the
steading before the betrothal was broken off at the behest of the lady Sigrid
Bjornsdottir, for this reason, that the man had a concubine and child at his
steading, and this concubine would not be persuaded to leave the steading
before the marriage." He looked at Thorstein, who was not far off, and
Thorstein nodded his head in approval.

"Now it happened that my wife, Steinunn Hrafnsdottir, showed
some winter distress at the steading of Solar Fell, for indeed, folk say that
this was an unusual winter, and hard for folk who are not accustomed to
it, and so she removed herself to Gardar and stayed with the priests, and
went to the cathedral every day for long prayers, and as a witness to this,
I have Sira Eindridi Andresson. And it is the case that my wife Steinunn
was much given to holy things, and so her desire to be at the seat of the
bishop, where the relic is, came as no surprise to me or to anyone else who
knows her. But it so happened that with great suddenness she began to go
with this Greenlander whom she had never before shown any knowledge
of. And for this knowledge, we have as witnesses Thorgrim Solvason and
Bork Snaebjornsson, and myself and Snorri Torfason, for we all came upon
them when they were together. And this behavior was accountable in only
one way: that is that she was seduced by witchcraft, such witchcraft as this
fellow, who goes about not as other men do, learned of from the Devil
himself in the waste places. And here is another sign of enchantment, that
after she was carried away from him, she fell into a stupor that still clings
to her, so that she can neither stand nor sit up, nor speak, nor eat much,
so that broth runs out between her lips and meat sits unchewed in her
mouth. It seems to me that she will die from this, and others agree with
me. And so we make our case, not upon the fact of seduction, but upon
the grounds of witchcraft, and we ask for this, that the man be burnt at
the stake, as those found guilty of witchcraft are treated in Norway and
Iceland and elsewhere in the north." And now Thorgrim held out his
hands, palms up, and showed that he had no weapons on him, and so
Gunnar, who was standing nearby, looked about at the Icelanders, but they
made no move toward their stock of weapons, and Gunnar saw that he
had prepared to counter the wrong strategy, and that the Icelanders had
no intention of breaking up the Thing with fighting. Now Thorgrim sat

down, and Bjorn Bollason called to Sira Eindridi to stand up, and come into the circle, and this is what Sira Eindridi said:

"All men must know that the Devil himself is always among us, that his minions swarm over the ground like mosquitoes in the summer, that they get into our eyes and our ears and our mouths without us knowing about them, and they carry their evil intentions into our hearts. The wastelands are home to these devils, for they find little rest among Christian men. Do we Greenlanders not see their creatures all about us, in the form of skraelings, who perform evil magic in their little boats? Who put spells upon the seals, and upon themselves, so that they may capture seals at their blow holes all winter? Think you that any man is safe against this evil, if he not strive against it with all his might? I tell you that he is not, and that once it gets into him, he brings it with him among others, a great contagion that dooms men to live among devils for all of eternity." And this is all that Sira Eindridi said, and he went out of the circle, and the shipmaster Snorri Torfason went into the circle, and described again the condition of the woman, and told how others he had seen in other places who had been the victims of witches had fallen into the same condition, sometimes dying and sometimes not, and he cited four cases of this, two in Iceland and two in Norway, exactly the same sort of thing, with no detail different. And he spoke carefully, and soberly, and those standing about were much moved by his tale, and the woman did indeed seem to have been enchanted, for nothing of the sort had ever happened before among the Greenlanders, had it?

Now there was a long pause, when Bjorn Bollason and the judges spoke among themselves, and then they called Kollgrim Gunnarsson into the circle, and they waited a long time for him to make his appearance.

Gunnar climbed the hillside to his booth, and inside he found Kollgrim, and Kollgrim was sleeping and difficult to awaken, although Gunnar called to him, and shook him, and at last pulled his hair. Now Kollgrim sat up, and Gunnar said, "My son, have you had a dream? For such a sleep as I have now aroused you from is a portentous one." But Kollgrim declared that he had had no dreams, and stood up and looked about him. There was no one else in the booth. Gunnar said, "Boy, they have made their case against you on the grounds of witchcraft, and have not elected to resort to fighting, as we expected. Instead they say that you have turned the woman's eyes to your face through evil artifice. You must make your case against this charge, and you have much hope in this, for it is a foolish charge, and the judges do not care to give it credit." Still Kollgrim looked about himself, as if little certain where he was. Now Gunnar went on, "My Kollgrim, you must gather your wits, for your life hangs upon your defense, and in such a case, no one can make it for you." Now Kollgrim turned his face to his father, and it seemed to Gunnar that his boy did not see him, although his eyes were as voracious as they had ever been. Kollgrim said, "What did they say of her?"

"I will not hide from you that she is ill and stupefied, and her state hasn't changed since last you saw her."

"Will she die?"

"They say so. Men cannot predict such things."

Now Kollgrim began to arrange his clothing and his hair, and as he did this, he moved restively about inside the booth, then stopped still, and stood staring at the ground. The flap of the booth twiched and opened. It was Jon Andres. He said, "The accused must defend himself or be lost. That is the law." And the two men began to lead Kollgrim down the hillside, one at each arm, and to Gunnar, Kollgrim's arm seemed hard and thick as a piece of driftwood, not a man's arm at all. The faces of the men below turned and peered up at them.

Now Kollgrim went into the circle, and the judges gazed upon him, and finally, one of them said, "How was it that you came to seduce the woman Steinunn Hrafnsdottir?"

The folk who were standing about stepped closer to the center of the circle, and listened eagerly to hear what Kollgrim would say. He looked up, toward the fjord, then down again. At length he said, "I don't know."

"Did you draw her affections to you by using such black arts as the Devil teaches folk?"

"I don't know."

"Did you learn such arts as these in the wastelands, from skraelings or other unaccountable folk as would be seen away from the dwellings of the Lord?"

"I know not."

"How was it that you first came to meet the woman?"

"I do not know these things. It may be as you say, if she is dying. It may be that the power of the Devil works through me. I know not."

And now the judges fell silent, looking at the man before them. At last, Bjorn Bollason spoke up and said, "Kollgrim Gunnarsson, the Icelanders ask for a cruel punishment for this crime, for the crime is not seduction, but witchcraft. You must make a defense against this charge, or by the law of the northern places, you must be burned at the stake."

"I know not of these matters. Is it not for the judges to decide?"

Now the judges spoke among themselves, and men stood about waiting for them to make up their minds. After a while, they called upon Sira Eindridi to come among them, and he did so. The twenty-four Icelanders stood together in a group, and their clothing was bright. All eyes were drawn to them, including those of Bjorn Bollason, who looked from them to the judges to Sira Eindridi and back to them, and seemed to Gunnar to be talking without listening, and looking without seeing. Sira Eindridi spoke at length and with vehemence. The judges regarded him gravely and nodded their heads. One by one, the judges, too, cast their eyes at the Icelanders, and at Bjorn Bollason, to whom most of them owed their offices, for he had put a lot of Brattahlid men into these judgeships after the great hunger. But, indeed, no one looked at Kollgrim, who stood with his eyes cast down, as immobile as a skraeling at the seal hole. But even though everyone looked at the Icelanders, they looked at no one, but only gazed resolutely out to the fjord, and across it to the clouds hanging above the mountains.

Now the sun began to drop in the sky, and Bjorn Bollason stood up and came into the center of the circle, and cleared his throat and announced the verdict of the judges, which was that Kollgrim Gunnarsson, for the crime of seducing the Icelandic woman, Steinunn Hrafnsdottir, through black arts, would be taken by the Icelanders and be burned at the stake on the last day of the Thing, for indeed, it would be a great sin to allow the fellow to walk among virtuous men for any longer than necessary, for it is the case that in his desperate last gasp, the Devil gains ten times his original strength, and pulls the souls of ten times as many men down along with him. And so, folk remarked, Larus' prophecy was fulfilled, and a devil was to be burned at the stake, and men began to talk about how this would release the Greenlanders from their long wait for a bishop, some news from Rome or Avignon, or even the pope of Jerusalem. Among themselves, the Icelanders smiled.

And here is how the Greenlanders went about burning Kollgrim Gunnarsson of Gunnars Stead in Vatna Hverfi district. They went down along the shore, and gathered what driftwood they were able to find, and one or two old boats were broken apart with axes, and men went across the fjord, and back into the birch woods that still stood in the clefts behind Steinstraumstead, and they cut some of this birch, although it was green and moist with summer. After that, the folk who lived nearby, at Brattahlid and behind there, these folk went into their steadings and found stools and such furniture as was broken apart or otherwise in need of repair, and they carried this to the spot. Two men went to their steadings, and found broken beams in buildings that had fallen down, and these, too, were carried to the spot, and so the pyre grew bigger, but Thorstein Olafsson and Snorri Torfason agreed that it is difficult to burn a man. Not so difficult, said Bjorn Bollason, if he is soaked in seal oil first, his clothing and his hair, and so this they also decided to do, for it did not look as though the man would resist such a thing.

The energy of many men makes quick work of most tasks, and this was no different, for the pyre grew through the night, and was ready on the next day, and many folk strolled about it and looked at it, for they had never seen such a thing, but mindful of Larus' prediction, they all contributed some little object to it, if not wood, then bone, for it is well known in Greenland that bone burns well enough for heat, if not for light, when there is nothing else. It happened that men were so drawn to this pile of objects that they forgot their morning meat and everything else in order to gaze upon it. All the other business of the Thing was completed, rather hurriedly, some folk said, and the judges came to the burning place, and stood about. The Icelanders brought forth Kollgrim Gunnarsson, who was their prisoner, and Sira Eindridi was with him, and he had shriven the fellow and given him his rites, and he led him to the pyre, and Kollgrim looked to Gunnar to be as blank and dead as he had ever seen him, until he saw the pile of objects and wood, and then his eyes leapt out of his head at the sight, and he quickened his step. The Icelanders stopped him, though, to pour seal oil over his clothing, and the stench of seal oil rose in the air.

Now Kollgrim stepped up onto the pyre, and embraced the beam that stood in the middle, and Thorstein tied his wrists together with a thong of seal gut so that it seemed to Gunnar that the boy's arms were nearly pulled out of their sockets. Now Gunnar went near to the pyre, and tried to gain Kollgrim's gaze, but Kollgrim looked not at him. Thorgrim Solvason went up behind Kollgrim with a torch that burned pale in the sunlight and set it against the seal oil–soaked pyre, and then stepped away. The fire crept among the bits and pieces for a little while, and Gunnar saw Kollgrim close his eyes, and he did not open them again after that. From some of the folk who were standing about, there came talking and moaning, but Kollgrim made no sound.

Soon enough Kollgrim was hanging off the beam in the midst of a great pale blaze that roared smokily around him, ate off his clothing, blackened his skin, chewed up his fingers and his eyebrows and his hair. Thick smoke smelling richly of seal oil hung in the air. Now the beam collapsed, and the flames rose higher with the new fuel, and then it seemed to Gunnar that Kollgrim's flesh and bones were burning, for the nature of the stench changed, and folk who had stood fascinated were driven away by it, but indeed, there was not much left to see, and the smoke was as thick as could be, so that folk's eyes teared with it, and they began to think of other business that they had to do.

Now it is usually the case that folk linger about the Thing field when they are taking down their booths, and making their arrangements to return to their own districts, for indeed, the opportunity to meet with folk and exchange news is a cherished one, and there is always the chance that some late bit of business will be carried out. But in this year, folk gathered up what belongings they could find, and carried them off, and many articles were left behind from the haste. At the last, when the pyre had fallen into ash and fragments, only Gunnar, Jon Andres, the Thorkelssons, and Sira Eindridi were standing about, and Gunnar saw that for once, Sira Eindridi did not know what to do, but kept looking over to him and looking away, but indeed, Gunnar himself knew not what to do, nor how to gather his strength to do it, and so they lingered into the late twilight.

At last, Jon Andres spoke, and said, "It seems to me that we must pour water upon the ashes, and then gather up what bones we might find of our brother, and bury them where it is proper to do so, according to the law of the Church and of the northern places." And he looked at Sira Eindridi. Sira Eindridi looked out toward the fjord, toward the ancient ruin of Thjodhilds church, that Erik the Red once built for his wife in the early days of the settlement, and he said, "Here at Brattahlid, there are men buried who never accepted Christ. These ashes may be put there," and so the Thorkelssons went off to a nearby steading and got some spades, and set about digging a hole on the north side of the little church. And because the spades were small and the day had been a long one, they dug for most of the night. Gunnar and Jon Andres gathered up what seemed to be pieces of bone and laid them on the moist grass to cool.

Now, after a short darkness the birds began to call again, and then the sky grew light, and Sira Eindridi and the Thorkelssons went into their booths and lay down for a short sleep, and Gunnar and Jon Andres sat down upon the hillside and began to talk. Jon Andres said, "I am little eager to bring this news to Helga, for we were not a little sanguine of the outcome before we came to the Thing field."

"Even so, it seems to me that she will hardly be surprised, and that my Birgitta will be less surprised. But indeed, there are times when a man knows not what to say of the will of the Lord, and such a time has come upon me."

"This is not the will of the Lord, but the will of men."

"The wish of Thorgrim, perhaps, who felt his injury so deeply."

"Do you not see that this Thorgrim is the dupe of the others? Men may go among the judges during the next winter or so, and gossip about this case," said Jon Andres. "Certainly it will be on everybody's tongue, and it will take little to put it on everybody's lips. I have a great curiosity about who said what and to whom, do you not?"

"Nay, my son. I have no curiosity at all."

"Evil has gone on here. We may at the least bring a case."

"Against whom?"

"That is what we will find out by careful gossip."

"This seems an ill course to me. I have never had luck in the law courts."

"But I have."

Gunnar said, "I will say to you what Greenlanders always say to each other, which is that you will do as you please in this as in all else." Now they sat quietly for a while, until the wife from a nearby steading brought them some bits of food for their morning meat, and then the Thorkelssons and Sira Eindridi got up, and the fragments of bone were cool, and these were placed in a sealskin bag, and buried among the remains of the unbaptized near Thjodhilds church, and the place of the burning was left through the summer, for no one cared to approach it or pick over the ashes.

Now Gunnar and the others went in the Gardar boat to the landing place that sits on the Eriks Fjord side of the Gardar neck, and they walked over the hill, and then Gunnar and Jon Andres and the Thorkelssons got into the Thorkelssons' boat, and set off down Einars Fjord, and the weather was calm and clear. None of the men spoke much among themselves, only to mention icebergs that were floating near, or such items of business that no one cared to hear about. It was the case that the sight that he had seen both recurred to Gunnar's thoughts and did not. The familiar snowy peaks and gray slopes with their skating black shadows passed on either side of the fjord in stately progression, apart from the effort of the rowers, who heaved and sweated just in front of where Gunnar was sitting. It occurred to Gunnar that such an event as had overtaken Kollgrim had never happened in the sight of these slopes before, for all the dangers of the hunt, and for all the pleasure Greenlanders took in fighting and killing each other, and for this reason it seemed not to have happened, in fact. Certainly he felt little grief and less anger. The punishment had fit the crime fantastically, like a huge man's robe on a tiny child. Gunnar knew not how to think of it, or to feel it, or, for that matter, to speak of it to Birgitta. Such were his idle thoughts as the boat slid nearer and nearer to the Ketils Stead landing. And it seemed to him that he felt the parting with his son-in-law and former enemy more than he felt the parting with his son, for indeed, tears came into his eyes to see the familiar supple figure and the well-known curly head turn away from the boat and begin to climb the grassy slope that led to the steading.

Now Gunnar took his place at the oars, and the mountains, darkening with nightfall, began to recede from his gaze and disappear, leaving only the light of the water and the glow of the icebergs floating here and there. Skeggi Thorkelsson said, "Gunnar, the long day is ending, and my father Thorkel will be pleased if we bring you to Hestur Stead for what remains of the night." But Gunnar refused this offer, and so some while later, they put him down at the landing, where folk who do not care to row around the wide spit of land that folds about Hvalsey begin their trek through the valley that leads to Lavrans Stead. And when they put him down here, the sky was as dark as it gets in midsummer, but light enough for him to see his way.

He was an old man, some fifty-six winters old, and he had repeated every step he was making myriad times before, and yet he was born like a baby into a new life, and each step toward Lavrans Stead was unsteady and frightening. Each glance ahead into the night was an effort to see into the future, which men cannot see, though they think to themselves that they can make familiar furniture out of the shapes before them. He stopped and looked about. A great storm of grief was waiting for him at his steading that he must lean into, as a man leans into the wind, and closes his eyes against the ice that flies in his face. As calm as this night was to him, threading his path between the mountains that rose on either side, just so violent would be this storm inside his steading, and it would lift him up and suck the breath from his corpus and set him down some other place, as another man, and though he walked eagerly, he also quailed before this storm. He saw that grief would be the gift that Birgitta would give him, as once before she had given him herself as a girl, then his own life, then his children, then herself again as an old woman. And it was the case that he must reach out his hands and take this gift with the same eagerness as any other gift. He came out at the top of the slope above the steading and saw that the sun was already brightening the sky above Hreiney. Now he paused for a moment, then he went on, and came to the steading.

Toward the feast of St. Lavrans, the old woman Birgitta Lavransdottir of Lavrans Stead took a long knife made of sharpened bone, and opened a great wound in her belly, although considering her age and her frailty, folk were much surprised that she had the strength to do this. She gave up much blood, and grew very ill after this incident, but lingered without dying, and then gained some of her strength back. Some folk considered that she performed this act out of grief over the death of Kollgrim Gunnarsson, and some considered that she performed it out of shame at his crime and execution. In the fall, she came into possession of a bird arrow and succeeded in driving it into her breast so that it pierced her heart and she died from this. Folk considered, as they do, that perhaps this was the best thing after all, if her grief was so great, although, of course, self-murder is a sin and affront to the Lord, and bars the soul from the hope of Heaven.

Now the winter came on, and it was much different from the previous one, being very snowy in every district. There was a great deal of visiting from steading to steading and district to district, for the fine days were still and pleasant for skiing. After Yule, Gunnar Asgeirsson and Johanna Gunnarsdottir piled all of their furnishings on a great sledge that could be pulled through the valley that leads to Einars Fjord, and they and some of their men servants pulled these things behind them. At the landing beside Einars Fjord, which was frozen, Skeggi Thorkelsson met them with three horses, and the horses pulled the sledge the rest of the way to Gunnars Stead, where Gunnar had decided to remove himself, and so it was that at the beginning of Lent some thirty-two winters after leaving, Gunnar returned to the steading of his fathers in Vatna Hverfi district. It seemed to him that although his daughter and his servants were with him, and his other daughter and her children were around the hillside at Ketils Stead, and the baggage and food they carried with them caused a great deal of annoyance and labor, he was returning to this steading a destitute fellow, and as it were giving himself up to it, that when he would open the ancient wooden door, coopered from Markland fir, he would enter and disappear. But of course, this did not happen. He only lit a seal oil lamp and looked about, then set up his parchment so that he might write something down if it came to him.

Jon Andres Erlendsson made many trips about the settlement in the course of the winter after the burning, and it seemed to folk that he wished to ingratiate himself with everyone in every district. Some folk declared that the burning was a great shame to him, but others did not know what to make of his actions, his smiles, his chat about sheep and cows and boats and all the business of the Greenlanders except the burning. But at the last, they all talked of this to him, too, for indeed, everyone wanted to know what the Gunnars Stead folk and the Ketils Stead folk were thinking, what had been done with the ashes, what had been said, what was planned. And so, though men vowed not to talk of this subject, Jon Andres was so agreeable and mild about it, that they did talk of it after all, and they did speculate about how it had come about that a man had been burned for such a little thing. What man had not gone with another's wife? or at least another's daughter or sister? If such things were to be punished in this wise, well, there would be no men left in Greenland, and that was a fact. Jon Andres nodded and smiled. He gave gifts, cheeses, dried sealmeat. He gave advice. He offered his rams and bull for breeding. He was a prosperous farmer and a well-known man. Folk were flattered at his attention. He came back to Gunnars Stead and he said to Gunnar, "It was Bjorn Bollason who suggested that they douse our brother in seal oil. If they had not done such a thing, there would not have been wood enough to carry out the burning."

"Who has told you this?"

"Folk speak of it everywhere."

"But perhaps only those who have something against Bjorn Bollason?"

"Nay, they praise him for it, though rather shamefacedly in front of me. They consider that he showed a little wit, as he did during the hunger, when he took provisions that had been stacked up at Gardar. Folk speak of him as an enterprising fellow, as good as the Icelanders in his way." Now Jon Andres smiled bitterly.

It seemed to Gunnar that this talk brought Kollgrim's death throes into his mind more vividly and with more completeness than when he had stood there as a witness to them, so vividly that the pictures took his breath away, and he felt the burning smoke in his eyes that Kollgrim must have felt, and his own flesh shrank as Kollgrim's must have shrunk from the heat, and this happened, also, that he felt a little flame in his innards that was the desire to crush Bjorn Bollason. And this desire came to him with as much urgency as any in his life—the desire to marry Birgitta, the desire to look upon his children, the desire to preserve Kollgrim from his fate. He said, "I have killed men twice in my life, and one of those times, the men who met their fates were your brothers. We dug that pit, and set the trap for them, and we were serious, but antic at the same time. It was a great chase, for deadly stakes, but our hearts were high with trickery, and running, and the secrecy of nighttime, and it might have been that they would have caught us and killed us and the contest would have gone the other way. When another man died, the Norwegian Skuli Gudmundsson, my foster brother Olaf and I went to the killing with heavy heart and more anger at the perfidy of women than at the fellow himself. Now I feel something else in my bosom that frightens me, and it is the will to make Bjorn Bollason suffer and suffer and suffer. To bring him into such agonies as a man should never know, to deny him shrift, to tear his flesh shred from shred. And how will I ever be forgiven for such a lust as this?"

Jon Andres looked Gunnar in the face, and Gunnar saw that his daughter's husband, a peaceful man, carried the same desire in his heart. The younger man shrugged his shoulders, and the two sat silently for some little time.

Now it became known among the Greenlanders that Larus the Prophet and Sira Eindridi Andresson were much seen together these days, with Larus going back and forth to Gardar in the small Gardar boat, and Sira Eindridi going to Larus Stead, and standing outside and looking in when Larus was carrying on one of his little services. After this, Sira Eindridi said nothing about it, neither for it nor against it, and so some folk were made bolder in their attendance at them. Larus pretended not to care one way or another, but went on, always in low rounded tones, always telling this bit or that bit of his visions, always having a little something to eat after. Where there used to be three women for every man who came to the services, now there were almost as many men as women, and folk spoke openly about these things, even when they were with others who did not participate in them. He and Ashild and little Tota dressed as simply as possible, all in the same sort of long robe woven and pieced together by some of the women who came to the services. They went bareheaded, and wore no hood nor headdress, but indeed, folk said that they were as unpretentious as could be. After the burning, everyone waited eagerly for the bishop's ship to come. Larus and Sira Eindridi were very assured about it, so assured that they did not look for it at all, but went about their business as if it weren't ever going to come.

The old mad priest, Sira Jon, died in this winter after the burning, and was carried out, wrapped in a fine silk shroud, and was as little as a child. The women who laid him out said among themselves that his hair had grown to his waist, and his eyebrows hung into his eyes, and his beard matted on his chest, and altogether, their duty had been an unpleasant one, for the lice jumped off him as lively as capelin jumping into the nets in summer. There was a great smell in his little chamber that had gotten into the very stones themselves, and the cook, not such a fastidious soul as a rule, said that nothing edible could be stored there, and so the door to the place was closed as tightly as it had been in the old fellow's life, and most folk forgot that he had died, and two or three times, the cook made up his dinner, as she was accustomed to doing, and left it by habit for Sira Pall Hallvardsson to take to him.

Sira Pall Hallvardsson was much crippled now, and had a boy who ran about for him, and either sat down or stood the whole time while he said the services in the cathedral.

It also happened to Sira Pall Hallvardsson that after the death of Sira Jon, he found his food so distasteful that it nearly gagged him to eat of it, although always before he had been of good appetite. It was a tenet of his preaching that whatever the Lord gave men for their nourishment was wholesome to them, and it was good for them to eat their fill of it, unless for some special penance they had engaged to fast for a brief time. He had also early gotten a taste for the foods of the Greenlanders, as sour and pungent as they were. But now the very odors of his meat brought nauseating juices into his mouth, or else his mouth grew so dry that he could not chew what he took between his teeth. Those about him urged him to eat, as he had always urged Sira Jon, and he found himself toying with it in the same wise as Sira Jon had always toyed with his meat.

He did not regret Sira Jon's death, for it is a sin to do so, when a man has been shriven and reconciled with the Lord and his friends may be confident that he has received his best reward. But it was also the case that there were many hours of the day to fill that had been filled before with something—carrying food, or talking, or sitting nearby, or whatever. These days, Sira Pall could not exactly remember what they had been filled with, but these days, also, he sat a great deal in the high seat of the great Gardar hall and looked about himself, or lay in his bed in the dark hours, sleepless, or sat in the cathedral, praying, sometimes energetically, sometimes idly, but always with the sense that while things needed to be done, there was nothing for him to do.

When he sat in the hall and looked about, it was his habit to remember the cathedral as it had once been, under the care of Bishop Alf, or even under the care of Sira Jon, a pleasant and well-kept spot, where folk took holy pleasure when they came. This was no longer the case. The floor was a mat of old and new rushes and leaves that gave off a rotting, dusty odor. The tapestries hung in blackened shreds, and no one dared to touch them, for the slightest pressure separated thread from thread, and they fell into bits on the floor. The altar furnishings were as black as could be, and dinted and bent. The high seat itself wobbled, for the joinings were coming apart, and the crucifix had a great crack now, that ran from the legend above His head, through His cheek, down the left side of His torso

and His leg, so that the leg was separated from the body, and then through
the lower limb of the crucifix. Once in a while a dream came to Sira Pall,
in which he was praying with great fervor, lying on the floor beneath the
crucifix, as he had not been able to do for some number of years, and the
very pressure of his praying split the crucifix in two, so that as he looked
up at it, it fell apart and toppled to the floor.

About the kitchen and the rest of the residence, things were in as
much disrepair as they were in the cathedral, or more. The cook and the
other servingfolk complained repeatedly of making do, of having little to
eat or wear, of being cold, of the dampness of their chambers. And the
storehouses were nearly empty. Here and there, some provisions, enough
for a day or so, were stacked in a corner. The fact was that none of the
tithes were collected any longer. During the hunger, Greenlanders had
gotten out of the habit of bringing their dues, and Sira Pall had not had
the patience or the heart to demand them when times improved. Now folk
expected Gardar, which anyway had the largest and best fields, to take care
of itself. Sira Pall thought that it might have, with a more practical man
in charge of things, but it had not. It had not taken care of itself at all.
These were his thoughts when he sat in the high seat in the hall.

Awake in bed in the dark of night, he thought not a little of Steinunn
Hrafnsdottir, who still lay close to death at Solar Fell, wasted and silent,
but alive. What sort of man might have saved her, and the boy Kollgrim
Gunnarsson? A harder man, such as Sira Eindridi, who would have bullied
her sins out of her? He saw now, had seen at once after the Icelanders broke
in, that she had been about to confess to him that day at the loom, when
he put his cloak about her shoulders. But what had he been thinking of?
Sira Jon, no doubt, who filled his mind always. It was the Lord's principle
that folk had choice in these matters, and Steinunn had had this choice as
well. She might have opened her heart to him, and she had chosen wrongly,
with poor judgment, to hug her sin unto her bosom, and not trust in the
Lord's forgiveness. It was hard to tell. It was always and ever hard to tell
with women why they chose one way and not another. Even so, it was
also the Lord's principle that His stewards on earth must see and hear and
act so that sin does not go forward, and result in more sin, and this little
sin, of adultery, had gone forward, and blossomed in the great sin of
wrongful death, or so Sira Pall thought, in spite of Sira Eindridi, who was
vocal in his approval of the measures that had been taken against the powers
of darkness, and Bjorn Bollason, who was less vocal, but no more doubtful.
As he lay on his pallet, Sira Pall thought of Kollgrim, too, a man of the
old style, full of fate, as lost as if he had worshiped the old gods and not

the True Lord. He turned over in his mind this thought, that there must be a language to speak to such folk, a hoard of words that they could hear, and would listen to.

But indeed, he had not found it in time, had he? He had not found it in time to save either the son or the mother, and it was with the greatest regret of all that thoughts of Birgitta Lavransdottir came to him, for she had always turned her gaze upon him with friendship and concern, had learned so quickly to read, in those early days, picking up words and sentences as if she were gathering little stones to keep, had mystified him always with her view of things that were unseen by others, had carried food and pieces of weaving to him at Hvalsey Fjord, making sure that he was comfortable and had some small pleasures to beguile himself with, always she had come after him, and peppered him with opinions, about the Lord, about himself, about the Greenlanders, about her own folk and the thoughts that came to her, opinions that he was drawn to attending, although it is well known that the views of women are worthless and false. He had made sure of her friendship, told her all the best things that he knew, spoken to her at length of the duties of folk on the earth, watched her as carefully as a shepherd may watch but one of his sheep, but then she, too, had sunk away from him, drawn to death by the deaths of her children, and now a self-murderer, unshriven, unforgiven.

How was it, Sira Pall sometimes thought in the darkness of his chamber, when the seal oil lamp had gone out, that the Lord gathered these folk together in one spot for only a long enough moment so that they came to love and depend on one another, and then wrested them apart for eternity, some to perdition, some to Heaven, some to bide their time in purgatory? And how could it be that the soul should endure perpetual separation, when even the little separations between deaths were hardly bearable? And it was also the case that he knew the answer to these questions, that men must love the Lord above all else, that these other loves must burn away in the fire of love for the Lord, a fire that should burn so hot that not even ash survives it. But although he knew the answer to these questions, he did not know how to make the answer part of himself.

When he sat on a bench in the church, praying, he prayed and thought about Sira Jon. Concerning this brother of his, he strove to feel no sorrow, for the man had been shriven and blessed, and had spoken all such words as were needful to assure himself of his heavenly reward. As at the death of Sira Audun, Sira Pall Hallvardsson saw that it was himself that he had to labor against, against his own regret and loneliness more than against sorrow for the departed soul. It was always a sin to sorrow for the departed soul, for it showed no real knowledge of God's grace. But even so, as he sat and prayed, or merely gazed upon the cloven face on the crucifix, his heart seemed a hole into which these comforting thoughts disappeared without a trace, a hole that breathed forth sorrow and despair, as vapors come out the earth in places like Iceland, for example. The real case of Sira Jon's death was somewhat different from appearances, and if Sira Pall Hallvardsson could see this, could not the Lord Himself, more readily, and without struggling to understand this sign and that mark?

For it was the case that although Sira Jon never spoke without speaking the proper words, such words as he had learned at his uncle's knee, and in school, such words as he had repeated over and over for the sixty-four winters of his life, the words were inflected in such a way as to cast doubt over everything he said. "Our Father, who art in Heaven." How many times had Jon said that? And how many times had a lifting of his voice thrown suspicion over one word or the other, slipping into Sira Pall's own thoughts the suspicion that some of us have no father, or that there is no father, or that such fathers as there are do not dwell in Heaven. How many times had the two priests' eyes flickered toward one another as such words were being spoken, and what had been communicated then, if not a sense of conspiracy, but a conspiracy that Sira Pall was not party to, and hardly recognized. He readily saw that he was a dull fellow in comparison to Sira Jon, hardly capable of dividing the Peter's pence from the tithes by throwing them into different chests, as he used to do in Hvalsey Fjord days. And he had been a dull fellow all along, never knowing what to do in the days of Sira Jon's madness, running after him when he was wild, hardly doing more than gaping with the servingfolk. After that, when his brother merely refused to eat, or wash or dress, he had been even more at a loss, sometimes thinking it best to force him, sometimes thinking it best to let him be, sometimes seeking the answers to these questions in the man's own words and actions, sometimes overlooking those words and actions completely. Oh, he was a dull fellow, indeed, and he sat on a bench in the cathedral, and looked away from His face, and cursed his own dullness. He was a dull fellow who stood with his hands outstretched before him, and what he wished to fall into them he had no idea of.

Here was another of his sins, that he longed to care for Sira Jon, still; that he would have called back the other man's suffering if he could have called back his life, so that he could have brought his meat to him, and held his arm under the other's head, and spooned his broth into his mouth, and smoothed the lengths of wadmal that were spread over his pallet, and carried him to the chamber pot, and done for him all the other services that had filled his days for so many years; so that he might have prayed with him more convincingly, and drained the other man's words of those doubting tones that he now thought of without ceasing, when he was sitting on a bench in the cathedral, and repeating those same prayers himself.

Sometimes, out of doors, looking at the dark faces of the mountains looming over the blue fjords and the green strips of pasture, he considered Erik the Red, who held onto his faith in the old gods until death, and it seemed to him that such events as had overtaken the Greenlanders would hardly have surprised him. Darkness, darkness. That's what Erik expected: Odin paid with his eye for a little insight, and the measure of the strength he gave away was the measure of how short he was to be when Fenrir snapped his chain and the powers of evil came forth to battle the Aesir. Old stories. Sira Pall Hallvardsson knew little about them, and cared not to think upon them.

Now the boy came to him with news that the cook was looking for him, and Sira Pall Hallvardsson lifted himself carefully, with the boy's help, and took his sticks, and made his way toward the kitchen. As difficult as it was sometimes to move, his very slowness passed the time, and the attention he must pay to his movements so as to mitigate the pain of them occupied his thoughts.

When he came out of the cathedral, Sira Pall Hallvardsson saw that Bjorn Bollason and Larus the Prophet had come, and that they and Sira Eindridi were deep in talk, but not so deep that Bjorn Bollason did not break off at once, and make his way across the grass to Sira Pall Hallvardsson. This was Bjorn Bollason's way, always to show respect and concern, and it was Sira Pall Hallvardsson's way always to be charmed by the other fellow's manner, charmed in spite of the distrust he felt for the lawspeaker. Now Bjorn Bollason came forward quickly, with a great grin upon his face, and he said, "Well met, Sira Pall Hallvardsson. I come to announce the betrothal of my daughter Sigrid, and indeed, may this be the last such announcement I have to make. The fellow seems to have enough resolution for the both of them, and he has subdued her with jokes and rhymes and merriment, so that she knows not what to think, or at least, what to say."

"That is a good state for a wife to be in, folk say."

"Few are, though. But Signy is pleased with this betrothal. The man is Thorstein Olafsson the Icelander."

"I cannot say that this bit of news surprises me." Sira Pall Hallvardsson saw that Bjorn was beside himself with pleasure at this news, and indeed, of all the Icelanders, only Snorri Torfason, the shipmaster, was a more powerful or respectable man. It was a marriage to please anyone, especially after the cloud cast upon Sigrid's marital prospects by the death of the man Kollgrim, even though that betrothal had been broken off long before his crime was committed. Sira Pall smiled, and said, "After many a storm, sometimes the little ship does come into harbor."

"And there is this, too. My son Bolli intends to take ship with the Icelanders and seek his fortune upon the sea. There is no reason why he cannot learn what there is to know from Snorri Torfason, and then bring a ship back to Greenland. The Greenlanders have been little enterprising in past years, compared to what they once were."

"Snorri seems to have made a prosperous life for himself upon the sea, and I am sure he is fond of the boy, for Bolli is a good boy."

"Yes, he is. I have four good boys." Bjorn said this with his usual self-congratulatory candor, and Sira Pall smiled. But, indeed, what circumstances had ever challenged Bjorn Bollason's opinion of himself or his good fortune?

"Things go well for you, Bjorn Bollason."

"It seems to me that it was a moment of great good luck for me when I first looked upon Snorri's ship in Einars Fjord, and that is the truth." And so he took some deep breaths, and his chest swelled in pride, and he parted from Sira Pall and went back to where Sira Eindridi and Larus were still having converse.

It was interesting to Sira Pall the way Eindridi and Larus had become friends, where they had once been as suspicious as two male dogs. Larus seemed to Sira Pall to be a sly little man, with his soft voice and his neatly delivered tales. Sira Audun would have appreciated him, Sira Pall thought. It was hard to believe now that Larus had been a servingman all of his life before the hunger: he spoke of everything, from the Virgin to the spoons on the table before him, with such mild fluency. He had the sort of voice that did not announce itself immediately, but caught the ear after a bit, and held it, dropping and dropping to a fascinating whisper, and folk were fascinated indeed at the tales he reported. Sira Pall did not himself know what to make of them, did not know whether the man was a true mystic or just an inventive fellow. Anything was possible, after all, and he had not the perspicacity to see into such things. Sira Eindridi was well meaning, but hard, with some verbal fluency of his own, though it was of a rather bombastic sort, and fascinated no one but Sira Eindridi himself. It was hard to know who had wooed whom, in this case, but these days Larus and Sira Eindridi were often together, and though Sira Eindridi always had the most to say, and spoke in the louder voice, and led the other man about, Sira Pall had little belief that the priest was the top dog. Now they both turned and came over to him, and spoke to him with the respect due to age, and asked after his health and his soul and his business, and the short result of it was that after but a few moments of this conversation, Sira Pall Hallvardsson conceived a great longing to go into his chamber and sleep like an old man.

The news of Birgitta Lavransdottir's self-murder came to Dyrnes shortly after Yule, with the folk who were returning from Solar Fell, where they had feasted with the Icelanders. Margret Asgeirsdottir had stayed in Dyrnes with Signy's brother's household after Sigrid went back to Solar Fell, because not only did she care little to go there, but she was little welcome there. Bjorn Bollason and Signy agreed that it was rather inconvenient, the way they had taken the woman up after the great hunger, considering how things had turned out, but it was not the way of such folk as themselves to turn her out of her place. In addition to this, Signy's mother rather liked having Margret in Dyrnes, as she was quiet and useful. Margret was much cast down by the news of Birgitta's death and kept very much to herself. During Lent, it occurred to her that she must now be some sixty-four winters old, as old as the nurse Ingrid had been in the year of her death. Still she was little afflicted with the joint ill. Only her finger joints and the joints of her big toes throbbed in wet weather. She thought often of Eyvind Eyvindsson, and less often of Skuli Gudmundsson.

But most often, she thought of Gunnar and Kollgrim, and mixed them in her mind. She remembered things she had said to one as if she had said them to the other. She remembered Kollgrim's fur clothing, but saw it in her mind upon the figure of Gunnar, who had never worn fur clothing. She remembered Gunnar in his bedcloset, still beneath the bearskin, but his face was Kollgrim's face. The child Gunnar, whom she had carried about on her back, she remembered as Kollgrim. The staring blue eyes of Kollgrim looked at her in her dreams out of the sockets of Gunnar. The mouth opened and spoke in Gunnar's tones, but said Kollgrim's words: "Folk say that sisters must be given up." When she overheard folk about the steading describing the burning, it was Gunnar's face she saw peering out of the smoke, his peculiar striped clothing that she saw going up in flames. It did not occur to many folk to avoid this talk when she was present. She had always been so silent that it hardly ever occurred to them that she was present.

When the spring came on, and the ice in Eriks Fjord broke up, and folk began going about in boats again, Margret put together some of her pieces of wadmal, the same number as she had brought with her to Solar Fell during the great hunger, and also a change of clothing, and she went to Signy's brother, who had a boat, and asked to be taken into Kambstead Fjord, where she could begin a trek to Hvalsey Fjord, for indeed, she longed to see her brother Gunnar with the longing of old people, that despairs, for lack of strength and time, to be fulfilled. Now Signy's brother went to Signy's mother, and spoke to her of this, because it seemed to him that the woman was too old to make such a trek, but Signy's mother said only, "It must be that she knows her own mind, and it is not for us to stop her." And so the man rowed her the long way around, into Kambstead Fjord, and set her down at the landing where folk begin the trek across to Hvalsey Fjord, which is a short and easy walk, although going around the edge of the fjord is tedious and lengthy.

Toward evening, Margret came to the door of the steading, and saw that the place had been abandoned. She pushed open the door and went inside, intending to spend the night. She was very tired from her long walk, and sat heavily on the bench against the wall of the steading. It was the case that she had depended upon his being here, that through her walk had made up the image of him standing in the doorway, then stepping forward to greet her, in such vivid colors that she had not thought of missing him. It was as if he had been given to her and taken from her all over again. She looked about the walls of the steading, at the broken or worthless objects left behind on the shelves and lost among the rushes on the floor, and then she laid her head down upon her arms on the table, and surrendered herself to such tears as she had never endured before, and as copious as they were, they seemed to be squeezed from her as water might be squeezed from stones, by the greatest crushing might, perhaps by the might of God Himself, from whom she had always turned her face.

Some little time later, Margret crept into one of the bedclosets, and lay there. Now what she had done seemed foolish and impossible to her, and she thought with longing of the round of work that she was accustomed to in Dyrnes and Solar Fell. Gunnar's face recurred to her over and over, not as it had done, but as she remembered it when he left her on the strand at Steinstraumstead, bitter and disapproving, his blue eyes as cool as water and distant as the vault of the sky. She saw now, lying in his bedcloset, as she had never seen before, that he was her implacable enemy. Always before she had thought of her own love for him as a child, or her annoyance with him after Asgeir died, or her jealousy of Birgitta. Never had she considered his feelings for her, but now as she lay where he had lain for so many nights, his thoughts seemed to be seeping into her, and it was not that he thought of her with antagonism, it was that he had no thoughts of her at all. He shunned thoughts of her. Had not Kollgrim been surprised, at their first meeting, even to be told that she was his father's sister? He had not even heard her name about the steading, as he would have had she died. It was Kollgrim's way to accept such things, and not to be curious, and Margret had thought little of his surprise at the time, especially in her pleasure at getting to know him, but now the meaning of such ignorance flooded her, and she shrank before it. It was not that she couldn't make the trip to Vatna Hverfi district, but that he would turn that same empty gaze upon her when she arrived. Wasn't she as implacable in her way? Couldn't she look into her own heart and recall how she had willed everything away—all grief, all desire, all hope—how she had worn herself down to a stone? Seeing that, could she expect any less from Gunnar?

Now she bethought herself of what she must do, for indeed, she could not go back to Dyrnes. They were happy enough to be rid of her. There would be steadings about Hvalsey Fjord where she might find tasks, but the district was a poor one, and getting poorer. She could stay at Lavrans Stead, for she longed for solitude, rather than feared it, but indeed, there was nothing there to start out with. She had only the food that Signy's mother had given her, and Gunnar had taken all of his stores. There were no sheep, either. Now she thought of this, that she might lie quietly in the bedcloset for some number of days, and let hunger take her. Certainly enough folk had done this in former days, and from her time with Eyvind Eyvindsson in Isafjord she knew that it was not so hard to do. Soon enough the body weakened so that there was not even the desire to seek food, and thoughts wandered over things that had not been turned up in many winters. It was even rather pleasant, or might be, if the end was desirable rather than fearful. With these thoughts, sleep came to her, and she slept far into the morning.

But in the morning she got up and put on her stockings and her shoes and her cloak, and gathered together her things, and went out of the steading. There was a boy with some sheep not far off, using the Lavrans Stead pasturage as if it were his own, and when she stepped out of the steading, he began to call to the sheep, as if to lead them off, but she stopped him, and asked him where the folk had gone, and he said that he knew not, but that his father Harald Hakonarson knew, and then he ran off, leaving her with the seven ewes and four lambs. Soon enough, this fellow Harald came peering after her, and as he answered her questions, saying that Gunnar had taken everything to Gunnars Stead in Vatna Hverfi district, he looked her frankly up and down, and at last said, "Old woman, why do you ask after these folk? Where do you come from? Are you some former servant of theirs?"

"Yes, indeed, a nurse. And I have lost my place in Dyrnes through a death, so I came seeking in Hvalsey Fjord."

"You have not so far to seek as Vatna Hverfi district, because we have need of a nurse around the hillside, there. My Gudny has four little ones besides this one here, and we have a good enough table as such things in Hvalsey Fjord go."

"But I am eager to see these folk, for they have been my favorites."

"Even so, the trek to the northern part of Vatna Hverfi district is a long one, and how is it that you will get across Einars Fjord?"

"There will be men with boats about, I am sure of that."

"Nay, old woman. It is unseemly for you to go about like this, looking here and there for help. I have a mind to take you to my steading with me, so you might see how happy you would be there, for my Gudny is a cheerful soul, and these boys and girls she has jump about with a great deal of liveliness."

"Even so—"

"These Lavrans Stead folk are an unlucky set. You must have heard that the old woman did away with herself, and I won't say, indeed, that I know the rights of the case. Folk say that there is more to these things than meets the eye. But I do know that they are all old and unhappy, and age needn't go with age, but should go with youth and good fortune. I am speaking of you, old woman. I mean it kindly."

"Indeed, Harald, I can see that you do, and that your household must be a pleasant one."

"You may come with me right now, if you please."

And it seemed to Margret that she did please. The boy was as bright as an egg, staring up at her, and Harald himself one of those round, red-bearded fellows who have much to say on every topic. She said, "Even so, I must see my nurslings before I die." And she stepped back from him and began to look about, and so at last he sighed and said, "You may go along the fjord there, and turn up through the valley, and come to Einars Fjord in a quick enough walk. But your journey, however hard it is, will be more agreeable than your arrival."

But her journey was agreeable after all, for the trek through the valley was an easy one, bright with sunlight and the newly greening turf. Although her conviction of Gunnar's coldness had not changed since the night before, still it seemed to her that she felt new life within her, and that she put her feet firmly on the path before her, although she had never walked it before in her life.

The sun was high in the sky when she came to the landing place, and there was a sturdy boat drawn up on the strand, and another, manned, some ways out in the fjord. Rather than hailing them, she sat down upon the hillside and opened her bag of provisions and began to eat some cheese she had with her. Soon enough a man came up to her where she was sitting, and asked her how she did, and she said, "I would do well enough if you or one of your fellows would take me across the fjord in your boat."

"Have you business in Vatna Hverfi district then?"

"Life and death business."

He looked her up and down, and she began to brush crumbs off her gown. "You carry nothing with you."

"I have nothing to carry except a few bits of weaving. I will give them all to you, at the end of the journey."

"I would rather you told me your business."

"Why is that?"

"We have been fishing for capelin many days now, and have run out of talk. We look at each other and say, 'well' and 'well' and 'well' again. We are nearly dead from the tedium of it."

"If you take me in your boat, I will tell you a tale that may or may not be the tale of my business." And so they got into the boat, and Margret told him the tale of Hauk Gunnarsson and the killing of the bear on Bear Island, which is two weeks sail from Herjolfsnes on the way to Markland, and after that she told them about Thorleif the Magnificent, and his great ship, and the wood and furs that were brought back from Markland in a single summer, and these men had never heard this tale before. They were so pleased by it that they took her far up the fjord, and let her out at a landing place not far over the hill from Gunnars Stead, and when they let her out, the owner of the boat said, "This is a fine tale, old woman, and hardly credible, although I do credit it, for you do not tell it with a practiced air, as folk tell tales who are used to telling lies. It seems to me that I will think upon this tale for a long time, for what you say of these distant places fires my soul."

"My brother, Gunnar Asgeirsson, can probably still show folk the bearskin that my uncle brought back with him, that is the truth of it."

"Someday I hope to see it, and that is the truth of that." And the man told Margret that his name was Harald Magnusson, of Nes, in Vatna Hverfi district, and he took her hand and helped her out of the boat, and a little ways up the path. The dusk was gathering, and she looked about herself, and saw that she knew just where she was, and she began to walk toward Gunnars Stead, and when she came within sight of it, in the pale summer darkness, she sat down and wrapped her cloak about her, and waited for the light, and then for folk to begin going about their morning business.

At Ketils Stead, little Gunnhild awakened with the light, and Helga got up with her, quietly, so as to let Jon Andres and the servants sleep. Gunnhild slept little these days, for she was learning to go about on her own two feet, and could not give up this activity even for food or for sleep. Helga took some bits of cheese into her pocket and followed the child out of the steading. Gunnhild's gait was such as Helga had never seen in a child before, already half a walk and half a run, as steady over uneven ground as over the floors of the steading. She was the image of her father, dark and wiry. It was a great pleasure to Helga to follow behind her, and to note that, as young as she was, a year and a winter, she never looked back.

Gunnhild directed her steps toward the path to Gunnars Stead, and Helga did not stop her, for she always had a longing to see her father, and even her sister, although Johanna was possessed of such a cool manner that Helga was unsure of her welcome. She let the child go before her as an offering, as Johanna was much taken with Gunnhild. Helga rather missed Elisabet Thorolfsdottir, who had been sent unhappily back to Hvalsey Fjord, to work for other folk there. Even in grief, Elisabet Thorolfsdottir had perked up with talk of cutting robes and making tablet weavings, and she had been very pretty, through everything. Now Gunnhild fell down and began to whimper, and Helga picked her up and carried her along the path. Soon enough she wiggled to get down again. Helga took some bits of cheese out of her pocket and began to eat them. The mist had cleared off; the morning was splendid. Little Unn, who had been born in the autumn, would be safely asleep, but Jon Andres would be getting up now. Helga felt a passing wish to be there with him, to run her hand down his back as he put his shirt on.

At Gunnars Stead, no one was stirring yet, and so Helga knew that Gunnhild had gotten her up even earlier than usual, and began to yawn. She paused, wondering whether to turn the child back toward Ketils Stead, but there seemed no reason for this. In fact, there seemed no reason for anything, except to follow the child here and there in the sunlight, to think of nothing and to feel no obligations. It seemed to Helga that everywhere Gunnhild stepped, she blessed the ground with her feet, and made a place for herself among the less happy ghosts whose steps she trod in. Kollgrim!

Kollgrim! Seized by tears, Helga paused to catch her balance, for she could see nothing in the watery glitter.

On the hillside, Margret sat up and threw off her cloak, for the sun was already warm upon her. Below her, she saw a woman and a child in the middle of the homefield, the child in a little white shirt, stumbling and running forward, its arms raised happily in the air. Its giggle rose on the breeze and came right into Margret's ear. Behind it, the mother, also in white, swayed in attentive pursuit, now smiling, now laughing at the child's antics. The child stumbled into a circle of flowers and fell down. The mother stepped forward and swept it into her arms and covered its neck with kisses, just below the ear, so that the child laughed out in glee. Now the mother put the child down, and lifted her sleeves to her face and wiped her eyes. Now she tossed her head, and she saw Margret and stopped dead in her tracks. Margret stood up.

With the distance, Helga could not tell who the woman on the hillside could be. Her hair was such a pale yellow that it might be white, and hung in braids in front of her shoulders, leading Helga to think that she must be an old woman. But she stepped with such firm grace that Helga thought she must be a young woman, and this look, of youth, of age, fascinated Helga and made her stare discourteously and stand still instead of going forward, as folk should do. But, of course, Gunnhild went forward, not toward the woman, but toward some flowers that attracted her gaze, and Helga could not help but follow her.

Now they were close enough to speak, but Helga knew not what to say, nor why she felt this hesitation.

Margret reached out her hand suddenly, and said, "You will be Helga. What is the child's name?" She knelt down and looked at the child, but did not stare, and kept her hands to herself, which made Gunnhild bold enough to step toward her.

"She is my daughter Gunnhild. I have another as well, Unn, but this one is up with the sun lately."

"Do you know who I am?"

"Nay, I do not, but it seems to me that I should."

"I am your father's sister."

"I know of you, though my father has never spoken of you. My brother Kollgrim said once that you lived inexplicably among those folk at Solar Fell." Her faced whitened, then reddened, and she cast her eyes down.

"Among your enemies, you are thinking."

"Nay, I know not what to think of them. They are not of our district, nor of our mind. Perhaps they have been bewitched by the Icelanders, who are so ready to cry out about witchcraft." But now she was agitated, casting her head about and wringing her hands, so Margret said, "They are ill to speak of. We should speak of Kollgrim, instead."

Helga's chest heaved. "There is no pleasure there, for he was a lost soul."

"Then let us talk of my brother, Gunnar, for I am eager to know about him, but little eager to see how he glances at me after so many winters. Is his hair white? Does he creep about, afflicted with the joint ill? Does he see and hear? Does he remember what happens from day to day?"

"He stands straight and suffers only from grief for my mother. He sits with his lamp over his parchment every day, and makes his marks, but hardly goes outside the steading. He is well enough. May I take you into the steading? My sister Johanna is there, too. She takes after you in the face, I see that now."

"Nay, I would rather sit upon the hillside, and perhaps look at the folk as they come out of the steading. You must go about your business, and pay me no attention, for now that the moment has come, I can hardly bear it. Later, perhaps, we will sit at the loom and talk to one another."

Not long after this, Gunnar came out of the steading to wash himself in the cistern, and his white hair stood up on end and he was wearing a peculiar particolored shirt, and he looked to Margret just as he had looked as a four-year-old child, with the same half discontented and half sleepy morning look on his face that he had worn then. He coughed and sniffed, and the sounds rose clearly on the breeze. Now he rubbed his eyes, and looked at the weather, and he saw her, and his gaze paused, and moved on, then moved back to her, and now it seemed to her that his blue eyes would never turn away from hers.

He had forgotten how tall she was, how gracefully she unfolded herself, and with what swaying strides she stepped forward. Her braids, he saw, were as thick as ever, and hung to her hips. Her gaze caught him, frightened him a little, as it always had, so unsmiling. She had aged so little, although she was twelve years older than his Birgitta, that she came toward him like a ghost from his youth. When she got closer, though, he saw the wrinkles in her face and the age of her hands—wrists and knuckles thickened with work. At this sight he remembered that he had done her many ill turns, and it seemed to him that she was due for revenge. He had no courtesy. He put his hands to his hair, and felt that it was standing on end, and he looked down at his shirt. He had put it on days before. When he looked up and met her gaze, she said, "My brother, have you made this shirt yourself?"

"It was about the steading, in an old chest." And these were the first words that they spoke to one another after thirty-four winters.

At Solar Fell, folk were as sanguine as they could be, and the entertainments and festivities of the betrothal went on for many days. Indeed, Thorstein had so many tales and rhymes and notions of things to do in his happiness that he seemed single-handedly to drive off the gloom that had lingered about the place for nearly a year. Thorgrim had taken Thorstein's place at Nes, and Steinunn still lay in her silent repose, much more wasted and nearer death than she had been, and folk spoke openly of their hope that she would die before the wedding was to take place. Her own sister Thorunn took the lead in this talk, for it was to her that care for the madwoman had fallen, and she had little taste for it, as it was laborious and had less than no effect on Steinunn's condition. It were better that she should die and receive her reward, whatever that might be, than linger as a burden to all, and a reminder of the frailty of women. This was what Thorunn said, that the Lord made sure that sin was too much for folk, and if the Lord made sure of that, then it was not for folk to go against His will. Whenever Sira Eindridi was about, he shrived and blessed the silent woman, and folk made the remark that perhaps this would be the last such time for him. And it was the case that she did die in the summer of this year, and the wedding was set for the early autumn, after the seal hunt, when there would be plenty of meat for the feast. This was also the case, that Sigrid set her heart upon having the wedding at St. Birgitta's church in Hvalsey Fjord, for that was much the nicest church in Greenland, nicer than the cathedral now, for it was newer, and the Hvalsey Fjorders had kept it in good repair.

The circumstances of Steinunn Hrafnsdottir's death did not pass without remark, and they were these, that one day in the summer, when folk were out of the steading going about their work, the living corpus of the woman was moved from one side of the bedcloset to another, and one of her legs and one of her hands were thrown over the side. But when folk came in for their evening meat, she was as still as ever, and these movements seemed unaccountable, except perhaps as evidence of her continued possession by the demons who had led her to her seduction. Thorunn went to her with her broth, and held up her head, and did what she could to get some nourishment into the woman, and these efforts were as fruitless as ever. On the next day, she had been moved again; this time she had been turned in a quarter circle from the straight way of the bedcloset, and at this, Bjorn Bollason went about to his sons and the servingfolk and asked who had been making sport at the poor woman's expense, but none would admit to such a thing. And for three days after this, there were no movements, and folk forgot about them. Now on the fourth day, it happened that the woman spoke aloud, as if in a dream, and she said, "Nay, it comes not so these days," as clearly as could be. Her speech was heard by two or three folk, including Signy, Bjorn Bollason's wife. Now folk began to chatter among themselves, and to look for Steinunn to revive and regain her health, but this did not happen. Instead, a day later, she let out a great groan that went like a knife into the hearts of those nearby, so full was it of agony, and when Thorunn ran to her bedcloset, she saw that Steinunn's eyes were open for the first time in many many months, and she said, "My sister, you are with us again." Steinunn's eyes filled with tears. But after this, her corpus twisted with pain, and soon after that she died.

And when the women went to lay her out, they saw that she was as wasted as folk had gotten during the hunger—with no breasts to speak of, and hipbones sticking up like spoons, and all of her ribs showing, and her knees larger than her thighs, and folk said that what she had died of was starvation, truly enough, just as if there hadn't been any food at all. Before her seduction she had been such a woman as Thorunn, broad and sturdy. She was buried in the graveyard at Solar Fell, which lies near the shrine of St. Olaf the Greenlander, and folk considered that she was more blessed in this circumstance of her death than she had been in life, for between the fires of volcanoes and the fires of evil seduction, she had gained no peace in her days, and must hope as best she could for her heavenly reward, such as it was.

It seemed to Bjorn Bollason that he had done all that was possible in these circumstances, and that things had turned out well enough, considering what might have happened, namely that there might have been a pitched battle at the Thing, where many Greenlanders would have gotten hurt or killed, or that Gunnar Asgeirsson might have sought revenge, as he had done in the past, or that the Icelanders might have somehow blamed him, Bjorn Bollason, for the circumstances of the woman's seduction and death. But Snorri Torfason was more than willing to take Bolli Bjornsson with him, and Thorstein Olafsson was as ardent a suitor as a man could be, and though Sigrid would find herself much farther off than Herjolfsnes,

Thorstein had so confused and subdued her that, if she thought of it, she did not complain of it. Back in Iceland, folk said, Thorstein was a well-known man from a powerful family, and might indeed be lawspeaker some day. Of cows and sheep and horses there was no telling how many wandered Thorstein's three steadings, and of goodly furnishings, well, there were articles from as far off as Damascus and Rome, as well as from Norway and England and Germany and Sweden. Thorstein's own mother's brother's daughter was a waiting maid at the court of Queen Margarethe, or had been some years before, though she might be married to a great Danish lord by now. And Thorstein had that Icelandic way with words that would lead him everywhere, to every success, as it had the great poets of the past, like Egil Skallagrimsson. All in all, Bjorn had never looked forward to the future with such a high heart, and not the least of these pleasures was that the troublesome Sigrid would be off his hands, and in the care of her husband.

As for Sigrid, it was her secret that once in a while a curious dream came to her, always the same dream. In it, she was standing in the doorway to the steading at Solar Fell, looking down the hillside toward the strand. The turf was green, but the fjord was white with ice, and the sky above the mountains was piled with clouds. These were shot with all colors of red and gold and purple, and looked not as the sky ever looked in Greenland, but as it was said that Heaven itself looked. In the first part of her dream, she only stood there, holding a trencher in her hand, and gazing upon the scene. After this, a man would appear, a stranger, and he would come toward her over the ice, and she would begin to float down the hillside toward him, holding out her trencher as an offering. But though she floated toward him, she was much afraid of him, and of how he would greet her. Even so, she could not stop herself, or turn back up the hillside. He came on skis, but not with the swinging laboring motions of a skier. He, too, was floating. And as he came closer, he did not become more familiar to her. He was always a stranger. Even so, when they met, he always took her in his arms and embraced her, and happiness rushed through her like a strong wind, and of itself, her body pressed against his, and then the dream was over, and she woke up. And this was also the case, that she awakened from this dream elated rather than despondent, and it seemed to her that as long as she held this dream secretly in her bosom, it would return to her again and again.

She was not unpleased with her marriage to Thorstein. It seemed to her that he had her firmly in his power, and that with him, she was out of danger. In addition to this, her wedding was to be at the loveliest church in Greenland, and her wedding clothes were as splendid as hands could make them—her hands, the hands of Margret Asgeirsdottir, the hands of all the women round about. First there would be the wedding, then there would be a little boat ride to Iceland, then there would be large farms with many sheep and cows and horses and servants, and then there would be such children as her brothers were, obedient, strong, lucky little boys, four or five or six. Snorri Torfason said, sometimes, that conditions in Iceland could not but surprise them, but were not the Icelanders possessed of many fine things? Did they not speak in such a way that pleased the ear? Did they not know more of the world, and of the entertainments of the world, than any Greenlander? And did they not think a great deal of her, Sigrid Bjornsdottir, though she was but a Greenlandic maid?

She did not hate Kollgrim Gunnarsson, though folk thought she must. She did not know exactly why they had parted, except that it was their fate to do so. One day he had come to Solar Fell, and found her in the steading doing some tablet weaving while the others were out or in other chambers, and he had sat down near her without touching her, but only looking into her face, and she had let the weaving fall from her hands, although it tangled the threads, and she had known without speaking that they were parted, that their marriage could not be, and she had known so clearly that in spite of their wills and desires something was stopping them, she had not even felt grief, only a sort of relief that greater grief was being avoided by this parting. She saw that he knew this, too, and that they were parting as friends. That was in the autumn, and in the winter her fears had been fulfilled with the seduction of the Icelandic woman. How was one to think of that? In spite of what she was told, by Thorstein and Bjorn Bollason and Thorunn, Sigrid held tightly to her incomprehension, and placed it in her bosom next to her secret dream.

And so it happened that she went through the summer, and through the preparations for her wedding and the feast as if spellbound. Sometimes Thorstein loomed near her, and sometimes he touched her, and sometimes he was far off, and she could hear his voice rising and falling, and laughter of folk that always followed him about. Her hands did their work of themselves—making cheeses, weaving, sewing in tiny stitches. They were busy and cozy with one another. Her lips opened and formed words that were suitable to every occasion, also of themselves, and the days passed in a stream. It is the case, her mother told her, that maidens are distracted by thoughts of their weddings, and their new lives. Certainly she had been very clumsy before marrying Bjorn Bollason, dropping everything, losing everything, until her own mother was ready to scream. And surely Sigrid had reason to be more distracted than most, for here she was getting ready to go off—Signy did not quite know what to make of this, her only daughter going off, perhaps never to return, or certainly never to return, and her boy Bolli as well. Signy dropped the spoon she was holding and put her sleeves to her eyes, and Sigrid turned to her, slowly, comprehending only with difficulty the significance of these actions. But now her arm went out, as a daughter's arm should do, and went about her mother's shoulders, and she made some noises, the proper noises, and when her mother had smiled again, and turned away from her, and picked up the spoon and gone about her business again, Sigrid forgot everything that had happened, although she could not have said what her thoughts returned to.

And so the day of the wedding came round, and the family and the Icelanders woke up in the priest's house in Hvalsey Fjord, and Sira Eindridi and Sira Pall Hallvardsson loomed before Sigrid, who found herself in her wedding robe, with the Solar Fell wedding garland on her head, and many trinkets that had been given to her by Thorstein on her hands and her arms and her neck. Now folk took her hands and her arms, and led her across the grass toward the church, and through the doorway, just briefly, she caught a glimpse of Thorstein, her fated husband, and it seemed to her that just for a moment she rose out of the spell that had held her for the entire course of the summer, and she saw the cut of his shirt, and the roundness of his cheeks, and the way his beard grew high on them, and then she saw his eyes turned upon her, evaluating her with approbation, but not, really, looking into her own eyes, and she remembered, just for a moment, how Kollgrim Gunnarsson had met her gaze with his own, and then, just for another moment, the thought came to her that Thorstein's gaze would always call forth in her thoughts the image of Kollgrim's gaze, from now on, until death should part her from both of them, and then for another moment, she had the sense to be greatly frightened, and then those who were leading her pulled her forward, and she fell again into the spell of the summer, and went into the church, and the service was spoken, and she was led out again, this time by Thorstein, and she wondered, now, if she was a happy woman at last, or an unhappy woman forever, and then someone spoke to her, and her lips formed a merry jest, and everyone went into the priest's house for the feast that had been laid for them, and some fifty guests, and more, sat about the tables, and ate their fill, for Bjorn Bollason the lawspeaker was a prosperous and a happy man.

Now the winter came on, and the first heavy snowfall, thick and wet, was on the ground before the cattle on most steadings were byred up, or the sealmeat was thoroughly dried from the autumn hunt. Shortly after this snowfall, a great, unseasonable wind picked up, and carried a deal of sand over the top of the snow, so that it melted in the sun and crusted, and men had to go about with their bone axes, and chop down to the grass, which, indeed, was still green, for the weather right up to the time of the snowfall had been warm enough. Now folk hurried to get their sheep in from the higher pastures and to slaughter those that would be used for winter meat, and to byre up their cattle, and the season was busy from the work, and unseasonably wet and uncomfortable from the snow. It also happened that around this time, Helga felt the quickening of another child in her belly, and she had suspected this for some time, for she had been ill off and on through the summer. The child did not seem to agree with her at all, and from the first quickening, seemed to roll about in her belly like a skiff in a storm. Sometime later, she began to feel so ill every day that she asked one of the women from Gunnars Stead to come and stay with her, for indeed, she had little strength for working about the steading and running after Unn and Gunnhild. It happened that Johanna came, and Helga saw that the two must learn to live together at last.

Now the first thing that Johanna did on the morning she brought her belongings around the hill was to throw all of the straw out of her bedcloset, and find herself newer straw. Then she made a ball out of the cloaks and furs that had lain in the bedcloset, and she set this outside the door, and then she laid her own cloaks and furs over the new straw, and she was at this for no little time, until Helga had to bite her tongue to keep from remarking about it. Johanna went about these tasks with hardly a word, and when Helga asked after their father, or their father's sister, or the others on the steading, Johanna only said, "He is well enough," and "She is quiet about the place." After making up her bed, Johanna took the ball of bed furnishings and unrolled it, and took out each piece and carried it into the light of the doorway, and fingered through the hairs of the furs, and some articles she threw down and others she only shook out and laid in a stack beside the door. Helga sat with her feet out of her bedcloset, and it seemed to her that her innards were going to rise up into her throat, but she swallowed hard, and at last she said, "What do you intend about those things, there?" Johanna gave them a kick, and said nothing. Now Gunnhild came into the steading, and her feet and stockings were covered with snow, and Johanna took her by the shoulders and turned her about without a word, and put her out again, and then went out after her, and brushed the sandy snow off her feet. Helga got up and went to the doorway, and saw that her sister held the child by the shoulder in a firm grasp, as if she were holding a sheep, and swept the snow off her with brisk strokes, and when Gunnhild wiggled out of her grasp, her hand shot out and clamped down upon the child, not roughly, but not tenderly, either. And now Helga's innards did rise into her mouth, and she staggered out the doorway and around the corner of the house to the midden, and vomited for the second time in that day.

Later it seemed to Helga that she might sit up at the loom for a while, and while she was at this, Johanna came up behind her and stood silently for a few moments. Then, wordless, she sniffed, and turned away, and soon after this, it seemed to Helga that the pattern she had chosen was not so pleasing after all, though she had liked it before, and she got up from the loom and sat on the bench beside the table. All trenchers and bowls and cups and other utensils, that usually lay about in a little disorder, were more than neatly stacked. All corners and handles were aligned on the shelves, and a piece of wadmal had been cut, hemmed, and hung across the lower shelf, to hide such pots and vats as there were there. Things were very neat, but Helga did not care for them. Now Johanna came in from the store-house, and she was wiping her hands on her robe, as if the storehouse were very dirty. When she saw Helga, she smiled one of her slow smiles, and said, "My sister, have you finished with your weaving already?"

"My sister, have you finished making over Ketils Stead to your own liking?"

Johanna said, mildly, "Indeed, there are other things to be done. But it may be that you would prefer that I not do them. When folk set out to please others, perhaps it is the case that they really set out to please themselves." She smiled her slow smile again.

"I know not what you mean, but I see that our ways here do not suit you."

"That is not what I was thinking. But I, too, have certain ways, for after all, I lived for a long time at Hestur Stead, and Jona's reputation was well known to all. I mean only to do as you wish."

Now Helga sat back and looked at her sister for a long moment, and then she smiled, and said, "Indeed, I do not know what I wish after all, except to feel myself again." Now she sighed, and looked about, and that was the first day that the two spent together, and it was a long time before they ceased to be uneasy with one another, for they were not only different in their habits, but also in their concerns, and for Helga's children Johanna cared not as Helga herself would, but with less tenderness and indulgence.

It happened that Helga felt her pains just at Yule, although she had not thought to feel them until nearly Lent, but they came on, and lasted for more than a day, and in the morning of the second day she was delivered of a boy, and toward the evening of that day, she was delivered of another boy, and where the first was tiny, the second was yet tinier, and neither of the two lived through the night. Helga herself gave forth much blood and other humors, and lay greatly weakened for many days, so weakened that she could barely speak or open her lips for nourishment, although Margret came every day around the hill to Ketils Stead, and made the girl strengthening drinks from herbs she had gathered the previous summer. Through this nursing, the women were much thrown together, and one day after Helga was able to sit up a little, Margret said to her in a low voice, "My Helga, it seems to me from this confinement and from what folk say of your confinement with Gunnhild, that you are little made for childbearing. You are like unto Helga Ingvadottir, your namesake and my mother, and you must take care that you preserve your life."

Helga whispered, "It is always a mischance and a peril to have twins."

"For most folk, the peril is to the children, not so much to the mother."

"Even so." She paused for a long moment. "Even so, such is the lot of wives, is it not?"

"They may stay apart from their husbands."

At this, Helga turned away her head, and Margret fell silent, and these words lay between them for the rest of the morning.

It seemed to Helga that Margret might take it upon herself to speak of this matter to Jon Andres, and so when the two were about the steading at the same time, she looked after them, to see if they were having talk with one another, but they did not appear to exchange more than friendly greetings, and truly, her father's sister was as silent as she was reputed to be. Still, after the exchange about childbearing, Helga was eager to have the older woman off the steading, and so she made herself sit up and smile, and throw her feet over the side of the bedcloset, and then to stand, although the color rushed out of her face, and she had to sit down again with a thump. She also forced whatever drinks and dishes that were offered her down her throat, whether they piqued her appetite or not. The result was that her strength seemed to return, as if by the power of her will, and she was up and about in the second week of Lent, and Margret stopped coming around the hill so often, and Johanna spoke once of going back to Gunnars Stead herself.

Helga saw it was the case that Jon Andres, whether he had been spoken to or not, was keeping much to himself. All winter, before Yule, and after he was certain that Helga was out of the danger of death, he had gone off many days and nights, and he said only that it had to do with a certain business that he and Gunnar Asgeirsson were carrying on together. It was also the case that he had named the two small boys, although they had lived but the shortest length of time, and were unbaptized, and the larger of these boys he had named Erlend, as was proper, and the smaller he had named Kollgrim, and he spoke of them a few times by name. When he was about the steading, he stayed apart from Helga, and had little to say to her, although also he was as kind to her as he could be. And Helga wondered what had parted them, after all her care. One day it happened that she awakened in the bedcloset, and felt that he was awake beside her, although it was very early morning, as yet before dawn. She lay quietly, as if still asleep, breathing deep, slow breaths, and allowed her hip to relax into his side. Now he let out a low, almost soundless groan, that seemed to Helga to be full of some sort of pain, and she could not keep herself from turning to him, but at once he stiffened in her arms, and sat up, and got out of the bedcloset in his shirt, and pulled on his leggings and went out of the steading, and so Helga thought that Margret must have spoken to him after all, outside, or in some moment when she, Helga, had been asleep, and she was bitterly disappointed, and angry with her father's sister, for she saw clearly that whatever the consequences were to be, she could not stay apart from her husband as long as she had breath in her body.

It was not the case that Margret had spoken with Jon Andres, but that he was so much taken up with the matter of Kollgrim Gunnarsson that he was afraid that if he began speaking to Helga in their usual fashion, he would speak of it to her, whether he wished to or not, and he and Gunnar had agreed that these affairs were to be secret, even, or especially, from the women about the steading. Gunnar could not have said where his fever for secrecy had come from, but it seemed the twin to his animus against Bjorn Bollason, and the guarantee that his resolution would not fail him, however long the Icelanders squatted at Solar Fell. For Jon Andres was also resolved, and his resolution was to abstain from all action until the Icelanders should leave, taking their swords and axes and other iron weapons with them. That was an easy resolution to maintain, but his promise to Gunnar never to speak of the business to Helga tried him every day, and every moment of every day. What he especially could not withstand was the slow turn of her head in his direction, and the slow lift of her eyelids, so that her gaze fell upon him with pleasure and sadness. Then his tongue seemed to come alive in his mouth, and to beat against his teeth, and it seemed to him that the stream of words was already half out of him. But Gunnar had impressed this secrecy upon him so utterly that he could not speak. He could only have dreams, as he did every so often, that he had told without meaning to, and in these dreams, chagrin burned him from feet to hairline. And so he fled from Helga and yearned for her at the same time. But it is well known that in such matters as honor and retaliation, women either weaken a man's perseverance with their cautious counsels, or they goad him forward too quickly with taunts, and so it is better for a man to keep his plans dark.

When he went about to other steadings, it was as it had been the year before. He talked about this and that with perfect candor. He allowed himself to be fed the best viands. He spoke of Helga and, after Yule, the sad case of the twin sons. He was one of the most powerful and wealthiest men in the district, and he dressed with careful richness, and always had two handsome servingmen with him, and when there was little snow on the ground, he rode his finest stud horse, and when there was much snow on the ground, he skied on carved skis. The first thing he did was let folk give him things and make him promises and speak to him of their business. The next thing he did was to make a few remarks concerning their business, always helpful, always canny about the ways of steadings or sheep or cows or men. The third thing he did was to settle little disputes, but carefully, so that both parties felt that the best possible thing had been done for them. He went from steading to steading, beginning with those steadings where he was little known, or known only to speak to. Then he went to steadings where he had visited in the past, or where the folk were under some small obligation to him. Then he went to his own steadings, where folk were his tenants. Then he went to the steadings of men nearly as prosperous and powerful as himself, men who considered themselves his faithful friends, and in every steading he counted the sons and the brothers and took note of what might be used for weapons, and in every steading he considered with care what was offered him, and he measured the constancy of the friendship he felt toward himself from the farmer. He weighed warmth against self-interest, generosity against dependability. He never once mentioned the name of Gunnar Asgeirsson. He was his own man, Jon Andres Erlendsson of Ketils Stead in Vatna Hverfi district, and to all appearances he was simply strengthening his position in the district, as men must do from time to time.

It happened that he went to Mosfell, the steading that was farmed by Ulfhild the widow, where once he and other men had nearly caught Ofeig, and Ulfhild and her sons welcomed him, as all folk in the district had done. Ulfhild set her best refreshments before him, and then, when he had eaten his fill, she took him out to the byre, and showed him the sheep he had given her, and also the horse he had sent to replace the horse that Ofeig had stolen. The new horse was a mare, and she had produced a rather nice young stud colt that was now a yearling. Jon Andres ran his hands over the back of the colt and down his legs, and he saw that someone had treated the animal with care, for it flinched not at his touch. He said, "He is a big fellow already, as big as a two-year-old and with a thick coat." He smiled. "I should have thought again before choosing to give you that Flosi mare. She will prove to be the best of what I had. Indeed, she is from the Hestur Stead line, and that's a fact."

Ulfhild spoke rather sourly. "And which of my sons will ride the beast when he is fully grown? Will you give me another to make it even between them?"

"You seem to like the little fellow, though you speak ill-naturedly. The two of them needn't ride the beast at the same time. There must be one boy about the steading to do some work."

"Why then and not now?"

Now Jon Andres laughed. "You are full of complaints, old woman," he said, "but affairs on your steading look to be as as prosperous as they have ever been since I have known you or your husband."

"They may be and they may not be. Such things depend not a little on you or such as you. The powerful men in the district have been quiet enough for the last few years. Something is hatching, it seems to me."

"What might that be?"

"That is for you to tell me. You didn't come here to eat at my table. If your own isn't better, then your wife is a poor stick. Nor did you come to look after this mare or sigh after this yearling colt. You came to look about, and to measure the height of my sons and the depth of their prowess. Nor is this the first steading you have visited. Do not think that though you go about by yourself, a train of talk does not follow behind you, my man."

"Greenlanders always talk, especially in the winter. They do not always know what they are speaking of."

"It is true that they speak highly of you, such a worthy fellow, so open and helpful, not so much like Erlend, nor yet like Vigdis, but perhaps of another strain."

"Folk say that of me all the time. It may be true, but at this date, there is little to tell one way or another."

"You are of the true Ketils Stead strain nonetheless, for when I was a girl, your father Erlend came about in just such a way as you are doing, and what he wanted was help in his case against Gunnar Asgeirsson. And it also seems to me that Gunnar Asgeirsson must figure in your comings and goings, somehow, since you have married his daughter."

"It must be, old woman, that you have no concerns of your own, since you consider mine so carefully."

"I am concerned with preserving my sons until they are strong enough to do something about the place. That is what I am concerned with. The great ones will bring us down in the end, and that is a fact."

"Nay, old woman. It is not a fact. Nothing that hasn't yet taken place is a fact."

"It is a fact that men love to fight, and pay for their pleasure with a few deaths or deadly injuries, and it is a fact that women can do little enough about it. If it comes to my sons to fight, then their hearts will fly to it as quickly as the hearts of any other men, though they are lazy enough about everything else."

"No one cares to fight." And at this, the old woman only smiled, and led Jon Andres back up the hill to the steading, where she offered him more refreshment, although he had eaten only a little while before. After dusk and moonrise, he mounted his horse and went on his way over the crusty snow, wondering about the talk of the district, and whether his plans lay as open to everyone as they did to him. He stayed at Ketils Stead for some time after this, and saw that Helga's confinement had turned her inward somehow, so that she had little to say to him, and he seemed to himself a much misused and isolated man.

Now the spring came on, and the ice broke up in the fjords, and folk were pleased enough, after a hard and snowy winter, to have what bits to eat they had left in their storehouses and cupboards, and at Easter they gave thanks for what there was to give thanks for, and otherwise prayed for better times. The Icelanders, with Sigrid Bjornsdottir and Bolli Bjornsson, made ready to depart, but at the last minute, Snorri Torfason the shipmaster changed his mind, and put off the departure for another season, much angering some of his folk, especially Thorstein Olafsson. But indeed, though he was a small, lazy man, it was the case that once Snorri had fixed

his mind on something, he would not, or could not change it, and he had
fixed his mind on staying with Bjorn Bollason yet another year, for living,
he surmised, was easier there than it would be back in Iceland, even if his
wife Gudrun were still alive, which, after eight winters, he somewhat
doubted. Bjorn Bollason was happy enough to have Snorri, and Thorstein,
and Sigrid, and Thorunn, for his enthusiasm for them never waned, but
Signy his wife could be heard to mutter under her breath from time to
time, for the case was that she and Thorunn were not such good friends
as they had been, but they were forced to live as sisters anyway.

Thorstein and some of the other Icelanders had gotten into the habit
of going on the seal hunt every spring and fall, and they were not so bad
at it, if a Greenlander with some experience was watching out for them.
Even so, most of the Greenlanders thought that trading these Icelanders,
even with their weapons, for such a hunter as Kollgrim Gunnarsson was
a poor bargain, especially since, in the two years since the burning, no ship
had arrived, and no bishop had walked among the folk gathered on the
strand and blessed them with real wheaten wafers and true wine. Indeed,
at every hunting gathering, the men could not forbear speaking of what
had been lost with Kollgrim Gunnarsson. Wasn't every man's portion less
now? And he had been such an inward fellow that he had never taught
much to others, such an inward fellow that it had never occurred to anyone
to seek his teaching. Some folk had never even heard him speak. But he
was gone now, and folk said among themselves that his burning was
unaccountable, and the circumstances of it grew cloudy in the memory.
Gunnar went on every hunt now, and that was remarkable, too, that the
father had so little knack for what the son did so well. But it was said that
the father wrote things down, as a priest does, and folk considered that such
a skill was like a deep hole into which other skills fell and were lost,
whether the man who wrote wished or not. Jon Andres went on every
hunt, as well, and he was as good as most men.

Helga was not glad to see the coming of the summer, with the seal
hunt and the Thing and much other traveling about to look forward to.
This strange state of unfriendship continued between herself and Jon
Andres all through the spring, so long that she ceased to wonder about it,
and began to resent him for prolonging it, and to turn away from him
herself. Whatever the reason for its beginning, the estrangement itself
became the reason for its continuation. Even so, Helga shrank from letting
him go off, for fear that he would be killed and never return. Certainty
that he would be taken from her for eternity, and her grief at this, beset
her every moment, from the time he mentioned that he would be going

off soon, to the time that he returned and lay stiffly in her bedcloset again, and this fear made her even more distant from him. It was as if she could not even shout to him, as folk shout across the fields, yet he was right beside her.

She shrank from letting him go off, but men go off, whatever the women about the steading have to say about it. There is business that must be done, and so Jon Andres went off to the seal hunt, and took his share, and the seal hunt went on for five days, with a day and a half for getting there and a day for getting back. And on the third of these days, Johanna and Helga went out into the yard beside the steading, and began to lay out the bedclothes to be beaten and aired. It could not be said that the two were easy with one another, but Johanna had not left Ketils Stead, although she spoke of it from time to time. The sky was high and sunny, with but the thinnest layer of pale cloud stretched out here and there. The grass had greened in the previous fortnight, and was dry and thick. The birch and willow scrub was beginning to bud out, and the angelica about the watercourses was beginning to unfold its rich, wide branches. In spite of her unhappiness, Helga was not immune to these signs, and she looked about her, and caught sight of her children playing at the edge of the homefield, and felt a certain pleasure and hope for the future. Jon Andres was a man some thirty-six winters of age, and he had gone on countless seal hunts, and returned unscathed every time, had he not? Johanna went in and out without smiling, as always, but it seemed to Helga that her sister, too, walked with a lighter tread, and sensed an end to unhappiness.

Now it was the case that this long summer day passed as such days do when folk have their work, and are sunk in their thoughts, so that they look up, now and again, and discover that the time for the morning meat has passed, or that some bits of washing have dried already, or that the sun has passed its zenith although the morning seems only to have begun. And it happened that Thormod, the shepherd, and his brother, Thorodd, whom Jon Andres had left behind to take care of the work about the place in his absence, came to Helga and received permission to take a flock of sheep over to Gunnars Stead, and spend the night there.

At the evening meat everyone was as sleepy as could be from breathing so much warm air. Gunnhild could hardly lift her spoon, and Unn could hardly swallow the meat Helga chewed for her. Even Johanna drooped where she sat, and the servingmaids, Thormod's wife Oddny, and the two others, had little enough to say, although usually they chattered over their food. Helga shooed them to their bedclosets as soon as the meal was over, and went to her own with Unn, but once there she lay awake for a long time, through the late dusk, thinking of Jon Andres with a peppery longing that set her to fidgeting among the cloaks and furs until her robe was all twisted about her once and then again. By then it was dark, and she began to think of all she might have done—sewing, or weaving, or spinning—when it was still light, instead of simply throwing herself about in futility. But she was reluctant to get up or light the seal oil lamp.

Now as she was speculating about what she might do, she heard a distinct swish and thump, so distinct that she could not dismiss it, but indeed, she little knew where it might be coming from, for it did not seem to be inside the steading. She lay silently. Now Johanna turned over in her bedcloset and hit her knee or her elbow on the side, and it seemed to Helga that the other might have been just such a sleeper's sound as this, except that Johanna was just there, across the room and to the left, and this other sound had no such particularity. She listened again to the silence, and considered the five women and two little girls in the steading, and after a few moments of this consideration, she sat up where she was, and rearranged the cloaks about her over Unn, so that she was more thoroughly hidden among them. Then she crept out of the bedcloset and began to feel her way toward Oddny's bedcloset, where Gunnhild slept, intending to do the same thing there, but just then there were a great many sounds— thumps and brushings, and she understood at once that they were coming from the roof of the steading, that someone was trying to get into the steading through the turves above them. Now she reached out her hand in the dark, and put it on the railing of Johanna's bedcloset, and then upon her sister's shoulder, which she shook, and then upon her mouth, so that she prevented the other woman from crying out as she woke. Now she turned and leaned into the bedcloset and said in a whisper, "Now we are hard put, for some bear or other beast is trying to get into this nest of women, and indeed, we have no weapons, for everything has been taken on the hunt, and I know not what to do."

Now Johanna sat up, and her face was pale in the gloom, and she listened to the sounds raining down with little bits of earth from the turves above them. She said, "That's what demons do in old tales, they ride the roof beam until the steading shakes under their weight."

"Well, the steading isn't shaking yet, and old tales aren't going to make us know what to do in this instance."

Johanna turned and put her feet over the side of the bedcloset and said, "It seems to me that we should arouse everyone and herd them into one of the other chambers."

"But this steading isn't like Gunnars Stead. There is only the one doorway here. The other rooms are blind, for warmth."

"May we not get into the cowbyre from inside the steading?"

"Vigdis closed off that passageway, for the smell, and the mess of the servants going back and forth."

"But we may open it again, if we have to. A hole to crawl through at the least." Now the noises came more loudly, and Helga looked up, afraid. Johanna stood up and began going about the bedclosets, rousing the servingwomen. Oddny got up with Gunnhild in her arms, and Helga heard Unn stir among the bedclothes with a muffled cry, and it seemed to her, in her growing panic, that the child must suffocate, and so she snatched her out of the bedcloset, and held her tightly in her arms. Now she could not remember what Johanna and she had thought of trying to do, and she stared at her younger sister for a long moment, and Johanna stared back at her, but then said, "From what chamber does the passage to the cowbyre go off?" And Helga gathered her wits, and put her arm around Oddny, and said, "This one, here——" but just then she was interrupted by the fall of a man's figure through the roof and onto the table. The table broke, and the man landed standing up. She saw in the moonlight that came in through the hole in the roof that the fellow was Ofeig Thorkelsson.

He was not so fat as he once had been, and in fact, his flesh was eked out over his long frame like the flesh of a cow at the end of winter. Bits of clothing hung about him, in no order, tied and wrapped with other bits to keep in some warmth. His hood was torn and mended with little skill, and he stood stoop-shouldered. His beard hung in thin locks to the middle of his chest. He was grinning, and he carried, for weapons, an ax and a small knife. Helga saw that his eyes, accustomed to the bright moonlight outside, could not yet make out who was about him, and she stepped back into the dark, and set Unn back into the bedcloset. But there was only that moment. The next moment, he grabbed Johanna's arm and twisted it behind her, and there was the distinct, low sound of a crack. Johanna gave a gasp of surprise, and stood as still as a rock. "Now, my girl," said Ofeig, "it would not ill please me to break it again, or, indeed, to break the other one, but I am a hungry fellow, and I long for some of the good, soft Ketils Stead cheese that I used to fill my belly with many years ago. So I will stand here with you, and the others will find me what they can."

Helga stepped forward, and out of the corner of her eye, she saw Oddny and Gunnhild disappear into Johanna's bedcloset. She did not know if Ofeig saw this, and so she said, "Ofeig, it is but the beginning of the summer, and such cheeses as we have are old and hard, but I will make up a trencher for you."

"You may fill it as you please, as long as it is plentiful and good. I don't want any garbage, like gnawed bones or offal, and if you give me any, I will jam it down this little one's throat here, for indeed, she has wandered into my power now, and everything that displeases me will cause her dissatisfaction." He jerked on Johanna's arm, and she gasped again, but did not cry out. Now Ofeig twisted her around so that he could see her. "Are you a servingmaid, or what? Tell me your name."

"Johanna Gunnarsdottir." Her voice was firm and cool, though Helga's had trembled when she spoke. Helga picked a trencher up off the floor, where the collapse of the table had thrown it, and began to go about, looking for what food there was to be had. Johanna said, "My Helga, there is wholesome dried sealmeat in that chest there," as if they were speaking of their evening meat. Helga lifted the lid of the chest with shaking fingers, and scooped almost all of the meat into the trencher. Then she cut some pieces of cheese, and held the trencher out to Ofeig, who said, "Stand here, and hold it while I eat. Now that I have caught this little one, I don't intend to let her go." And he jerked her arm again. And Johanna said, "If you are Ofeig Thorkelsson, then folk say that you are the devil himself, and it must be the case that prayer is our only hope." And she began to pray in a firm voice, "Hail Mary, Mother of God." He jerked her arm again, harder, and said, "I like this praying little," but Johanna continued, "Blessed art thou among women——" until Helga herself put her hand over Johanna's mouth and stopped her. Ofeig said, "The Devil is a powerful fellow, I have heard, and he doesn't go from steading to steading, as I do, being satisfied with a bit of this and a bit of that. I will tell you this, that the Greenlanders are a niggardly lot, and I hate them as much as the Devil does. Indeed, it is a poor part of the earth that we live in, bitter cold and waste, and the wind bites the flesh like a dog. Give me some more of that." And Helga took the trencher and began looking about for other things to serve him. Johanna said, as coolly as before, "There is sourmilk in the near storeroom, a big vat of it, and some pickled blubber and some svid, as well." He gave her arm another jerk, and this time, expecting it, she made no sound at all. He went on, "And I'll tell you another thing, I hate these Gunnars Stead folk. I hear they burned up the one, the staring one who used to follow us about. That rejoiced me, indeed. But you must be his sister. I see somewhat of the same stare about you, now that I've had something to eat and can look about me. Why don't you light a lamp here?

I'd like to see what's about the place. Indeed, I hate this steading. I hate every place I've ever been in this godforsaken land, and that's a fact."

Helga said, "I haven't a flint. On these long days, we don't light the lamps." She fingered the flint in her pocket, and prayed that Unn would make no sound behind her. It seemed to her that the darkness was her only salvation, and also that she must give up her sister to preserve her daughters, and her heart sank within her so that she could hardly keep on her feet. Johanna seemed to be two people to her—this doomed, pale creature, standing stock-still in the streaming moonlight, and also that sunlit figure of the smooth countenance and firm tread whom she had watched go in and out of the steading all morning long. And it was the case that she repented with all her heart of the annoyance she had felt during the winter and the spring, and she saw that whatever Johanna lacked of softness, she had in extra measure of goodness and grace. Now Johanna said, in her clear, firm voice, "Have you finished eating, Ofeig Thorkelsson? For indeed, I remember something else that might please you, and that is dried capelin with some bits of sour butter."

"Now I see that this little one really does wish to please me. It seems to me that I have such a hunger that I could eat you out of this steading, and it has been no little time since I have had such a treat."

And Johanna said to Helga, "In the back of the near storeroom. You can feel with your hands where the butter and the dried sealmeat are. And there are other things, too. Some dried reindeer meat, and some mutton, and a round of cheese." And Helga went out, trembling, and felt about the storeroom in the dark with clumsy fingers, and returned with what she had found, and then she stood again beside Ofeig, and held the trencher while he ate from it. Now he sat down upon the bench, with Johanna on his lap, with her arm still twisted behind her, and he let out two mighty belches, and then he began to lay his hand upon Johanna's belly and breasts, and Helga saw her sister close her eyes, and move her lips in prayer. Helga said, "You have eaten much savory food, Ofeig Thorkelsson. Are you not dry, as well?"

"Give me the day's milking, for I am dry enough, now that you mention it."

Now Helga opened the door of the steading, and reached for a vat of ewe's milk from the evening milking, for it was the case that everyone had been so weary from the day's tasks that the vats had not been carried to the dairy, and she brought it into the steading and dipped up two cups full for Ofeig. He took his hand off Johanna's breast and drank them down, and then two more, and then he let out another belch and put his hand on his belly. And it seemed to Helga that he had eaten a prodigious amount, more than any three men. And now there was a whimper from Unn, a whimper followed by a cry, and Helga stepped back suddenly, and put her hand into the bedcloset. Ofeig began to stand up, Johanna still with him, and he opened his mouth to speak, but then he suddenly clutched for his belly with both hands, and doubled over on the bench. He let out a groan, and now he began to vomit all of the food he had gorged himself upon, and it spewed out everywhere, all over Johanna, and the broken table, and the floor, and a little bit on the hem of Helga's robe, and Johanna, her arm free, jumped away and grabbed the ax and the knife he had laid down for the tasks of eating and fondling her. And she said, "Ofeig Thorkelsson, you are the Devil indeed, and it is manifest in your hatred and your gluttony, and now you are cast down, through the grace of the Lord and the intercession of our prayers."

And now Ofeig began rolling about in the agony of a big feeding after a long fast, which every Greenlander is wary of, and the serving-women came forth out of the bedclosets, where they had been hiding, and they began to beat upon Ofeig with trenchers and other utensils, about the head and the shoulders. Johanna even lifted the ax, but indeed, he had more strength than they thought, for suddenly he scrabbled to his feet and threw himself out the door, and the last they saw of him, he was running off in the moonlight.

Through the broken-down roof, Helga saw that the sky was lightening toward dawn. She sat down upon the bench, and looked at the others gathered about her. Gunnhild sat upon Oddny's lap, and Unn sat upon Thordis' lap, and Johanna sat with a smile on her face, and with her arm limp at her side, and Helga said, "Your arm must hurt you more than a little, for I fear that this demon has broken it."

"We will walk over to Gunnars Stead after our morning meat, and Margret Asgeirsdottir will set it for me." And that was all she had to say on the subject. And Ofeig was not seen again in that district, although Helga looked for him each night until the return of Jon Andres and the other men. But Johanna did not, and went to bed in faith and trust every evening.

Now it happened that the end of the seventh day came round, and Jon Andres failed to return, and the end of the eighth day as well, and Gunnar Asgeirsson, too, stayed away, although all of the servingfolk came back to Gunnars Stead, and the result of this was that on the ninth day, when Jon Andres did return, much dirtied and fatigued by the hunt, the tale that Helga had hoped to make of her adventure with Ofeig was stopped in her mouth, and the wish that she had had, to speak of this, and then speak of other things, that were nearer to her heart, was unfulfilled, and the silence between herself and her husband continued unabated. Jon Andres heard the story from Oddny and probed Johanna about it. He was much disturbed by it, but Helga did not mention it, though he gave her the chance more than once. Then he vowed not to speak of it to Helga if she had no care to mention it to him, and so things went on between them for the rest of the summer, and Margret's proscription was fulfilled, and Helga had nothing to do with her husband that might endanger her life. In the summer, Johanna moved back to Gunnars Stead, and Helga was much cast down to see her go, and she considered Johanna a great friend of hers, although the two women never spoke of this.

At Gunnars Stead, Johanna found things to be much the same as they had been for many years; that was, it seemed to her now, very elderly. At Ketils Stead, she had conceived an affection for Gunnhild and Unn that she had not felt before. It seemed to her that children must wear into one, that a bit of fellowship with them was more than enough, but constant fellowship with them was less than enough. She was some twenty-four winters in age, not so much past the time of marrying for a Gunnars Stead maiden, and it occurred to her that her father might take her to the Thing this year, or might go himself, and seek about for a husband for her, but when she thought of this, it was not just any husband or any establishment that she felt this bit of longing for, but what was to be found at Ketils Stead, and so she held her peace. Gunnar and Margret were pleasant to her, and her footsteps about the place, and her pauses to look upon their work, one at her loom and the other at his parchment, were refreshing to them and long missed. Gunnar saw that she was his favorite child, as untroubling to him and as pure as water from tarns high in the mountains, and it also seemed to him, since her defeat of Ofeig, that she must outlive him, for which he felt simple gratitude.

At the spring seal hunt, Gunnar and Jon Andres had listened to many men, to many complaints of the absence of Kollgrim Gunnarsson, that issued from the mouths of men who themselves had tossed some wooden trinket upon the pyre that burned him. Gunnar and Jon Andres had nodded, had recalled, once in a while, how Kollgrim once killed forty-two seals in an afternoon, how he rowed his boat as quickly and as agilely as a skraeling, how he had preserved the life of Hrafnkel Snaefelsson when his boat was lost, so that he barely got his legs wet. Indeed, they had an ally in Hrafnkel himself, who was something of a blowhard, and always ready to tell the tale of his near drowning, and how he had felt himself all at once lost and saved, with Kollgrim's arm, "like a roof beam, that big and hard, about my arms and chest." The Icelanders, when they were about, cast a silence over the Greenlanders, a silence in which the cheerful tones of Bjorn Bollason and his sons rang like bells. The seal hunt had not been so prosperous as some, not so meager as some. No boats had been lost and no man killed. After it, the Thing came on, and then the rest of the summer, and folk went about their work as they had always done, in Greenland, and it seemed they would always do.

One day shortly after the next Yule, Snorri Torfason got out of the bedcloset where he had established himself for most of the previous four years, and he said that he would like to see his farms in Iceland, and after he said this he was as a demon of energy. That very day, he took some of his men and went on skis to Gardar, where their ship was drawn up on rollers, and pulled off such coverings as were over it and surveyed what damage there was to be repaired. There were a few staved-in boards, and some rot along the keel, and the steppings for the mast were split. These difficulties, which had seemed too tedious to rectify when Snorri didn't really want to return to Iceland, now seemed inconsequential. Snorri went straight to Sira Eindridi and began quizzing him that evening about such resources as were available for the repair of the ship. After that, the Icelanders went around on skis, trading for such wood as they needed, and seal oil, which is not so good as pitch for spreading over the outside of the ship, but must do where there is no pitch to be had. The short case of it was that as soon as the ice broke up and blew out of Einars Fjord after the feast of St. Erik, the Icelanders, with Sigrid Bjornsdottir and Bolli Bjornsson, were gone. And one day after this departure, Gunnar Asgeirsson and Jon Andres Erlendsson went about Vatna Hverfi district and Hvalsey Fjord and called witnesses to hear that they were pressing a case at the Thing, against Bjorn Bollason the lawspeaker, for the untimely death of Kollgrim Gunnarsson. And most Greenlanders who were the least bit knowledgeable of the law said that they had never heard of such a case being made against the lawspeaker himself, but indeed, folk may press any case that they wish, if they can make the judges hear it.

Bjorn Bollason did not quite know what to do about this. He went to his friends in Brattahlid district, and talked to them about it, and to Sira Eindridi, but all said that he was the lawspeaker, and therefore had the laws at the tip of his tongue, and so he must make up his own defense, which, indeed, did not seem as if it would be so hard to do. And Gunnar Asgeirsson had never won a case at the Thing in his life, and Jon Andres Erlendsson was not a litigious man, having only had to defend himself once, and never having pressed a case. But still the lawspeaker was flurried and dismayed, for the Icelanders were gone, and he saw that those friends among the Greenlanders that he had once had were somewhat more remote than he remembered them being, and he regretted that he had not cultivated his status more industriously in late years. After going to Brattahlid district, he went to Dyrnes and spoke to folk there, but Hoskuld, his foster father, had died in the previous year, and Hoskuld's own sons, who were powerful men as folk in Dyrnes go, were also a bit reserved, with, they said, difficulties of their own. Bjorn Bollason saw that, indeed, they were in some sense his enemies, because while they would not lift a hand against him, for the sake of long acquaintance, they would also not lift a hand for him, for Hoskuld had lifted his hand to help Bjorn Bollason perhaps too many times in the past, at the expense of his own sons. A man need only to sit across from them at evening meat, and watch the way they glanced out the door or across the room whenever Bjorn Bollason looked them in the face, to know this. And so he came back to Solar Fell, which was after all not really in any special district, but set off by itself, somewhat cast down.

Now the Thing came on, and it was thickly attended, for everyone in all the nearest districts wanted to see how these men acquitted themselves. All thought well of Gunnar Asgeirsson, but considered that he had always had ill enough luck. Bjorn Bollason was spoken of as the lesser man with the greater luck, and it was said that such distinctions between the two might never have been made if this case had not come up, for it is in these conflicts that the worth of men is measured by their neighbors. And that is why the Greenlanders always chatter of the concerns of others, for it is in the nature of folk to ask of themselves as well as of the Lord, how is each man to be judged? And when there are few enough men and women about, as there are in Greenland, then each one is seen more often, but the wealth of opinion is so diverse that no man is seen whole, or, indeed, seen as he wishes to be.

Jon Andres Erlendsson set up his booth, which was a rich one, in the very center of the Thing field, and about his booth, in a great wheel, were some twelve other booths, larger and smaller, from Vatna Hverfi district and Hvalsey Fjord district. Booths from the other districts were scattered about these, so that men had to walk through these in order to get to the others. The flaps of these twelve booths were always open, and men and boys, some of whom hadn't been to many Things before, or any, were always milling about them. And if they hadn't many provisions, then Jon Andres had food for them, as Bjorn Bollason had always fed everyone who came by in the early days, when he was just become lawspeaker. Gunnar Asgeirsson set up his booth in his usual spot, a little ways above the Thing field, and he had nothing to say at all.

Now Bjorn Bollason began, on the first morning of the Thing, to say out the laws, and this lasted almost until the end of the day, with some repetitions and muddlings, but indeed, few enough of the older folk knew to correct even one or two of these. There were six cases to be decided, with the case against Bjorn Bollason, and these were as follows: A man in Herjolfsnes claimed driftage rights over some wood that came to his strand, and then drifted off in the night and came to his neighbor's strand, and he had beaten a servant of his neighbor's when the servant had begun to carry off the wood, so that the servant had lost use of his arm and shoulder, and was therefore of less value to his master. Two fishermen, who were brothers, had built a boat together, and then fallen out, so that each claimed the boat. A man from Dyrnes had set to beating his wife, but had ended up killing her instead of chastising her. Two boys from the southern part of Vatna Hverfi district had gone about stealing from various store-houses, so that they amassed some thirty-six whole rounds of cheese, and instead of eating it, they had broken it up and left it to rot in Antler Lake. A man and his wife from Brattahlid laid claim to a farm abandoned by their brother, although the brother himself had made a present of the farm to his concubine. Such were the cases that occupied the Thing in this year, and as usual, many complained that most of these disputes might have been settled in the households, or the districts. In this way the Greenlanders were accustomed to complain of their long journeys and the trouble they had in setting up their booths.

On the afternoon of the second day of the Thing, it came to Jon Andres to make the case against Bjorn Bollason, and he strode into the circle among the judges, where cases were made, and his many followers pressed around, Gunnar among them. And it was the case that in the years since Jon Andres had defended himself against Gunnar Asgeirsson, he had lost none of his eloquence or grace, but only gained a certain confidence of manner, such as men have that boys don't have, and so now, as then, all eyes were riveted upon him. His smile flashed, and then his face grew as sober as could be, and he spoke as follows:

"What man among us does not have a brother or a son or a cousin who acts as he pleases, whether folk agree with his ways or not? Indeed, what man himself acts as he knows he should every moment of his life? What man is not led by desire or fear into stumbling? If he is starving, does he not bend down to pick some berries that are growing in the pathway, though the pathway may be through his neighbor's field? And when the priest comes to his district church, the man confesses his sin, and the priest gives him penance, and he is forgiven for this sin. If he says that he stretched his hand out for the berries, then other men may understand his action, for, indeed, every man himself has done such a thing in his time, and so, through our own sin, we come to understand the sinner. For does not the Lord Himself say that you must love the sinner, though you hate the sin?

"Now all men know that there are other sins that are not so trivial as eating a few berries. Stealing another man's lamb is one of these sins, or stealing the affections of his wife, and such sins must also be confessed, and the penance is greater, but there is forgiveness for these sins as well, is there not? For if there were not, we would surely all be condemned to Hell, and have no hope of salvation, and who among us here can say that he has no hope of salvation? The Greenlanders are great fighting men, are they not? And it sometimes happens in a fight that a man is killed, and those who have killed him must recognize their sin, and do penance, but indeed, are they barred from all hope of salvation for their deed? Well," said Jon Andres, "it is the case that no one knows the answer to this question, who is barred from Heaven and who is not, for Christ has not come among us to separate the sheep from the goats, has He?" And he spoke all of these things in a quiet, even tone that men strained to hear. Everything that he said seemed just and true.

Now, he said, "I too had a brother whose ways were not mine. Once upon a time, I acted toward this man as if he were my enemy, and I caused him great injury, and those folk who knew him before and after the injury say that he was never again quite himself, but was subject to confusion of mind, and forever after this injury, and as I came to know this man as my brother, I was heartily sorry and remorseful for this injury that I had done him, the more that I saw that he did not really forgive me in his heart, although he acted as a brother to me in all things. And so it happened that I came to love him who had once been my enemy, and my heart went out to him in his confusion of mind, for I saw that life was too much for him, and that many times he knew not how to direct his steps in the best possible fashion. The habit of wayward willfulness was so strong in him that he always took counsel in a contrary fashion. Even so, he was a strong and useful fellow, with talents of a certain nature such as no other man among the Greenlanders can claim, and this man was Kollgrim Gunnarsson of Gunnars Stead in Vatna Hverfi district. But who among us does not have a brother or a cousin or a son who seems as though he cannot be helped to do right, but must always find his own way through the thickest undergrowth, although the clear path be near by? Who among us does not sometimes grow angry and sometimes grow bitter and sometimes grow melancholy at the ways of such folk?

"Now it happened that my brother stumbled, and came to desire a woman that was wedded to an Icelander, but who was living by herself for a time. It may be said about this woman that she, too, was of an unusual and melancholy temperament, for when others were laughing, she might only smile, and when others were smiling, she might look down at her hands in her lap, and when others were listening, she might be dumb with her own thoughts. Was it so unusual that these two melancholy folk, who set themselves apart from others, should meet on some common footing that is not readily apparent to the rest of men? For it is also the case that the ways in which a man and a woman come together are multifarious and even laughable to the rest of folk.

"At any rate, they did not come together for very long, for they were discovered in right good time by the husband and his friends, and they were parted then, with some grief on both sides. Perhaps it may be said that they were parted with no little grief, for the case was that they were of the grieving sort. And it happened that the husband brought an action against my brother Kollgrim for this adultery, and all the Greenlanders laughed privily at this, for if every man were brought to the Thing for adultery, then indeed we would be here for a fortnight every summer.

"But the Icelanders got up a strange case, having to do with practices that Greenlanders know little of, though of course all Christian men are aware of how the Devil works in the world, and all men fear his power. And it happened that my brother, whom no one could outdo with weapons, was brought into this circle here, in much confusion of mind, and full of melancholy waywardness, and he knew so little of the matter that he was charged with—that is, witchcraft—that he knew not how to answer the questions that were presented to him, and said, even, that if the judges spoke of things in a certain way, then they must be that way. Do these sound like the words of the Devil? Can a man be so full of guile that he betrays himself into the fire through feigning ignorance? I was here, myself looking on, and what I saw then was not a devil or a witch or even a man, but a dumb beast, a bear wounded unto death, who stumbles and looks blindly about, tossing his head in pain, seeking he knows not what, for he is only a dumb beast. And does not the Lord require us to show mercy to those weaker than ourselves? Might not the judges, if not the Icelanders, have seen the pain and confusion on his countenance, and shown my brother mercy? They might have. It seemed to me then and it seems to me now that they might have." Here Jon Andres paused and looked around, and took a deep breath, and closed his eyes for a moment.

Now he went on, "By the laws of Greenland, in the absence of a representative of the king, men are outlawed and sent into the wilds, and there their enemies may hunt them down, and do them such damage as they can. But it was the case that no one could have done my brother damage in this way, for the wilds were his natural home, and prowess his natural talent. Whose table has not been a little lighter after the seal hunts and the reindeer hunts since the killing of Kollgrim Gunnarsson? And who is to say that these hunts as we've had won't be harder and less prosperous in the future? They have been in the past. Who has a child who might not live or die, someday, on the balance of a bit of meat, such as Kollgrim Gunnarsson might have furnished? Never once did my brother take as his share more than a quarter of his catch. Is the wealth of the Greenlanders so great that they can afford to lose a boat, or some arrows and spears, or a man? Nay, indeed, the Greenlanders are like six men in a four-man boat, who see that the sea comes to a fingerspan of the gunwales, who may sink in the next moment, or float, depending upon that fingerspan of freeboard.

"But these men did not follow the laws of Greenland. Who is to know what laws they followed? Laws said to exist in other northern places, but only they said this. We Greenlanders have little means of knowing the laws of other places. Even so, my brother was summarily hauled to that part of the field over there"—he waved his hand in the direction of the site of the pyre—"and put to death by burning. No Greenlander has ever been put to death by burning before. It seems to me that those who witnessed this death must hope that no Greenlander suffers the same fate again. I should choose, myself, freezing or starving over this death, or an ax blow to the head. But even so, there is one other thing that we know. We know that mercy might have been shown at the last, when it looked as if the Greenlanders might not be able to gather enough wood to support the burning. Hearts might have failed in this devilish undertaking right then and there. My brother might have been outlawed, then. But a certain person, the object of this case, said unto his accomplices, 'Soak him with seal oil.' And that is what they did, and when the seal oil had burned off him in a great conflagration, he was dead." Jon Andres scowled blackly in the direction of the lawspeaker. "So it is that I say to you that the lawspeaker himself was the murderer of my brother, and should suffer outlawry and loss of his property for this crime, unusual though it may be. What if the lawspeaker had sneaked up on my brother in the night, and delivered him his death blow with an ax? This is no different. A man may kill another with the strength of his arm, or he may kill another with the strength of his cleverness. He may kill him as a man or in the guise of lawspeaker, but the man who is killed is equally dead either way, and equally mourned, and equally lost to the good of folk who depend upon him. And now I demand a judgment of full outlawry and deprivation of property against Bjorn Bollason, exile into the wastelands, loss of his position as lawspeaker, and any other punishments as self-judgment might allow us to ask for." And he stopped speaking and looked carefully about the circle, at each of his followers, and at each of the lookers-on, and at each of the judges, and finally at Bjorn Bollason himself, and folk stood still for this staring.

Now Bjorn Bollason strode into the circle, and he was very richly dressed, in layers of white wadmal, with a great seal of St. Olaf the Greenlander dangling on his chest. He wore a number of ornaments that the Icelanders had given him as gifts, and he looked proud and imposing. And it was the case that he did not look at anyone, neither those standing about, nor Jon Andres, nor the judges, but only looked off, over the fjord, once, and up toward the mountains once. And then he began to speak in a proud voice, and he said, "I, Bjorn Bollason, have been lawspeaker of the Greenlanders for many summers, and before that, my foster father Hoskuld had great knowledge of the law. Never in the memory of men has such a case been brought before the Thing, where a man who is a judge has been threatened with outlawry for carrying out the laws as they were decided upon. This action is absurd at the least and dangerous at the most, for in this way every decision of the judges can be challenged whenever and for as long as men wish to challenge it, and that is all I have to say in the matter." And he strode out of the circle as proudly as he had strode into it. And now it was getting on toward the evening meat, and so the judges retired to make their decision, and what they decided was not unexpected by anyone, including Gunnar and Jon Andres. Folk gathered about, pressing hard upon the little circle, and the chief judge below Bjorn Bollason, a man from Brattahlid named Bessi Hallsteinsson, announced that the case could not be made, and that the lawspeaker had committed no crime, and indeed, would have committed a crime had he not endeavored his utmost to carry out the punishment that had been decided upon.

Now a great shouting arose, and some men began to press backwards from the circle where the judges had their places, and others began to press forwards, from where the booths were set up, and folk saw that the men from Hvalsey Fjord and Vatna Hverfi district were much more numerous than it had seemed before, and that, all at once, they were armed with axes and clubs and bows and arrows. The men from Brattahlid and Dyrnes who were Bjorn Bollason's supporters, and Bjorn and his sons, as well, ran from the Thing field to the place where weapons were laid down on the first day of the Thing, and they grabbed everything they could find, whether it belonged to them or not, and they turned and made their stand at that place, for the Vatna Hverfi men were upon them almost at once.

It seemed to Gunnar Asgeirsson that the shouting at the verdict arose around him, but then he understood that his own mouth was stretched open, and his own throat was pouring forth curses upon the heads of Bjorn Bollason and his hand-picked judges. Had someone told him that his hair was in flames, he would not have been surprised to hear it, so hotly did the rage and enmity burn within him. Bjorn Bollason had not deigned to look at the assembled folk, so proud was he, so ostentatiously clothed in white, and just that, that turn of the head, as he looked from Eriks Fjord to the mountains behind, drew all of Gunnar's anger forth, like meltwater pouring off the glacier in spring. When the Vatna Hverfi men came up behind him, as had been planned in the case of such a verdict, Gunnar received his ax in his hand, but he could not have said who gave it to him, for his eyes were all for Bjorn Bollason, who had turned, and staggered, and was now running toward the pile of weapons, and Gunnar ran after him. In the crowd of men, with folk before him and after him, he never lost sight of Bjorn Bollason for a moment, nor felt his rage diminish for a part of a moment. Indeed, such rage as he felt in one moment was as nothing to what he felt in the next, and it was his fixed intention not merely to kill Bjorn Bollason, but to make him feel in his bones every ache and torment that Kollgrim had felt, and also that he, Gunnar Asgeirsson, had felt in the time since that death, every moment of fury and of grief. Could he visit upon the man, through blows, the sight of Birgitta Lavransdottir with her innards half showing through her self-inflicted cuts, and then, the sight of her lifeless corpus rolled against a stone by the side of the steading, the bird arrow jutting bloodily from her breast? Could he make the lawspeaker hear the sound of such screams and weeping as filled his steading and his ears for days on end at his return from the Thing field? She had needed no one to tell her the news, for it had come to her through her second sight, or through her maternal flesh, the news of Kollgrim's death, and she had greeted him at the door to his steading as a madwoman might, undone by grief, twisted with the joint ill, yet standing, stiff with agony, to meet him. There were the others, too, not least Elisabet Thorolfsdottir, who tore the hair from her head, and Helga, who simply moaned and clutched her child to her breast, and Jon Andres, that man of peace, who planned, coldly, and step by knowing step, every move to this moment, the moment of crushing and destroying Bjorn Bollason and his sons. With that proud turn of the head, Gunnar could see and hear Bjorn Bollason say what he must have said, "He could be soaked with seal oil," and it seemed to him that the fire in him would burn hotter and hotter until Bjorn Bollason lay still on the ground, unrecognizable, torn piece from bloody piece.

The Brattahlid men drew themselves up in a ragged line, their weapons raised, and the Vatna Hverfi men fell upon them with the full force of their speed, so that some men ran through the line and found themselves behind their adversaries, while others were stopped in their flight by the strength of the enemy. The Brattahlid men were much outnumbered, but in fact they were better armed, for the other men had left a few of their weapons, for appearance' sake, on the pile. Now there was the sound of grunting and huffing and the fall of blows and the screams of injury, as men set to fighting in earnest.

At first, Bjorn Bollason hung back, in a kind of surprise. Indeed, he did not know how things had come to this pass, nor quite what to do about it. And his belly had grown so broad with the good Solar Fell meat that running from the judges' circle to the weapon pile had shortened his breath and made him considerably dizzy. And then it happened that he was knocked down on his knees, and kicked in the head, so that he fell forward onto his face, and this surprised him so that it did not occur to him to lie still, as if dead, but he strove to arise again, and to turn and look at his attacker, for indeed, it surprised him that he, such a popular and lucky man, should be attacked at all. But as soon as he got to his knees again, a club fell, first on his shoulder, a glancing blow, and then on his back, and a pain seared through him, so that it seemed better to lie down, after all, but still he tried to turn over, to see who was afflicting him like this, but indeed, he could not turn over, until a hand grasped him by the hair and wrenched him onto his back, and he saw the face of Jon Andres Erlendsson, and behind him, the face of Gunnar Asgeirsson, and that was the last thing he saw, for each then struck him an ax blow on the head and one of these was his death blow, although it could not be said clearly which one, and that was part of Jon Andres Erlendsson's plan, as well.

And here was the toll of death after this battle: in addition to Bjorn Bollason, his two sons, Sigurd and Hoskuld, were killed on the field, and the third, Arni, was carried off with his death wound. Another man on the Brattahlid side was killed with an arrow shot, and the eye of a man from Dyrnes was gouged out. Of the Vatna Hverfi men, one, Karl, the second son of the widow Ulfhild, of Mosfell, was killed outright, and another man had an ax sunk so deeply in his thigh that he died the following Yule. There were many bruises and cuts, and other painful hurts, and many of the fighters were hard put after this battle to recover themselves. The Thing was broken up without deciding any more cases, and the judges went home to their steadings, as if in flight. Indeed, everyone there went home as if in flight, for they knew not how to regain the normal ways that had been lost through this event.

Gunnar and Jon Andres escaped without injury, and returned to Vatna Hverfi district, and it was generally agreed that they had been strongly provoked in this case, and were not to be blamed too harshly for what had come about, for men must avenge the injuries done to them, if they are strong enough to do it. If those whom they avenge themselves upon are, in their turn, not strong enough to exact payment from them, then justice has been done.

Now on the evening of this battle, Sira Pall Hallvardsson was sitting in his accustomed place in the cathedral, looking upon the split visage of the Lord that hung over the altar, and no one had as yet brought in the seal oil lamps, and so the place was not a little gloomy. As he was sitting there, the door to the hall was flung open, and Sira Eindridi and Larus the Prophet came into the cathedral in a great flurry. And they stopped in the darkness, and looked about until Sira Pall announced his whereabouts, and then Sira Eindridi came to him, panting, and told him the news of the battle at Brattahlid, and Sira Pall listened in silence, and then said, calmly, "These are grievous tidings indeed, and I must rise and go to my chamber and think upon them," and he held out his arm so that Sira Eindridi might lift him and help him to his sticks, but just in this moment, the old priest let out a great moan, and fell forward so that Sira Eindridi had not the strength to prevent him from falling, and as he fell he hit his head upon the bench. And it happened shortly after this that it was discovered that Sira Pall Hallvardsson was dead, and it was considered that although Sira Eindridi had not administered his rites to him, since he was praying at the time of his death, then he was assured of entrance into Heaven. This was the view of Larus the Prophet. Afterward, folk spoke of Sira Pall as a casualty of the Brattahlid battle as much as any of the others, for, they said, his heart broke at the news, and none could prove that it had not.

One day in this summer, Gunnar was sitting on the pleasant hillside outside the steading at Gunnars Stead, and Margret was walking back and forth in front of him, spinning. He watched her spindle twirl and drop as she walked in one direction, and then he watched her wind the yarn upon it as she walked in the other direction and it seemed to him that the spindle and the lengthening thread cast a spell over him, and that this spell led him to speak in a way that he had never spoken before. He said, "How do men journey back from passion?" He looked up at her face, and it was as if he were a child again, and she his older sister, and he had just asked her how butter is made, or how the Lord knows who is good and who is not—such was the innocence that he felt behind his question, after a long and sinful life. Margret paused in her pacing and looked down upon him, and she said, "It seems to me that most do not." And Gunnar saw at once that this was the case, but he said, "What will happen next?" And Margret stopped again in her progress and looked down upon him again, and said, "Certainly we will die, though perhaps it will not be us who die of this very passion."

Now Gunnar said, "Did you ever think of our father Asgeir's travels to Norway and Iceland? Men elsewhere must live differently than Greenlanders do."

"When I was living among the Icelanders, Snorri Torfason always used to say that the Greenlanders sin with the pride of thinking themselves the worst off until they hear news of other folk, then they sin with the pride of thinking themselves the best."

"When I dealt Bjorn Bollason his death blow, it seemed to me that I had done a little thing, for it passed in a moment. My passion ran on beyond it, and was unfulfilled. Now it still seems to me a little thing, but a little thing like a snag, upon which my robe has caught. But instead of disentangling myself from this little snag, every thought and every movement nets me more and more tightly to it, so that sooner or later I will be strangled upon it."

"The lawspeaker's supporters will be glad to hear this, since that will relieve them of the burden of retaliation." And Margret began pacing back and forth again, as deliberately as before, and so she went on for a while, with the spindle twirling and the thread lengthening, and Gunnar watched as he had before, and the sun shone brightly on the homefield, as it had for nearly half a millennium, since the time of Erik the Red, and the first Gunnar who had farmed this steading, and first fenced the homefield and fertilized it with the manure of his cows and sheep and horses. Then he said, "My sister, what is it that you seek in the world?" And Margret said, "It has always seemed to me that I seek to be as a stone, and when I was a young woman, it seemed to me that such was the progress toward death—a hardening that would come over the flesh bit by bit, until the corpus lay there in the bedcloset, or was thrown out into the snow to await burial in the spring. Now it seems to me that the flesh quivers with still more life in every year, and that I will never achieve what I seek. I fear, indeed, that death is not death, but life everlasting after all." And she resumed her pacing and her spinning, and some time later, Johanna came to them and said that the evening meat was upon the table.

During the autumn seal hunt and through the fall, there were many discussions and arguments among the Greenlanders about who would be the new lawspeaker, or whether there would be any new lawspeaker at all, and it was the case that Bjorn Bollason had not sought to teach the body of the law to anyone, except perhaps, to Sigurd Bjornsson, who had died with his father at Brattahlid, and this was accountable to folk only through the speculation that Bjorn Bollason had considered himself such a lucky fellow that he would never die, as other men do. Or, perhaps, folk said, he had not as yet gotten around to it, for there were many things that Bjorn Bollason was more interested in than sitting down and going over the laws. Such entertainments as had been the rule at Solar Fell, especially in the years when the Icelanders lived there, must have filled a great deal of the lawspeaker's time, after all. It was also the case that Bjorn Bollason could be said not to have learned the laws especially well himself, since the telling of them had shrunk in his time from a three-day cycle to less than a one-day cycle.

And to this, some folk said, what did it matter, after all? Such cases as had been going to the Thing were better decided in the districts, or among the folk who were principals in the cases, and if they were decided with blows, once in a while, was that so different from what had happened to Bjorn Bollason himself? The case had been decided in his favor, and yet he was dead with no one to avenge his death, since the foster brothers in Dyrnes had spoken not a word about it all summer, even though Signy had gone to live with them. To go to the Thing, especially as it was at Brattahlid, was a considerable inconvenience these days, when there were so few men about every steading to keep up with the work. There had been a time when the Thing lasted seven days, or more, with all the laws and all the cases, but now it seemed as though as soon as a man had put up his booth, it was time to take it down again, and so folk talked about this all fall and all winter, and no move was made, by Sira Eindridi or anyone else, to replace the lawspeaker. Though no one knew all of the laws, did not everyone know, in a general way, what was to be expected of one another? And if they did not, then Sira Eindridi might be consulted, since folk had to go to Gardar anyway. And now some of the older folk remembered the time of the bishop and of Sira Jon, when hardly anyone had gone to the Thing at all. Such times come and go, they said. Men will always find a way to govern themselves. And so the winter passed, and the spring came on, and with it the spring seal hunt, and nothing was decided, except that when the Thing should be held again, it should not be held at Brattahlid, but at Gardar, as it had been, but no Thing was held in this year, though a few men showed up at Gardar during the regular Thing time, and spoke to Sira Eindridi Andresson about their concerns, and he advised them, and also consulted with Larus the Prophet, who had cast off Ashild and little Tota, and lived celibately at Gardar in the chamber that Sira Audun had once had for himself.

And so for most of the Greenlanders in the year after the great battle at the Brattahlid Thing, a sort of peace descended, for the hunts were prosperous enough, the winter snowy and cold enough for easy travel, the summer warm and moist enough for a good crop of hay in almost every homefield. The sheep went from upper pasture to lower pasture, and the cows from field to byre, and the folk from table to bedcloset to field, from steading to storehouse, from loom to dairy, from snaring ptarmigan to slaughtering sheep, and things had not changed with the burning of Kollgrim Gunnarsson or the killing of Bjorn Bollason.

Only it seemed to Larus the Prophet that they had changed, and changed for the better, if one seeks a way to rid the world of evil, and prepare folk for their imminent meeting with the Lord. It happened that on the feast day of St. Nikolaus, Larus was standing in the cathedral, thinking of little except that his feet were beginning to grow cold on the stone floor. And just as this feeling came to him, he felt the cold of the stones rise through his feet and calves and thighs and trunk, and he knew that behind him there was such a presence as only he was capable of welcoming among the Greenlanders, and he fell to shivering where he stood, but still he could not turn around until he was commanded to do so. Now the cold ran all through him, and he looked up at the riven crucifix and said with his lips, "Lord, let me not run away from Thee," as he always said in such moments, and then he fell upon the stones of the floor, which was also his habit.

Now a humble man approached him closely, whose robe was of a dark, roughly woven wadmal, and whose face was shaded, so that Larus could not make out his countenance, and the man said, "It is I, Lazarus, who was raised from the dead, who comes before you in this spot, and I come to bring you not light, but darkness, for indeed, Larus, such darkness spreads over this land as no man has ever known in the deepest winter night, even among the cows in the walled-up byre. That darkness is as a blinding light to the darkness I bring to you." And this Lazarus put his finger upon Larus' forehead, and a stream of blackness seemed to flow into him, filling every corner of his being.

It was just after the morning meat that these things came to Larus, and after them he lay on the floor of the cathedral, insensible, for most of the day, until two servingmen, who were looking for him, found him there and came near to see what had struck him down. As they approached, he roused himself, and sat up. He put his hands to his face, and his flesh felt doughy and bloodless. He said to the men, "Indeed, my children, I have been lost today," but he smiled upon them, as he always did, for his demeanor was always mild and welcoming, and for this folk liked him, in spite of his peculiar talk. Now he got to his knees, and said, "We must pray," and the servingmen knelt, as well, and all three now prayed in the usual way for a short while, then the men went off, and Larus went to find Sira Eindridi, for that had been the message of the men, that Sira Eindridi was in the horse pasture, and needed Larus to come to him there.

It happened, of course, that before he became a prophet, Larus had been a cowman in Brattahlid district, and had been somewhat well known for his knowledge of livestock, and it was this knowledge that enabled him to leave serving other men after the hunger and claim his own steading. Upon becoming a prophet, he had not lost this knowledge, and so Sira Eindridi considered him a useful fellow to have about the place, for he himself had no skill in this. In fact, Sira Eindridi considered that he had done well all around with Larus. Without making the fellow a priest he had made him an ally of the Church, and such tirades as the one he had delivered at Sira Pall Hallvardsson's famous service were in the past now. Sira Eindridi had no fear of being interrupted. In addition to this, those services about his steading table that Larus had fallen into conducting for some years were also ended. Folk sought him out, but they came to Gardar to do it, and when they were there, whatever they spoke to him of privily, the cathedral, and the face of the Lord, and the relics of St. Olaf looked down upon them, and their thoughts could not stray far into dangerous channels. Sira Eindridi was certain of that. Wasn't it the case that holy places gave off an invisible radiance that recalled the minds of men from such idiosyncrasies as they were prone to, back to the true faith as the consensus of souls dictated it? Someone had told him of this power, perhaps Sira Pall Hallvardsson, perhaps not. At any rate, to have a horse go badly lame, and then to call upon Larus to look at the beast, and to have Larus come out at once and see that the horse had been kicked in a pasture fight, but that no bones were broken, was reassuring in any number of ways. Neither then nor later that day did Larus mention how Lazarus had come to him, or what conclusions were to be drawn from that vision. It seemed to him that this Lazarus would come to him as often as he could bear it, and that he would be a hard master, indeed.

Shortly after this, near to Yule, news came from Vatna Hverfi district that the corpus of Ofeig Thorkelsson had been found on an abandoned farmstead in Alptafjord. To all appearances, the devil had been dead for some time, and perhaps had died of starvation, for the flesh on him was wasted and meager, and hardly like the flesh of a man, being leathery and dry and stretched over the bones. Perhaps, folk said, remembering his great size, Satan had sucked the life out of him, leaving but this shell of a man. He was dead, and there was nothing to fear from him anymore, or there wouldn't be, when precautions were taken. Skeggi Thorkelsson, who sent the message, respectfully requested Sira Eindridi Andresson or Sira Andres Eindridason to journey to Hestur Stead and perform such rites as were necessary to assure the ghost, and his potential victims about the steading and the district, of peace. And after the feast of the Epiphany, Sira Andres went out with some servingmen, on skis, and came to Hestur Stead.

Sira Andres was a good-looking youth, tall and fair, with a lively countenance, and he was not unaware of his effect on maidens, who always preferred to make their confessions to him, or to converse with him, or to walk along a little ways with him, or even to touch him on the sleeve. Some folk laughed and said that he was a priest in the old style, the style of Sira Nikolaus, whose "wife" had lived with him at Undir Hofdi church for sixty or a hundred winters, and to whom he had not been uniformly faithful over the years. But such priests have their uses, too, and so folk did not consider that Sira Andres was doing especial damage with his unorthodox ways.

Although Thorkel Gellison was a very old man, much bent with the joint ill and entirely deaf and confined for the most part to his bedcloset, Hestur Stead was still a great steading, large enough for Skeggi, Ingolf, and Ogmund, Thorkel's sons, all to live upon it with their wives and children, and among these children were a number of daughters, so Sira Andres was happy in where he found himself at the end of his journey. On the morning after his arrival, which was welcoming and festive, with a great deal of food and talk, Skeggi Thorkelsson got up, and aroused Sira Andres, and said, "Now, priest, you must perform your office, and bury this man, but, indeed, you must bury him so that he does not get up again, for if any man were ever to walk after death, our brother Ofeig is such a one."

The shrunken corpus of Ofeig was wrapped in lengths of wadmal and stored in an empty storehouse, and since the ground was frozen, it had been decided to put it in a cairn, rather than saving it for spring burial, and this cairn had been built for the most part. All it needed was for Sira Andres to pronounce the proper formulas, and then the corpus would be put in place, and the cairn would be completed with such heavy stones that even Ofeig should not be able to push them aside. Now Sira Andres put on his robes, his cope and his chasuble, and the other garments, and he went out, and somberly pronounced the customary burial services. When he was finished, he looked about, expecting folk to commence with the completion of the cairn, but all those gathered about looked back at him. Skeggi nodded, as if to encourage him to say something more, and Sira Andres realized that something special was expected of him, but indeed, he did not know what this should be. He smiled in his lively way, and Skeggi frowned at him, and after a moment, said, "Are you not going to lay the evil spirit, as well? We have great fear of this, that the soul of our brother Ofeig will not depart the earth, and will torment the folk about the steading. You must say the phrases that will prevent this." Sira Andres continued to smile, for indeed, he did not know what else to do. Now Skeggi turned to Ingolf and said, in rather a low voice, "It seems to me that the boy does not know what to say, and that this visit is in vain." And Ingolf leaned toward him, and whispered something, and then went off to the steading.

Now the folk stood about the cairn and waited, and Sira Andres began to feel a little discomfited. After a little while, Ingolf returned with an old woman by the arm, and he was leading her, for she was blind and bent, and when he brought her into the circle, he said to Sira Andres, "This is our cousin, our mother's cousin, whose name is Borghild, and though her voice is old and cracking, if you listen closely, she will tell you the words to say, and if you say them after her, the deed will be done." And this Borghild came very close to Sira Andres, and his nose turned, for indeed, she was very old and incontinent. She spoke in a wheeze, and Sira Andres listened as well as he could, and spoke after her, "Lord hear our plea in this matter. We commend to Thy charge our son, Ofeig, who has sinned often in his life. His crimes are legion, and he has given himself as a home to the minions of the Devil. We ask You to take him from us now and forever, and to forbid that he walk among us, for we are Thy faithful servants. And this is what we ask of You: that over him You put the earth, and the stones of the earth, and the waters of the earth, and all of these in such quantities that only You in Your infinite wisdom can find him." And so Sira Andres said all of these things. Now Skeggi handed the priest a handful of earth, and Sira Andres threw it upon the corpus, then Skeggi handed him a stone, and Sira Andres threw this upon the corpus, and now Skeggi handed him a dipperful of water, and Sira Andres threw this upon the corpus, and then all made the sign of the cross and the Thorkelssons began to pile the stones upon the corpus, and the others turned away and went back to the steading.

Sira Andres did not think much more about this ceremony after that, and he stayed another two nights, and he found the Thorkelssons very pleasant company, and agreed to return on clerical business sometime during Lent, and his journey to the southern parishes. But it happened that when he got back to Gardar, he was sitting at his evening meat with his father and Larus the Prophet, and it occurred to him to relate, for their entertainment, what the old woman had said to him, and what he had done with the earth and the stone and the water. And Sira Eindridi said little, only went on with his meat, but Larus the Prophet looked up suddenly, and then looked away, and after a few moments, he asked Sira Andres to repeat what he had said, word for word, and Sira Andres did so. After that Larus fell silent, and said no more for the rest of the evening.

Sometime after this, in the course of the spring, another thing happened in the southern part of Vatna Hverfi district that came to Larus' attention, and that was this. A cow that had been bred at Hestur Stead, to the Hestur Stead bull, and then had been returned to her owner, gave birth to a calf with five legs and three eyes, and indeed, part of a second head growing out of the first head. And this calf lived as a normal calf might, for some days, until the farmer decided that it would bring him ill luck, and so he slaughtered it. But the birth of this weird beast was indeed unlucky to the cow, for she sickened and died not long after the calf was slaughtered, and the farmer was not a little annoyed to lose both, since the cow had been one of his best milkers, and now folk began to talk idly of whether their own cows might suffer the same fate if they were bred to the Hestur Stead bull, who was a fine bull, but had just come into maturity, and had not produced many calves other than this one. One might go to the Ketils Stead bull, or one of the other bulls in Vatna Hverfi, or indeed, one might take one's cows in a boat to Gardar, and breed to the Gardar bulls, which were the finest in Greenland. The talk went about, and the breeding season came on, and men could not decide what to do.

The Thorkelssons made a number of jokes about the bull, saying that in his first year he had produced one and a half calves per cow, so surely in the second season every cow would twin, and every farmer would be that much richer, and then the talk subsided, and all the farmers made their own decisions about which bulls to breed to.

About this time, Larus was found insensible again, this time on the greensward outside the cathedral, and when he was revived, he spoke at last, privily, to Sira Eindridi, of this saint, Lazarus, who came to him and spoke to him and filled him, he said, with the darkness of the sin that was to be found among the Greenlanders, and because of this calf business in Vatna Hverfi district, Sira Eindridi and Larus spoke at length, long into the night, of what these portents might mean, and in the morning, they called Sira Andres to them again, and asked him about the words that the old woman had said to him, and what he had done with the earth and the stone and the water and the corpus of Ofeig Thorkelsson. And between them, Sira Eindridi and Larus the Prophet decided that they were being guided by the saint, Lazarus, to see that this woman, Borghild Finnkelsdottir, was a witch, for she was said to have been the nurse of Ofeig Thorkelsson, she had known this old ceremony without hesitation, the Hestur Stead folk were cousins to the Gunnars Stead folk, who had produced the known witch, Kollgrim Gunnarsson, and now the Hestur Stead bull was itself cursed.

What happened in their conversation was this, that Larus set the evidence before Sira Eindridi in his usual mild way, just as he had often related the substance of his visions in the past. And Sira Eindridi looked at him, and at length he said, "Men of God must act without hesitation in such things, and I am well known as a hard and direct person. It is always better to act, for the Lord will take care of the judgments." And so they sent a messenger to Hestur Stead, asking for the woman Borghild Finnkelsdottir, to present herself at Gardar, and to this message Skeggi Thorkelsson replied with disbelief that such a thing would be demanded at this time of the year, when the fjords were just freezing over, and as treacherous as possible. And after that, the woman would be unable to come, for she was too old to ski, and Skeggi and his brothers saw no reason to bring her on a sledge. Skeggi finished by saying that he would bring the woman himself in the Hestur Stead boat after the breakup of the ice in the spring.

Now Sira Eindridi was greatly exercised with wrath, for he detected in Skeggi's message an undertone of contempt, and he sent back another message that the woman must indeed come, at peril of her soul, and Skeggi himself must bring her. Skeggi received this message, and sent the messenger back without a reply, and so Sira Eindridi expected him any day, but the winter passed, and he never came, and Sira Eindridi was deeply angered at this, for he saw that all of those folk, all of the Vatna Hverfi folk, but especially those allied with Gunnar of Gunnars Stead and Jon Andres Erlendsson of Ketils Stead, were not a little wayward and in great peril of their souls. And it is well known to all men that the soul must be saved, even through the destruction of the flesh, for the soul belongs to the Lord above, and He is jealous of His belongings.

It happened that Larus the Prophet entertained the visitations of the saint, Lazarus, two more times in the course of this winter, and each time it was borne in upon him more clearly and with greater pain that an enormous darkness loomed over the Greenlanders, and their fate could not be averted, except through the sternest measures, and in the spring after these visions, which now numbered four, he began speaking of them privily to some of the women and men who came to Gardar to see him, and whereas his visions of Jesus, and the Virgin, and the Angel Gabriel had been freely spoken of in years past, folk were somewhat afraid to talk of what they now heard from him, and it could not be said that they did not hear of the Thorkelssons and Borghild Finnkelsdottir. They heard of her in confidence, it is true, but as the Greenlanders say, as men breathe, so they speak what they are thinking of.

At the end of the winter, toward the feast of St. Joseph, the woman died, and Skeggi sent this in a message to Sira Eindridi with the further message that it was his conviction that this should be the end of the matter. At this, Sira Eindridi sent a message back to Skeggi saying that the man was taking a very high-handed position with the Lord, and it was possible that he, and others, would come to regret it. And Skeggi sent the messenger back with word that there were plenty of weapons at Hestur Stead, and plenty of men to wield them. And so relations were very bad between Hestur Stead and Gardar.

At Ketils Stead, Helga Gunnarsdottir was preparing herself for another confinement, for indeed, the fight at the Thing three years before had borne in upon her that wives must give up the pride of their enmity, and consign their wills to their husbands, for it is always the case in Greenland that the husband may return to the steading a dead man. For Jon Andres, as well, there was the relief of giving up his secret to the breezes, and when Helga turned her slow gaze once more upon him, he turned his quick one upon her, and for three years they were very content with one another. The pregnancy went no more ill, although no better, than any of the others, and Margret Asgeirsdottir came to the steading every day with strengthening food and drinks, and Johanna cared for the work about the place and for Gunnhild, and little Unn. It seemed to Helga that the child would be a boy, and she was very happy.

One day when Helga was lying in her bedcloset and the others were outside, or in other chambers of the steading, she heard a man's footstep in the chamber outside the bedcloset. Knowing that this would be Jon Andres, of whom she had just been thinking, she sat up, and looked out of the opening. And indeed, there was a male figure inside the steading, with his back turned to her, but he was not wearing Jon Andres' sheepskin vest, but rich furs of blue fox. When he turned to face her, she saw that it was Kollgrim, and that he was beaming upon her with the same melancholy smile as he had always had for her, in the old days, when they lived together at Gunnars Stead, before she went away as a married woman. And it seemed to her that she was his after all, entirely his, only lent for a brief while to the others. And when Margret Asgeirsdottir came in sometime later to speak with her, Helga told her of this dream, and Margret said nothing, but they both knew how to interpret it, and so it came to pass that Helga Gunnarsdottir died in childbirth, and the child, whose name was Kollgrim, died as well, some little while after his mother. And it was the case that Helga was buried near the north wall of Undir Hofdi church, near the grave of Helga Ingvadottir and not far from the graves of Hauk Gunnarsson and Asgeir Gunnarsson, and all of the other folk of their lineage. She was thirty-eight winters of age. After Helga's death, Johanna stayed on at Ketils Stead and cared for Gunnhild and Unn, and though her ways with them were always brisk rather than gentle, the two girls grew accustomed to her.

In this year, once again, no Thing was held, although there was some talk during the spring seal hunt of reinstituting it, but the Greenlanders would have to make up a whole new set of laws for a new lawspeaker to learn, and this seemed both an impossible task and an unnecessary one, since almost everyone agreed on what actions were the proper ones and what were the improper ones. And there were always Sira Eindridi and Larus the Prophet to speak to, and Gardar was a more convenient place to go than Brattahlid, and folk had to go there anyway, to breed their sheep to the Gardar rams, or to breed their cows to the Gardar bulls. On this seal hunt, there was some talk of Skeggi Thorkelsson and of the trouble Sira Eindridi was having with him, and some folk considered that Skeggi was much provoked, and some folk considered that he had always been a stiff-necked fellow, proud of his father's rich steading and complacent in his relations to other farmers in the district.

In the summer after this seal hunt, shortly before the feast of St. Margaret, Larus received the saint, Lazarus, again, and was insensible for a whole day and a whole night, and could on no account be roused. He fell down in the kitchen, as he was talking to the cook, and stayed there the whole time, for the servingfolk, and Sira Eindridi, were afraid to move him. He lay as if dead, and from time to time the cook wet her finger and put it under his nose, to see if he still breathed. When he finally roused himself, folk saw that he was much weakened by this spell, more so than he had been in the past, and for a day afterward, he could hardly shuffle from place to place, and his face was white as a newly washed fleece. When Sira Eindridi questioned him about these matters, he could hardly speak of them so as to be understood, and finally Sira Eindridi said to him, "Larus, my friend, I see that this Lazarus bears down hard upon you, but that is the sign that you and only you have the strength to bear up underneath his weight." And Larus nodded, for he had considered this as well.

Now, on the very next day after Sira Eindridi said these words, a woman from Brattahlid came to Gardar, and her name was Gunndis, and she had been one of Larus' first women. She had sewed garments for him and been many times to his table, and she knew many of his visions as well as he did, and in almost the very same words. He received her with pleasure, and she spoke to him for a long time, and the result was that he saw that the prophecy of the day before, that "the north will be as the south, the east as the west, and evil will rise up on all sides as the waves rise around a tiny boat" was fulfilled.

In Brattahlid, said Gunndis, there were a man and a woman casting spells over their neighbors, so that cattle and sheep all about their farm were falling ill, but theirs were not, and the reason for these spells was this—this man and this woman were in conflict with neighbors on two sides over the size of their holdings, and had tried through other means to gain more pasturage, and now they were trying by this means. Gunndis herself lived far from the couple, but her cousin's daughter lived at one of the afflicted farms, and could not see her way out of the affliction, except through the intercession, which Gunndis had suggested, of Larus the Prophet. Larus told her he had expected something of this kind, and then, privily, of the visitation of Lazarus, the saint, and he sent her off, and it could not be said that she kept these matters to herself when she got back to Brattahlid, but everyone she told, she also asked to keep these things in their breasts as secrets.

Also in this summer, the news came to Larus the Prophet that a great storm had spread over the southern part of Vatna Hverfi district, and that in this storm, the Hestur Stead bull, who had been standing in his field, was struck by lightning. It seemed to Larus that this event spoke for itself, and that he need not speak for it, except to Skeggi Thorkelsson, and so he sent him the following message: "Thy pride shall be thy abasement, and the tongue in thy mouth shall speak against itself." Skeggi returned no reply to this message, and things went on quietly for the rest of the summer, except that the man and woman from Brattahlid who had brought disease to their neighbors' sheep and cows were called to Gardar, where they humbled themselves, and were sent home again, but indeed, they were intransigent in their evil, for the deaths of neighboring cows continued unabated. Larus and Sira Eindridi had some discussion about what their next course of action should be, and they remained undecided. These things were much discussed at the autumn seal hunt.

Toward the end of the summer half year, Ashild came to Gardar with little Tota, who was some seventeen winters old now, but still known as little Tota. Ashild had been living on her farm, Larus Stead, between Brattahlid district and Solar Fell with a man, Gerd, to whom she was not married. Larus was not a little pleased to see her, and gave her a kiss on each cheek, which was, he said, the Kiss of Everlasting Virtue. He told her that although he never longed for her as flesh longs for flesh, there were times when he longed to be in the presence of her purified nature, and she said that this was the case for her as well, and they agreed that the early days on Larus Stead, after the first visions, when folk were just beginning to come to them, to eat with them, and to hear what Larus had to say, had been contented and peaceful times. Ashild suggested that she might come to Gardar as a pilgrim, and do the lowliest forms of labor there, and perhaps meet with Larus from time to time, but Larus said that she must not think of this. And so they got on to the real tale of her visit.

Ashild said of herself that she was much frightened, and often longed for the comfort of Larus' presence, for there were malevolent powers abroad in the world, and these had been unleashed, perhaps, at the burning of Kollgrim Gunnarsson. One could not say, interrupted Larus, where the devils would lodge who had fled the burning man, and many had watched the burning. Ashild nodded. She herself had seen a portent that night, in the form of a glowing bubble in the water of Eriks Fjord, down toward Solar Fell, somewhat to the Brattahlid side of the shrine of St. Olaf the Greenlander, though she had not known what it was at the time, and had not thought much of it. But since then it came to her over and over, as if the meaning of it must press itself into her thoughts in spite of her ignorance. Larus nodded. Since that time, Ashild had kept her eyes open, and had noticed many things. And it was also true that because of her long association with Larus, people looked on her with favor, and often came to her for counsel, which she tried to give them as Larus himself might. Larus nodded. But indeed, went on Ashild, the Devil keeps himself well hidden, and it is only the sharpest eyes that can make out the tip of his horn, or the print of his cloven foot in the earth.

A servingmaid had fallen into a spell at the end of winter, and had spoken roughly in another tongue, and another voice, as well, and though the mistress had beaten her for this, she had sworn that she could not remember what she had said and done. Ashild had believed her. This was at the house of Ragnleif Isleifsson, where Margret Asgeirsdottir had once been a servingmaid, too. That was one thing. A boy at another steading had unaccountably awakened in the night, and climbed out of his bed-closet, although it was the dead of winter, and gone out of the steading, where he saw, he said, a cross of fiery stars in the sky, and blood pouring from it. And he could not be moved from the details of his story. He was some twelve winters old, Ashild guessed. Old enough to speak of what he saw. That was another thing. And the third thing was this. A certain woman named Asta Bjartsdottir had come to Ashild three times, and each time she had told her privily of a vision she had had. For, the old woman said, of all the folk in the district, Ashild had lived the longest with Larus the Prophet, and Larus had had the most visions, and if Ashild had learned nothing of this from their time together, she must be a fool. The first vision was of men on fine horses, such horses as are found only at Hestur Stead, trampling some children to death beneath the feet of their horses, and laughing all the while. The second vision was of Kollgrim Gunnarsson, whom the woman had seen at the time of the trial and the burning, and he was sitting with dark clothed men, laughing, too, and there was a red glow behind him. And the third vision was of Larus the Prophet himself, and he was standing on a hillside, in a white garment, and a herd of reindeer were galloping toward him, and as the woman watched, these deer changed first into a swell of water, then into an avalanche, and then into a raging fire, and the fire seemed to burn Larus up where he stood. And the woman was greatly afraid, and asked Ashild to be sure that Larus was warned of this vision.

Now Larus felt himself exalted by this news, and he took Ashild's hands into his own, and he told her the whole tale of Lazarus, and everything that Lazarus had told him about the fate that awaited the Greenlanders through their sinful natures and their intransigent ways. And a dire fate it was, for steadings would be broken up, and houses and byres would fall down, and sheep and cows would be scattered into the wilds, and grass would grow everywhere, and sand would fly in and cover everything, and the people would vanish from the face of the earth, leaving behind themselves only bits of tools and broken toys and shards of bone, and the land would be so accursed that even the accursed skraelings would avoid the places of the Greenlanders. These visions that all were seeing in Brattahlid were intimations of this fate, and also the Lord's warning to men to reform themselves, and allow themselves to be led out of the darkness. For Larus could save the Greenlanders, he told Ashild, if the Greenlanders would allow themselves to be saved.

Ashild asked how this might be done, and Larus sat up hungrily, and looked into her face, and said, "Skeggi Thorkelsson must be burned at the stake as Kollgrim Gunnarsson was, and these two intransigent witches in Brattahlid must also be burned at the stake, and the folk of Vatna Hverfi in general must give up their pride and much of their wealth to Gardar, for their wealth is the fruit of sinful waywardness. All households, no matter how far off they are, must send pilgrims on foot to Gardar and to Solar Fell, to kneel before the relics of St. Olaf. And in addition to these things, all the Greenlanders must accept the will of the Lord, as it comes through Lazarus, the saint, to Larus the Prophet. And those who don't must be killed. And the church services, as well, are to be modified, for the pope of Jerusalem is at hand." These words poured out of Larus in a torrent, and Ashild felt herself much uplifted by them, and after they had talked a while longer, she went back to her steading, and she published these tales all about the district, as busily as she could. And though Larus had told her these things in confidence, and there were among them things he had never told anyone before, he did not mind so much that they were out, for as Lazarus was pressing hard upon him, so it was time for him to press hard upon the Greenlanders.

All winter, folk in Brattahlid district talked of these things, and compared them to other things Larus had said. Toward the end of Lent it happened that some men broke into the steading of that man and that woman who had been accused of bringing disease to the livestock of their neighbors, and clubbed them to death where they stood, and the peculiar thing about this was that the men who did the killing never announced it, as is customary in Greenland, and, as with Jon Andres Erlendsson and Gunnar Asgeirsson, these men were never punished or outlawed. Indeed, the Thing no longer met, and no one knew the laws, so it was not possible to outlaw them. When this news became general at the spring seal hunt, folk from other districts did not know what to make of it, except to say that the Brattahlid folk had always done things in their own way, since the time of Erik the Red. When Skeggi Thorkelsson heard that Larus the Prophet prescribed burning at the stake for his case, he could not be made to stop laughing.

But the seal hunt went ill. Two boats were lost, and three men, and few seals were taken, and men fell to blaming each other and all looked forward to a hungry summer. One of the men lost was Skeggi Thorkelsson. Afterward, Larus called the wave that swamped the Hestur Stead boat the Corrective Wave of the Righteous Lord. And after the seal hunt, many folk in many districts were afraid, and no longer spoke to one another as Greenlanders once had, in open jest about many things. During that summer, Sira Eindridi allowed Larus the Prophet to change the mass slightly, in accordance with the formulas that Lazarus had dictated to him, and Larus taught these formulas to Sira Eindridi himself and to Sira Andres.

One day in the summer, after all these events had taken place, Gunnar Asgeirsson went on horseback to Hestur Stead, to see Thorkel Gellison, for it seemed to him that the old man would soon die. Gunnar was also much cast down by the death of Skeggi Thorkelsson, and by the tales that attached themselves to it. When he got to Hestur Stead, he saw that Thorkel was indeed a dying man, and that his life might stretch to a matter of days, but no longer than that, and for a while he sat beside Thorkel's bedcloset while Thorkel slept. Then Thorkel woke up, and Gunnar said, "It is I, Gunnar Asgeirsson, come to seek your counsel for the last time." And Thorkel said nothing, so Gunnar thought that perhaps he could not hear him, but he went on talking anyway, about sheep and cows and the hunt and the weather, and such other matters as Greenlanders like to speak of, but suddenly, Thorkel spoke up and said in a clear voice, "Gunnar Asgeirsson, you have spread your bad luck over the whole of Greenland," and he fell silent again. Now Gunnar did not know what to say, for what Thorkel said seemed to him to be true, and so he sat silently for a while. And then Thorkel spoke again, and said, "Even so, you are always welcome at Hestur Stead, for men do not choose their friends for their good luck, nor do they betray them for their ill luck. In this as in all things, men are foolish enough." And he was much weakened by these speeches, and soon fell asleep again. Gunnar stayed for two days, and talked to Thorkel twice more, and then returned to Gunnars Stead, and some days later he had the news of Thorkel's death.

Now in this summer, which was according to most calendars the summer of 1415, another thing happened that was worth talking about, and that was that some men who had a large boat, large enough for twenty rowers, declared that they intended to leave Greenland and seek Markland and Vinland. These were Brattahlid men and Dyrnes men for the most part, and one of them was the fellow Harald Magnusson, who had carried Margret across Einars Fjord when she was on her way to Gunnars Stead. The boat would carry, it was said, fifteen men and five women, and necessary household furnishings and lambs and calves past the weaning stage, and it was not intended that these folk would return to Greenland, and that was the unaccountable thing about it. Folk speculated for a long time as to whether Harald and his friends would carry out their boast, and it happened that they did, and after they were gone, folk looked for them to return all through the summer, or for the pieces of their boat to be washed up on some strand or another, but such a thing never happened, and so folk did not ever learn of the fate of Harald Magnusson and his little boat, except through such dreams as they had from time to time. Such tales as folk remembered of Erik the Red and his son Leif the Lucky, and the bishop Erik, and Thorleif the Magnificent, and Hauk Gunnarsson, and others who had made the Markland journey through the years were brought out and renewed, and folk were disquieted by them, for indeed, Vinland is a great paradise of forests and vines and self-sown wheat, where men may rest from their labors from time to time, and all folk long for such a place if they are brought to think of it.

It may be said that things went on quietly now for some years. Larus the Prophet was the lord at Gardar, and Sira Eindridi and Sira Andres were his servants, no more than that, and though these two continued going out to the churches in the winter, as priests had always done, folk were less inclined to attend the services, so changed were they from what had been. Many said that now there was no hope of salvation, for a man might do anything and be in the wrong. There was no way to tell. It was better to stay on the steading and mind the cows and be content with such days as are left to one and cease to wonder about life everlasting. If disputes arose, then men must settle them or fight about them, and if men are killed in these fights, then the disputes are settled in that way. Some folk even stayed away from the seal hunts, if they felt like it, because it could not be said whether the seal hunts were profitable or not. The Brattahlid folk nowadays always brought the ill luck of their witchcraft controversies with them, and it seemed to many that they bewitched the seals, or the boats, or the other men, so that something was always lost. It was better to keep one's boat at home. There were few enough of them, after all. But it was true that every farmstead was the hungrier for not going to the seal hunt, and every Lent the longer, and every family the more hard put.

The folk at Gunnars Stead grew older. Jon Andres Erlendsson married Johanna Gunnarsdottir, and she gave birth to two children. It seemed to Gunnar that folk were thinly scattered over the ground these days, and he began to think that Birgitta Lavransdottir had been right, that the end of the world was upon the Greenlanders, at least. Perhaps it was upon every nation and people, but indeed, there was no way of finding out, except through such dreams as came to folk. In Brattahlid, folk were embroiled in conflicts and killings, and this was true to a degree in Dyrnes, also. Vatna Hverfi folk shunned contact with these others.

In Vatna Hverfi all was peace. The sun rose each morning, and shone upon the riot of flowers that grew around the middens, and blanketed the homefield. It turned the fjord green and the lakes blue, and a man could stand at the edge of these and see the shimmering copper of their bottoms glowing up through the depths. The grass grew thick and long, and bent this way and that in the breeze, for there is always a breeze in Greenland. The black mountains with their sparkling summits changed shape in the light, but were changeless. Each summer, the angelica sprouted overnight, and unfolded its branches like the palms of men open in supplication. Among its roots, the low rushing sound of water was unceasing. Men and women arose, went in and out of their steadings, looked about themselves, and lay down again for sleep.

It seemed to Gunnar, perhaps because he was an old man now, that these years passed as in a spell. Margret grew very old, he saw, but she went every day as far as she could into the hills. She did not look for anything, or bring anything back. She simply could not abide spending the day in the steading. One of these days she came back smiling a little, and he asked her her news, and she said, "Indeed, there were skraelings upon Einars Fjord, numbers of them in their skin boats, and they were fat and prosperous, and it seems to me that I saw Sigurd Kolsson among them, and he was tall and sturdy and had two wives." Gunnar himself sat beside his parchment. His eyes were good, and his hands were unafflicted with the joint ill, and sometimes he wrote a sentence or two. News came: Sira Eindridi died of a stomach ill. Other news came: two ships had been sighted entering Einars Fjord. They were much unlike any ships that the Greenlanders had ever seen before. Folk went down to the strand, curious. The ships moved slowly up the fjord. They were wide and heavy-looking, with many sails. Ungraceful, but exceedingly large, as if carrying a great cargo. The faces of men, oddly deformed and silvery, stared over the gunwales.

The ships sailed on, past the staring Greenlanders, and this is what happened when they got to Gardar. The men upon them disembarked in a great rush, and ran through the water, and up the strand, and they were wearing plate metal armor and helmets, and carrying various iron weapons, not only swords, but shields and pikes and halberds, and they at once set about slaughtering all of the animals that they could see about the cathedral compound, and when the steward, whose name was Odd, came to them and told them that they were on Church land, they killed him. Now other servingfolk came out, and were standing about, and of course, Larus the Prophet, and Sira Andres as well. And these sailors at once set about preparing to cook and eat the animals that they had killed, for it is always the case that folk who travel to Greenland arrive hungry. But there was little or no wood to be had, except some driftage and some small stocks in the kitchen at Gardar, and these men were so enraged by this that they set about killing the servingfolk, at random, or beating them, or, in the case of women, raping them and then beating them.

Now Larus the Prophet approached them with his hands out in front of him, to show that he had no weapons, and he began to expostulate with them in his usual way, namely by calling on the saints and other holy folk who were his friends to witness that these things being done were great evils, and that the Lord would exact his due punishment against these devils. It happened that one of these sailors spoke a bit of Norse, from travels to Norway and Denmark, and he understood some of what Larus was saying, so in the midst of the turmoil, he shouted, "What is your name, then?" in the Norse tongue, and Larus shouted, "I am Larus the Prophet!" and when the sailor heard this, he began to laugh, and to relay this information to his fellows, who also laughed, and Larus was much put out, and repeated his words about the Lord's punishment. The sailor said, "The Lord may find us if he can, then!"

Now Larus said, "What manner of men are these, O Lord, that they plunder us without mercy?"

"We are Bristol men!" shouted the sailor. "And we are unpleased to find ourselves in Greenland so late in the year, you may be sure of that!"

Larus did not know what Bristol men were, but it was evident to everyone that they must be such marauders as folk had never known before, for after they had slaughtered all of the cattle and horses they could find, they pursued the Greenlanders into the cathedral, where they had taken refuge, and they stole whatever was to be had there, and beat or killed anyone who tried to prevent them, and one of the folk that they killed was Larus himself, and this is what happened. Larus ran as fast as he could into the cathedral, to put away the altar furnishings. Some of these sailors ran after him and found him taking down the crucifix that hung above the altar. He was standing on the altar to do it. As he took it down, it broke into two pieces, and one of these dropped on the floor, causing Larus to let out a great moan, and then the sailors were about him, teasing him where he stood upon the altar, and he clasped the larger part of the crucifix to his bosom, and began to yell. He yelled, "Lord! Lord! Rain thy fire and darkness upon these devils! Crush them and rend them with sharp wheels, wheels of iron spikes, for they have come upon us as a horde of marauders, and they undo us and outrage Thee in Thy consecrated house!" and one of the sailors reached out and poked him with his pike, enough to draw blood, and Larus raised the broken crucifix above him as a weapon, and brought it down with no little force on that man's helmeted head, so that in spite of his helmet he fell down on the stones beside the altar. Now Larus began to shout that the Lord's victory was his, and just then he was pushed off the altar, and stabbed and hacked and poked to death by the others who were standing around. And that was the death of Larus the Prophet.

It seemed that these Bristol men were seized with a frenzy, for they rampaged through all the buildings in Gardar, stealing everything that was fine, and breaking up everything that did not interest them. From the cathedral they got the wooden benches, and carried them outside, and built some fires with them, and began to cook their meat over these fires, and with this meat, they drank such wine and ale and other intoxicating beverages as they had with them, and after this feast, they tore through the buildings again, carrying torches, looking for the Lord Himself knew not what. Those Greenlanders who escaped scattered in every direction with this news, but many did not. Eight men and four women were killed outright, and four more men and two more women, including the Gardar cook, died after some days of their injuries. And it must be said that during the days when these injured folk lay about with their injuries, the Bristol men heeded not their cries for water or mercy or aid, but only ate their meat and drank their drink and slept the stupefied sleep of the intoxicated.

Soon enough there was nothing left at Gardar, and the Bristol men went on to their ships, and began to sail out of Einars Fjord, and as they went, they stopped in many places along the strand, where there were steadings on the hillsides, and they raided these places, as well, and one of these steadings was Ketils Stead. All of the animals were stolen, and all of the furnishings stolen or destroyed, and the turves torn from the walls of the buildings, and the stores in the storehouses taken or fouled or tipped out of their vats. Jon Andres had not hoped to defend his steading, for he had no weapons and no men for it, but he stood in the hills and looked down upon the devastation, and wondered at the ferocity of the Bristol men. And though it was the case that Ketils Stead had belonged to someone of his lineage since the time of Erik the Red, he watched the destruction rather coolly, and it seemed to him that the death of Helga had tempered his spirit and prepared him to endure any other loss.

Gunnars Stead, where Johanna and the servingfolk had gone with the children, was far enough from the fjord so as not to attract the gaze or the interest of the Bristol men, and so escaped untouched, but there was this misadventure. On that day when the Bristol men plundered Ketils Stead, Margret Asgeirsdottir went out of the steading for her usual venture into the hills, and no one thought to stop her, for indeed, with the children and the servingfolk from Ketils Stead, everything was in great disarray. When Jon Andres returned to Gunnars Stead with the news of what had been taken or demolished on his steading, there was much consternation, so that it was not until nightfall that Gunnar thought to seek Margret in the hills, and even then he did not think much about it, for danger is hard to see even when it is upon one. But now, in the long blue twilight, he donned his vest and went with one of the servingmen in the direction Margret was used to going, and as soon as he set his foot on this path, he realized that it could easily have taken her to the strand, and toward the Ketils Stead lands, and he was sorely afraid, and began to run.

Now he and the servingman looked frantically among the birch and willow scrub, and paused from time to time to listen for cries or moans, but at first they saw nothing and heard nothing. Soon enough, they had a view of the fjord, where white icebergs floated silently in the dark water, and then they had a view of the remains of Ketils Stead, and still they saw nothing, and Gunnar was tempted to have hope, and he sent the servingman back to Gunnars Stead to see if Margret had returned. But, indeed, there was her cloak, dark in the gathering dusk, and beneath was her corpus, and much had been done to it in the way of hacking and poking. Even so, her head was still upon her neck, and her face was whole and recognizable, and her long braids coiled about her in the grass. Now he knelt down in the grass and willow scrub, and he wept as only old men weep who have no hope left.

And it was the case that in his weeping, he cursed the hearts of the Bristol men, that gave them to do such injury. And after that he cursed his own heart, for he, too, had turned his mind and his strength to such killing as this. Eight men had fallen by his hand, and through his enmity, and he made himself think carefully upon their names: Skuli Gudmundsson, Ketil the Unlucky, Hallvard Erlendsson, Kollbein Erlendsson, Bjorn Bollason, Sigurd Bjornsson, Hoskuld Bjornsson, and Arni Bjornsson, and then he fell upon his face in the grass, and he wept for these eight men, all of them his enemies, all of them who had done him injury, but all of them men. And then he saw what he was, an old man, ready to die, pressed against the Greenland earth, as small as an ash berry on the face of a mountain, and he did the only thing that men can do when they know themselves, which was to weep and weep and weep.

EPILOGUE

After the destruction of Gardar and of most of the steadings that looked upon the fjords of the south, news between the districts was slow, and every district turned in upon itself. Cattle and sheep that had been few enough were fewer still, and the same was true of men and boats. Some things were said: that women and children in Hvalsey Fjord had been left without men entirely, and had gone off with the skraelings; that the conflicts in Brattahlid district intensified after the visitation of the Bristol men, and all the families were in a turmoil of accusations and retaliations; that if the coming winter was a hard one, few households would get through it, but indeed, this was said every year, and no man could judge in advance whether it would be true or not.

Margret Asgeirsdottir was buried with as much of a ceremony as Jon Andres and Gunnar between them could remember, next to Helga Gunnarsdottir in the lee of Undir Hofdi church, though no services had been held there in six or eight winters. Jon Andres and Johanna and their children and servingfolk reclaimed such belongings as they could from Ketils Stead, and moved to Gunnars Stead. Folk no longer considered it lucky to live in view of the fjord, in case the Bristol men should return. Gunnars Stead prospered well enough. The fields were wide, still, and well watered, though folk were on their own now, without support from Gardar, and without many neighbors. Inside, there was the rubbing of elbows that many people on one steading have with one another. Gunnar was not sanguine. One winter or another, he thought, would surely kill them all. Onto his parchment he wrote such sentences as occurred to him.

In the winter, as always in Greenland, every day was much the same, and every night. About the eaves, the snowy wind howled, but was muffled by the turfing. Snow mounded against the door, pressing it closed so that two men, or three, must press it open in the morning. The children sat in the bedcloset, by the light of a seal oil lamp, and played or slept. Jon Andres and Johanna sat over the chessboard, for folk may not contemplate their fates all the time, and must play as well as work. The great loom, upon which Margret Asgeirsdottir had woven her lengths of wadmal, and before her Helga Ingvadottir, and before her Maria Steinsdottir, and before her Asta Palssdottir, and many generations of wives before them, cast its black shadow across the wall. In front of Gunnar, on the table, the small seal oil lamp that he used flickered and burned for a moment more dimly and for a moment more brightly. He thought of going to his bedcloset and huddling under the old bearskin that his uncle Hauk Gunnarsson had left him, but then Johanna looked up from the game, with her cool and serious countenance, and said, "My father, it is very silent, except for the wind. You might enliven us with a tale." And the children peeped out of the bedcloset, and Gunnar told his tale.

A NOTE ABOUT THE AUTHOR

Jane Smiley was born in Los Angeles, grew up in St. Louis, and studied at Vassar and the University of Iowa, where she received her Ph.D. She is the author of three novels—*Barn Blind, At Paradise Gate,* and *Duplicate Keys*—a story collection, *The Age of Grief,* which was nominated for the National Book Critics Circle Award, and one non-fiction book, *Catskill Crafts.* She teaches at Iowa State University and lives in Ames, Iowa.

A NOTE ON THE TYPE

The text of this book was set in a digitized version of Bembo, a well-known Monotype face. Named for Pietro Bembo, the celebrated Renaissance writer and humanist scholar who was made a cardinal and served as secretary to Pope Leo X, the original cutting of Bembo was made by Francesco Griffo of Bologna only a few years after Columbus discovered America

Sturdy, well balanced, and finely proportioned, Bembo is a face of rare beauty, extremely legible in all of its sizes.

Composed by the Haddon Craftsmen, Inc., Scranton, Pennsylvania from a standard IBM tape supplied by the author through the VAX System at Iowa State University. Printed and bound by Fairfield Graphics, Fairfield, Pennsylvania.

Map art by David Lindroth

Calligraphy in text and maps by Carole Lowenstein

Designed by Virginia Tan